ARCHIE HORROR PRESENTS

# CHILLING ADVENTURES IN SORCERY®

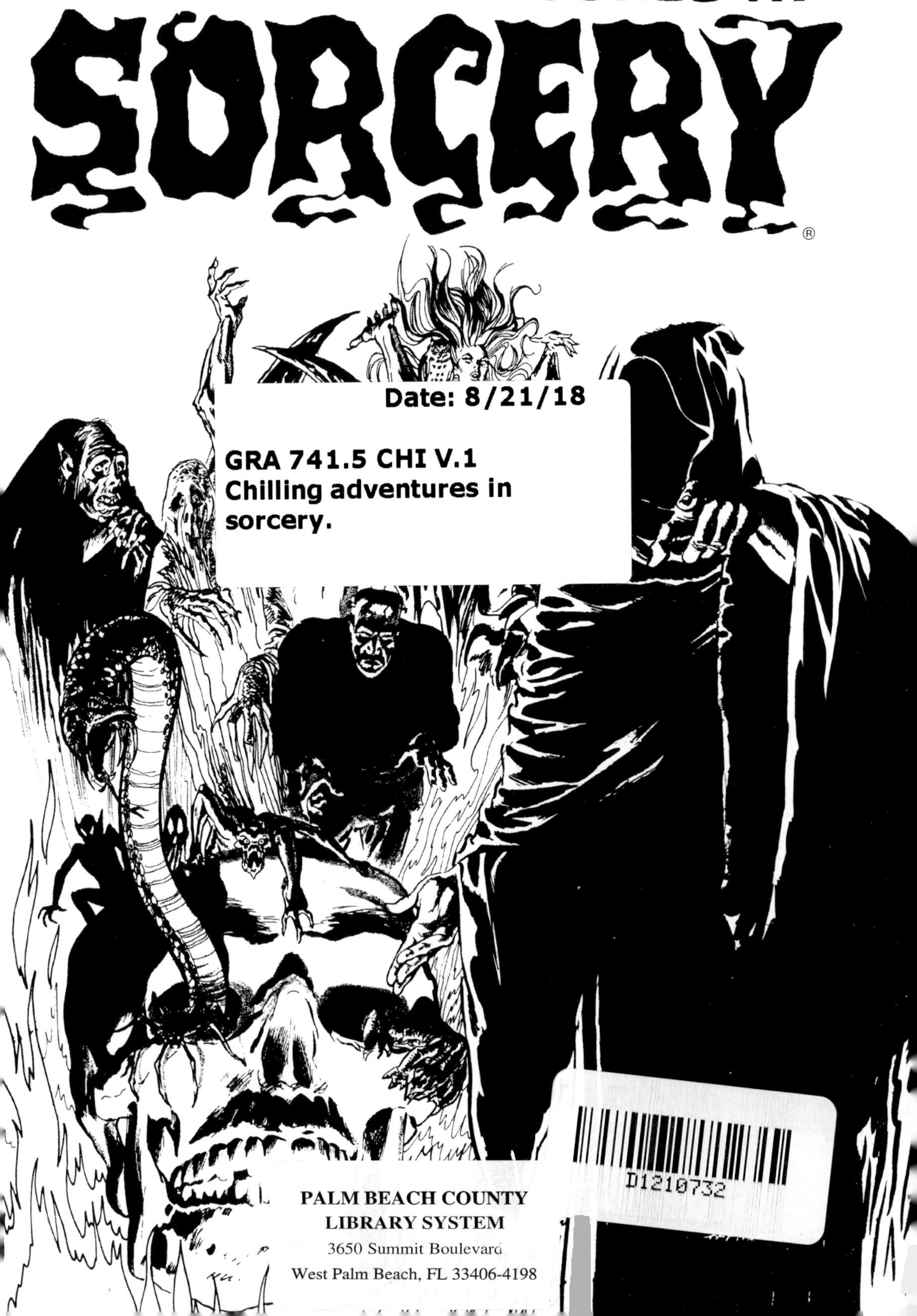

# CHILLING ADVENTURES IN SORCERY

FEATURING THE TALENTS OF

**GRAY MORROW, ALEX TOTH, FRANK THORNE, MARVIN CHANNING, VICENTE ALCAZAR, DICK GIORDANO, HOWARD CHAYKIN, DAN DECARLO, JIM DECARLO, BILL YOSHIDA, FRANK DOYLE, JON D'AGOSTINO, STAN GOLDBERG, MARIO ACQUAVIVA, DON GLUT, PHIL SEULING, CAROLE SEULING, LARRY HAMA, RUDY LAPICK, STEVE SKEATES, MARY SKRENES, ED DAVIS, T. CASEY BRENNAN, CARLOS PINO, HENRY SCARPELLI, BRUCE JONES**

REMASTERED LETTERING BY

**JACK MORELLI** (ISSUES 1 & 2)

EDITOR-IN-CHIEF

**VICTOR GORELICK**

EDITOR/GRAPHIC DESIGN

**VINCENT LOVALLO**

PUBLISHER

**JON GOLDWATER**

This book contains some material that was originally created in a less socially sensitive time in our society and reflects attitudes that may be interpreted as being unacceptable today. The stories are reprinted here without alteration for historical reference.

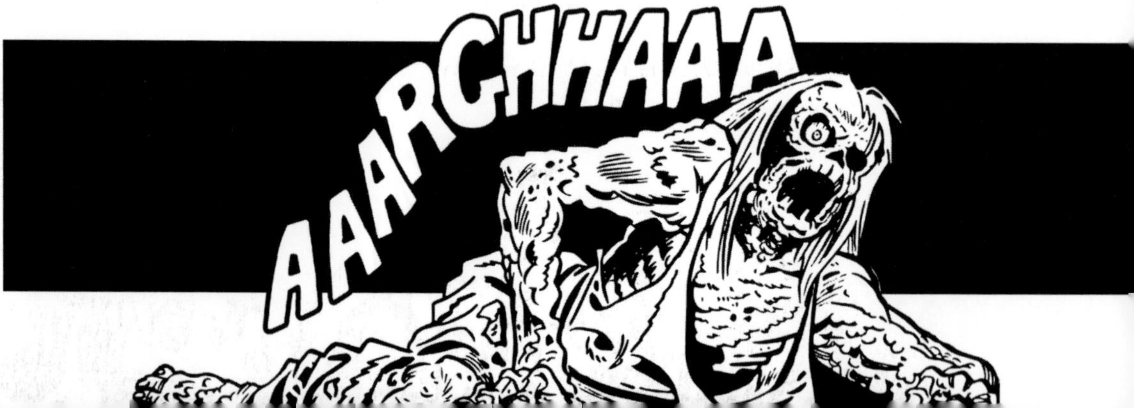
AAARCHHAAA

# INTRODUCTION

The summer I was seven I was obsessed with Moon Landings, Miracle Mets... and MONSTERS! August of that year, my parents rented a small "cabana" at a blue collar beach club called Breezy Point. They were little more than attached tool sheds built on piers in the sand, at what seemed like a mile from any water. Ours came furnished with a tattered couch, rocking chair, and an old foot locker for a coffee table. But when I cracked the lid to peek inside, I discovered that it was actually a treasure chest. Some careless previous occupant had left behind a big stack of comics. MONSTER COMICS!

Many of them were early *Archie's Madhouse* books, and boy, was I in heaven! The frighteningly fun depictions of all the classic monsters, along with ghouls, goblins, aliens and witches, plus the entire Archie gang having every manner of mayhem visited upon them, mesmerized me. I'd lay about on the musty, sandy throw rug and read all day. Mom would literally have to sweep me out of the place with a broom to my backside and the command "Go play!" but I'd just spirit the prized periodicals out under my shirt and slip beneath the boardwalk to continue. Down there among that perfectly creepy backdrop of dark pilings and crossbeams, I would lurk and lurch about, pretending to be the dreadful creatures I'd been marveling over, a la Calvin sans his Hobbes.

Three years later, Archie began publishing *Chilling Adventures in Sorcery*, as told by Sabrina (who actually debuted the same month and year as yours truly!). Each Tuesday, which was the new comics day in my neighborhood, I would fly home from school, swap out my uniform for a pair of Buddy Lee's, and race on my bike to the newsstand at the entrance to the elevated subway. Finding the latest *Chilling Adventures* was like hitting the lotto. The tales were as tantalizing as the art was terrifying. From the gothic Poe set-ups, to the moving O'Henry pay-offs, the stories seemed to be penned just for me. With every gruesome ghoul casting such long, crawling shadows, I could never make it all the way home without stopping en route to read at least one.

They never failed to fuel my imagination, but the one thing I could have never imagined was that by decade's end I would actually be working in the industry that produced them. And even more incredible, that FOUR decades later I would be so impossibly lucky as to be part of the sensational re-launch of the legendary Archie Horror and Madhouse lines. After this long in comics, and having bounced around a bit like a pinball, working on these titles with the likes of Roberto Aquirre-Sacasa, Francesco Francavilla, Robert Hack, Frank Tieri, the Kennedy brothers and Joe Eisma has me humming the Vanessa Williams tune "Save the Best for Last" each morning at my desk.

And now, when editor Vincent Lovallo asked me to play a part in this project, I jumped at what would be a true labor of love. Each story, every image in this volume is for me akin to French author Proust's Madeleine moment in *Remembrance of Things Past*, where a single bite of a fabulous cookie transports him on a magical journey of memory through his youth to the time when he had first tasted one.

We in this business all stand on the shoulders of the titanic talent who built it and who inspired us. I for one can never repay the debt owed the creators whose work is featured here.

So, fright fans, join us as we climb into the Way-Back machine, and set the dial for a time when it was summer, I was seven, and obsessed...

Jack Morelli,
Letterer, *Afterlife with Archie*,
*Chilling Adventures of Sabrina*,
*Jughead the Hunger*

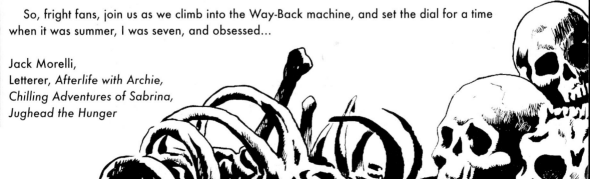

# ISSUE ONE

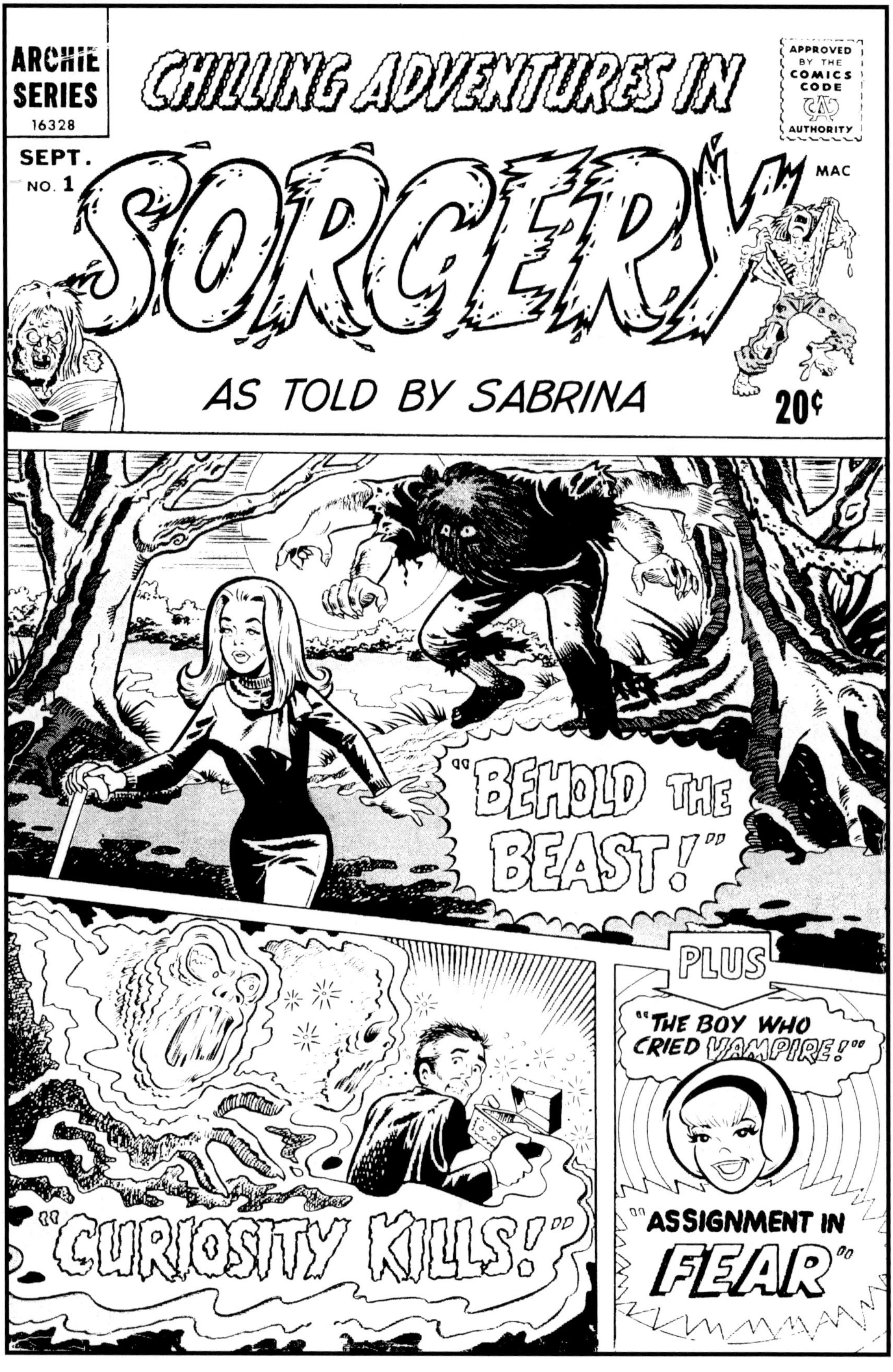
ARCHIE SERIES
16328
APPROVED BY THE COMICS CODE AUTHORITY
CHILLING ADVENTURES IN
SEPT.
NO. 1
SORCERY
MAC
AS TOLD BY SABRINA
20¢
"BEHOLD THE BEAST!"
PLUS
"THE BOY WHO CRIED VAMPIRE!"
"CURIOSITY KILLS!"
"ASSIGNMENT IN FEAR"

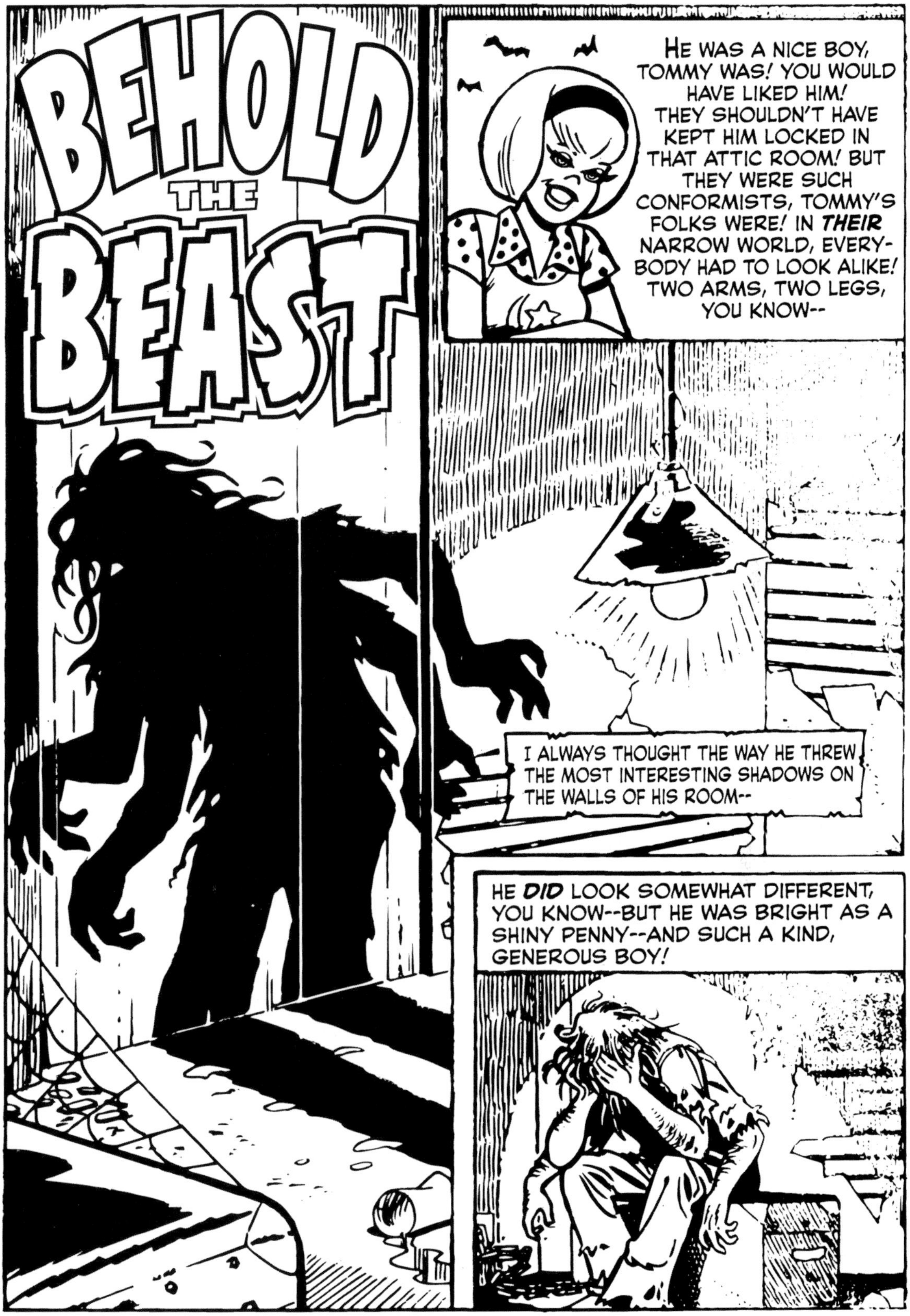
BEHOLD THE BEAST
HE WAS A NICE BOY, TOMMY WAS! YOU WOULD HAVE LIKED HIM! THEY SHOULDN'T HAVE KEPT HIM LOCKED IN THAT ATTIC ROOM! BUT THEY WERE SUCH CONFORMISTS, TOMMY'S FOLKS WERE! IN ***THEIR*** NARROW WORLD, EVERY-BODY HAD TO LOOK ALIKE! TWO ARMS, TWO LEGS, YOU KNOW--
I ALWAYS THOUGHT THE WAY HE THREW THE MOST INTERESTING SHADOWS ON THE WALLS OF HIS ROOM--
HE ***DID*** LOOK SOMEWHAT DIFFERENT, YOU KNOW--BUT HE WAS BRIGHT AS A SHINY PENNY--AND SUCH A KIND, GENEROUS BOY!

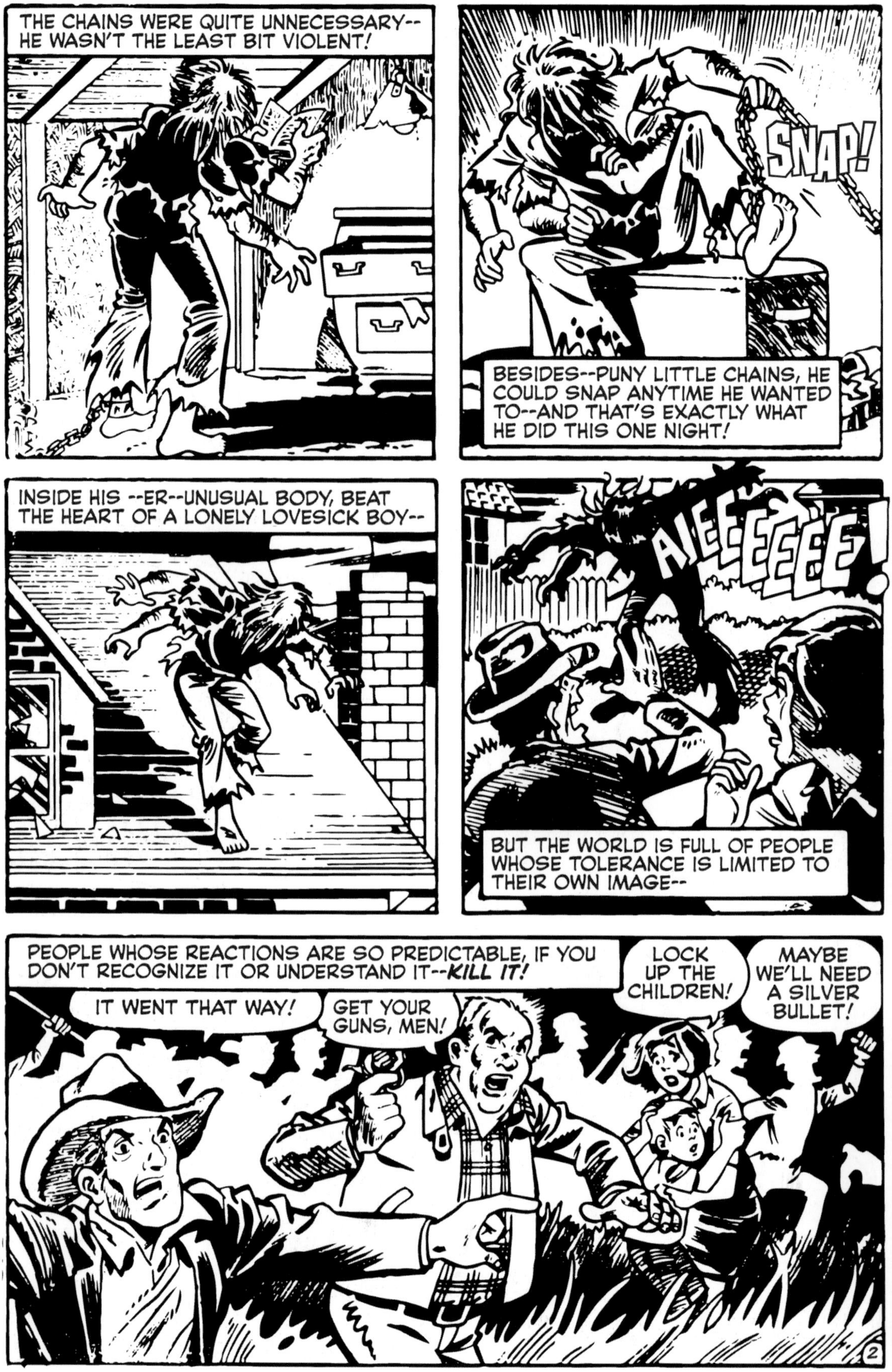

THE CHAINS WERE QUITE UNNECESSARY-- HE WASN'T THE LEAST BIT VIOLENT!
SNAP!
BESIDES--PUNY LITTLE CHAINS, HE COULD SNAP ANYTIME HE WANTED TO--AND THAT'S EXACTLY WHAT HE DID THIS ONE NIGHT!
INSIDE HIS --ER--UNUSUAL BODY, BEAT THE HEART OF A LONELY LOVESICK BOY--
AIEEEEEEE!
BUT THE WORLD IS FULL OF PEOPLE WHOSE TOLERANCE IS LIMITED TO THEIR OWN IMAGE--
PEOPLE WHOSE REACTIONS ARE SO PREDICTABLE, IF YOU DON'T RECOGNIZE IT OR UNDERSTAND IT--*KILL IT!*
IT WENT THAT WAY!
GET YOUR GUNS, MEN!
LOCK UP THE CHILDREN!
MAYBE WE'LL NEED A SILVER BULLET!

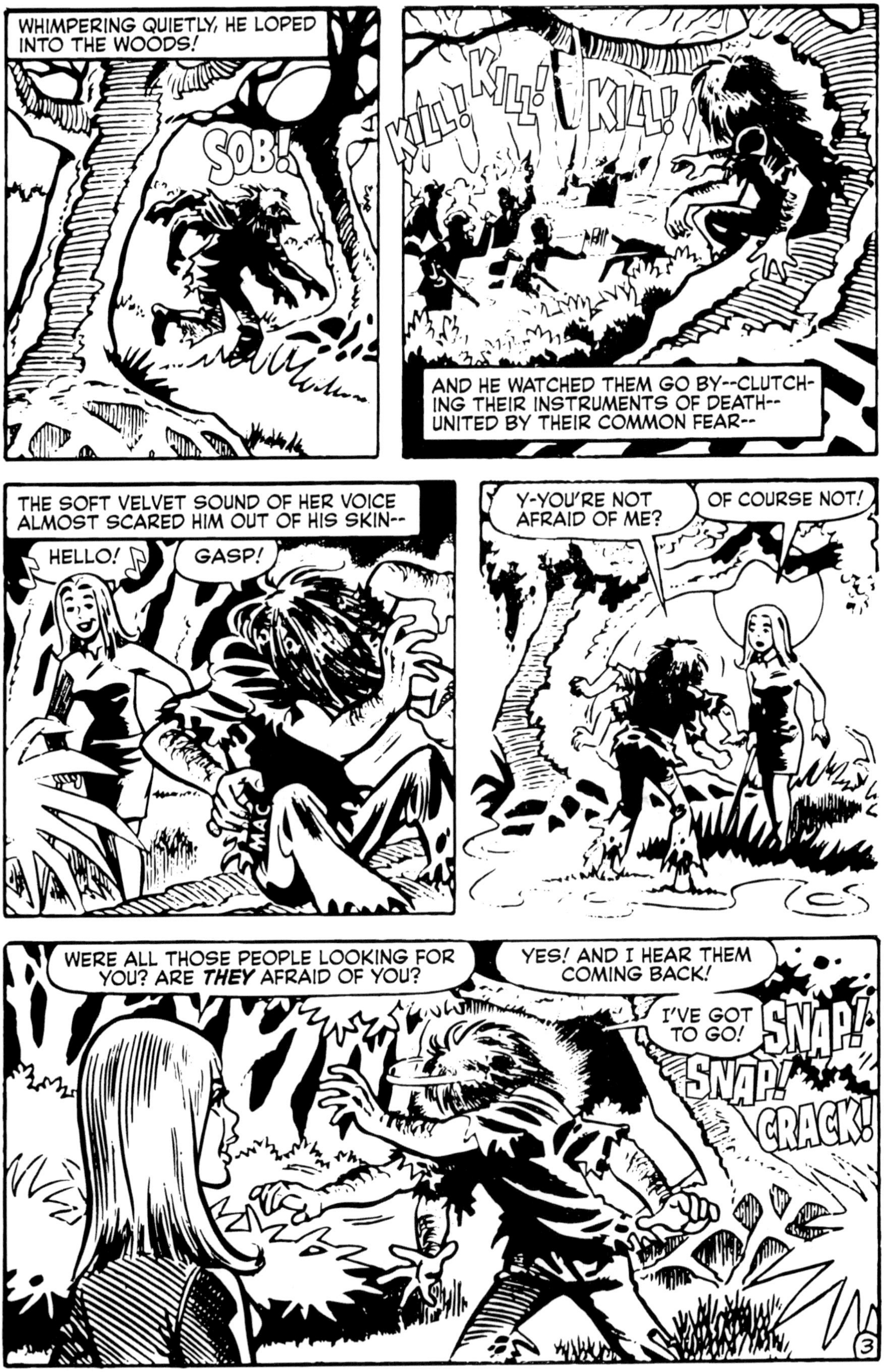

WHIMPERING QUIETLY, HE LOPED INTO THE WOODS!
SOB!
KILL! KILL! KILL!
AND HE WATCHED THEM GO BY--CLUTCHING THEIR INSTRUMENTS OF DEATH--UNITED BY THEIR COMMON FEAR--
THE SOFT VELVET SOUND OF HER VOICE ALMOST SCARED HIM OUT OF HIS SKIN--
HELLO!
GASP!
MAC
Y-YOU'RE NOT AFRAID OF ME?
OF COURSE NOT!
WERE ALL THOSE PEOPLE LOOKING FOR YOU? ARE *THEY* AFRAID OF YOU?
YES! AND I HEAR THEM COMING BACK!
I'VE GOT TO GO!
SNAP!
SNAP!
CRACK!
3

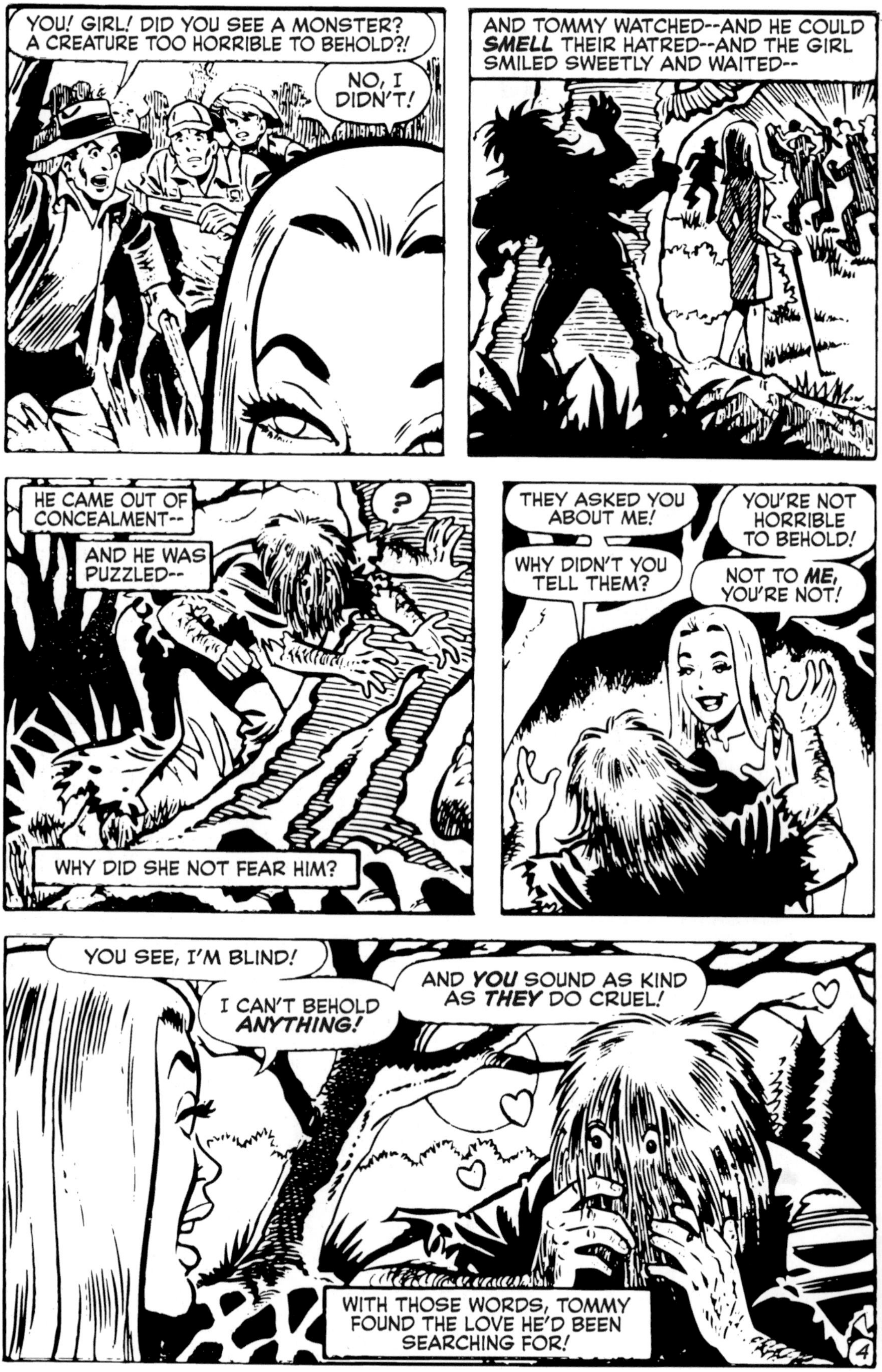
YOU! GIRL! DID YOU SEE A MONSTER? A CREATURE TOO HORRIBLE TO BEHOLD?!
NO, I DIDN'T!
AND TOMMY WATCHED--AND HE COULD SMELL THEIR HATRED--AND THE GIRL SMILED SWEETLY AND WAITED--
HE CAME OUT OF CONCEALMENT--
AND HE WAS PUZZLED--
?
WHY DID SHE NOT FEAR HIM?
THEY ASKED YOU ABOUT ME!
WHY DIDN'T YOU TELL THEM?
YOU'RE NOT HORRIBLE TO BEHOLD!
NOT TO ME, YOU'RE NOT!
YOU SEE, I'M BLIND!
I CAN'T BEHOLD ANYTHING!
AND YOU SOUND AS KIND AS THEY DO CRUEL!
WITH THOSE WORDS, TOMMY FOUND THE LOVE HE'D BEEN SEARCHING FOR!
4

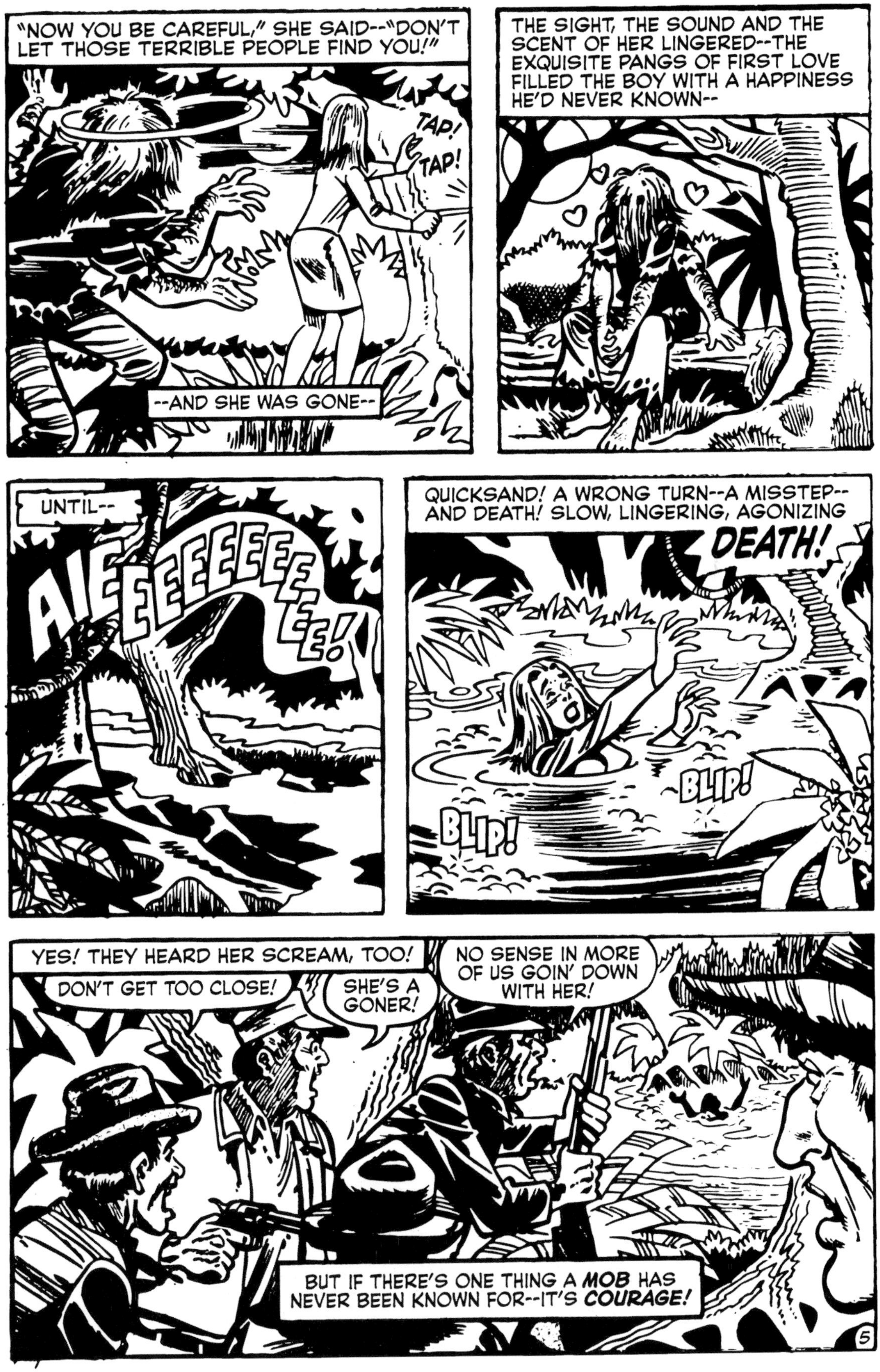
"NOW YOU BE CAREFUL," SHE SAID--"DON'T LET THOSE TERRIBLE PEOPLE FIND YOU!"
TAP! TAP!
--AND SHE WAS GONE--
THE SIGHT, THE SOUND AND THE SCENT OF HER LINGERED--THE EXQUISITE PANGS OF FIRST LOVE FILLED THE BOY WITH A HAPPINESS HE'D NEVER KNOWN--
UNTIL--
AIEEEEEEEEEEE!
QUICKSAND! A WRONG TURN--A MISSTEP--AND DEATH! SLOW, LINGERING, AGONIZING DEATH!
BLIP!
BLIP!
YES! THEY HEARD HER SCREAM, TOO!
DON'T GET TOO CLOSE!
SHE'S A GONER!
NO SENSE IN MORE OF US GOIN' DOWN WITH HER!
BUT IF THERE'S ONE THING A MOB HAS NEVER BEEN KNOWN FOR--IT'S COURAGE!
5

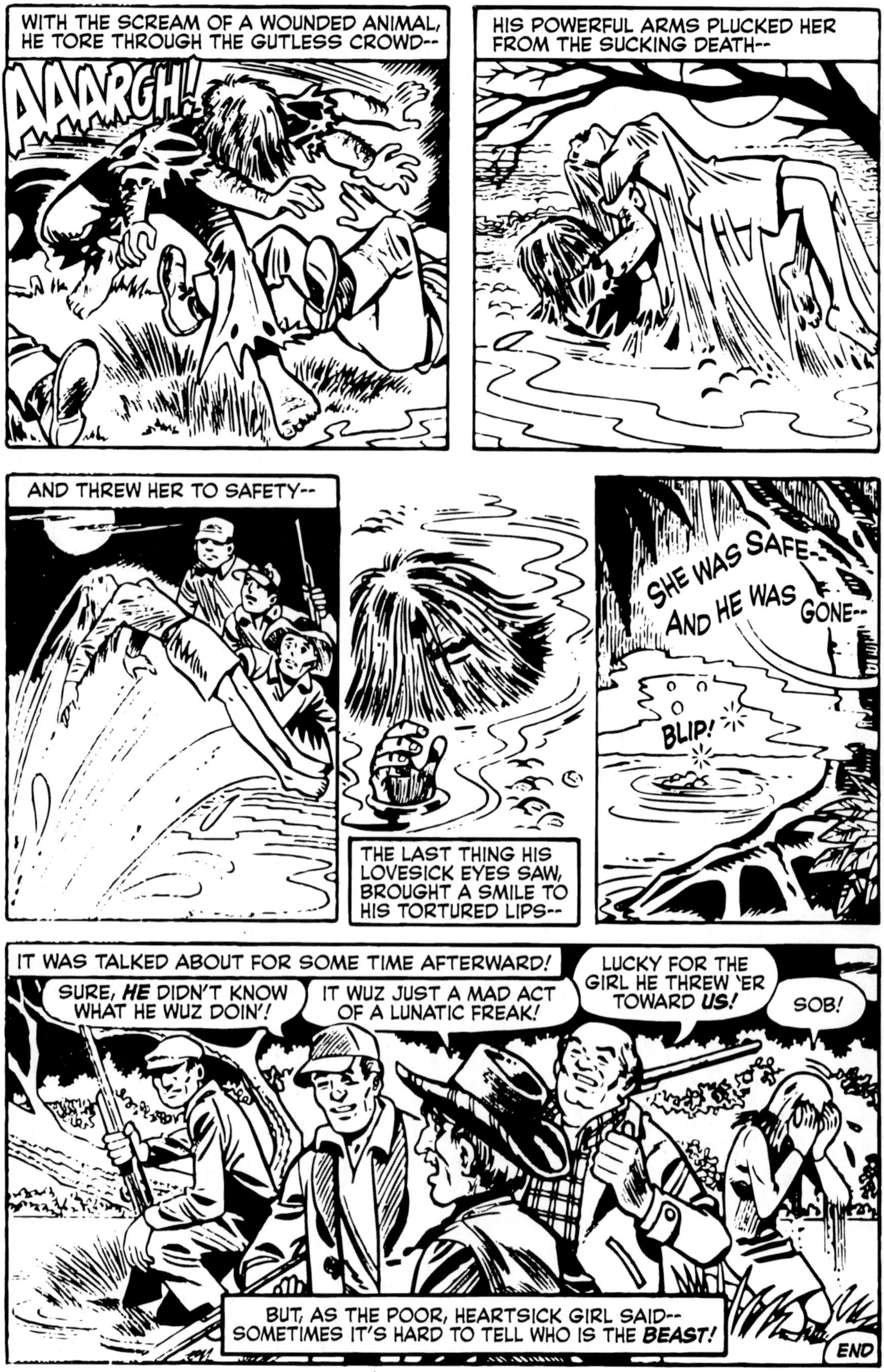
WITH THE SCREAM OF A WOUNDED ANIMAL, HE TORE THROUGH THE GUTLESS CROWD--
AAARGH!
HIS POWERFUL ARMS PLUCKED HER FROM THE SUCKING DEATH--
AND THREW HER TO SAFETY--
THE LAST THING HIS LOVESICK EYES SAW, BROUGHT A SMILE TO HIS TORTURED LIPS--
SHE WAS SAFE--
AND HE WAS GONE--
BLIP!
IT WAS TALKED ABOUT FOR SOME TIME AFTERWARD!
SURE, HE DIDN'T KNOW WHAT HE WUZ DOIN'!
IT WUZ JUST A MAD ACT OF A LUNATIC FREAK!
LUCKY FOR THE GIRL HE THREW 'ER TOWARD US!
SOB!
BUT, AS THE POOR, HEARTSICK GIRL SAID-- SOMETIMES IT'S HARD TO TELL WHO IS THE BEAST!
END

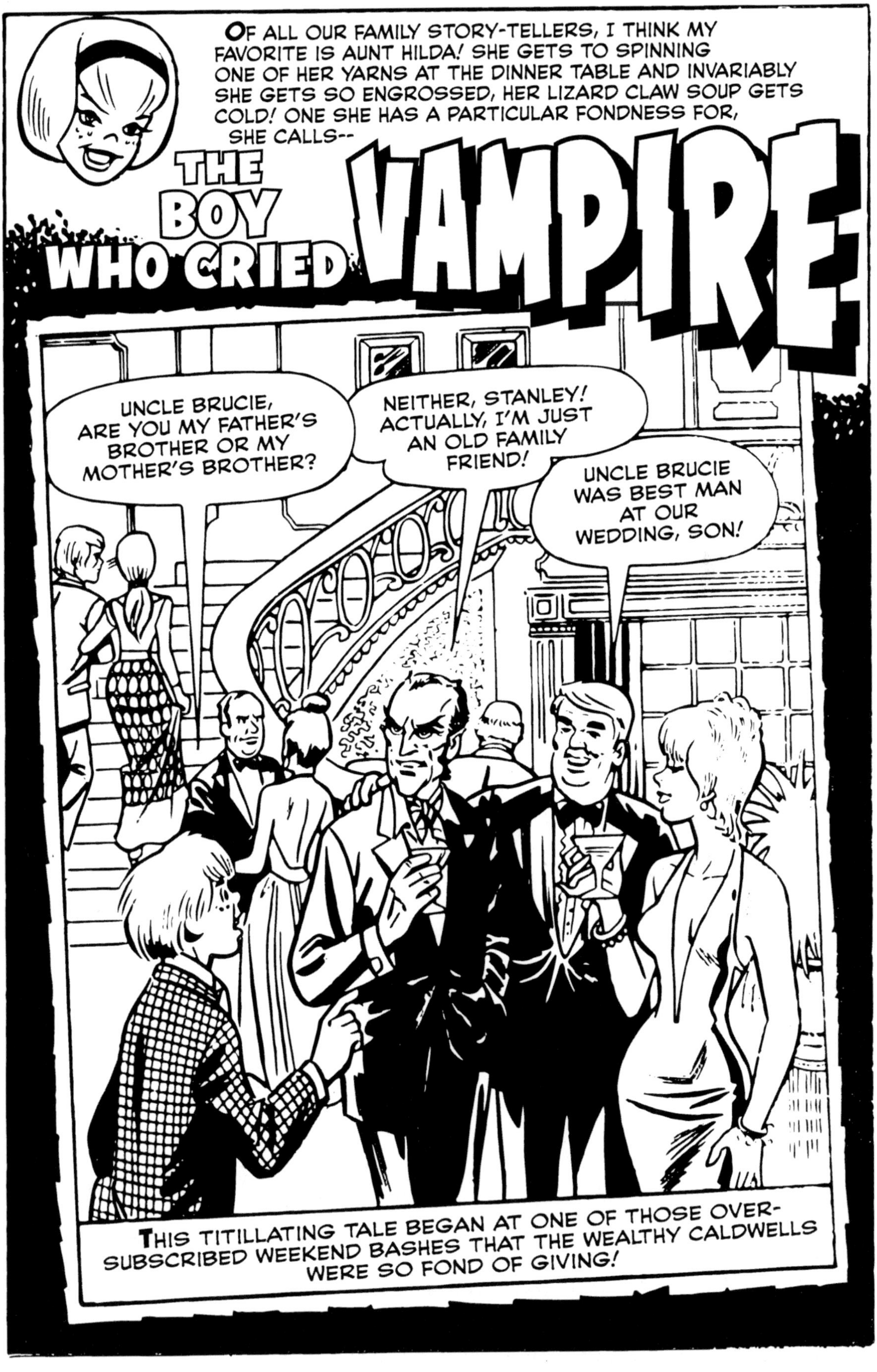

OF ALL OUR FAMILY STORY-TELLERS, I THINK MY FAVORITE IS AUNT HILDA! SHE GETS TO SPINNING ONE OF HER YARNS AT THE DINNER TABLE AND INVARIABLY SHE GETS SO ENGROSSED, HER LIZARD CLAW SOUP GETS COLD! ONE SHE HAS A PARTICULAR FONDNESS FOR, SHE CALLS--
THE BOY WHO CRIED VAMPIRE
UNCLE BRUCIE, ARE YOU MY FATHER'S BROTHER OR MY MOTHER'S BROTHER?
NEITHER, STANLEY! ACTUALLY, I'M JUST AN OLD FAMILY FRIEND!
UNCLE BRUCIE WAS BEST MAN AT OUR WEDDING, SON!
THIS TITILLATING TALE BEGAN AT ONE OF THOSE OVER-SUBSCRIBED WEEKEND BASHES THAT THE WEALTHY CALDWELLS WERE SO FOND OF GIVING!

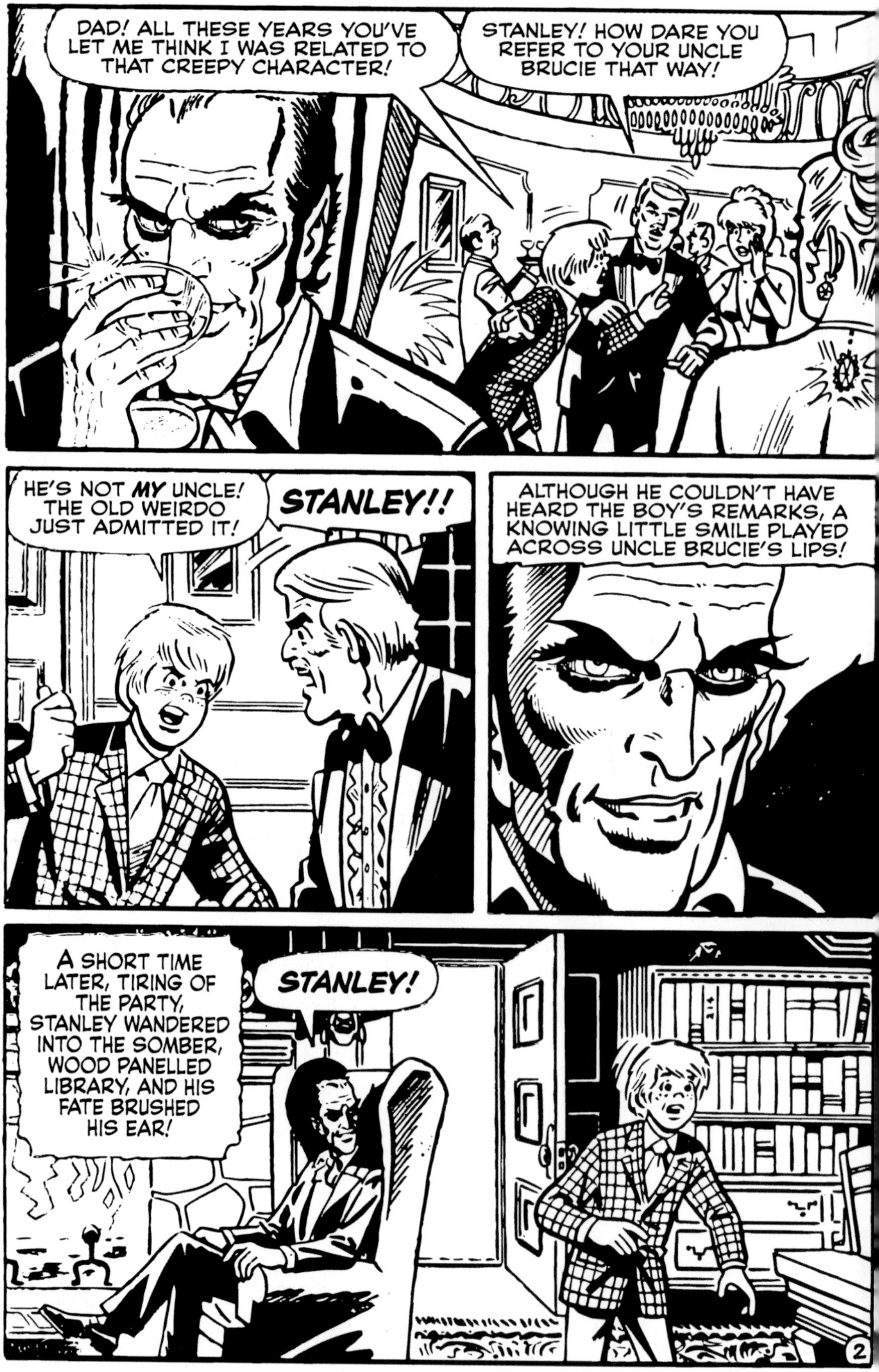
DAD! ALL THESE YEARS YOU'VE LET ME THINK I WAS RELATED TO THAT CREEPY CHARACTER!
STANLEY! HOW DARE YOU REFER TO YOUR UNCLE BRUCIE THAT WAY!
HE'S NOT *MY* UNCLE! THE OLD WEIRDO JUST ADMITTED IT!
STANLEY!!
ALTHOUGH HE COULDN'T HAVE HEARD THE BOY'S REMARKS, A KNOWING LITTLE SMILE PLAYED ACROSS UNCLE BRUCIE'S LIPS!
A SHORT TIME LATER, TIRING OF THE PARTY, STANLEY WANDERED INTO THE SOMBER, WOOD PANELLED LIBRARY, AND HIS FATE BRUSHED HIS EAR!
STANLEY!
2

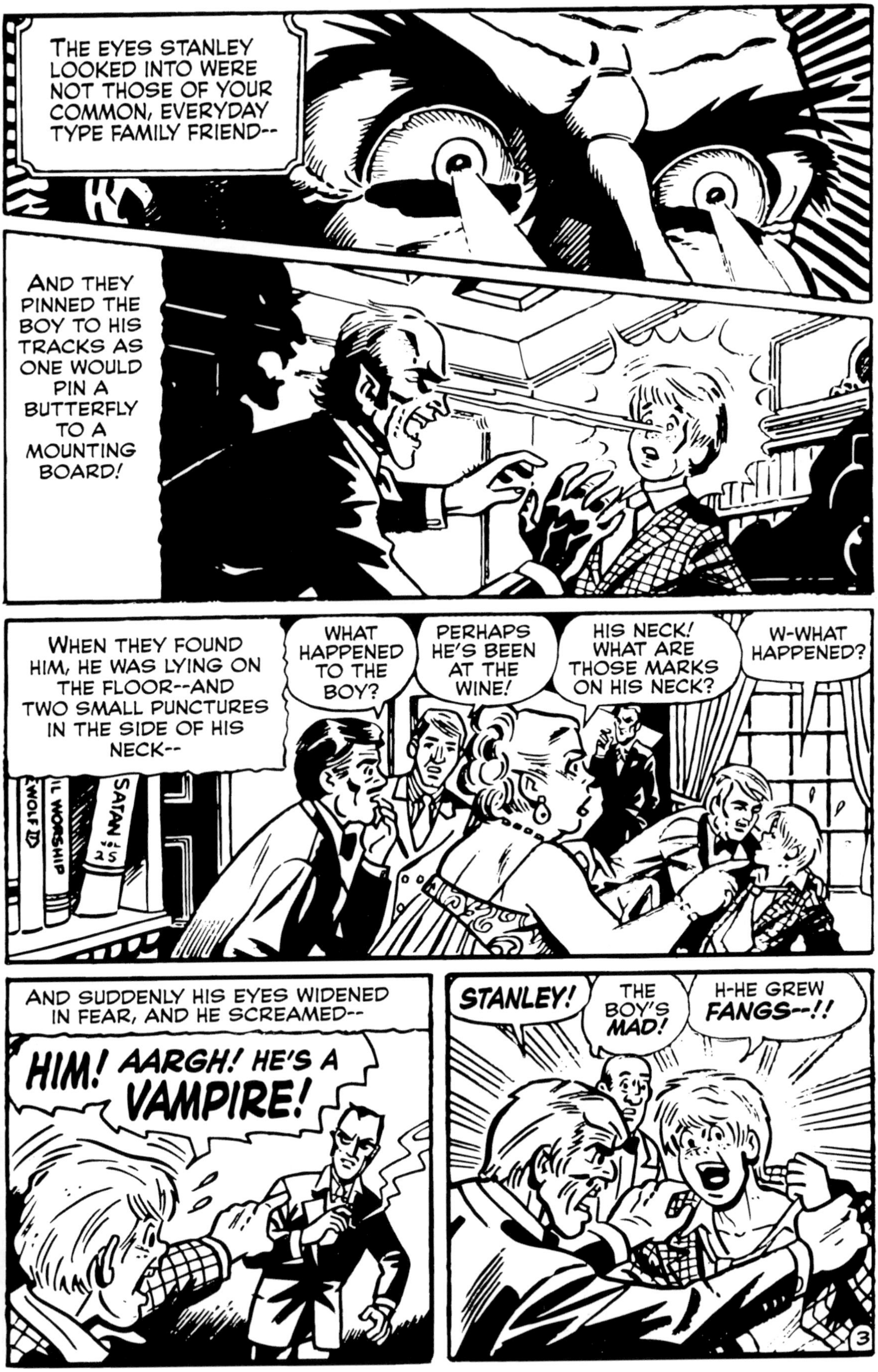
THE EYES STANLEY LOOKED INTO WERE NOT THOSE OF YOUR COMMON, EVERYDAY TYPE FAMILY FRIEND--
AND THEY PINNED THE BOY TO HIS TRACKS AS ONE WOULD PIN A BUTTERFLY TO A MOUNTING BOARD!
WHEN THEY FOUND HIM, HE WAS LYING ON THE FLOOR--AND TWO SMALL PUNCTURES IN THE SIDE OF HIS NECK--
WHAT HAPPENED TO THE BOY?
PERHAPS HE'S BEEN AT THE WINE!
HIS NECK! WHAT ARE THOSE MARKS ON HIS NECK?
W-WHAT HAPPENED?
SATAN
AND SUDDENLY HIS EYES WIDENED IN FEAR, AND HE SCREAMED--
HIM! AARGH! HE'S A VAMPIRE!
STANLEY!
THE BOY'S MAD!
H-HE GREW FANGS--!!

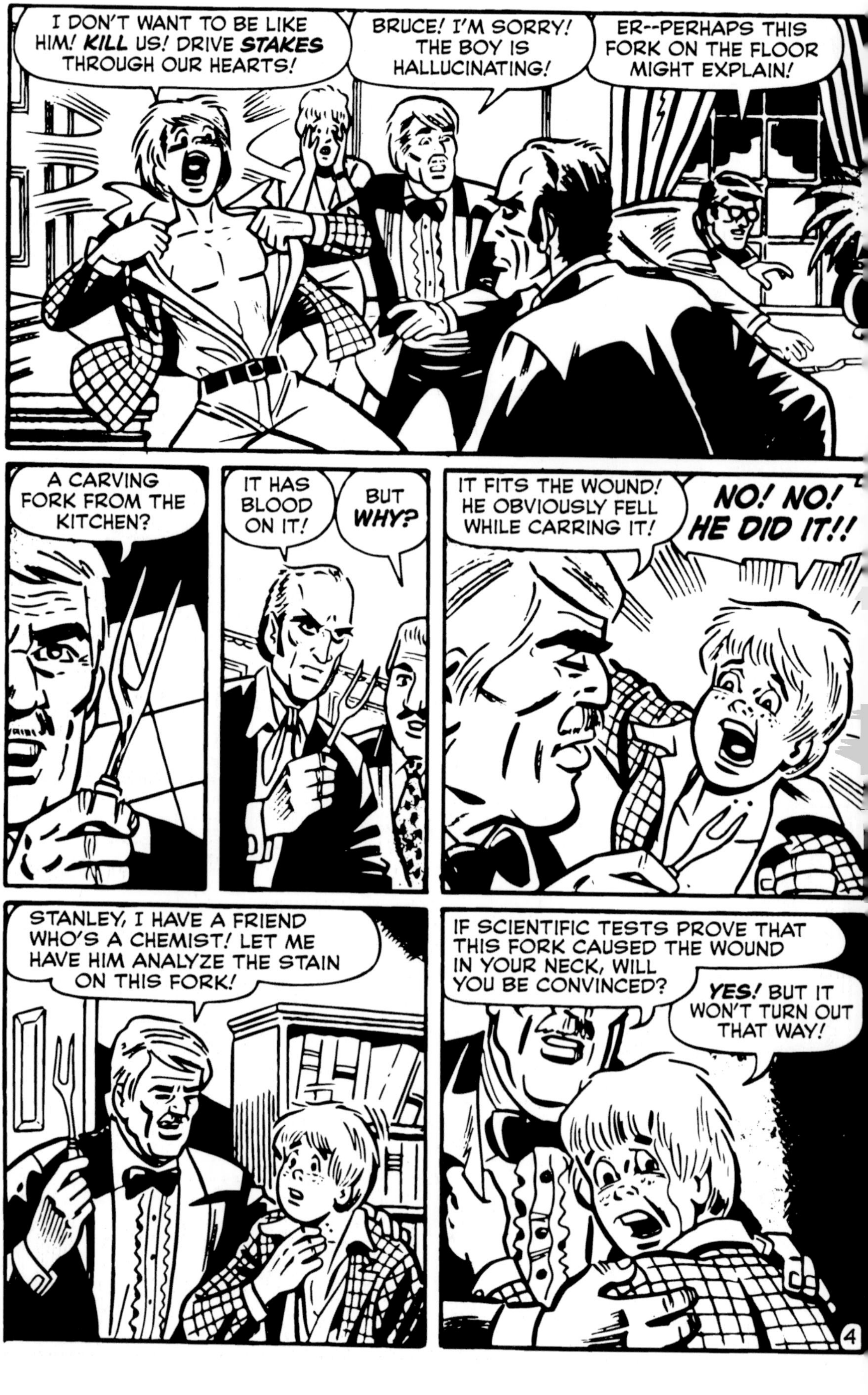
I DON'T WANT TO BE LIKE HIM! KILL US! DRIVE STAKES THROUGH OUR HEARTS!
BRUCE! I'M SORRY! THE BOY IS HALLUCINATING!
ER--PERHAPS THIS FORK ON THE FLOOR MIGHT EXPLAIN!
A CARVING FORK FROM THE KITCHEN?
IT HAS BLOOD ON IT!
BUT WHY?
IT FITS THE WOUND! HE OBVIOUSLY FELL WHILE CARRING IT!
NO! NO! HE DID IT!!
STANLEY, I HAVE A FRIEND WHO'S A CHEMIST! LET ME HAVE HIM ANALYZE THE STAIN ON THIS FORK!
IF SCIENTIFIC TESTS PROVE THAT THIS FORK CAUSED THE WOUND IN YOUR NECK, WILL YOU BE CONVINCED?
YES! BUT IT WON'T TURN OUT THAT WAY!
4

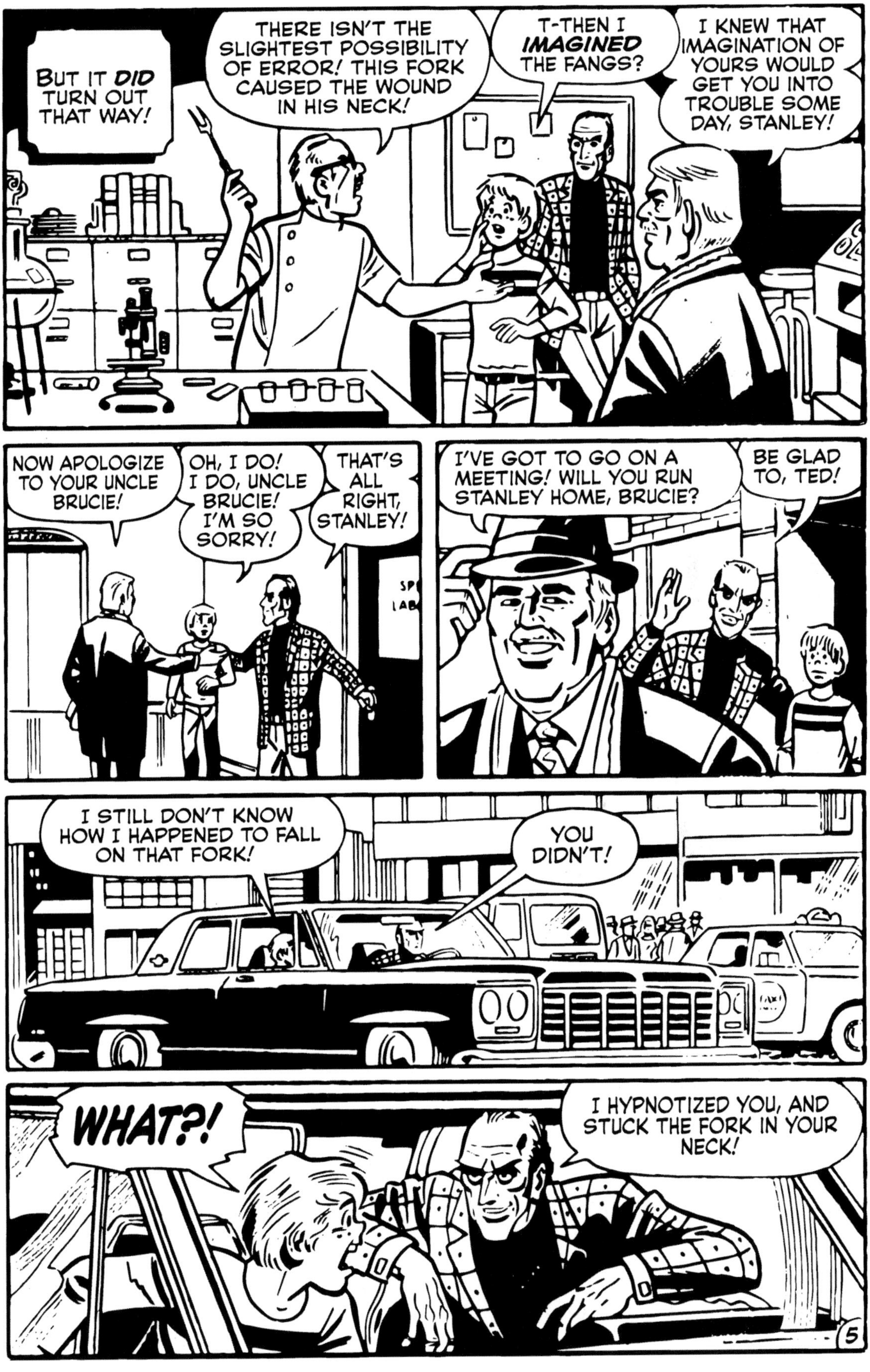

BUT IT DID TURN OUT THAT WAY!
THERE ISN'T THE SLIGHTEST POSSIBILITY OF ERROR! THIS FORK CAUSED THE WOUND IN HIS NECK!
T-THEN I IMAGINED THE FANGS?
I KNEW THAT IMAGINATION OF YOURS WOULD GET YOU INTO TROUBLE SOME DAY, STANLEY!
NOW APOLOGIZE TO YOUR UNCLE BRUCIE!
OH, I DO! I DO, UNCLE BRUCIE! I'M SO SORRY!
THAT'S ALL RIGHT, STANLEY!
I'VE GOT TO GO ON A MEETING! WILL YOU RUN STANLEY HOME, BRUCIE?
BE GLAD TO, TED!
I STILL DON'T KNOW HOW I HAPPENED TO FALL ON THAT FORK!
YOU DIDN'T!
WHAT?!
I HYPNOTIZED YOU, AND STUCK THE FORK IN YOUR NECK!
5

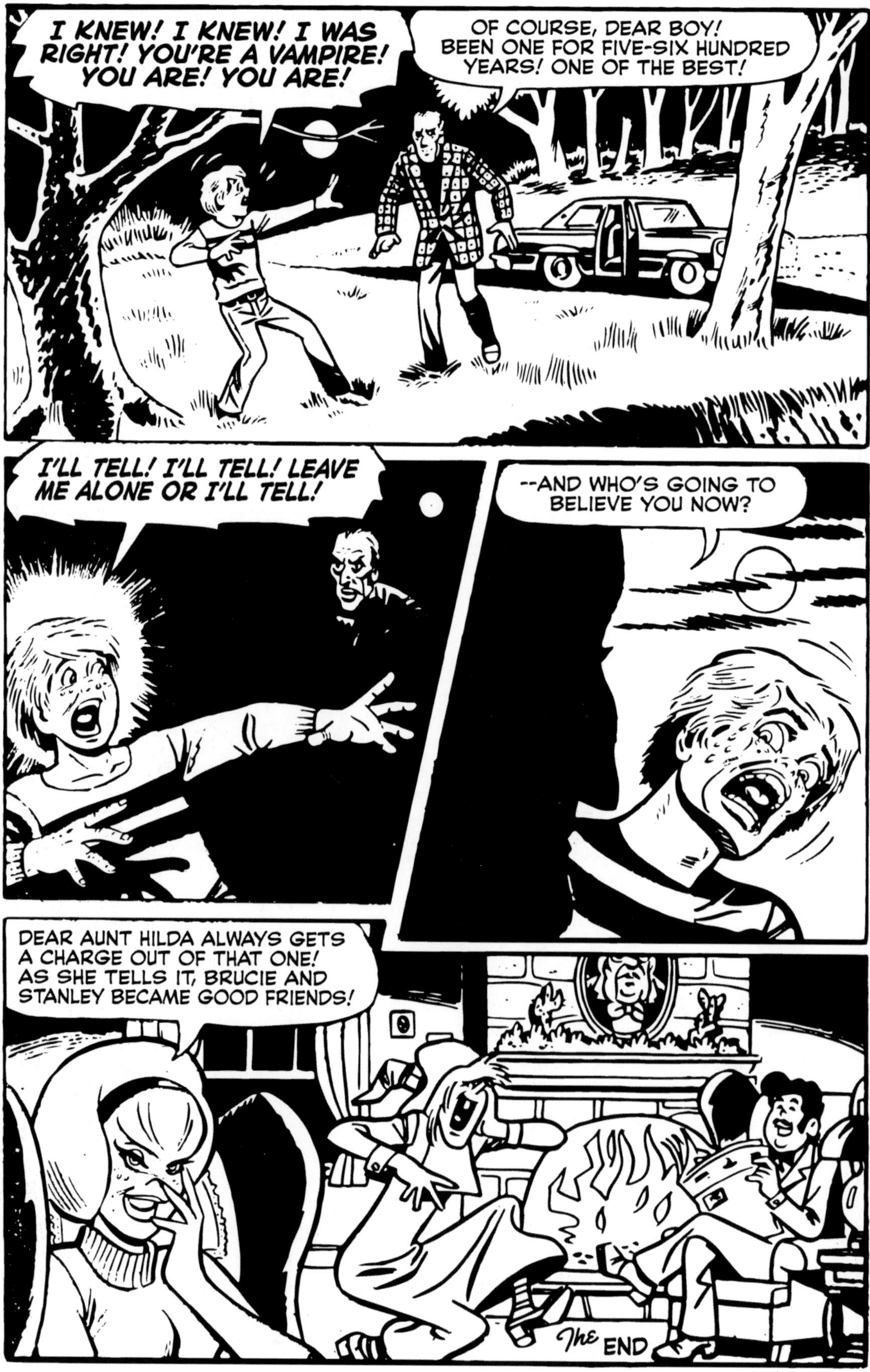
I KNEW! I KNEW! I WAS RIGHT! YOU'RE A VAMPIRE! YOU ARE! YOU ARE!
OF COURSE, DEAR BOY! BEEN ONE FOR FIVE-SIX HUNDRED YEARS! ONE OF THE BEST!
I'LL TELL! I'LL TELL! LEAVE ME ALONE OR I'LL TELL!
--AND WHO'S GOING TO BELIEVE YOU NOW?
DEAR AUNT HILDA ALWAYS GETS A CHARGE OUT OF THAT ONE! AS SHE TELLS IT, BRUCIE AND STANLEY BECAME GOOD FRIENDS!
The END

## CHILLING ADVENTURES IN SORCERY

# ASSIGNMENT IN FEAR

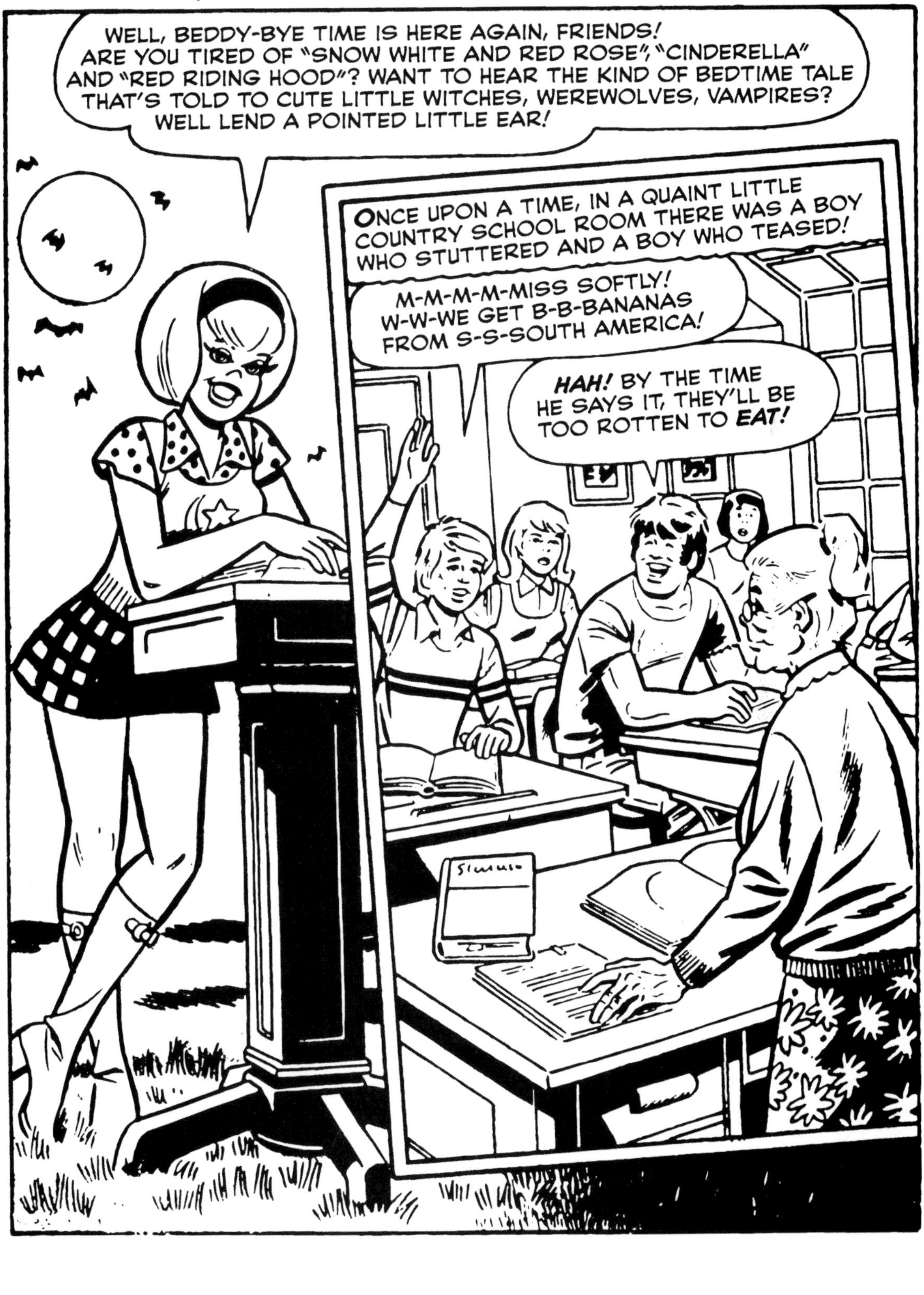
WELL, BEDDY-BYE TIME IS HERE AGAIN, FRIENDS! ARE YOU TIRED OF "SNOW WHITE AND RED ROSE", "CINDERELLA" AND "RED RIDING HOOD"? WANT TO HEAR THE KIND OF BEDTIME TALE THAT'S TOLD TO CUTE LITTLE WITCHES, WEREWOLVES, VAMPIRES? WELL LEND A POINTED LITTLE EAR!
ONCE UPON A TIME, IN A QUAINT LITTLE COUNTRY SCHOOL ROOM THERE WAS A BOY WHO STUTTERED AND A BOY WHO TEASED!
M-M-M-M-MISS SOFTLY! W-W-WE GET B-B-BANANAS FROM S-S-SOUTH AMERICA!
HAH! BY THE TIME HE SAYS IT, THEY'LL BE TOO ROTTEN TO EAT!

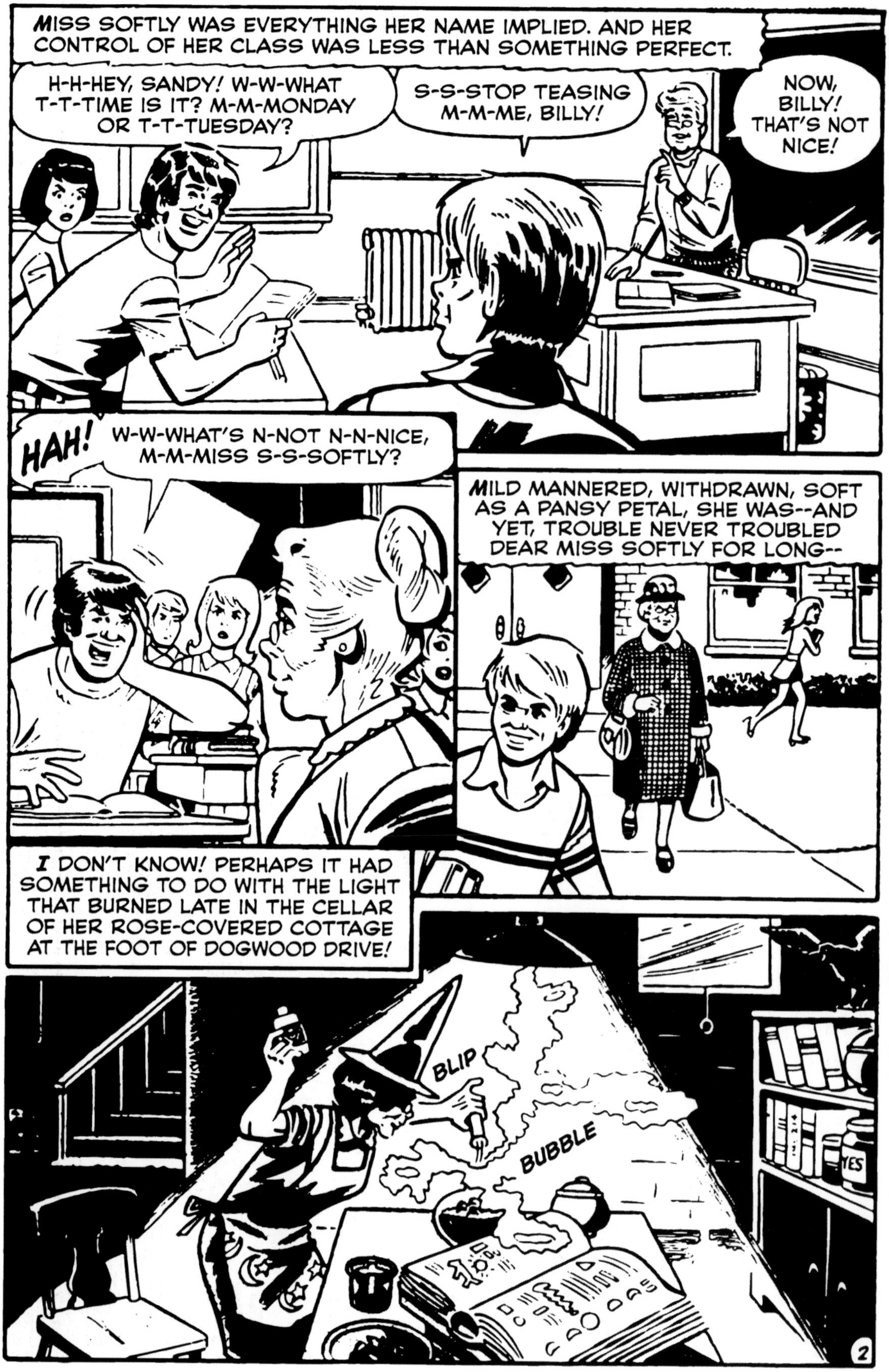
MISS SOFTLY WAS EVERYTHING HER NAME IMPLIED. AND HER CONTROL OF HER CLASS WAS LESS THAN SOMETHING PERFECT.
H-H-HEY, SANDY! W-W-WHAT T-T-TIME IS IT? M-M-MONDAY OR T-T-TUESDAY?
S-S-STOP TEASING M-M-ME, BILLY!
NOW, BILLY! THAT'S NOT NICE!
HAH!
W-W-WHAT'S N-NOT N-N-NICE, M-M-MISS S-S-SOFTLY?
MILD MANNERED, WITHDRAWN, SOFT AS A PANSY PETAL, SHE WAS--AND YET, TROUBLE NEVER TROUBLED DEAR MISS SOFTLY FOR LONG--
I DON'T KNOW! PERHAPS IT HAD SOMETHING TO DO WITH THE LIGHT THAT BURNED LATE IN THE CELLAR OF HER ROSE-COVERED COTTAGE AT THE FOOT OF DOGWOOD DRIVE!
BLIP
BUBBLE
YES
2

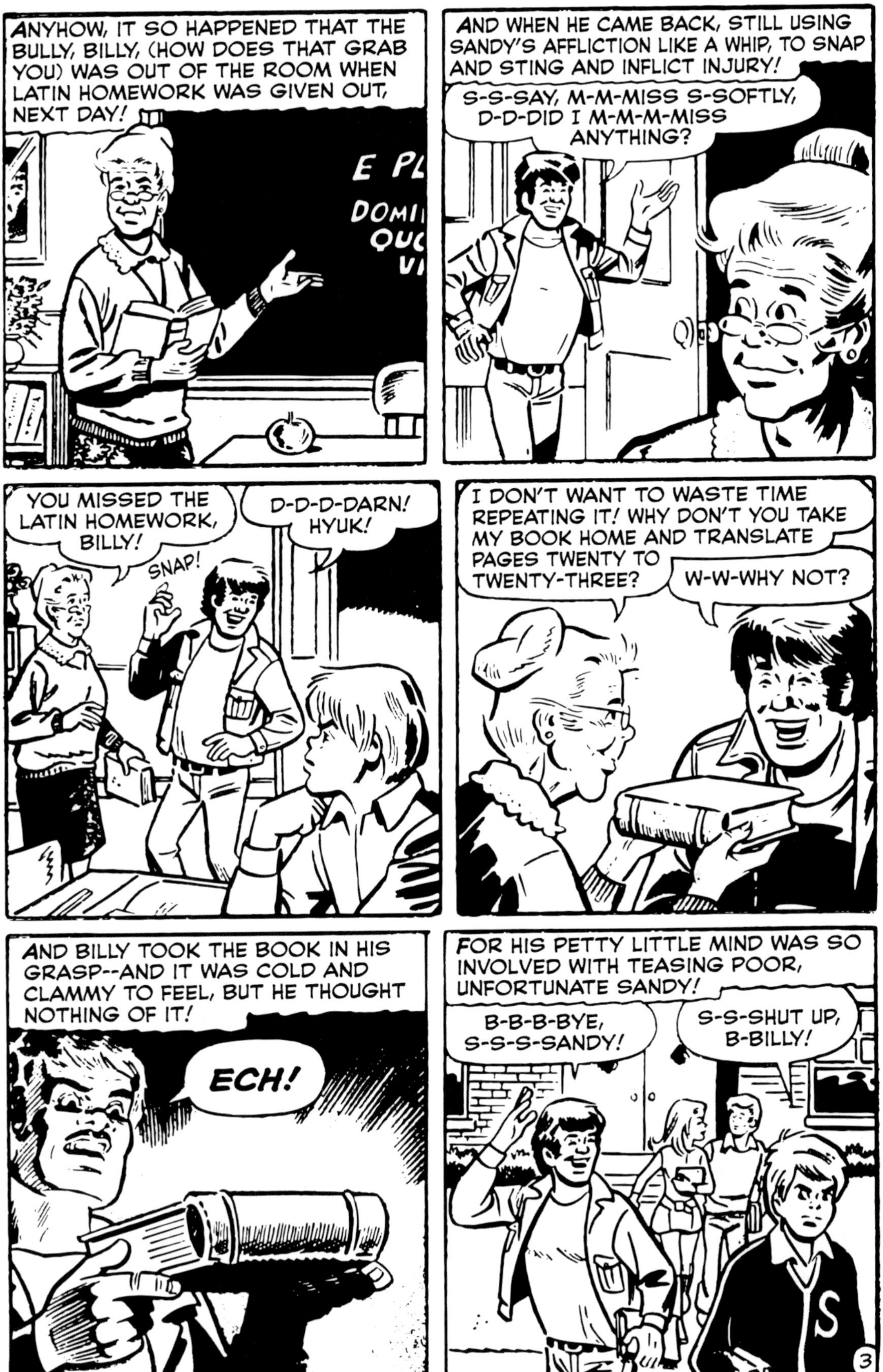
ANYHOW, IT SO HAPPENED THAT THE BULLY, BILLY, (HOW DOES THAT GRAB YOU) WAS OUT OF THE ROOM WHEN LATIN HOMEWORK WAS GIVEN OUT, NEXT DAY!
AND WHEN HE CAME BACK, STILL USING SANDY'S AFFLICTION LIKE A WHIP, TO SNAP AND STING AND INFLICT INJURY!
S-S-SAY, M-M-MISS S-SOFTLY, D-D-DID I M-M-M-MISS ANYTHING?
YOU MISSED THE LATIN HOMEWORK, BILLY!
SNAP!
D-D-D-DARN! HYUK!
I DON'T WANT TO WASTE TIME REPEATING IT! WHY DON'T YOU TAKE MY BOOK HOME AND TRANSLATE PAGES TWENTY TO TWENTY-THREE?
W-W-WHY NOT?
AND BILLY TOOK THE BOOK IN HIS GRASP--AND IT WAS COLD AND CLAMMY TO FEEL, BUT HE THOUGHT NOTHING OF IT!
ECH!
FOR HIS PETTY LITTLE MIND WAS SO INVOLVED WITH TEASING POOR, UNFORTUNATE SANDY!
B-B-B-BYE, S-S-S-SANDY!
S-S-SHUT UP, B-BILLY!
S

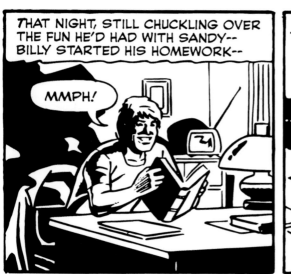

THAT NIGHT, STILL CHUCKLING OVER THE FUN HE'D HAD WITH SANDY-- BILLY STARTED HIS HOMEWORK--

MMPH!

AND AS HE TRANSLATED THE LATIN FROM THE MUSTY OLD TOME--

"AND THE EVIL WITHIN SHALL BUBBLE AND BOIL--"

"THE SULPHUROUS FUMES OF BEELZEBUB SHALL RISE TO THE SURFACE--"

"AND THE MARK OF THE DEVIL SHALL BE UPON THE FLESH!"

AAARGHHAAA

SOB

4

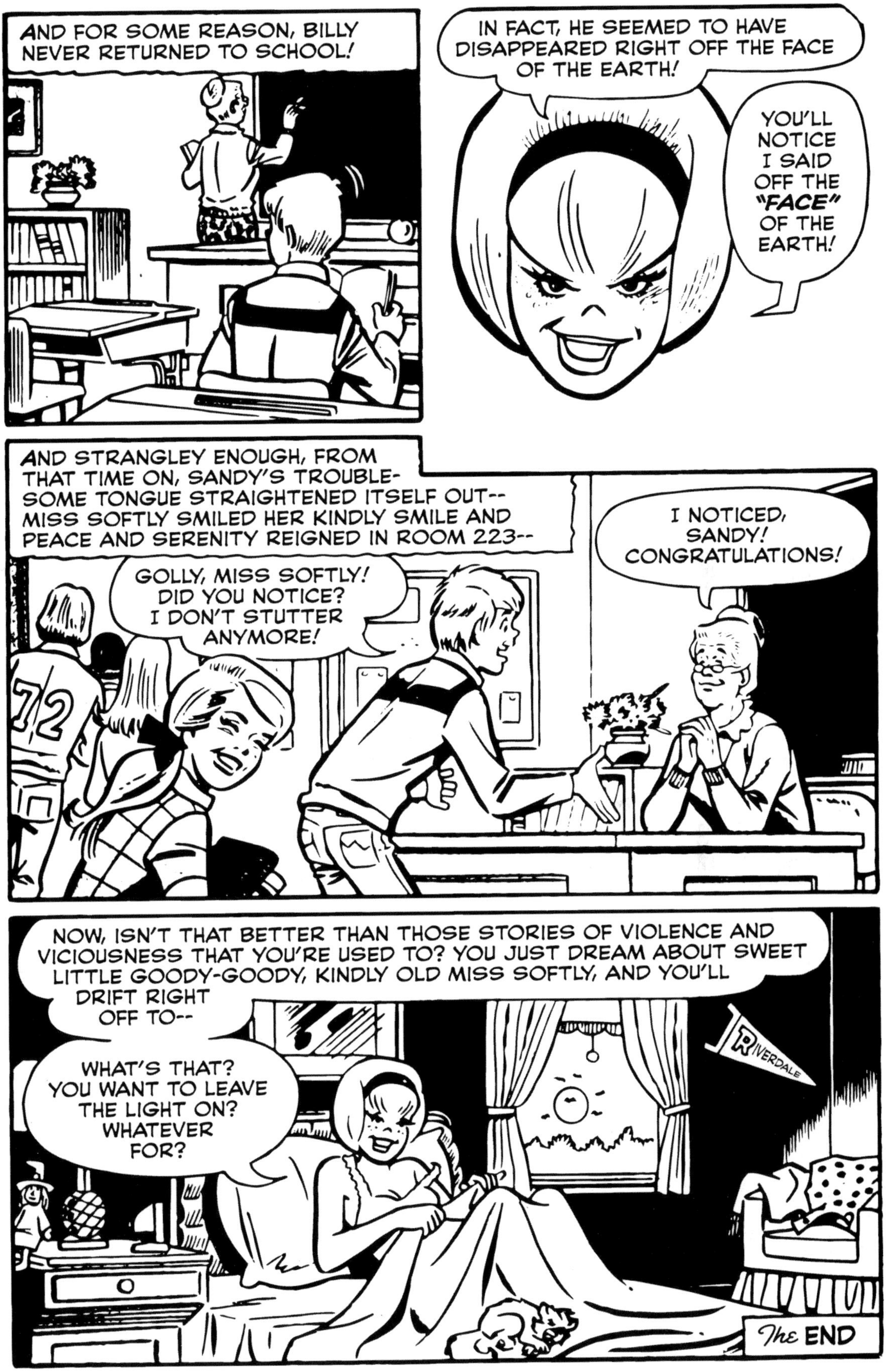
AND FOR SOME REASON, BILLY NEVER RETURNED TO SCHOOL!
IN FACT, HE SEEMED TO HAVE DISAPPEARED RIGHT OFF THE FACE OF THE EARTH!
YOU'LL NOTICE I SAID OFF THE "FACE" OF THE EARTH!
AND STRANGLEY ENOUGH, FROM THAT TIME ON, SANDY'S TROUBLE-SOME TONGUE STRAIGHTENED ITSELF OUT-- MISS SOFTLY SMILED HER KINDLY SMILE AND PEACE AND SERENITY REIGNED IN ROOM 223--
GOLLY, MISS SOFTLY! DID YOU NOTICE? I DON'T STUTTER ANYMORE!
I NOTICED, SANDY! CONGRATULATIONS!
72
NOW, ISN'T THAT BETTER THAN THOSE STORIES OF VIOLENCE AND VICIOUSNESS THAT YOU'RE USED TO? YOU JUST DREAM ABOUT SWEET LITTLE GOODY-GOODY, KINDLY OLD MISS SOFTLY, AND YOU'LL DRIFT RIGHT OFF TO--
WHAT'S THAT? YOU WANT TO LEAVE THE LIGHT ON? WHATEVER FOR?
RIVERDALE
The END

# CHILLING ADVENTURES IN SORGERY

# A REAL HOT TALENT

Jugglin' is what I wished I coulda' done. Ol' Charlie Thornwell—he could juggle up a storm. Man, that ol' Charlie was good all right. He'd take three apples, or oranges, or tennis balls, or anything, an' he could keep them goin' in the air somethin' fierce.

Andy Fortunato could spit and nail a fly on the wall every time.

Even girls—like Sally Crenshaw. There wasn't nobody could walk on their hands like Sally. She could even climb a ladder on her hands if she was a mind to. Honest! I ain't puttin' you on. I seen her do that with my own eyes.

Talent? Everybody had some kind of talent they could show off with; be a big shot with; have everybody look at them bug-eyed and say, "Golly, I wish I could do that!" Everybody but me, that is. There wasn't nothin' I could do to call attention to myself.

Except think fire.

When I was maybe two-three years old, the kid in the next apartment—he got this real neat truck and he wouldn't let me play with it. He was mean, that kid. Mean and selfish. I wanted to touch that truck, and play with it so bad—

That was the first time. I remember it so clear! I clenched my fists until the knuckles turned white. The mad was in me so fierce, that I thought I'd bust right open and the hate for that rotten kid seemed to fill the whole room where we was playin' and I wished his lousy truck would burn up right in front of his selfish fat face and he let out a yelp and pulled his hand back and the truck glowed kinda red and a little smoke came from it and, poof!

When his mother dumped a pot of water on it, there wasn't nothin' left but a black, twisted mess of metal. We both caught it for that, because nobody would believe we wasn't playing with matches. But I didn't care. It was worth it. I giggled all night, listening to him cryin' in the next apartment. Next time maybe he'd learn not to be so selfish. Especially with me!

But, look, you got a talent for settin' fire to anything just by thinkin' about it, right? So who you gonna brag to? Y'see what I mean? This ain't jugglin', or spittin', or walkin' on your hands. Once they learnt about this little—uh—knack of mine, they'd be pickin' me up every time some joker flipped a cigarette butt.

So I watched the other kids get the applause and be the heroes and take the bows. It wasn't easy. I wanted appreciation so much I could taste it. What I could do was better than what any of them could do, but I couldn't let 'em know.

I got better at it, too—practicin' in secret all the time like I had to. I got to control it real good. I could light a toothpick at forty feet, or set a whole wall ablaze. But it was miserable, not havin' anyone know how good I was. I had to have some sort of recognition.

Shucks, I didn't hurt nobody. But it was nice to see my fires in the papers. A patch of scrub pine; an old, abandoned shack; a stripped car beside the parkway. Once a whole big factory building that was gonna be tore down anyway. That one was a real beauty.

But I never got no credit.

You just can't go on never gettin' no credit no time.

The day that dumb old Miss Patrick came up with the dumb idea for a dumb talent show for our class was the day the trouble started. First she asks for volunteers an' she gets Charlie with his jugglin' and Sally walkin' on her hands. Andy wanted to spit for her, but she just looked kinda sick and said, "No."

Most everybody in the class either volunteered or was dragged up by ol' lady Patrick and she finally come to me. I told her I couldn't do nothin' and she woulda tooken my word for it, but then some of them wise kids started makin' fun and callin' me a no-talent slob and all like that. And I stand there gettin' mad and thinkin' of what I can do that'd make all their stupid little tricks look real dumb. And the more they tease the more mad I get. The more mad I get, the more they tease.

I snap my fingers and the homework assignment on the blackboard is written in fire. I charcoal broil two desks in the front row. The window shades go up in smoke. Pete Zuccini's history book burns right through his desk like a hot coal, the dumb girls start screamin' like stuck pigs and ol' Miss Patrick keels over in a dead faint.

They remember me back in that ol' school, you betcha. When Mom comes to visit me she says they still talk about it, but lots of them don't really believe it happened. It's the kind of thing you gotta see to believe. Like last week when the head shrink here is talkin' to me in his office with me lyin' on the couch an' all. And he laughs kinda, when he tells me this whole funny farm is fireproofed so good they don't have to worry about me, and I says, kinda quiet like—

"Let me think on that, doc!"

They're rebuilding the west wing, now.....

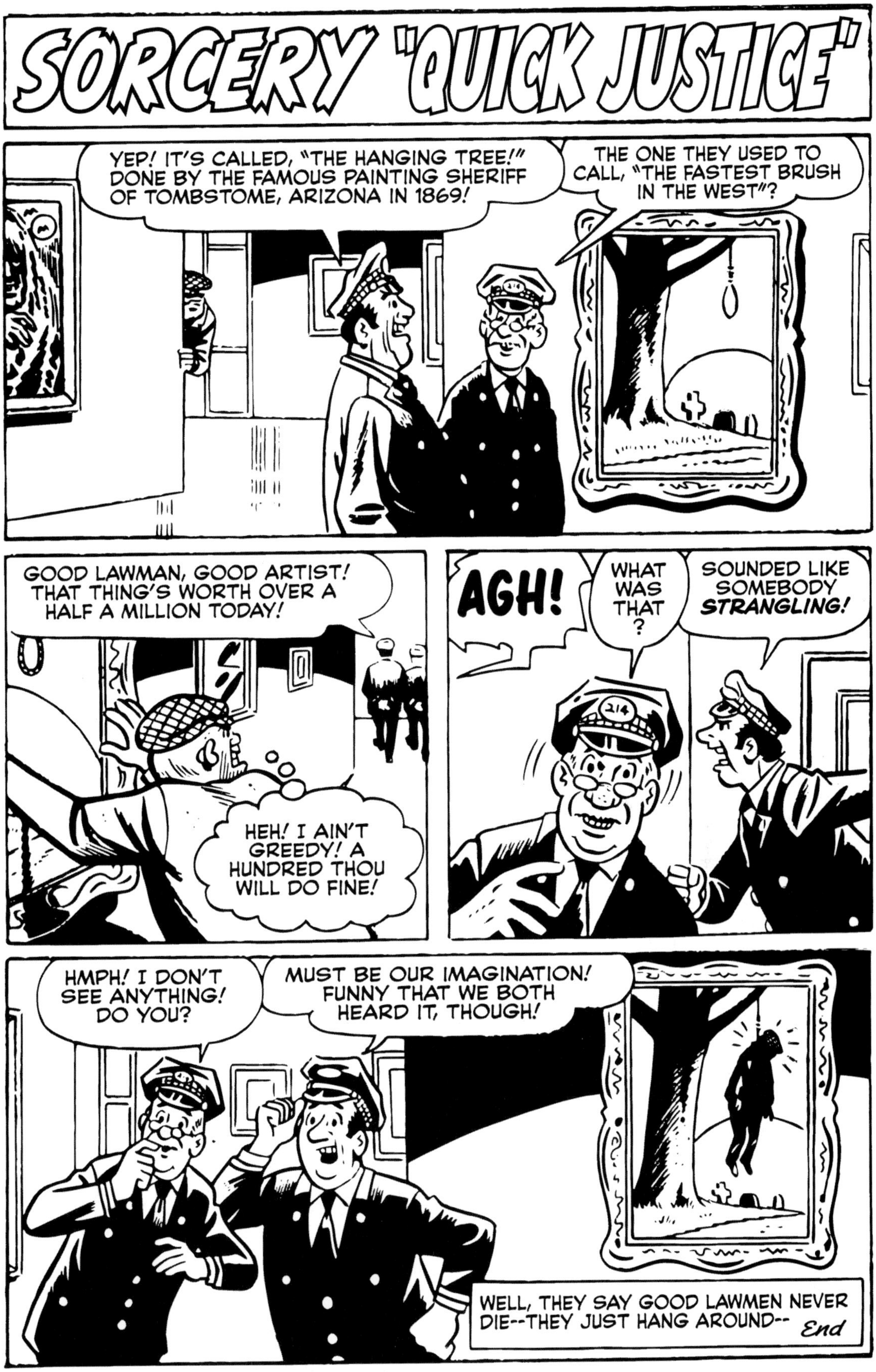
SORCERY "QUICK JUSTICE"
YEP! IT'S CALLED, "THE HANGING TREE!" DONE BY THE FAMOUS PAINTING SHERIFF OF TOMBSTOME, ARIZONA IN 1869!
THE ONE THEY USED TO CALL, "THE FASTEST BRUSH IN THE WEST"?
GOOD LAWMAN, GOOD ARTIST! THAT THING'S WORTH OVER A HALF A MILLION TODAY!
HEH! I AIN'T GREEDY! A HUNDRED THOU WILL DO FINE!
AGH!
WHAT WAS THAT ?
SOUNDED LIKE SOMEBODY STRANGLING!
HMPH! I DON'T SEE ANYTHING! DO YOU?
MUST BE OUR IMAGINATION! FUNNY THAT WE BOTH HEARD IT, THOUGH!
WELL, THEY SAY GOOD LAWMEN NEVER DIE--THEY JUST HANG AROUND--
End

# CURIOSITY KILLS

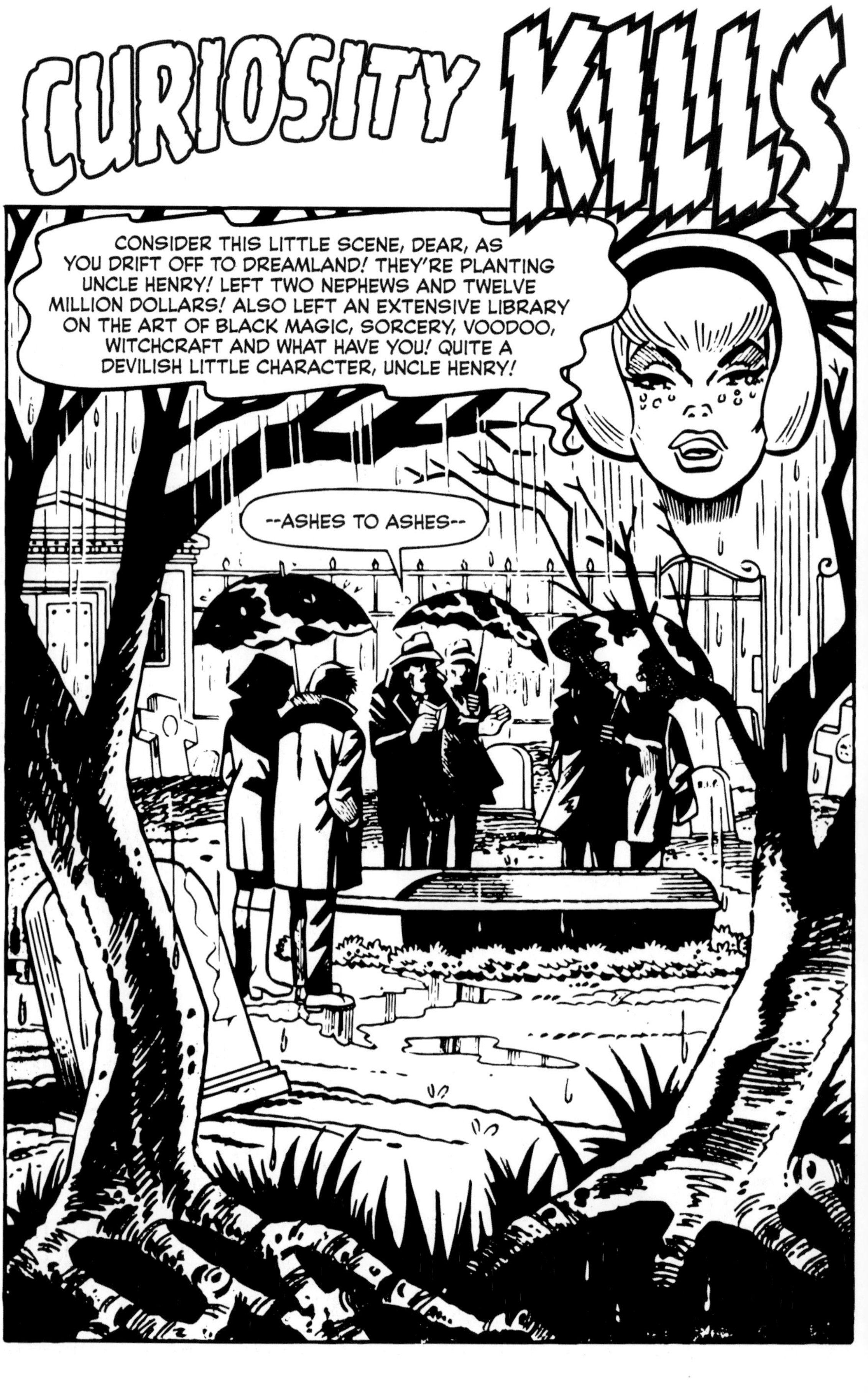
CONSIDER THIS LITTLE SCENE, DEAR, AS YOU DRIFT OFF TO DREAMLAND! THEY'RE PLANTING UNCLE HENRY! LEFT TWO NEPHEWS AND TWELVE MILLION DOLLARS! ALSO LEFT AN EXTENSIVE LIBRARY ON THE ART OF BLACK MAGIC, SORCERY, VOODOO, WITCHCRAFT AND WHAT HAVE YOU! QUITE A DEVILISH LITTLE CHARACTER, UNCLE HENRY!
--ASHES TO ASHES--

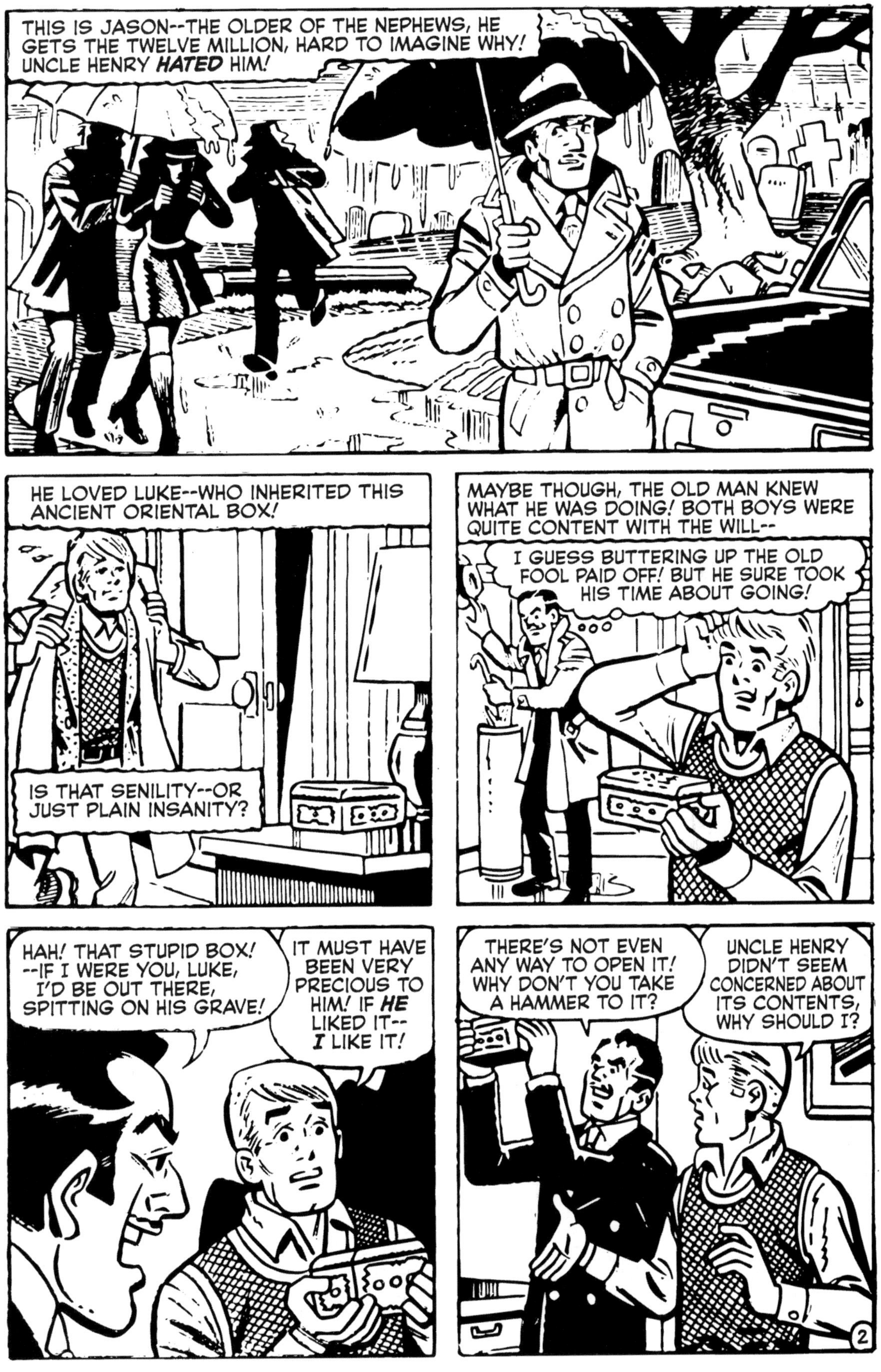
THIS IS JASON--THE OLDER OF THE NEPHEWS, HE GETS THE TWELVE MILLION, HARD TO IMAGINE WHY! UNCLE HENRY HATED HIM!
HE LOVED LUKE--WHO INHERITED THIS ANCIENT ORIENTAL BOX!
IS THAT SENILITY--OR JUST PLAIN INSANITY?
MAYBE THOUGH, THE OLD MAN KNEW WHAT HE WAS DOING! BOTH BOYS WERE QUITE CONTENT WITH THE WILL--
I GUESS BUTTERING UP THE OLD FOOL PAID OFF! BUT HE SURE TOOK HIS TIME ABOUT GOING!
HAH! THAT STUPID BOX! --IF I WERE YOU, LUKE, I'D BE OUT THERE, SPITTING ON HIS GRAVE!
IT MUST HAVE BEEN VERY PRECIOUS TO HIM! IF HE LIKED IT-- I LIKE IT!
THERE'S NOT EVEN ANY WAY TO OPEN IT! WHY DON'T YOU TAKE A HAMMER TO IT?
UNCLE HENRY DIDN'T SEEM CONCERNED ABOUT ITS CONTENTS, WHY SHOULD I?
2

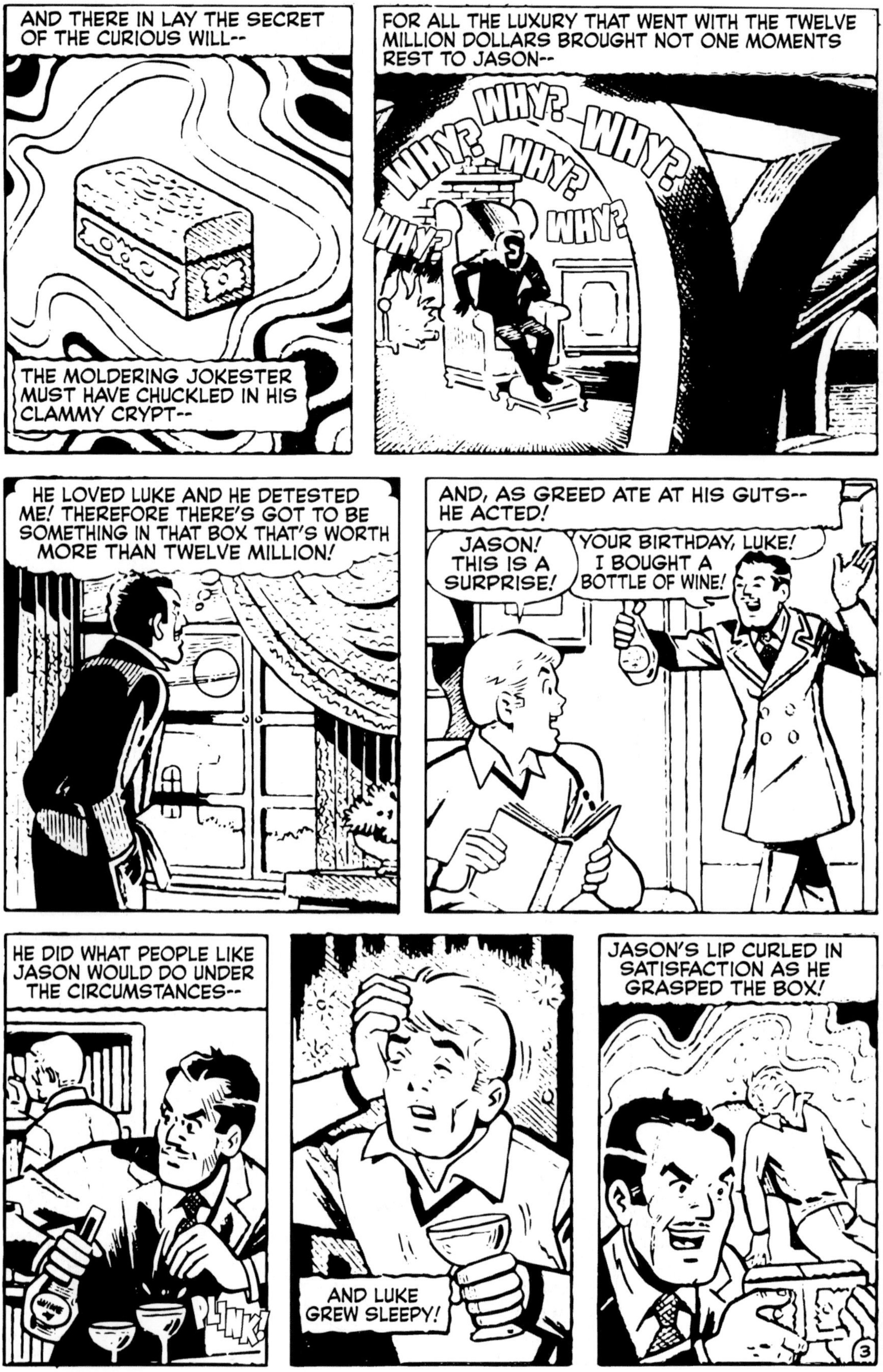
AND THERE IN LAY THE SECRET OF THE CURIOUS WILL--
THE MOLDERING JOKESTER MUST HAVE CHUCKLED IN HIS CLAMMY CRYPT--
FOR ALL THE LUXURY THAT WENT WITH THE TWELVE MILLION DOLLARS BROUGHT NOT ONE MOMENTS REST TO JASON--
WHY? WHY? WHY? WHY? WHY? WHY?
HE LOVED LUKE AND HE DETESTED ME! THEREFORE THERE'S GOT TO BE SOMETHING IN THAT BOX THAT'S WORTH MORE THAN TWELVE MILLION!
AND, AS GREED ATE AT HIS GUTS-- HE ACTED!
JASON! THIS IS A SURPRISE!
YOUR BIRTHDAY, LUKE! I BOUGHT A BOTTLE OF WINE!
HE DID WHAT PEOPLE LIKE JASON WOULD DO UNDER THE CIRCUMSTANCES--
PLINK!
AND LUKE GREW SLEEPY!
JASON'S LIP CURLED IN SATISFACTION AS HE GRASPED THE BOX!

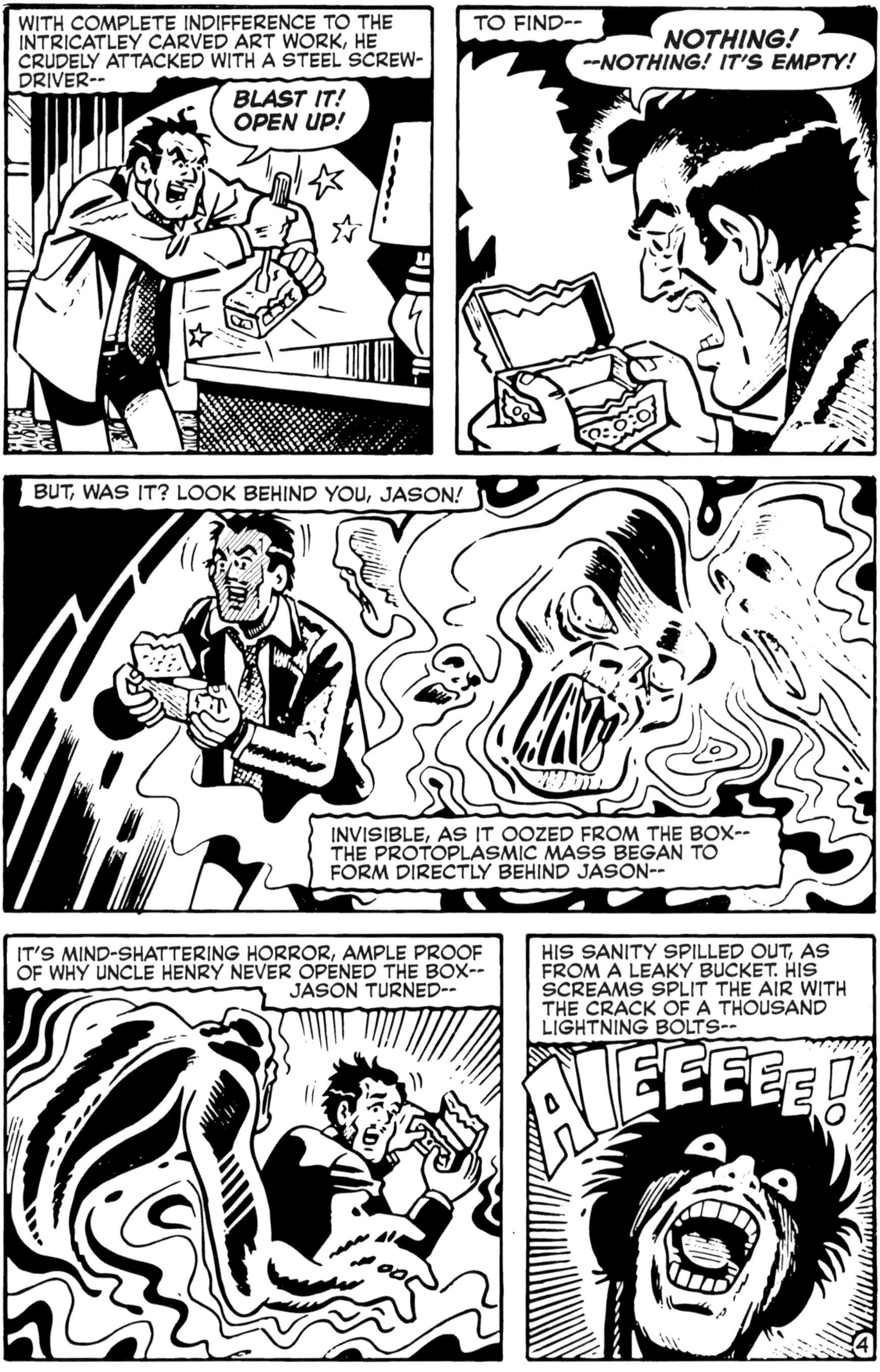
WITH COMPLETE INDIFFERENCE TO THE INTRICATLEY CARVED ART WORK, HE CRUDELY ATTACKED WITH A STEEL SCREW-DRIVER--
BLAST IT! OPEN UP!
TO FIND--
NOTHING! --NOTHING! IT'S EMPTY!
BUT, WAS IT? LOOK BEHIND YOU, JASON!
INVISIBLE, AS IT OOZED FROM THE BOX-- THE PROTOPLASMIC MASS BEGAN TO FORM DIRECTLY BEHIND JASON--
IT'S MIND-SHATTERING HORROR, AMPLE PROOF OF WHY UNCLE HENRY NEVER OPENED THE BOX-- JASON TURNED--
HIS SANITY SPILLED OUT, AS FROM A LEAKY BUCKET. HIS SCREAMS SPLIT THE AIR WITH THE CRACK OF A THOUSAND LIGHTNING BOLTS--
AIEEEEEE!
4

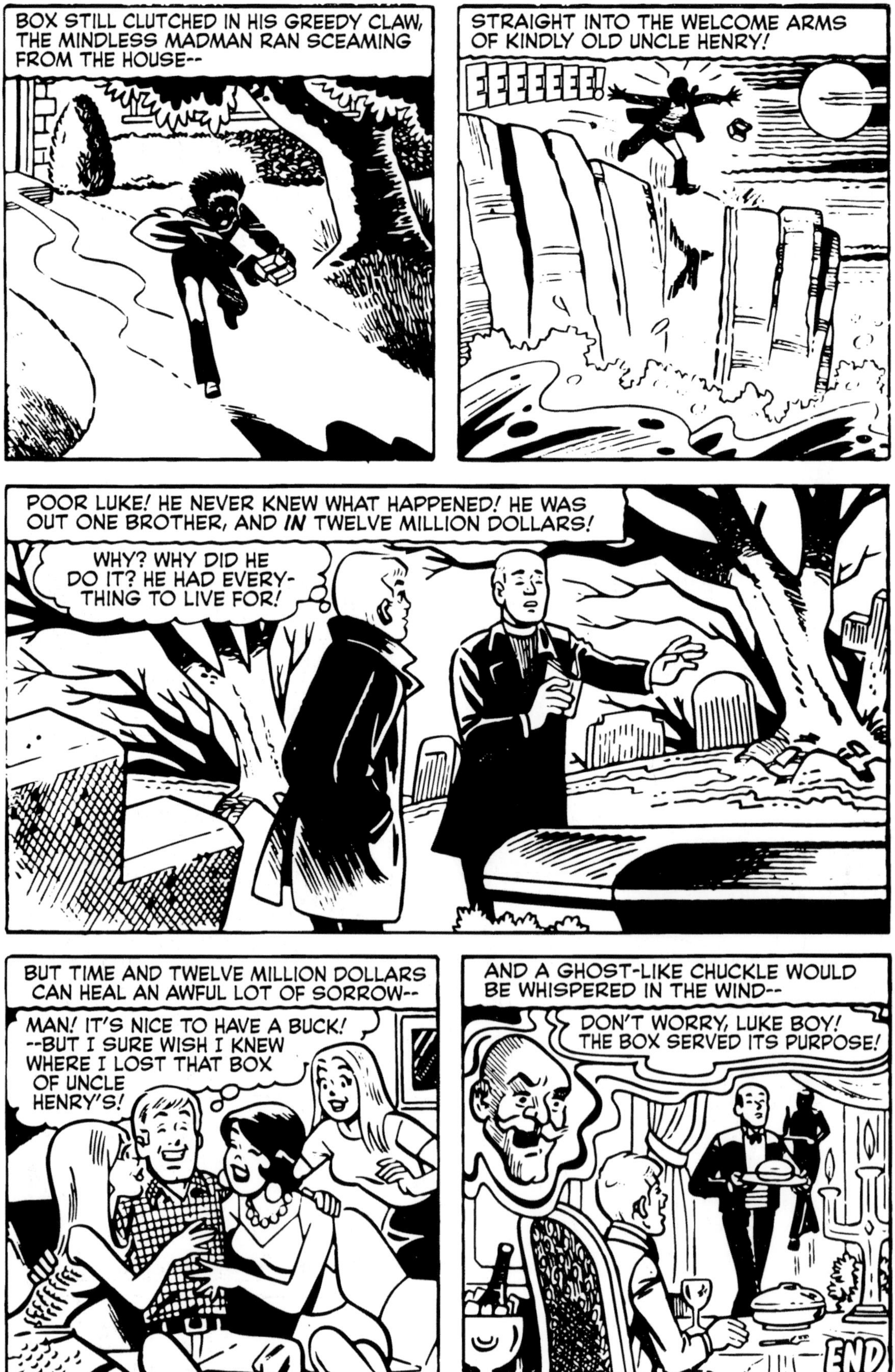
BOX STILL CLUTCHED IN HIS GREEDY CLAW, THE MINDLESS MADMAN RAN SCEAMING FROM THE HOUSE--
STRAIGHT INTO THE WELCOME ARMS OF KINDLY OLD UNCLE HENRY!
EEEEEEE!
POOR LUKE! HE NEVER KNEW WHAT HAPPENED! HE WAS OUT ONE BROTHER, AND IN TWELVE MILLION DOLLARS!
WHY? WHY DID HE DO IT? HE HAD EVERY-THING TO LIVE FOR!
BUT TIME AND TWELVE MILLION DOLLARS CAN HEAL AN AWFUL LOT OF SORROW--
MAN! IT'S NICE TO HAVE A BUCK! --BUT I SURE WISH I KNEW WHERE I LOST THAT BOX OF UNCLE HENRY'S!
AND A GHOST-LIKE CHUCKLE WOULD BE WHISPERED IN THE WIND--
DON'T WORRY, LUKE BOY! THE BOX SERVED ITS PURPOSE!
END

# ISSUE TWO

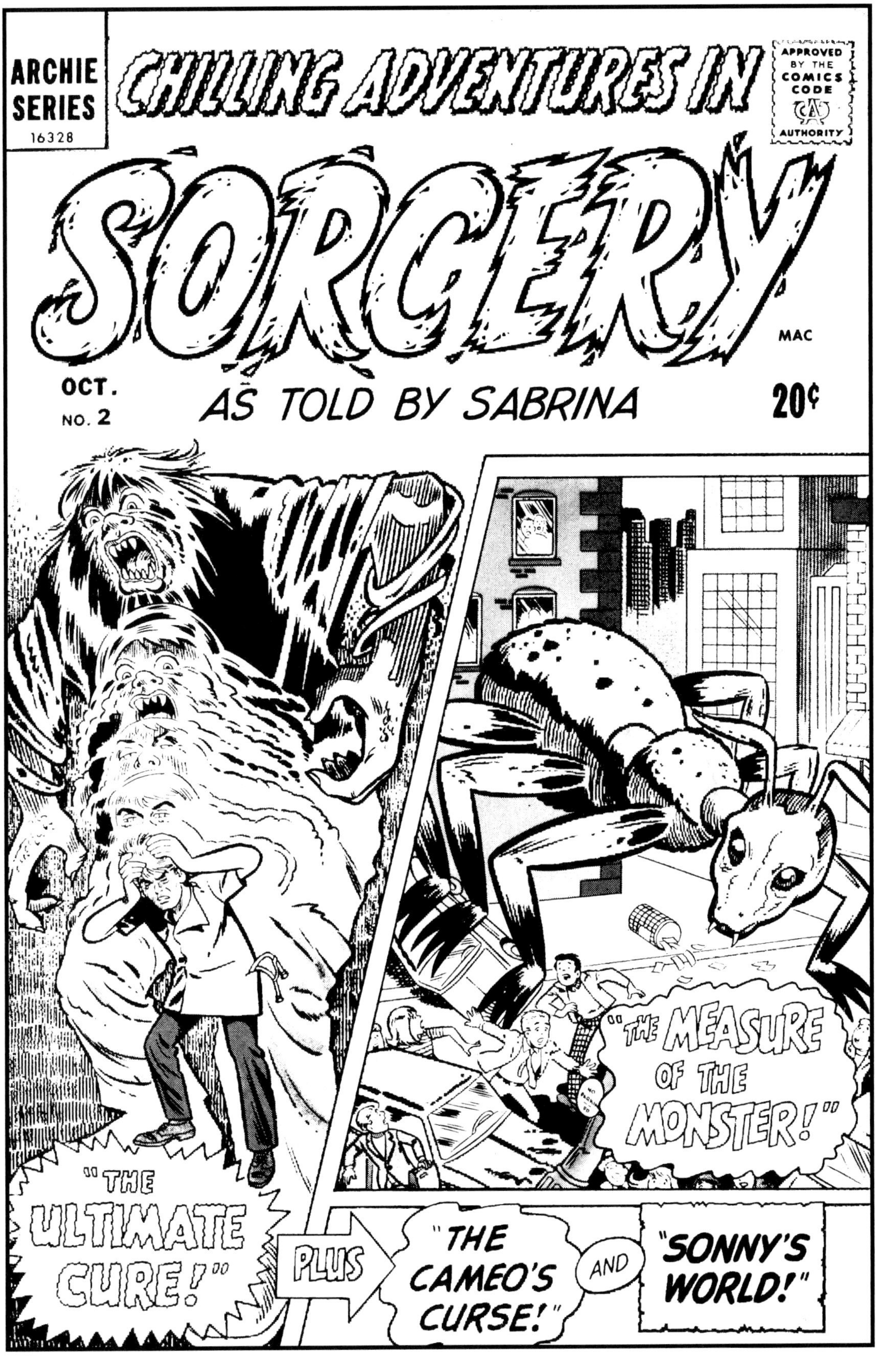

ARCHIE SERIES
16328
CHILLING ADVENTURES IN
SORCERY
APPROVED BY THE COMICS CODE AUTHORITY
MAC
OCT.
NO. 2
AS TOLD BY SABRINA
20¢
"THE MEASURE OF THE MONSTER!"
"THE ULTIMATE CURE!"
PLUS
"THE CAMEO'S CURSE!"
AND
"SONNY'S WORLD!"

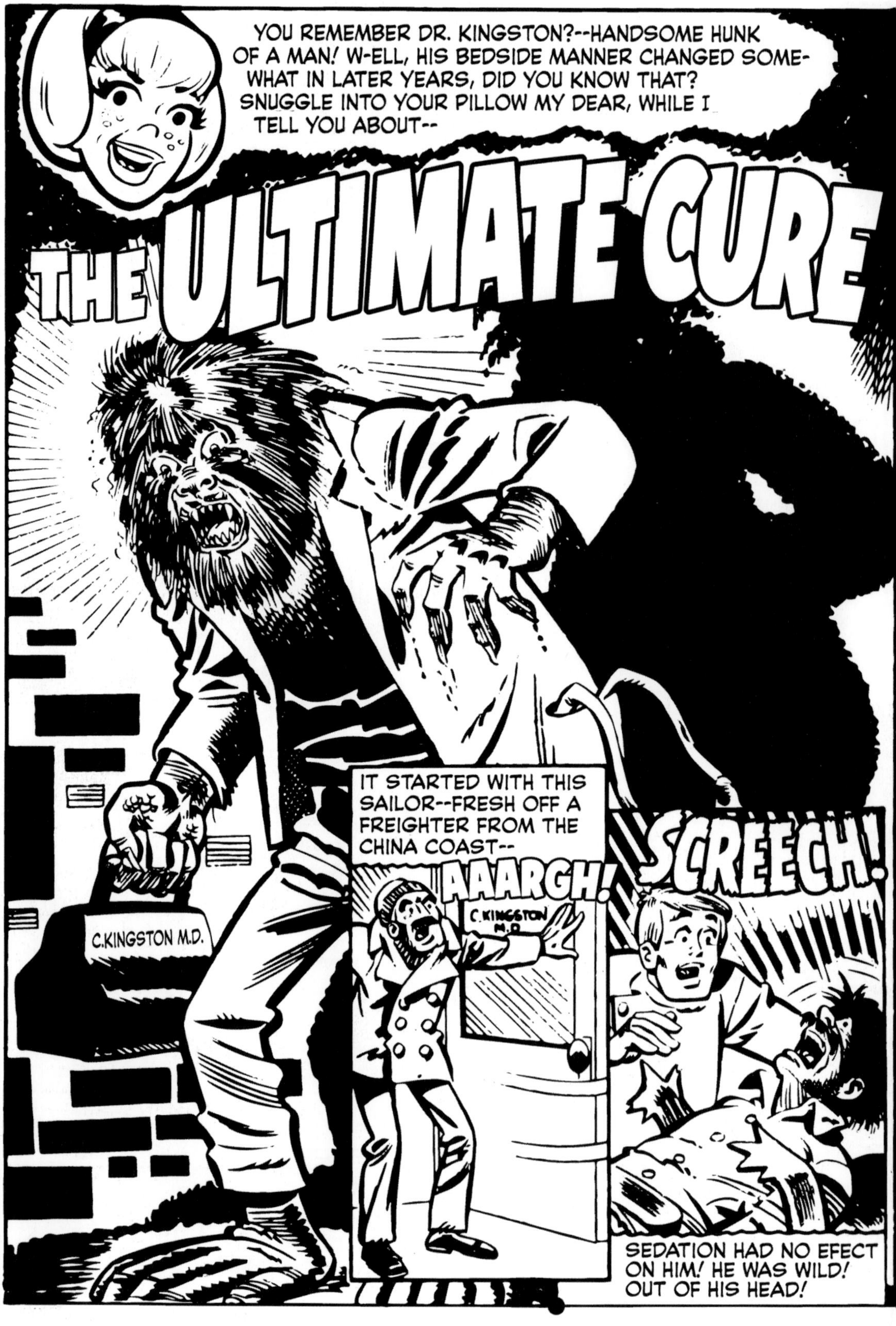

YOU REMEMBER DR. KINGSTON?--HANDSOME HUNK OF A MAN! W-ELL, HIS BEDSIDE MANNER CHANGED SOMEWHAT IN LATER YEARS, DID YOU KNOW THAT? SNUGGLE INTO YOUR PILLOW MY DEAR, WHILE I TELL YOU ABOUT--
THE ULTIMATE CURE
C.KINGSTON M.D.
IT STARTED WITH THIS SAILOR--FRESH OFF A FREIGHTER FROM THE CHINA COAST--
AAARGH!
C.KINGSTON M.D.
SCREECH!
SEDATION HAD NO EFECT ON HIM! HE WAS WILD! OUT OF HIS HEAD!

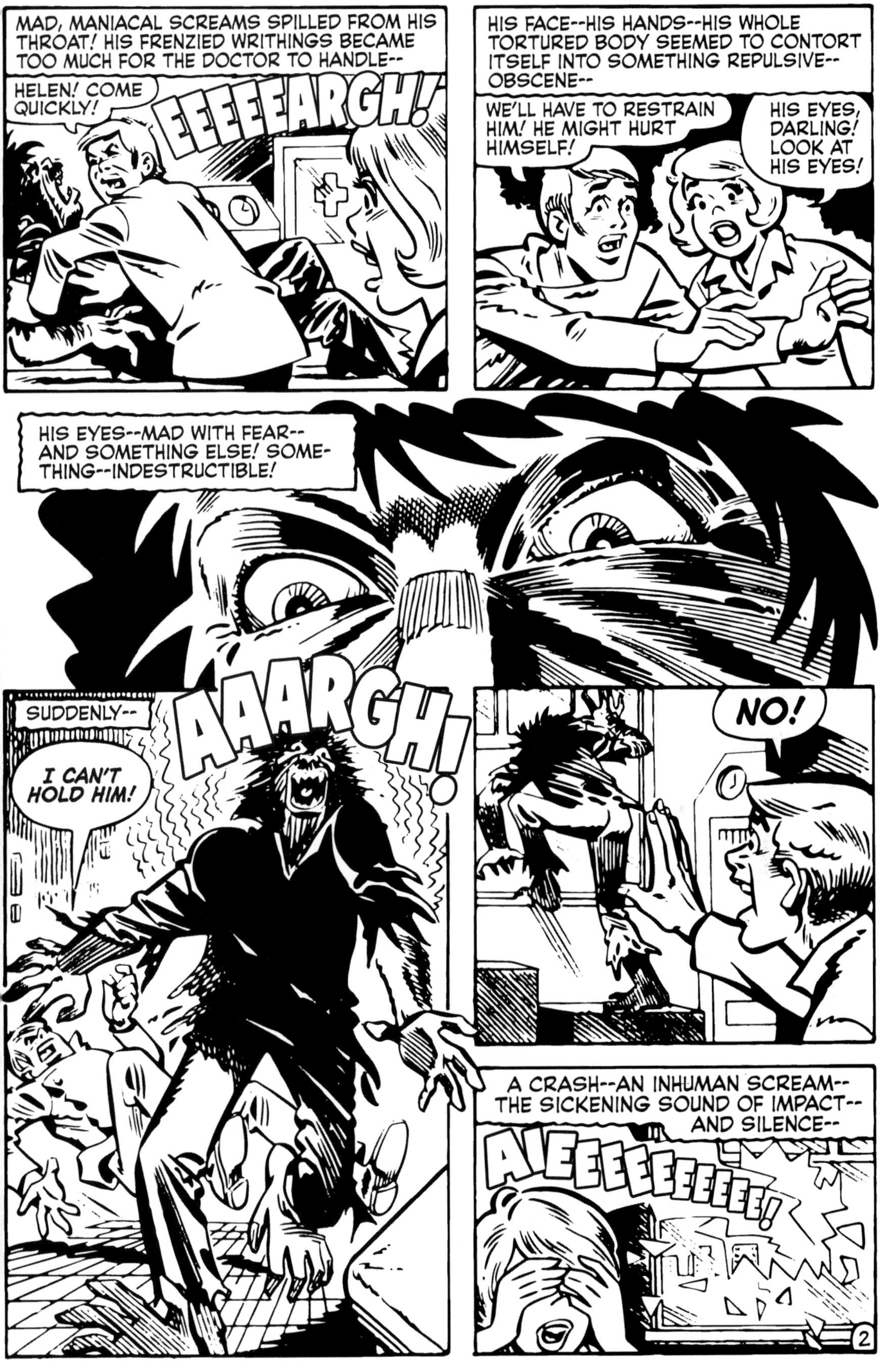
MAD, MANIACAL SCREAMS SPILLED FROM HIS THROAT! HIS FRENZIED WRITHINGS BECAME TOO MUCH FOR THE DOCTOR TO HANDLE--
HELEN! COME QUICKLY!
EEEEEARGH!
HIS FACE--HIS HANDS--HIS WHOLE TORTURED BODY SEEMED TO CONTORT ITSELF INTO SOMETHING REPULSIVE--OBSCENE--
WE'LL HAVE TO RESTRAIN HIM! HE MIGHT HURT HIMSELF!
HIS EYES, DARLING! LOOK AT HIS EYES!
HIS EYES--MAD WITH FEAR--AND SOMETHING ELSE! SOMETHING--INDESTRUCTIBLE!
SUDDENLY--
AAARGH!
I CAN'T HOLD HIM!
NO!
A CRASH--AN INHUMAN SCREAM--THE SICKENING SOUND OF IMPACT--AND SILENCE--
AIEEEEEEEEEE!
2

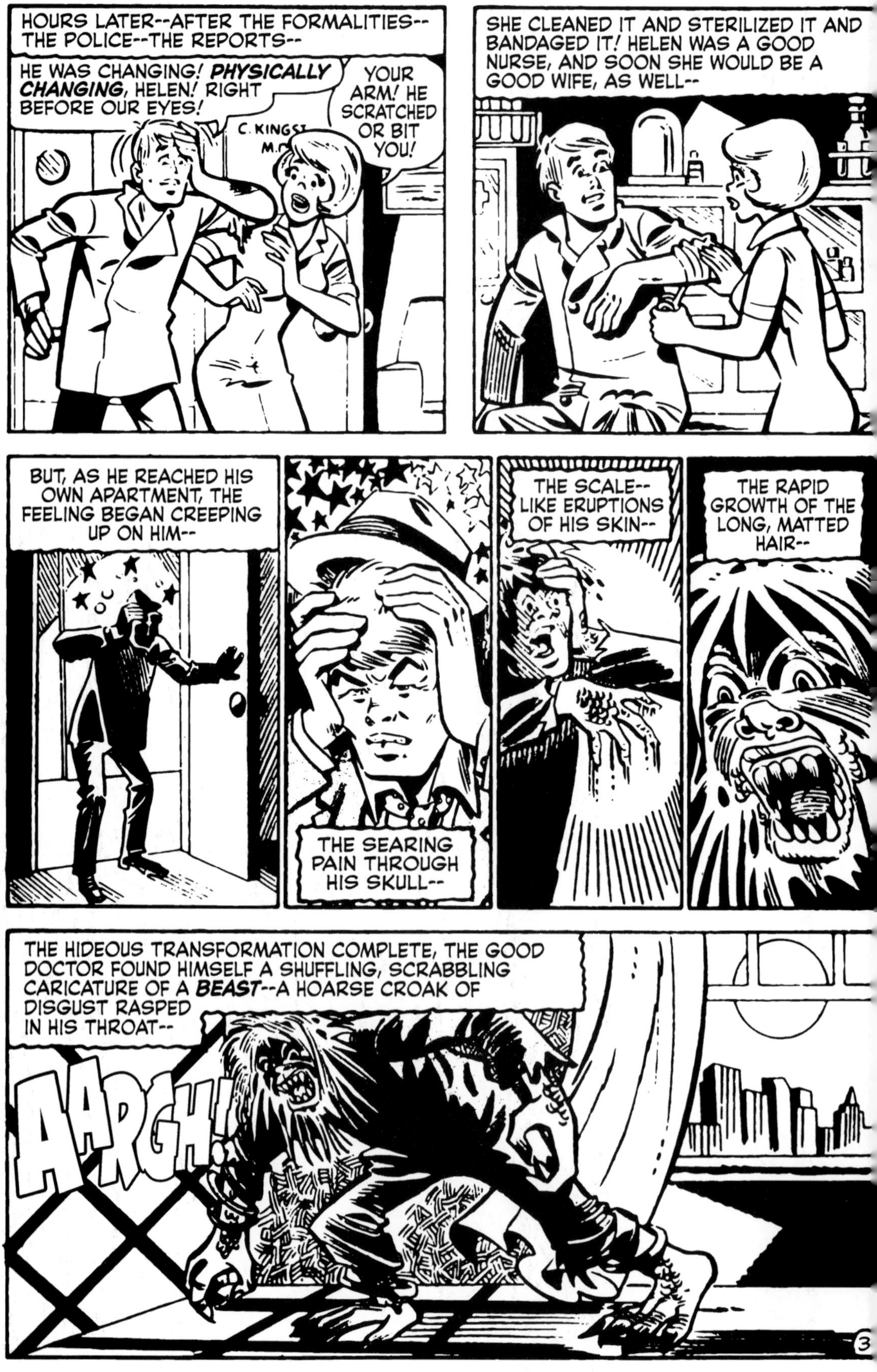

HOURS LATER--AFTER THE FORMALITIES-- THE POLICE--THE REPORTS--
HE WAS CHANGING! PHYSICALLY CHANGING, HELEN! RIGHT BEFORE OUR EYES!
YOUR ARM! HE SCRATCHED OR BIT YOU!
C. KINGS
M.D.
SHE CLEANED IT AND STERILIZED IT AND BANDAGED IT! HELEN WAS A GOOD NURSE, AND SOON SHE WOULD BE A GOOD WIFE, AS WELL--
BUT, AS HE REACHED HIS OWN APARTMENT, THE FEELING BEGAN CREEPING UP ON HIM--
THE SEARING PAIN THROUGH HIS SKULL--
THE SCALE--LIKE ERUPTIONS OF HIS SKIN--
THE RAPID GROWTH OF THE LONG, MATTED HAIR--
THE HIDEOUS TRANSFORMATION COMPLETE, THE GOOD DOCTOR FOUND HIMSELF A SHUFFLING, SCRABBLING CARICATURE OF A BEAST--A HOARSE CROAK OF DISGUST RASPED IN HIS THROAT--
AARGH!
3

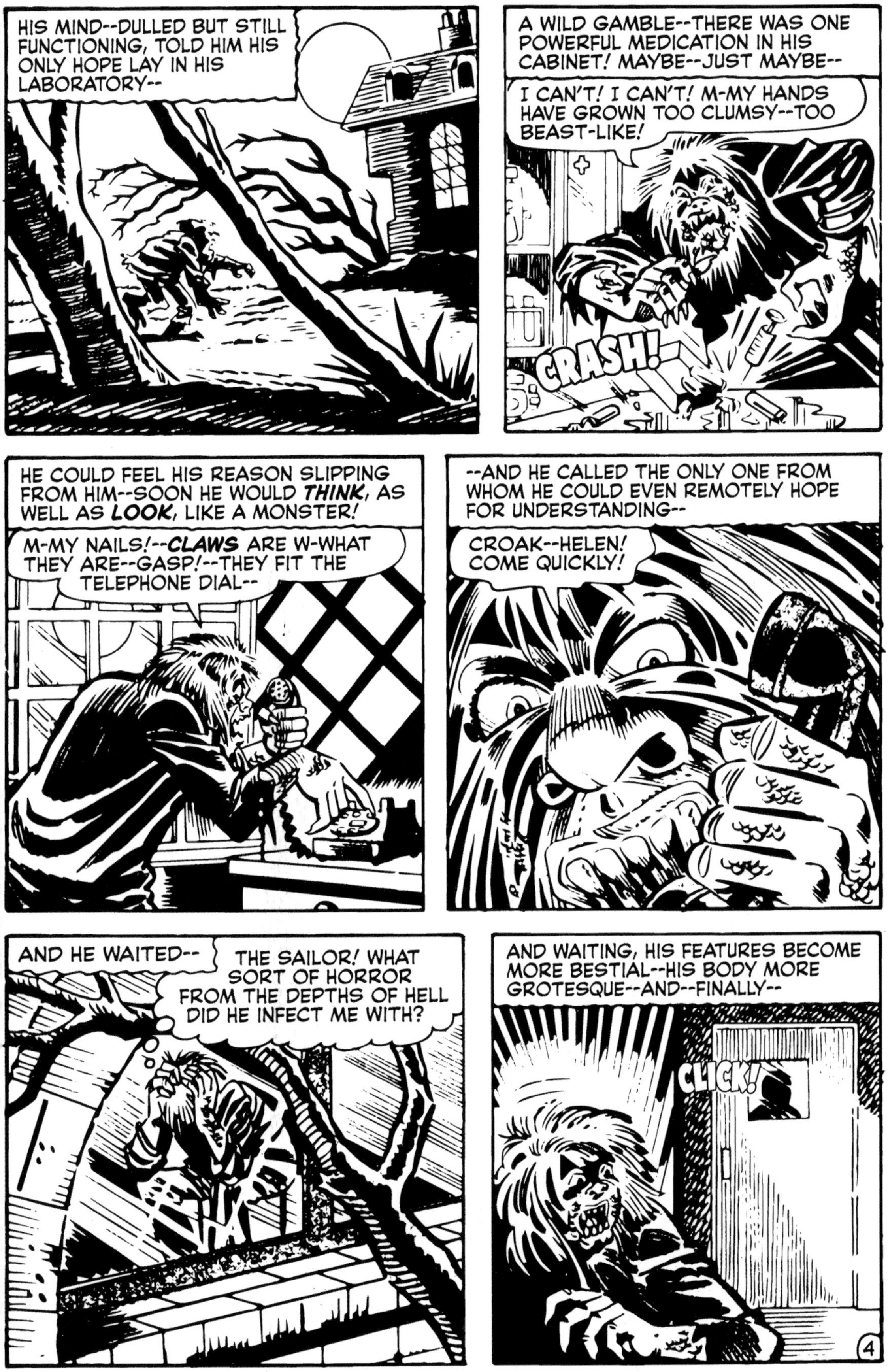
HIS MIND--DULLED BUT STILL FUNCTIONING, TOLD HIM HIS ONLY HOPE LAY IN HIS LABORATORY--
A WILD GAMBLE--THERE WAS ONE POWERFUL MEDICATION IN HIS CABINET! MAYBE--JUST MAYBE--
I CAN'T! I CAN'T! M-MY HANDS HAVE GROWN TOO CLUMSY--TOO BEAST-LIKE!
CRASH!
HE COULD FEEL HIS REASON SLIPPING FROM HIM--SOON HE WOULD THINK, AS WELL AS LOOK, LIKE A MONSTER!
M-MY NAILS!--CLAWS ARE W-WHAT THEY ARE--GASP!--THEY FIT THE TELEPHONE DIAL--
--AND HE CALLED THE ONLY ONE FROM WHOM HE COULD EVEN REMOTELY HOPE FOR UNDERSTANDING--
CROAK--HELEN! COME QUICKLY!
AND HE WAITED--
THE SAILOR! WHAT SORT OF HORROR FROM THE DEPTHS OF HELL DID HE INFECT ME WITH?
AND WAITING, HIS FEATURES BECOME MORE BESTIAL--HIS BODY MORE GROTESQUE--AND--FINALLY--
CLICK!
4

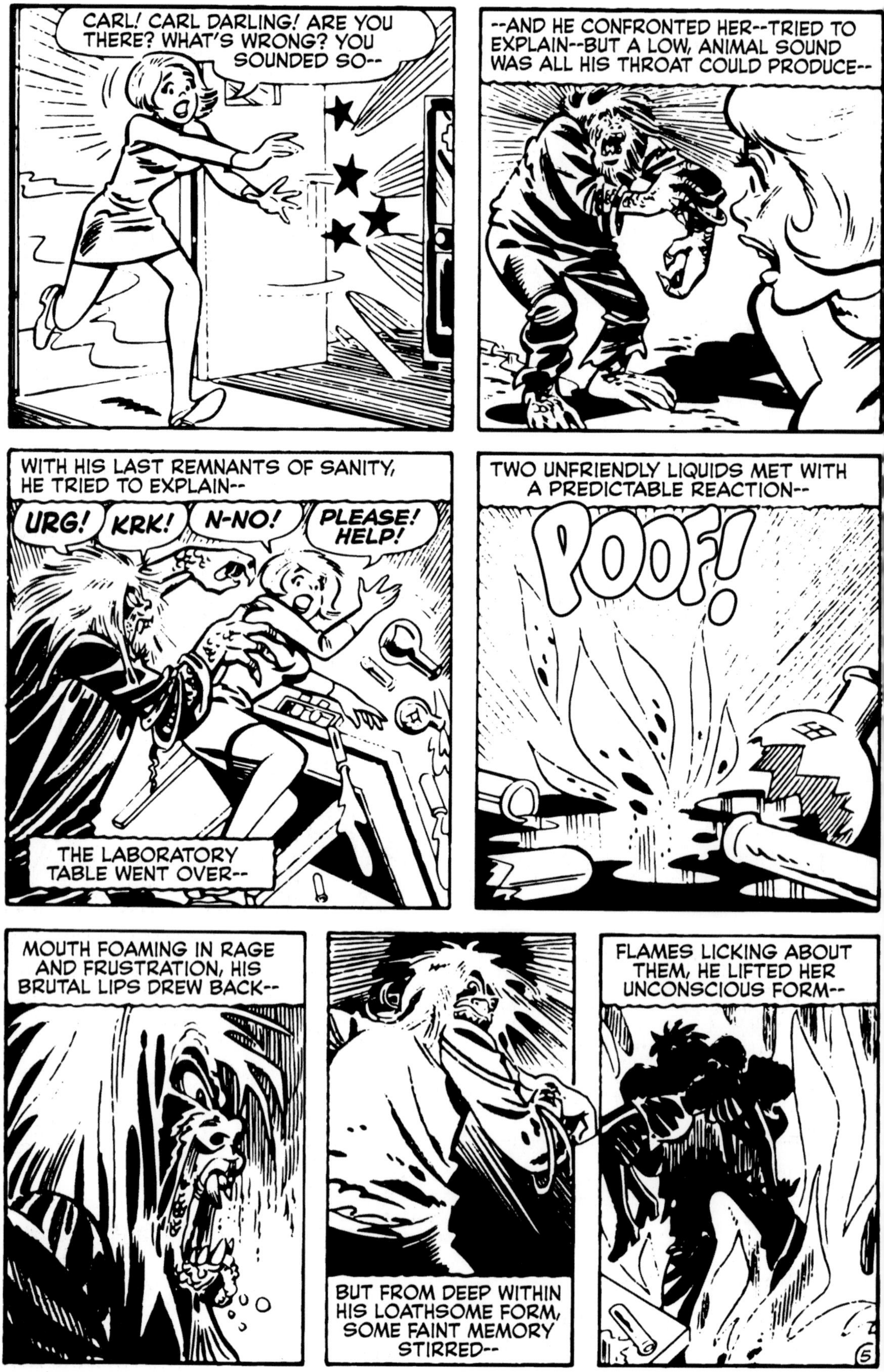
CARL! CARL DARLING! ARE YOU THERE? WHAT'S WRONG? YOU SOUNDED SO--
--AND HE CONFRONTED HER--TRIED TO EXPLAIN--BUT A LOW, ANIMAL SOUND WAS ALL HIS THROAT COULD PRODUCE--
WITH HIS LAST REMNANTS OF SANITY, HE TRIED TO EXPLAIN--
URG!
KRK!
N-NO!
PLEASE! HELP!
THE LABORATORY TABLE WENT OVER--
TWO UNFRIENDLY LIQUIDS MET WITH A PREDICTABLE REACTION--
POOF!
MOUTH FOAMING IN RAGE AND FRUSTRATION, HIS BRUTAL LIPS DREW BACK--
BUT FROM DEEP WITHIN HIS LOATHSOME FORM, SOME FAINT MEMORY STIRRED--
FLAMES LICKING ABOUT THEM, HE LIFTED HER UNCONSCIOUS FORM--
5

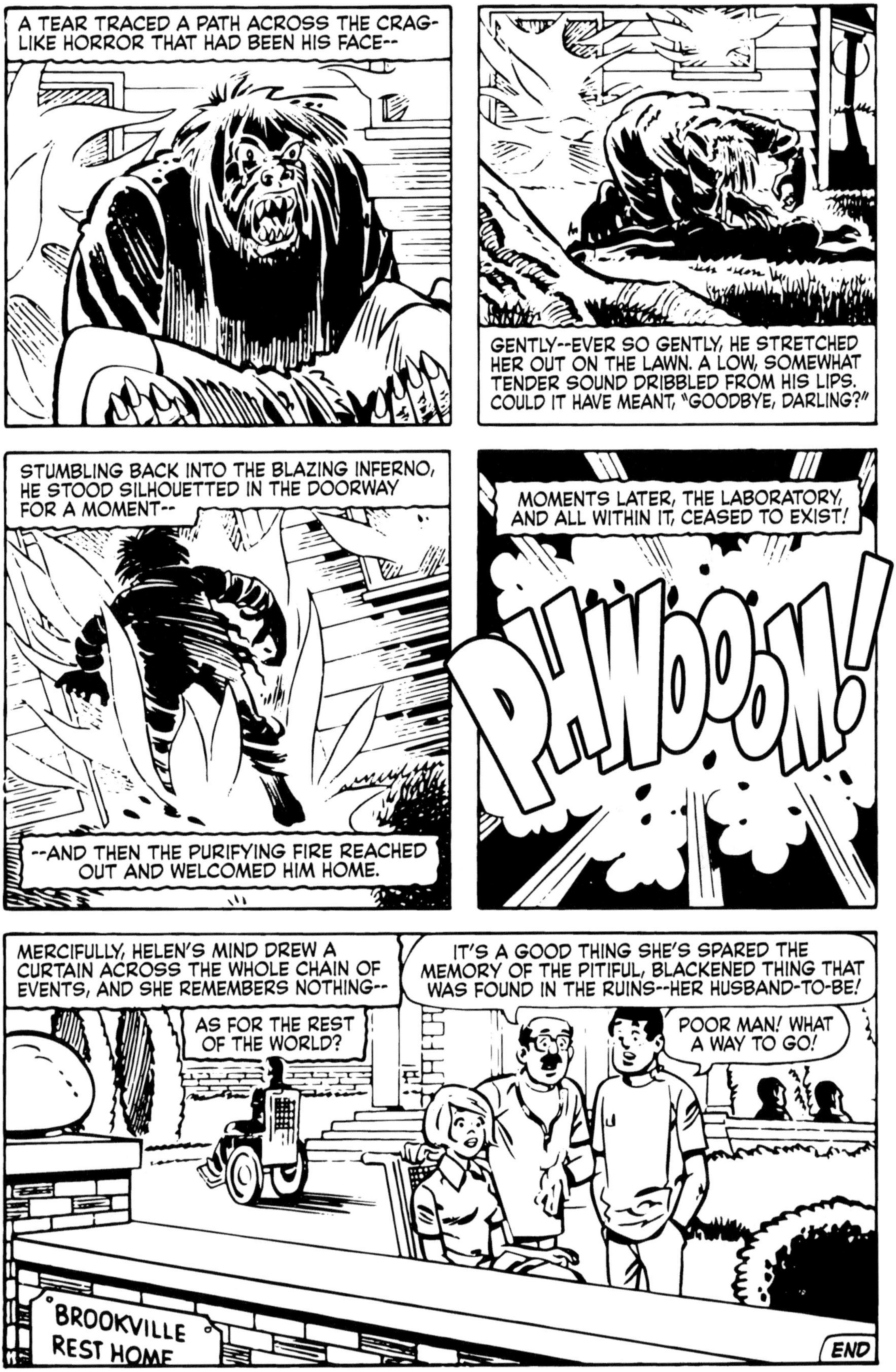

A TEAR TRACED A PATH ACROSS THE CRAG-LIKE HORROR THAT HAD BEEN HIS FACE--
GENTLY--EVER SO GENTLY, HE STRETCHED HER OUT ON THE LAWN. A LOW, SOMEWHAT TENDER SOUND DRIBBLED FROM HIS LIPS. COULD IT HAVE MEANT, "GOODBYE, DARLING?"
STUMBLING BACK INTO THE BLAZING INFERNO, HE STOOD SILHOUETTED IN THE DOORWAY FOR A MOMENT--
--AND THEN THE PURIFYING FIRE REACHED OUT AND WELCOMED HIM HOME.
MOMENTS LATER, THE LABORATORY, AND ALL WITHIN IT, CEASED TO EXIST!
PHWOOOM!
MERCIFULLY, HELEN'S MIND DREW A CURTAIN ACROSS THE WHOLE CHAIN OF EVENTS, AND SHE REMEMBERS NOTHING--
AS FOR THE REST OF THE WORLD?
IT'S A GOOD THING SHE'S SPARED THE MEMORY OF THE PITIFUL, BLACKENED THING THAT WAS FOUND IN THE RUINS--HER HUSBAND-TO-BE!
POOR MAN! WHAT A WAY TO GO!
BROOKVILLE REST HOME
END

# CHILLING ADVENTURES IN SORCERY

# LOOK UPON YOUR LEGACY

The sound was moist—wet—somehow almost obscene. A juicy, slapping footstep in the darkened hallway outside his room. A cold, clammy sweat beaded his brow as he sat upright in the strange bed and strained his ears to hear the next frightening footfall. In his vivid imagination, he saw some unholy, indescribable horror rising from the fetid swamp that lay just south of the house.

It rose slowly, in his mind's eye, and the strands of green slime that covered the polluted waters hung down across what might have been a face, and glistened wetly in the moonlight. It seemed to move almost painfully as it strove to pull its grotesque bulk from the creamy-thick mire. One large, misshapen foot groped and finally found solid ground. A gurgling sound that might have passed for satisfaction emanated from somewhere within the bestial creature. It heaved mightily and the other foot pulled free of the muck with a loud, smacking noise that seemed to punctuate the reluctance of the filthy bog to let its victim go.

It hung there on the edge of the swamp for a moment; pulsating like some immense, malformed organ. A foul smelling puddle formed on the grass beneath its feet, and it shuffled slowly toward the house.

Harrison Watts trembled like an aspen leaf in a high wind. His ears listened for the next sloshing sound of the unknown terror in the blackness of the unfamiliar hall. His tongue ran nervously over his lips and he swallowed convulsively. The dryness in his mouth was the dryness of death.

The candles on the bedside table flickered erratically, and his twisted imagination saw—in the changing shadows on the wall—a replay of the events of that morning and his final triumph over miserly, niggardly, thankfully deceased Uncle Thaddeus.

Senile old fool; his aging mind crumbling like a stale cracker. Sitting on, who knows—forty, fifty million dollars—and lasting, with his usual greed, well past the three score and ten years allotted to him.

Waiting for the miserly old goat to pack it in, was hard enough, but watching that beautiful money being dribbled away on superstitious rot was more than Harrison could bear.

The Occult. Sorcery. Black Magic, Voodoo. Witchcraft. Togas and turbans. Incense and incantations. Mutterings in strange tongues. Symbols on the walls and circles on the floor. Hooded figures in long robes gliding about. Ritualistic mumbo-jumbo sounding through the halls at all hours of night.

And all the while the precious money disappearing down the drain like water from a leaking faucet.

But this morning changed all that.

Harrison had arrived quite early and, for the first time in many months found no one in the mansion but uncle. The servants had bolted ages ago when the first wave of conjurers, broomstick riders and assorted hokus pokus merchants had infiltrated their sacred domain.

And then it came!

A cup clattered to the floor and the strangled cry from the library, suddenly snapped the whole scene for Harrison into crystal clarity.

A heart attack! The bony hand clutching at the dressing gown pocket for the life saving pills. The bottle dropping to the floor. Harrison snatching it up and stepping back. The look in the eyes; first pleading—then accusing. The last, gasping words . . . sing song . . . gibberish . . . like some language from another age . . . another time . . . and then, nothing. Frozen, like a figure in a wax museum; the eyes still staring, still accusing . . . but lifeless.

Harrison laughing. A curse! A dying man's stupid, superstitious curse! Mad as a hatter to the end. Tears of laughter and relief rolling down Harrison's cheek as he tucked the pill bottle back in the dressing gown pocket and left the house. Let his occult buddies find the body. Maybe they'd whisk him away to some never-never land of goblins and ghoulies and things that go bump in the night, and the old fool could play at being a spook for all eternity.

And then the drive to put distance between himself and the house. The sudden storm. The car breaking down in front of this place. The old couple kindly putting him up for the night. And now . . . the thing in the hall.

The thing that moved wetly outside his door. The thing that came closer . . . closer . . . closer. A sound in the night, like heavy, labored breathing. Not a sound really, but a . . . a feeling. A pulsing pressure that filled the room and seemed to penetrate Harrison's skull. A stench . . . putrifying, eye burning, acrid stench of death . . . decay . . . like rotting flesh, seeped through the door and seared his nostrils like a branding iron.

His eyes bulged, staring at the door as the wet spot appeared in the center and began to grow . . and grow . . . and take form . . . and ooze toward the bed. The strands of green slime parted momentarily and the scream rose in Harrison's throat as he looked upon the evil that Uncle Thaddeus had called down upon him . . . and, as no mortal can look upon that which Uncle Thaddeus had wished upon him . . . the scream never came.

They found him in the morning. The bright, sunlit morning. The birds sang, the air was fresh and clear. A water lily bloomed in the swamp, just south of the house. No slime, no wetness on the hall carpet, no stench of death and decay.

Just Harrison. Or what he left behind when he went away to that never-never land of goblins and ghoulies and things that go bump in the night.

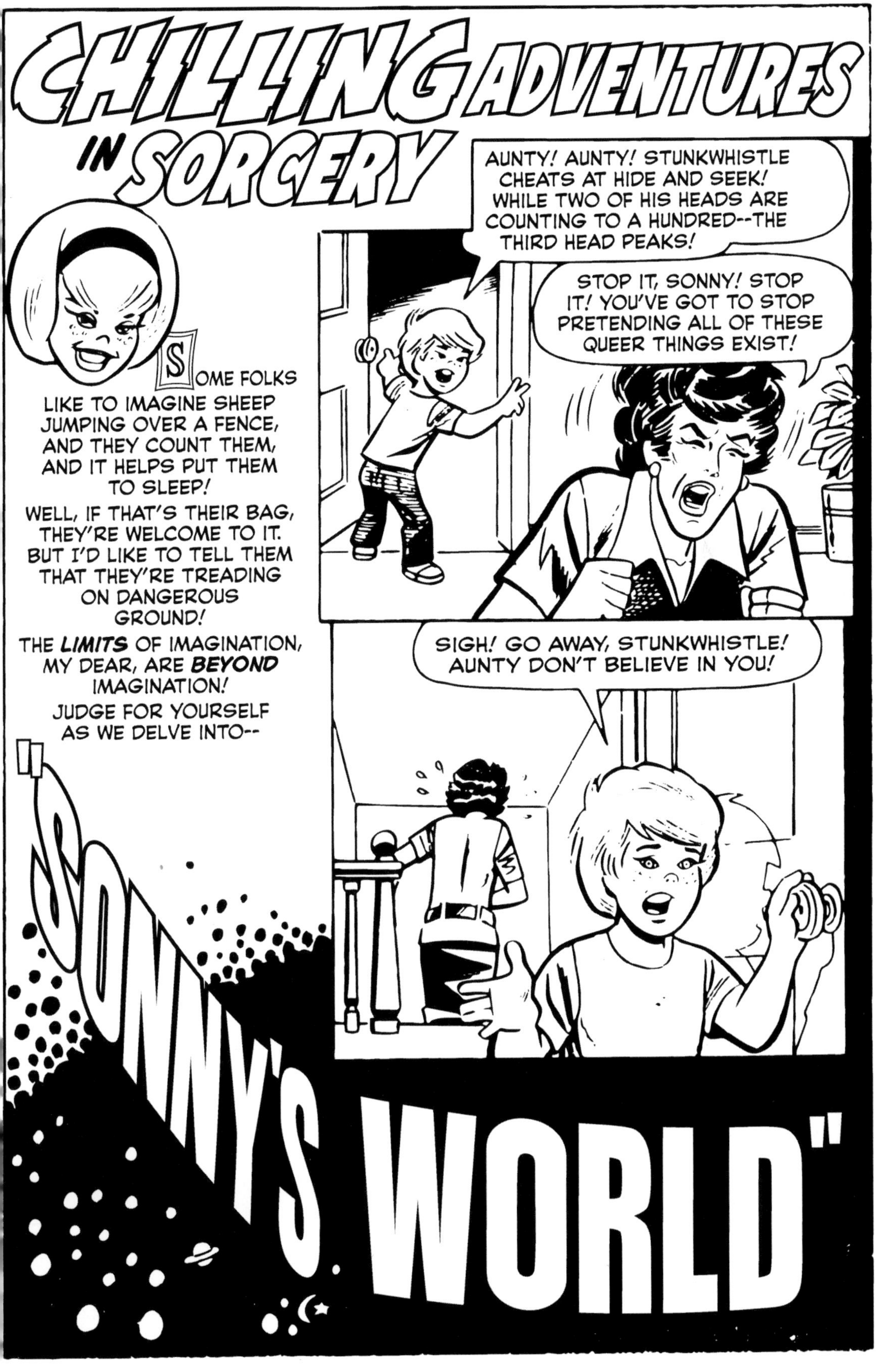
CHILLING ADVENTURES IN SORCERY
SOME FOLKS LIKE TO IMAGINE SHEEP JUMPING OVER A FENCE, AND THEY COUNT THEM, AND IT HELPS PUT THEM TO SLEEP!
WELL, IF THAT'S THEIR BAG, THEY'RE WELCOME TO IT. BUT I'D LIKE TO TELL THEM THAT THEY'RE TREADING ON DANGEROUS GROUND!
THE LIMITS OF IMAGINATION, MY DEAR, ARE BEYOND IMAGINATION!
JUDGE FOR YOURSELF AS WE DELVE INTO--
"SONNY'S WORLD"
AUNTY! AUNTY! STUNKWHISTLE CHEATS AT HIDE AND SEEK! WHILE TWO OF HIS HEADS ARE COUNTING TO A HUNDRED--THE THIRD HEAD PEAKS!
STOP IT, SONNY! STOP IT! YOU'VE GOT TO STOP PRETENDING ALL OF THESE QUEER THINGS EXIST!
SIGH! GO AWAY, STUNKWHISTLE! AUNTY DON'T BELIEVE IN YOU!

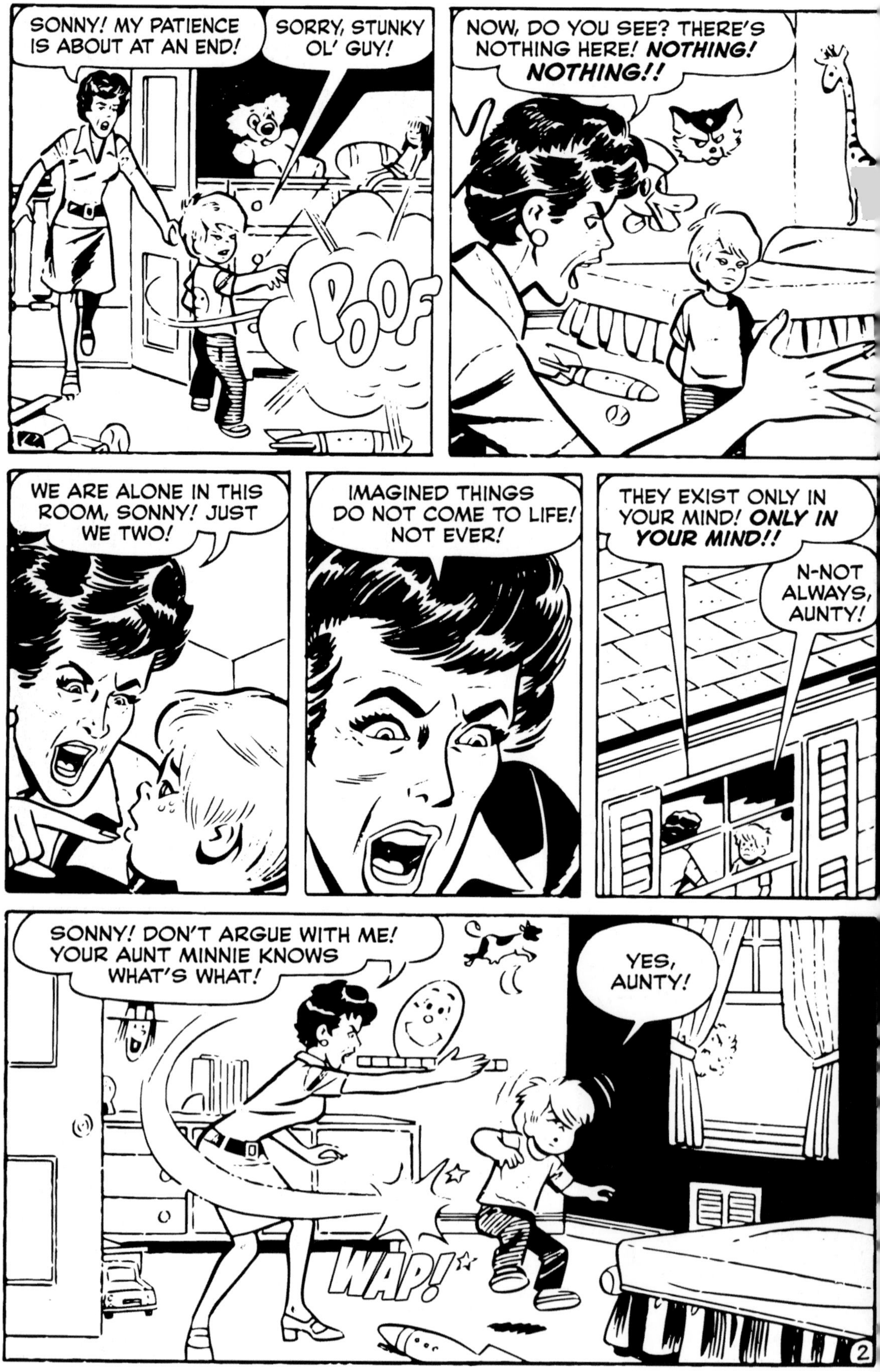

SONNY! MY PATIENCE IS ABOUT AT AN END!
SORRY, STUNKY OL' GUY!
POOF
NOW, DO YOU SEE? THERE'S NOTHING HERE! NOTHING! NOTHING!!
WE ARE ALONE IN THIS ROOM, SONNY! JUST WE TWO!
IMAGINED THINGS DO NOT COME TO LIFE! NOT EVER!
THEY EXIST ONLY IN YOUR MIND! ONLY IN YOUR MIND!!
N-NOT ALWAYS, AUNTY!
SONNY! DON'T ARGUE WITH ME! YOUR AUNT MINNIE KNOWS WHAT'S WHAT!
YES, AUNTY!
WAP!

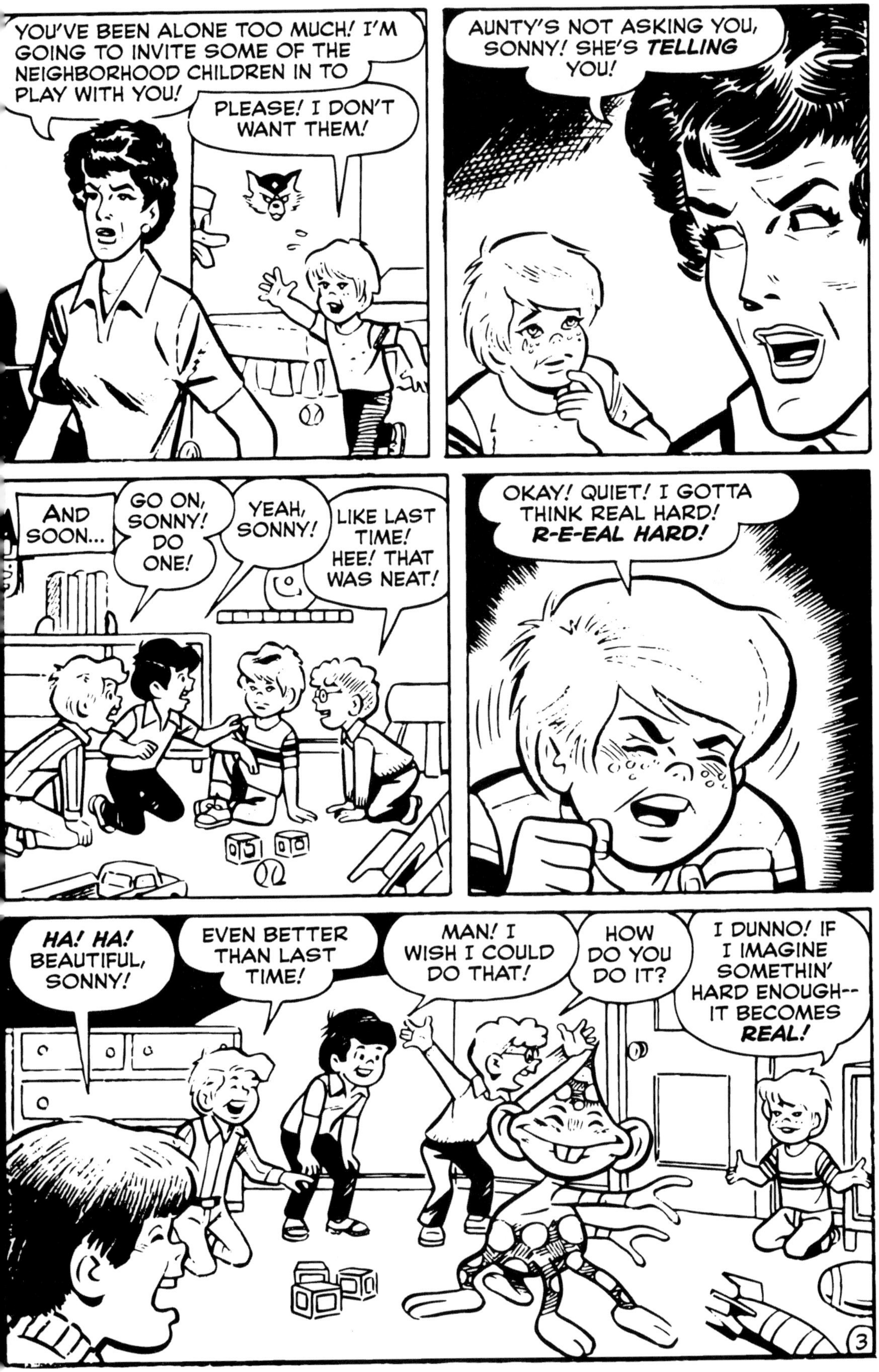

YOU'VE BEEN ALONE TOO MUCH! I'M GOING TO INVITE SOME OF THE NEIGHBORHOOD CHILDREN IN TO PLAY WITH YOU!
PLEASE! I DON'T WANT THEM!
AUNTY'S NOT ASKING YOU, SONNY! SHE'S TELLING YOU!
AND SOON...
GO ON, SONNY! DO ONE!
YEAH, SONNY!
LIKE LAST TIME! HEE! THAT WAS NEAT!
OKAY! QUIET! I GOTTA THINK REAL HARD! R-E-EAL HARD!
HA! HA! BEAUTIFUL, SONNY!
EVEN BETTER THAN LAST TIME!
MAN! I WISH I COULD DO THAT!
HOW DO YOU DO IT?
I DUNNO! IF I IMAGINE SOMETHIN' HARD ENOUGH-- IT BECOMES REAL!

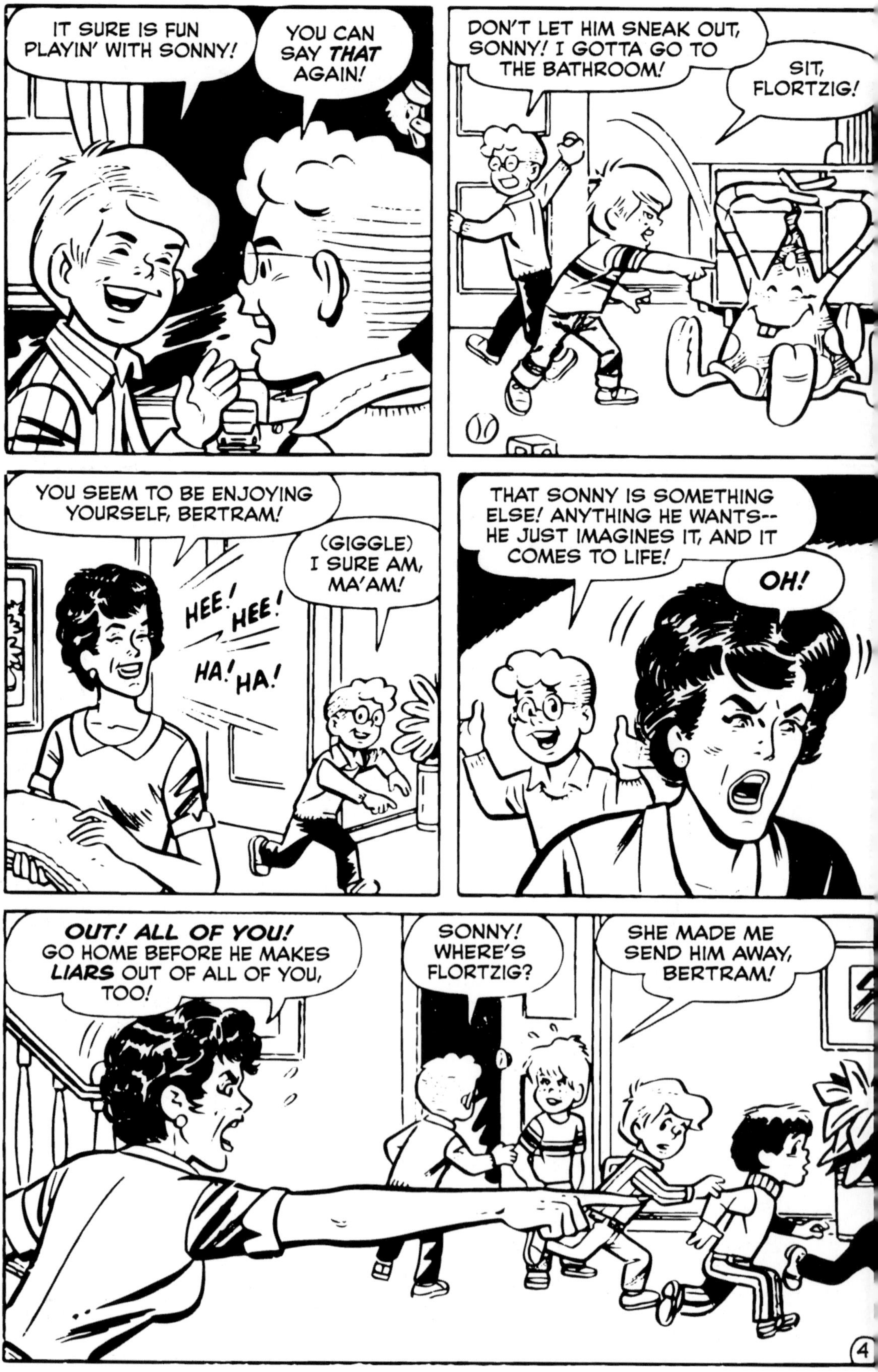
IT SURE IS FUN PLAYIN' WITH SONNY!
YOU CAN SAY THAT AGAIN!
DON'T LET HIM SNEAK OUT, SONNY! I GOTTA GO TO THE BATHROOM!
SIT, FLORTZIG!
YOU SEEM TO BE ENJOYING YOURSELF, BERTRAM!
HEE! HEE! HA! HA!
(GIGGLE) I SURE AM, MA'AM!
THAT SONNY IS SOMETHING ELSE! ANYTHING HE WANTS-- HE JUST IMAGINES IT, AND IT COMES TO LIFE!
OH!
OUT! ALL OF YOU! GO HOME BEFORE HE MAKES LIARS OUT OF ALL OF YOU, TOO!
SONNY! WHERE'S FLORTZIG?
SHE MADE ME SEND HIM AWAY, BERTRAM!
4

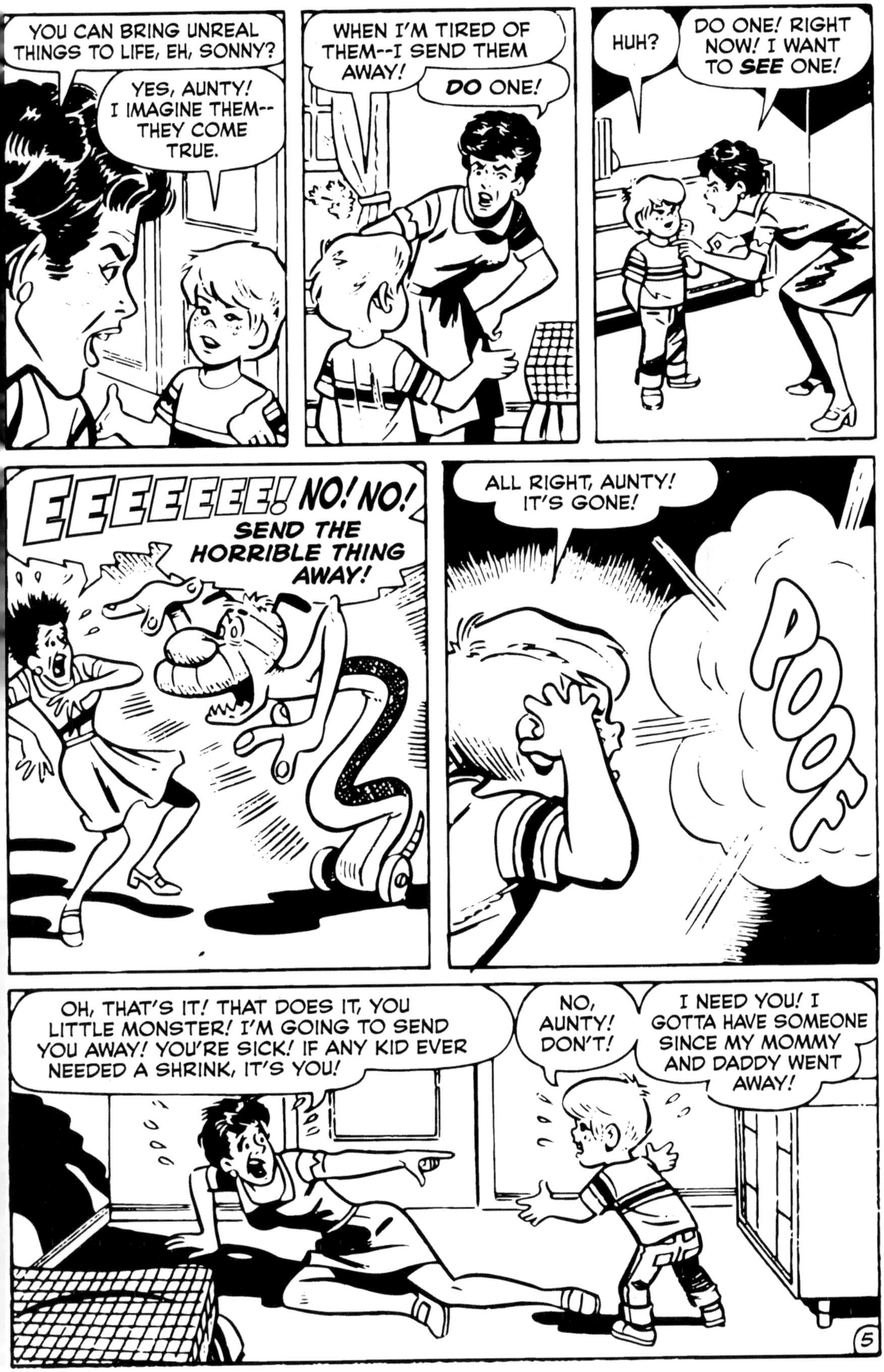
YOU CAN BRING UNREAL THINGS TO LIFE, EH, SONNY?
YES, AUNTY! I IMAGINE THEM--THEY COME TRUE.
WHEN I'M TIRED OF THEM--I SEND THEM AWAY!
DO ONE!
HUH?
DO ONE! RIGHT NOW! I WANT TO SEE ONE!
EEEEEEE! NO! NO! SEND THE HORRIBLE THING AWAY!
ALL RIGHT, AUNTY! IT'S GONE!
POOF
OH, THAT'S IT! THAT DOES IT, YOU LITTLE MONSTER! I'M GOING TO SEND YOU AWAY! YOU'RE SICK! IF ANY KID EVER NEEDED A SHRINK, IT'S YOU!
NO, AUNTY! DON'T!
I NEED YOU! I GOTTA HAVE SOMEONE SINCE MY MOMMY AND DADDY WENT AWAY!
5

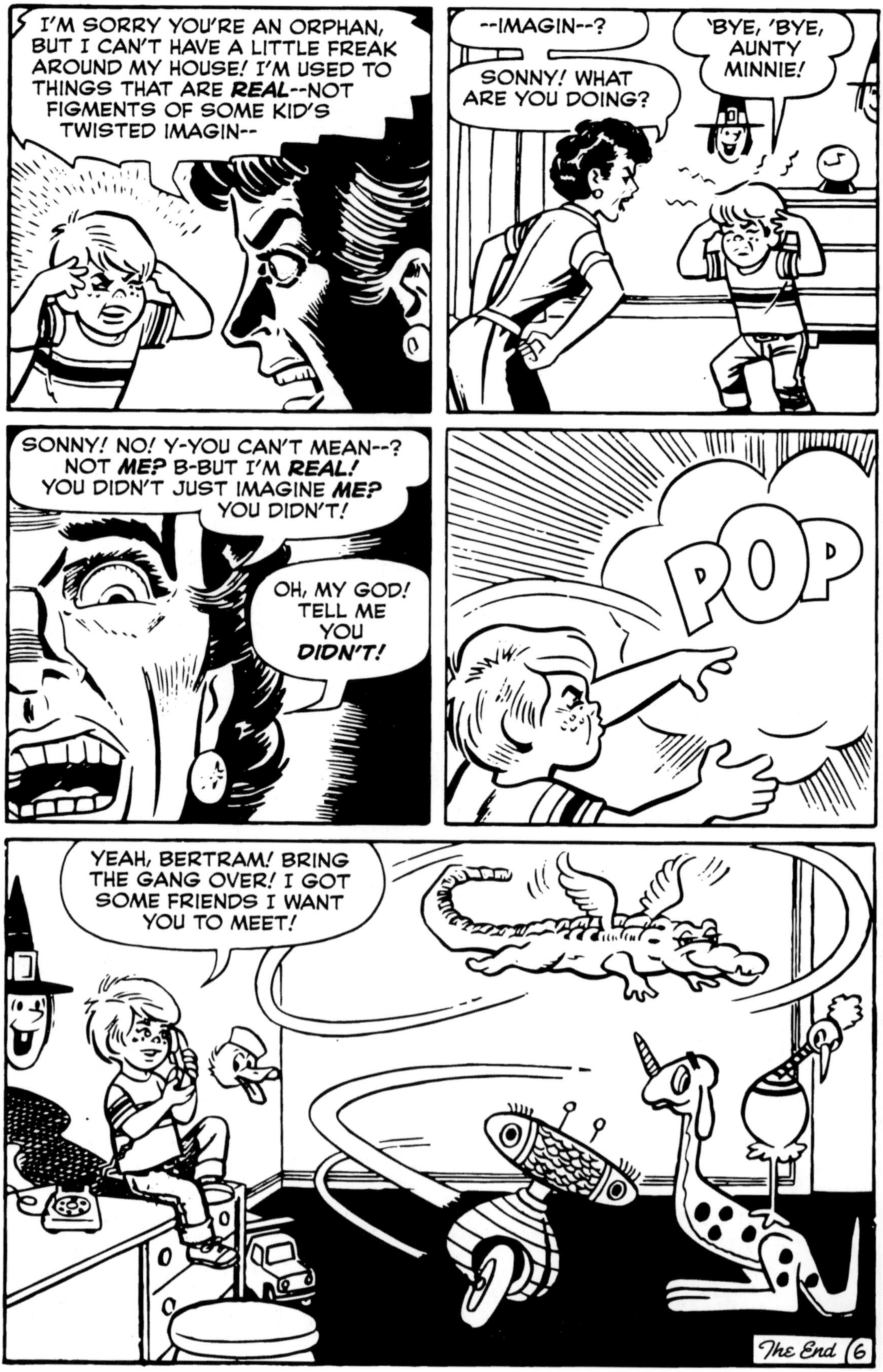
I'M SORRY YOU'RE AN ORPHAN, BUT I CAN'T HAVE A LITTLE FREAK AROUND MY HOUSE! I'M USED TO THINGS THAT ARE REAL--NOT FIGMENTS OF SOME KID'S TWISTED IMAGIN--
--IMAGIN--?
SONNY! WHAT ARE YOU DOING?
'BYE, 'BYE, AUNTY MINNIE!
SONNY! NO! Y-YOU CAN'T MEAN--? NOT ME? B-BUT I'M REAL! YOU DIDN'T JUST IMAGINE ME? YOU DIDN'T!
OH, MY GOD! TELL ME YOU DIDN'T!
POP
YEAH, BERTRAM! BRING THE GANG OVER! I GOT SOME FRIENDS I WANT YOU TO MEET!
The End
6

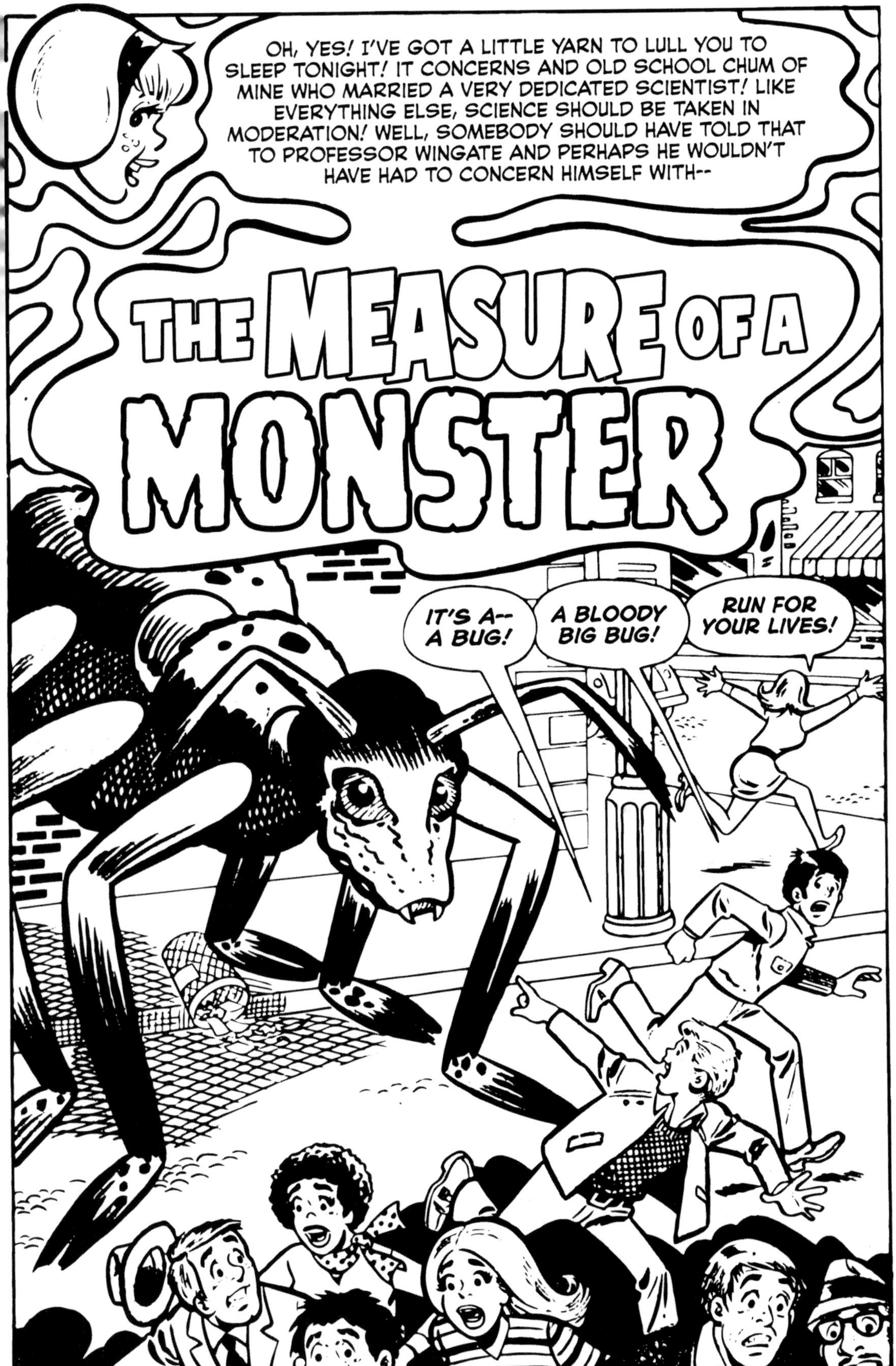
OH, YES! I'VE GOT A LITTLE YARN TO LULL YOU TO SLEEP TONIGHT! IT CONCERNS AND OLD SCHOOL CHUM OF MINE WHO MARRIED A VERY DEDICATED SCIENTIST! LIKE EVERYTHING ELSE, SCIENCE SHOULD BE TAKEN IN MODERATION! WELL, SOMEBODY SHOULD HAVE TOLD THAT TO PROFESSOR WINGATE AND PERHAPS HE WOULDN'T HAVE HAD TO CONCERN HIMSELF WITH--
THE MEASURE OF A MONSTER
IT'S A-- A BUG!
A BLOODY BIG BUG!
RUN FOR YOUR LIVES!

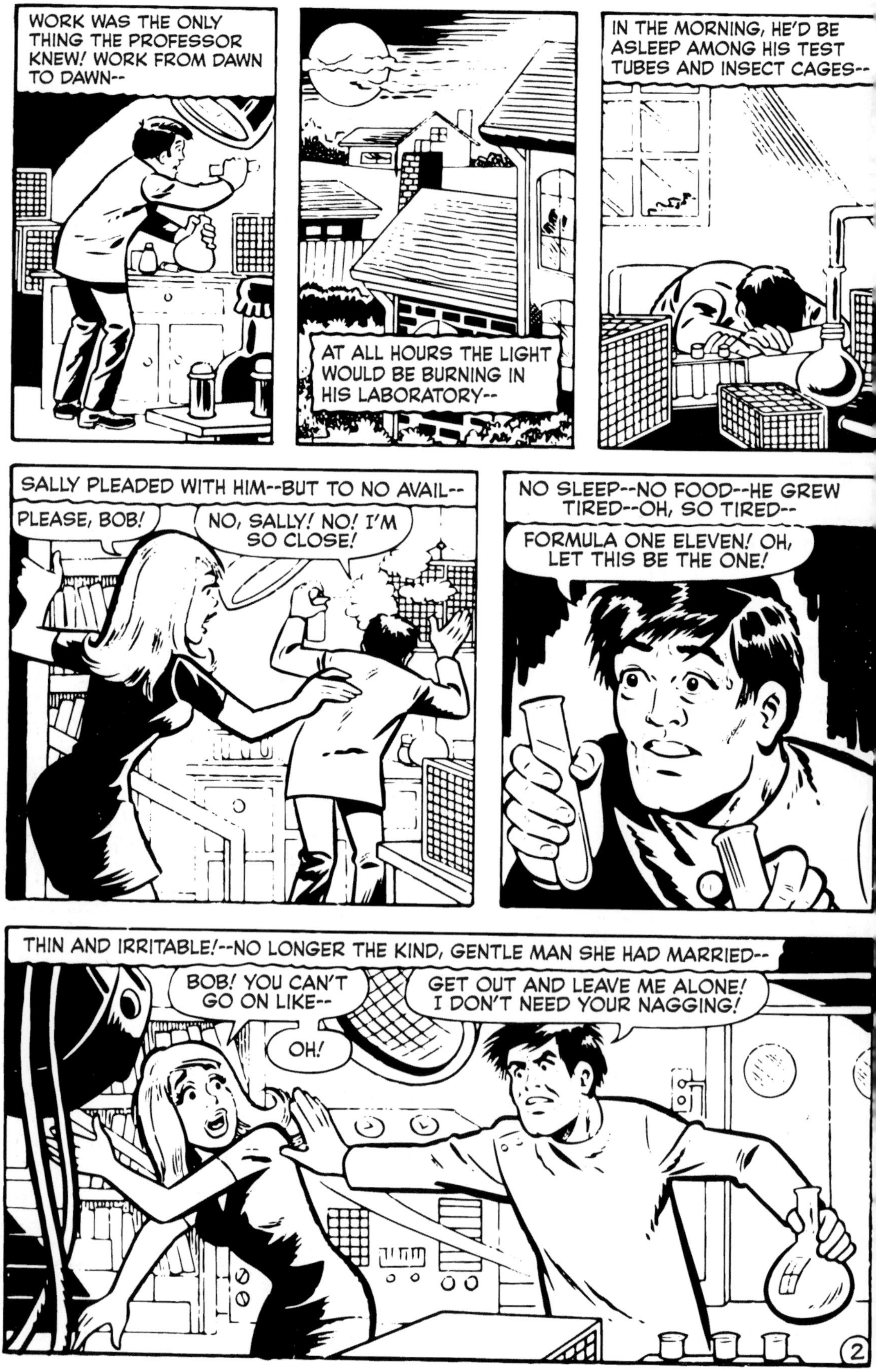

WORK WAS THE ONLY THING THE PROFESSOR KNEW! WORK FROM DAWN TO DAWN--
AT ALL HOURS THE LIGHT WOULD BE BURNING IN HIS LABORATORY--
IN THE MORNING, HE'D BE ASLEEP AMONG HIS TEST TUBES AND INSECT CAGES--
SALLY PLEADED WITH HIM--BUT TO NO AVAIL--
PLEASE, BOB!
NO, SALLY! NO! I'M SO CLOSE!
NO SLEEP--NO FOOD--HE GREW TIRED--OH, SO TIRED--
FORMULA ONE ELEVEN! OH, LET THIS BE THE ONE!
THIN AND IRRITABLE!--NO LONGER THE KIND, GENTLE MAN SHE HAD MARRIED--
BOB! YOU CAN'T GO ON LIKE--
GET OUT AND LEAVE ME ALONE! I DON'T NEED YOUR NAGGING!
OH!
2

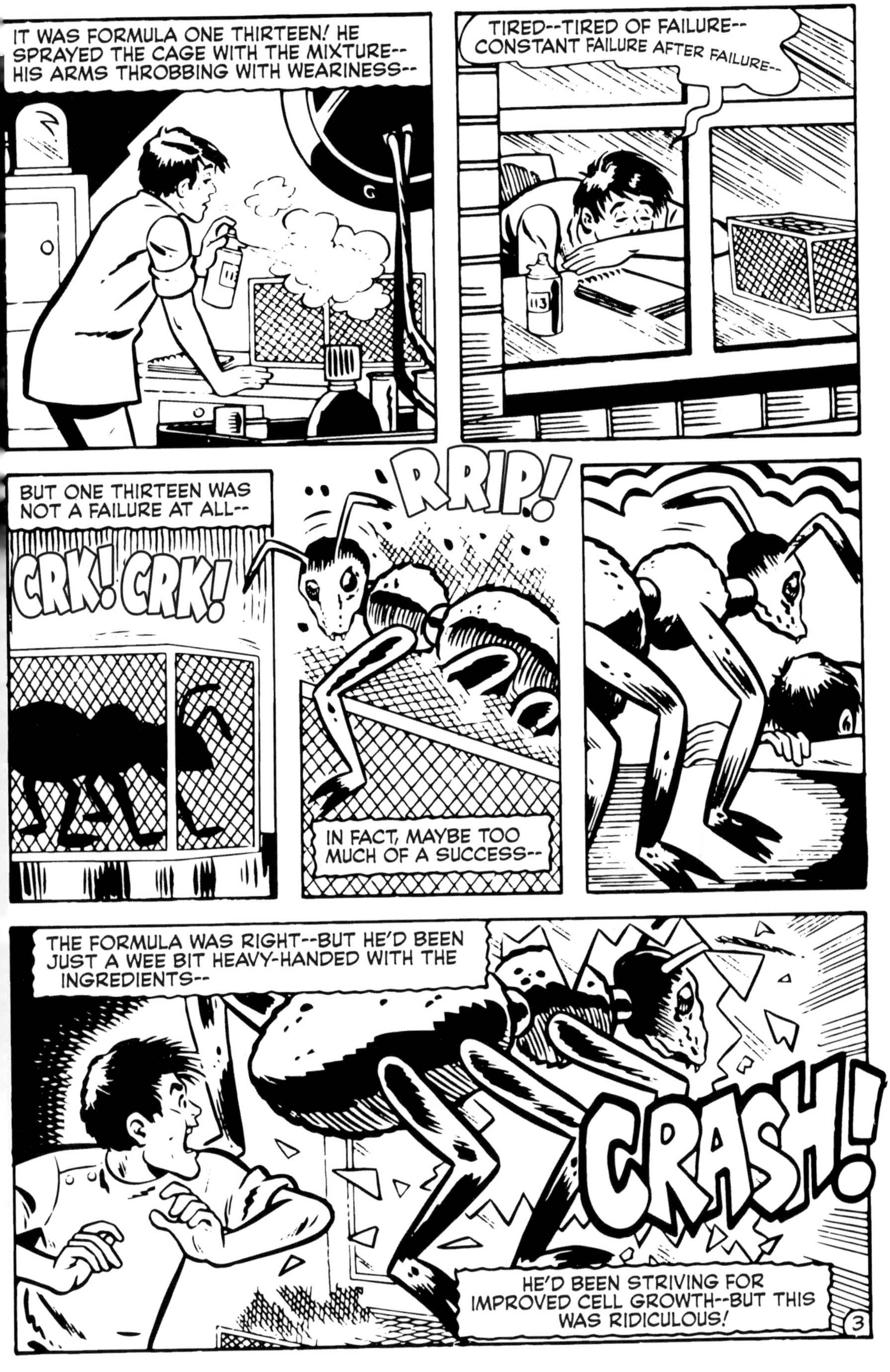
IT WAS FORMULA ONE THIRTEEN! HE SPRAYED THE CAGE WITH THE MIXTURE-- HIS ARMS THROBBING WITH WEARINESS--
113
TIRED--TIRED OF FAILURE-- CONSTANT FAILURE AFTER FAILURE--
113
BUT ONE THIRTEEN WAS NOT A FAILURE AT ALL--
CRK! CRK!
RRIP!
IN FACT, MAYBE TOO MUCH OF A SUCCESS--
THE FORMULA WAS RIGHT--BUT HE'D BEEN JUST A WEE BIT HEAVY-HANDED WITH THE INGREDIENTS--
CRASH!
HE'D BEEN STRIVING FOR IMPROVED CELL GROWTH--BUT THIS WAS RIDICULOUS!
3

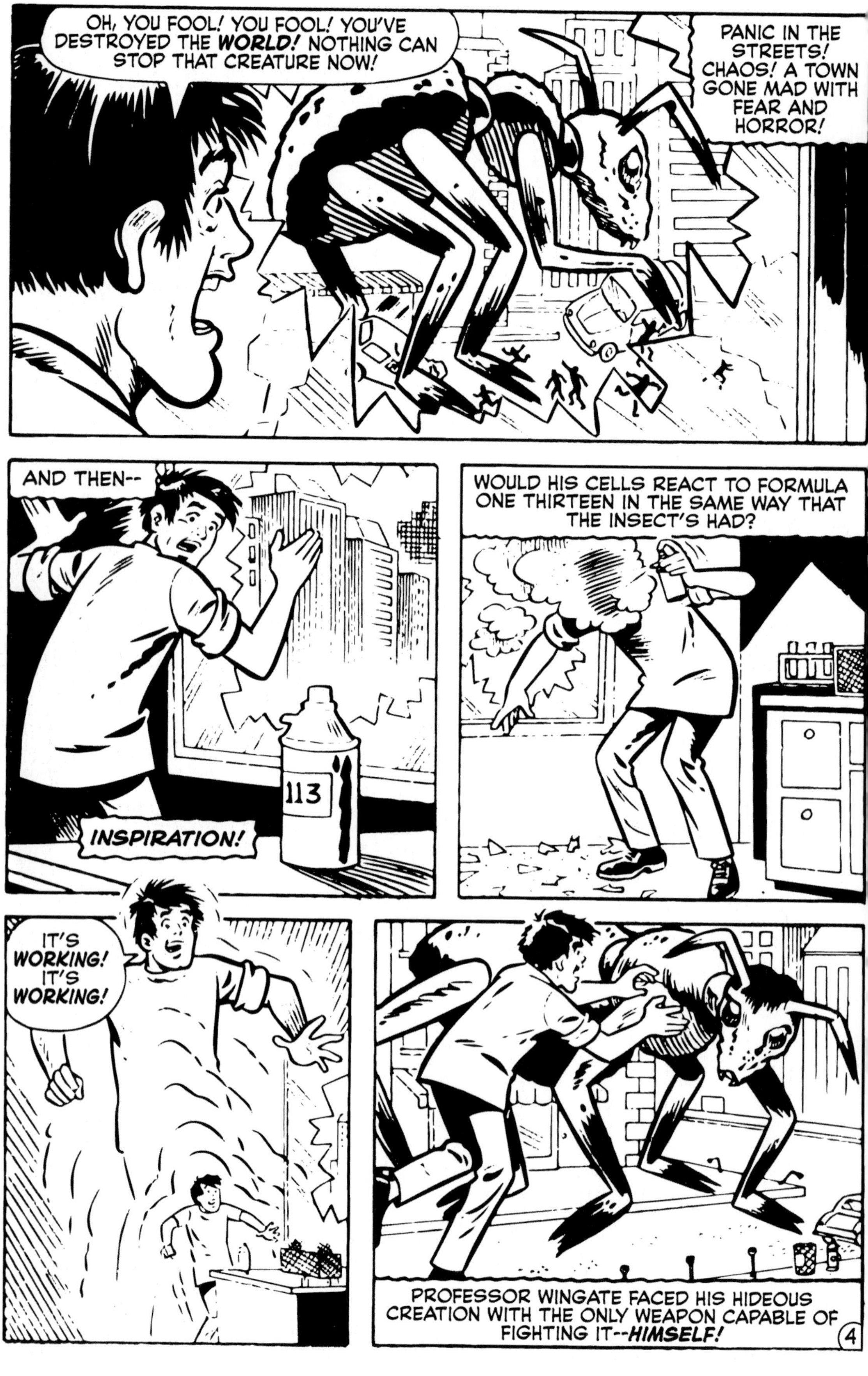

OH, YOU FOOL! YOU FOOL! YOU'VE DESTROYED THE WORLD! NOTHING CAN STOP THAT CREATURE NOW!
PANIC IN THE STREETS! CHAOS! A TOWN GONE MAD WITH FEAR AND HORROR!
AND THEN--
113
INSPIRATION!
WOULD HIS CELLS REACT TO FORMULA ONE THIRTEEN IN THE SAME WAY THAT THE INSECT'S HAD?
IT'S WORKING! IT'S WORKING!
PROFESSOR WINGATE FACED HIS HIDEOUS CREATION WITH THE ONLY WEAPON CAPABLE OF FIGHTING IT--HIMSELF!

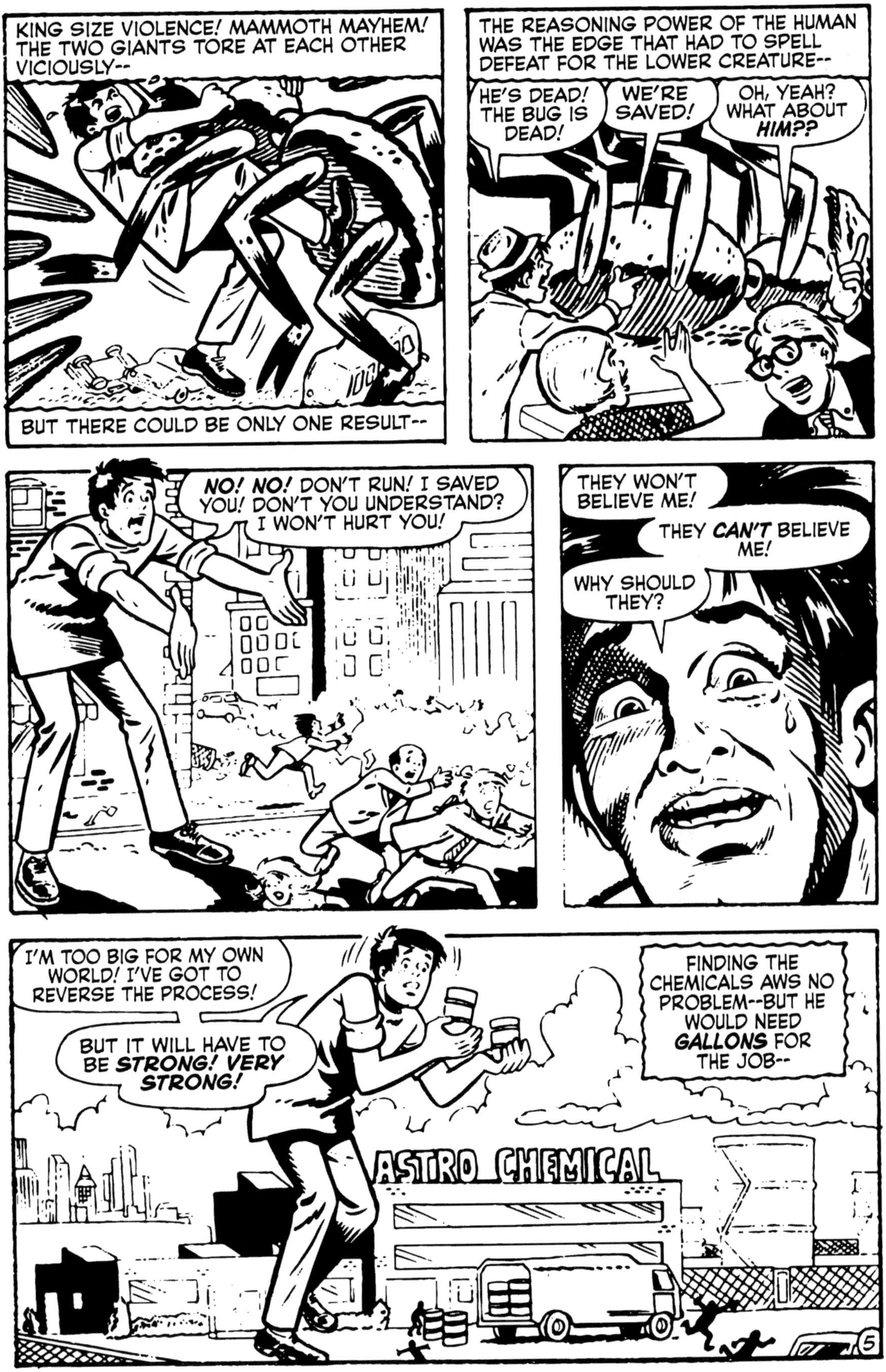
KING SIZE VIOLENCE! MAMMOTH MAYHEM! THE TWO GIANTS TORE AT EACH OTHER VICIOUSLY--
BUT THERE COULD BE ONLY ONE RESULT--
THE REASONING POWER OF THE HUMAN WAS THE EDGE THAT HAD TO SPELL DEFEAT FOR THE LOWER CREATURE--
HE'S DEAD! THE BUG IS DEAD!
WE'RE SAVED!
OH, YEAH? WHAT ABOUT HIM??
NO! NO! DON'T RUN! I SAVED YOU! DON'T YOU UNDERSTAND? I WON'T HURT YOU!
THEY WON'T BELIEVE ME!
THEY CAN'T BELIEVE ME!
WHY SHOULD THEY?
I'M TOO BIG FOR MY OWN WORLD! I'VE GOT TO REVERSE THE PROCESS!
BUT IT WILL HAVE TO BE STRONG! VERY STRONG!
FINDING THE CHEMICALS AWS NO PROBLEM--BUT HE WOULD NEED GALLONS FOR THE JOB--
ASTRO CHEMICAL
5

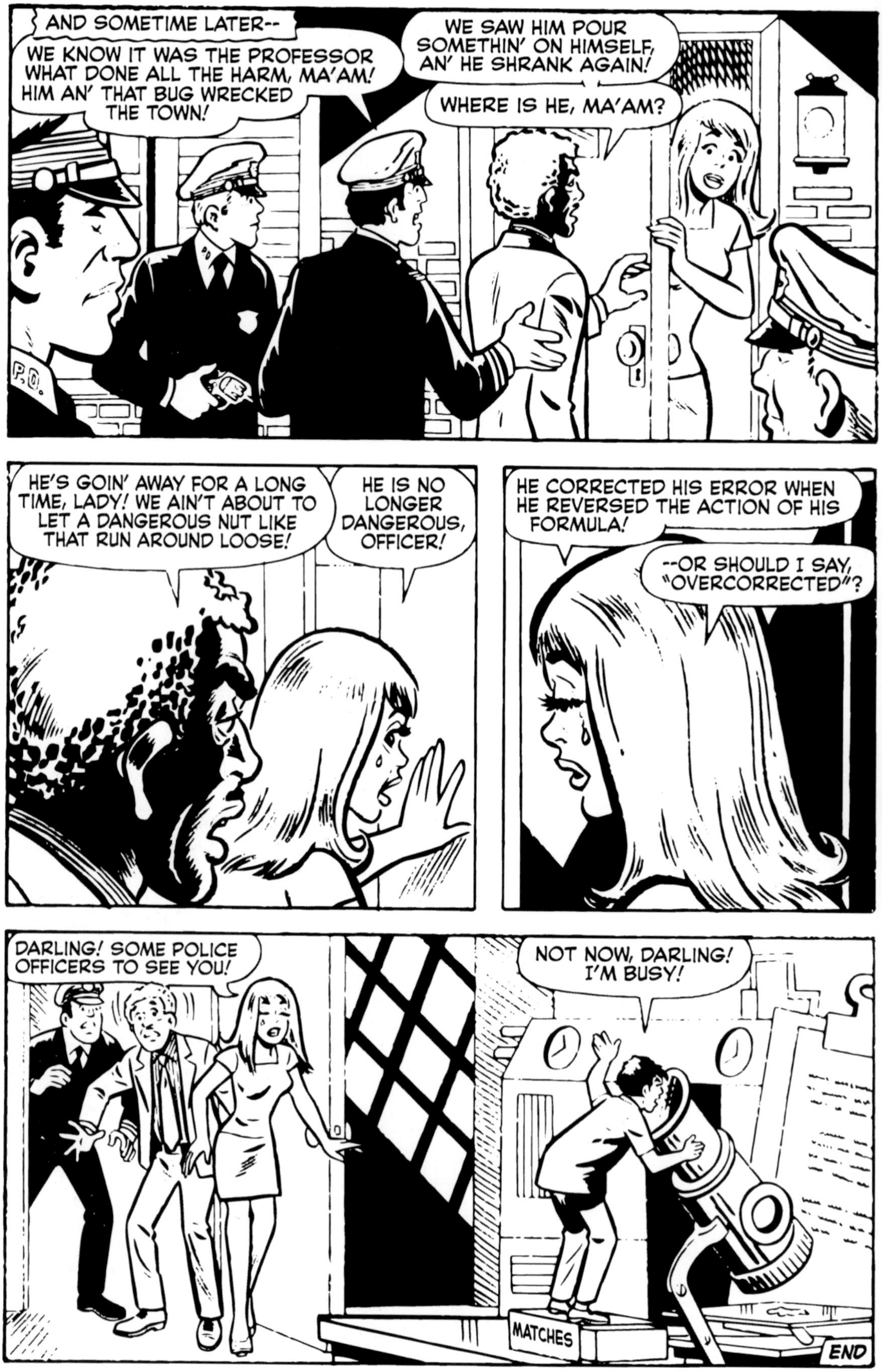
AND SOMETIME LATER--
WE KNOW IT WAS THE PROFESSOR WHAT DONE ALL THE HARM, MA'AM! HIM AN' THAT BUG WRECKED THE TOWN!
WE SAW HIM POUR SOMETHIN' ON HIMSELF, AN' HE SHRANK AGAIN!
WHERE IS HE, MA'AM?
P.D.
HE'S GOIN' AWAY FOR A LONG TIME, LADY! WE AIN'T ABOUT TO LET A DANGEROUS NUT LIKE THAT RUN AROUND LOOSE!
HE IS NO LONGER DANGEROUS, OFFICER!
HE CORRECTED HIS ERROR WHEN HE REVERSED THE ACTION OF HIS FORMULA!
--OR SHOULD I SAY, "OVERCORRECTED"?
DARLING! SOME POLICE OFFICERS TO SEE YOU!
NOT NOW, DARLING! I'M BUSY!
MATCHES
END

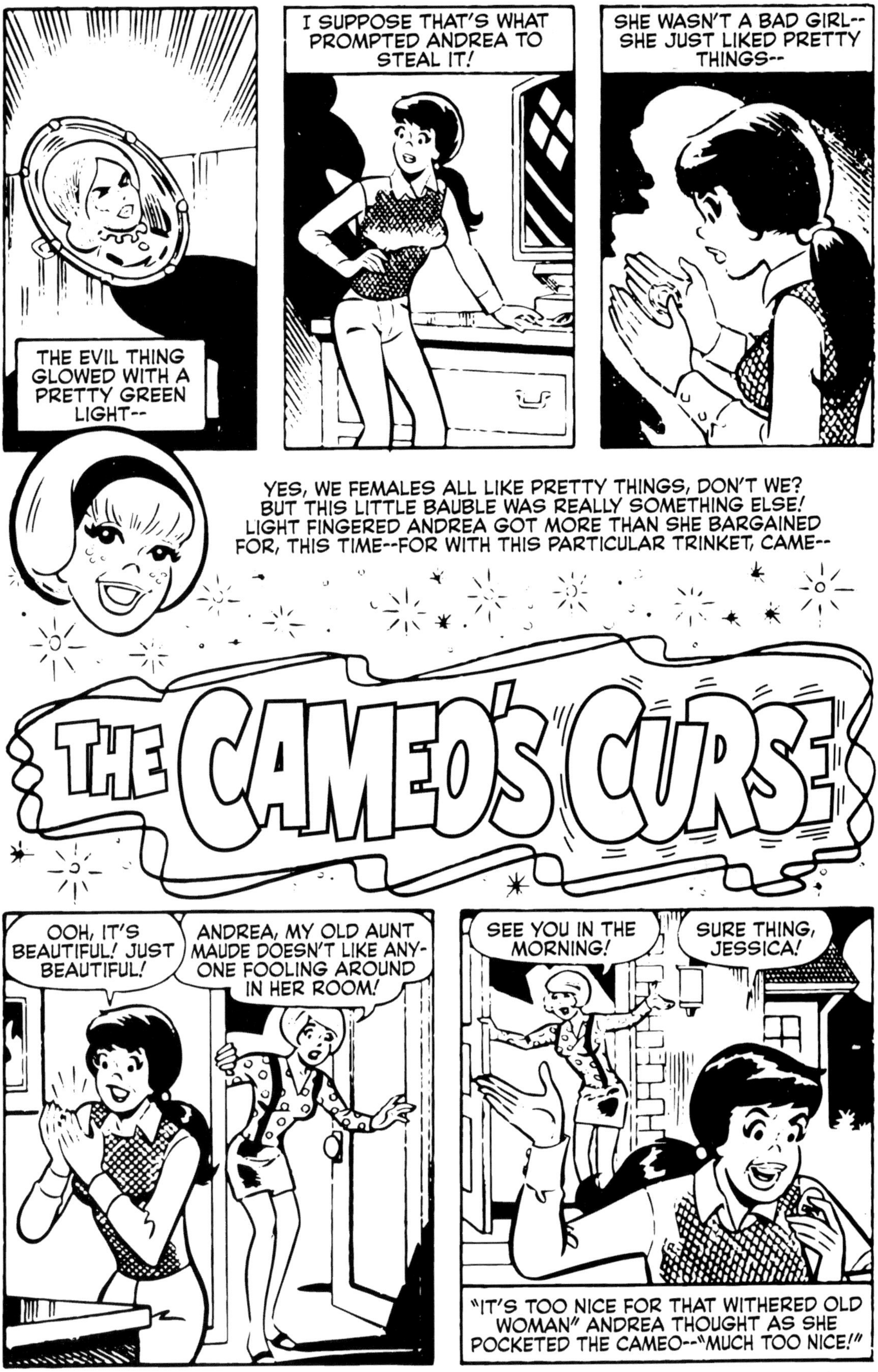
THE EVIL THING GLOWED WITH A PRETTY GREEN LIGHT--
I SUPPOSE THAT'S WHAT PROMPTED ANDREA TO STEAL IT!
SHE WASN'T A BAD GIRL--SHE JUST LIKED PRETTY THINGS--
YES, WE FEMALES ALL LIKE PRETTY THINGS, DON'T WE? BUT THIS LITTLE BAUBLE WAS REALLY SOMETHING ELSE! LIGHT FINGERED ANDREA GOT MORE THAN SHE BARGAINED FOR, THIS TIME--FOR WITH THIS PARTICULAR TRINKET, CAME--
THE CAMEO'S CURSE
OOH, IT'S BEAUTIFUL! JUST BEAUTIFUL!
ANDREA, MY OLD AUNT MAUDE DOESN'T LIKE ANY-ONE FOOLING AROUND IN HER ROOM!
SEE YOU IN THE MORNING!
SURE THING, JESSICA!
"IT'S TOO NICE FOR THAT WITHERED OLD WOMAN" ANDREA THOUGHT AS SHE POCKETED THE CAMEO--"MUCH TOO NICE!"

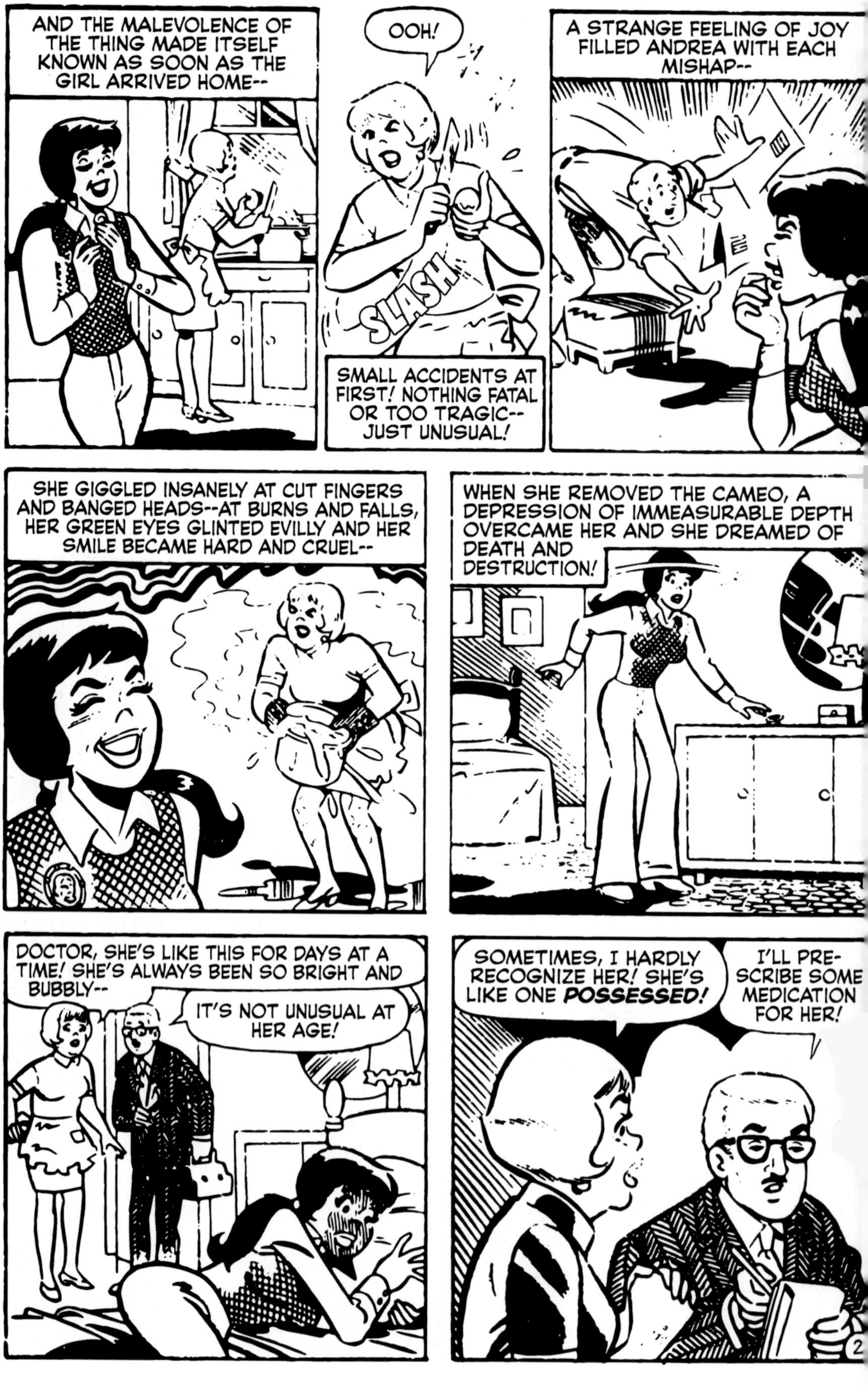
AND THE MALEVOLENCE OF THE THING MADE ITSELF KNOWN AS SOON AS THE GIRL ARRIVED HOME--
OOH!
SLASH
SMALL ACCIDENTS AT FIRST! NOTHING FATAL OR TOO TRAGIC-- JUST UNUSUAL!
A STRANGE FEELING OF JOY FILLED ANDREA WITH EACH MISHAP--
SHE GIGGLED INSANELY AT CUT FINGERS AND BANGED HEADS--AT BURNS AND FALLS, HER GREEN EYES GLINTED EVILLY AND HER SMILE BECAME HARD AND CRUEL--
WHEN SHE REMOVED THE CAMEO, A DEPRESSION OF IMMEASURABLE DEPTH OVERCAME HER AND SHE DREAMED OF DEATH AND DESTRUCTION!
DOCTOR, SHE'S LIKE THIS FOR DAYS AT A TIME! SHE'S ALWAYS BEEN SO BRIGHT AND BUBBLY--
IT'S NOT UNUSUAL AT HER AGE!
SOMETIMES, I HARDLY RECOGNIZE HER! SHE'S LIKE ONE POSSESSED!
I'LL PRE-SCRIBE SOME MEDICATION FOR HER!
2

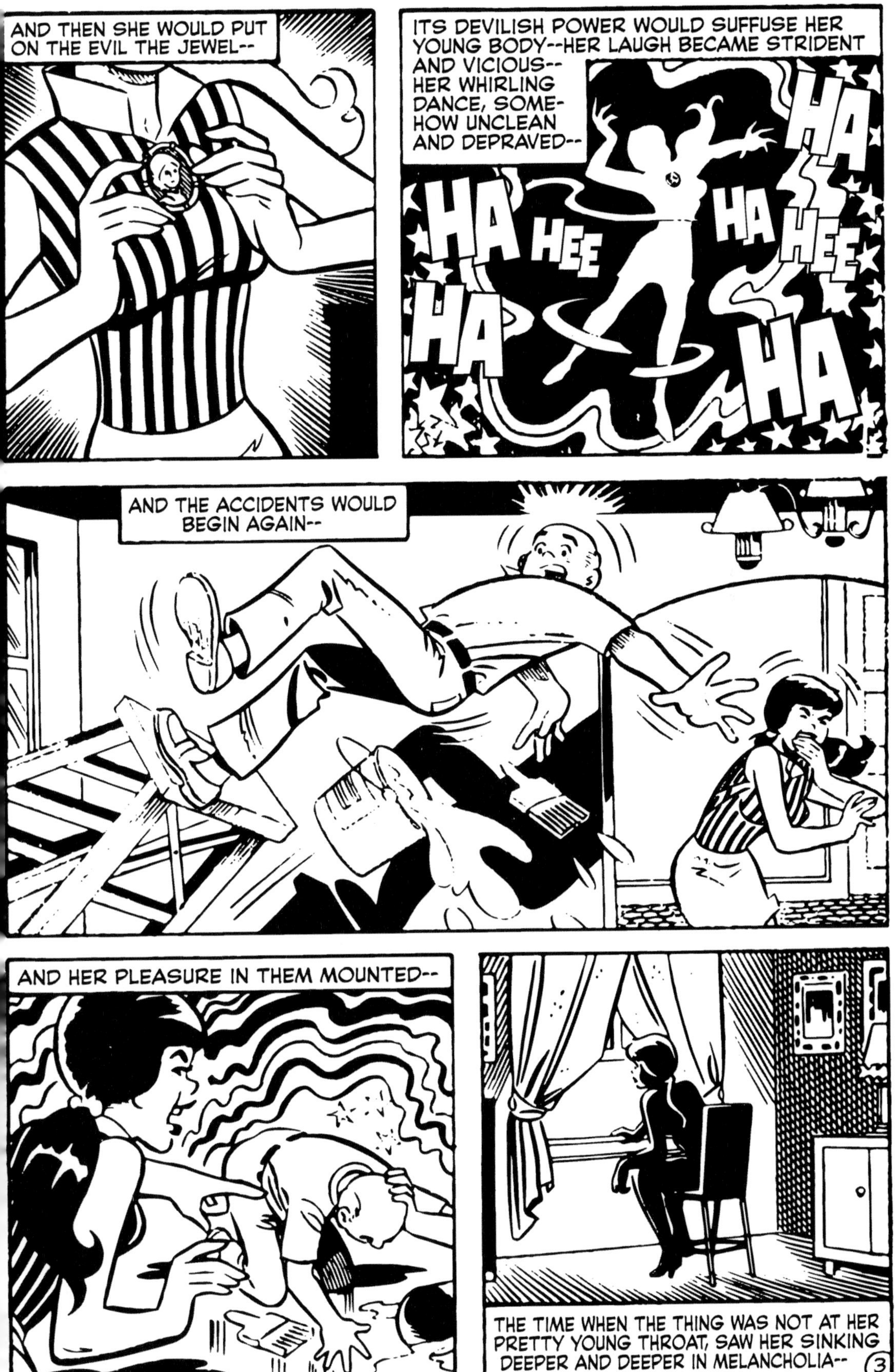
AND THEN SHE WOULD PUT ON THE EVIL THE JEWEL--
ITS DEVILISH POWER WOULD SUFFUSE HER YOUNG BODY--HER LAUGH BECAME STRIDENT AND VICIOUS--
HER WHIRLING DANCE, SOMEHOW UNCLEAN AND DEPRAVED--
HA
HA
HEE
HA
HA
HA
HEE
HA
AND THE ACCIDENTS WOULD BEGIN AGAIN--
AND HER PLEASURE IN THEM MOUNTED--
THE TIME WHEN THE THING WAS NOT AT HER PRETTY YOUNG THROAT, SAW HER SINKING DEEPER AND DEEPER IN MELANCHOLIA--

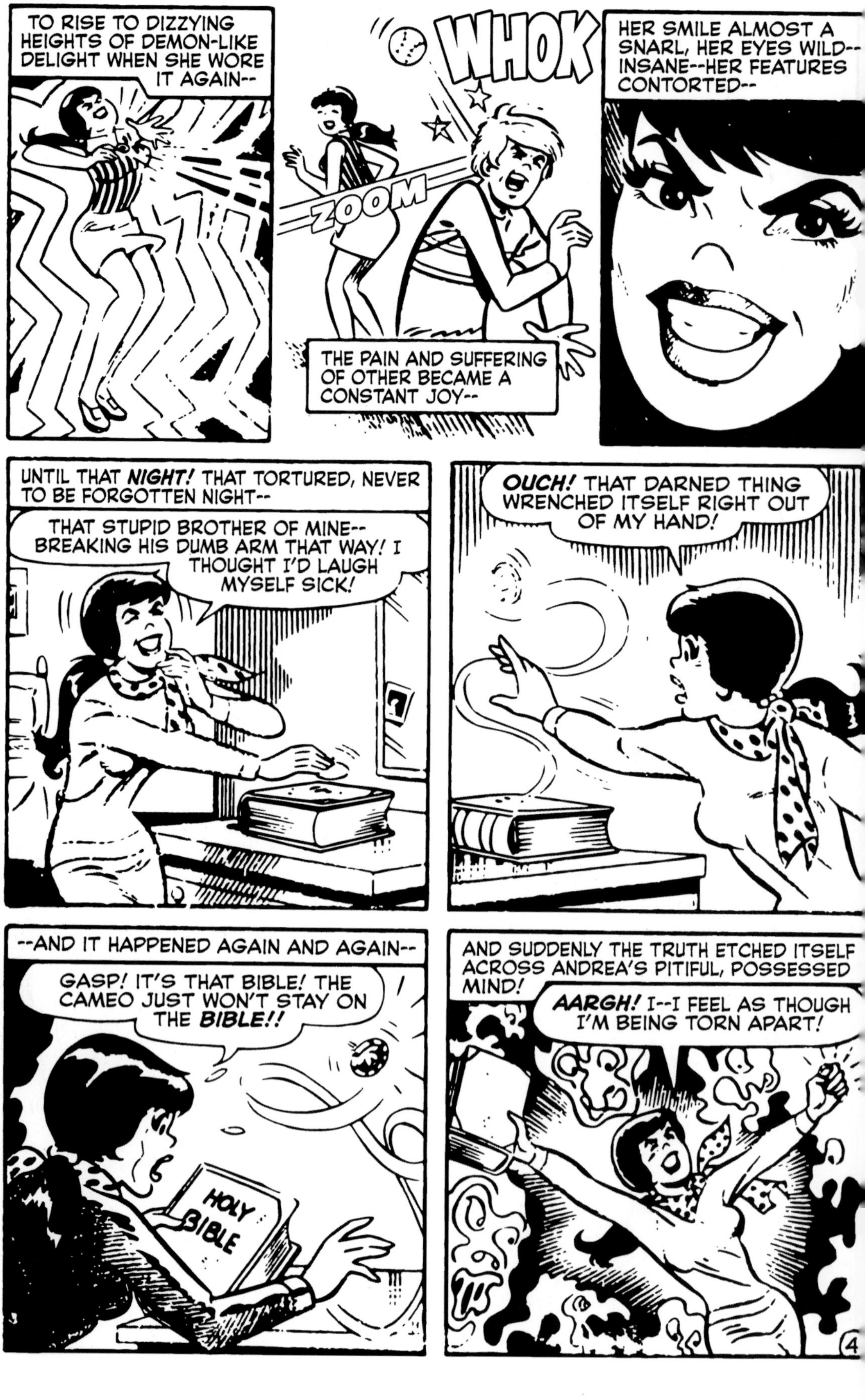
TO RISE TO DIZZYING HEIGHTS OF DEMON-LIKE DELIGHT WHEN SHE WORE IT AGAIN--
WHOK
ZOOM
THE PAIN AND SUFFERING OF OTHER BECAME A CONSTANT JOY--
HER SMILE ALMOST A SNARL, HER EYES WILD--INSANE--HER FEATURES CONTORTED--
UNTIL THAT NIGHT! THAT TORTURED, NEVER TO BE FORGOTTEN NIGHT--
THAT STUPID BROTHER OF MINE--BREAKING HIS DUMB ARM THAT WAY! I THOUGHT I'D LAUGH MYSELF SICK!
OUCH! THAT DARNED THING WRENCHED ITSELF RIGHT OUT OF MY HAND!
--AND IT HAPPENED AGAIN AND AGAIN--
GASP! IT'S THAT BIBLE! THE CAMEO JUST WON'T STAY ON THE BIBLE!!
HOLY BIBLE
AND SUDDENLY THE TRUTH ETCHED ITSELF ACROSS ANDREA'S PITIFUL, POSSESSED MIND!
AARGH! I--I FEEL AS THOUGH I'M BEING TORN APART!
4

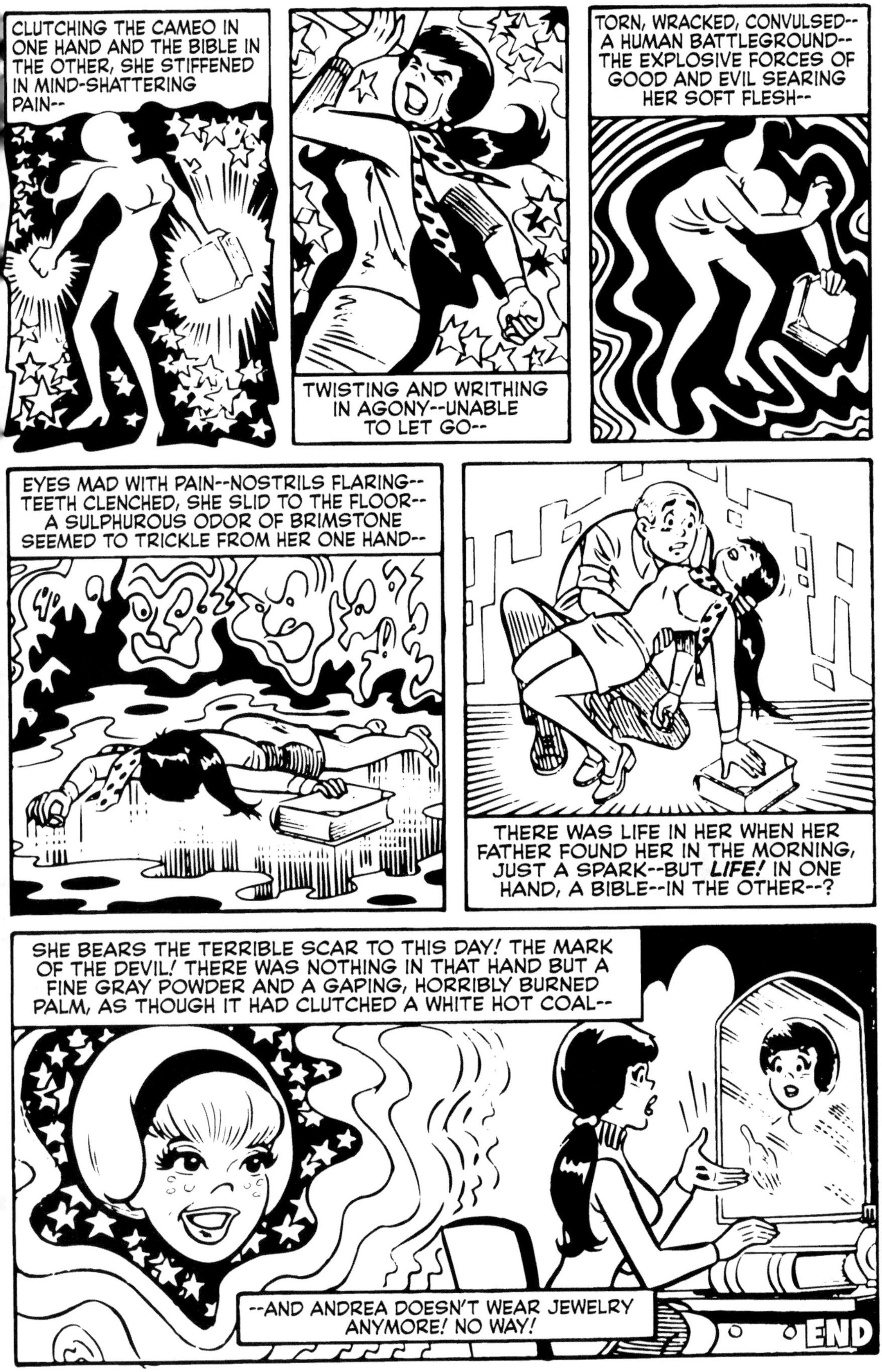
CLUTCHING THE CAMEO IN ONE HAND AND THE BIBLE IN THE OTHER, SHE STIFFENED IN MIND-SHATTERING PAIN--
TWISTING AND WRITHING IN AGONY--UNABLE TO LET GO--
TORN, WRACKED, CONVULSED--A HUMAN BATTLEGROUND--THE EXPLOSIVE FORCES OF GOOD AND EVIL SEARING HER SOFT FLESH--
EYES MAD WITH PAIN--NOSTRILS FLARING--TEETH CLENCHED, SHE SLID TO THE FLOOR--A SULPHUROUS ODOR OF BRIMSTONE SEEMED TO TRICKLE FROM HER ONE HAND--
THERE WAS LIFE IN HER WHEN HER FATHER FOUND HER IN THE MORNING, JUST A SPARK--BUT *LIFE!* IN ONE HAND, A BIBLE--IN THE OTHER--?
SHE BEARS THE TERRIBLE SCAR TO THIS DAY! THE MARK OF THE DEVIL! THERE WAS NOTHING IN THAT HAND BUT A FINE GRAY POWDER AND A GAPING, HORRIBLY BURNED PALM, AS THOUGH IT HAD CLUTCHED A WHITE HOT COAL--
--AND ANDREA DOESN'T WEAR JEWELRY ANYMORE! NO WAY!
END

# ISSUE THREE

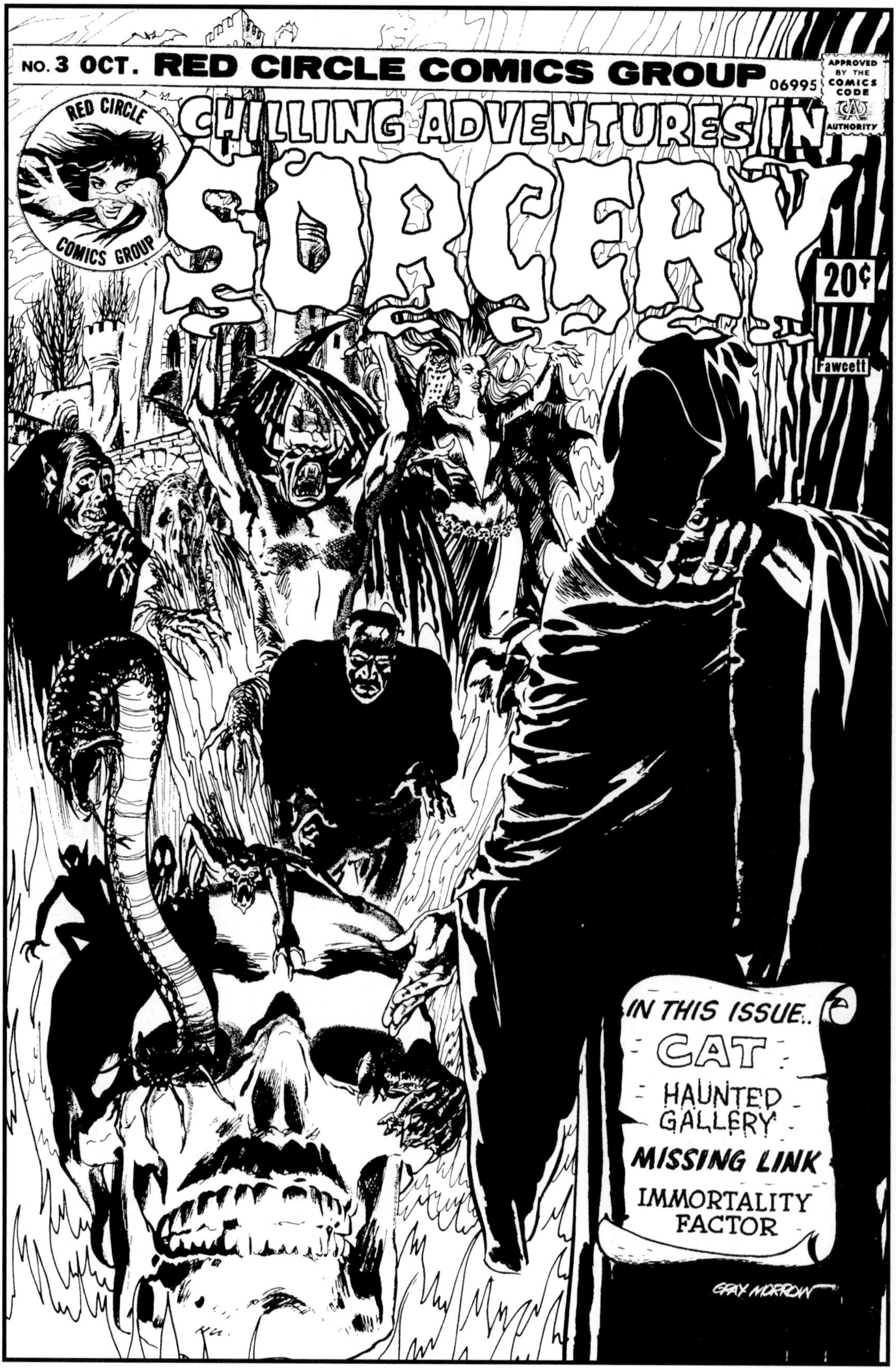
NO. 3 OCT. RED CIRCLE COMICS GROUP
06995
APPROVED BY THE COMICS CODE AUTHORITY
RED CIRCLE COMICS GROUP
CHILLING ADVENTURES IN
SORCERY
20¢
Fawcett
IN THIS ISSUE..
CAT
HAUNTED GALLERY
MISSING LINK
IMMORTALITY FACTOR
GRAY MORROW

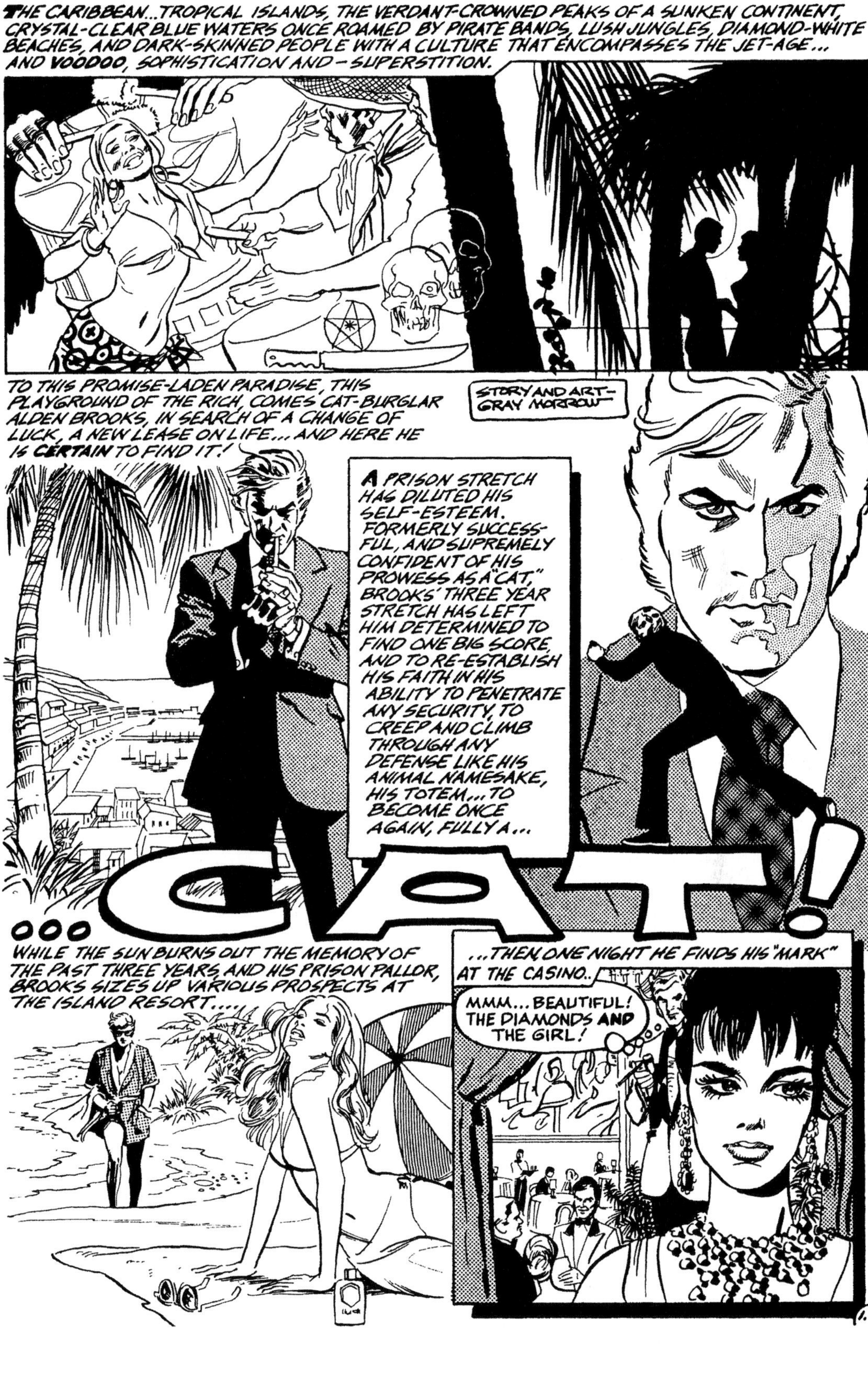

THE CARIBBEAN...TROPICAL ISLANDS, THE VERDANT-CROWNED PEAKS OF A SUNKEN CONTINENT, CRYSTAL-CLEAR BLUE WATERS ONCE ROAMED BY PIRATE BANDS, LUSH JUNGLES, DIAMOND-WHITE BEACHES, AND DARK-SKINNED PEOPLE WITH A CULTURE THAT ENCOMPASSES THE JET-AGE... AND VOODOO, SOPHISTICATION AND -- SUPERSTITION.
TO THIS PROMISE-LADEN PARADISE, THIS PLAYGROUND OF THE RICH, COMES CAT-BURGLAR ALDEN BROOKS, IN SEARCH OF A CHANGE OF LUCK, A NEW LEASE ON LIFE... AND HERE HE IS CERTAIN TO FIND IT!
STORY AND ART-- GRAY MORROW
A PRISON STRETCH HAS DILUTED HIS SELF-ESTEEM. FORMERLY SUCCESSFUL, AND SUPREMELY CONFIDENT OF HIS PROWESS AS A "CAT," BROOKS' THREE YEAR STRETCH HAS LEFT HIM DETERMINED TO FIND ONE BIG SCORE, AND TO RE-ESTABLISH HIS FAITH IN HIS ABILITY TO PENETRATE ANY SECURITY, TO CREEP AND CLIMB THROUGH ANY DEFENSE LIKE HIS ANIMAL NAMESAKE, HIS TOTEM... TO BECOME ONCE AGAIN, FULLY A...
CAT!
OOO
WHILE THE SUN BURNS OUT THE MEMORY OF THE PAST THREE YEARS AND HIS PRISON PALLOR, BROOKS SIZES UP VARIOUS PROSPECTS AT THE ISLAND RESORT....
...THEN, ONE NIGHT HE FINDS HIS "MARK" AT THE CASINO..
MMM... BEAUTIFUL! THE DIAMONDS AND THE GIRL!
1.

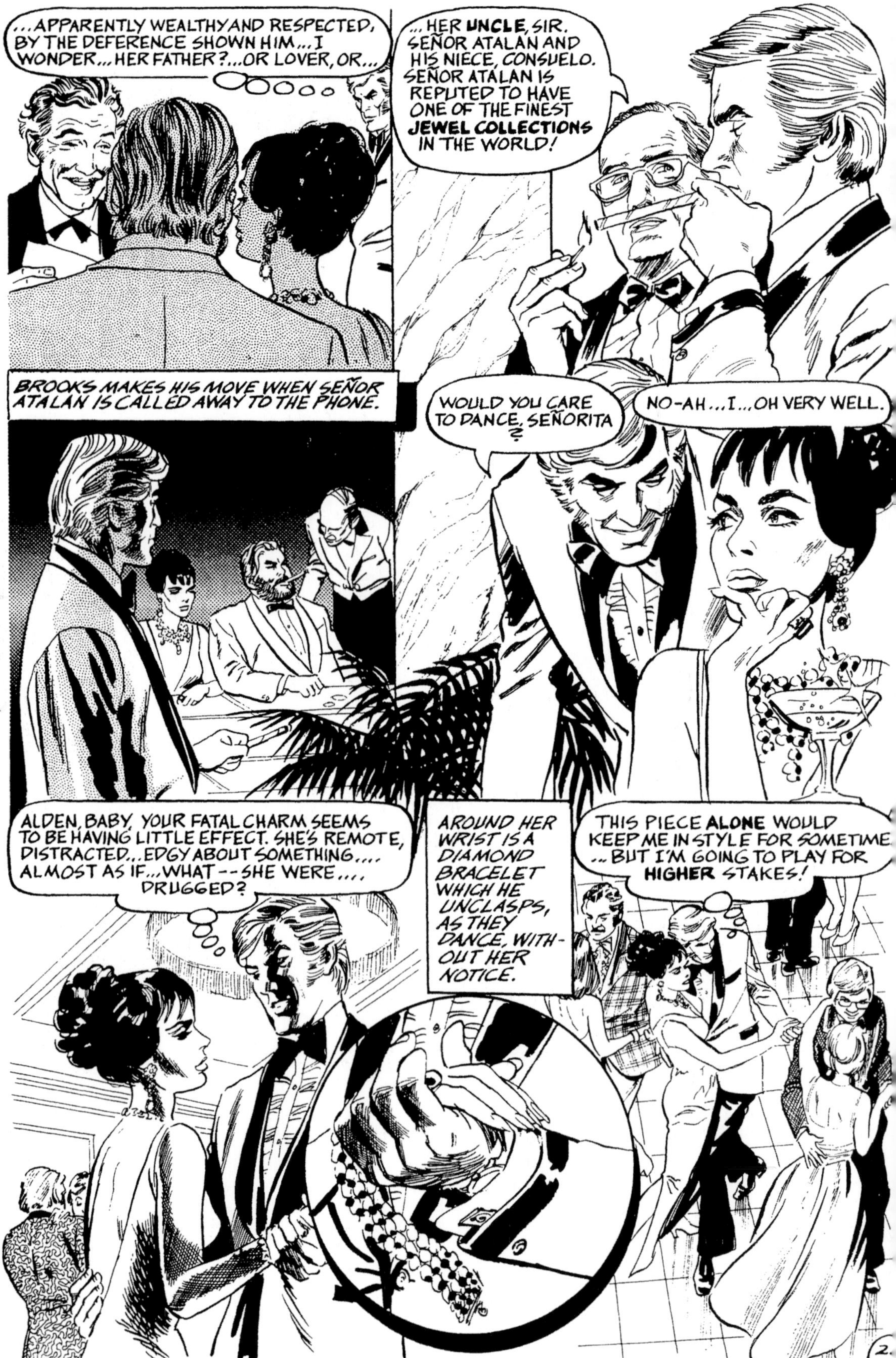
...APPARENTLY WEALTHY AND RESPECTED, BY THE DEFERENCE SHOWN HIM... I WONDER... HER FATHER?...OR LOVER, OR...
...HER UNCLE, SIR. SEÑOR ATALAN AND HIS NIECE, CONSUELO. SEÑOR ATALAN IS REPUTED TO HAVE ONE OF THE FINEST JEWEL COLLECTIONS IN THE WORLD!
BROOKS MAKES HIS MOVE WHEN SEÑOR ATALAN IS CALLED AWAY TO THE PHONE.
WOULD YOU CARE TO DANCE, SEÑORITA?
NO-AH ...I... OH VERY WELL.
ALDEN, BABY, YOUR FATAL CHARM SEEMS TO BE HAVING LITTLE EFFECT. SHE'S REMOTE, DISTRACTED... EDGY ABOUT SOMETHING.... ALMOST AS IF... WHAT -- SHE WERE.... DRUGGED?
AROUND HER WRIST IS A DIAMOND BRACELET WHICH HE UNCLASPS, AS THEY DANCE, WITHOUT HER NOTICE.
THIS PIECE ALONE WOULD KEEP ME IN STYLE FOR SOMETIME ...BUT I'M GOING TO PLAY FOR HIGHER STAKES!

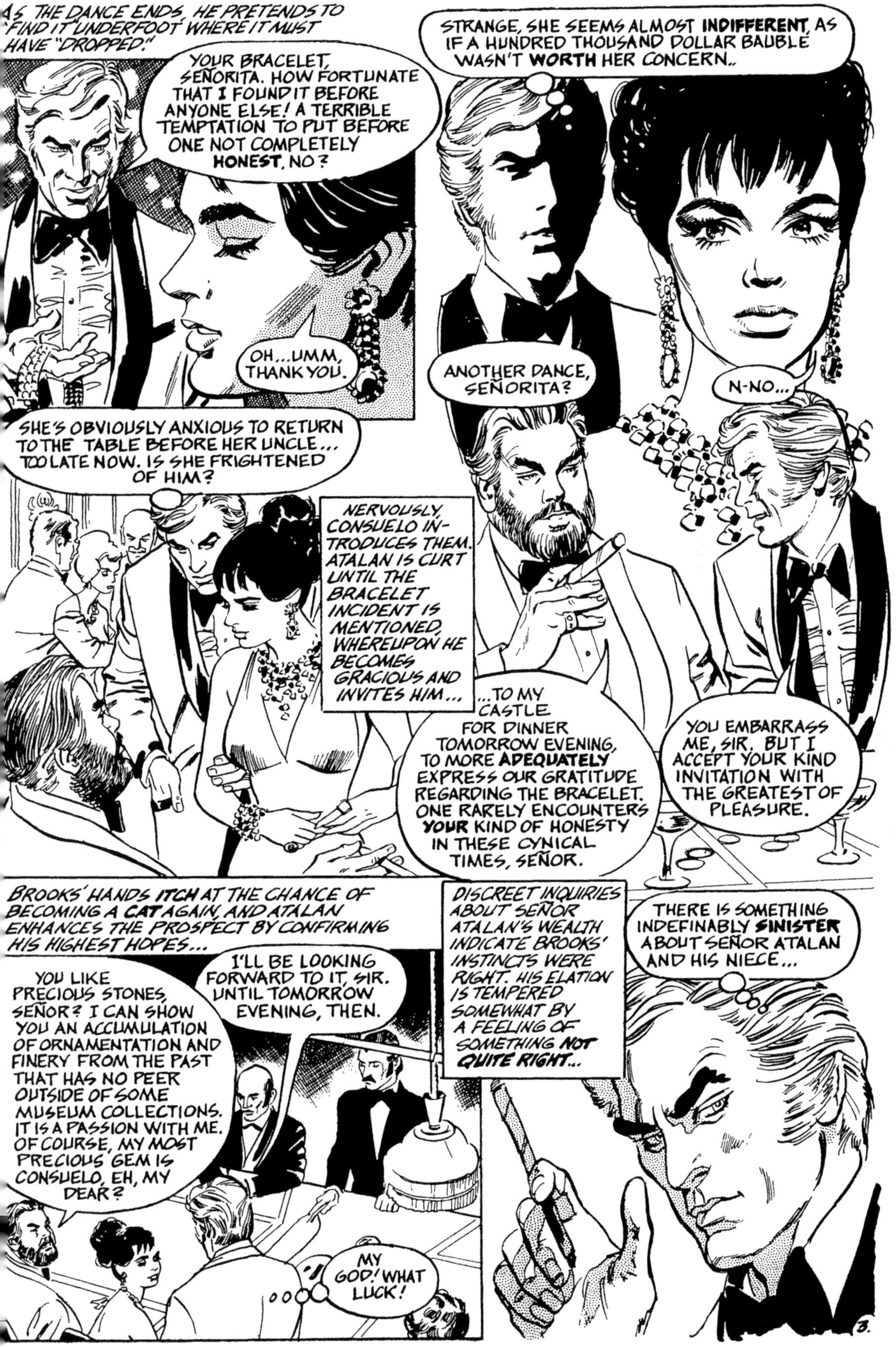
AS THE DANCE ENDS, HE PRETENDS TO "FIND IT" UNDERFOOT WHERE IT MUST HAVE "DROPPED."
YOUR BRACELET, SEÑORITA. HOW FORTUNATE THAT I FOUND IT BEFORE ANYONE ELSE! A TERRIBLE TEMPTATION TO PUT BEFORE ONE NOT COMPLETELY HONEST, NO?
OH...UMM, THANK YOU.
STRANGE, SHE SEEMS ALMOST INDIFFERENT, AS IF A HUNDRED THOUSAND DOLLAR BAUBLE WASN'T WORTH HER CONCERN..
ANOTHER DANCE, SEÑORITA?
N-NO...
SHE'S OBVIOUSLY ANXIOUS TO RETURN TO THE TABLE BEFORE HER UNCLE... TOO LATE NOW. IS SHE FRIGHTENED OF HIM?
NERVOUSLY, CONSUELO INTRODUCES THEM. ATALAN IS CURT UNTIL THE BRACELET INCIDENT IS MENTIONED, WHEREUPON HE BECOMES GRACIOUS AND INVITES HIM...
...TO MY CASTLE FOR DINNER TOMORROW EVENING, TO MORE ADEQUATELY EXPRESS OUR GRATITUDE REGARDING THE BRACELET. ONE RARELY ENCOUNTERS YOUR KIND OF HONESTY IN THESE CYNICAL TIMES, SEÑOR.
YOU EMBARRASS ME, SIR, BUT I ACCEPT YOUR KIND INVITATION WITH THE GREATEST OF PLEASURE.
BROOKS' HANDS ITCH AT THE CHANCE OF BECOMING A CAT AGAIN, AND ATALAN ENHANCES THE PROSPECT BY CONFIRMING HIS HIGHEST HOPES...
YOU LIKE PRECIOUS STONES, SEÑOR? I CAN SHOW YOU AN ACCUMULATION OF ORNAMENTATION AND FINERY FROM THE PAST THAT HAS NO PEER OUTSIDE OF SOME MUSEUM COLLECTIONS. IT IS A PASSION WITH ME. OF COURSE, MY MOST PRECIOUS GEM IS CONSUELO, EH, MY DEAR?
I'LL BE LOOKING FORWARD TO IT, SIR. UNTIL TOMORROW EVENING, THEN.
MY GOD! WHAT LUCK!
DISCREET INQUIRIES ABOUT SEÑOR ATALAN'S WEALTH INDICATE BROOKS' INSTINCTS WERE RIGHT. HIS ELATION IS TEMPERED SOMEWHAT BY A FEELING OF SOMETHING NOT QUITE RIGHT...
THERE IS SOMETHING INDEFINABLY SINISTER ABOUT SEÑOR ATALAN AND HIS NIECE...
3.

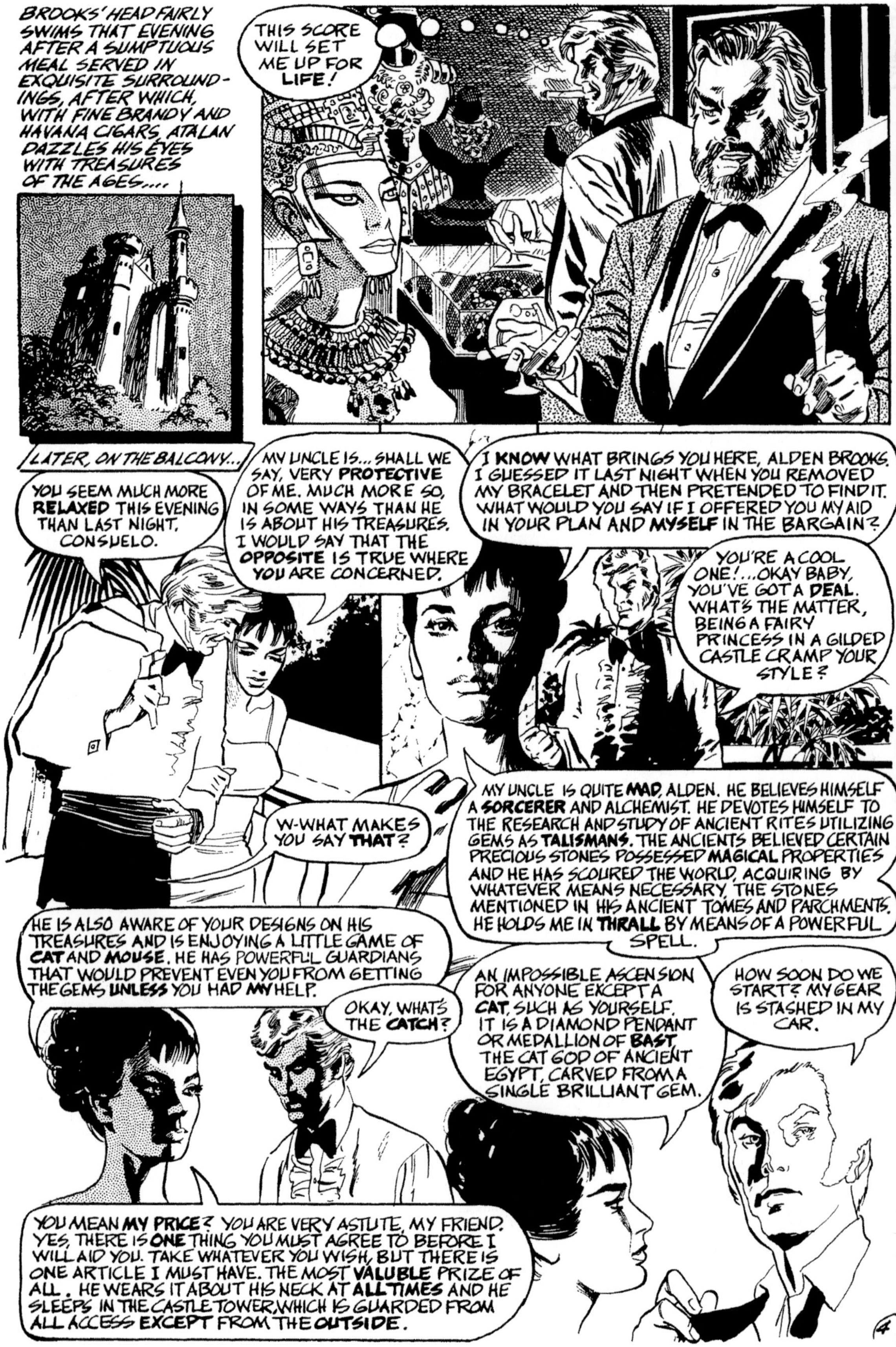
BROOKS' HEAD FAIRLY SWIMS THAT EVENING AFTER A SUMPTUOUS MEAL SERVED IN EXQUISITE SURROUNDINGS, AFTER WHICH, WITH FINE BRANDY AND HAVANA CIGARS, ATALAN DAZZLES HIS EYES WITH TREASURES OF THE AGES....
THIS SCORE WILL SET ME UP FOR LIFE!
LATER, ON THE BALCONY...
YOU SEEM MUCH MORE RELAXED THIS EVENING THAN LAST NIGHT, CONSUELO.
MY UNCLE IS... SHALL WE SAY, VERY PROTECTIVE OF ME. MUCH MORE SO, IN SOME WAYS THAN HE IS ABOUT HIS TREASURES. I WOULD SAY THAT THE OPPOSITE IS TRUE WHERE YOU ARE CONCERNED.
W-WHAT MAKES YOU SAY THAT?
I KNOW WHAT BRINGS YOU HERE, ALDEN BROOKS. I GUESSED IT LAST NIGHT WHEN YOU REMOVED MY BRACELET AND THEN PRETENDED TO FIND IT. WHAT WOULD YOU SAY IF I OFFERED YOU MY AID IN YOUR PLAN AND MYSELF IN THE BARGAIN?
YOU'RE A COOL ONE!... OKAY BABY, YOU'VE GOT A DEAL. WHAT'S THE MATTER, BEING A FAIRY PRINCESS IN A GILDED CASTLE CRAMP YOUR STYLE?
MY UNCLE IS QUITE MAD, ALDEN. HE BELIEVES HIMSELF A SORCERER AND ALCHEMIST. HE DEVOTES HIMSELF TO THE RESEARCH AND STUDY OF ANCIENT RITES UTILIZING GEMS AS TALISMANS. THE ANCIENTS BELIEVED CERTAIN PRECIOUS STONES POSSESSED MAGICAL PROPERTIES AND HE HAS SCOURED THE WORLD, ACQUIRING BY WHATEVER MEANS NECESSARY, THE STONES MENTIONED IN HIS ANCIENT TOMES AND PARCHMENTS. HE HOLDS ME IN THRALL BY MEANS OF A POWERFUL SPELL.
HE IS ALSO AWARE OF YOUR DESIGNS ON HIS TREASURES AND IS ENJOYING A LITTLE GAME OF CAT AND MOUSE. HE HAS POWERFUL GUARDIANS THAT WOULD PREVENT EVEN YOU FROM GETTING THE GEMS UNLESS YOU HAD MY HELP.
OKAY, WHAT'S THE CATCH?
YOU MEAN MY PRICE? YOU ARE VERY ASTUTE, MY FRIEND. YES, THERE IS ONE THING YOU MUST AGREE TO BEFORE I WILL AID YOU. TAKE WHATEVER YOU WISH, BUT THERE IS ONE ARTICLE I MUST HAVE. THE MOST VALUBLE PRIZE OF ALL. HE WEARS IT ABOUT HIS NECK AT ALL TIMES AND HE SLEEPS IN THE CASTLE TOWER, WHICH IS GUARDED FROM ALL ACCESS EXCEPT FROM THE OUTSIDE.
AN IMPOSSIBLE ASCENSION FOR ANYONE EXCEPT A CAT, SUCH AS YOURSELF. IT IS A DIAMOND PENDANT OR MEDALLION OF BAST, THE CAT GOD OF ANCIENT EGYPT, CARVED FROM A SINGLE BRILLIANT GEM.
HOW SOON DO WE START? MY GEAR IS STASHED IN MY CAR.
4

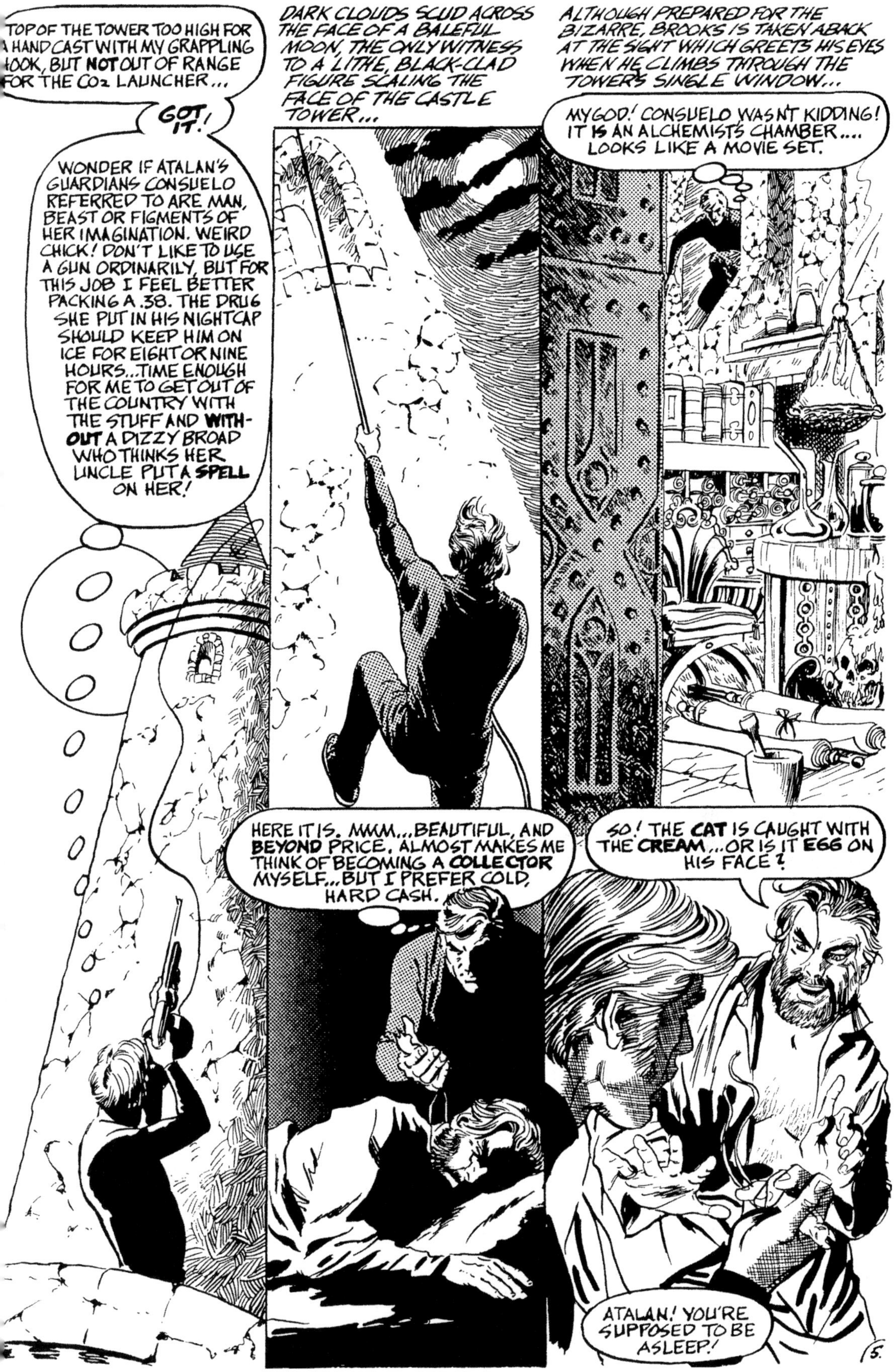
TOP OF THE TOWER TOO HIGH FOR A HAND CAST WITH MY GRAPPLING HOOK, BUT NOT OUT OF RANGE FOR THE CO2 LAUNCHER...
GOT IT!
WONDER IF ATALAN'S GUARDIANS CONSUELO REFERRED TO ARE MAN, BEAST OR FIGMENTS OF HER IMAGINATION. WEIRD CHICK! DON'T LIKE TO USE A GUN ORDINARILY, BUT FOR THIS JOB I FEEL BETTER PACKING A .38. THE DRUG SHE PUT IN HIS NIGHTCAP SHOULD KEEP HIM ON ICE FOR EIGHT OR NINE HOURS...TIME ENOUGH FOR ME TO GET OUT OF THE COUNTRY WITH THE STUFF AND WITHOUT A DIZZY BROAD WHO THINKS HER UNCLE PUT A SPELL ON HER!
DARK CLOUDS SCUD ACROSS THE FACE OF A BALEFUL MOON, THE ONLY WITNESS TO A LITHE, BLACK-CLAD FIGURE SCALING THE FACE OF THE CASTLE TOWER...
ALTHOUGH PREPARED FOR THE BIZARRE, BROOKS IS TAKEN ABACK AT THE SIGHT WHICH GREETS HIS EYES WHEN HE CLIMBS THROUGH THE TOWER'S SINGLE WINDOW...
MY GOD! CONSUELO WASN'T KIDDING! IT IS AN ALCHEMIST'S CHAMBER.... LOOKS LIKE A MOVIE SET.
HERE IT IS. MMM...BEAUTIFUL, AND BEYOND PRICE. ALMOST MAKES ME THINK OF BECOMING A COLLECTOR MYSELF...BUT I PREFER COLD, HARD CASH.
SO! THE CAT IS CAUGHT WITH THE CREAM...OR IS IT EGG ON HIS FACE?
ATALAN! YOU'RE SUPPOSED TO BE ASLEEP!
5.

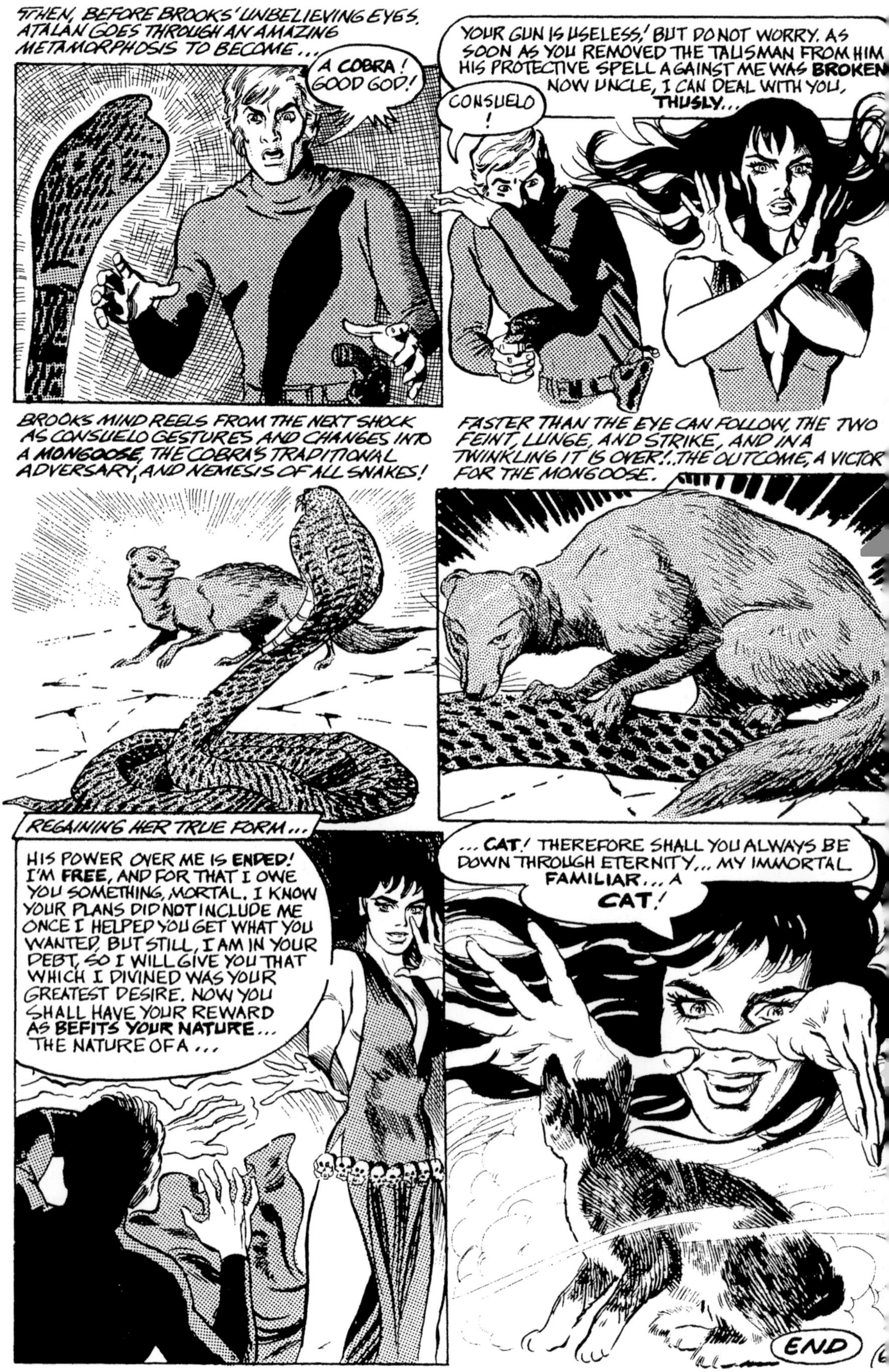

THEN, BEFORE BROOKS' UNBELIEVING EYES, ATALAN GOES THROUGH AN AMAZING METAMORPHOSIS TO BECOME...
A COBRA! GOOD GOD!
YOUR GUN IS USELESS! BUT DO NOT WORRY. AS SOON AS YOU REMOVED THE TALISMAN FROM HIM HIS PROTECTIVE SPELL AGAINST ME WAS BROKEN. NOW UNCLE, I CAN DEAL WITH YOU, THUSLY...
CONSUELO!
BROOKS MIND REELS FROM THE NEXT SHOCK AS CONSUELO GESTURES AND CHANGES INTO A MONGOOSE, THE COBRA'S TRADITIONAL ADVERSARY, AND NEMESIS OF ALL SNAKES!
FASTER THAN THE EYE CAN FOLLOW, THE TWO FEINT, LUNGE, AND STRIKE, AND IN A TWINKLING IT IS OVER!..THE OUTCOME, A VICTOR FOR THE MONGOOSE.
REGAINING HER TRUE FORM...
HIS POWER OVER ME IS ENDED! I'M FREE, AND FOR THAT I OWE YOU SOMETHING, MORTAL. I KNOW YOUR PLANS DID NOT INCLUDE ME ONCE I HELPED YOU GET WHAT YOU WANTED, BUT STILL, I AM IN YOUR DEBT, SO I WILL GIVE YOU THAT WHICH I DIVINED WAS YOUR GREATEST DESIRE. NOW YOU SHALL HAVE YOUR REWARD AS BEFITS YOUR NATURE... THE NATURE OF A...
...CAT! THEREFORE SHALL YOU ALWAYS BE DOWN THROUGH ETERNITY,.. MY IMMORTAL FAMILIAR... A CAT!
END

# A STAB IN THE DARK

"Someone is trying to kill me! And it is by witch-craft, I tell you! What more evidence do you need?" The woman's bony hand held the doctor's arm as she screeched her fears at him.

"Please calm down, woman!" pleaded the doctor. "Your story is too far-fetched even if I did believe in sorcery and devilment! How could you be 'set up' for murder by the mere words of a letter?"

"You don't believe, but I do!" she grated. "If a witch sees her death described in detail three times, then all she owns belongs to the one who makes it come true! And I have *seen* it three times! Someone wants my money! Someone knows I have it!"

The doctor drew back, away from the frail old woman on the hospital bed. Who would have believed this dirty, ragged old woman had money? It was perhaps easier to believe she was a witch than to believe she was wealthy! Yet, she had been carrying twenty hundred-dollar bills in her rags. It was certainly amazing how such an outcast from modern civilization could accumulate so much of civilization's wealth!

"Here!" she insisted. "Read this!"

The doctor took the paper from her as she thrust it at him. It was wrinkled and dirty from being carried around for a week. The words, in red ink, said:

The light of the night
Will see death enter
Through metal sharp and bright
Into the body's center.

"Please stay calm," said the doctor. "Nothing will happen! These words have no power!"

"But things have happened," she wailed. "Two nights ago I was walking home past an apartment building when there was a loud clatter behind me! Someone had dropped a pair of scissors out of a window just as I was passing in the light in front of the building entrance!

The doctor protested. "That was obviously an accident. A terrible accident, of course, but why do you think it was witchcraft? Because of the light and the sharp metal? Mere coincidence!"

"No, no!" pleaded the old woman. "I too am a witch, and I know the signs! And tonight when I was attacked it was not by coincidence! Look at my shoulder where I was stabbed! And it was beneath a street light! . . . a street light!"

The doctor opened his black bag. It would not pay to have her remain in this hysterical state. Suppose others heard her talk of witches and spells? He reassured the woman that all would be well.

"Nothing can happen to you here in the hospital, woman! There are no street thugs to attack you with knives, or scissors to fall on you from open windows! How did your little poem go?

'The light of the night
Will see death enter.

Well, if you will lean back and close your eyes now, I will shut out the lights in this room!"

The woman seemed to consider a moment. Then, slowly, she leaned back. Her heavy lids closed, adding a few more wrinkles to her face. The doctor shut off the lights.

'Through metal sharp and bright
Into the body's center'

The doctor continued. "All knives and scissors are gone. There's not a sharp piece of metal to be seen." In the darkened room, the doctor reached in to his bag for a small bottle which he had never believed he would actually use.

"I'm going to help you sleep now," he said. "Are you all right?"

There was no answer, but he could hear her breathing more heavily now. She was probably asleep already, from exhaustion. He did not blame her. He walked to the window and re-arranged the window blinds. He could see her dimly in outline in the darkness. She slept in the trust the doctor had given her. He had convinced her of her safety and that she had no cause for fears.

And she had also convinced him. He now believed that she had money, and that soon it would be his. He was also convinced that if he could fulfill the words of the little poem, he might be ridding the world of a witch! And that wasn't a bad thing! In fact, it might even deserve a reward!

He waited until the moonlight coming through the window lighted the sleeping woman. It was quite bright. It glistened on the sharp metal point of the lethal hypodermic needle in his hand as he approached the bed.

**THE END**

HAYDEN BURRIS IS ON THE THRESHOLD OF UNRAVELING ONE OF THE GREATEST MYSTERIES OF THIS PLANET.... THE ENIGMA OF MANKIND'S EVOLUTION FROM THE STOOPED APE-LIKE **NEANDERTHAL** INTO THE UPRIGHT FORERUNNER OF MODERN MAN, THE **CRO-MAGNON**. IN OTHER WORDS, THE MUCH DISCUSSED, CONTROVERSIAL, AND AS YET, UNSUBSTANTIATED....

# MISSING LINK!

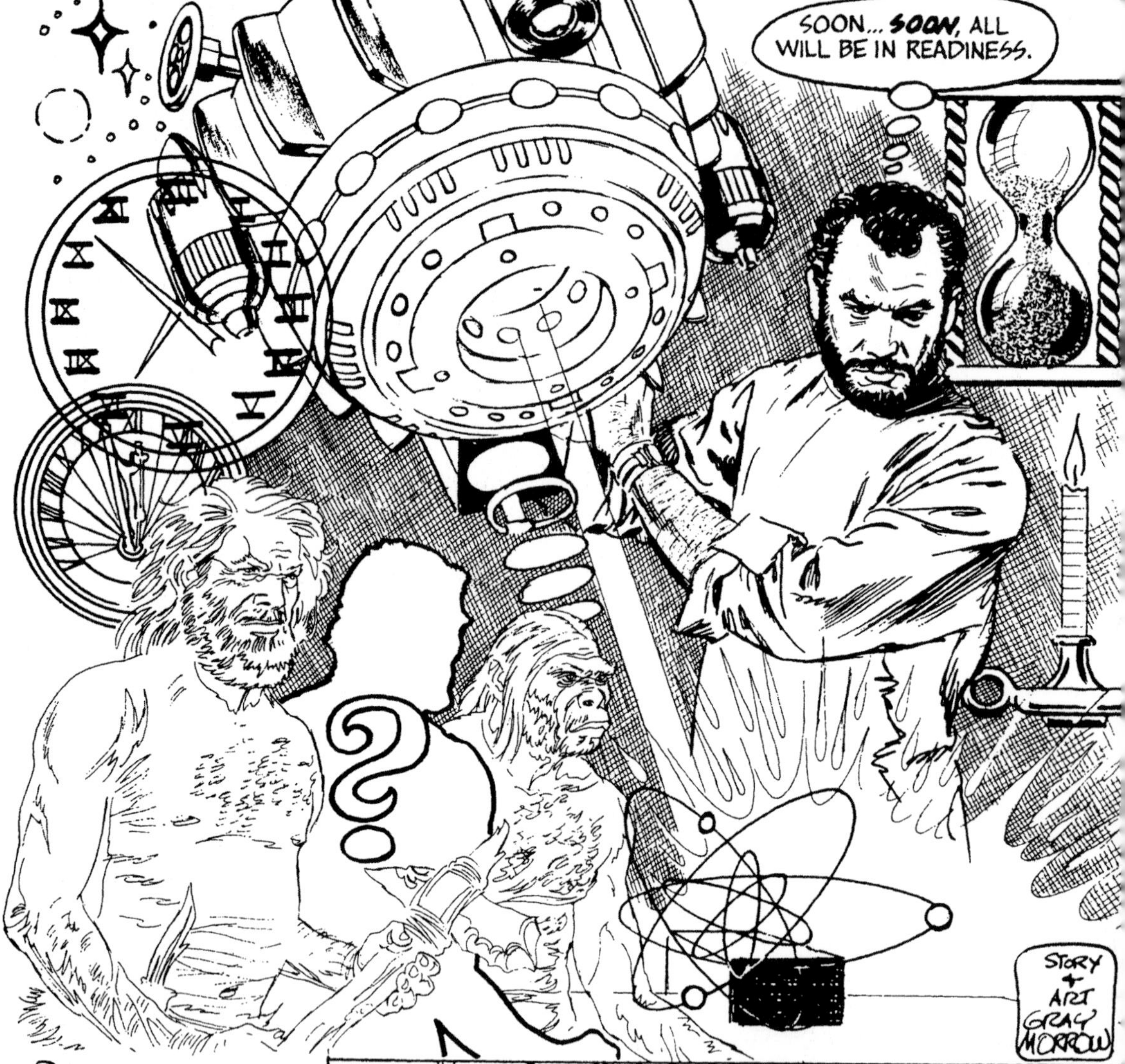
SOON... **SOON**, ALL WILL BE IN READINESS.
STORY + ART GRAY MORROW

DR. BURRIS, WITHOUT THE UNIVERSITY'S KNOWLEDGE OR SANCTION, IS ABOUT TO DEPART ON A LITTLE SABBATICAL... TO THE **PREHISTORIC PAST!** HAVING CHANNELED CERTAIN FUNDS ALLOCATED FOR A MORE MUNDANE KIND OF RESEARCH TO A PET PROJECT OF HIS **OWN**, HE HAS CONSTRUCTED AND OUTFITTED A **TIME MACHINE** TO SPAN THE CENTURIES AND SOLVE THE RIDDLES OF THE AGES.

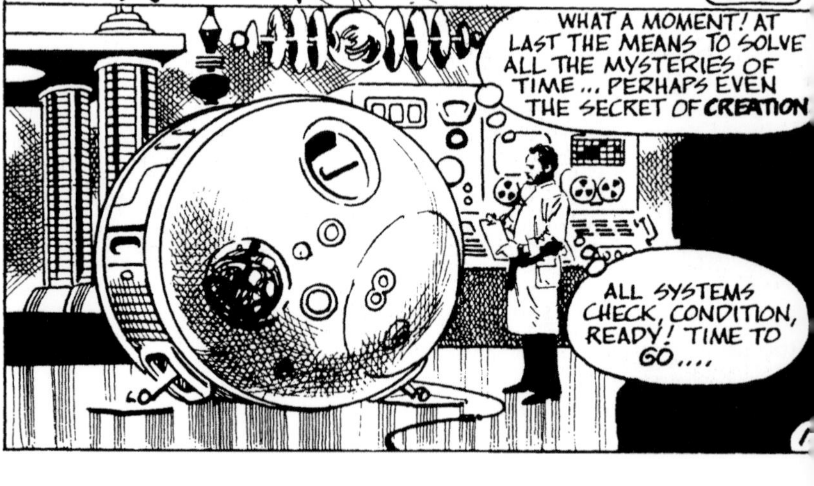
WHAT A MOMENT! AT LAST THE MEANS TO SOLVE ALL THE MYSTERIES OF TIME ... PERHAPS EVEN THE SECRET OF **CREATION**
ALL SYSTEMS CHECK, CONDITION, READY! TIME TO **GO**....

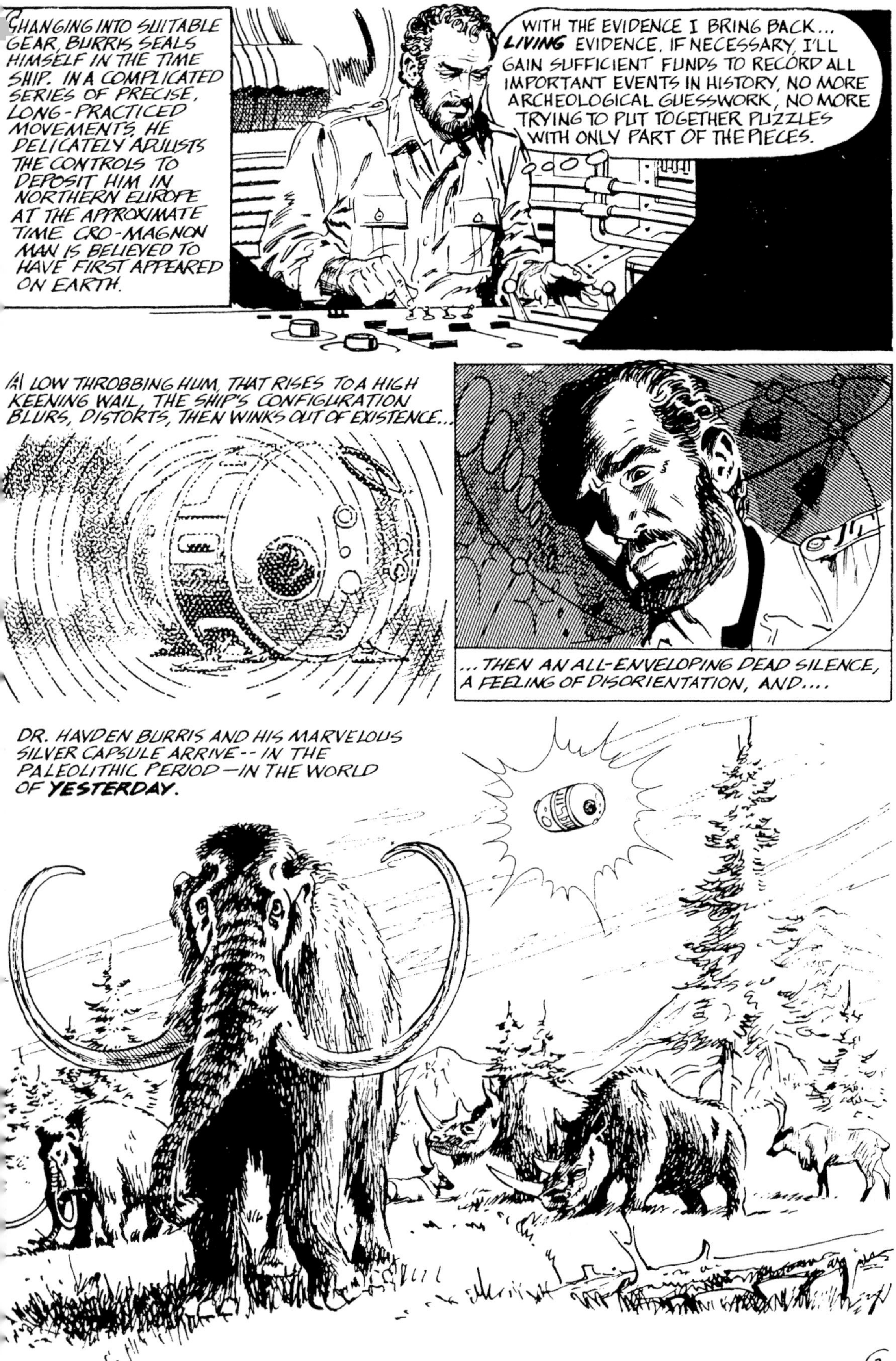
CHANGING INTO SUITABLE GEAR, BURRIS SEALS HIMSELF IN THE TIME SHIP. IN A COMPLICATED SERIES OF PRECISE, LONG-PRACTICED MOVEMENTS, HE DELICATELY ADJUSTS THE CONTROLS TO DEPOSIT HIM IN NORTHERN EUROPE AT THE APPROXIMATE TIME CRO-MAGNON MAN IS BELIEVED TO HAVE FIRST APPEARED ON EARTH.
WITH THE EVIDENCE I BRING BACK... LIVING EVIDENCE, IF NECESSARY, I'LL GAIN SUFFICIENT FUNDS TO RECORD ALL IMPORTANT EVENTS IN HISTORY, NO MORE ARCHEOLOGICAL GUESSWORK, NO MORE TRYING TO PUT TOGETHER PUZZLES WITH ONLY PART OF THE PIECES.
A LOW THROBBING HUM, THAT RISES TO A HIGH KEENING WAIL, THE SHIP'S CONFIGURATION BLURS, DISTORTS, THEN WINKS OUT OF EXISTENCE...
...THEN AN ALL-ENVELOPING DEAD SILENCE, A FEELING OF DISORIENTATION, AND....
DR. HAYDEN BURRIS AND HIS MARVELOUS SILVER CAPSULE ARRIVE-- IN THE PALEOLITHIC PERIOD—IN THE WORLD OF YESTERDAY.

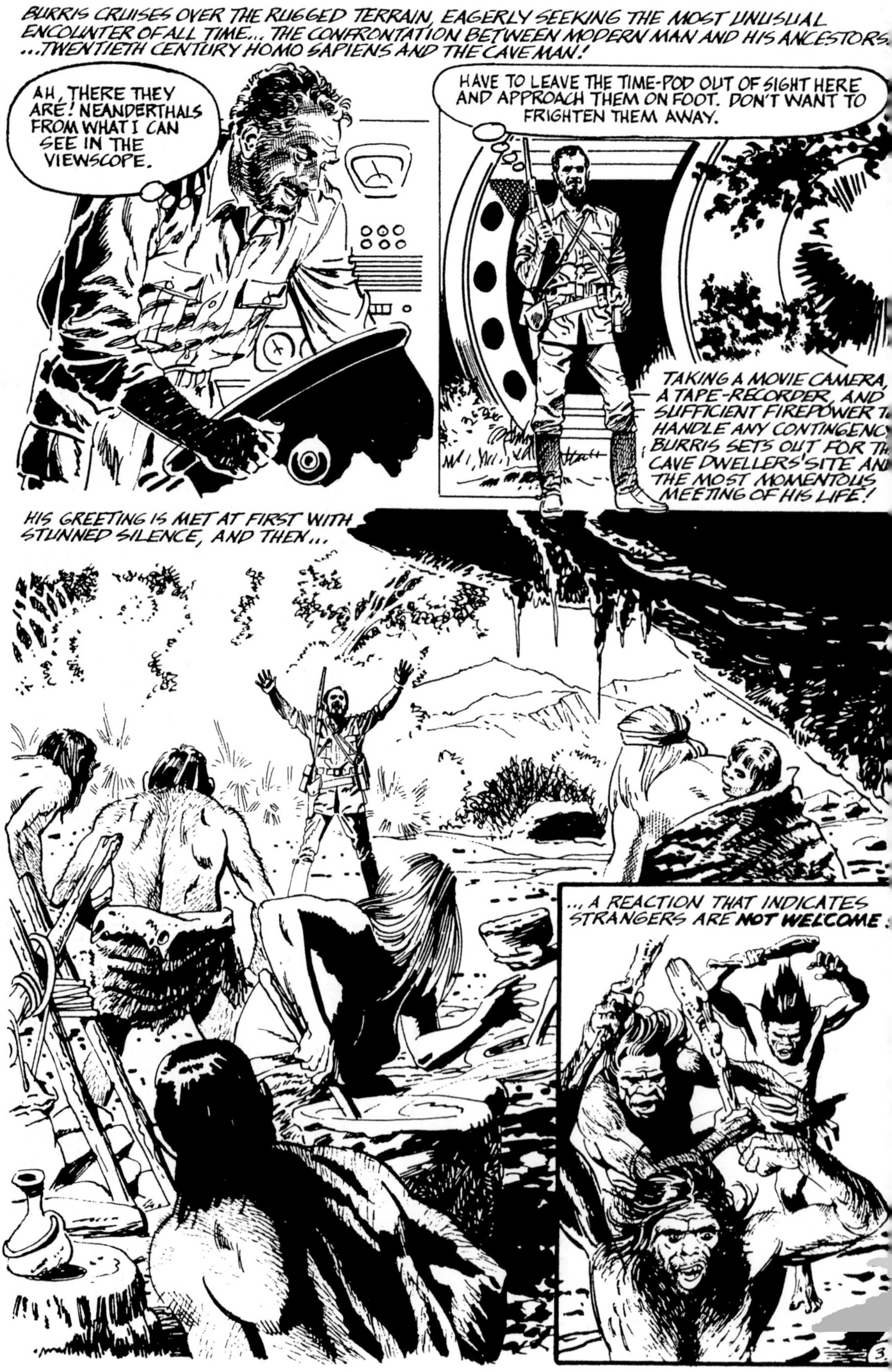
BURRIS CRUISES OVER THE RUGGED TERRAIN, EAGERLY SEEKING THE MOST UNUSUAL ENCOUNTER OF ALL TIME... THE CONFRONTATION BETWEEN MODERN MAN AND HIS ANCESTORS ...TWENTIETH CENTURY HOMO SAPIENS AND THE CAVE MAN!
AH, THERE THEY ARE! NEANDERTHALS FROM WHAT I CAN SEE IN THE VIEWSCOPE.
HAVE TO LEAVE THE TIME-POD OUT OF SIGHT HERE AND APPROACH THEM ON FOOT. DON'T WANT TO FRIGHTEN THEM AWAY.
TAKING A MOVIE CAMERA, A TAPE-RECORDER, AND SUFFICIENT FIREPOWER T HANDLE ANY CONTINGENC BURRIS SETS OUT FOR TH CAVE DWELLERS' SITE AN THE MOST MOMENTOUS MEETING OF HIS LIFE!
HIS GREETING IS MET AT FIRST WITH STUNNED SILENCE, AND THEN...
...A REACTION THAT INDICATES STRANGERS ARE **NOT WELCOME**.

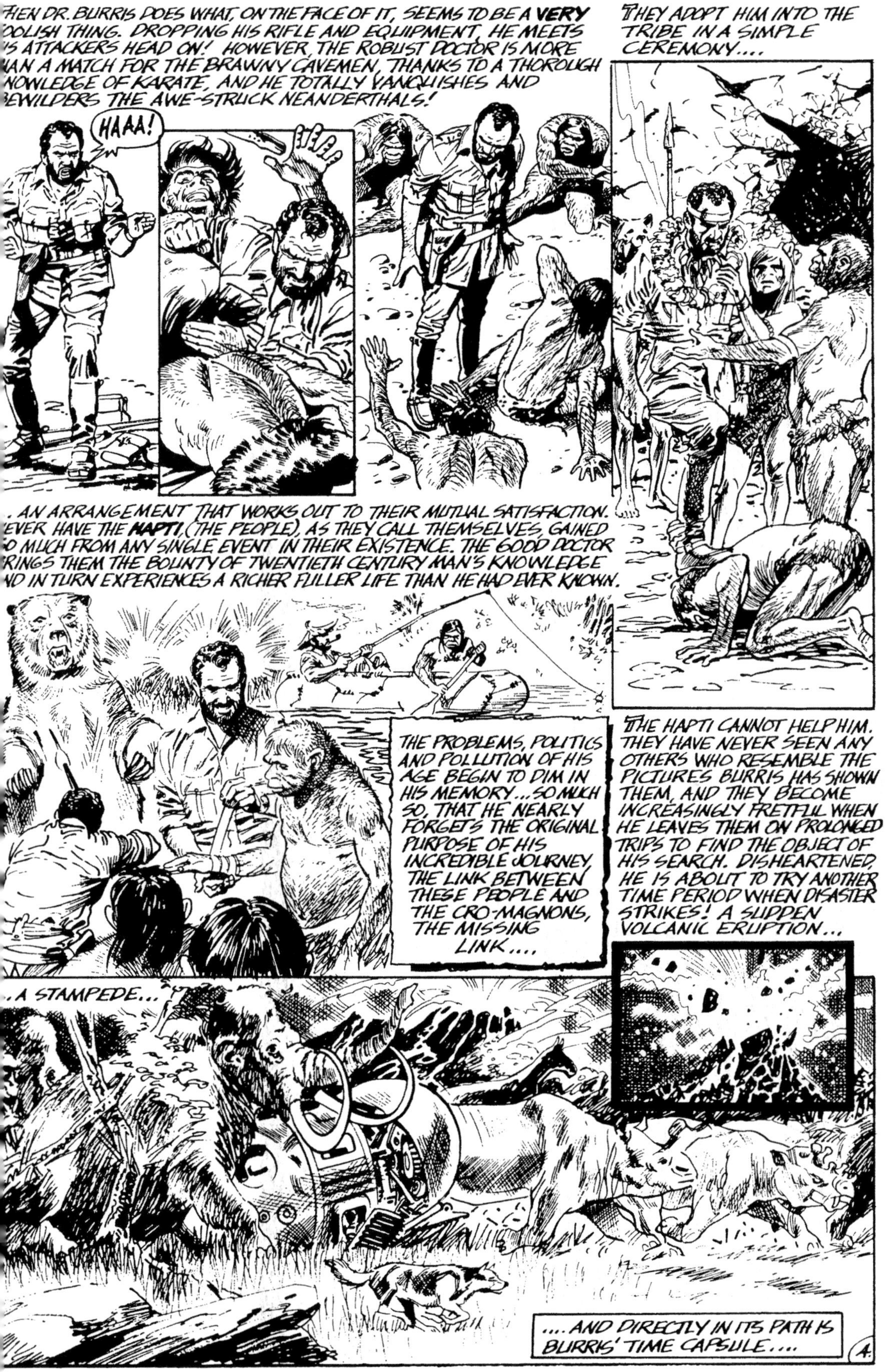
THEN DR. BURRIS DOES WHAT, ON THE FACE OF IT, SEEMS TO BE A VERY FOOLISH THING. DROPPING HIS RIFLE AND EQUIPMENT, HE MEETS HIS ATTACKERS HEAD ON! HOWEVER, THE ROBUST DOCTOR IS MORE THAN A MATCH FOR THE BRAWNY CAVEMEN, THANKS TO A THOROUGH KNOWLEDGE OF KARATE, AND HE TOTALLY VANQUISHES AND BEWILDERS THE AWE-STRUCK NEANDERTHALS!
HAAA!
THEY ADOPT HIM INTO THE TRIBE IN A SIMPLE CEREMONY....
... AN ARRANGEMENT THAT WORKS OUT TO THEIR MUTUAL SATISFACTION. NEVER HAVE THE HAPTI, (THE PEOPLE), AS THEY CALL THEMSELVES, GAINED SO MUCH FROM ANY SINGLE EVENT IN THEIR EXISTENCE. THE GOOD DOCTOR BRINGS THEM THE BOUNTY OF TWENTIETH CENTURY MAN'S KNOWLEDGE AND IN TURN EXPERIENCES A RICHER FULLER LIFE THAN HE HAD EVER KNOWN.
THE PROBLEMS, POLITICS AND POLLUTION OF HIS AGE BEGIN TO DIM IN HIS MEMORY... SO MUCH SO, THAT HE NEARLY FORGETS THE ORIGINAL PURPOSE OF HIS INCREDIBLE JOURNEY, THE LINK BETWEEN THESE PEOPLE AND THE CRO-MAGNONS, THE MISSING LINK....
THE HAPTI CANNOT HELP HIM. THEY HAVE NEVER SEEN ANY OTHERS WHO RESEMBLE THE PICTURES BURRIS HAS SHOWN THEM, AND THEY BECOME INCREASINGLY FRETFUL WHEN HE LEAVES THEM ON PROLONGED TRIPS TO FIND THE OBJECT OF HIS SEARCH. DISHEARTENED, HE IS ABOUT TO TRY ANOTHER TIME PERIOD WHEN DISASTER STRIKES! A SUDDEN VOLCANIC ERUPTION...
... A STAMPEDE...
.... AND DIRECTLY IN ITS PATH IS BURRIS' TIME CAPSULE....
4.

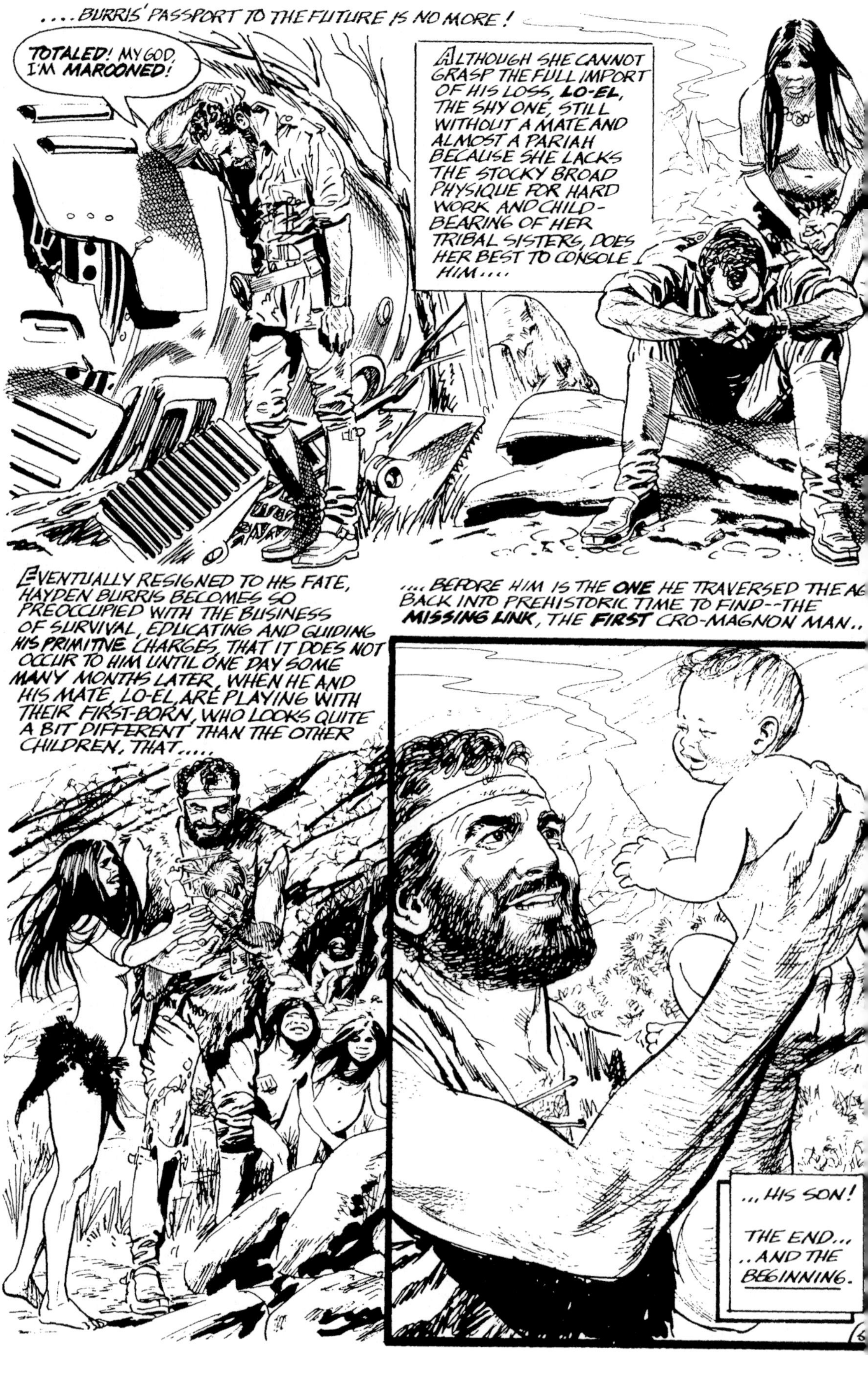

....BURRIS' PASSPORT TO THE FUTURE IS NO MORE!
TOTALED! MY GOD, I'M MAROONED!
ALTHOUGH SHE CANNOT GRASP THE FULL IMPORT OF HIS LOSS, LO-EL, THE SHY ONE, STILL WITHOUT A MATE AND ALMOST A PARIAH BECAUSE SHE LACKS THE STOCKY BROAD PHYSIQUE FOR HARD WORK AND CHILD-BEARING OF HER TRIBAL SISTERS, DOES HER BEST TO CONSOLE HIM....
EVENTUALLY RESIGNED TO HIS FATE, HAYDEN BURRIS BECOMES SO PREOCCUPIED WITH THE BUSINESS OF SURVIVAL, EDUCATING AND GUIDING HIS PRIMITIVE CHARGES, THAT IT DOES NOT OCCUR TO HIM UNTIL ONE DAY SOME MANY MONTHS LATER, WHEN HE AND HIS MATE, LO-EL, ARE PLAYING WITH THEIR FIRST-BORN, WHO LOOKS QUITE A BIT DIFFERENT THAN THE OTHER CHILDREN, THAT.....
....BEFORE HIM IS THE ONE HE TRAVERSED THE AG BACK INTO PREHISTORIC TIME TO FIND--THE MISSING LINK, THE FIRST CRO-MAGNON MAN..
...HIS SON!
THE END... ..AND THE BEGINNING.

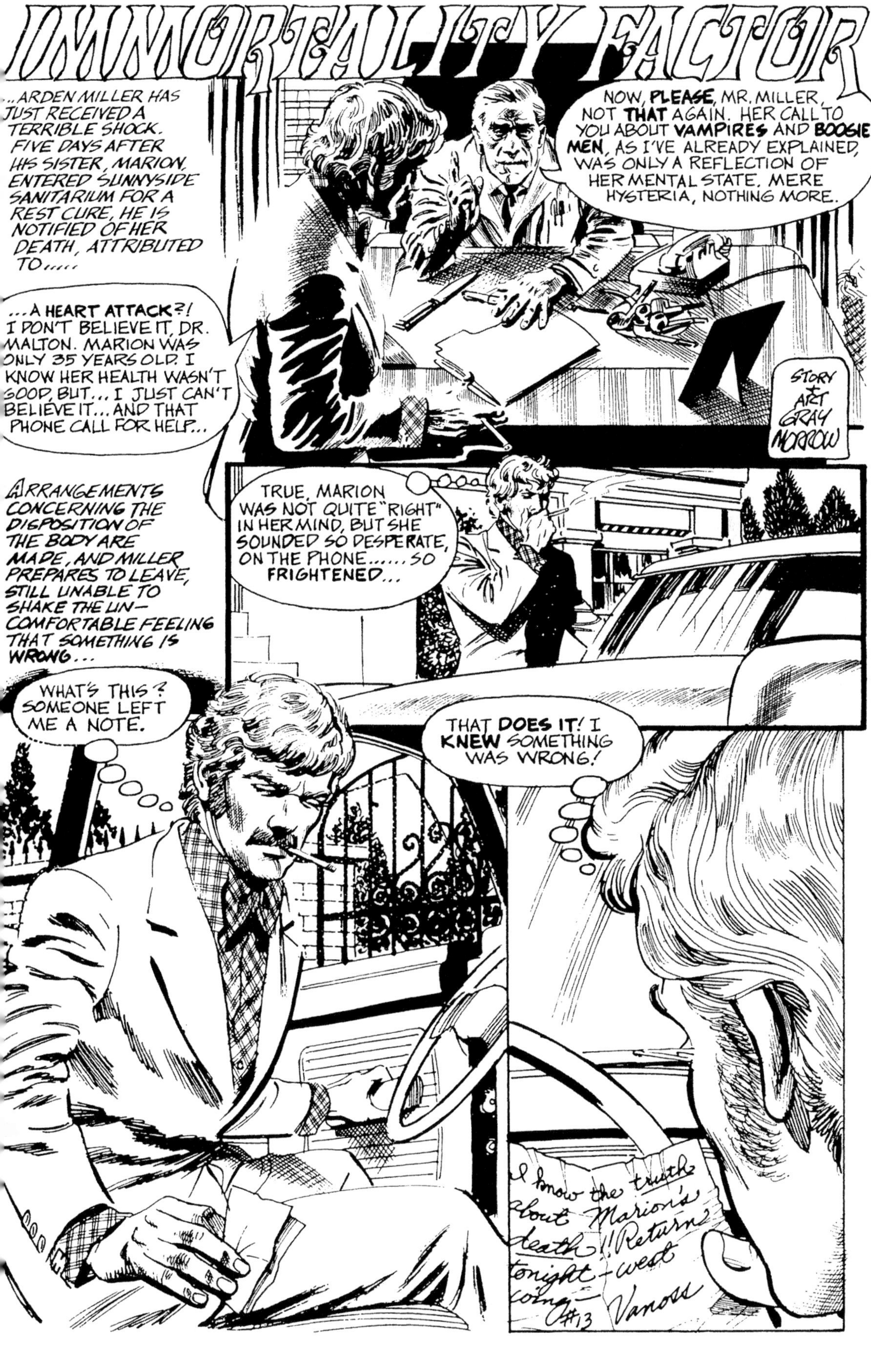
IMMORTALITY FACTOR
...ARDEN MILLER HAS JUST RECEIVED A TERRIBLE SHOCK. FIVE DAYS AFTER HIS SISTER, MARION, ENTERED SUNNYSIDE SANITARIUM FOR A REST CURE, HE IS NOTIFIED OF HER DEATH, ATTRIBUTED TO.....
...A HEART ATTACK?! I DON'T BELIEVE IT, DR. MALTON. MARION WAS ONLY 35 YEARS OLD. I KNOW HER HEALTH WASN'T GOOD, BUT... I JUST CAN'T BELIEVE IT... AND THAT PHONE CALL FOR HELP...
NOW, PLEASE, MR. MILLER, NOT THAT AGAIN. HER CALL TO YOU ABOUT VAMPIRES AND BOOGIE MEN, AS I'VE ALREADY EXPLAINED, WAS ONLY A REFLECTION OF HER MENTAL STATE. MERE HYSTERIA, NOTHING MORE.
STORY + ART GRAY MORROW
ARRANGEMENTS CONCERNING THE DISPOSITION OF THE BODY ARE MADE, AND MILLER PREPARES TO LEAVE, STILL UNABLE TO SHAKE THE UN-COMFORTABLE FEELING THAT SOMETHING IS WRONG...
TRUE, MARION WAS NOT QUITE "RIGHT" IN HER MIND, BUT SHE SOUNDED SO DESPERATE, ON THE PHONE...... SO FRIGHTENED...
WHAT'S THIS? SOMEONE LEFT ME A NOTE.
THAT DOES IT! I KNEW SOMETHING WAS WRONG!
I know the truth
bout Marion's
eath!! Return
tonight - west
ing — #13
Vanoss

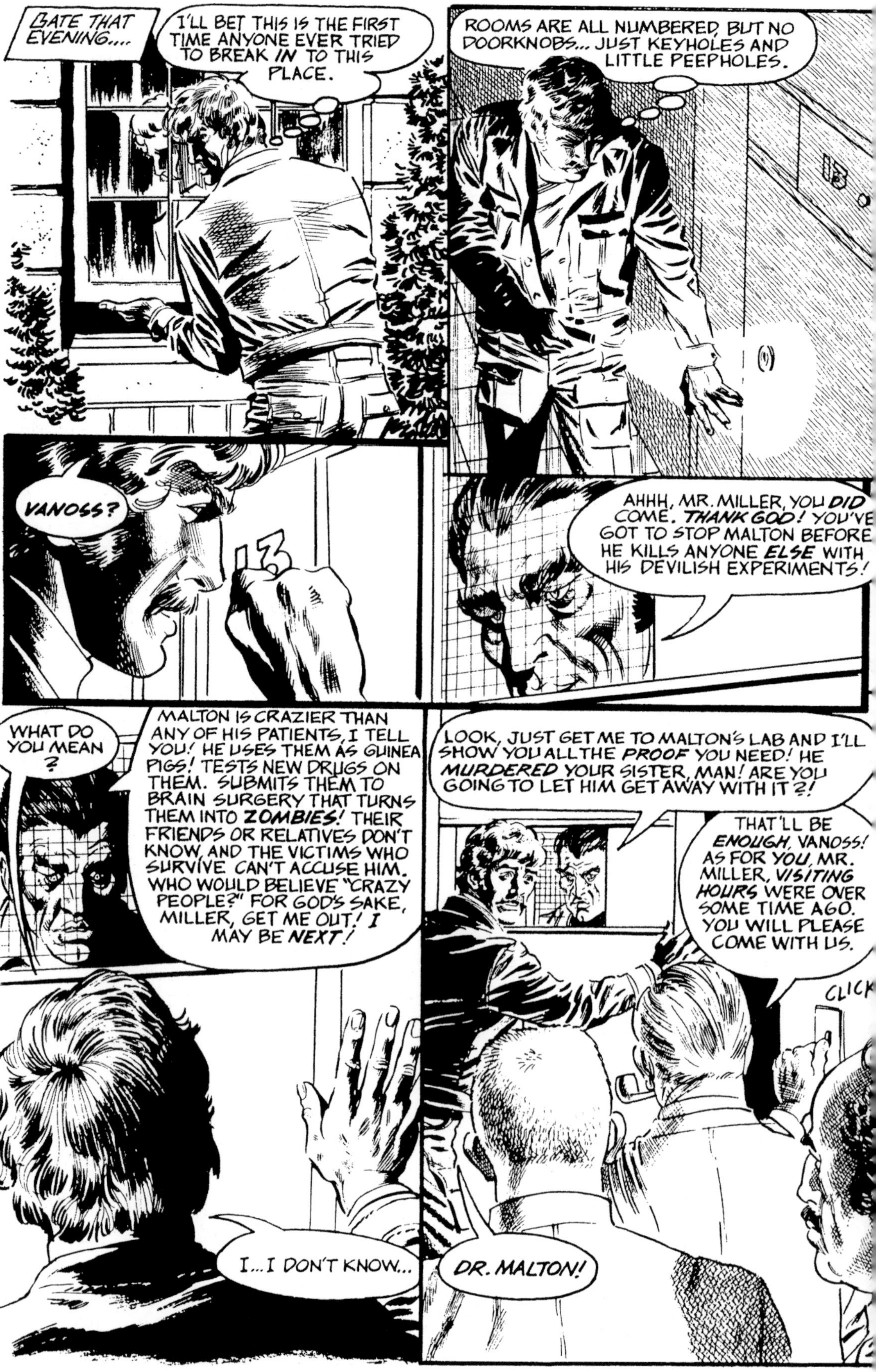
LATE THAT EVENING....
I'LL BET THIS IS THE FIRST TIME ANYONE EVER TRIED TO BREAK IN TO THIS PLACE.
ROOMS ARE ALL NUMBERED BUT NO DOORKNOBS... JUST KEYHOLES AND LITTLE PEEPHOLES.
13
VANOSS?
AHHH, MR. MILLER, YOU DID COME. THANK GOD! YOU'VE GOT TO STOP MALTON BEFORE HE KILLS ANYONE ELSE WITH HIS DEVILISH EXPERIMENTS!
WHAT DO YOU MEAN ?
MALTON IS CRAZIER THAN ANY OF HIS PATIENTS, I TELL YOU! HE USES THEM AS GUINEA PIGS! TESTS NEW DRUGS ON THEM. SUBMITS THEM TO BRAIN SURGERY THAT TURNS THEM INTO ZOMBIES! THEIR FRIENDS OR RELATIVES DON'T KNOW, AND THE VICTIMS WHO SURVIVE CAN'T ACCUSE HIM. WHO WOULD BELIEVE "CRAZY PEOPLE?" FOR GOD'S SAKE, MILLER, GET ME OUT! I MAY BE NEXT!
I...I DON'T KNOW...
LOOK, JUST GET ME TO MALTON'S LAB AND I'LL SHOW YOU ALL THE PROOF YOU NEED! HE MURDERED YOUR SISTER, MAN! ARE YOU GOING TO LET HIM GET AWAY WITH IT?!
THAT'LL BE ENOUGH, VANOSS! AS FOR YOU, MR. MILLER, VISITING HOURS WERE OVER SOME TIME AGO. YOU WILL PLEASE COME WITH US.
CLICK
DR. MALTON!

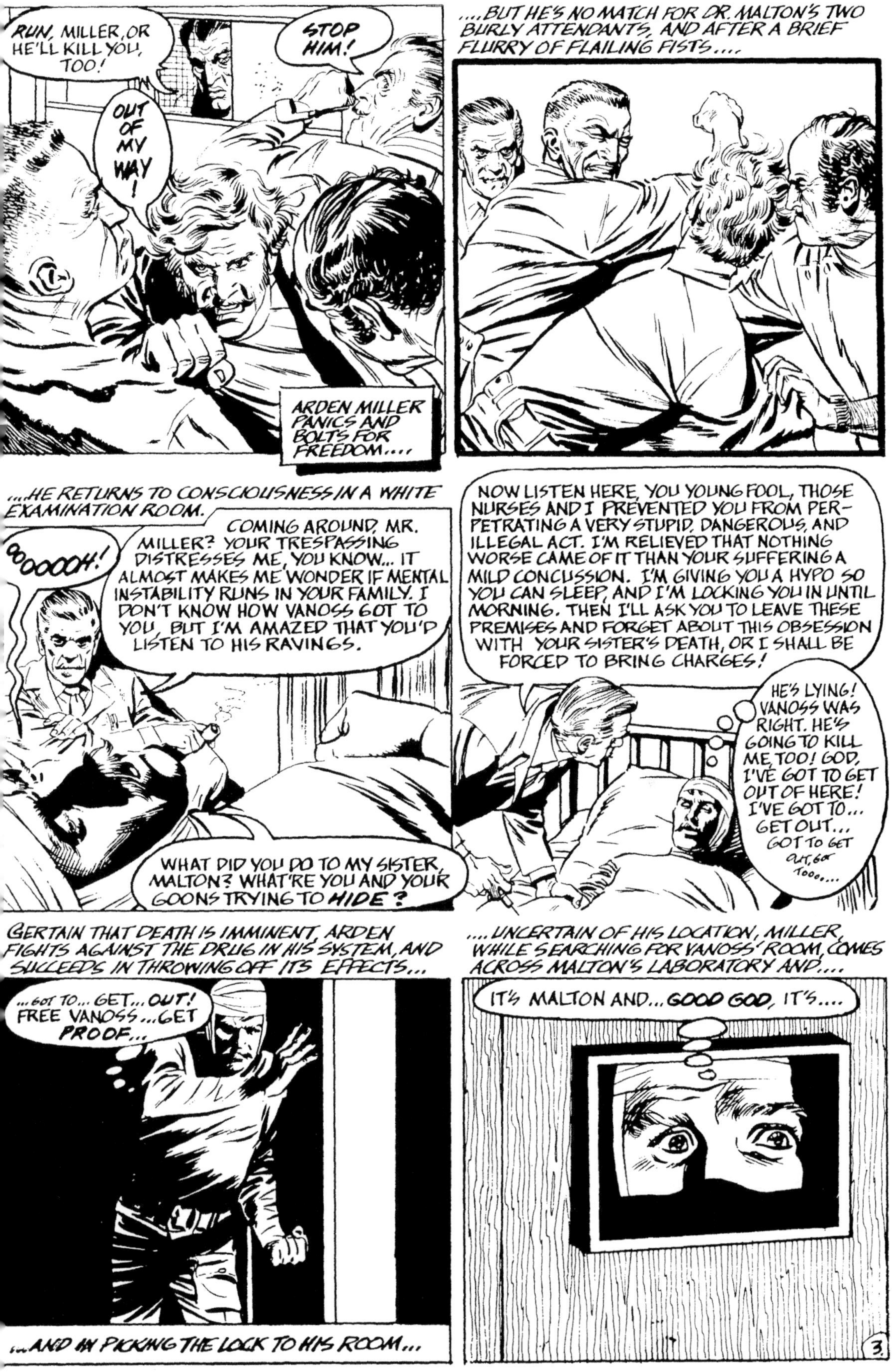
RUN, MILLER, OR HE'LL KILL YOU, TOO!
STOP HIM!
OUT OF MY WAY!
ARDEN MILLER PANICS AND BOLTS FOR FREEDOM....
....BUT HE'S NO MATCH FOR DR. MALTON'S TWO BURLY ATTENDANTS, AND AFTER A BRIEF FLURRY OF FLAILING FISTS....
...HE RETURNS TO CONSCIOUSNESS IN A WHITE EXAMINATION ROOM.
OOOOOOH!
COMING AROUND, MR. MILLER? YOUR TRESPASSING DISTRESSES ME, YOU KNOW... IT ALMOST MAKES ME WONDER IF MENTAL INSTABILITY RUNS IN YOUR FAMILY. I DON'T KNOW HOW VANOSS GOT TO YOU, BUT I'M AMAZED THAT YOU'D LISTEN TO HIS RAVINGS.
WHAT DID YOU DO TO MY SISTER, MALTON? WHAT'RE YOU AND YOUR GOONS TRYING TO HIDE?
NOW LISTEN HERE, YOU YOUNG FOOL, THOSE NURSES AND I PREVENTED YOU FROM PERPETRATING A VERY STUPID, DANGEROUS, AND ILLEGAL ACT. I'M RELIEVED THAT NOTHING WORSE CAME OF IT THAN YOUR SUFFERING A MILD CONCUSSION. I'M GIVING YOU A HYPO SO YOU CAN SLEEP, AND I'M LOCKING YOU IN UNTIL MORNING. THEN I'LL ASK YOU TO LEAVE THESE PREMISES AND FORGET ABOUT THIS OBSESSION WITH YOUR SISTER'S DEATH, OR I SHALL BE FORCED TO BRING CHARGES!
HE'S LYING! VANOSS WAS RIGHT. HE'S GOING TO KILL ME, TOO! GOD, I'VE GOT TO GET OUT OF HERE! I'VE GOT TO... GET OUT... GOT TO GET OUT, GOT TOOO....
CERTAIN THAT DEATH IS IMMINENT, ARDEN FIGHTS AGAINST THE DRUG IN HIS SYSTEM, AND SUCCEEDS IN THROWING OFF ITS EFFECTS...
...GOT TO... GET... OUT! FREE VANOSS... GET PROOF...
...AND IN PICKING THE LOCK TO HIS ROOM...
....UNCERTAIN OF HIS LOCATION, MILLER, WHILE SEARCHING FOR VANOSS' ROOM, COMES ACROSS MALTON'S LABORATORY AND....
IT'S MALTON AND... GOOD GOD, IT'S....
3

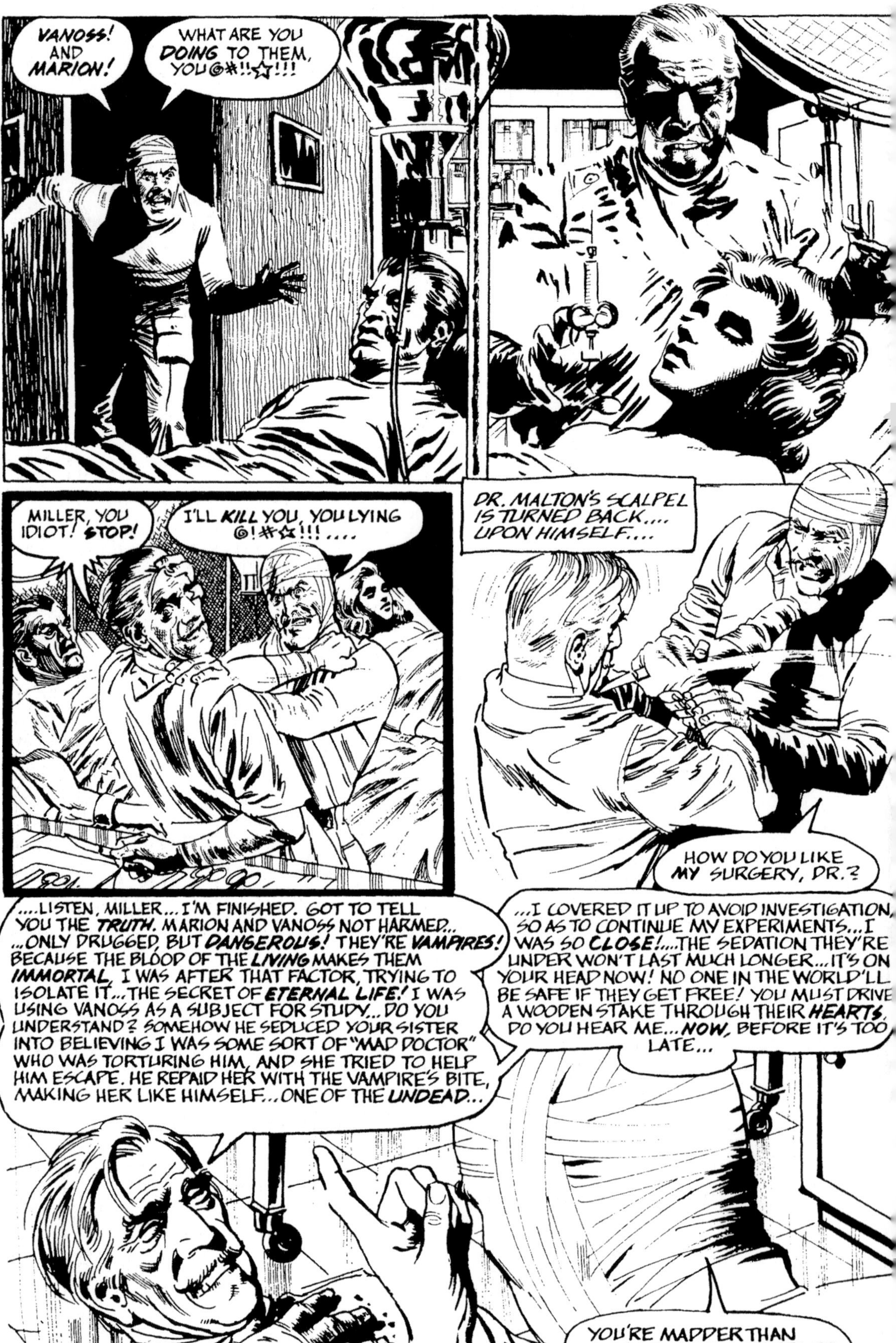

VANOSS! AND MARION!
WHAT ARE YOU DOING TO THEM, YOU @#!!☆!!!
MILLER, YOU IDIOT! STOP!
I'LL KILL YOU, YOU LYING @!#☆!!!....
DR. MALTON'S SCALPEL IS TURNED BACK.... UPON HIMSELF....
HOW DO YOU LIKE MY SURGERY, DR.?
....LISTEN, MILLER... I'M FINISHED. GOT TO TELL YOU THE TRUTH. MARION AND VANOSS NOT HARMED... ...ONLY DRUGGED, BUT DANGEROUS! THEY'RE VAMPIRES! BECAUSE THE BLOOD OF THE LIVING MAKES THEM IMMORTAL. I WAS AFTER THAT FACTOR, TRYING TO ISOLATE IT... THE SECRET OF ETERNAL LIFE! I WAS USING VANOSS AS A SUBJECT FOR STUDY... DO YOU UNDERSTAND? SOMEHOW HE SEDUCED YOUR SISTER INTO BELIEVING I WAS SOME SORT OF "MAD DOCTOR" WHO WAS TORTURING HIM, AND SHE TRIED TO HELP HIM ESCAPE. HE REPAID HER WITH THE VAMPIRE'S BITE, MAKING HER LIKE HIMSELF... ONE OF THE UNDEAD...
...I COVERED IT UP TO AVOID INVESTIGATION, SO AS TO CONTINUE MY EXPERIMENTS... I WAS SO CLOSE!....THE SEDATION THEY'RE UNDER WON'T LAST MUCH LONGER... IT'S ON YOUR HEAD NOW! NO ONE IN THE WORLD'LL BE SAFE IF THEY GET FREE! YOU MUST DRIVE A WOODEN STAKE THROUGH THEIR HEARTS, DO YOU HEAR ME... NOW, BEFORE IT'S TOO LATE...
YOU'RE MADDER THAN ANY OF YOUR INMATES, DR.

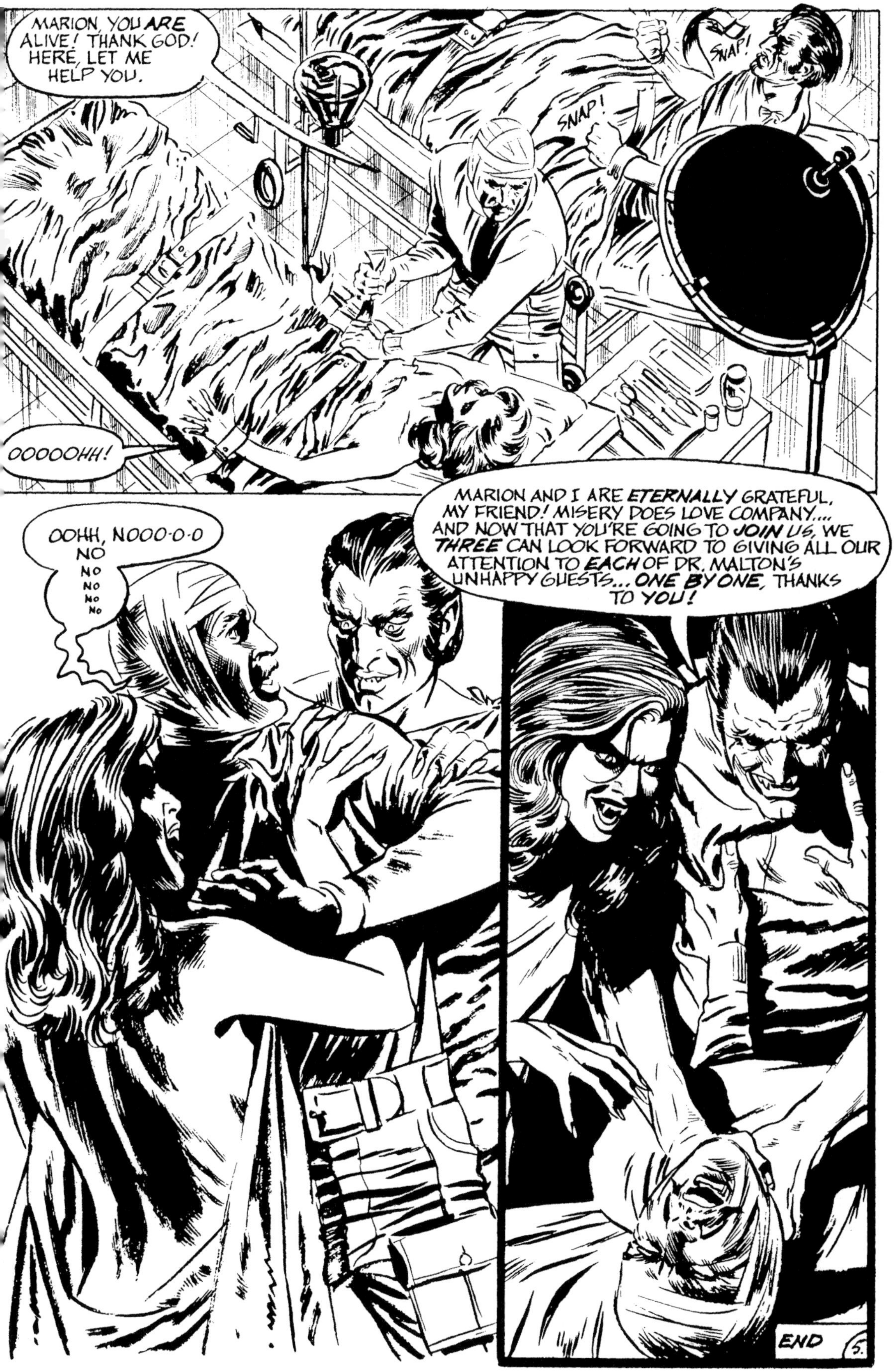
MARION, YOU ARE ALIVE! THANK GOD! HERE, LET ME HELP YOU.
SNAP!
SNAP!
OOOOOHH!
OOHH, NOOO-O-O NO NO NO NO NO
MARION AND I ARE ETERNALLY GRATEFUL, MY FRIEND! MISERY DOES LOVE COMPANY.... AND NOW THAT YOU'RE GOING TO JOIN US, WE THREE CAN LOOK FORWARD TO GIVING ALL OUR ATTENTION TO EACH OF DR. MALTON'S UNHAPPY GUESTS... ONE BY ONE, THANKS TO YOU!
END
5.

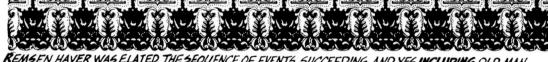

# HAUNTED GALLERY

REMSEN HAVER WAS ELATED. THE SEQUENCE OF EVENTS SUCCEEDING, AND YES, **INCLUDING** OLD MAN GAINESFORD'S **TIMELY** DEATH, HAD ALL GONE **EXACTLY** ACCORDING TO PLAN —**HIS** PLAN....

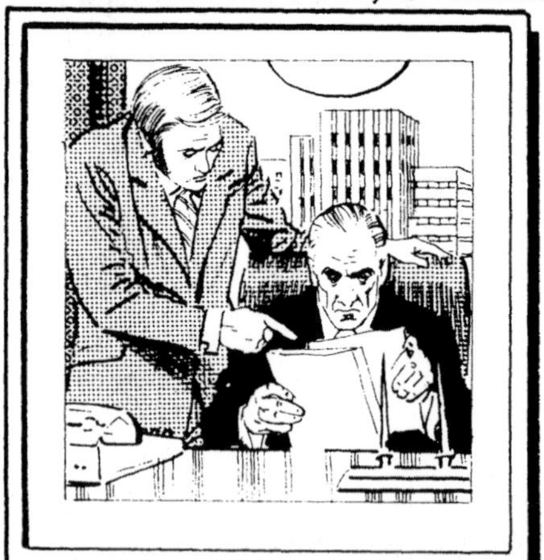

...AS HIS LAWYER, HAVER HAD MANAGED ELIAS GAINESFORD'S AFFAIRS FOR A NUMBER OF YEARS...

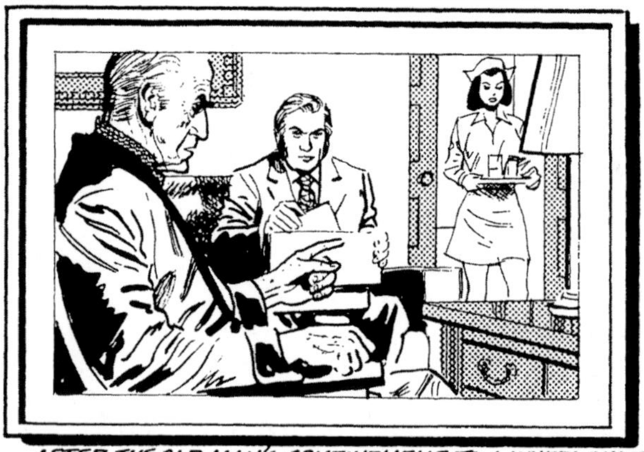

...AFTER THE OLD MAN'S CONFINEMENT TO A WHEELCHAIR, THE RESULT OF HIS COMBINING FAST DRIVING WITH HIS HEAVY DRINKING, REMSEN BECAME EVEN MORE INVOLVE IN HANDLING THE GAINESFORD INTERESTS, AND IN TIME ALMOST A MEMBER OF THE HOUSEHOLD...

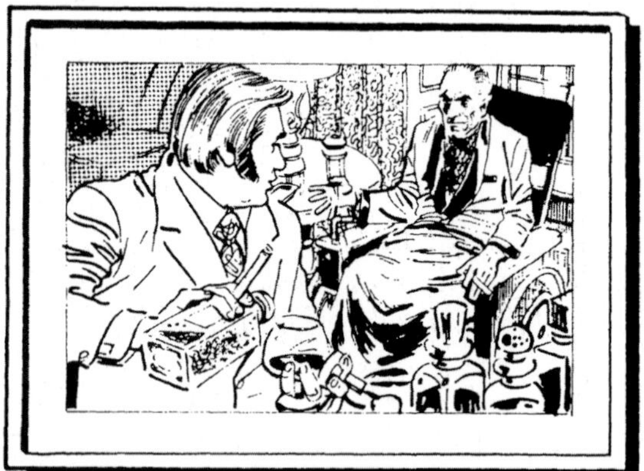

...IT WAS **EASY** AFTER THAT TO ARRANGE THE FINAL STEPS IN HIS CAMPAIGN TO CONTROL THE GAINESFORD MILLIONS...

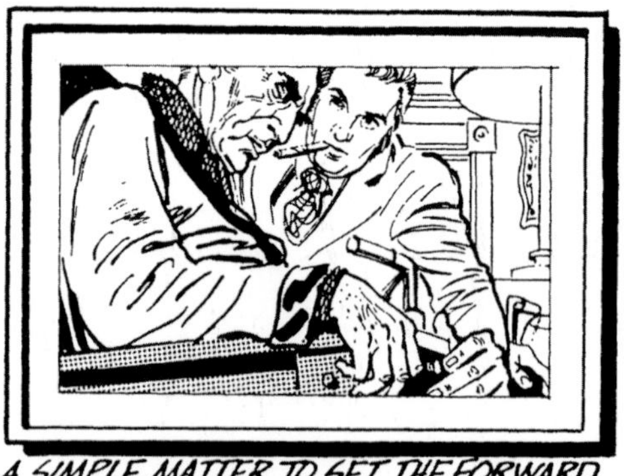

...A SIMPLE MATTER TO SET THE FORWARD SPEED CONTROL ON THE OLD MAN'S ELECTRIC-POWERED WHEELCHAIR ONE NIGHT AFTER HE'D IMBIBED SEVERAL TOO MANY BRANDIES, FALLEN ASLEEP AS HE WAS OFTEN KNOWN TO DO, AND...

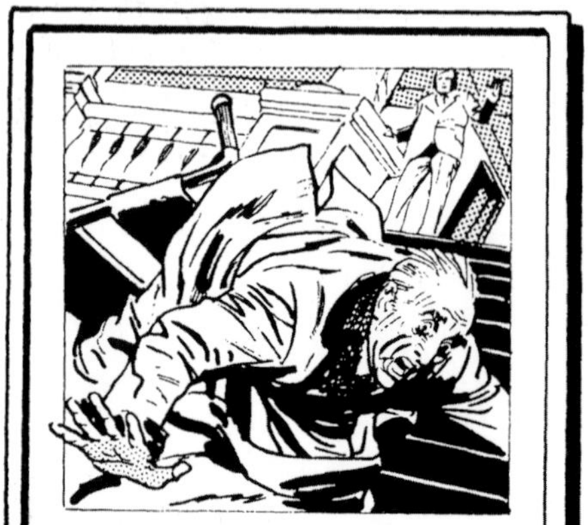

..SEND IT CRASHING DOWN A LONG FLIGHT OF STAIRS! DEATH DUE TO...

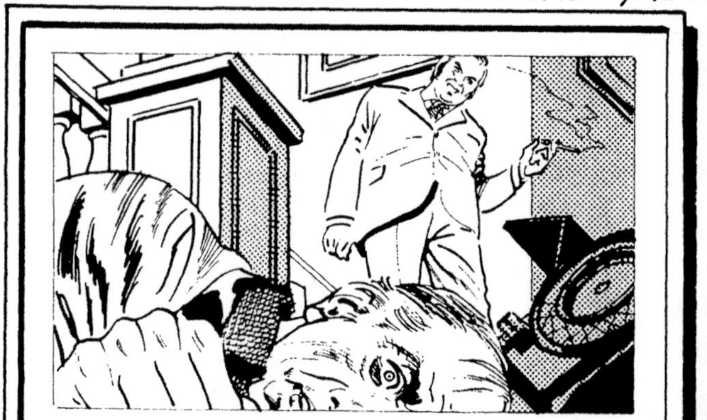

....DRUNKEN DRIVING! REMSEN HAD TO LAUGH AT THAT...

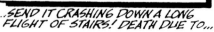

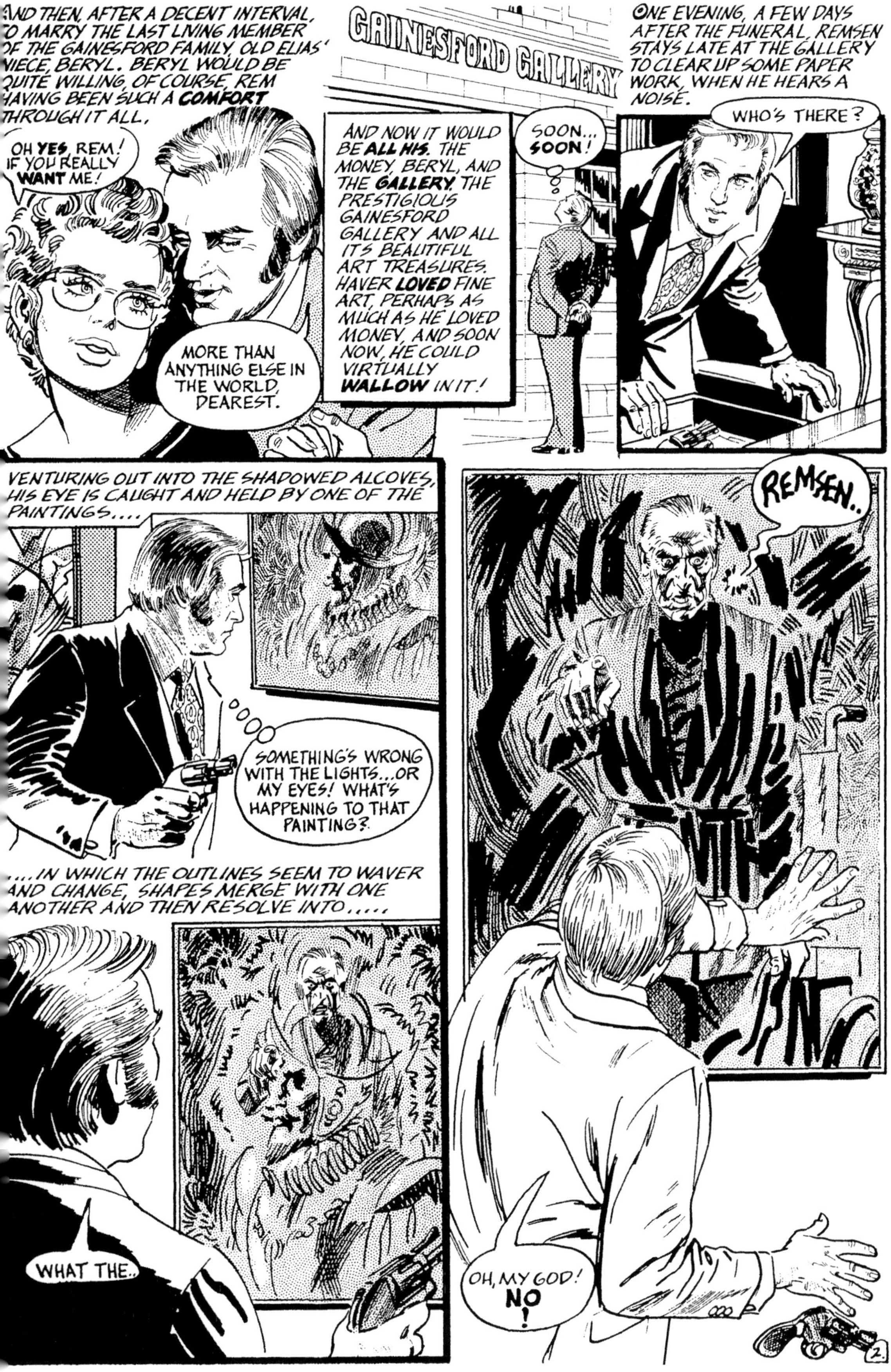
AND THEN, AFTER A DECENT INTERVAL, TO MARRY THE LAST LIVING MEMBER OF THE GAINESFORD FAMILY, OLD ELIAS' NIECE, BERYL. BERYL WOULD BE QUITE WILLING, OF COURSE, REM HAVING BEEN SUCH A COMFORT THROUGH IT ALL.
OH YES, REM! IF YOU REALLY WANT ME!
MORE THAN ANYTHING ELSE IN THE WORLD, DEAREST.
GAINESFORD GALLERY
AND NOW IT WOULD BE ALL HIS. THE MONEY, BERYL, AND THE GALLERY. THE PRESTIGIOUS GAINESFORD GALLERY AND ALL ITS BEAUTIFUL ART TREASURES. HAVER LOVED FINE ART, PERHAPS AS MUCH AS HE LOVED MONEY, AND SOON NOW, HE COULD VIRTUALLY WALLOW IN IT!
SOON... SOON!
ONE EVENING, A FEW DAYS AFTER THE FUNERAL, REMSEN STAYS LATE AT THE GALLERY TO CLEAR UP SOME PAPER WORK, WHEN HE HEARS A NOISE.
WHO'S THERE?
VENTURING OUT INTO THE SHADOWED ALCOVES, HIS EYE IS CAUGHT AND HELD BY ONE OF THE PAINTINGS....
SOMETHING'S WRONG WITH THE LIGHTS...OR MY EYES! WHAT'S HAPPENING TO THAT PAINTING?
....IN WHICH THE OUTLINES SEEM TO WAVER AND CHANGE, SHAPES MERGE WITH ONE ANOTHER AND THEN RESOLVE INTO.....
WHAT THE..
REMSEN..
OH, MY GOD! NO!
2.

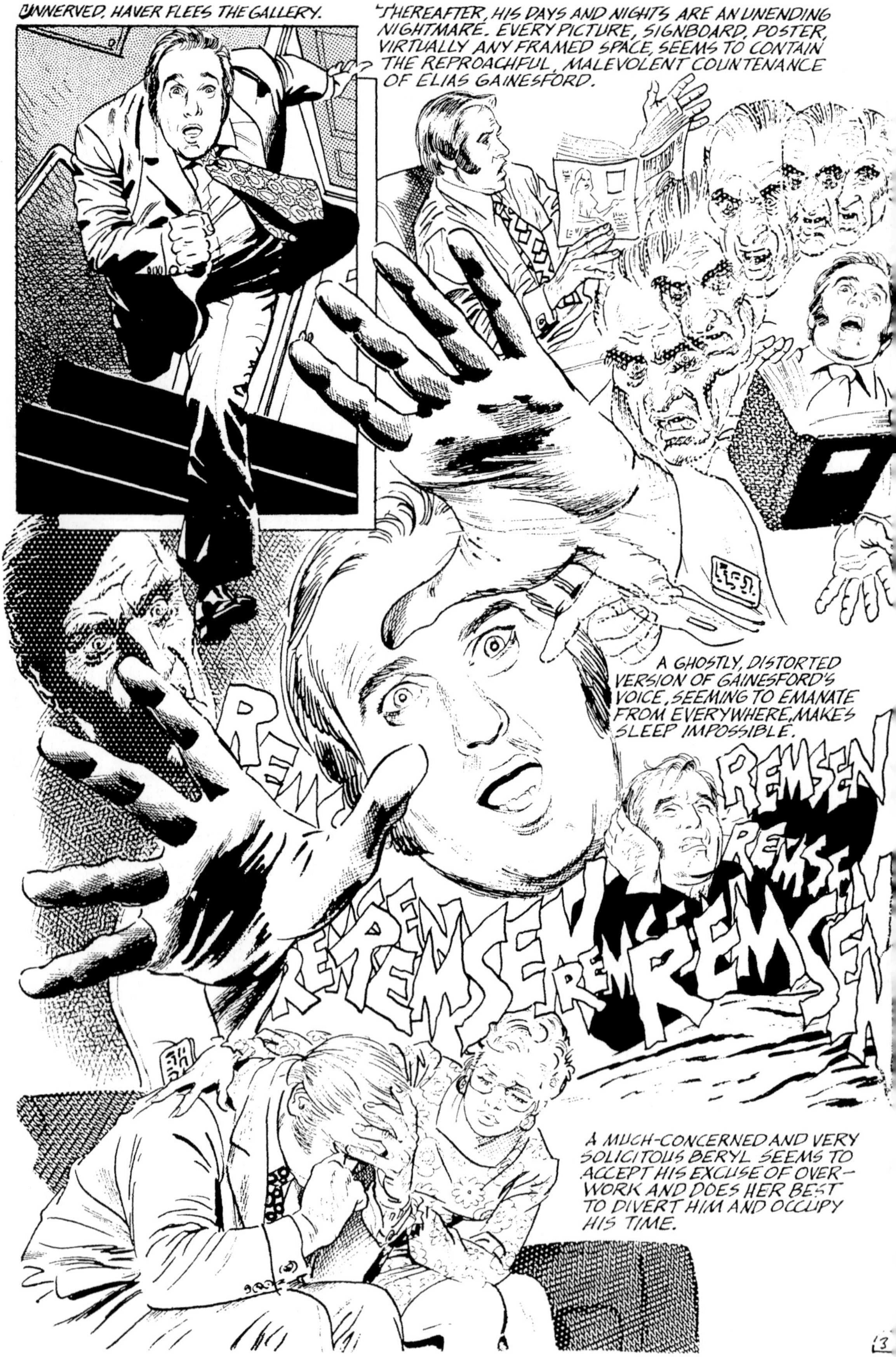
UNNERVED, HAVER FLEES THE GALLERY.
THEREAFTER, HIS DAYS AND NIGHTS ARE AN UNENDING NIGHTMARE. EVERY PICTURE, SIGNBOARD, POSTER, VIRTUALLY ANY FRAMED SPACE, SEEMS TO CONTAIN THE REPROACHFUL, MALEVOLENT COUNTENANCE OF ELIAS GAINESFORD.
A GHOSTLY, DISTORTED VERSION OF GAINESFORD'S VOICE, SEEMING TO EMANATE FROM EVERYWHERE, MAKES SLEEP IMPOSSIBLE.
REMSEN
REMSEN
REMSEN
REMSEN
A MUCH-CONCERNED AND VERY SOLICITOUS BERYL SEEMS TO ACCEPT HIS EXCUSE OF OVER-WORK AND DOES HER BEST TO DIVERT HIM AND OCCUPY HIS TIME.

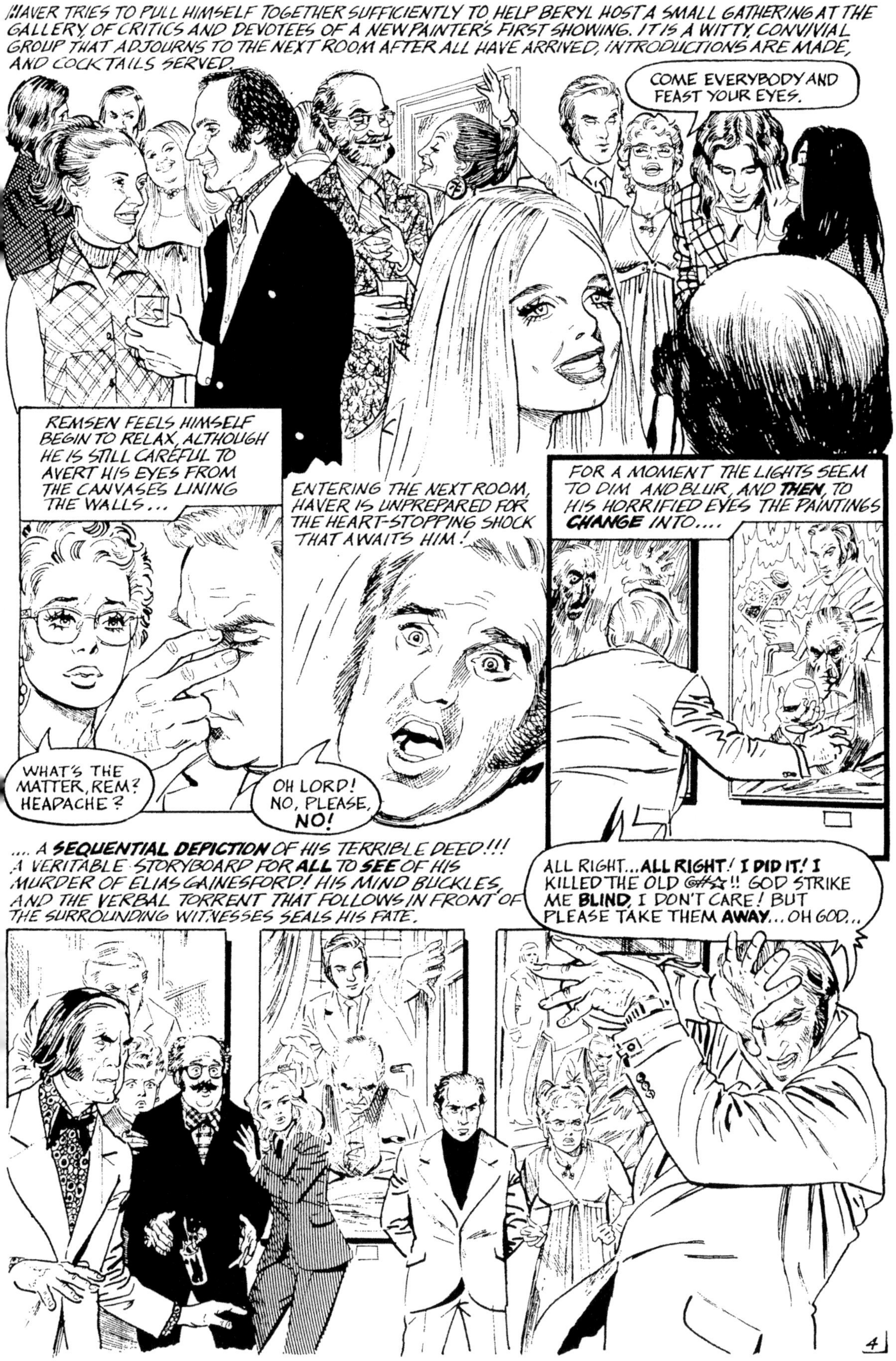
HAVER TRIES TO PULL HIMSELF TOGETHER SUFFICIENTLY TO HELP BERYL HOST A SMALL GATHERING AT THE GALLERY OF CRITICS AND DEVOTEES OF A NEW PAINTER'S FIRST SHOWING. IT IS A WITTY, CONVIVIAL GROUP THAT ADJOURNS TO THE NEXT ROOM AFTER ALL HAVE ARRIVED, INTRODUCTIONS ARE MADE, AND COCKTAILS SERVED.
COME EVERYBODY AND FEAST YOUR EYES.
REMSEN FEELS HIMSELF BEGIN TO RELAX, ALTHOUGH HE IS STILL CAREFUL TO AVERT HIS EYES FROM THE CANVASES LINING THE WALLS...
WHAT'S THE MATTER, REM? HEADACHE?
ENTERING THE NEXT ROOM, HAVER IS UNPREPARED FOR THE HEART-STOPPING SHOCK THAT AWAITS HIM!
OH LORD! NO, PLEASE, NO!
FOR A MOMENT THE LIGHTS SEEM TO DIM AND BLUR, AND THEN, TO HIS HORRIFIED EYES THE PAINTINGS CHANGE INTO....
.... A SEQUENTIAL DEPICTION OF HIS TERRIBLE DEED!!! A VERITABLE STORYBOARD FOR ALL TO SEE OF HIS MURDER OF ELIAS GAINESFORD! HIS MIND BUCKLES, AND THE VERBAL TORRENT THAT FOLLOWS IN FRONT OF THE SURROUNDING WITNESSES SEALS HIS FATE.
ALL RIGHT... ALL RIGHT! I DID IT! I KILLED THE OLD @#☆!! GOD STRIKE ME BLIND, I DON'T CARE! BUT PLEASE TAKE THEM AWAY... OH GOD...
4

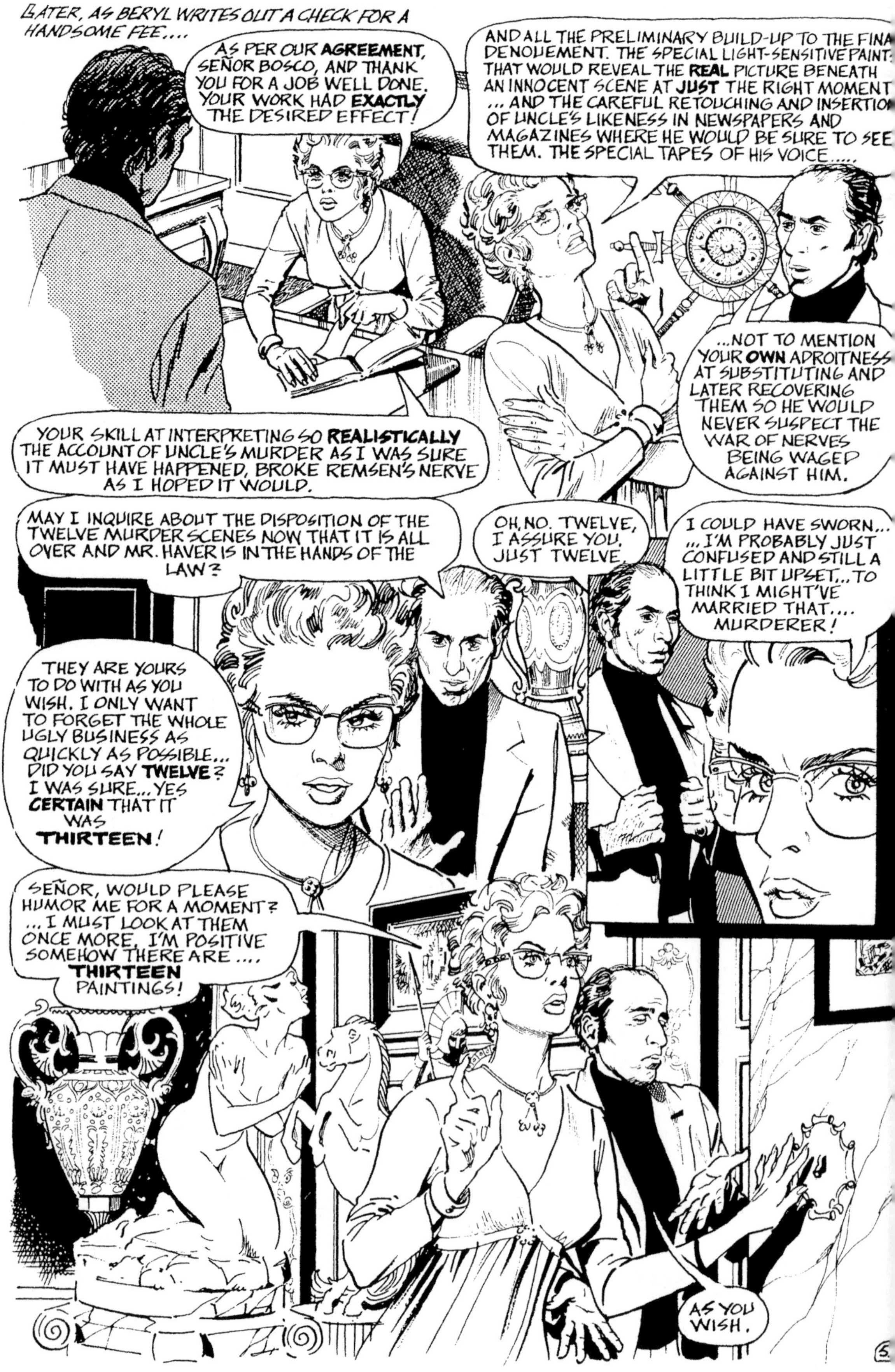
LATER, AS BERYL WRITES OUT A CHECK FOR A HANDSOME FEE....
AS PER OUR AGREEMENT, SEÑOR BOSCO, AND THANK YOU FOR A JOB WELL DONE. YOUR WORK HAD EXACTLY THE DESIRED EFFECT!
YOUR SKILL AT INTERPRETING SO REALISTICALLY THE ACCOUNT OF UNCLE'S MURDER AS I WAS SURE IT MUST HAVE HAPPENED, BROKE REMSEN'S NERVE AS I HOPED IT WOULD.
AND ALL THE PRELIMINARY BUILD-UP TO THE FINA DENOUEMENT. THE SPECIAL LIGHT-SENSITIVE PAINT THAT WOULD REVEAL THE REAL PICTURE BENEATH AN INNOCENT SCENE AT JUST THE RIGHT MOMENT ... AND THE CAREFUL RETOUCHING AND INSERTIO OF UNCLE'S LIKENESS IN NEWSPAPERS AND MAGAZINES WHERE HE WOULD BE SURE TO SEE THEM. THE SPECIAL TAPES OF HIS VOICE.....
...NOT TO MENTION YOUR OWN ADROITNESS AT SUBSTITUTING AND LATER RECOVERING THEM SO HE WOULD NEVER SUSPECT THE WAR OF NERVES BEING WAGED AGAINST HIM.
MAY I INQUIRE ABOUT THE DISPOSITION OF THE TWELVE MURDER SCENES NOW THAT IT IS ALL OVER AND MR. HAVER IS IN THE HANDS OF THE LAW?
THEY ARE YOURS TO DO WITH AS YOU WISH. I ONLY WANT TO FORGET THE WHOLE UGLY BUSINESS AS QUICKLY AS POSSIBLE... DID YOU SAY TWELVE? I WAS SURE... YES CERTAIN THAT IT WAS THIRTEEN!
OH, NO. TWELVE, I ASSURE YOU, JUST TWELVE.
I COULD HAVE SWORN... ... I'M PROBABLY JUST CONFUSED AND STILL A LITTLE BIT UPSET... TO THINK I MIGHT'VE MARRIED THAT.... MURDERER!
SEÑOR, WOULD PLEASE HUMOR ME FOR A MOMENT? ... I MUST LOOK AT THEM ONCE MORE. I'M POSITIVE SOMEHOW THERE ARE .... THIRTEEN PAINTINGS!
AS YOU WISH.

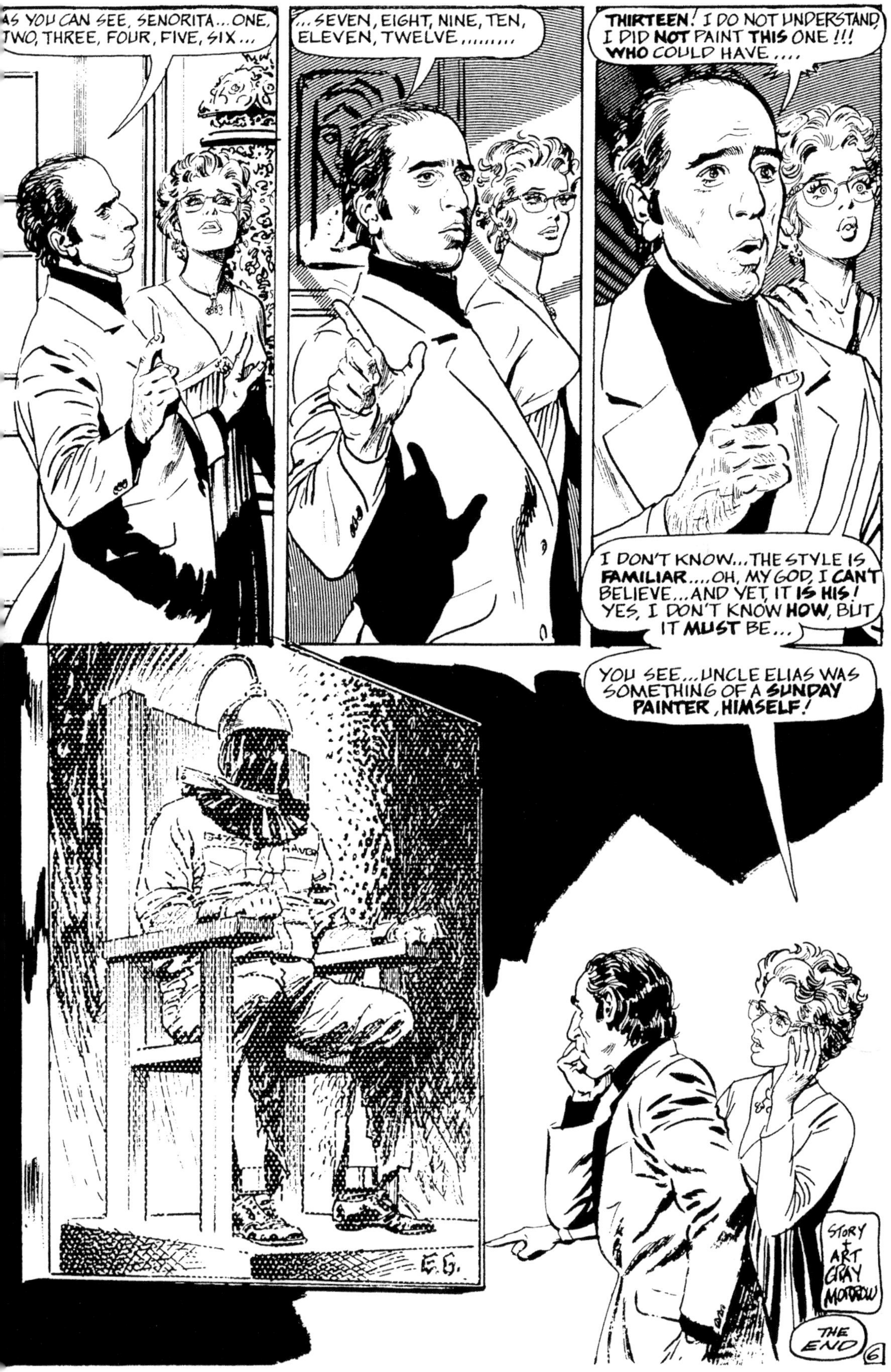
AS YOU CAN SEE, SENORITA... ONE, TWO, THREE, FOUR, FIVE, SIX...
...SEVEN, EIGHT, NINE, TEN, ELEVEN, TWELVE.........
THIRTEEN! I DO NOT UNDERSTAND, I DID NOT PAINT THIS ONE!!! WHO COULD HAVE....
I DON'T KNOW... THE STYLE IS FAMILIAR....OH, MY GOD, I CAN'T BELIEVE... AND YET, IT IS HIS! YES, I DON'T KNOW HOW, BUT IT MUST BE...
YOU SEE... UNCLE ELIAS WAS SOMETHING OF A SUNDAY PAINTER, HIMSELF!
E.G.
STORY + ART GRAY MORROW
THE END
6

# ESSAYS INTO THE SUPERNATURAL

TEXT: PHIL SUELING

ART: GRAY MORROW

WHEN MEN STILL LIVED IN TRIBES, MAGIC RULED HIS WORLD. HE FEARED THE ELEMENTS OF STORM AND FIRE, AND ADMIRED THE CREATURES WITH GOOD SURVIVAL TECHNIQUES. HE ASSOCIATED HIS GODS WITH THE STRENGTH OF A LION, OR THE CRAFTINESS OF A FOX, OR THE SPEED AND NOBILITY OF A STAG,

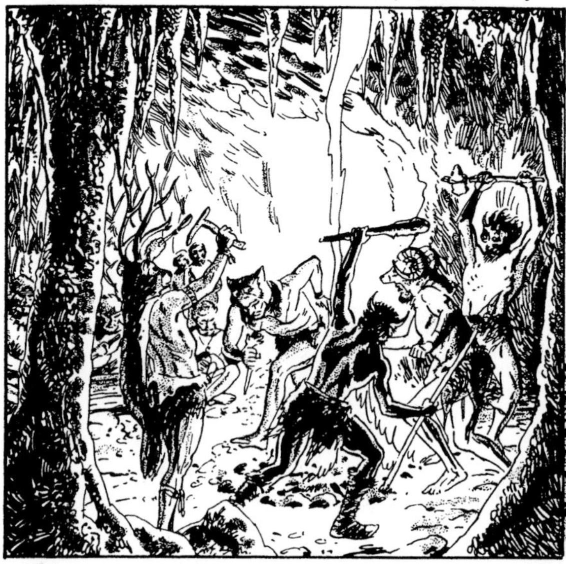

THROUGH RITUAL AND REPETITION, AND OVER THE COURSE OF CENTURIES, GOD AND CREATURE GREW CLOSER IN MAN'S MIND. BUT NEW RELIGIONS AROSE AND TO THEM, THE OLD GODS WERE EVIL. THE GODS OF THE OLD RELIGION BECAME THE DEVILS OF THE NEW. THE OLD GODS AND THEIR ASSOCIATE ANIMAL-SERVANTS WERE DRIVEN INTO HIDING.

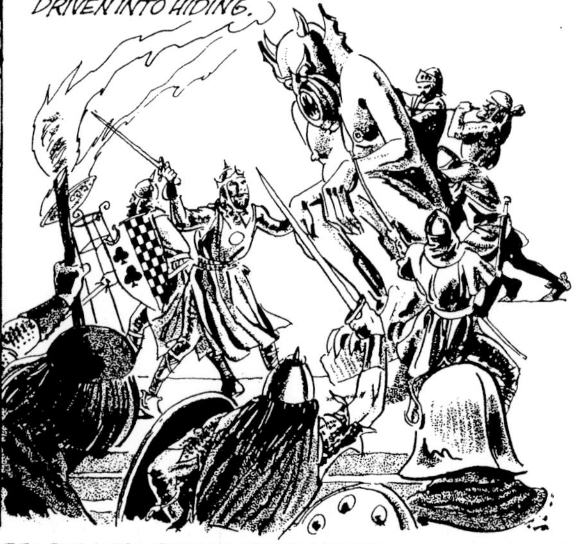

HOW COULD A LOYAL FOLLOWER LOCATE AND WORSHIP THE OUTLAWED GODS? HOW COULD THE OLD CHERISHED RELIGION BE PRACTICED? THE ANSWER WAS SECRECY, AND TOWNSPEOPLE WHISPERED AMONG THEMSELVES ABOUT "DEVILS" AND "BLACK RITES" AND "WITCHES." AND THE LINKS BETWEEN THE OLD GOD-DEVILS AND THEIR WITCH-SUBJECTS WERE THE SYMBOLIC ANIMALS.

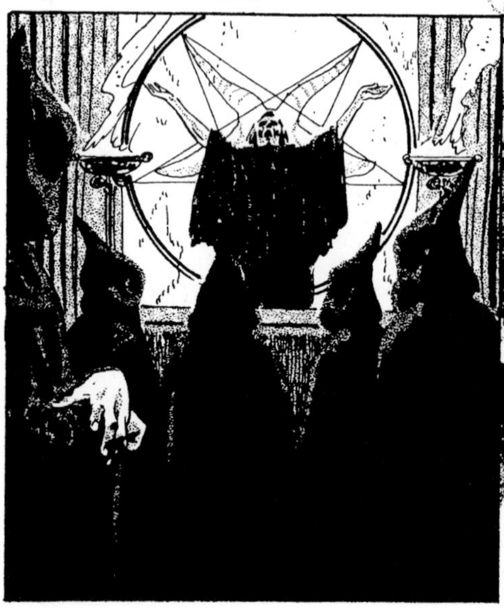

THE PEOPLE WHO FEARED THEM LEARNED TO RECOGNIZE THESE OUTCAST "WITCHES" BY THEIR FAMILIARS. THESE FAMILIARS WERE ANIMALS WHICH (IT WAS BELIEVED) DID THE EVIL BIDDING AND ASSISTED IN THE BLACK MAGIC OF THE WITCH-MASTER. THE FAMILIAR WAS MOST OFTEN A CAT, FROG, OR OWL. BUT ANY CREATURE WOULD DO.

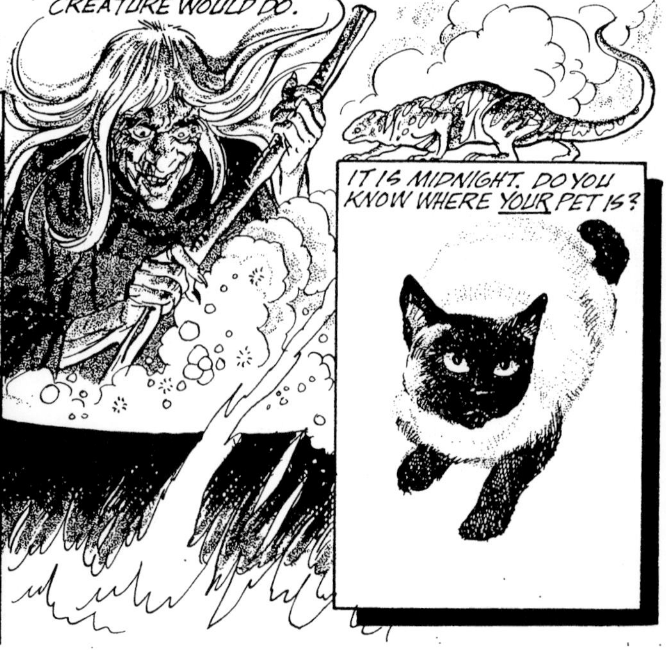
IT IS MIDNIGHT. DO YOU KNOW WHERE YOUR PET IS?

# ISSUE FOUR

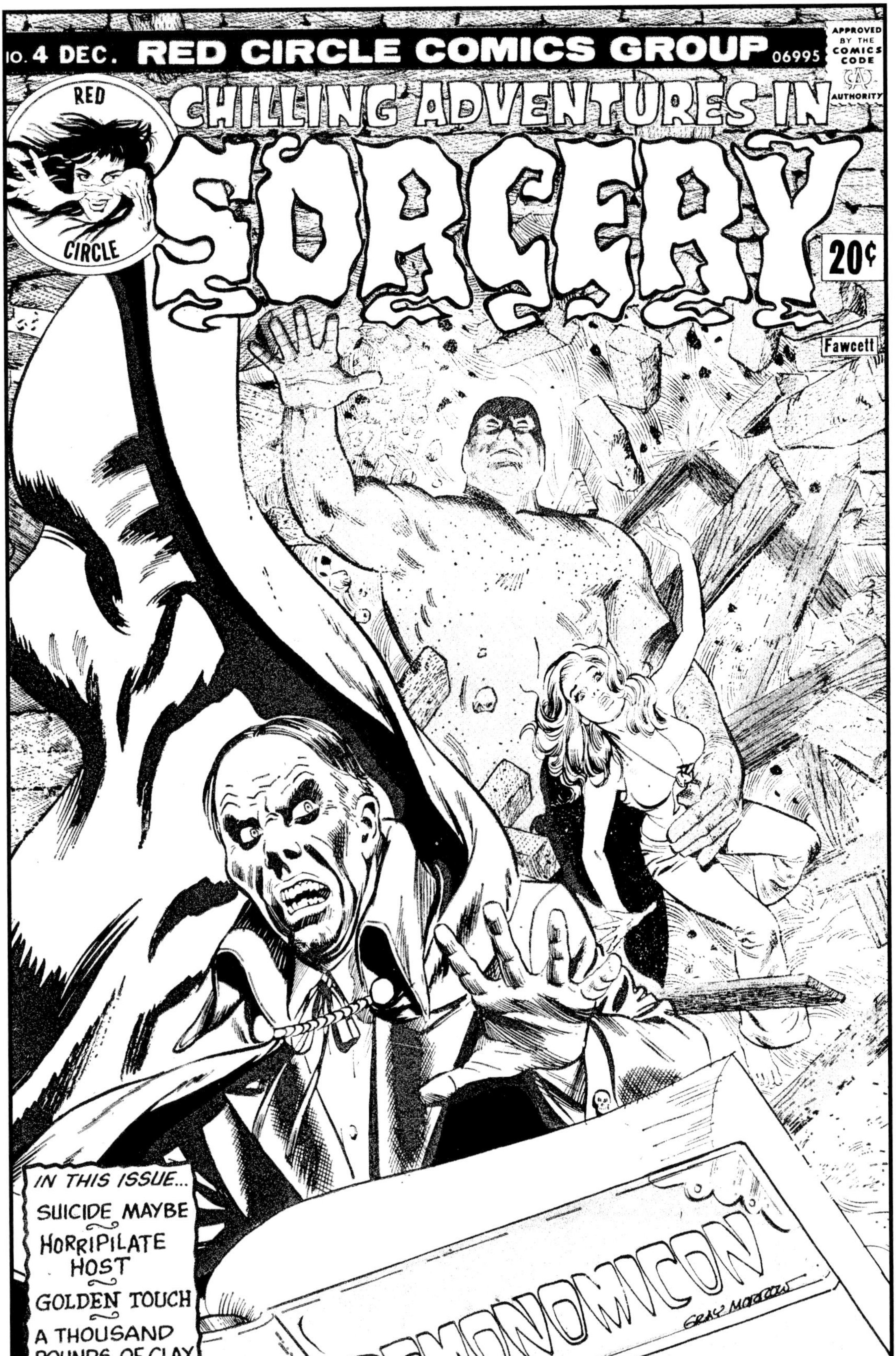

IO. 4 DEC.
RED CIRCLE COMICS GROUP
06995
APPROVED BY THE COMICS CODE AUTHORITY
RED CIRCLE
CHILLING ADVENTURES IN
SORCERY
20¢
Fawcett
IN THIS ISSUE...
SUICIDE MAYBE
HORRIPILATE HOST
GOLDEN TOUCH
A THOUSAND POUNDS OF CLAY
DEMONOMICON
GRAY MORROW

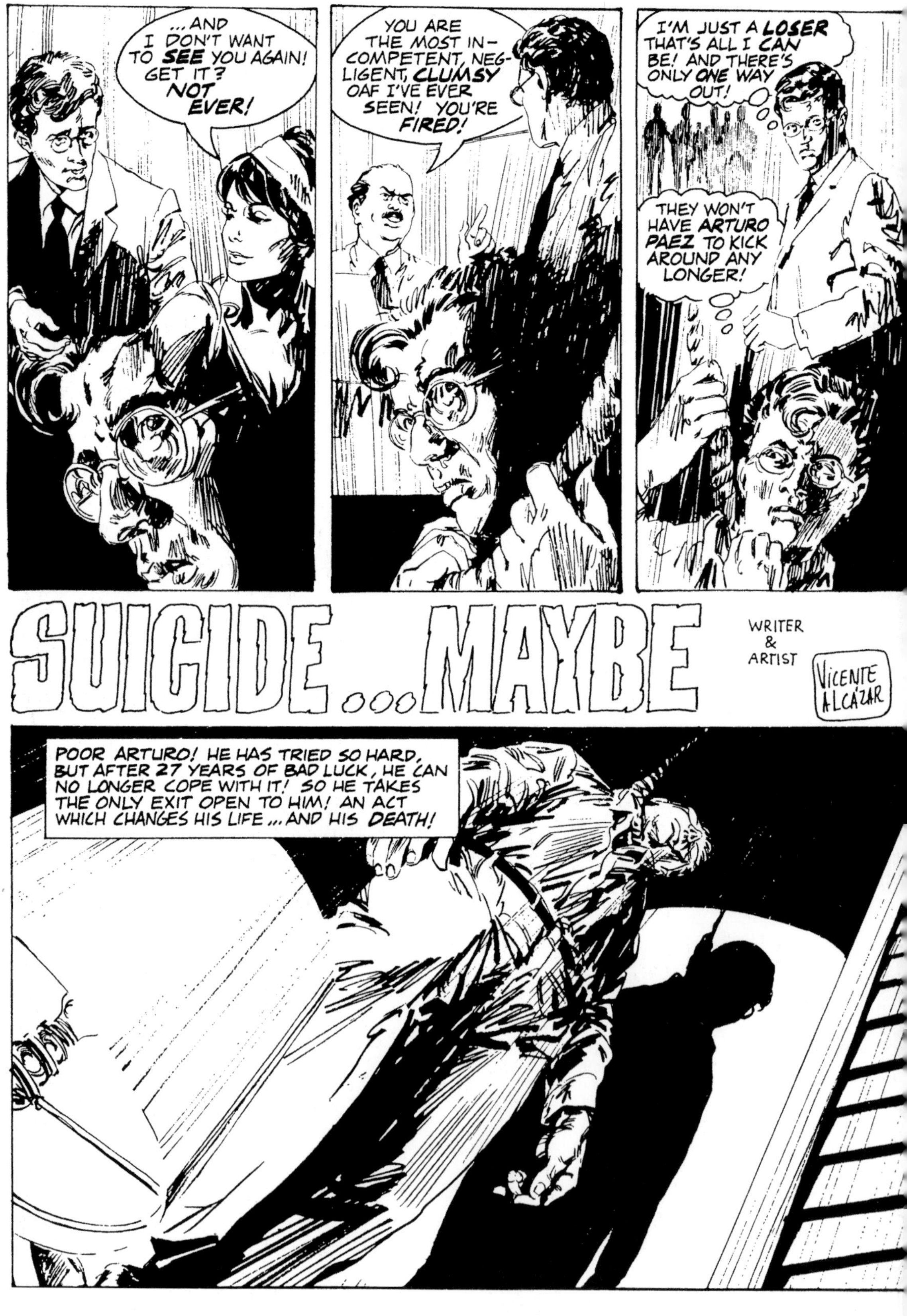
...AND I DON'T WANT TO SEE YOU AGAIN! GET IT? NOT EVER!
YOU ARE THE MOST IN-COMPETENT, NEG-LIGENT, CLUMSY OAF I'VE EVER SEEN! YOU'RE FIRED!
I'M JUST A LOSER THAT'S ALL I CAN BE! AND THERE'S ONLY ONE WAY OUT!
THEY WON'T HAVE ARTURO PAEZ TO KICK AROUND ANY LONGER!
SUICIDE...MAYBE
WRITER & ARTIST
VICENTE ALCÁZAR
POOR ARTURO! HE HAS TRIED SO HARD, BUT AFTER 27 YEARS OF BAD LUCK, HE CAN NO LONGER COPE WITH IT! SO HE TAKES THE ONLY EXIT OPEN TO HIM! AN ACT WHICH CHANGES HIS LIFE... AND HIS DEATH!

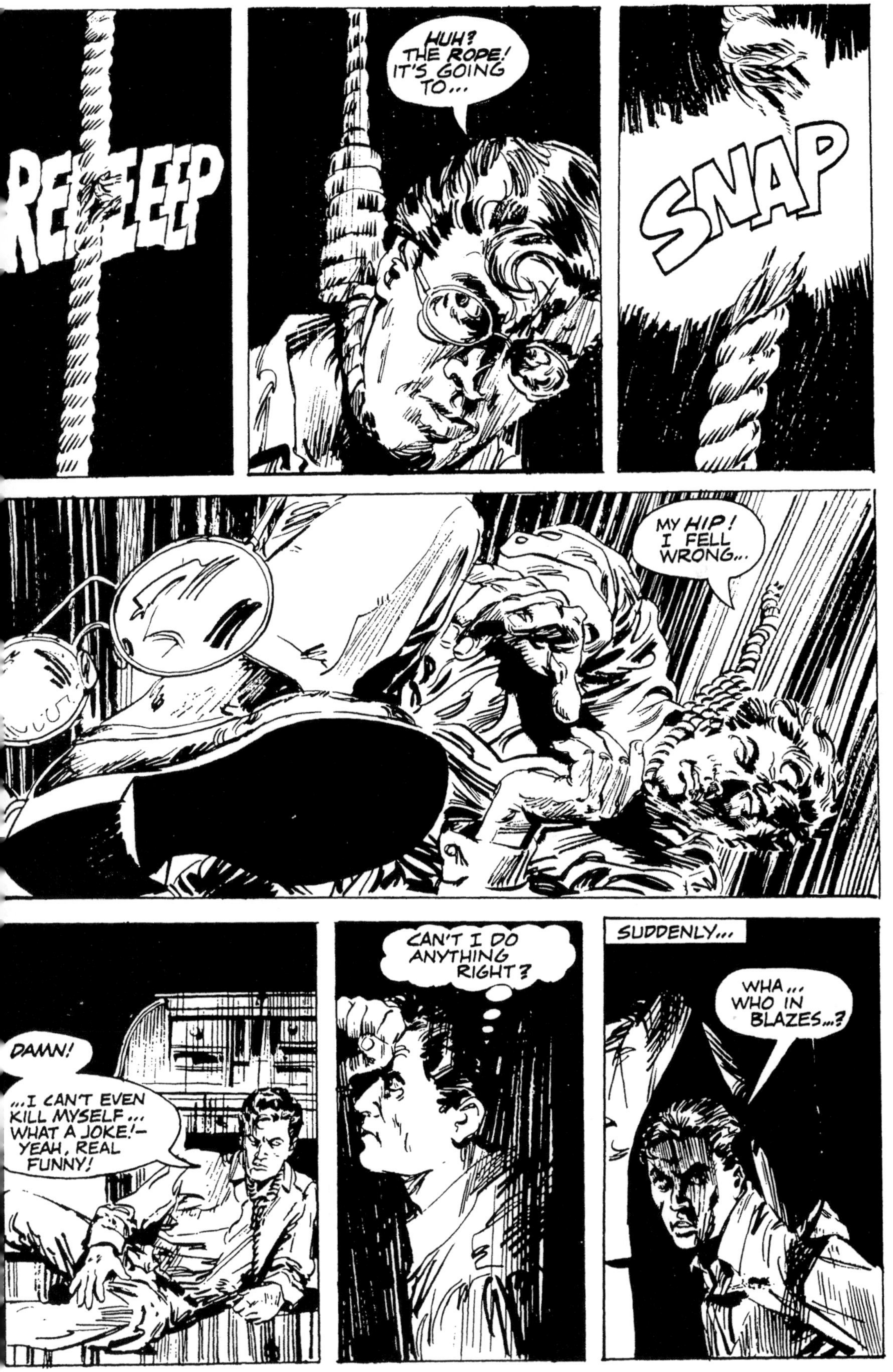
REEEEP
HUH? THE ROPE! IT'S GOING TO...
SNAP
MY HIP! I FELL WRONG...
DAMN!
...I CAN'T EVEN KILL MYSELF... WHAT A JOKE!— YEAH, REAL FUNNY!
CAN'T I DO ANYTHING RIGHT?
SUDDENLY...
WHA... WHO IN BLAZES...?

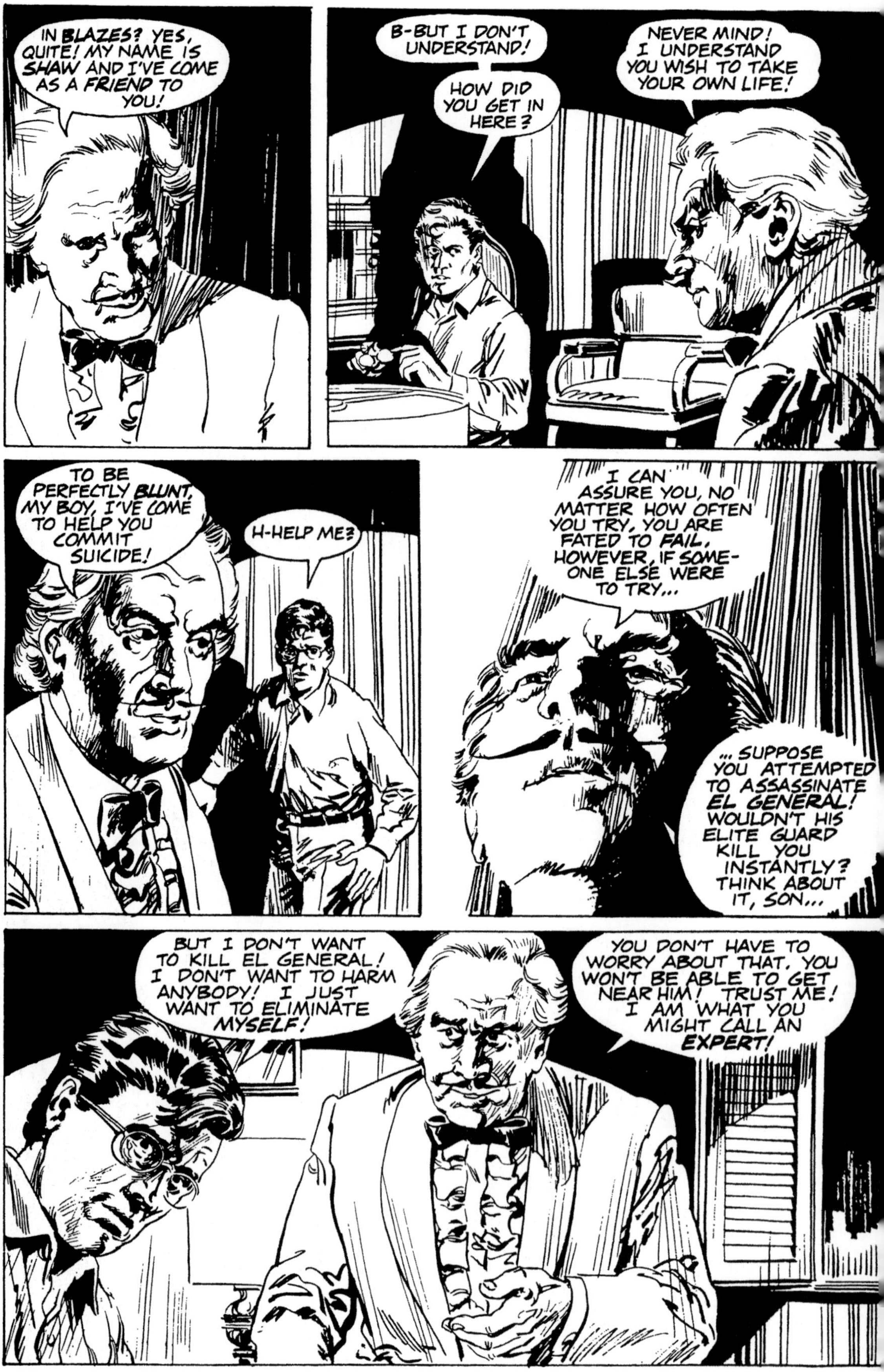
IN BLAZES? YES, QUITE! MY NAME IS SHAW AND I'VE COME AS A FRIEND TO YOU!
B-BUT I DON'T UNDERSTAND!
HOW DID YOU GET IN HERE?
NEVER MIND! I UNDERSTAND YOU WISH TO TAKE YOUR OWN LIFE!
TO BE PERFECTLY BLUNT, MY BOY, I'VE COME TO HELP YOU COMMIT SUICIDE!
H-HELP ME?
I CAN ASSURE YOU, NO MATTER HOW OFTEN YOU TRY, YOU ARE FATED TO FAIL. HOWEVER, IF SOME-ONE ELSE WERE TO TRY...
...SUPPOSE YOU ATTEMPTED TO ASSASSINATE EL GENERAL! WOULDN'T HIS ELITE GUARD KILL YOU INSTANTLY? THINK ABOUT IT, SON...
BUT I DON'T WANT TO KILL EL GENERAL! I DON'T WANT TO HARM ANYBODY! I JUST WANT TO ELIMINATE MYSELF!
YOU DON'T HAVE TO WORRY ABOUT THAT. YOU WON'T BE ABLE TO GET NEAR HIM! TRUST ME! I AM WHAT YOU MIGHT CALL AN EXPERT!

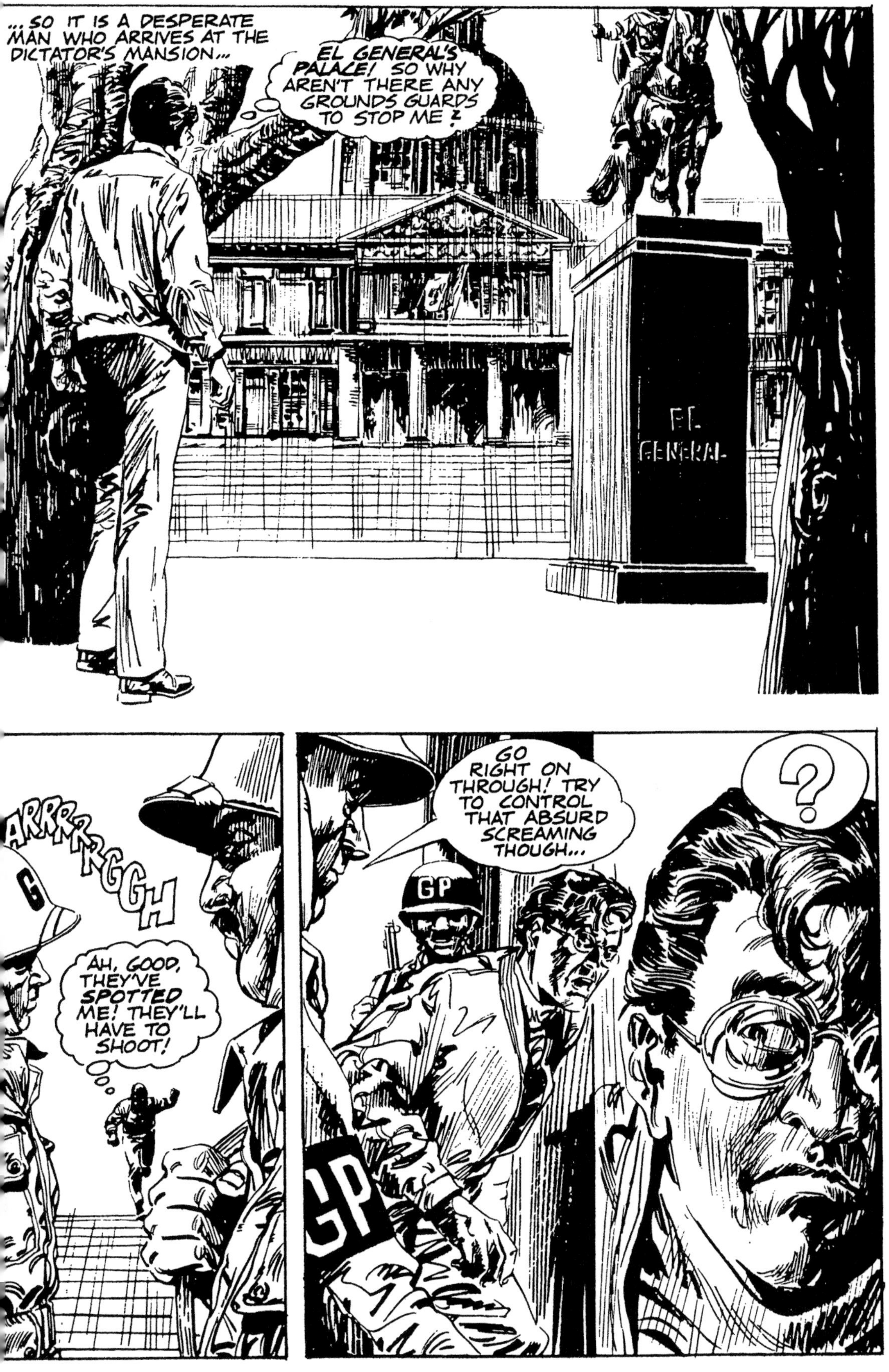

...SO IT IS A DESPERATE MAN WHO ARRIVES AT THE DICTATOR'S MANSION...
EL GENERAL'S PALACE! SO WHY AREN'T THERE ANY GROUNDS GUARDS TO STOP ME?
EL GENERAL
ARRRRRRGGH
AH, GOOD, THEY'VE SPOTTED ME! THEY'LL HAVE TO SHOOT!
GO RIGHT ON THROUGH! TRY TO CONTROL THAT ABSURD SCREAMING THOUGH...
GP
GP
?

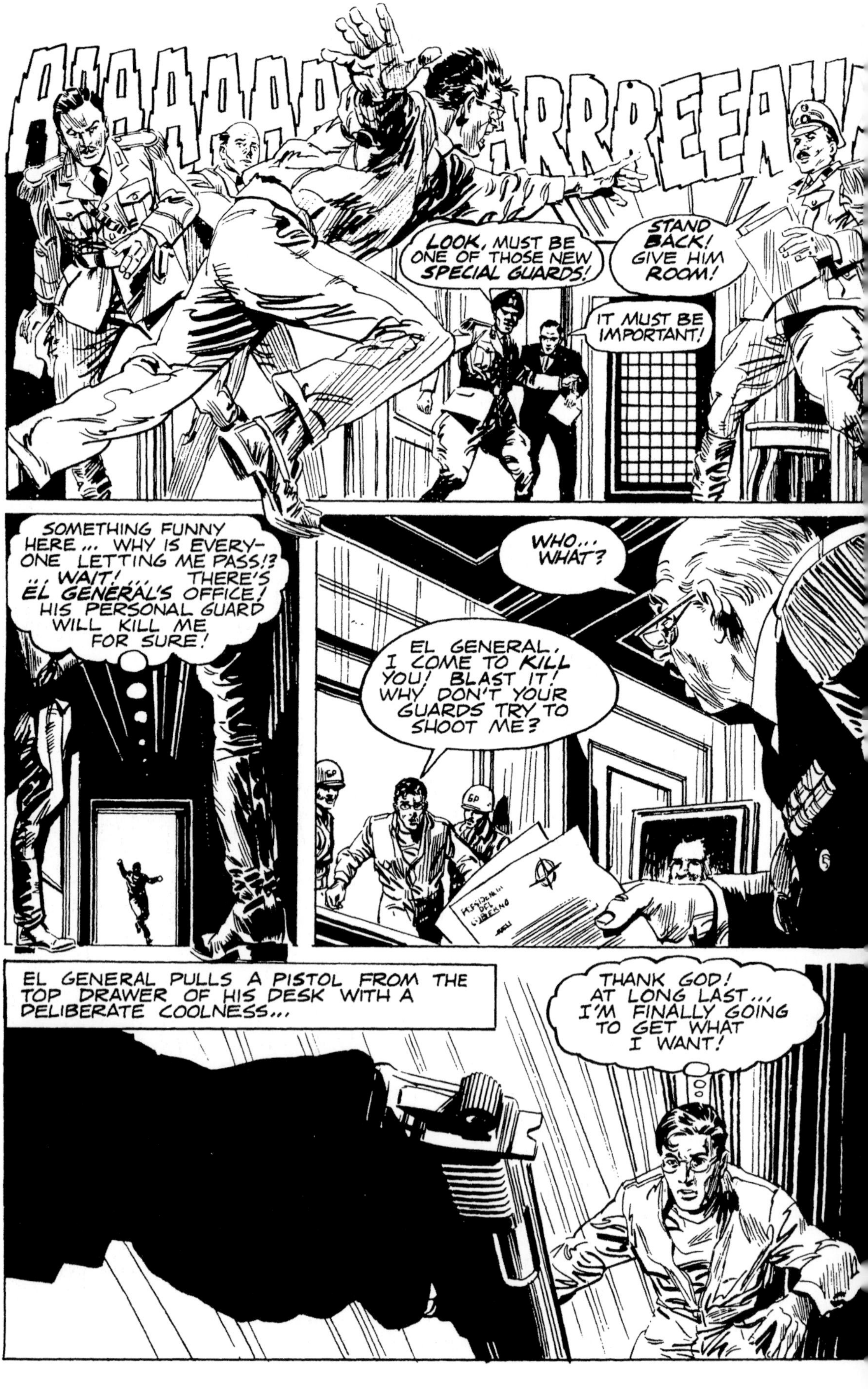
AAAAAAARRRREEAA
LOOK, MUST BE ONE OF THOSE NEW SPECIAL GUARDS!
STAND BACK! GIVE HIM ROOM!
IT MUST BE IMPORTANT!
SOMETHING FUNNY HERE... WHY IS EVERY-ONE LETTING ME PASS!? .. WAIT! ... THERE'S EL GENERAL'S OFFICE! HIS PERSONAL GUARD WILL KILL ME FOR SURE!
WHO... WHAT?
EL GENERAL, I COME TO KILL YOU! BLAST IT! WHY DON'T YOUR GUARDS TRY TO SHOOT ME?
EL GENERAL PULLS A PISTOL FROM THE TOP DRAWER OF HIS DESK WITH A DELIBERATE COOLNESS...
THANK GOD! AT LONG LAST... I'M FINALLY GOING TO GET WHAT I WANT!

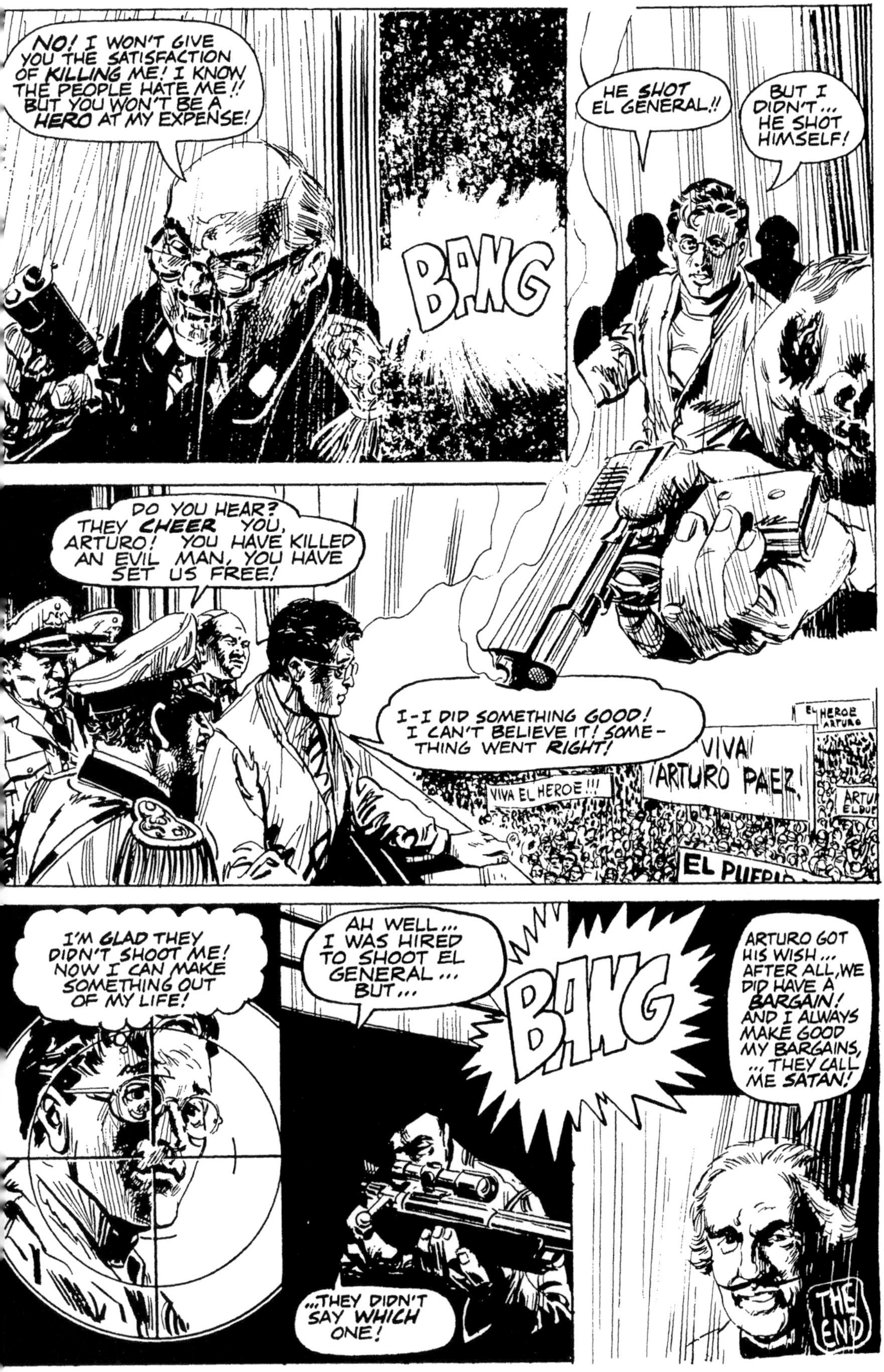
NO! I WON'T GIVE YOU THE SATISFACTION OF KILLING ME! I KNOW THE PEOPLE HATE ME!! BUT YOU WON'T BE A HERO AT MY EXPENSE!
BANG
HE SHOT EL GENERAL!!
BUT I DIDN'T... HE SHOT HIMSELF!
DO YOU HEAR? THEY CHEER YOU, ARTURO! YOU HAVE KILLED AN EVIL MAN, YOU HAVE SET US FREE!
I-I DID SOMETHING GOOD! I CAN'T BELIEVE IT! SOMETHING WENT RIGHT!
EL HEROE ARTURO
VIVA ARTURO PAEZ
VIVA EL HEROE!!!
I'M GLAD THEY DIDN'T SHOOT ME! NOW I CAN MAKE SOMETHING OUT OF MY LIFE!
AH WELL... I WAS HIRED TO SHOOT EL GENERAL... BUT...
BANG
...THEY DIDN'T SAY WHICH ONE!
ARTURO GOT HIS WISH... AFTER ALL, WE DID HAVE A BARGAIN! AND I ALWAYS MAKE GOOD MY BARGAINS, ...THEY CALL ME SATAN!
THE END

CHILLING ADVENTURES IN SORCERY

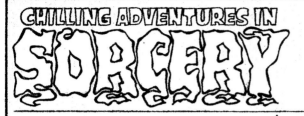

# LOOPHOLE

Jerome Hayley couldn't resist a bargain. He was sharp, shrewd and always ready to, "make a deal," rarely to his disadvantage. Thus, when the opportunity came to negotiate the biggest deal of his life, *a pact with the Devil,* it's not surprising that he hedged a bit, looking for loopholes.

"Looks okay, but my lawyer will have to check it out," he said, squinting at the parchment proferred him by *Lucifer's* claw-like hand.

"So sorry, no third party may be involved. This is strictly between you and I," said the Devil. "After all, you summoned *me,* so please make up your mind . . . and would you please turn off that air-conditioning? It's freezing in here!"

. . . "Wait, what about this clause? 'Wherein the party of the first part, meaning me, shall receive his heart's desire in all things; health, wealth, power and influence, etc., for a period not to exceed seven years, at which time this contract terminates and I forfeit my eternal soul to the party of the second part, meaning you, who shall be waiting behind a *Green Door* with *Fire* and *Damnation!*' I've heard how tricky you are! Suppose I walk through a Green Door before the seven years are up? You grab me, right? Or, suppose you strike me blind or use some other devious device to walk through that door before my time is up? What about it?"

"My dear sir, you wound me! Of course, such behavior on my part would render our agreement null and void. You mortals are always looking for the loophole. An escape clause. A way to bail yourself out at the eleventh hour. Certainly if you do not pass through the Green Door, I cannot collect and you do not have to honor the contract, yes? I always include such a clause; makes it more interesting. Rather sporting of me, don't you think? Obviously, you have no faith in inhuman nature. Now, do we have a deal, sir?" the Devil sniffed.

"I-I-I guess so."

"Excellent! Now the signature please."

"Don't I have to sign in blood?"

"I assure you our agreement is just as binding if you use this ball point pen. Please do hurry," he sniffed. "I think I'm catching cold, change of climate you know." He shuddered, and drew his scarlet cloak more closely about him.

Finally satisfied, Hayley scratched his name on the bottom line, certain that for at least seven glorious years, he would live like a king. The price . . . merely his soul . . . Well, just maybe there was a way around that. Contracts had been broken before. . .

"Achoo! Thank you. A bargain, believe me, and a real pleasure doing business with you. Until we meet again . . . *Achoo!* I mean adieu!"

So saying, Lucifer took his leave in his traditional puff of smoke, with one last gusty sneer.

The Devil certainly lived up to his end of the deal from the very first day. Overnight Jerome Hayley became fabulously wealthy, traveled in only the best circles, was politically influential, never had a sick day, or even suffered so much as the annoyance of a hangnail. In fact, he enjoyed what can only be described as a totally carefree existence. With one *exception.* When the expiration date of the pact began to draw closer by a few years time, it began to nag at him. He had to outfox the Devil. There *had* to be a way! He began to formulate a plan.

He needed someone in his corner, a powerful ally. So, he began a campaign to enlist the aid of Lucifer's old adversary, the Church. First came a series of heavy contributions to all of his favorite charities. Actually, it was his only favorite charity, but the recipients of his largesse didn't know or care about that. Outwardly, at least, he soon became a thoroughly devout follower of his faith and famous for his good works.

Then, after the revelation of his predicament to the holiest of the many holy men he'd come to know, he secured their sacred promise of help. On the final day, in a church, surrounded by Godly men employing their prayers and rites of exorcism, he began to know a growing sense of security. The devil had been beaten before, and would be *this time,* too! He, Jerome Hayley, would beat the Devil at his own game.

Hayley's confident ruminations were scattered like leaves by an Autumn wind when the Priest's litany was interrupted by a hoarse shout from one of them as he pointed to the smoke curling from under the door. *Fire!* En mass, they rushed to and from the windowless room and shouldered their way into the smoke-filled hall. Panicked, eyes stinging, Hayley groped his way down the corridor, seeking escape from the roaring holocaust that seemed to engulf him. . . .

"Never saw a blaze quite like it. Seems to have been confined to just that one wing of the building. No evidence of arson." The fire chief was discussing the incident with one of the priests.

"Only one casualty. Can't understand why this Hayley guy didn't save himself. Must've been overcome by the smoke. Ironic isn't it? He was only a few steps from salvation.

"How do you mean?"

"We found his body only a few feet from the fire exit door."

"Which door. . . ?"

"You know, the *Green* fire exit door.

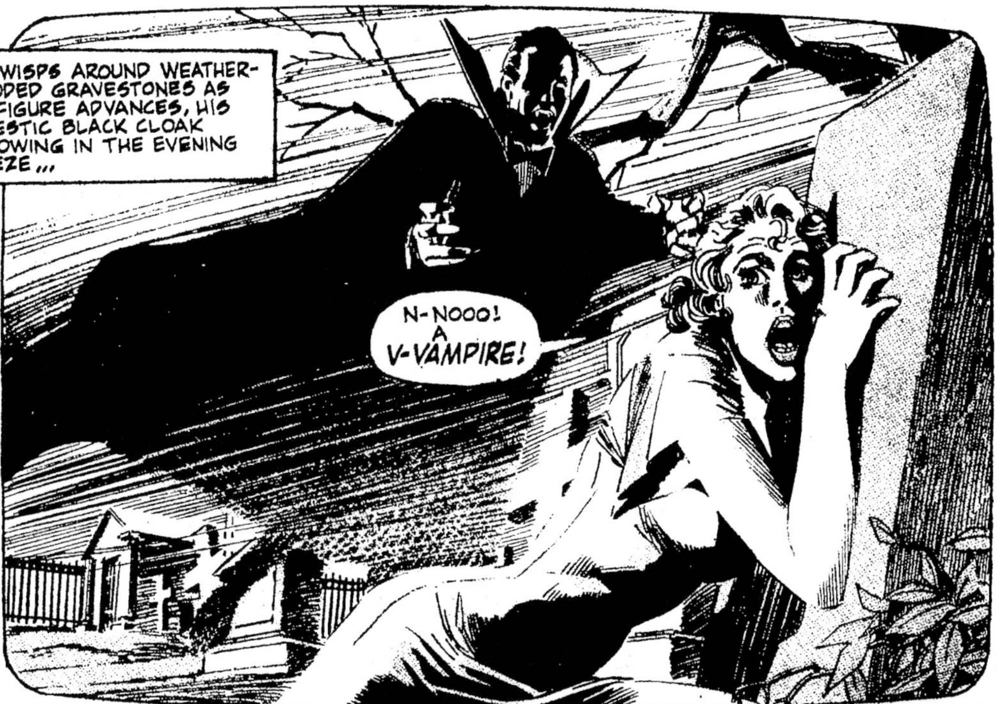
FOG WISPS AROUND WEATHER-ERODED GRAVESTONES AS THE FIGURE ADVANCES, HIS MAJESTIC BLACK CLOAK BILLOWING IN THE EVENING BREEZE...
N-NOOO! A V-VAMPIRE!

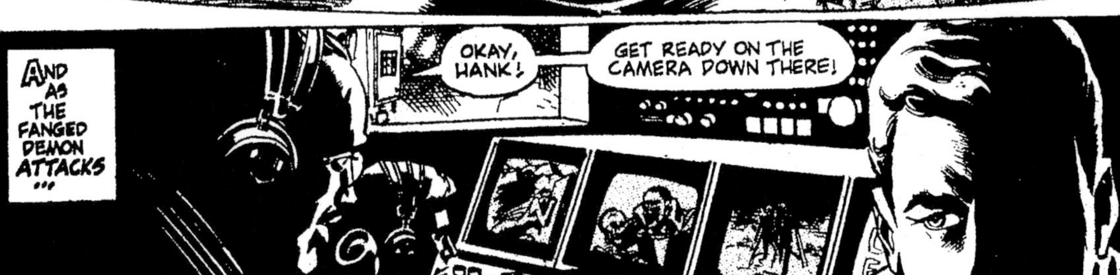
AND AS THE FANGED DEMON ATTACKS...
OKAY, HANK!
GET READY ON THE CAMERA DOWN THERE!

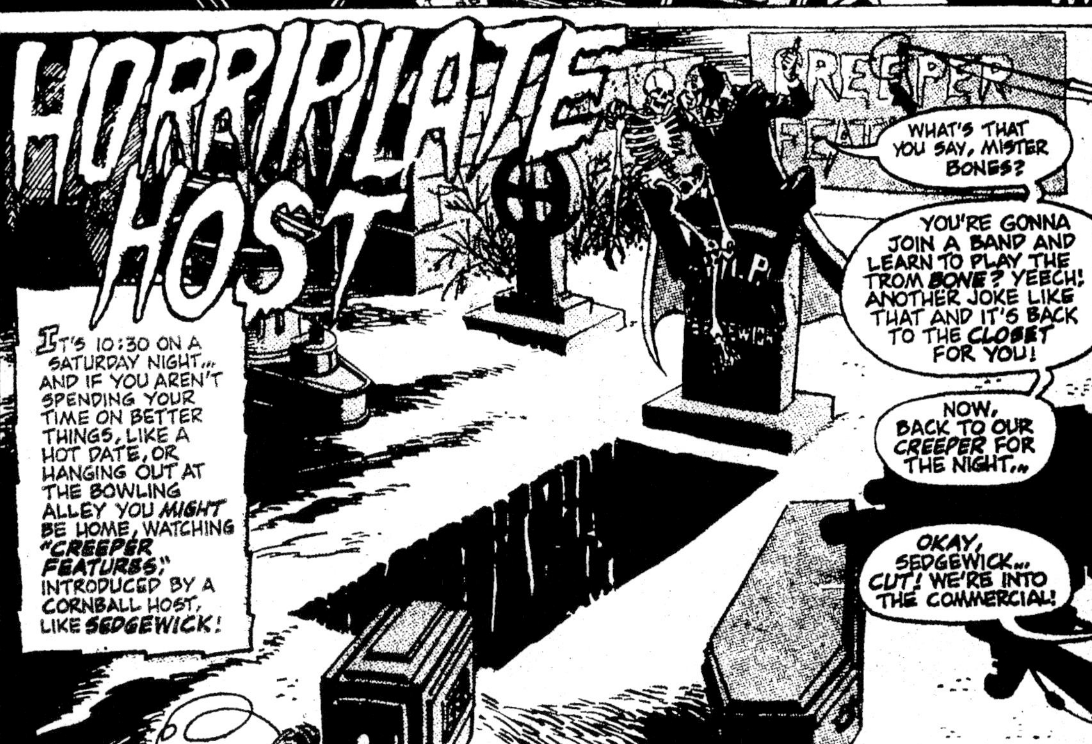
HORRIPLATE HOST
IT'S 10:30 ON A SATURDAY NIGHT... AND IF YOU AREN'T SPENDING YOUR TIME ON BETTER THINGS, LIKE A HOT DATE, OR HANGING OUT AT THE BOWLING ALLEY YOU MIGHT BE HOME, WATCHING "CREEPER FEATURES," INTRODUCED BY A CORNBALL HOST, LIKE SEDGEWICK!
CREEPER
WHAT'S THAT YOU SAY, MISTER BONES?
YOU'RE GONNA JOIN A BAND AND LEARN TO PLAY THE TROMBONE? YEECH! ANOTHER JOKE LIKE THAT AND IT'S BACK TO THE CLOSET FOR YOU!
NOW, BACK TO OUR CREEPER FOR THE NIGHT...
OKAY, SEDGEWICK... CUT! WE'RE INTO THE COMMERCIAL!

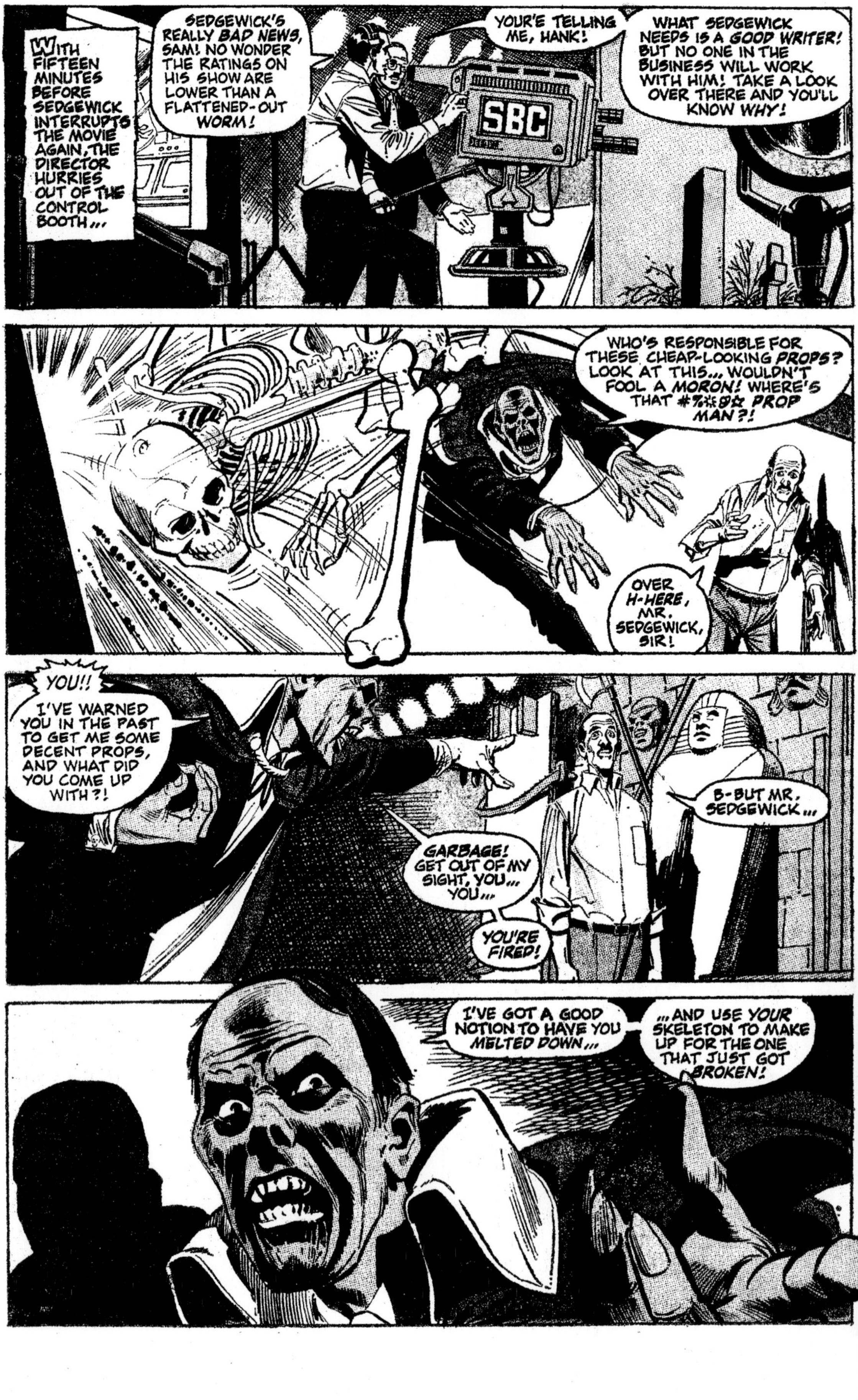
WITH FIFTEEN MINUTES BEFORE SEDGEWICK INTERRUPTS THE MOVIE AGAIN, THE DIRECTOR HURRIES OUT OF THE CONTROL BOOTH...
SEDGEWICK'S REALLY BAD NEWS, SAM! NO WONDER THE RATINGS ON HIS SHOW ARE LOWER THAN A FLATTENED-OUT WORM!
YOUR'E TELLING ME, HANK!
WHAT SEDGEWICK NEEDS IS A GOOD WRITER! BUT NO ONE IN THE BUSINESS WILL WORK WITH HIM! TAKE A LOOK OVER THERE AND YOU'LL KNOW WHY!
SBC
WHO'S RESPONSIBLE FOR THESE CHEAP-LOOKING PROPS? LOOK AT THIS... WOULDN'T FOOL A MORON! WHERE'S THAT #%*@☆ PROP MAN?!
OVER H-HERE, MR. SEDGEWICK, SIR!
YOU!! I'VE WARNED YOU IN THE PAST TO GET ME SOME DECENT PROPS, AND WHAT DID YOU COME UP WITH?!
B-BUT MR. SEDGEWICK...
GARBAGE! GET OUT OF MY SIGHT, YOU... YOU...
YOU'RE FIRED!
I'VE GOT A GOOD NOTION TO HAVE YOU MELTED DOWN...
...AND USE YOUR SKELETON TO MAKE UP FOR THE ONE THAT JUST GOT BROKEN!

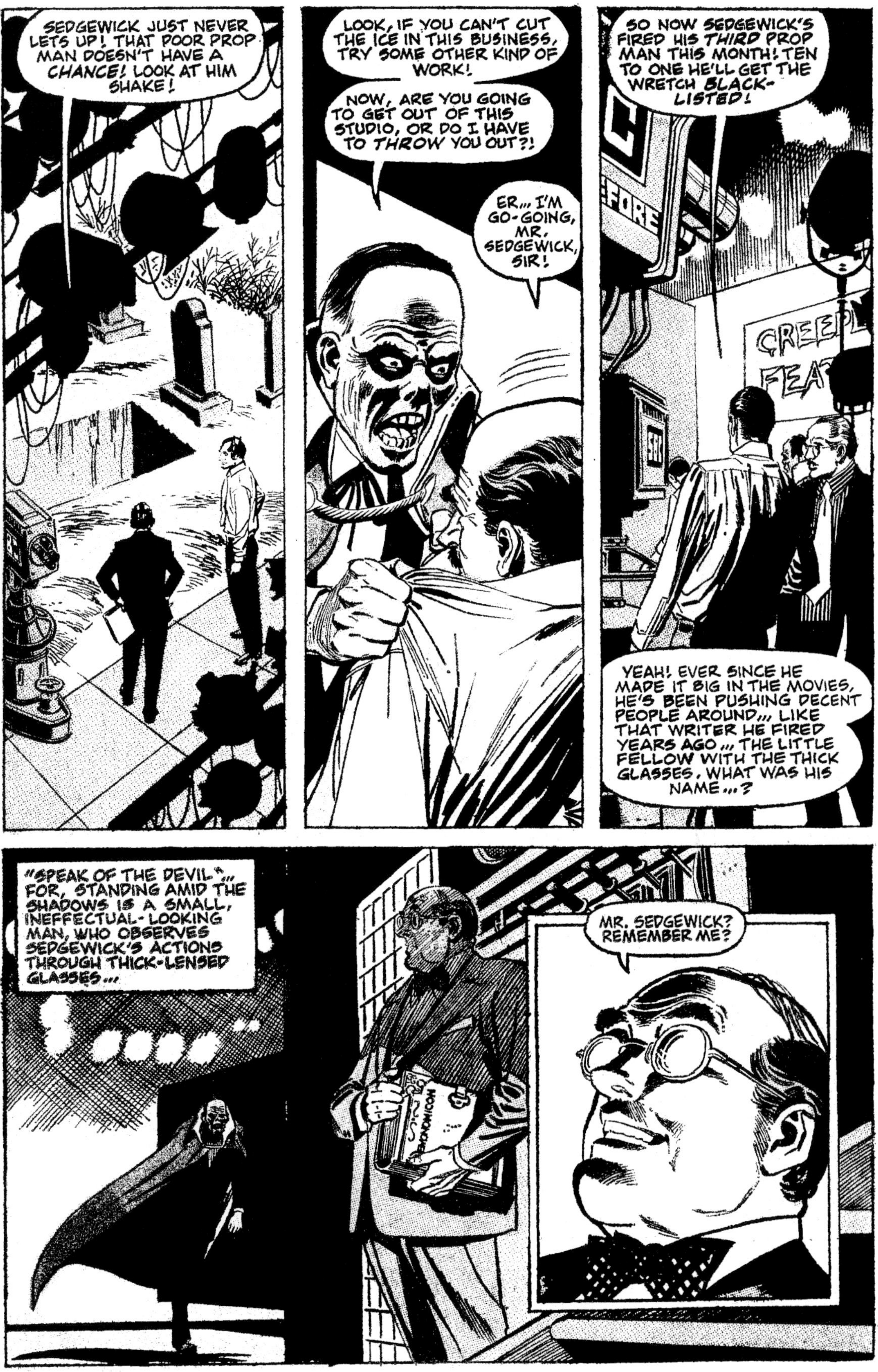
SEDGEWICK JUST NEVER LETS UP! THAT POOR PROP MAN DOESN'T HAVE A CHANCE! LOOK AT HIM SHAKE!
LOOK, IF YOU CAN'T CUT THE ICE IN THIS BUSINESS, TRY SOME OTHER KIND OF WORK!
NOW, ARE YOU GOING TO GET OUT OF THIS STUDIO, OR DO I HAVE TO THROW YOU OUT?!
ER... I'M GO-GOING, MR. SEDGEWICK, SIR!
SO NOW SEDGEWICK'S FIRED HIS THIRD PROP MAN THIS MONTH! TEN TO ONE HE'LL GET THE WRETCH BLACK-LISTED!
YEAH! EVER SINCE HE MADE IT BIG IN THE MOVIES, HE'S BEEN PUSHING DECENT PEOPLE AROUND... LIKE THAT WRITER HE FIRED YEARS AGO... THE LITTLE FELLOW WITH THE THICK GLASSES. WHAT WAS HIS NAME...?
"SPEAK OF THE DEVIL"... FOR, STANDING AMID THE SHADOWS IS A SMALL, INEFFECTUAL-LOOKING MAN, WHO OBSERVES SEDGEWICK'S ACTIONS THROUGH THICK-LENSED GLASSES...
MR. SEDGEWICK? REMEMBER ME?

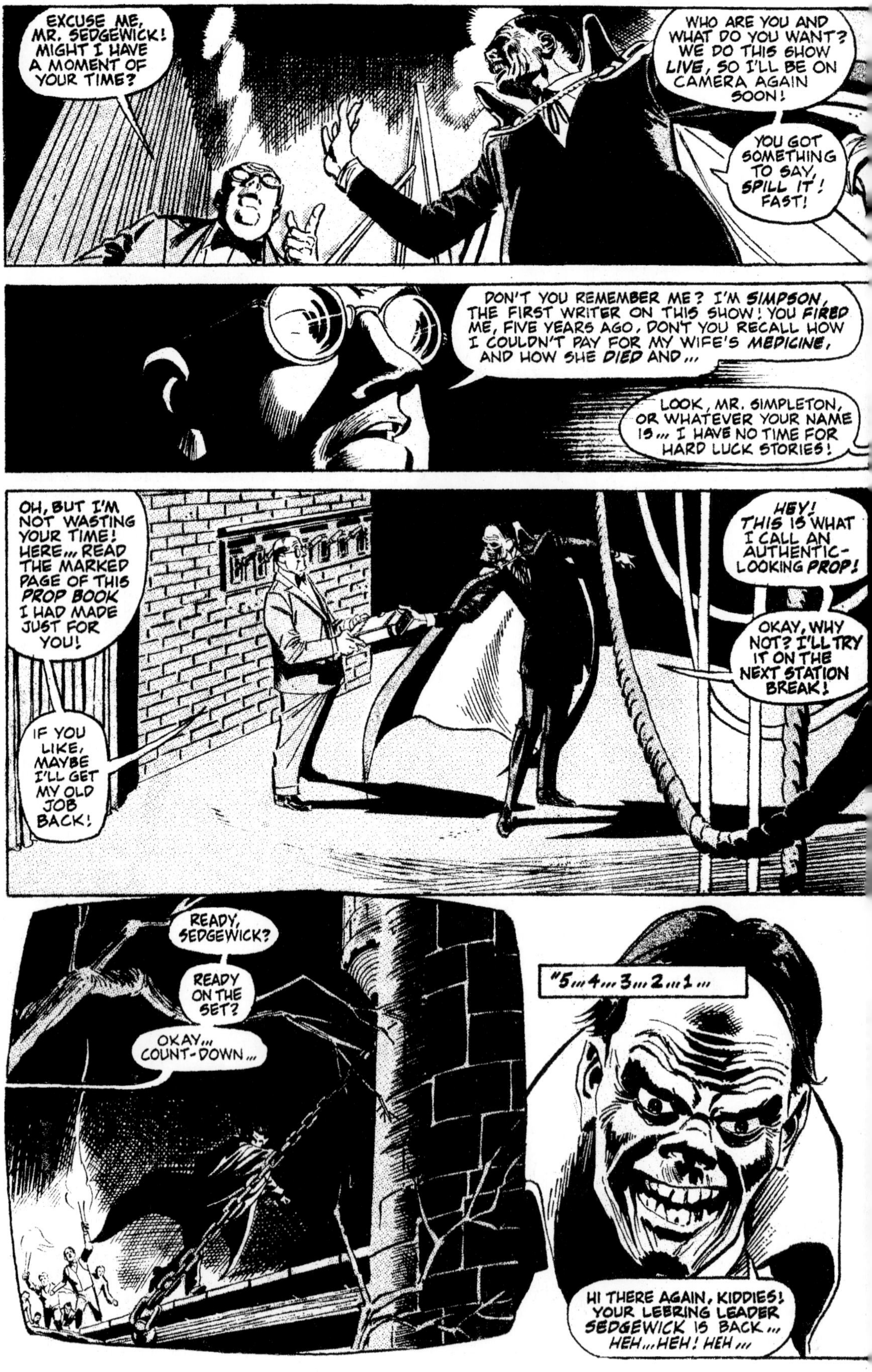

EXCUSE ME, MR. SEDGEWICK! MIGHT I HAVE A MOMENT OF YOUR TIME?
WHO ARE YOU AND WHAT DO YOU WANT? WE DO THIS SHOW LIVE, SO I'LL BE ON CAMERA AGAIN SOON!
YOU GOT SOMETHING TO SAY, SPILL IT! FAST!
DON'T YOU REMEMBER ME? I'M SIMPSON, THE FIRST WRITER ON THIS SHOW! YOU FIRED ME, FIVE YEARS AGO. DON'T YOU RECALL HOW I COULDN'T PAY FOR MY WIFE'S MEDICINE, AND HOW SHE DIED AND...
LOOK, MR. SIMPLETON, OR WHATEVER YOUR NAME IS... I HAVE NO TIME FOR HARD LUCK STORIES!
OH, BUT I'M NOT WASTING YOUR TIME! HERE... READ THE MARKED PAGE OF THIS PROP BOOK I HAD MADE JUST FOR YOU!
IF YOU LIKE, MAYBE I'LL GET MY OLD JOB BACK!
HEY! THIS IS WHAT I CALL AN AUTHENTIC-LOOKING PROP!
OKAY, WHY NOT? I'LL TRY IT ON THE NEXT STATION BREAK!
READY, SEDGEWICK?
READY ON THE SET?
OKAY... COUNT-DOWN...
"5...4...3...2...1...
HI THERE AGAIN, KIDDIES! YOUR LEERING LEADER SEDGEWICK IS BACK... HEH...HEH! HEH...

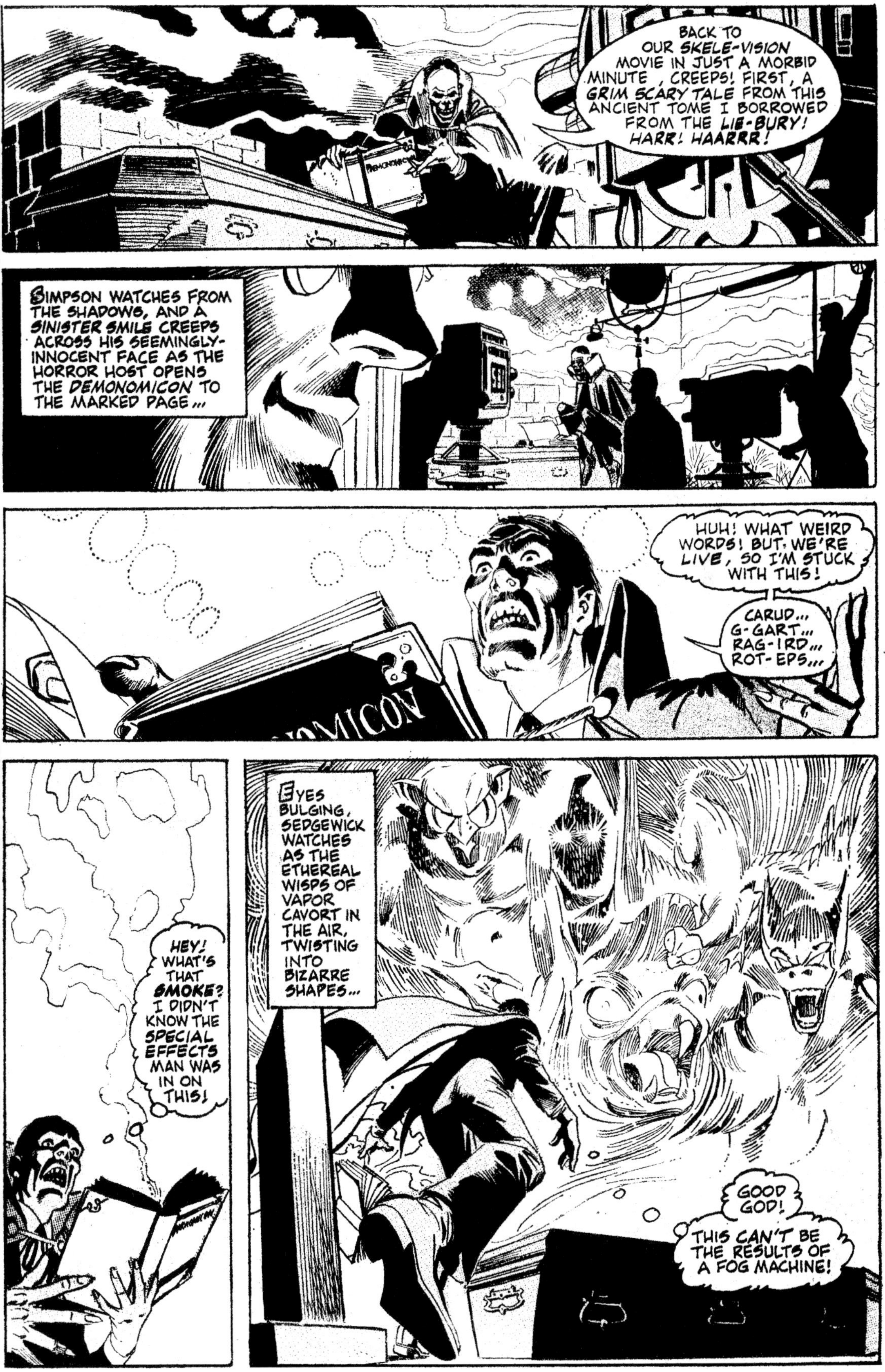
BACK TO OUR SKELE-VISION MOVIE IN JUST A MORBID MINUTE, CREEPS! FIRST, A GRIM SCARY TALE FROM THIS ANCIENT TOME I BORROWED FROM THE LIE-BURY! HARR! HAARRR!
DEMONOMICON
SIMPSON WATCHES FROM THE SHADOWS, AND A SINISTER SMILE CREEPS ACROSS HIS SEEMINGLY-INNOCENT FACE AS THE HORROR HOST OPENS THE DEMONOMICON TO THE MARKED PAGE...
HUH! WHAT WEIRD WORDS! BUT, WE'RE LIVE, SO I'M STUCK WITH THIS!
CARUD... G-GART... RAG-IRD... ROT-EPS...
NOMICON
HEY! WHAT'S THAT SMOKE? I DIDN'T KNOW THE SPECIAL EFFECTS MAN WAS IN ON THIS!
EYES BULGING, SEDGEWICK WATCHES AS THE ETHEREAL WISPS OF VAPOR CAVORT IN THE AIR, TWISTING INTO BIZARRE SHAPES...
GOOD GOD!
THIS CAN'T BE THE RESULTS OF A FOG MACHINE!

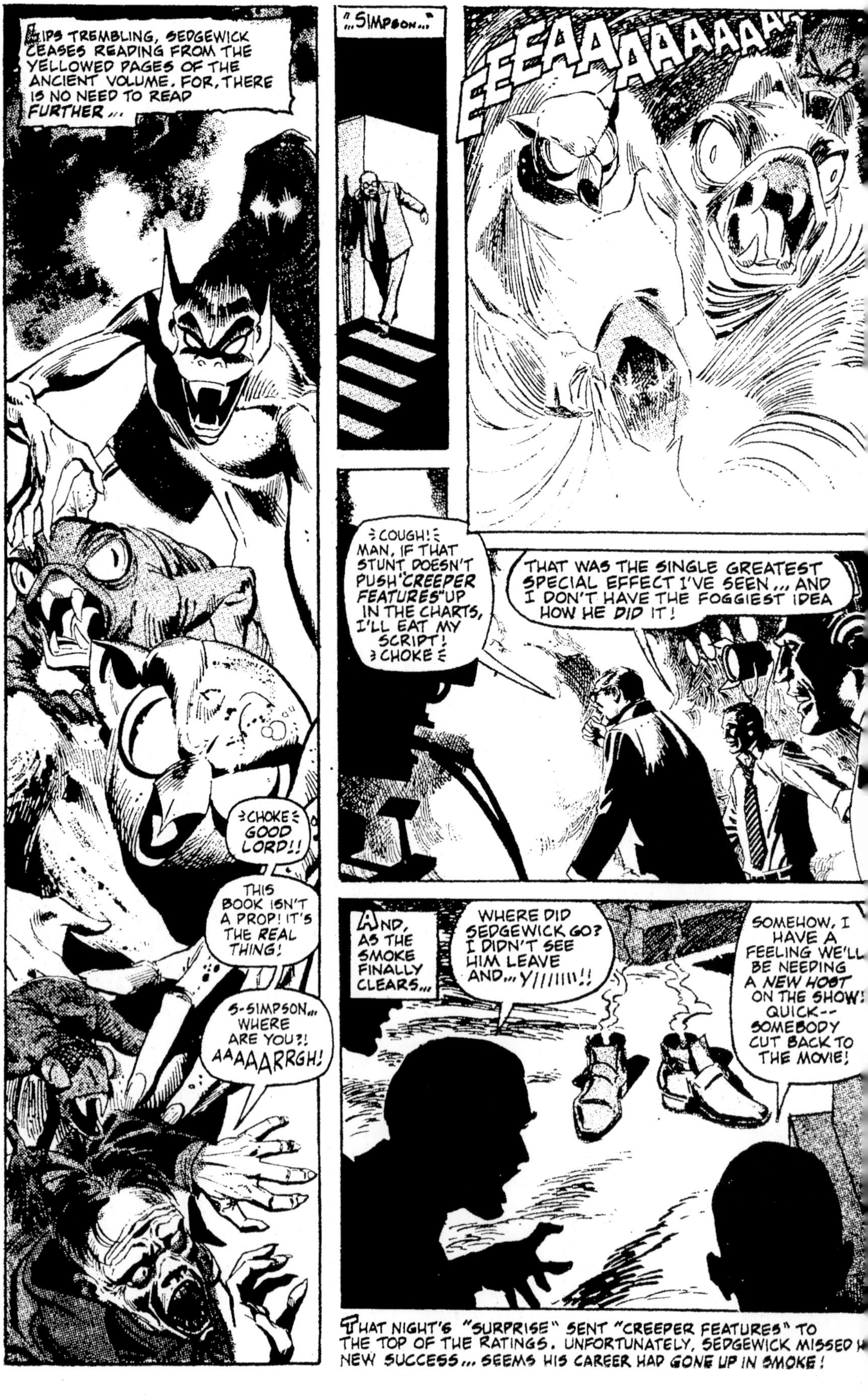
LIPS TREMBLING, SEDGEWICK CEASES READING FROM THE YELLOWED PAGES OF THE ANCIENT VOLUME. FOR, THERE IS NO NEED TO READ FURTHER...
CHOKE GOOD LORD!!
THIS BOOK ISN'T A PROP! IT'S THE REAL THING!
S-SIMPSON... WHERE ARE YOU?! AAAAARRGH!
"...SIMPSON..."
EEEAAAAAAAA
COUGH! MAN, IF THAT STUNT DOESN'T PUSH "CREEPER FEATURES" UP IN THE CHARTS, I'LL EAT MY SCRIPT! CHOKE
THAT WAS THE SINGLE GREATEST SPECIAL EFFECT I'VE SEEN... AND I DON'T HAVE THE FOGGIEST IDEA HOW HE DID IT!
AND, AS THE SMOKE FINALLY CLEARS...
WHERE DID SEDGEWICK GO? I DIDN'T SEE HIM LEAVE AND... YIIIIII!!
SOMEHOW, I HAVE A FEELING WE'LL BE NEEDING A NEW HOST ON THE SHOW! QUICK-- SOMEBODY CUT BACK TO THE MOVIE!
THAT NIGHT'S "SURPRISE" SENT "CREEPER FEATURES" TO THE TOP OF THE RATINGS. UNFORTUNATELY, SEDGEWICK MISSED H NEW SUCCESS... SEEMS HIS CAREER HAD GONE UP IN SMOKE!

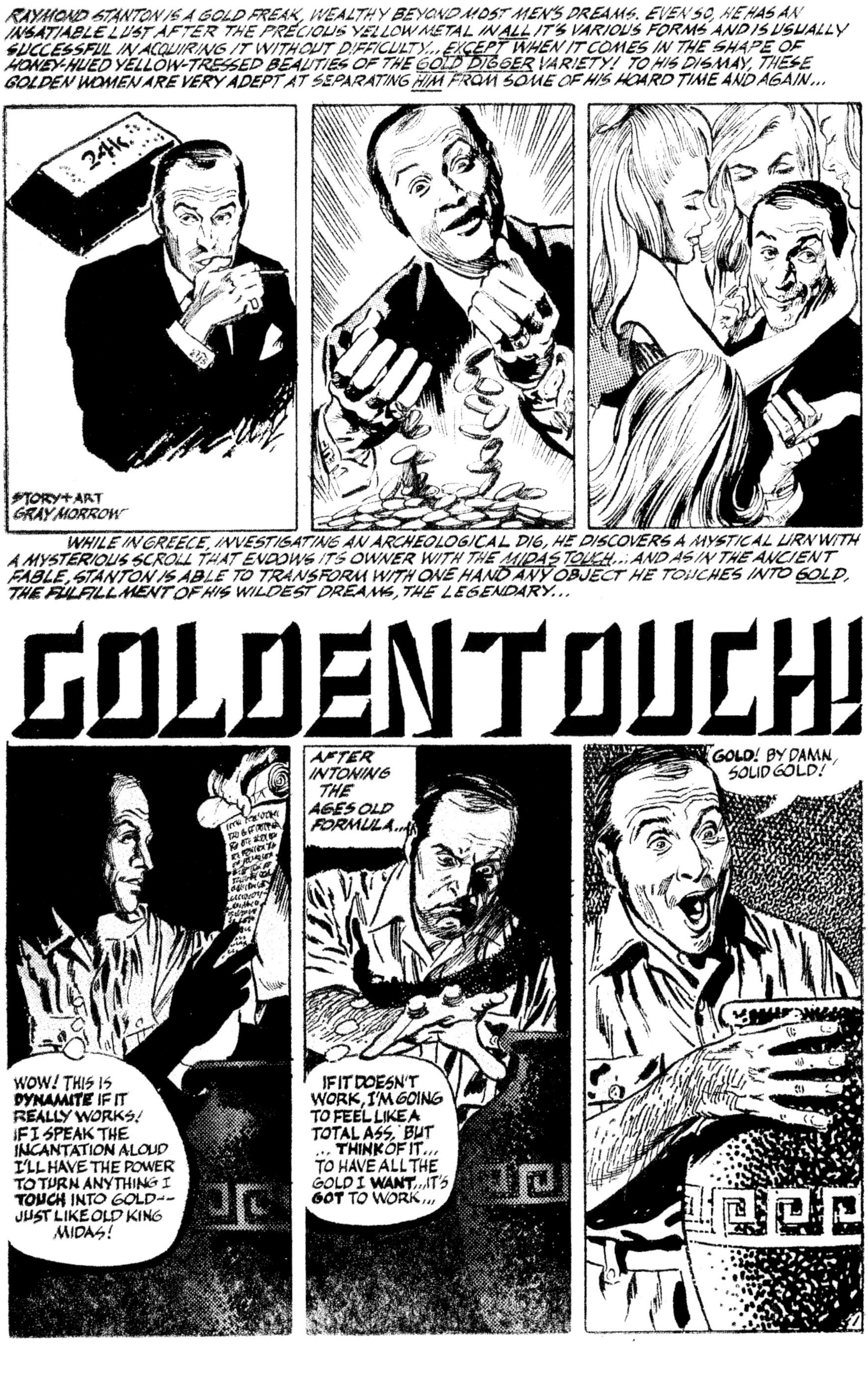
RAYMOND STANTON IS A GOLD FREAK, WEALTHY BEYOND MOST MEN'S DREAMS. EVEN SO, HE HAS AN INSATIABLE LUST AFTER THE PRECIOUS YELLOW METAL IN ALL IT'S VARIOUS FORMS AND IS USUALLY SUCCESSFUL IN ACQUIRING IT WITHOUT DIFFICULTY... EXCEPT WHEN IT COMES IN THE SHAPE OF HONEY-HUED YELLOW-TRESSED BEAUTIES OF THE GOLD DIGGER VARIETY! TO HIS DISMAY, THESE GOLDEN WOMEN ARE VERY ADEPT AT SEPARATING HIM FROM SOME OF HIS HOARD TIME AND AGAIN...
24K
STORY+ART GRAY MORROW
WHILE IN GREECE, INVESTIGATING AN ARCHEOLOGICAL DIG, HE DISCOVERS A MYSTICAL URN WITH A MYSTERIOUS SCROLL THAT ENDOWS IT'S OWNER WITH THE MIDAS TOUCH... AND AS IN THE ANCIENT FABLE, STANTON IS ABLE TO TRANSFORM WITH ONE HAND ANY OBJECT HE TOUCHES INTO GOLD, THE FULFILLMENT OF HIS WILDEST DREAMS, THE LEGENDARY...
GOLDEN TOUCH!
WOW! THIS IS DYNAMITE IF IT REALLY WORKS! IF I SPEAK THE INCANTATION ALOUD I'LL HAVE THE POWER TO TURN ANYTHING I TOUCH INTO GOLD-- JUST LIKE OLD KING MIDAS!
AFTER INTONING THE AGES OLD FORMULA...
IF IT DOESN'T WORK, I'M GOING TO FEEL LIKE A TOTAL ASS, BUT ... THINK OF IT... TO HAVE ALL THE GOLD I WANT... IT'S GOT TO WORK...
GOLD! BY DAMN, SOLID GOLD!

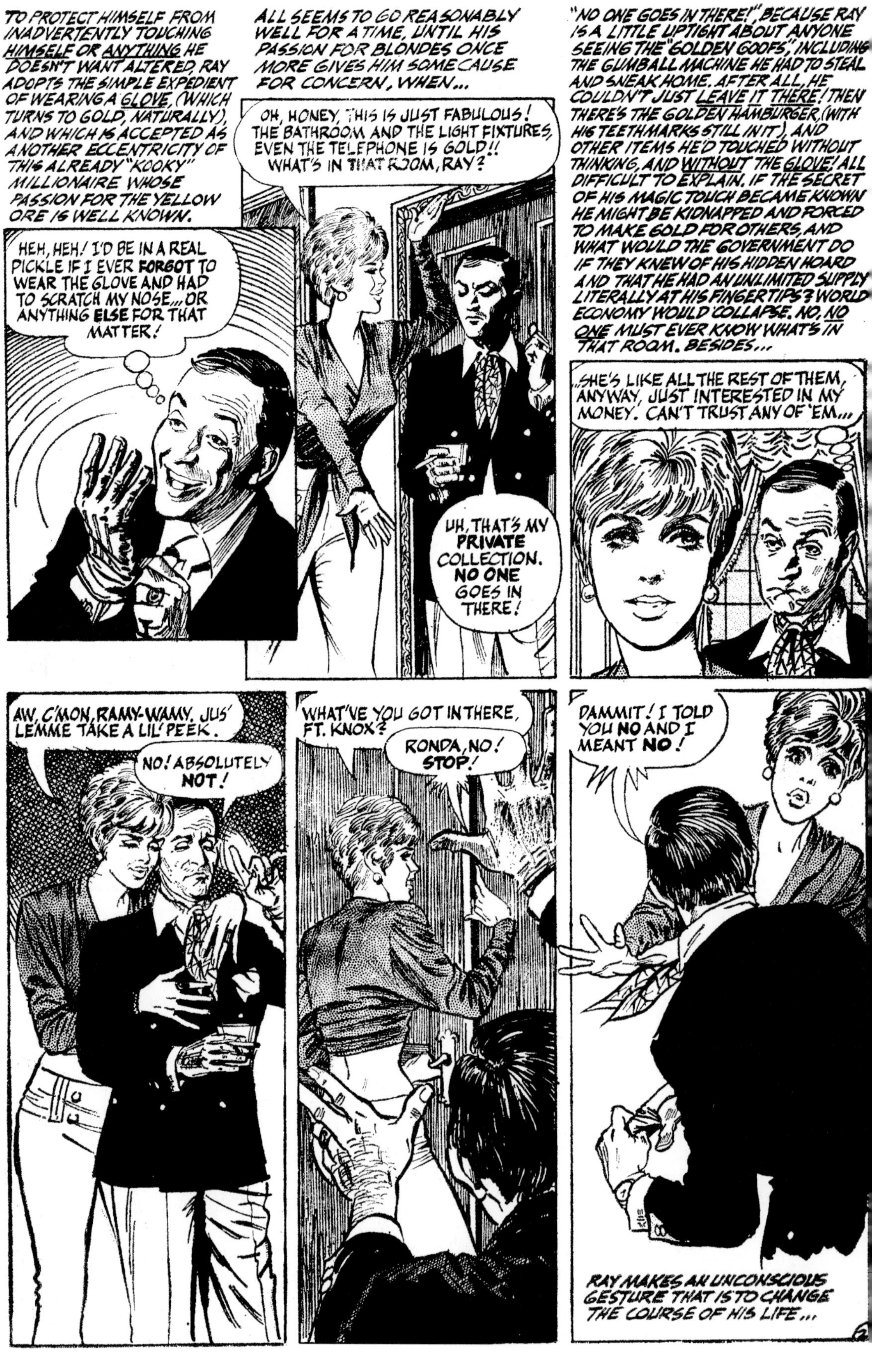
TO PROTECT HIMSELF FROM INADVERTENTLY TOUCHING HIMSELF OR ANYTHING HE DOESN'T WANT ALTERED, RAY ADOPTS THE SIMPLE EXPEDIENT OF WEARING A GLOVE, (WHICH TURNS TO GOLD, NATURALLY), AND WHICH IS ACCEPTED AS ANOTHER ECCENTRICITY OF THIS ALREADY "KOOKY" MILLIONAIRE WHOSE PASSION FOR THE YELLOW ORE IS WELL KNOWN.
HEH, HEH! I'D BE IN A REAL PICKLE IF I EVER FORGOT TO WEAR THE GLOVE AND HAD TO SCRATCH MY NOSE... OR ANYTHING ELSE FOR THAT MATTER!
ALL SEEMS TO GO REASONABLY WELL FOR A TIME, UNTIL HIS PASSION FOR BLONDES ONCE MORE GIVES HIM SOME CAUSE FOR CONCERN, WHEN...
OH, HONEY, THIS IS JUST FABULOUS! THE BATHROOM AND THE LIGHT FIXTURES, EVEN THE TELEPHONE IS GOLD!! WHAT'S IN THAT ROOM, RAY?
UH, THAT'S MY PRIVATE COLLECTION. NO ONE GOES IN THERE!
"NO ONE GOES IN THERE!", BECAUSE RAY IS A LITTLE UPTIGHT ABOUT ANYONE SEEING THE "GOLDEN GOOFS", INCLUDING THE GUMBALL MACHINE HE HAD TO STEAL AND SNEAK HOME. AFTER ALL, HE COULDN'T JUST LEAVE IT THERE! THEN THERE'S THE GOLDEN HAMBURGER, (WITH HIS TEETHMARKS STILL IN IT), AND OTHER ITEMS HE'D TOUCHED WITHOUT THINKING, AND WITHOUT THE GLOVE! ALL DIFFICULT TO EXPLAIN. IF THE SECRET OF HIS MAGIC TOUCH BECAME KNOWN HE MIGHT BE KIDNAPPED AND FORCED TO MAKE GOLD FOR OTHERS, AND WHAT WOULD THE GOVERNMENT DO IF THEY KNEW OF HIS HIDDEN HOARD AND THAT HE HAD AN UNLIMITED SUPPLY LITERALLY AT HIS FINGERTIPS? WORLD ECONOMY WOULD COLLAPSE. NO, NO ONE MUST EVER KNOW WHAT'S IN THAT ROOM. BESIDES...
...SHE'S LIKE ALL THE REST OF THEM, ANYWAY, JUST INTERESTED IN MY MONEY. CAN'T TRUST ANY OF 'EM...
AW, C'MON, RAMY-WAMY, JUS' LEMME TAKE A LIL' PEEK.
NO! ABSOLUTELY NOT!
WHAT'VE YOU GOT IN THERE, FT. KNOX?
RONDA, NO! STOP!
DAMMIT! I TOLD YOU NO AND I MEANT NO!
RAY MAKES AN UNCONSCIOUS GESTURE THAT IS TO CHANGE THE COURSE OF HIS LIFE...

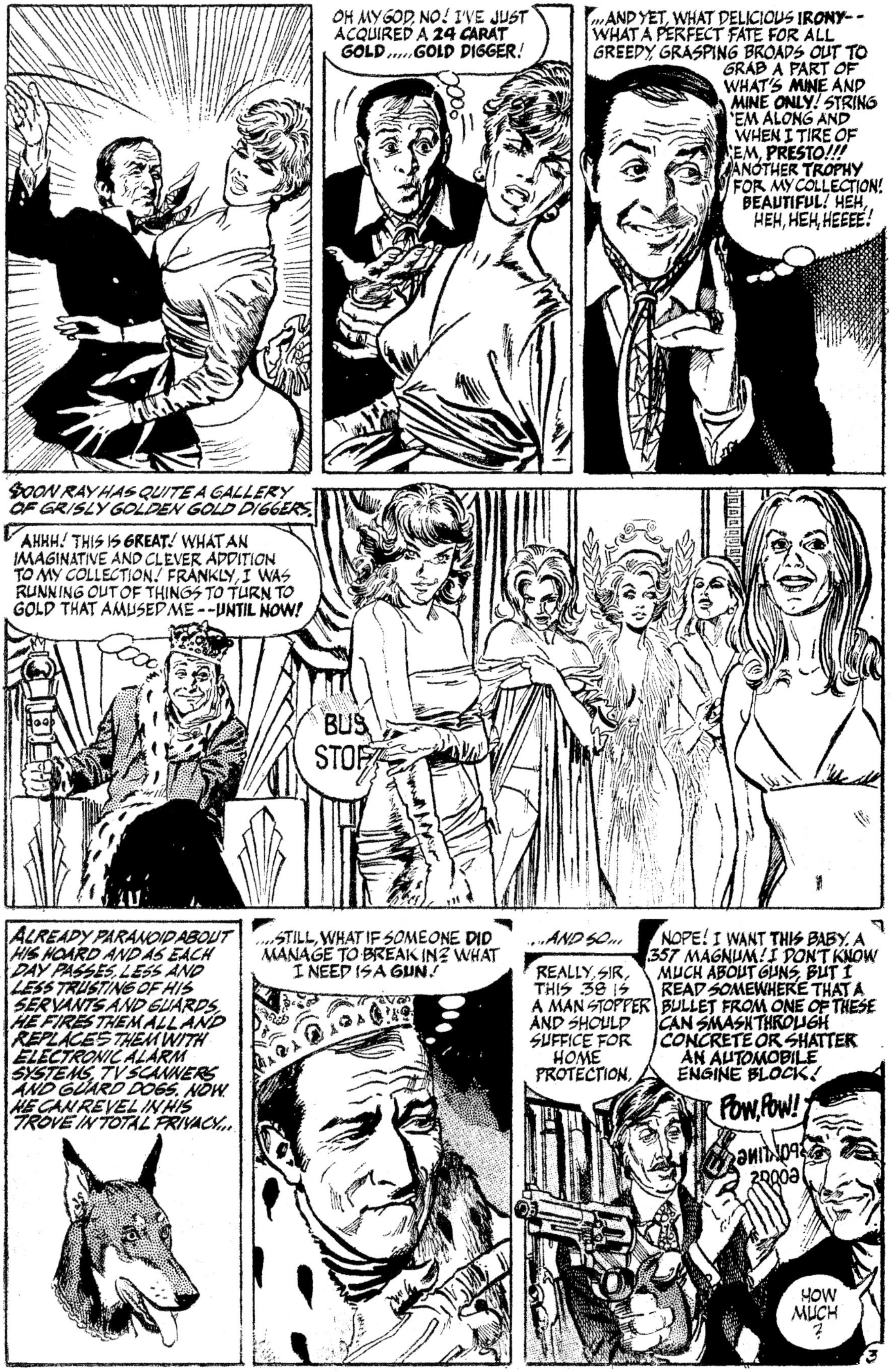

OH MY GOD, NO! I'VE JUST ACQUIRED A 24 CARAT GOLD.....GOLD DIGGER!
...AND YET, WHAT DELICIOUS IRONY-- WHAT A PERFECT FATE FOR ALL GREEDY, GRASPING BROADS OUT TO GRAB A PART OF WHAT'S MINE AND MINE ONLY! STRING 'EM ALONG AND WHEN I TIRE OF 'EM, PRESTO!!! ANOTHER TROPHY FOR MY COLLECTION! BEAUTIFUL! HEH, HEH, HEH, HEEEE!
SOON RAY HAS QUITE A GALLERY OF GRISLY GOLDEN GOLD DIGGERS.
AHHH! THIS IS GREAT! WHAT AN IMAGINATIVE AND CLEVER ADDITION TO MY COLLECTION! FRANKLY, I WAS RUNNING OUT OF THINGS TO TURN TO GOLD THAT AMUSED ME--UNTIL NOW!
BUS STOP
ALREADY PARANOID ABOUT HIS HOARD AND AS EACH DAY PASSES, LESS AND LESS TRUSTING OF HIS SERVANTS AND GUARDS, HE FIRES THEM ALL AND REPLACES THEM WITH ELECTRONIC ALARM SYSTEMS, TV SCANNERS AND GUARD DOGS. NOW HE CAN REVEL IN HIS TROVE IN TOTAL PRIVACY...
...STILL, WHAT IF SOMEONE DID MANAGE TO BREAK IN? WHAT I NEED IS A GUN!
...AND SO...
REALLY, SIR, THIS .38 IS A MAN STOPPER AND SHOULD SUFFICE FOR HOME PROTECTION.
NOPE! I WANT THIS BABY. A .357 MAGNUM! I DON'T KNOW MUCH ABOUT GUNS, BUT I READ SOMEWHERE THAT A BULLET FROM ONE OF THESE CAN SMASH THROUGH CONCRETE OR SHATTER AN AUTOMOBILE ENGINE BLOCK!
POW, POW!
HOW MUCH ?

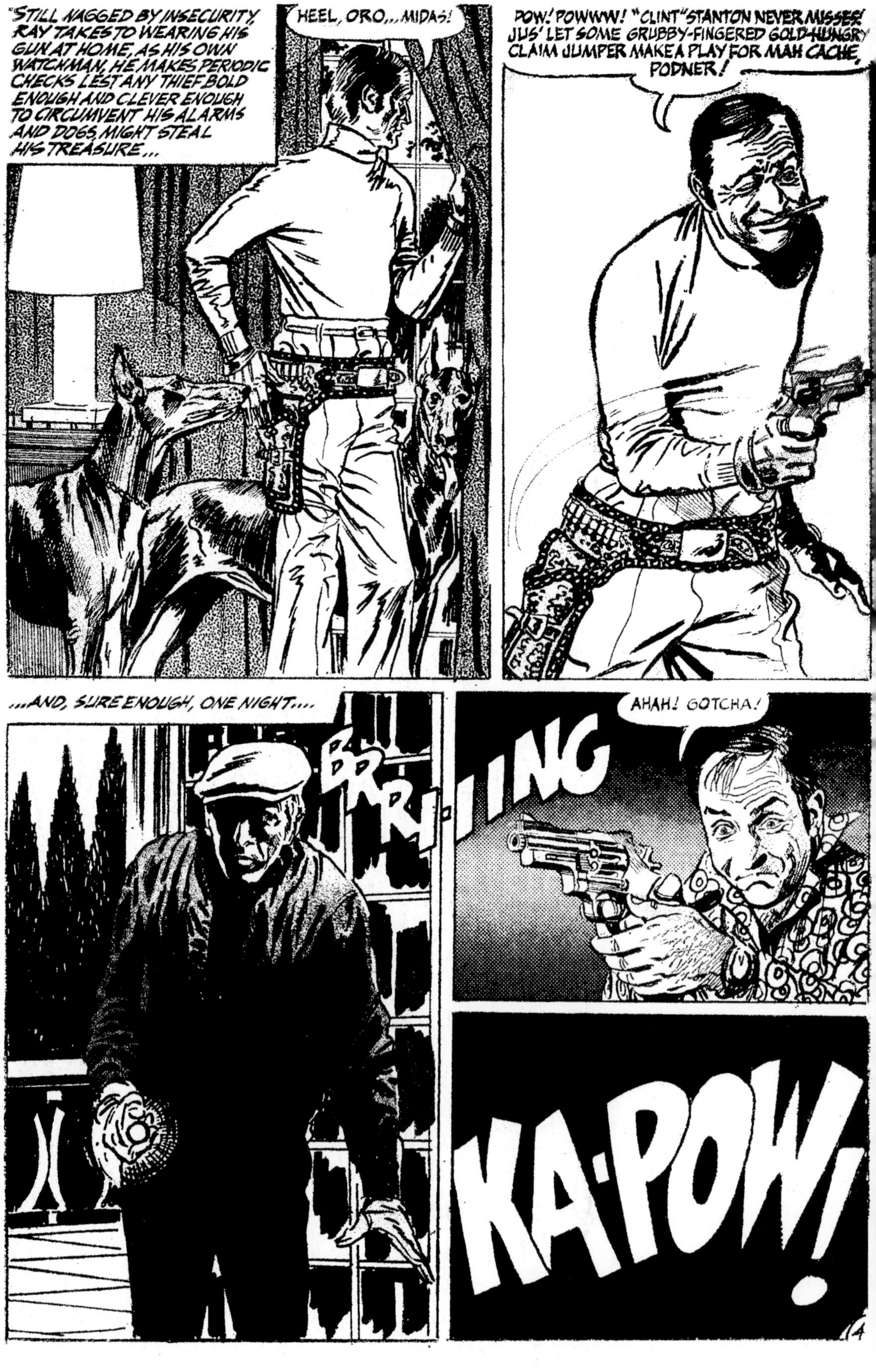
"STILL NAGGED BY INSECURITY, RAY TAKES TO WEARING HIS GUN AT HOME, AS HIS OWN WATCHMAN. HE MAKES PERIODIC CHECKS LEST ANY THIEF BOLD ENOUGH AND CLEVER ENOUGH TO CIRCUMVENT HIS ALARMS AND DOGS, MIGHT STEAL HIS TREASURE...
HEEL, ORO... MIDAS!
POW! POWWW! "CLINT" STANTON NEVER MISSES! JUS' LET SOME GRUBBY-FINGERED GOLD-HUNGRY CLAIM JUMPER MAKE A PLAY FOR MAH CACHE, PODNER!
...AND, SURE ENOUGH, ONE NIGHT....
BRRRIIING
AHAH! GOTCHA!
KA-POW!
4

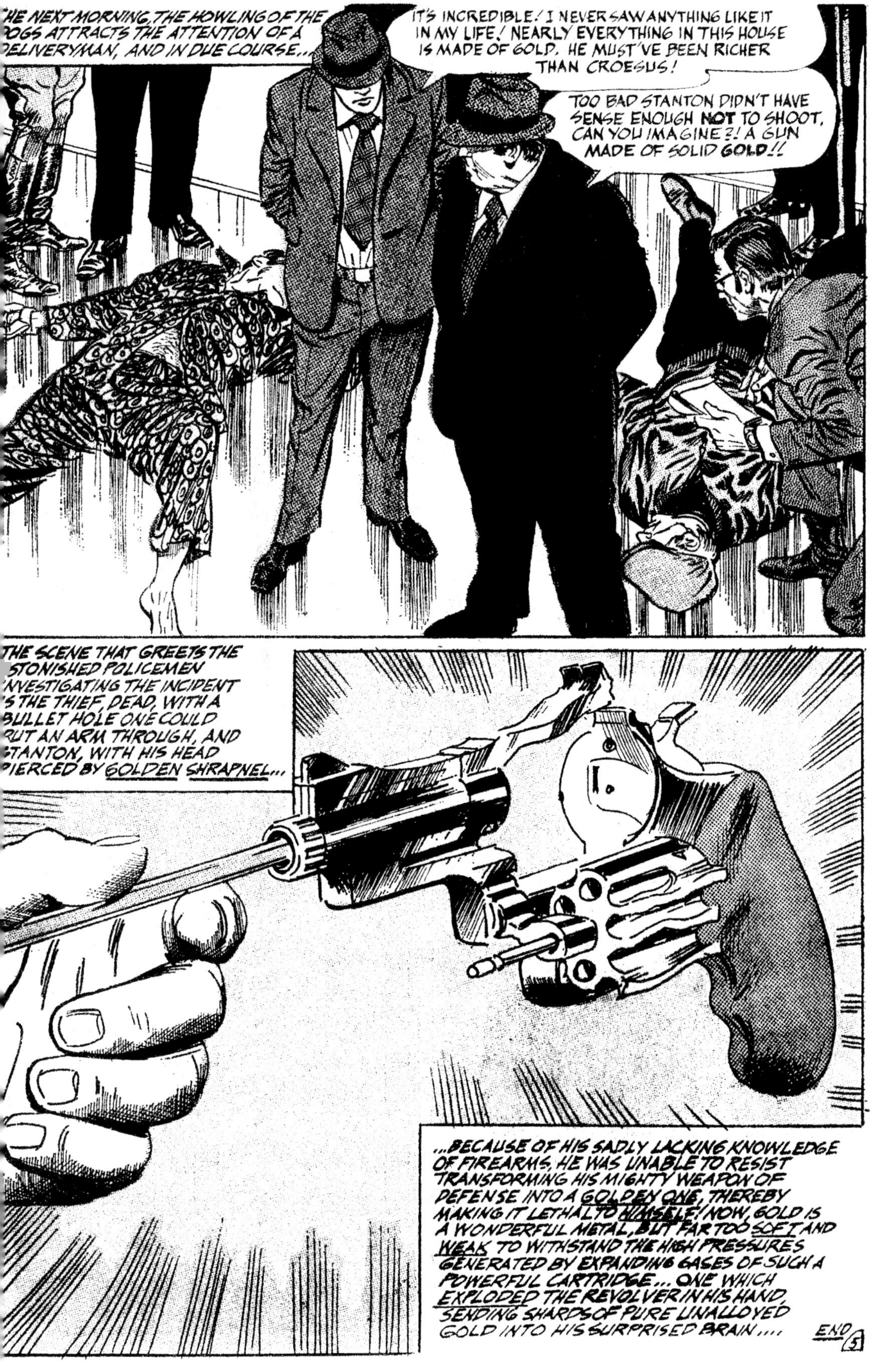
THE NEXT MORNING, THE HOWLING OF THE DOGS ATTRACTS THE ATTENTION OF A DELIVERYMAN, AND IN DUE COURSE...
IT'S INCREDIBLE! I NEVER SAW ANYTHING LIKE IT IN MY LIFE! NEARLY EVERYTHING IN THIS HOUSE IS MADE OF GOLD. HE MUST'VE BEEN RICHER THAN CROESUS!
TOO BAD STANTON DIDN'T HAVE SENSE ENOUGH NOT TO SHOOT. CAN YOU IMAGINE?! A GUN MADE OF SOLID GOLD!!
THE SCENE THAT GREETS THE ASTONISHED POLICEMEN INVESTIGATING THE INCIDENT IS THE THIEF, DEAD, WITH A BULLET HOLE ONE COULD PUT AN ARM THROUGH, AND STANTON, WITH HIS HEAD PIERCED BY GOLDEN SHRAPNEL...
...BECAUSE OF HIS SADLY LACKING KNOWLEDGE OF FIREARMS, HE WAS UNABLE TO RESIST TRANSFORMING HIS MIGHTY WEAPON OF DEFENSE INTO A GOLDEN ONE, THEREBY MAKING IT LETHAL TO HIMSELF! NOW, GOLD IS A WONDERFUL METAL, BUT FAR TOO SOFT AND WEAK TO WITHSTAND THE HIGH PRESSURES GENERATED BY EXPANDING GASES OF SUCH A POWERFUL CARTRIDGE... ONE WHICH EXPLODED THE REVOLVER IN HIS HAND, SENDING SHARDS OF PURE UNALLOYED GOLD INTO HIS SURPRISED BRAIN....
END
5

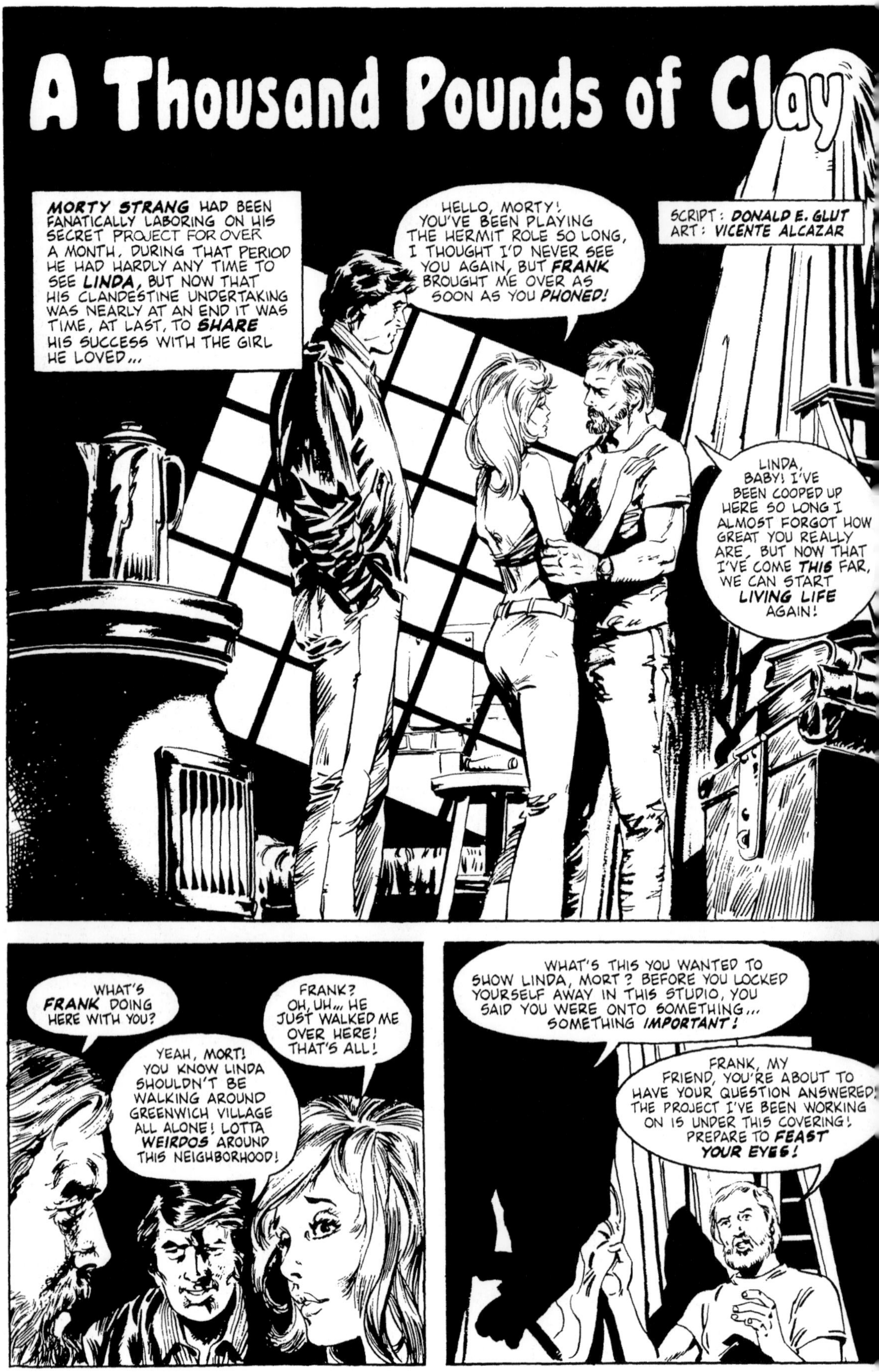

A Thousand Pounds of Clay
MORTY STRANG HAD BEEN FANATICALLY LABORING ON HIS SECRET PROJECT FOR OVER A MONTH. DURING THAT PERIOD HE HAD HARDLY ANY TIME TO SEE LINDA, BUT NOW THAT HIS CLANDESTINE UNDERTAKING WAS NEARLY AT AN END IT WAS TIME, AT LAST, TO SHARE HIS SUCCESS WITH THE GIRL HE LOVED...
HELLO, MORTY! YOU'VE BEEN PLAYING THE HERMIT ROLE SO LONG, I THOUGHT I'D NEVER SEE YOU AGAIN, BUT FRANK BROUGHT ME OVER AS SOON AS YOU PHONED!
SCRIPT: DONALD E. GLUT
ART: VICENTE ALCAZAR
LINDA, BABY! I'VE BEEN COOPED UP HERE SO LONG I ALMOST FORGOT HOW GREAT YOU REALLY ARE, BUT NOW THAT I'VE COME THIS FAR, WE CAN START LIVING LIFE AGAIN!
WHAT'S FRANK DOING HERE WITH YOU?
FRANK? OH, UH... HE JUST WALKED ME OVER HERE! THAT'S ALL!
YEAH, MORT! YOU KNOW LINDA SHOULDN'T BE WALKING AROUND GREENWICH VILLAGE ALL ALONE! LOTTA WEIRDOS AROUND THIS NEIGHBORHOOD!
WHAT'S THIS YOU WANTED TO SHOW LINDA, MORT? BEFORE YOU LOCKED YOURSELF AWAY IN THIS STUDIO, YOU SAID YOU WERE ONTO SOMETHING... SOMETHING IMPORTANT!
FRANK, MY FRIEND, YOU'RE ABOUT TO HAVE YOUR QUESTION ANSWERED! THE PROJECT I'VE BEEN WORKING ON IS UNDER THIS COVERING! PREPARE TO FEAST YOUR EYES!

CATCHING THE BREEZE THAT ISSUES THROUGH THE STUDIO WINDOW, THE CLOTH BILLOWS TO THE FLOOR... EXPOSING SOMETHING WHICH CAUSES THE TWO VISITORS TO GAZE IN WONDER AT THE LOOMING GIANT... A SILENT, YET FORBIDDING CREATURE OF CLAY...

"OVER 400 YEARS AGO, A CERTAIN *RABBI LOEW* BUILT HIS OWN CLAY GOLEM... THEN, BY MEANS OF AN ANCIENT *RITUAL* AND MAGIC *INSCRIPTIONS* CARVED INTO THE FIGURE'S FOREHEAD, BROUGHT HIS CREATURE TO *LIFE*. THE GOLEM *OBEYED* HIS CREATOR AND *MASTER* AND PROCEEDED TO SMASH HIS WAY THROUGH *PRAGUE*, FREEING THE RABBI'S OPRESSED PEOPLE FROM THEIR GHETTO..."

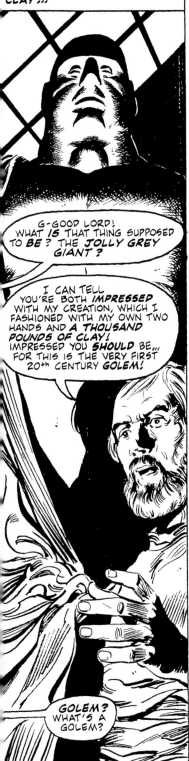

G-GOOD LORD! WHAT *IS* THAT THING SUPPOSED TO *BE*? THE *JOLLY GREY GIANT*?

I CAN TELL YOU'RE BOTH *IMPRESSED* WITH MY CREATION, WHICH I FASHIONED WITH MY OWN TWO HANDS AND *A THOUSAND POUNDS OF CLAY!* IMPRESSED YOU *SHOULD* BE... FOR THIS IS THE VERY FIRST 20th CENTURY *GOLEM!*

GOLEM? WHAT'S A GOLEM?

YOU ACTUALLY *BELIEVE* THAT OLD FAIRY TALE, MORT?

NOT ONLY BELIEVE IT, BUT WILL *PROVE* IT! TONIGHT, WHEN THE *MOON* IS *FULL*, I'M GOING TO PERFORM THE RITUAL WRITTEN IN THE ANCIENT MANUSCRIPT!

EVEN IF IT *DID* WORK, MORTY, WHY WOULD YOU WANT A... A GOLEM?

WHY?! BECAUSE I'VE *ALWAYS* BEEN TREATED LIKE *DIRT* BY THE *ESTABLISHMENT*! FORCED TO LIVE IN *FILTH*... *KICKED AROUND* ...ALL BECAUSE I WON'T *CONFORM* TO THE *MAN'S* STYLE OF EXISTENCE! WELL, THIS GOLEM IS MY *OUT!* AND JUST AS THE GOLEM OF OLD SAVED THE PEOPLE OF PRAGUE, THIS ONE WILL CRUSH *MY* ENEMIES BEFORE THEY DESTROY *ME!*

I'VE KNOWN YOU A LONG TIME, MORT, AND I HATE TO HURT YOUR FEELINGS BUT I'M AFRAID YOU'VE *FLIPPED!* YOU'RE A TOTAL *PARANOID!* I THINK LINDA AND I SHOULD *GO!*

WAIT! DON'T YOU WANT TO SEE HIM COME TO *LIFE?*

I'M SORRY, MORT... I'LL... ER... TALK TO YOU *LATER!*

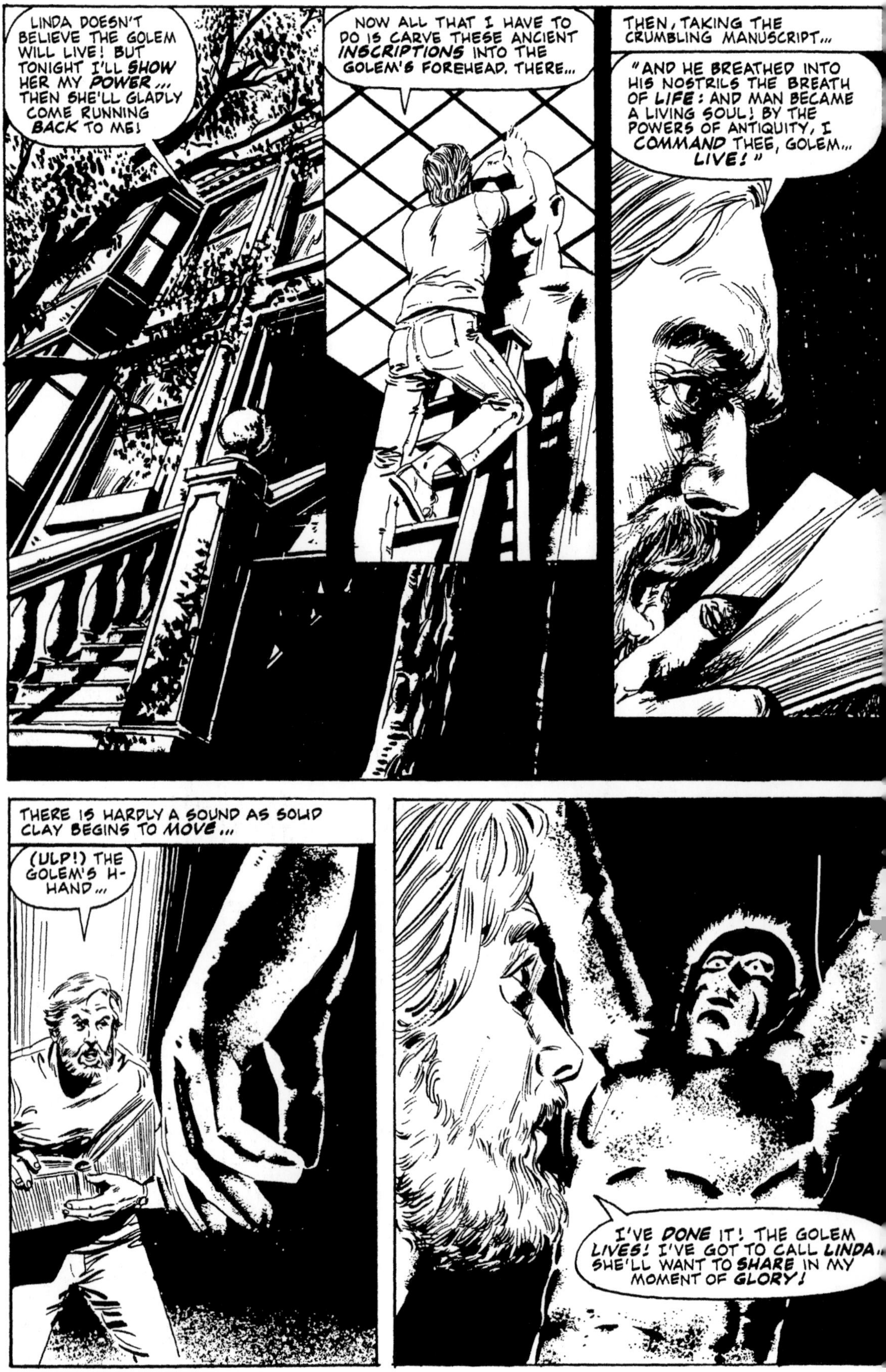
LINDA DOESN'T BELIEVE THE GOLEM WILL LIVE! BUT TONIGHT I'LL SHOW HER MY POWER... THEN SHE'LL GLADLY COME RUNNING BACK TO ME!
NOW ALL THAT I HAVE TO DO IS CARVE THESE ANCIENT INSCRIPTIONS INTO THE GOLEM'S FOREHEAD. THERE...
THEN, TAKING THE CRUMBLING MANUSCRIPT...
"AND HE BREATHED INTO HIS NOSTRILS THE BREATH OF LIFE: AND MAN BECAME A LIVING SOUL! BY THE POWERS OF ANTIQUITY, I COMMAND THEE, GOLEM... LIVE!"
THERE IS HARDLY A SOUND AS SOLID CLAY BEGINS TO MOVE...
(ULP!) THE GOLEM'S H-HAND...
I'VE DONE IT! THE GOLEM LIVES! I'VE GOT TO CALL LINDA... SHE'LL WANT TO SHARE IN MY MOMENT OF GLORY!

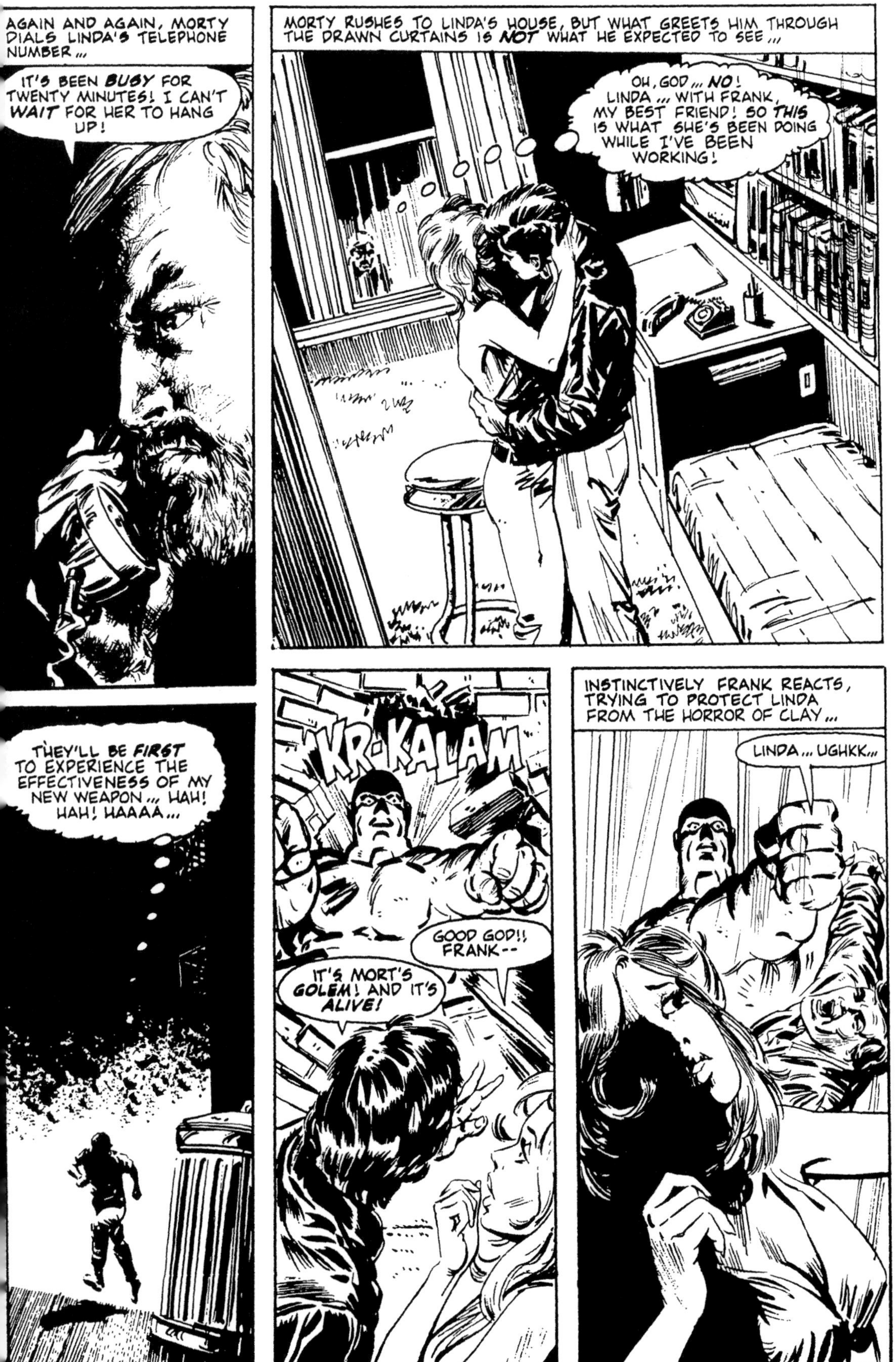
AGAIN AND AGAIN, MORTY DIALS LINDA'S TELEPHONE NUMBER...
IT'S BEEN BUSY FOR TWENTY MINUTES! I CAN'T WAIT FOR HER TO HANG UP!
MORTY RUSHES TO LINDA'S HOUSE, BUT WHAT GREETS HIM THROUGH THE DRAWN CURTAINS IS NOT WHAT HE EXPECTED TO SEE...
OH, GOD... NO! LINDA... WITH FRANK, MY BEST FRIEND! SO THIS IS WHAT SHE'S BEEN DOING WHILE I'VE BEEN WORKING!
THEY'LL BE FIRST TO EXPERIENCE THE EFFECTIVENESS OF MY NEW WEAPON... HAH! HAH! HAAAA...
KR-KALAM
GOOD GOD!! FRANK--
IT'S MORT'S GOLEM! AND IT'S ALIVE!
INSTINCTIVELY FRANK REACTS, TRYING TO PROTECT LINDA FROM THE HORROR OF CLAY...
LINDA... UGHKK...

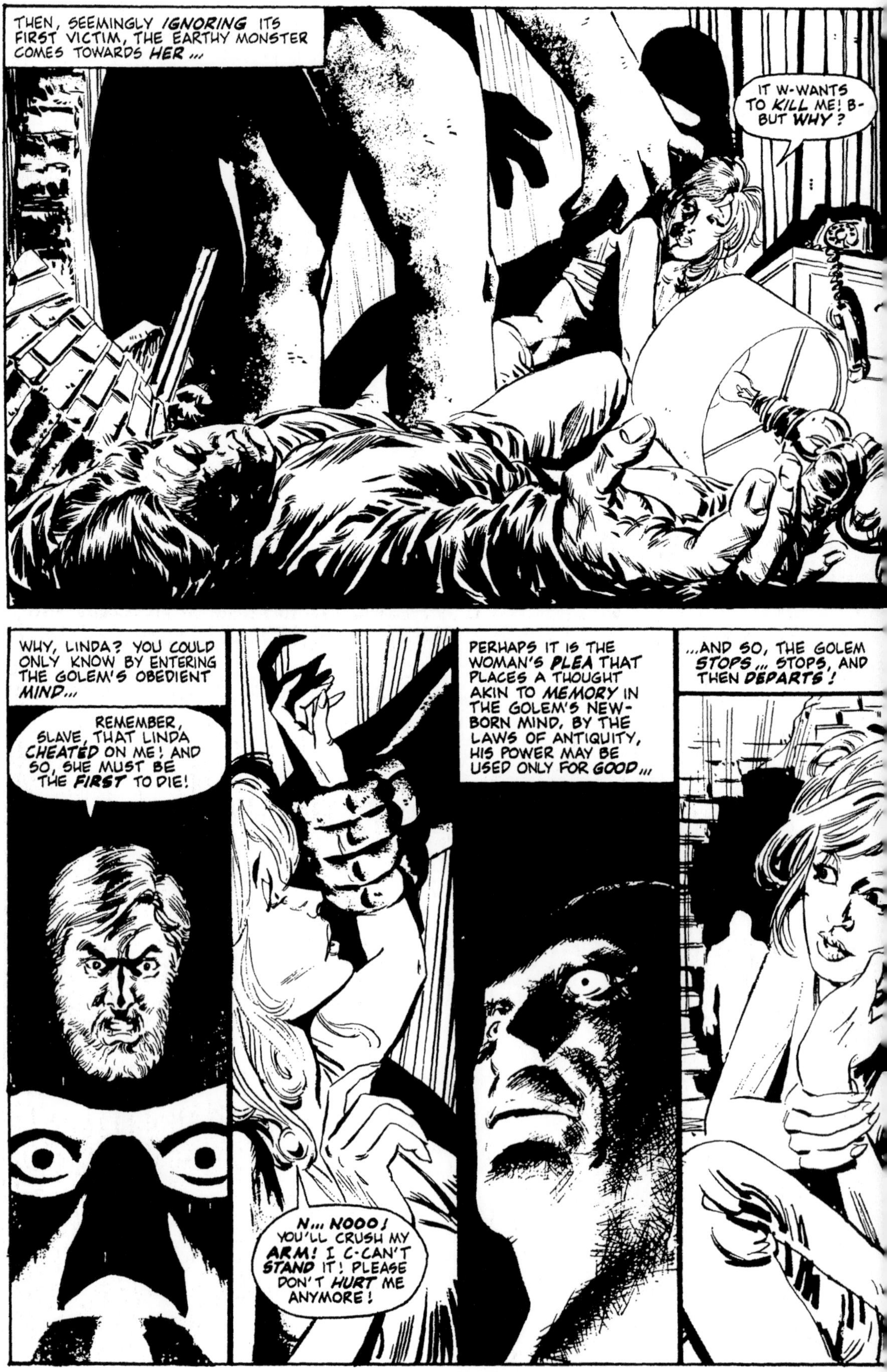
THEN, SEEMINGLY IGNORING ITS FIRST VICTIM, THE EARTHY MONSTER COMES TOWARDS HER ...
IT W-WANTS TO KILL ME! B-BUT WHY?
WHY, LINDA? YOU COULD ONLY KNOW BY ENTERING THE GOLEM'S OBEDIENT MIND...
REMEMBER, SLAVE, THAT LINDA CHEATED ON ME! AND SO, SHE MUST BE THE FIRST TO DIE!
N... NOOO! YOU'LL CRUSH MY ARM! I C-CAN'T STAND IT! PLEASE DON'T HURT ME ANYMORE!
PERHAPS IT IS THE WOMAN'S PLEA THAT PLACES A THOUGHT AKIN TO MEMORY IN THE GOLEM'S NEW-BORN MIND, BY THE LAWS OF ANTIQUITY, HIS POWER MAY BE USED ONLY FOR GOOD...
...AND SO, THE GOLEM STOPS... STOPS, AND THEN DEPARTS!

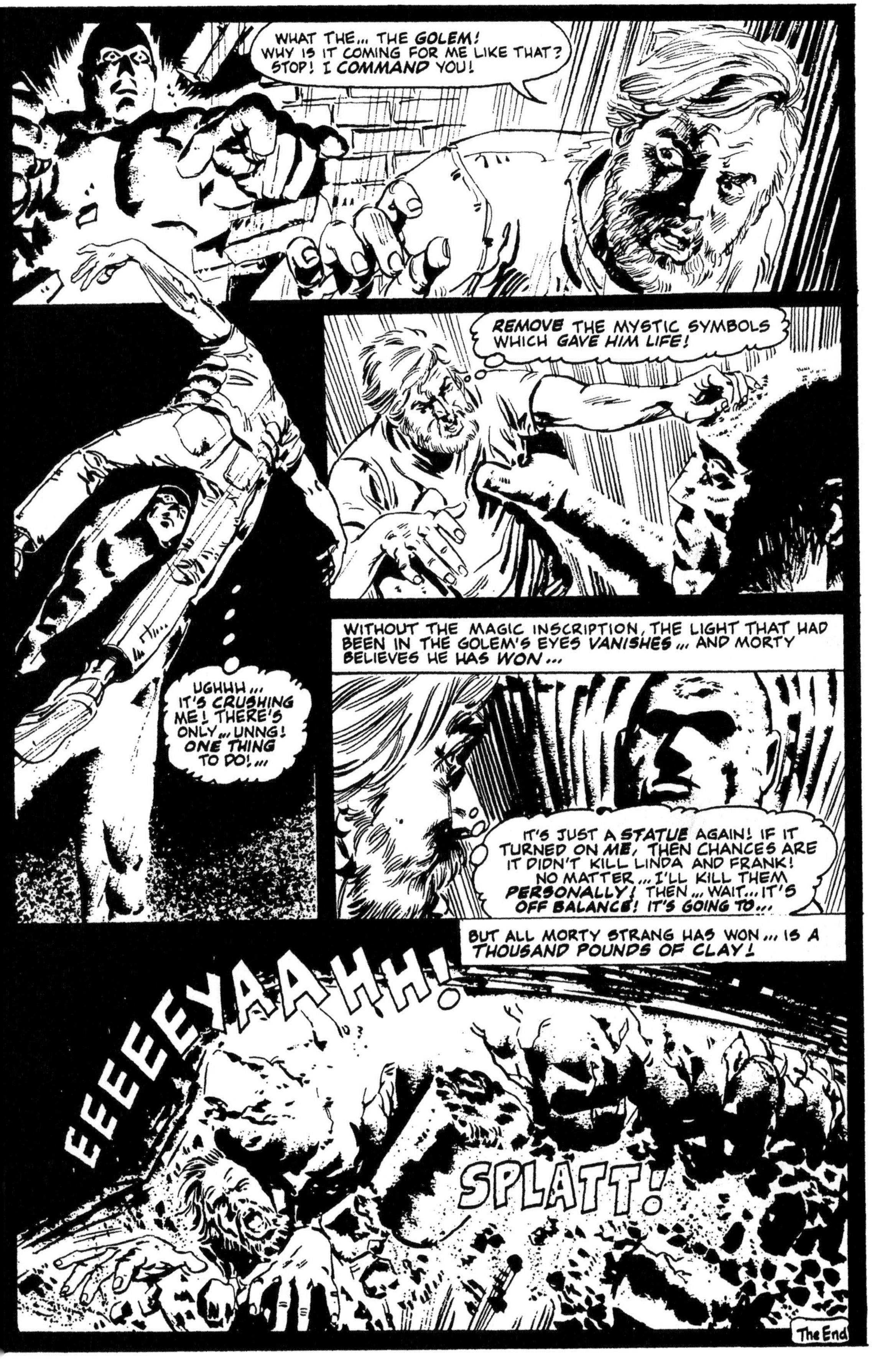
WHAT THE... THE GOLEM! WHY IS IT COMING FOR ME LIKE THAT? STOP! I COMMAND YOU!
REMOVE THE MYSTIC SYMBOLS WHICH GAVE HIM LIFE!
UGHHH... IT'S CRUSHING ME! THERE'S ONLY... UNNG! ONE THING TO DO!...
WITHOUT THE MAGIC INSCRIPTION, THE LIGHT THAT HAD BEEN IN THE GOLEM'S EYES VANISHES... AND MORTY BELIEVES HE HAS WON...
IT'S JUST A STATUE AGAIN! IF IT TURNED ON ME, THEN CHANCES ARE IT DIDN'T KILL LINDA AND FRANK! NO MATTER... I'LL KILL THEM PERSONALLY! THEN... WAIT... IT'S OFF BALANCE! IT'S GOING TO...
BUT ALL MORTY STRANG HAS WON... IS A THOUSAND POUNDS OF CLAY!
EEEEEYAAHH!
SPLATT!
The End

# ESSAYS INTO THE SUPERNATURAL

# THE WITCH!

DOWN THROUGH THE AGES, ARTISTS HAVE BEEN FASCINATED BY WITCHCRAFT. HARDLY SURPRISING, WHEN ONE CONSIDERS HOW THE SUBJECT CAN STILL ARREST ATTENTION TODAY, WHETHER IT BE TREATED AS ESCAPIST FARE IN BOOKS AND FILMS, OR NOTED IN THE NEWS MEDIA REGARDING IT'S AMAZING GROWTH IN THIS ATOMIC AGE. IN RECENT TIMES, IT HAS COME UNDER CLOSER SCRUTINY BY SERIOUS RESEARCHERS AS A PHENOMENON HAVING IT'S ROOTS IN OUR PREHISTORIC PAST, YET RETAINING ITS CHARACTER AND BASIC RITUALS UNCHANGED. ALSO UNCHANGED, IT'S CENTRAL FIGURE, THE WITCH HERSELF, HAS MOST POPULARLY, AND LEAST ACCURATELY, BEEN PORTRAYED AS THE OLD CRONE IN BLACK WITH POINTED HAT, ASTRIDE HER BROOMSTICK...

...YET HISTORY SHOWS THAT ATTRACTIVE YOUNG WOMEN HAVE ALWAYS BEEN INVOLVED IN THE DARK ARTS. VIRGIL MENTIONS THE BEAUTIFUL LIBYAN SORCERESS WHO COULD BEWITCH, "WITH BOTH HER CHARMS AND HER MAGIC," AND OVID RHAPSODIZES OVER THE OCCULT POWERS OF COLCHIAN MEDEA. THE OBVIOUS ATTRACTION OF SUCH WOMEN GAVE THEM GREATER INFLUENCE OVER MEN THAN EITHER THE MALE WITCHES OR THEIR OLD HAG COUNTERPARTS.

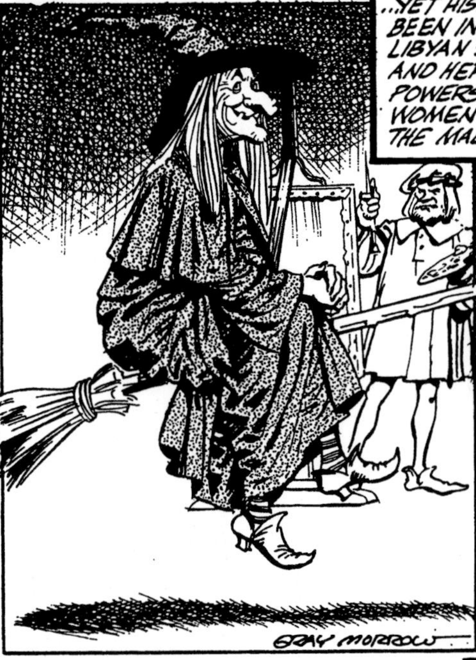
GRAY MORROW

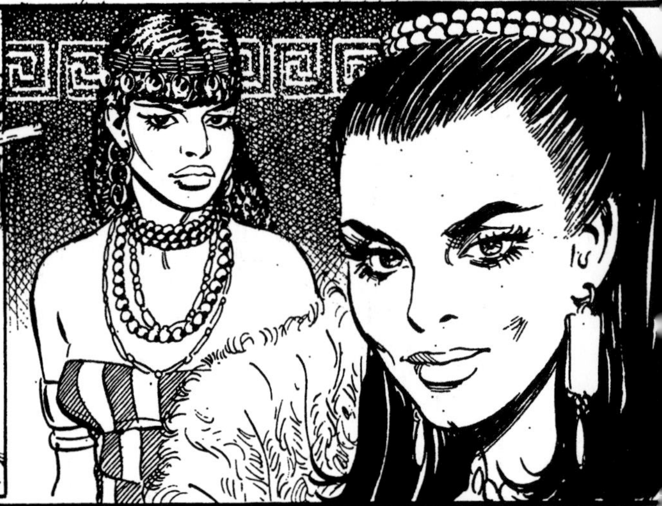

WITCHES HAVE ALWAYS COME FROM ALL WALKS OF LIFE, AND THERE IS NO REASON WHY SOME SHOULD NOT HAVE BEEN MORE BEAUTEOUS THAN OTHERS. AFTER ALL, WHY SHOULD THE DEVIL HAVE HAD TO SETTLE FOR SECOND BEST WHERE BEAUTY IS CONCERNED...?

... OR THE AVERAGE MAN FOR THAT MATTER? EVEN THE MOST CYNICAL NON-BELIEVER UNWITTINGLY SPEAKS OF BEING BEWITCHED BY A PRETTY GIRL. THERE'S PERHAPS A BIT OF THE SORCERESS IN ALL WOMEN AND THE ARTIST STILL SUCCUMBS TO HER ENCHANTMENTS. THE NICE THING ABOUT IT ALL, IS ONE DOESN'T HAVE TO BE EITHER A BELIEVER IN MAGIC OR AN ARTIST TO BE CHARMED BY THIS VERY REAL... WITCHCRAFT!

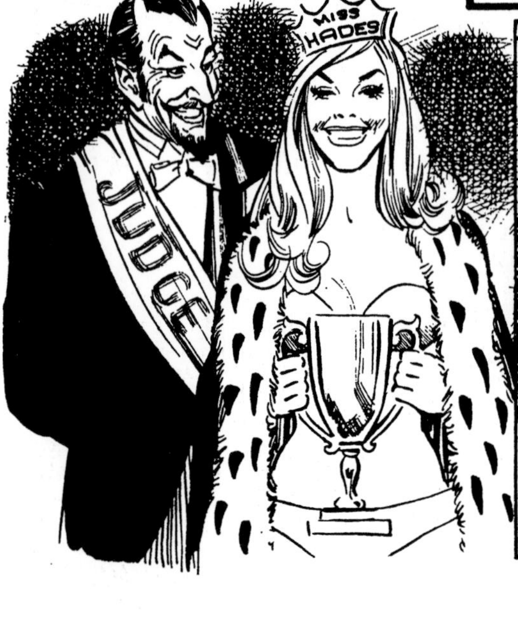
MISS HADES
JUDGE

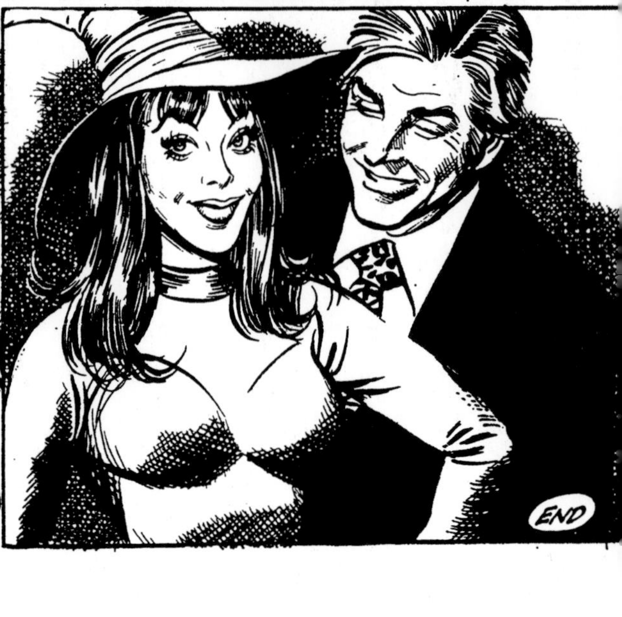
END

# ISSUE FIVE

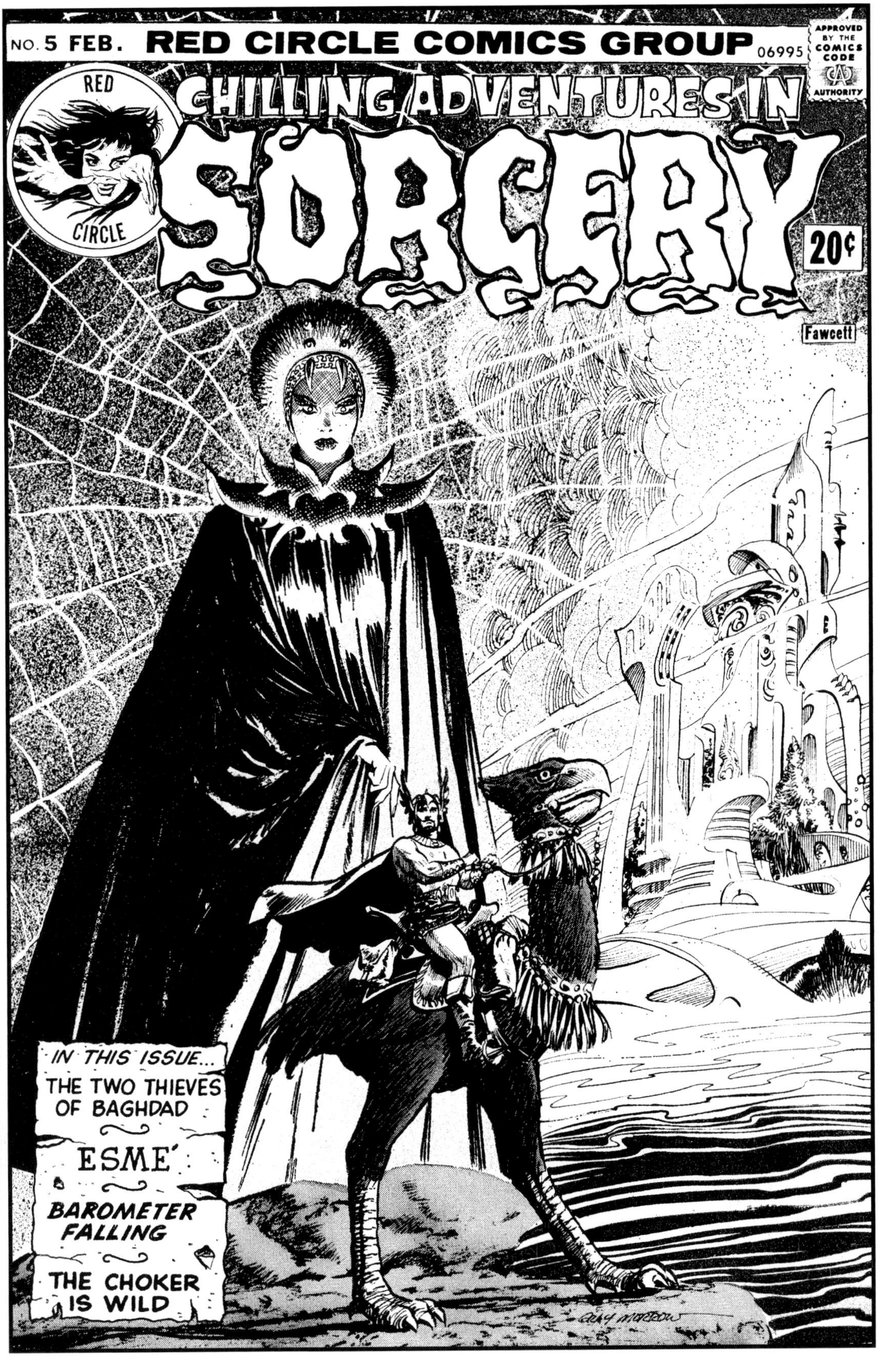
NO. 5 FEB.
RED CIRCLE COMICS GROUP
06995
APPROVED BY THE COMICS CODE AUTHORITY
RED CIRCLE
CHILLING ADVENTURES IN
SORCERY
20¢
Fawcett
IN THIS ISSUE...
THE TWO THIEVES OF BAGHDAD
ESME'
BAROMETER FALLING
THE CHOKER IS WILD

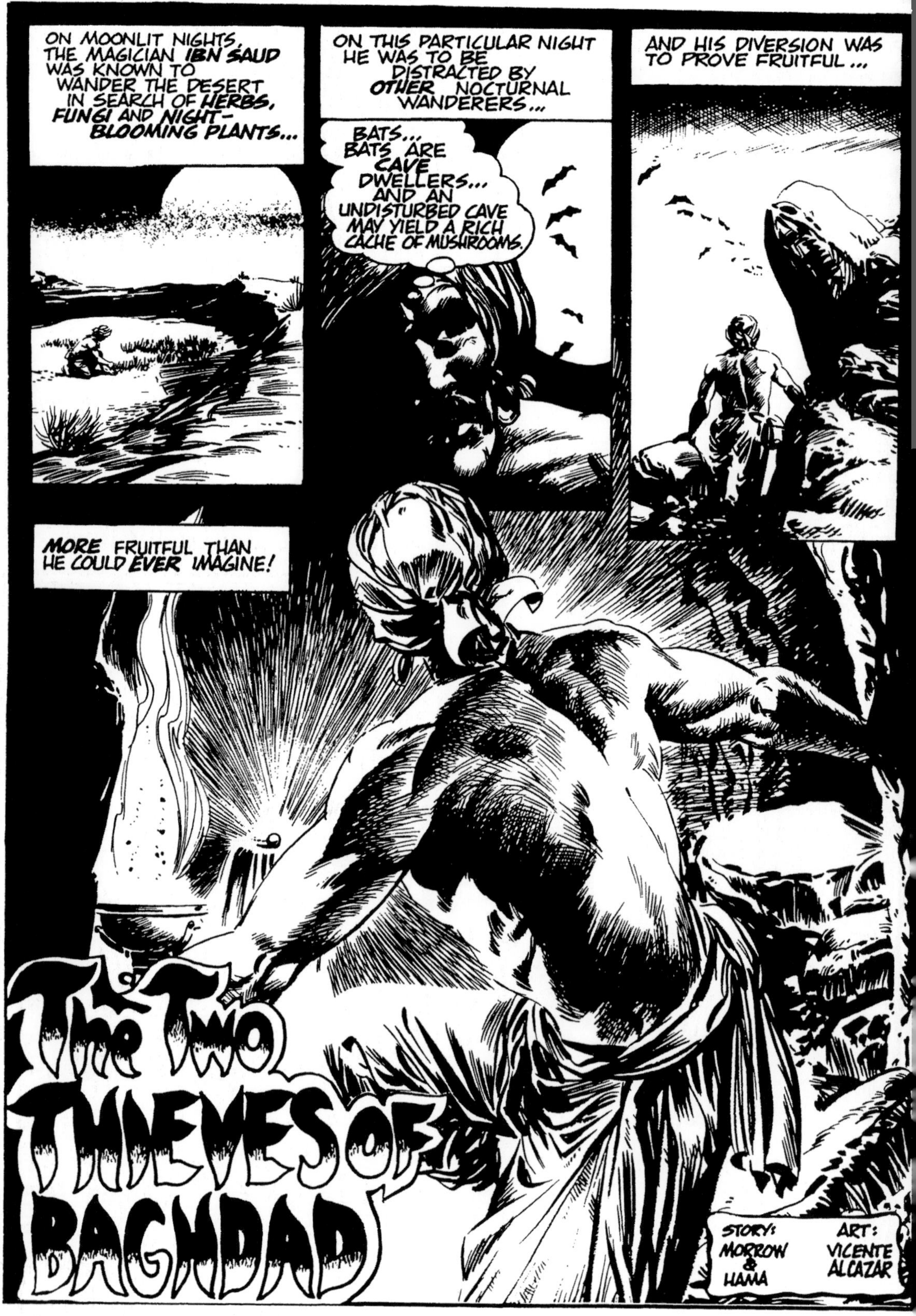
ON MOONLIT NIGHTS, THE MAGICIAN IBN SAUD WAS KNOWN TO WANDER THE DESERT IN SEARCH OF HERBS, FUNGI AND NIGHT-BLOOMING PLANTS...
ON THIS PARTICULAR NIGHT HE WAS TO BE DISTRACTED BY OTHER NOCTURNAL WANDERERERS...
BATS... BATS ARE CAVE DWELLERS... AND AN UNDISTURBED CAVE MAY YIELD A RICH CACHE OF MUSHROOMS.
AND HIS DIVERSION WAS TO PROVE FRUITFUL...
MORE FRUITFUL THAN HE COULD EVER IMAGINE!
The Two THIEVES OF BAGHDAD
STORY: MORROW & HAMA
ART: VICENTE ALCAZAR

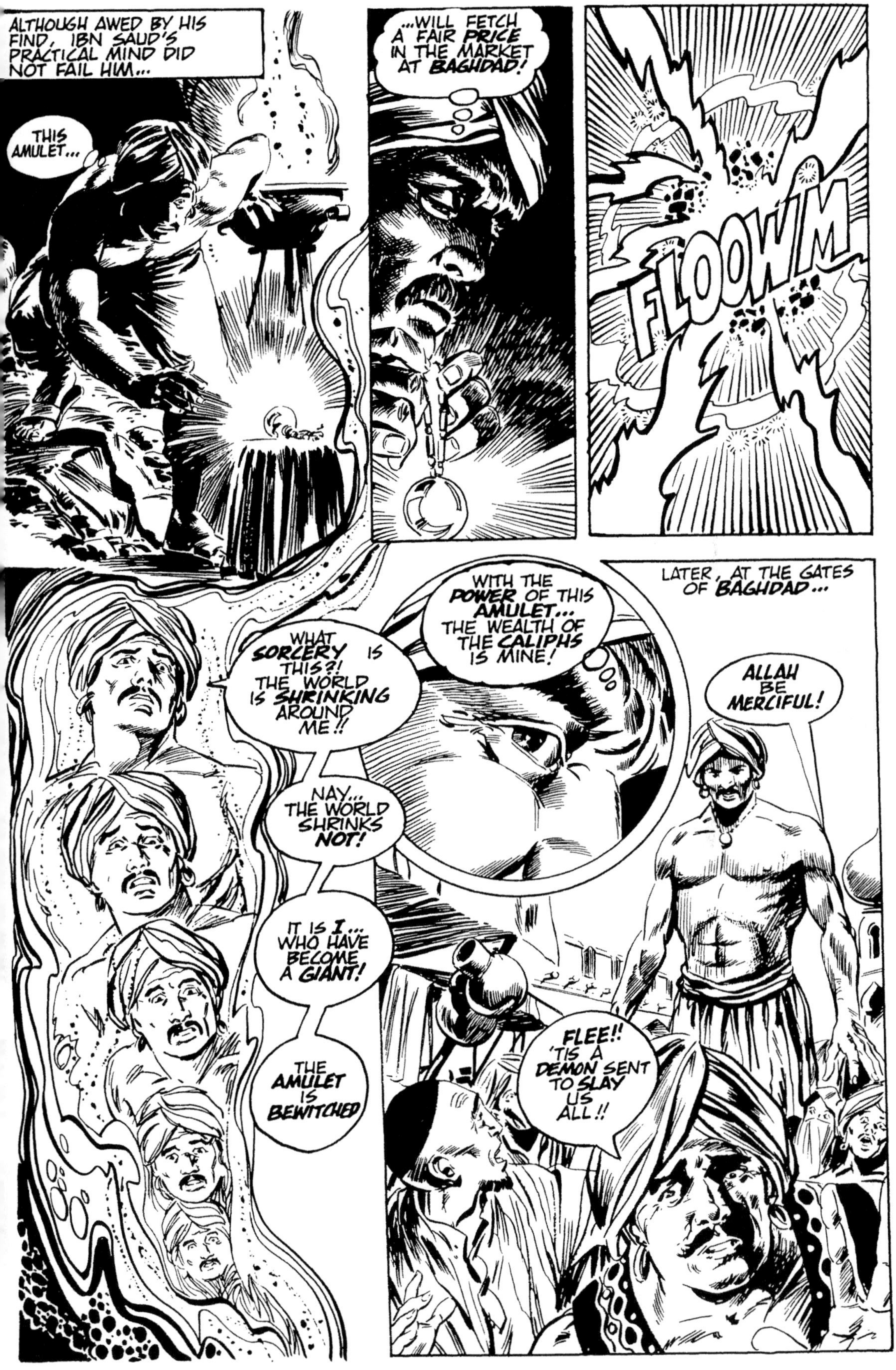
ALTHOUGH AWED BY HIS FIND, IBN SAUD'S PRACTICAL MIND DID NOT FAIL HIM...
THIS AMULET...
...WILL FETCH A FAIR PRICE IN THE MARKET AT BAGHDAD!
FLOOWM
WHAT SORCERY IS THIS?! THE WORLD IS SHRINKING AROUND ME!!
NAY... THE WORLD SHRINKS NOT!
IT IS I... WHO HAVE BECOME A GIANT!
THE AMULET IS BEWITCHED
WITH THE POWER OF THIS AMULET... THE WEALTH OF THE CALIPHS IS MINE!
LATER, AT THE GATES OF BAGHDAD...
ALLAH BE MERCIFUL!
FLEE!! 'TIS A DEMON SENT TO SLAY US ALL!!

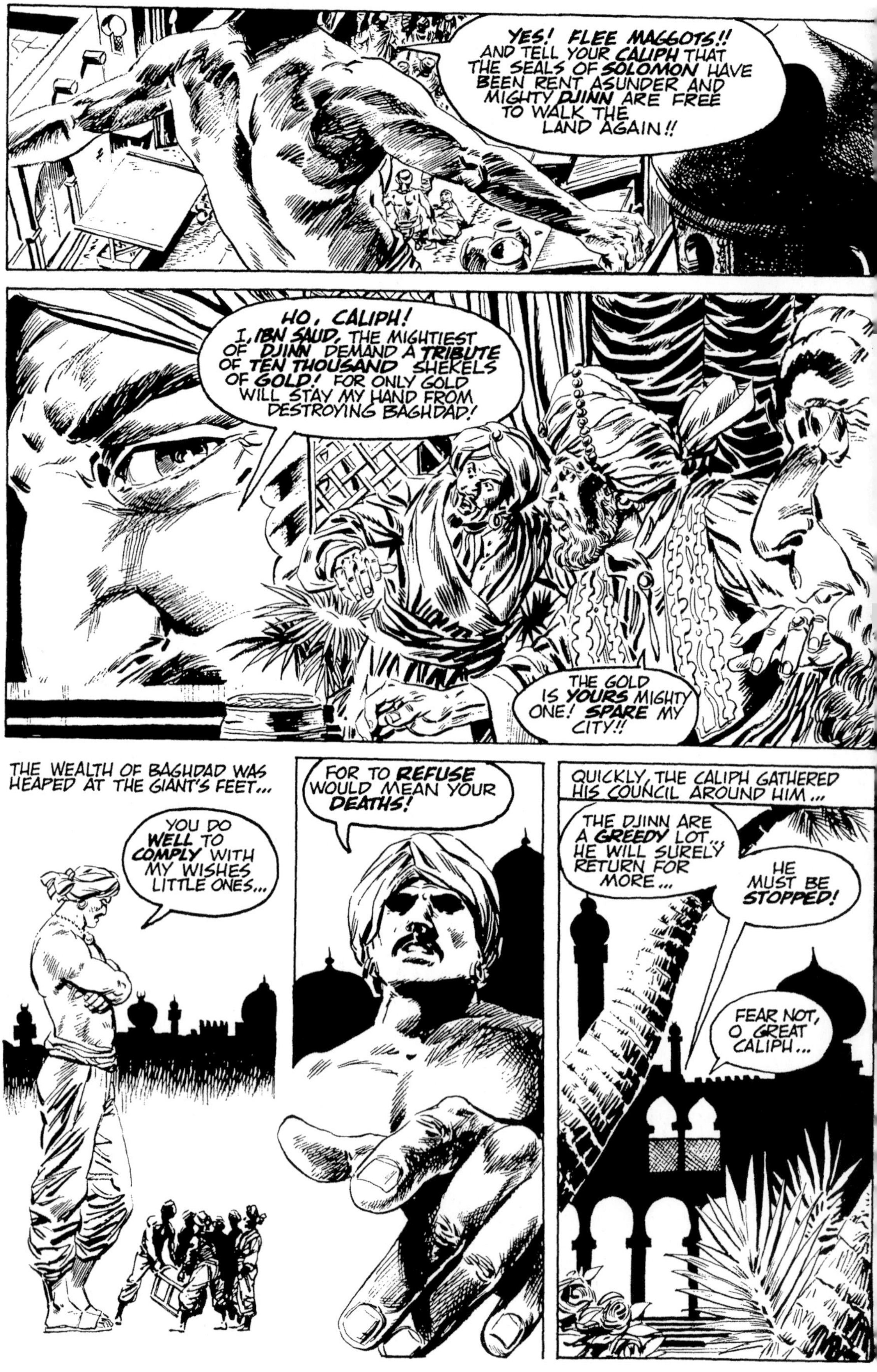
YES! FLEE MAGGOTS!! AND TELL YOUR CALIPH THAT THE SEALS OF SOLOMON HAVE BEEN RENT ASUNDER AND MIGHTY DJINN ARE FREE TO WALK THE LAND AGAIN!!
HO, CALIPH! I, IBN SAUD, THE MIGHTIEST OF DJINN DEMAND A TRIBUTE OF TEN THOUSAND SHEKELS OF GOLD! FOR ONLY GOLD WILL STAY MY HAND FROM DESTROYING BAGHDAD!
THE GOLD IS YOURS MIGHTY ONE! SPARE MY CITY!!
THE WEALTH OF BAGHDAD WAS HEAPED AT THE GIANT'S FEET...
YOU DO WELL TO COMPLY WITH MY WISHES LITTLE ONES...
FOR TO REFUSE WOULD MEAN YOUR DEATHS!
QUICKLY, THE CALIPH GATHERED HIS COUNCIL AROUND HIM...
THE DJINN ARE A GREEDY LOT... HE WILL SURELY RETURN FOR MORE...
HE MUST BE STOPPED!
FEAR NOT, O GREAT CALIPH...

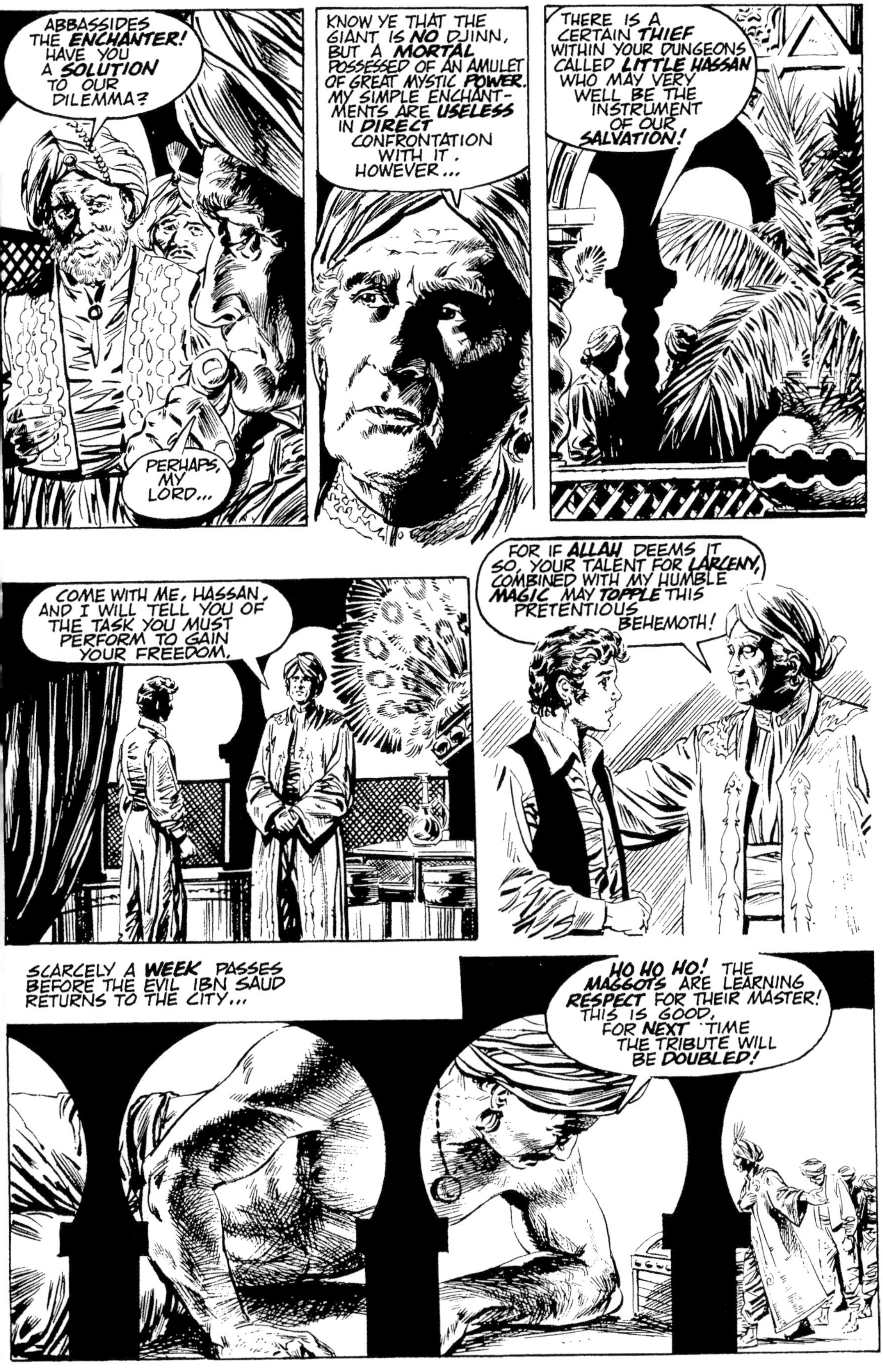
ABBASSIDES THE ENCHANTER! HAVE YOU A SOLUTION TO OUR DILEMMA?
PERHAPS, MY LORD...
KNOW YE THAT THE GIANT IS NO DJINN, BUT A MORTAL POSSESSED OF AN AMULET OF GREAT MYSTIC POWER. MY SIMPLE ENCHANTMENTS ARE USELESS IN DIRECT CONFRONTATION WITH IT. HOWEVER...
THERE IS A CERTAIN THIEF WITHIN YOUR DUNGEONS CALLED LITTLE HASSAN WHO MAY VERY WELL BE THE INSTRUMENT OF OUR SALVATION!
COME WITH ME, HASSAN, AND I WILL TELL YOU OF THE TASK YOU MUST PERFORM TO GAIN YOUR FREEDOM.
FOR IF ALLAH DEEMS IT SO, YOUR TALENT FOR LARCENY, COMBINED WITH MY HUMBLE MAGIC MAY TOPPLE THIS PRETENTIOUS BEHEMOTH!
SCARCELY A WEEK PASSES BEFORE THE EVIL IBN SAUD RETURNS TO THE CITY...
HO HO HO! THE MAGGOTS ARE LEARNING RESPECT FOR THEIR MASTER! THIS IS GOOD, FOR NEXT TIME THE TRIBUTE WILL BE DOUBLED!

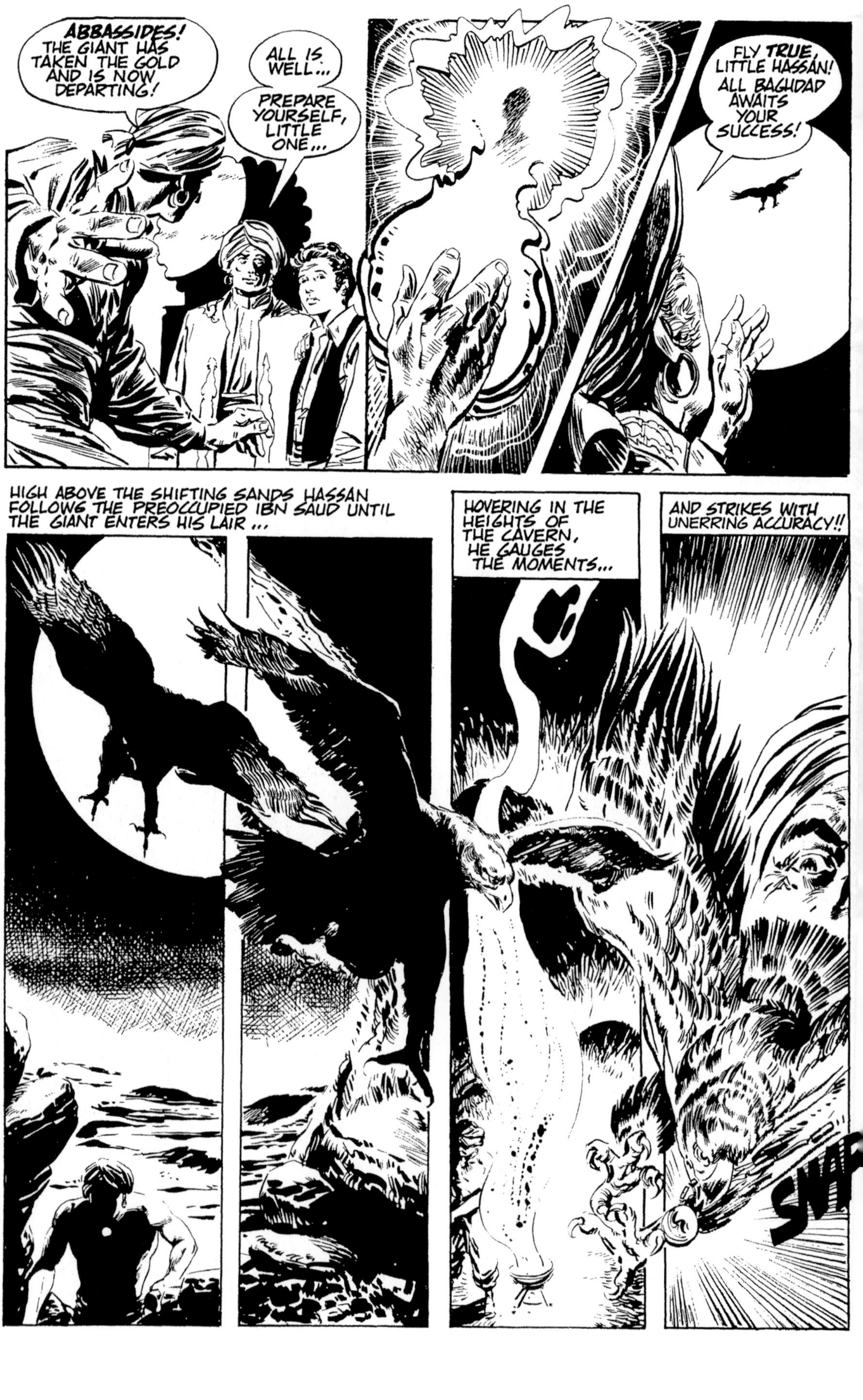
ABBASSIDES! THE GIANT HAS TAKEN THE GOLD AND IS NOW DEPARTING!
ALL IS WELL...
PREPARE YOURSELF, LITTLE ONE...
FLY TRUE, LITTLE HASSAN! ALL BAGHDAD AWAITS YOUR SUCCESS!
HIGH ABOVE THE SHIFTING SANDS HASSAN FOLLOWS THE PREOCCUPIED IBN SAUD UNTIL THE GIANT ENTERS HIS LAIR...
HOVERING IN THE HEIGHTS OF THE CAVERN, HE GAUGES THE MOMENTS...
AND STRIKES WITH UNERRING ACCURACY!!

WITH THE CATALYTIC AMULET SWEPT AWAY... THE MYSTIC FORCES WITHIN THE CAVE RAGE AND BOIL IN FURIOUS TURMOIL!

...UNTIL THE VERY ROCKS GIVE WAY BEFORE IT'S POWER!

RUMBLE RUMBLE

...AND THROUGH THE SWIRLING DUST, A LONE BIRD WINGS A STEADY COURSE TOWARDS BAGHDAD...

...TO UNDERGO A STARTLING TRANSFORMATION AT THE GATES AND RECIEVE A HERO'S WELCOME!

RUMBLE RUMBLE

BAGHDAD RETURNED TO IT'S PEACEFUL EXISTANCE... BUT FROM TIME TO TIME THE FOOT HILLS IN THE DESERT WERE SEEN TO SHIFT AND TREMBLE... AS IF A GIANT STIRRED IN IT'S SLEEP BELOW THE EARTH... AND WATCHING QUIETLY, A BOY NAMED HASSAN WOULD DREAM OF A TIME WHEN HE HAD WINGS TO SOAR...

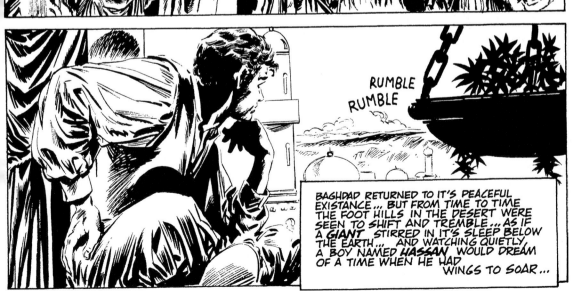

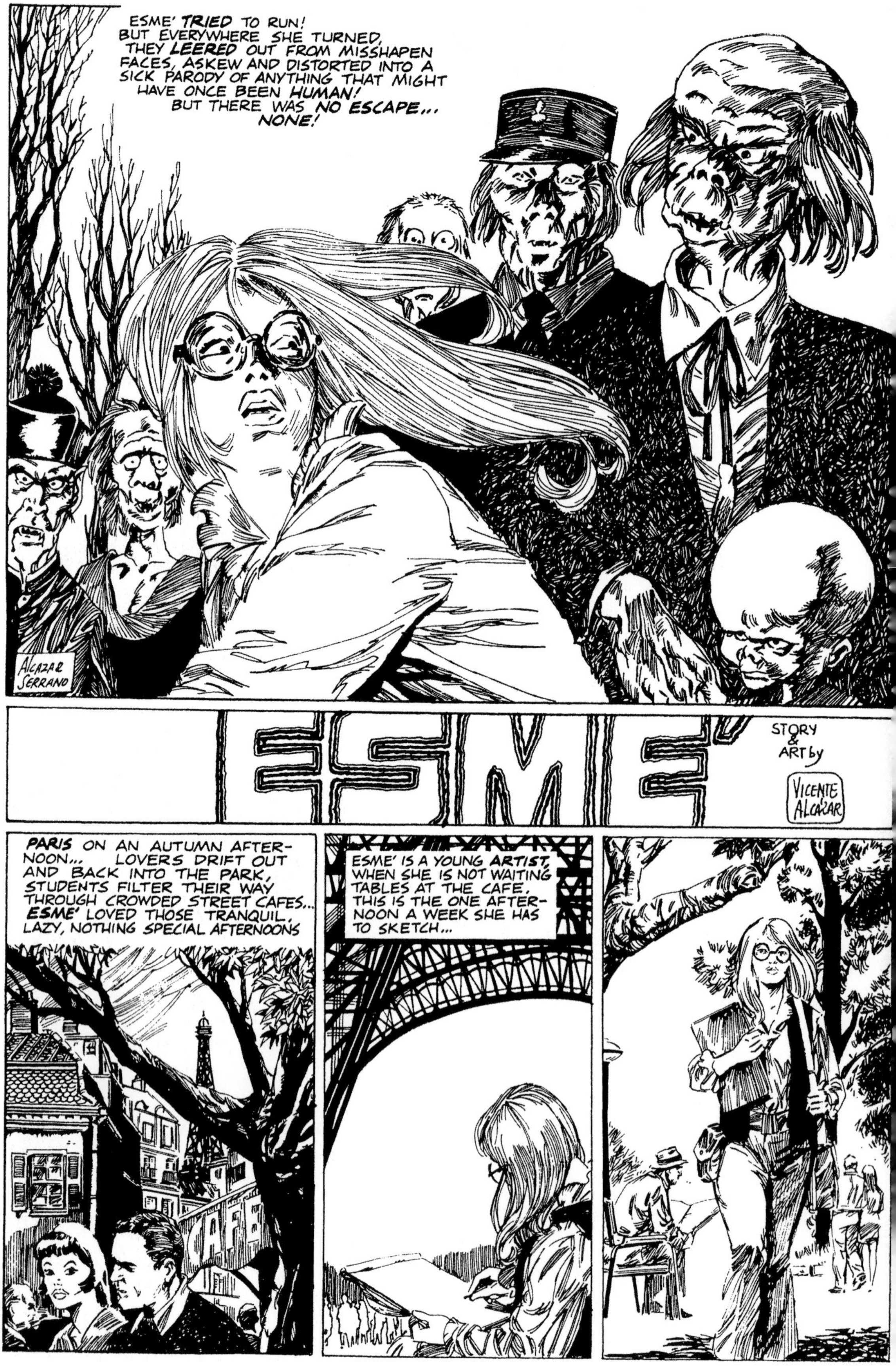
ESME' TRIED TO RUN! BUT EVERYWHERE SHE TURNED, THEY LEERED OUT FROM MISSHAPEN FACES, ASKEW AND DISTORTED INTO A SICK PARODY OF ANYTHING THAT MIGHT HAVE ONCE BEEN HUMAN! BUT THERE WAS NO ESCAPE... NONE!
ALCAZAR SERRANO
ESME'
STORY & ART by VICENTE ALCAZAR
PARIS ON AN AUTUMN AFTERNOON... LOVERS DRIFT OUT AND BACK INTO THE PARK, STUDENTS FILTER THEIR WAY THROUGH CROWDED STREET CAFES... ESME' LOVED THOSE TRANQUIL, LAZY, NOTHING SPECIAL AFTERNOONS
ESME' IS A YOUNG ARTIST, WHEN SHE IS NOT WAITING TABLES AT THE CAFE. THIS IS THE ONE AFTERNOON A WEEK SHE HAS TO SKETCH...

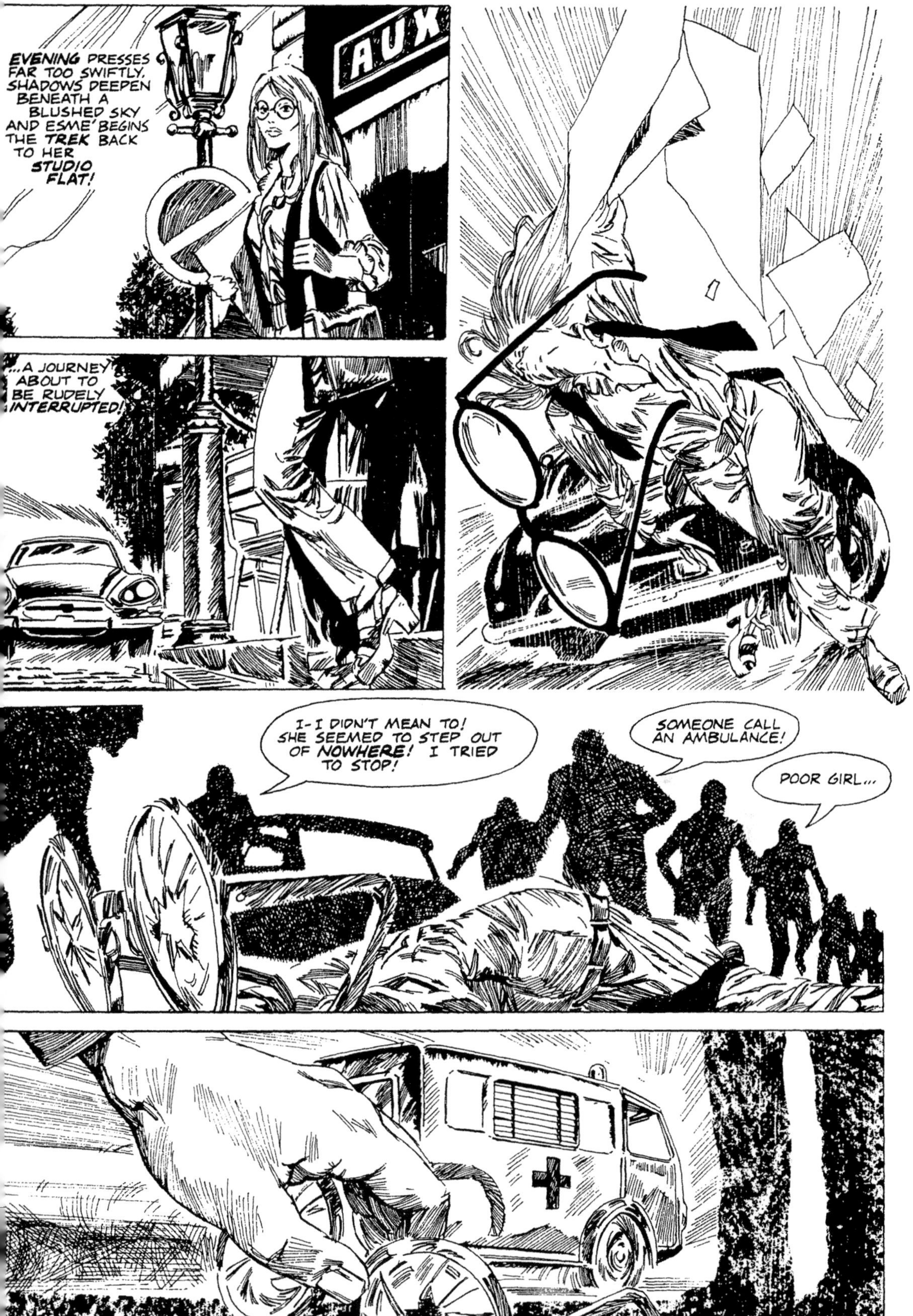
EVENING PRESSES FAR TOO SWIFTLY. SHADOWS DEEPEN BENEATH A BLUSHED SKY AND ESME' BEGINS THE TREK BACK TO HER STUDIO FLAT!
AUX
...A JOURNEY ABOUT TO BE RUDELY INTERRUPTED!
I-I DIDN'T MEAN TO! SHE SEEMED TO STEP OUT OF NOWHERE! I TRIED TO STOP!
SOMEONE CALL AN AMBULANCE!
POOR GIRL...

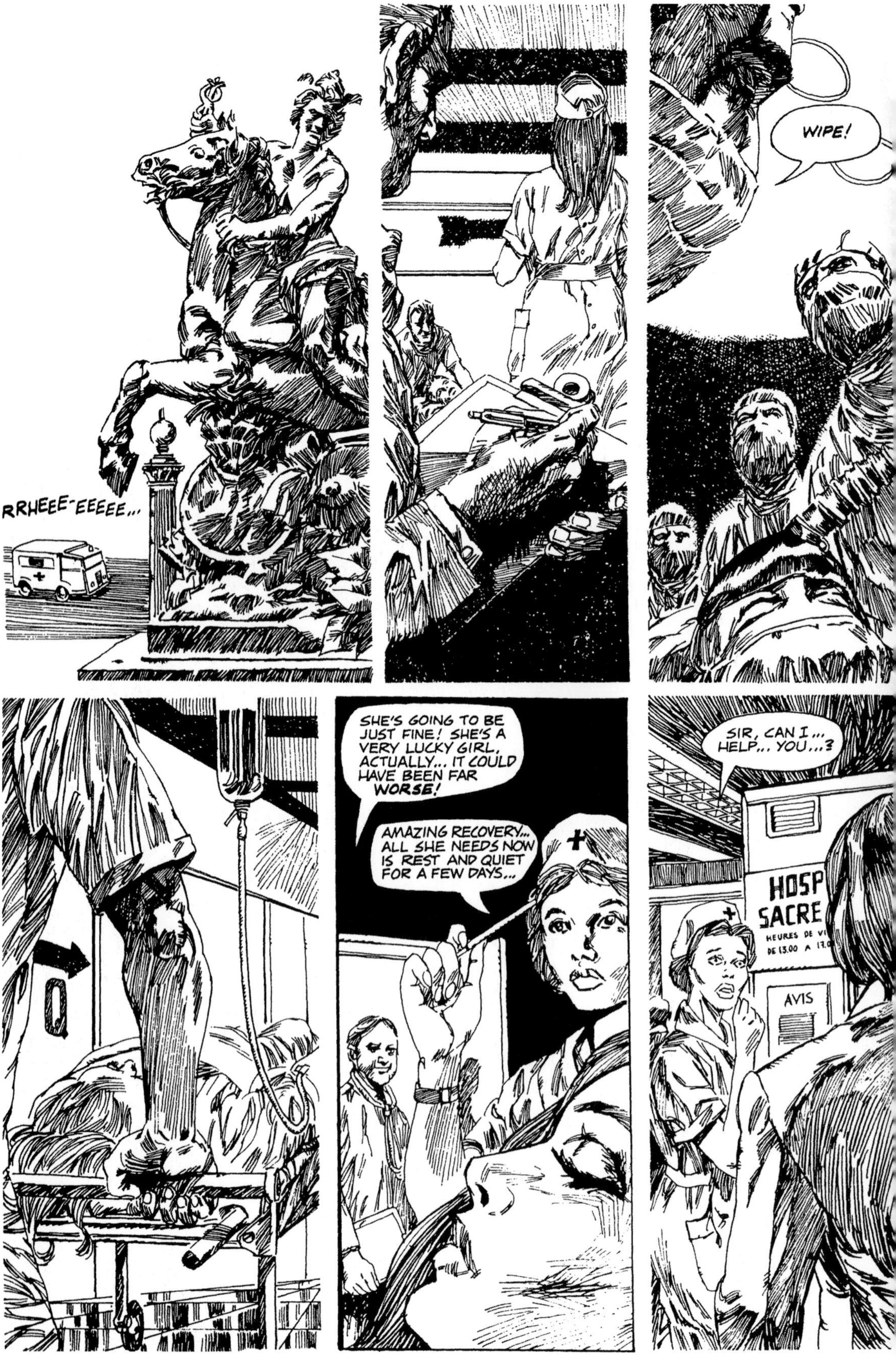
RRHEEE-EEEEE...
WIPE!
SHE'S GOING TO BE JUST FINE! SHE'S A VERY LUCKY GIRL, ACTUALLY... IT COULD HAVE BEEN FAR WORSE!
AMAZING RECOVERY... ALL SHE NEEDS NOW IS REST AND QUIET FOR A FEW DAYS...
SIR, CAN I... HELP... YOU...?
HOSP
SACRE
AVIS

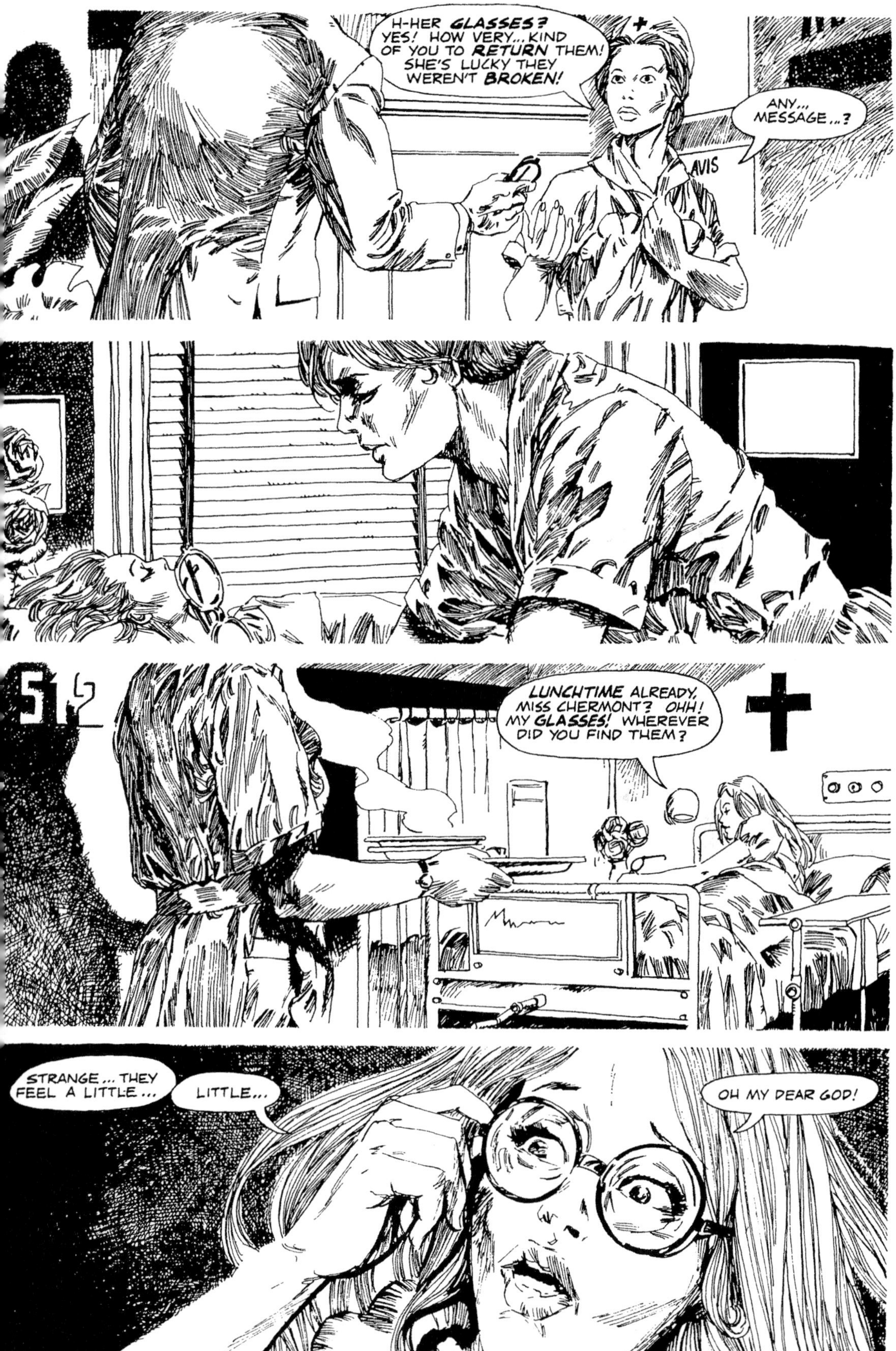
H-HER GLASSES? YES! HOW VERY... KIND OF YOU TO RETURN THEM! SHE'S LUCKY THEY WEREN'T BROKEN!
ANY... MESSAGE...?
AVIS
LUNCHTIME ALREADY, MISS CHERMONT? OHH! MY GLASSES! WHEREVER DID YOU FIND THEM?
STRANGE... THEY FEEL A LITTLE...
LITTLE...
OH MY DEAR GOD!

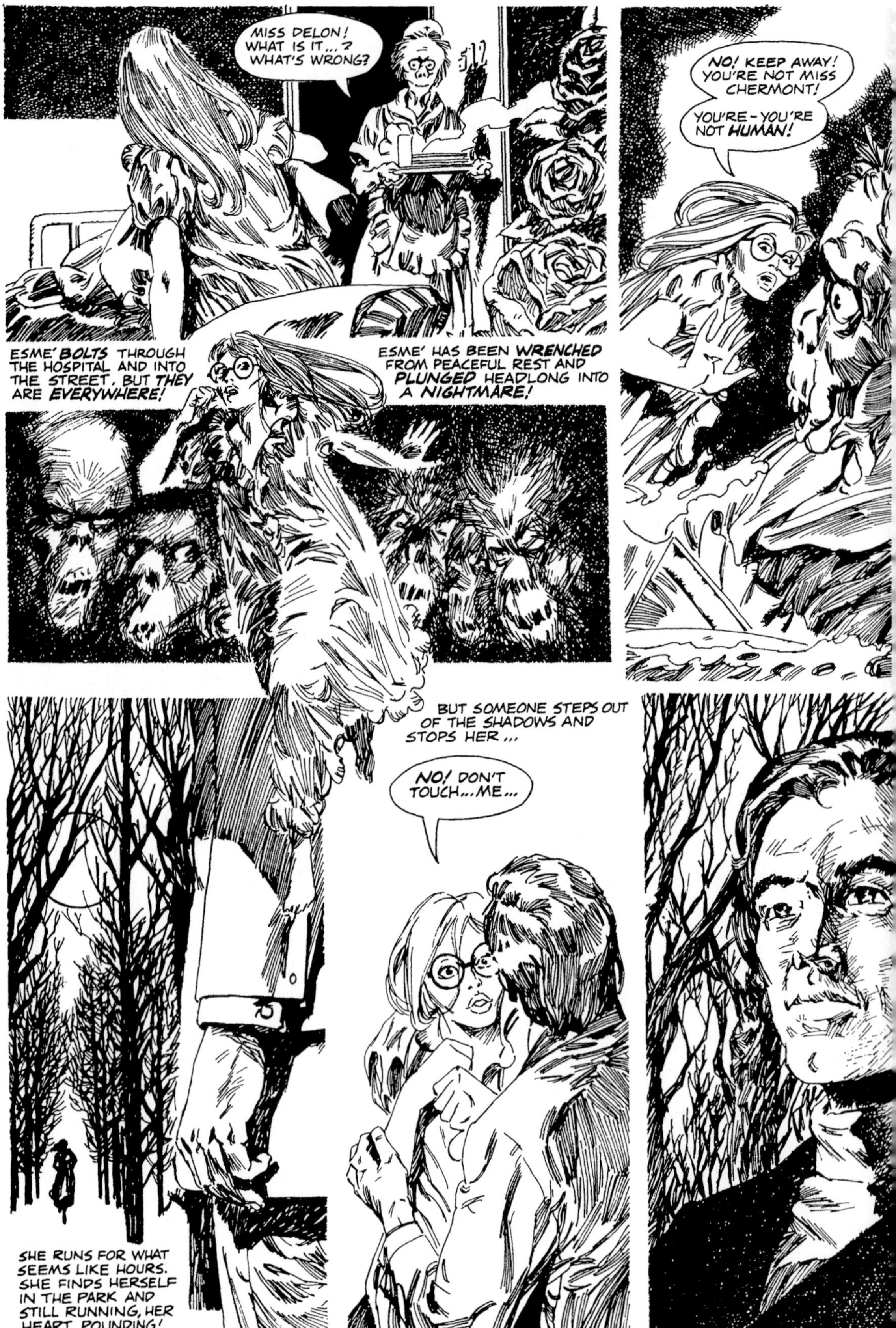
MISS DELON! WHAT IS IT...? WHAT'S WRONG?
NO! KEEP AWAY! YOU'RE NOT MISS CHERMONT!
YOU'RE - YOU'RE NOT HUMAN!
ESME' BOLTS THROUGH THE HOSPITAL AND INTO THE STREET. BUT THEY ARE EVERYWHERE!
ESME' HAS BEEN WRENCHED FROM PEACEFUL REST AND PLUNGED HEADLONG INTO A NIGHTMARE!
SHE RUNS FOR WHAT SEEMS LIKE HOURS. SHE FINDS HERSELF IN THE PARK AND STILL RUNNING, HER HEART POUNDING!
BUT SOMEONE STEPS OUT OF THE SHADOWS AND STOPS HER...
NO! DON'T TOUCH... ME...

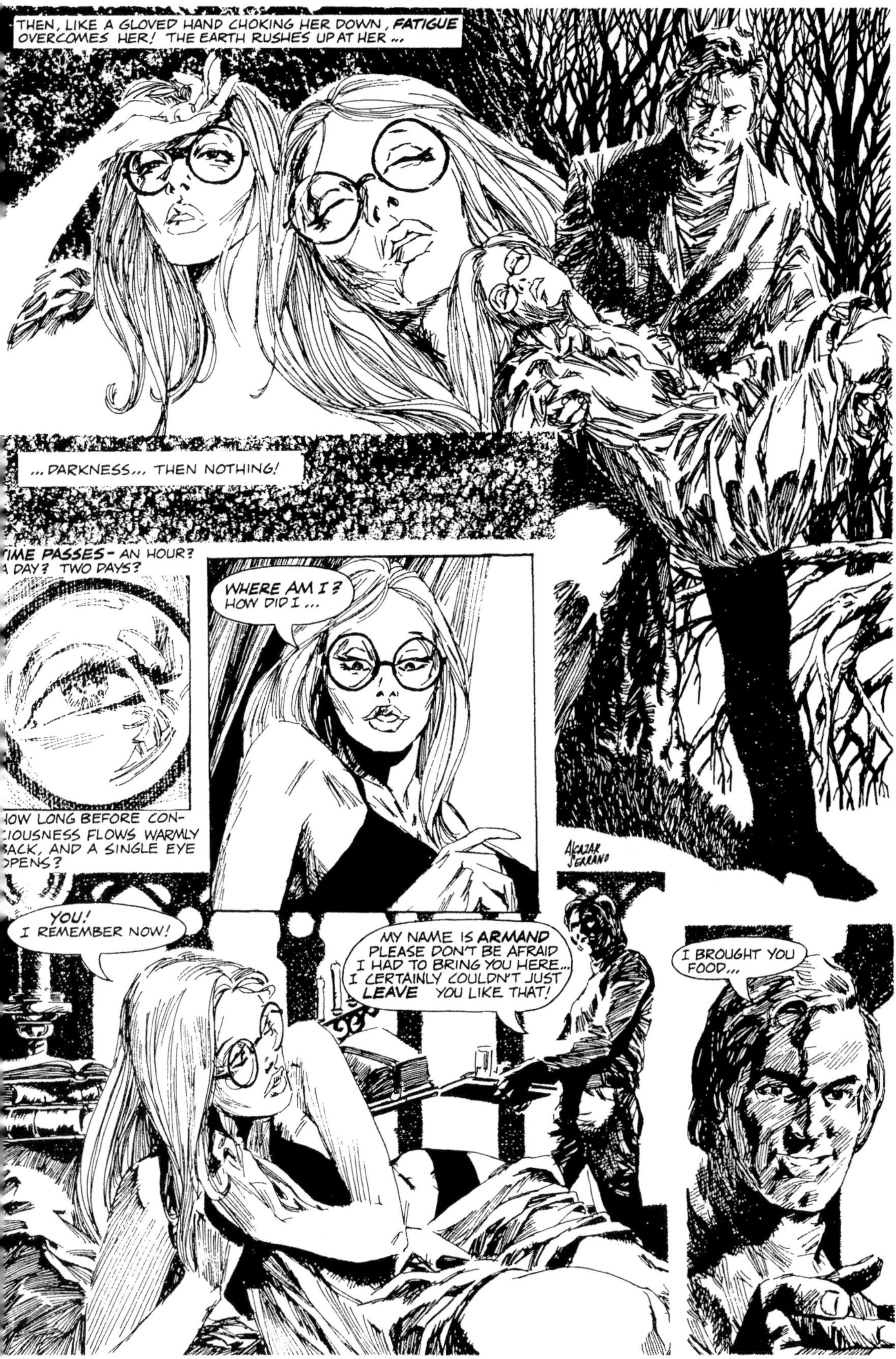
THEN, LIKE A GLOVED HAND CHOKING HER DOWN, FATIGUE OVERCOMES HER! THE EARTH RUSHES UP AT HER ...
... DARKNESS ... THEN NOTHING!
TIME PASSES - AN HOUR? A DAY? TWO DAYS?
HOW LONG BEFORE CONCIOUSNESS FLOWS WARMLY BACK, AND A SINGLE EYE OPENS?
WHERE AM I? HOW DID I ...
ALCAZAR SERRANO
YOU! I REMEMBER NOW!
MY NAME IS ARMAND PLEASE DON'T BE AFRAID I HAD TO BRING YOU HERE... I CERTAINLY COULDN'T JUST LEAVE YOU LIKE THAT!
I BROUGHT YOU FOOD...

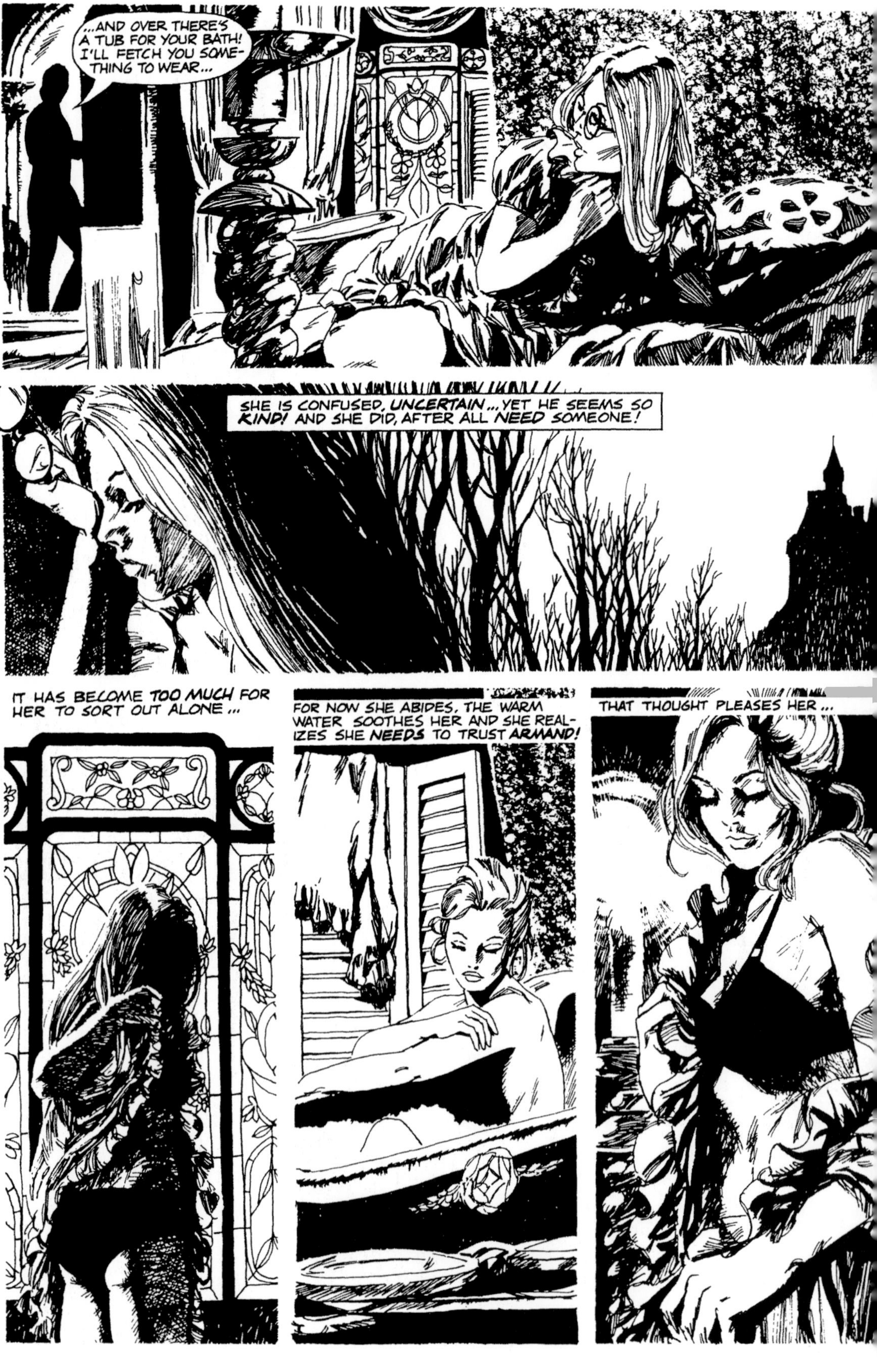
...AND OVER THERE'S A TUB FOR YOUR BATH! I'LL FETCH YOU SOMETHING TO WEAR...
SHE IS CONFUSED, UNCERTAIN... YET HE SEEMS SO KIND! AND SHE DID, AFTER ALL NEED SOMEONE!
IT HAS BECOME TOO MUCH FOR HER TO SORT OUT ALONE...
FOR NOW SHE ABIDES. THE WARM WATER SOOTHES HER AND SHE REALIZES SHE NEEDS TO TRUST ARMAND!
THAT THOUGHT PLEASES HER...

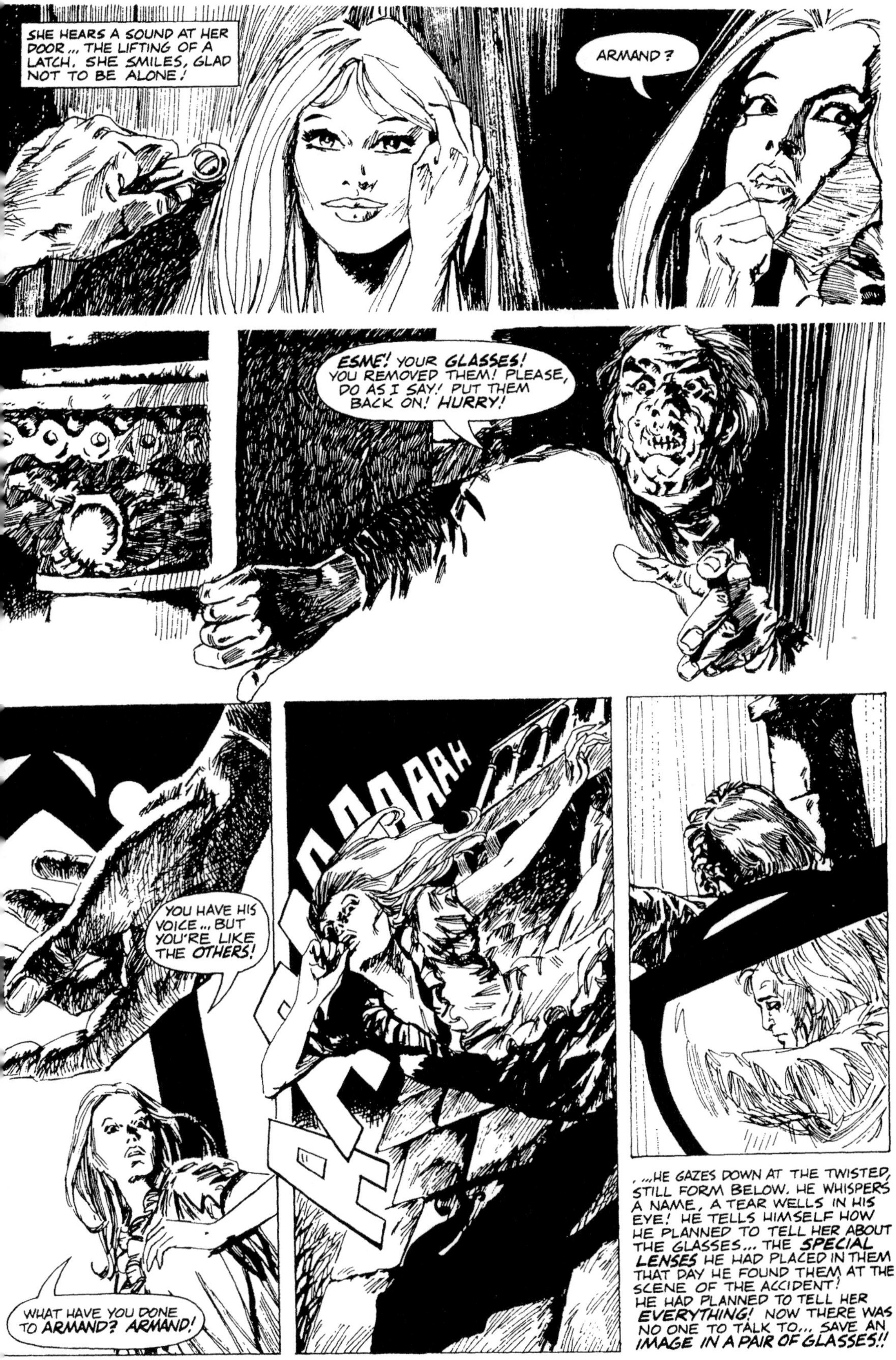
SHE HEARS A SOUND AT HER DOOR... THE LIFTING OF A LATCH. SHE SMILES, GLAD NOT TO BE ALONE!
ARMAND?
ESME! YOUR GLASSES! YOU REMOVED THEM! PLEASE, DO AS I SAY! PUT THEM BACK ON! HURRY!
YOU HAVE HIS VOICE... BUT YOU'RE LIKE THE OTHERS!
WHAT HAVE YOU DONE TO ARMAND? ARMAND!
AAAAAAAH
...HE GAZES DOWN AT THE TWISTED, STILL FORM BELOW. HE WHISPERS A NAME, A TEAR WELLS IN HIS EYE! HE TELLS HIMSELF HOW HE PLANNED TO TELL HER ABOUT THE GLASSES... THE SPECIAL LENSES HE HAD PLACED IN THEM THAT DAY HE FOUND THEM AT THE SCENE OF THE ACCIDENT! HE HAD PLANNED TO TELL HER EVERYTHING! NOW THERE WAS NO ONE TO TALK TO... SAVE AN IMAGE IN A PAIR OF GLASSES!!

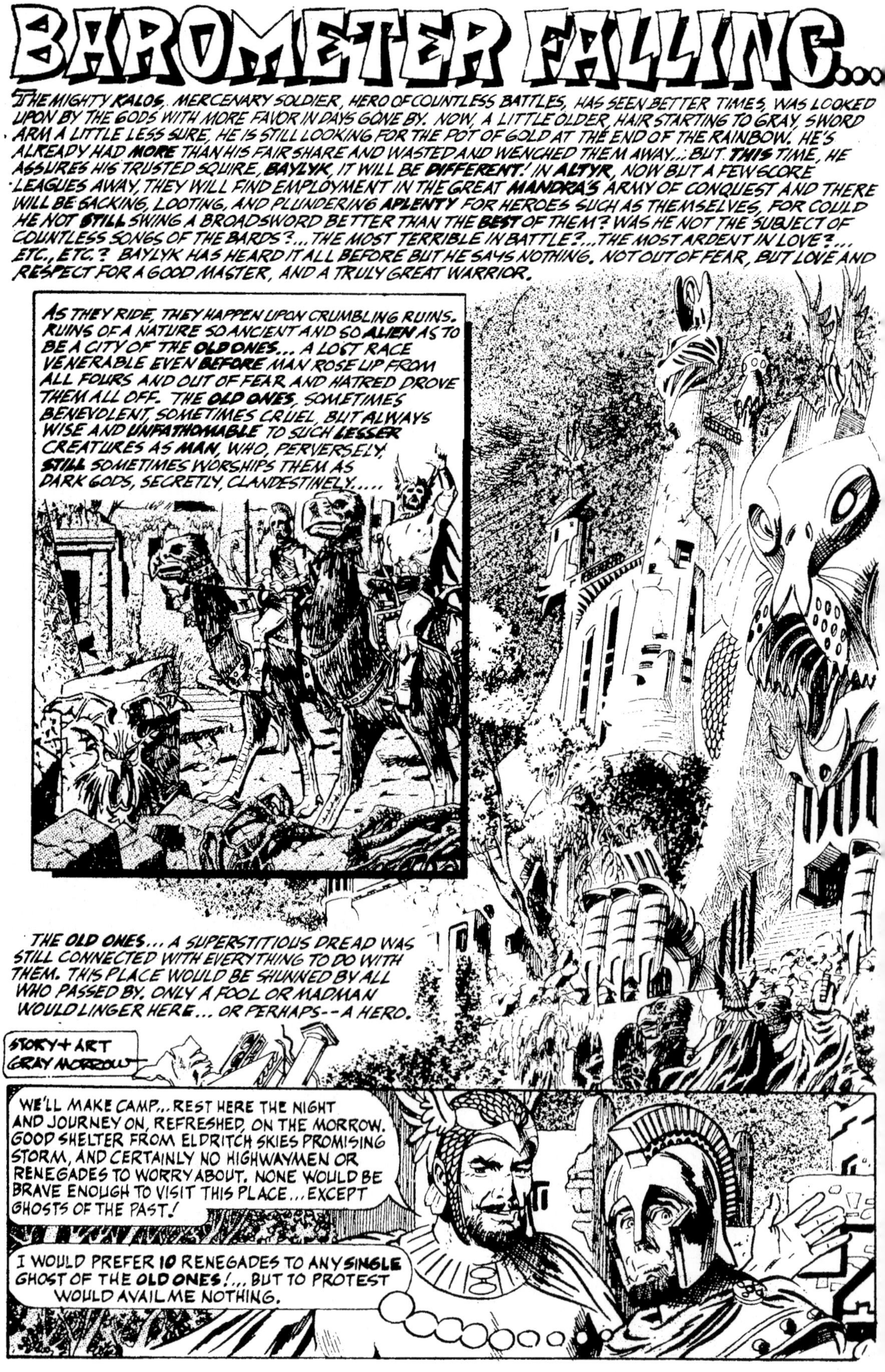
BAROMETER FALLING...
THE MIGHTY KALOS, MERCENARY SOLDIER, HERO OF COUNTLESS BATTLES, HAS SEEN BETTER TIMES, WAS LOOKED UPON BY THE GODS WITH MORE FAVOR IN DAYS GONE BY. NOW, A LITTLE OLDER, HAIR STARTING TO GRAY, SWORD ARM A LITTLE LESS SURE, HE IS STILL LOOKING FOR THE POT OF GOLD AT THE END OF THE RAINBOW. HE'S ALREADY HAD MORE THAN HIS FAIR SHARE AND WASTED AND WENCHED THEM AWAY... BUT THIS TIME, HE ASSURES HIS TRUSTED SQUIRE, BAYLYK, IT WILL BE DIFFERENT! IN ALTYR, NOW BUT A FEW SCORE LEAGUES AWAY, THEY WILL FIND EMPLOYMENT IN THE GREAT MANDRA'S ARMY OF CONQUEST AND THERE WILL BE SACKING, LOOTING, AND PLUNDERING APLENTY FOR HEROES SUCH AS THEMSELVES, FOR COULD HE NOT STILL SWING A BROADSWORD BETTER THAN THE BEST OF THEM? WAS HE NOT THE SUBJECT OF COUNTLESS SONGS OF THE BARDS?... THE MOST TERRIBLE IN BATTLE?... THE MOST ARDENT IN LOVE?... ETC., ETC.? BAYLYK HAS HEARD IT ALL BEFORE BUT HE SAYS NOTHING. NOT OUT OF FEAR, BUT LOVE AND RESPECT FOR A GOOD MASTER, AND A TRULY GREAT WARRIOR.
AS THEY RIDE, THEY HAPPEN UPON CRUMBLING RUINS. RUINS OF A NATURE SO ANCIENT AND SO ALIEN AS TO BE A CITY OF THE OLD ONES... A LOST RACE VENERABLE EVEN BEFORE MAN ROSE UP FROM ALL FOURS AND OUT OF FEAR AND HATRED DROVE THEM ALL OFF. THE OLD ONES, SOMETIMES BENEVOLENT, SOMETIMES CRUEL, BUT ALWAYS WISE AND UNFATHOMABLE TO SUCH LESSER CREATURES AS MAN, WHO, PERVERSELY, STILL SOMETIMES WORSHIPS THEM AS DARK GODS, SECRETLY, CLANDESTINELY....
THE OLD ONES... A SUPERSTITIOUS DREAD WAS STILL CONNECTED WITH EVERYTHING TO DO WITH THEM. THIS PLACE WOULD BE SHUNNED BY ALL WHO PASSED BY. ONLY A FOOL OR MADMAN WOULD LINGER HERE... OR PERHAPS--A HERO.
STORY + ART GRAY MORROW
WE'LL MAKE CAMP... REST HERE THE NIGHT AND JOURNEY ON, REFRESHED, ON THE MORROW. GOOD SHELTER FROM ELDRITCH SKIES PROMISING STORM, AND CERTAINLY NO HIGHWAYMEN OR RENEGADES TO WORRY ABOUT. NONE WOULD BE BRAVE ENOUGH TO VISIT THIS PLACE... EXCEPT GHOSTS OF THE PAST!
I WOULD PREFER 10 RENEGADES TO ANY SINGLE GHOST OF THE OLD ONES!... BUT TO PROTEST WOULD AVAIL ME NOTHING.

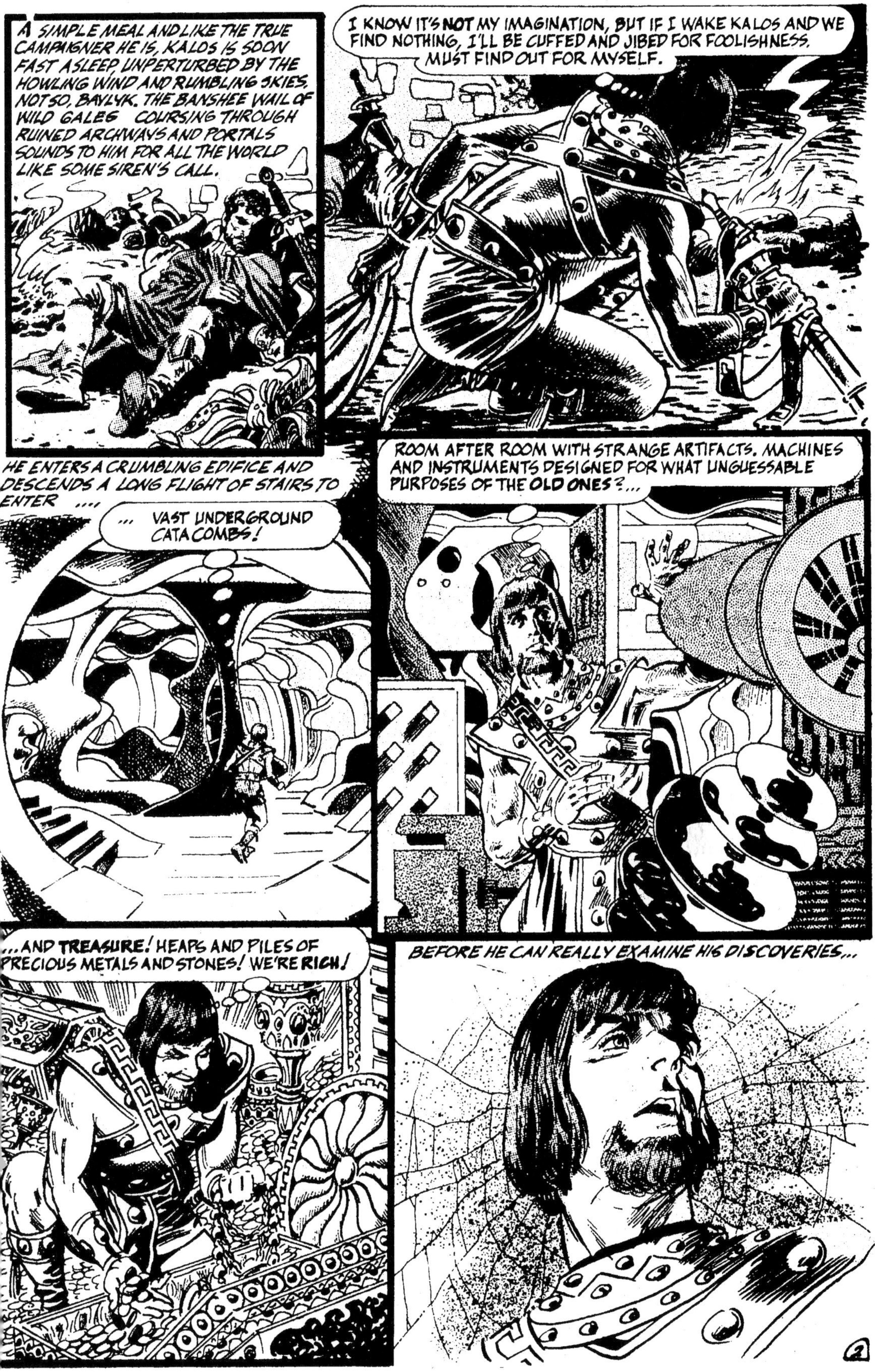
A SIMPLE MEAL AND LIKE THE TRUE CAMPAIGNER HE IS, KALOS IS SOON FAST ASLEEP, UNPERTURBED BY THE HOWLING WIND AND RUMBLING SKIES. NOT SO, BAYLYK. THE BANSHEE WAIL OF WILD GALES COURSING THROUGH RUINED ARCHWAYS AND PORTALS SOUNDS TO HIM FOR ALL THE WORLD LIKE SOME SIREN'S CALL.
I KNOW IT'S NOT MY IMAGINATION, BUT IF I WAKE KALOS AND WE FIND NOTHING, I'LL BE CUFFED AND JIBED FOR FOOLISHNESS. MUST FIND OUT FOR MYSELF.
HE ENTERS A CRUMBLING EDIFICE AND DESCENDS A LONG FLIGHT OF STAIRS TO ENTER ....
... VAST UNDERGROUND CATACOMBS!
ROOM AFTER ROOM WITH STRANGE ARTIFACTS. MACHINES AND INSTRUMENTS DESIGNED FOR WHAT UNGUESSABLE PURPOSES OF THE OLD ONES?...
...AND TREASURE! HEAPS AND PILES OF PRECIOUS METALS AND STONES! WE'RE RICH!
BEFORE HE CAN REALLY EXAMINE HIS DISCOVERIES...
2

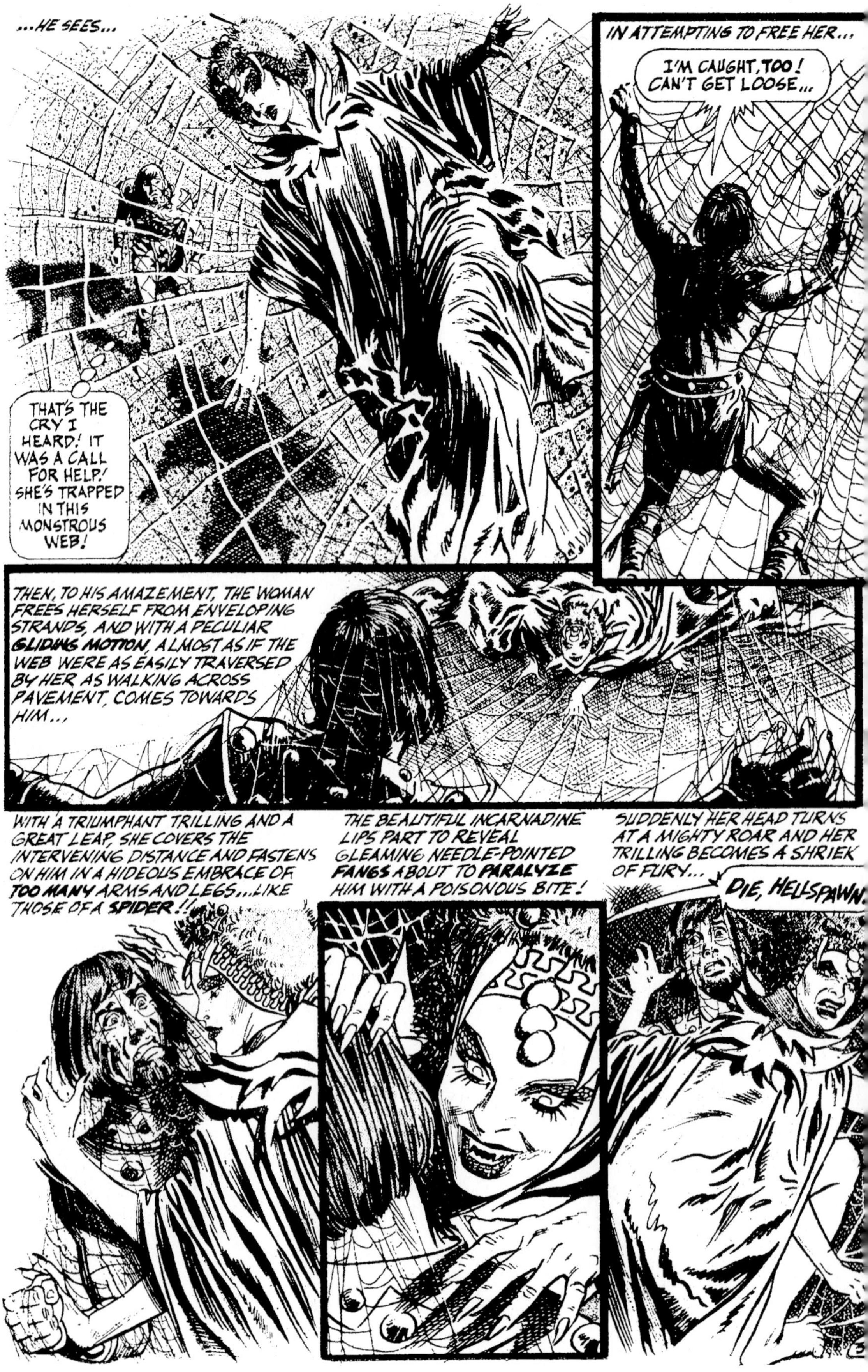
...HE SEES...
THAT'S THE CRY I HEARD! IT WAS A CALL FOR HELP! SHE'S TRAPPED IN THIS MONSTROUS WEB!
IN ATTEMPTING TO FREE HER...
I'M CAUGHT, TOO! CAN'T GET LOOSE...
THEN, TO HIS AMAZEMENT, THE WOMAN FREES HERSELF FROM ENVELOPING STRANDS, AND WITH A PECULIAR GLIDING MOTION, ALMOST AS IF THE WEB WERE AS EASILY TRAVERSED BY HER AS WALKING ACROSS PAVEMENT, COMES TOWARDS HIM...
WITH A TRIUMPHANT TRILLING AND A GREAT LEAP, SHE COVERS THE INTERVENING DISTANCE AND FASTENS ON HIM IN A HIDEOUS EMBRACE OF TOO MANY ARMS AND LEGS...LIKE THOSE OF A SPIDER!!
THE BEAUTIFUL INCARNADINE LIPS PART TO REVEAL GLEAMING NEEDLE-POINTED FANGS ABOUT TO PARALYZE HIM WITH A POISONOUS BITE!
SUDDENLY HER HEAD TURNS AT A MIGHTY ROAR AND HER TRILLING BECOMES A SHRIEK OF FURY...
DIE, HELLSPAWN!
3

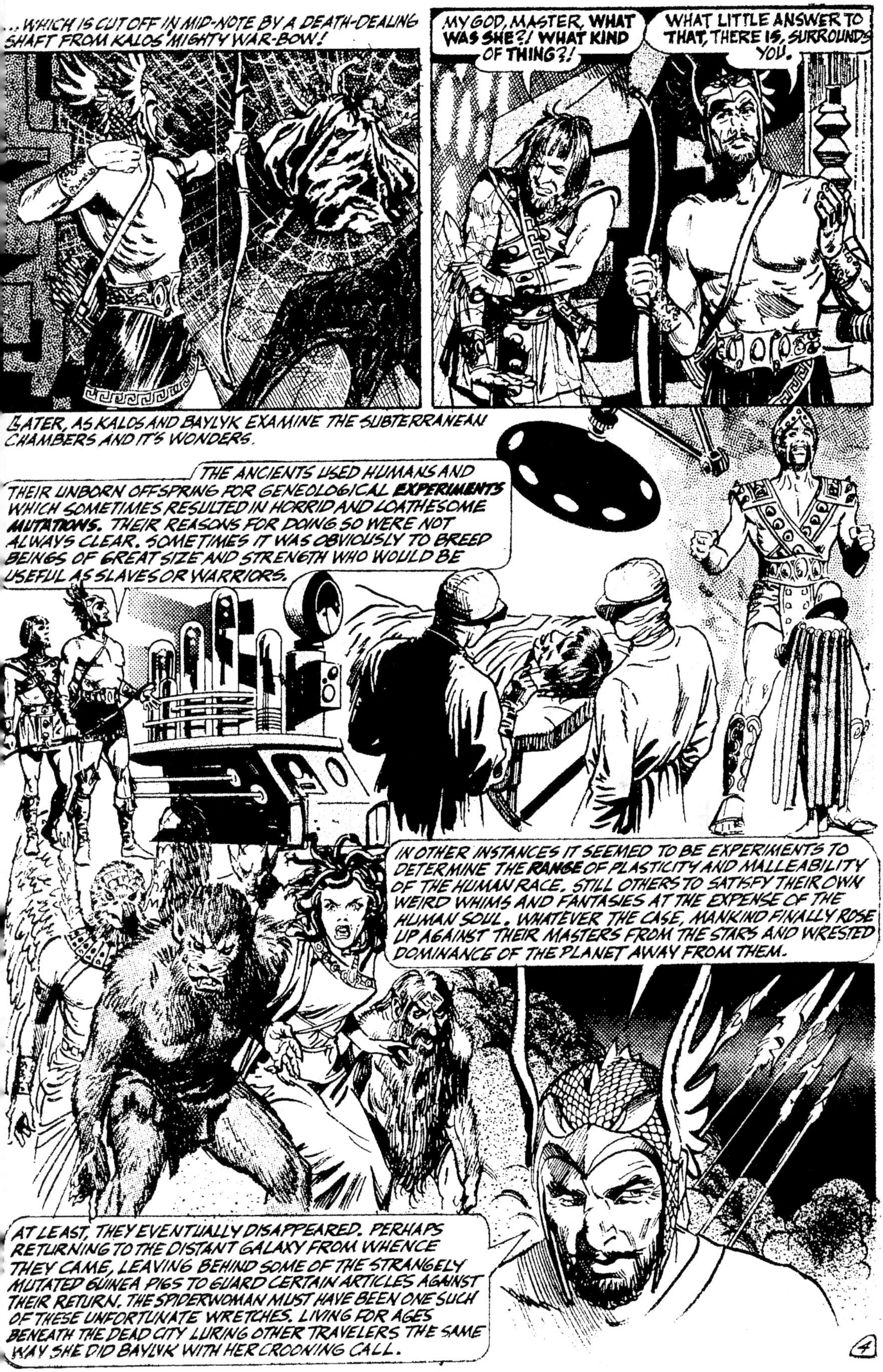

..WHICH IS CUT OFF IN MID-NOTE BY A DEATH-DEALING SHAFT FROM KALOS' MIGHTY WAR-BOW!
MY GOD, MASTER, WHAT WAS SHE?! WHAT KIND OF THING?!
WHAT LITTLE ANSWER TO THAT, THERE IS, SURROUNDS YOU.
LATER, AS KALOS AND BAYLYK EXAMINE THE SUBTERRANEAN CHAMBERS AND IT'S WONDERS.
THE ANCIENTS USED HUMANS AND THEIR UNBORN OFFSPRING FOR GENEOLOGICAL EXPERIMENTS WHICH SOMETIMES RESULTED IN HORRID AND LOATHESOME MUTATIONS. THEIR REASONS FOR DOING SO WERE NOT ALWAYS CLEAR. SOMETIMES IT WAS OBVIOUSLY TO BREED BEINGS OF GREAT SIZE AND STRENGTH WHO WOULD BE USEFUL AS SLAVES OR WARRIORS.
IN OTHER INSTANCES IT SEEMED TO BE EXPERIMENTS TO DETERMINE THE RANGE OF PLASTICITY AND MALLEABILITY OF THE HUMAN RACE. STILL OTHERS TO SATISFY THEIR OWN WEIRD WHIMS AND FANTASIES AT THE EXPENSE OF THE HUMAN SOUL. WHATEVER THE CASE, MANKIND FINALLY ROSE UP AGAINST THEIR MASTERS FROM THE STARS AND WRESTED DOMINANCE OF THE PLANET AWAY FROM THEM.
AT LEAST, THEY EVENTUALLY DISAPPEARED. PERHAPS RETURNING TO THE DISTANT GALAXY FROM WHENCE THEY CAME, LEAVING BEHIND SOME OF THE STRANGELY MUTATED GUINEA PIGS TO GUARD CERTAIN ARTICLES AGAINST THEIR RETURN. THE SPIDERWOMAN MUST HAVE BEEN ONE SUCH OF THESE UNFORTUNATE WRETCHES. LIVING FOR AGES BENEATH THE DEAD CITY LURING OTHER TRAVELERS THE SAME WAY SHE DID BAYLYK WITH HER CROONING CALL.

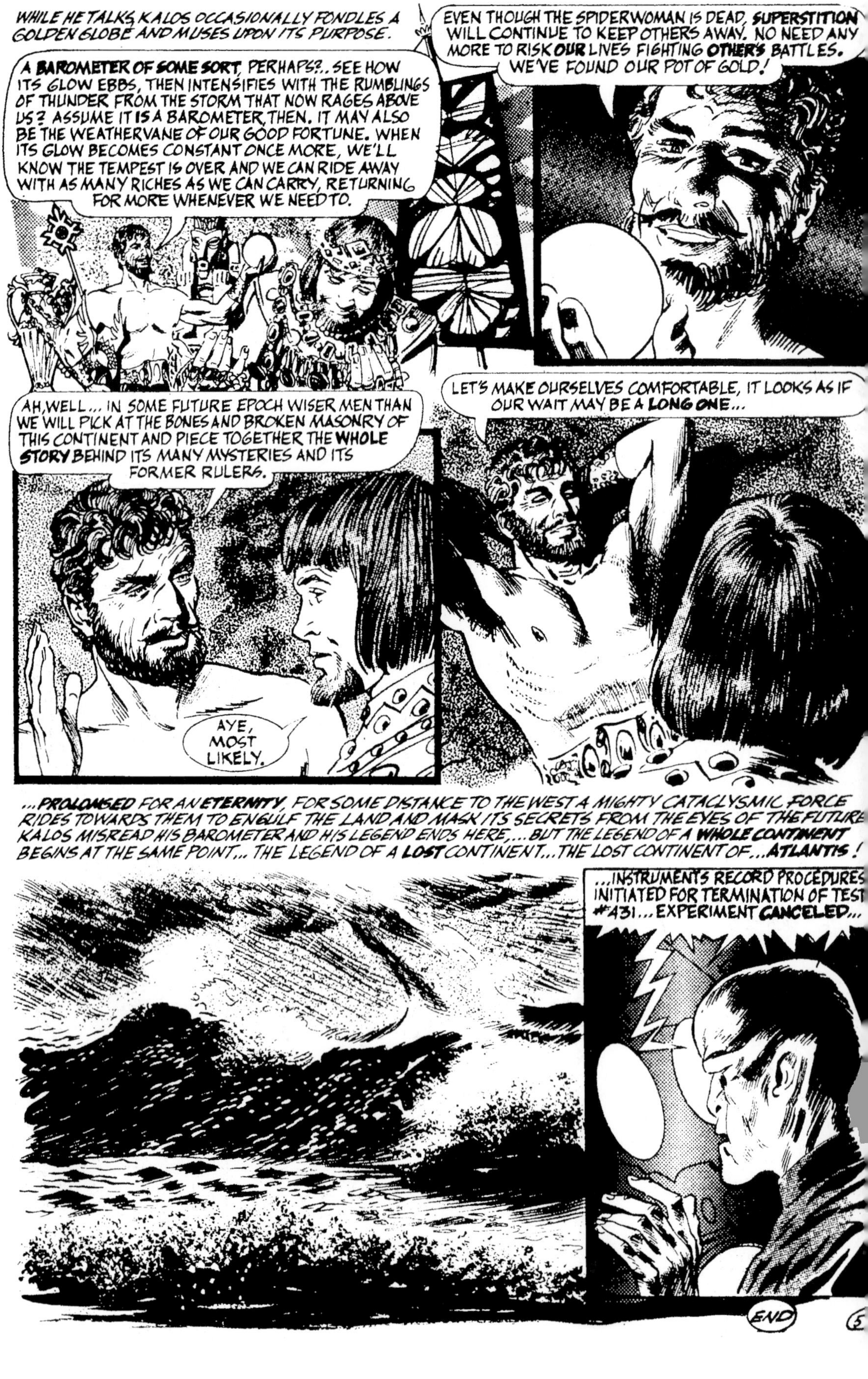

WHILE HE TALKS, KALOS OCCASIONALLY FONDLES A GOLDEN GLOBE AND MUSES UPON ITS PURPOSE.
A BAROMETER OF SOME SORT, PERHAPS?.. SEE HOW ITS GLOW EBBS, THEN INTENSIFIES WITH THE RUMBLINGS OF THUNDER FROM THE STORM THAT NOW RAGES ABOVE US? ASSUME IT IS A BAROMETER, THEN. IT MAY ALSO BE THE WEATHERVANE OF OUR GOOD FORTUNE. WHEN ITS GLOW BECOMES CONSTANT ONCE MORE, WE'LL KNOW THE TEMPEST IS OVER AND WE CAN RIDE AWAY WITH AS MANY RICHES AS WE CAN CARRY, RETURNING FOR MORE WHENEVER WE NEED TO.
EVEN THOUGH THE SPIDERWOMAN IS DEAD, SUPERSTITION WILL CONTINUE TO KEEP OTHERS AWAY. NO NEED ANY MORE TO RISK OUR LIVES FIGHTING OTHER'S BATTLES. WE'VE FOUND OUR POT OF GOLD!
AH, WELL... IN SOME FUTURE EPOCH WISER MEN THAN WE WILL PICK AT THE BONES AND BROKEN MASONRY OF THIS CONTINENT AND PIECE TOGETHER THE WHOLE STORY BEHIND ITS MANY MYSTERIES AND ITS FORMER RULERS.
AYE, MOST LIKELY.
LET'S MAKE OURSELVES COMFORTABLE, IT LOOKS AS IF OUR WAIT MAY BE A LONG ONE...
...PROLONGED FOR AN ETERNITY, FOR SOME DISTANCE TO THE WEST A MIGHTY CATACLYSMIC FORCE RIDES TOWARDS THEM TO ENGULF THE LAND AND MASK ITS SECRETS FROM THE EYES OF THE FUTURE. KALOS MISREAD HIS BAROMETER AND HIS LEGEND ENDS HERE,... BUT THE LEGEND OF A WHOLE CONTINENT BEGINS AT THE SAME POINT... THE LEGEND OF A LOST CONTINENT... THE LOST CONTINENT OF... ATLANTIS!
...INSTRUMENTS RECORD PROCEDURES INITIATED FOR TERMINATION OF TEST #431... EXPERIMENT CANCELED...
END

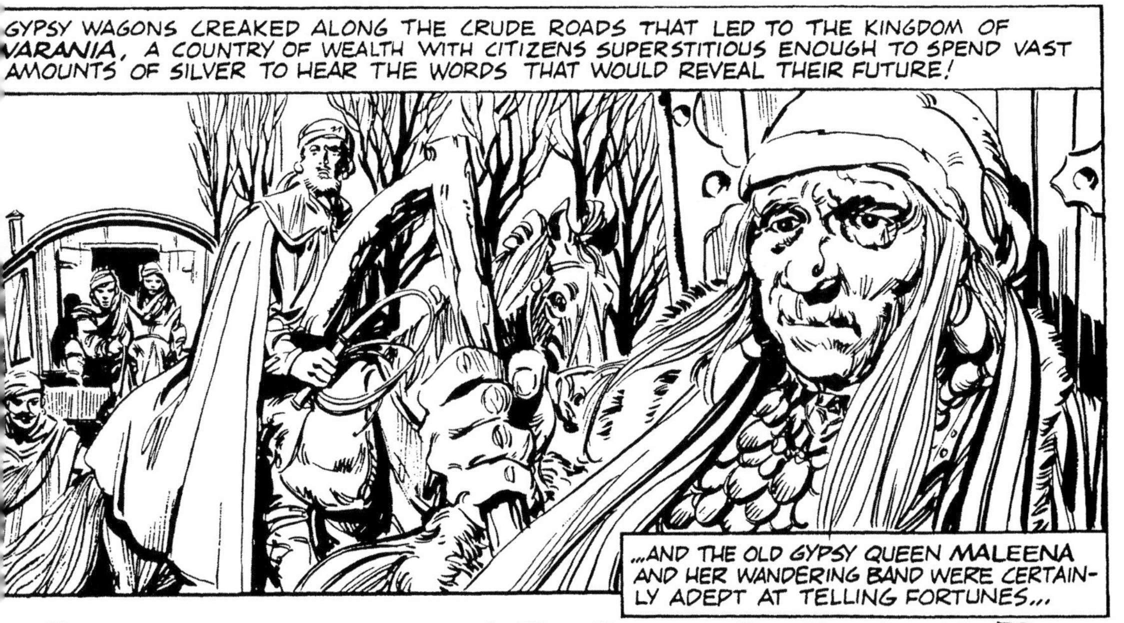
GYPSY WAGONS CREAKED ALONG THE CRUDE ROADS THAT LED TO THE KINGDOM OF VARANIA, A COUNTRY OF WEALTH WITH CITIZENS SUPERSTITIOUS ENOUGH TO SPEND VAST AMOUNTS OF SILVER TO HEAR THE WORDS THAT WOULD REVEAL THEIR FUTURE!
...AND THE OLD GYPSY QUEEN MALEENA AND HER WANDERING BAND WERE CERTAINLY ADEPT AT TELLING FORTUNES...

# THE CHOKER IS WILD

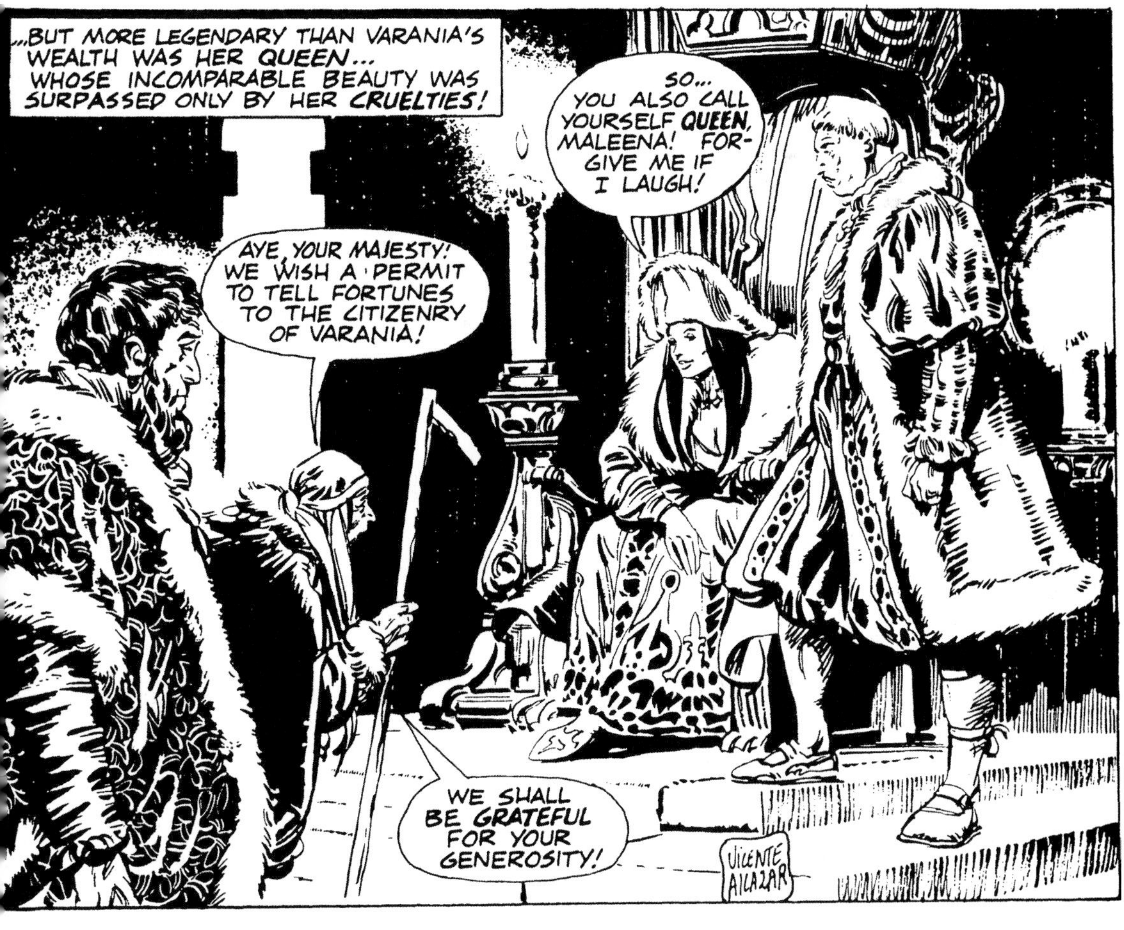
...BUT MORE LEGENDARY THAN VARANIA'S WEALTH WAS HER QUEEN... WHOSE INCOMPARABLE BEAUTY WAS SURPASSED ONLY BY HER CRUELTIES!
SO... YOU ALSO CALL YOURSELF QUEEN, MALEENA! FORGIVE ME IF I LAUGH!
AYE, YOUR MAJESTY! WE WISH A PERMIT TO TELL FORTUNES TO THE CITIZENRY OF VARANIA!
WE SHALL BE GRATEFUL FOR YOUR GENEROSITY!
VICENTE ALCAZAR

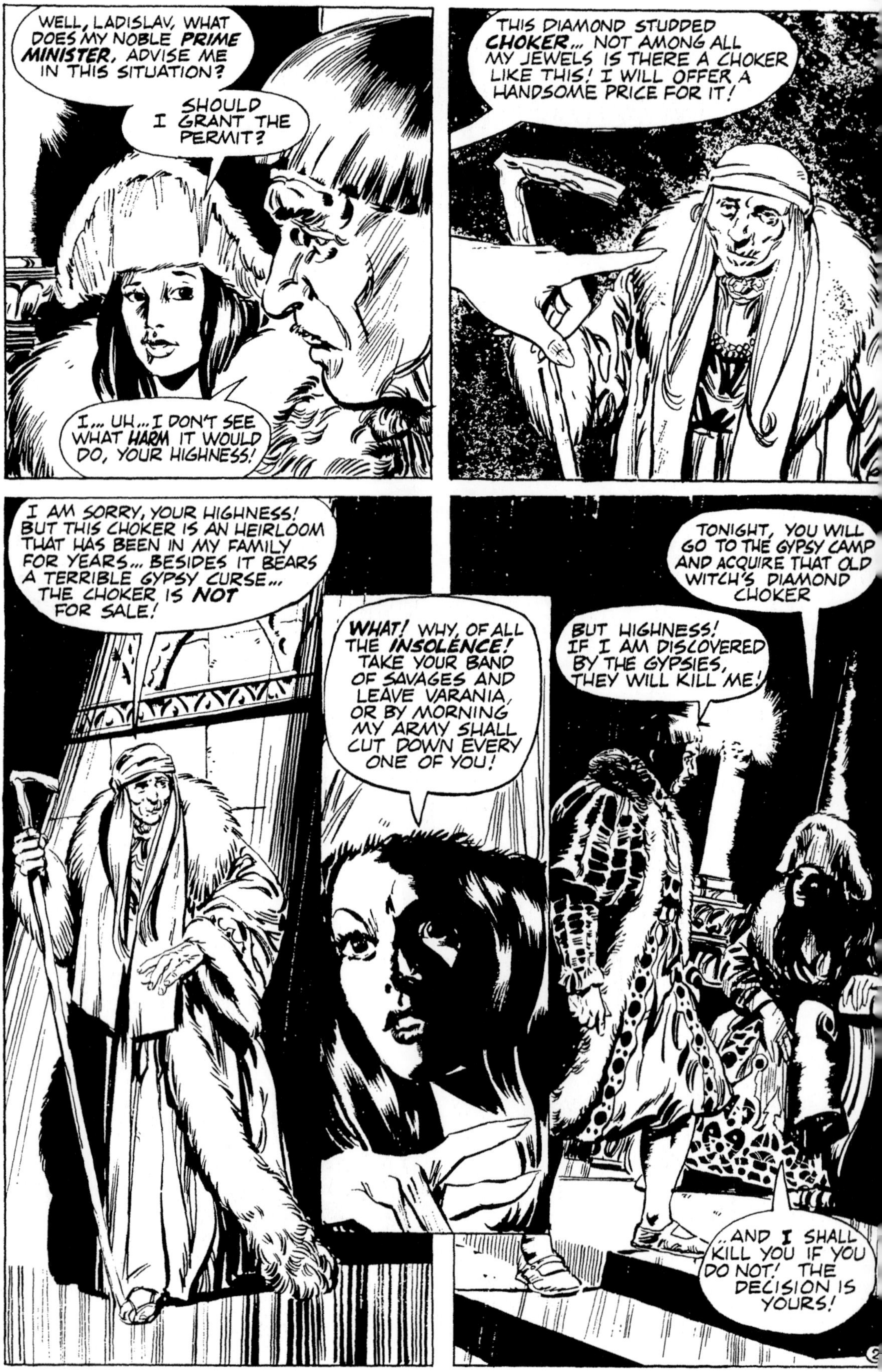
WELL, LADISLAV, WHAT DOES MY NOBLE PRIME MINISTER, ADVISE ME IN THIS SITUATION?
SHOULD I GRANT THE PERMIT?
I... UH... I DON'T SEE WHAT HARM IT WOULD DO, YOUR HIGHNESS!
THIS DIAMOND STUDDED CHOKER... NOT AMONG ALL MY JEWELS IS THERE A CHOKER LIKE THIS! I WILL OFFER A HANDSOME PRICE FOR IT!
I AM SORRY, YOUR HIGHNESS! BUT THIS CHOKER IS AN HEIRLOOM THAT HAS BEEN IN MY FAMILY FOR YEARS... BESIDES IT BEARS A TERRIBLE GYPSY CURSE... THE CHOKER IS NOT FOR SALE!
WHAT! WHY, OF ALL THE INSOLENCE! TAKE YOUR BAND OF SAVAGES AND LEAVE VARANIA, OR BY MORNING MY ARMY SHALL CUT DOWN EVERY ONE OF YOU!
TONIGHT, YOU WILL GO TO THE GYPSY CAMP AND ACQUIRE THAT OLD WITCH'S DIAMOND CHOKER
BUT HIGHNESS! IF I AM DISCOVERED BY THE GYPSIES, THEY WILL KILL ME!
...AND I SHALL KILL YOU IF YOU DO NOT! THE DECISION IS YOURS!

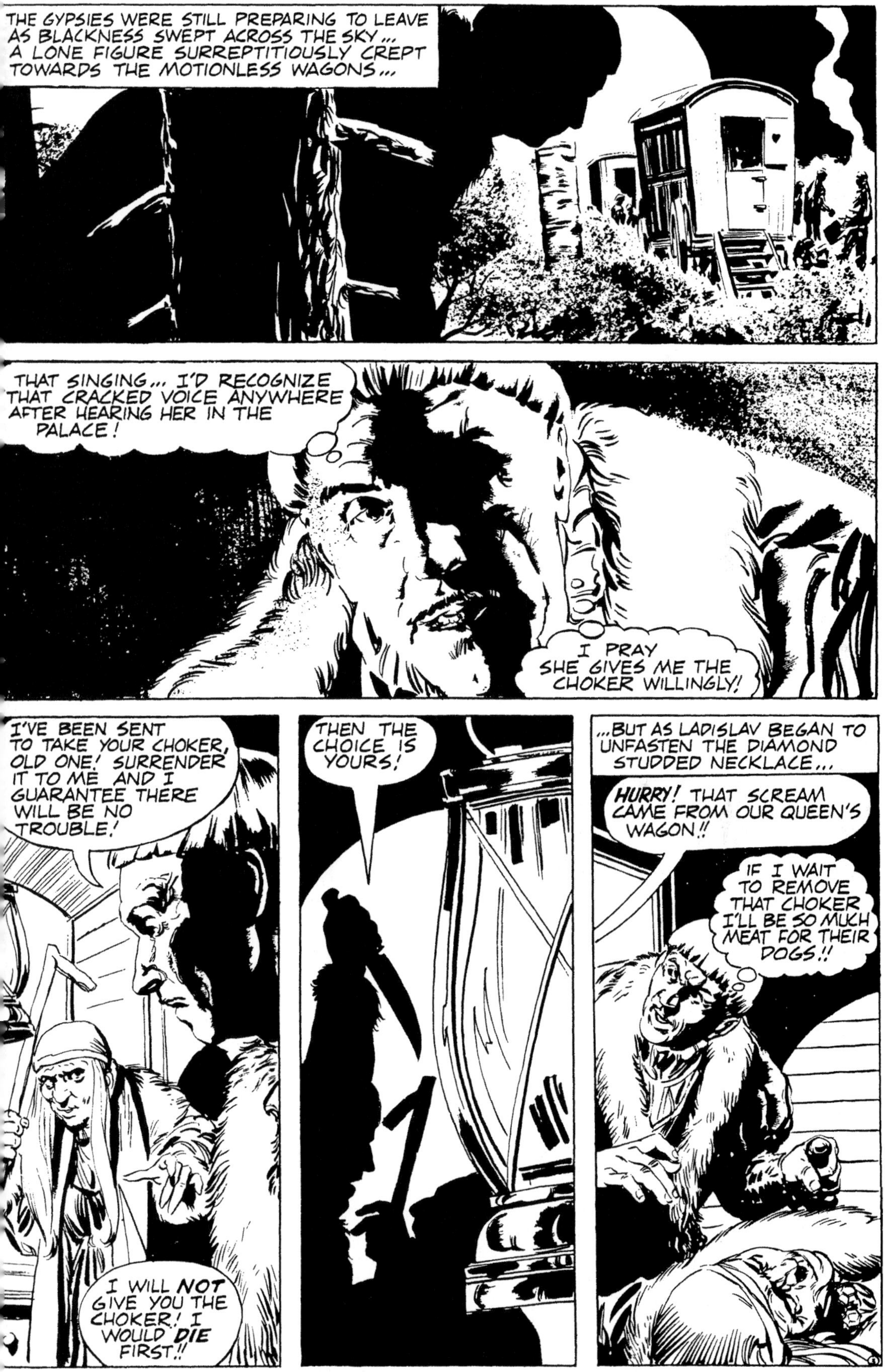
THE GYPSIES WERE STILL PREPARING TO LEAVE AS BLACKNESS SWEPT ACROSS THE SKY... A LONE FIGURE SURREPTITIOUSLY CREPT TOWARDS THE MOTIONLESS WAGONS...
THAT SINGING... I'D RECOGNIZE THAT CRACKED VOICE ANYWHERE AFTER HEARING HER IN THE PALACE!
I PRAY SHE GIVES ME THE CHOKER WILLINGLY!
I'VE BEEN SENT TO TAKE YOUR CHOKER, OLD ONE! SURRENDER IT TO ME AND I GUARANTEE THERE WILL BE NO TROUBLE!
I WILL **NOT** GIVE YOU THE CHOKER! I WOULD **DIE** FIRST!!
THEN THE CHOICE IS YOURS!
...BUT AS LADISLAV BEGAN TO UNFASTEN THE DIAMOND STUDDED NECKLACE...
**HURRY!** THAT SCREAM CAME FROM OUR QUEEN'S WAGON!!
IF I WAIT TO REMOVE THAT CHOKER I'LL BE SO MUCH MEAT FOR THEIR DOGS!!

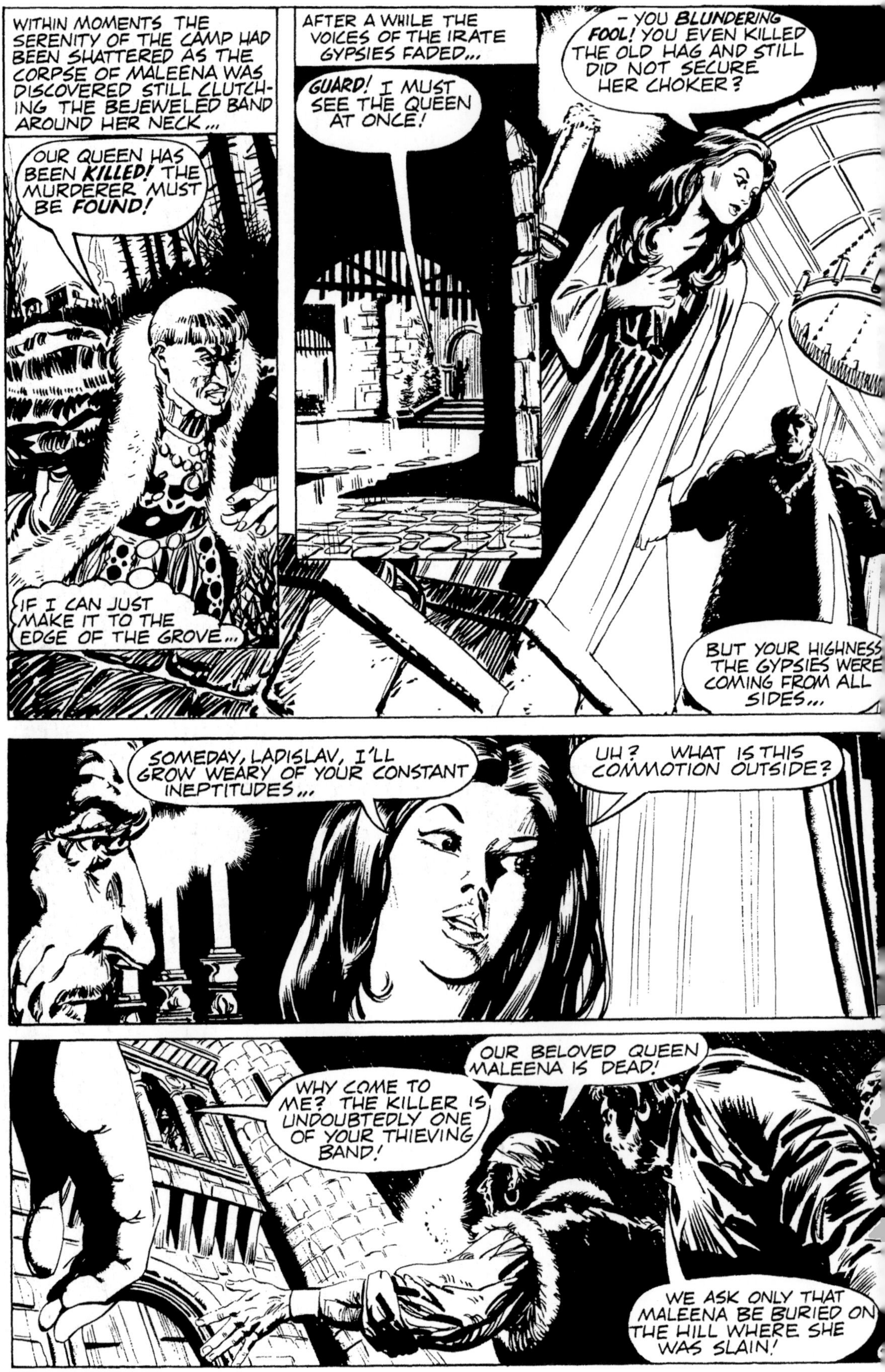
WITHIN MOMENTS THE SERENITY OF THE CAMP HAD BEEN SHATTERED AS THE CORPSE OF MALEENA WAS DISCOVERED STILL CLUTCHING THE BEJEWELED BAND AROUND HER NECK...
OUR QUEEN HAS BEEN **KILLED!** THE MURDERER MUST BE **FOUND!**
IF I CAN JUST MAKE IT TO THE EDGE OF THE GROVE...
AFTER A WHILE THE VOICES OF THE IRATE GYPSIES FADED...
**GUARD!** I MUST SEE THE QUEEN AT ONCE!
- YOU **BLUNDERING FOOL!** YOU EVEN KILLED THE OLD HAG AND STILL DID NOT SECURE HER CHOKER?
BUT YOUR HIGHNESS THE GYPSIES WERE COMING FROM ALL SIDES...
SOMEDAY, LADISLAV, I'LL GROW WEARY OF YOUR CONSTANT INEPTITUDES...
UH? WHAT IS THIS COMMOTION OUTSIDE?
OUR BELOVED QUEEN MALEENA IS DEAD!
WHY COME TO ME? THE KILLER IS UNDOUBTEDLY ONE OF YOUR THIEVING BAND!
WE ASK ONLY THAT MALEENA BE BURIED ON THE HILL WHERE SHE WAS SLAIN!

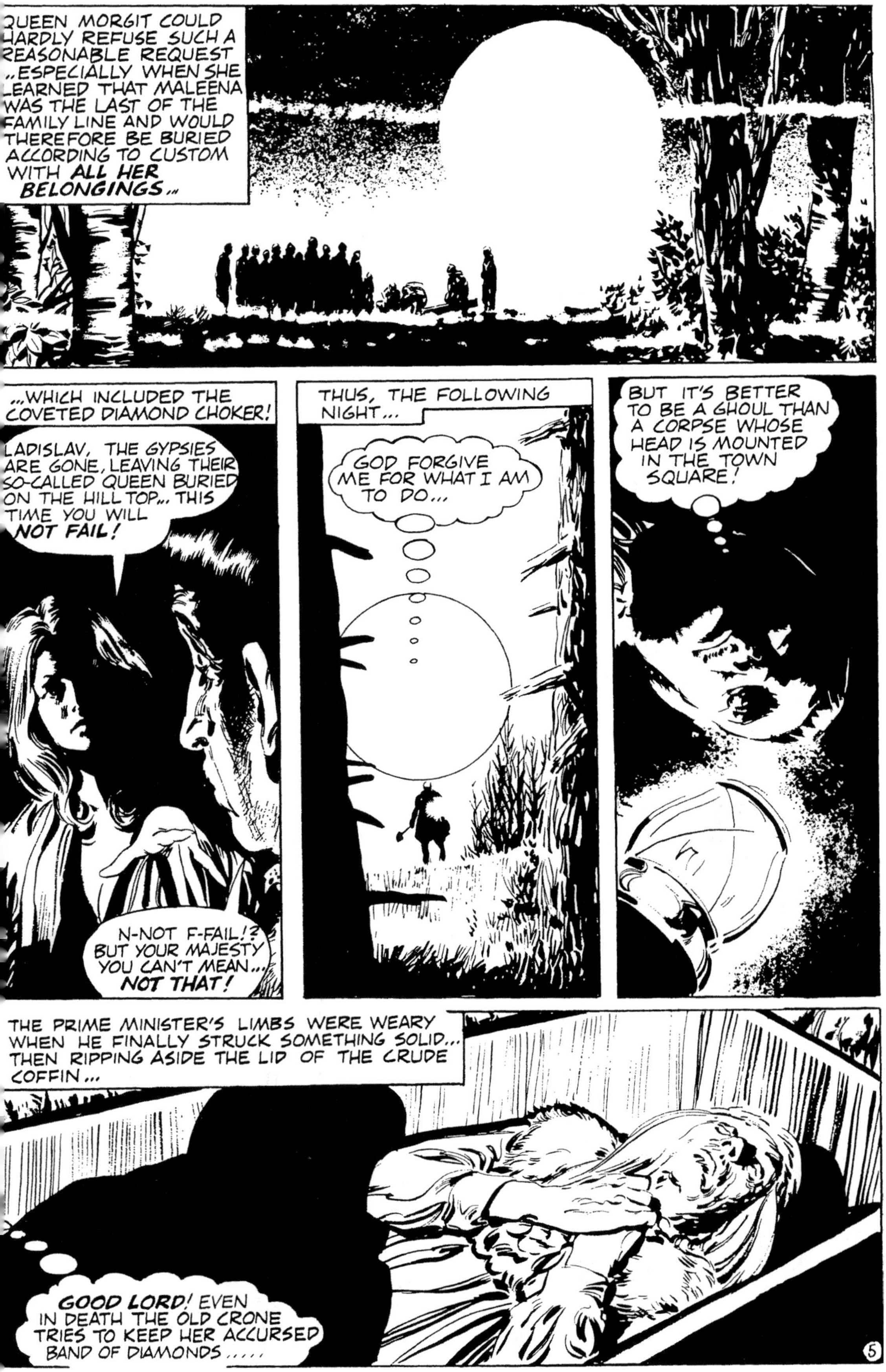
QUEEN MORGIT COULD HARDLY REFUSE SUCH A REASONABLE REQUEST ..ESPECIALLY WHEN SHE LEARNED THAT MALEENA WAS THE LAST OF THE FAMILY LINE AND WOULD THEREFORE BE BURIED ACCORDING TO CUSTOM WITH ALL HER BELONGINGS...
...WHICH INCLUDED THE COVETED DIAMOND CHOKER!
LADISLAV, THE GYPSIES ARE GONE, LEAVING THEIR SO-CALLED QUEEN BURIED ON THE HILL TOP... THIS TIME YOU WILL NOT FAIL!
N-NOT F-FAIL!? BUT YOUR MAJESTY YOU CAN'T MEAN... NOT THAT!
THUS, THE FOLLOWING NIGHT...
GOD FORGIVE ME FOR WHAT I AM TO DO...
BUT IT'S BETTER TO BE A GHOUL THAN A CORPSE WHOSE HEAD IS MOUNTED IN THE TOWN SQUARE!
THE PRIME MINISTER'S LIMBS WERE WEARY WHEN HE FINALLY STRUCK SOMETHING SOLID... THEN RIPPING ASIDE THE LID OF THE CRUDE COFFIN...
GOOD LORD! EVEN IN DEATH THE OLD CRONE TRIES TO KEEP HER ACCURSED BAND OF DIAMONDS.....
5

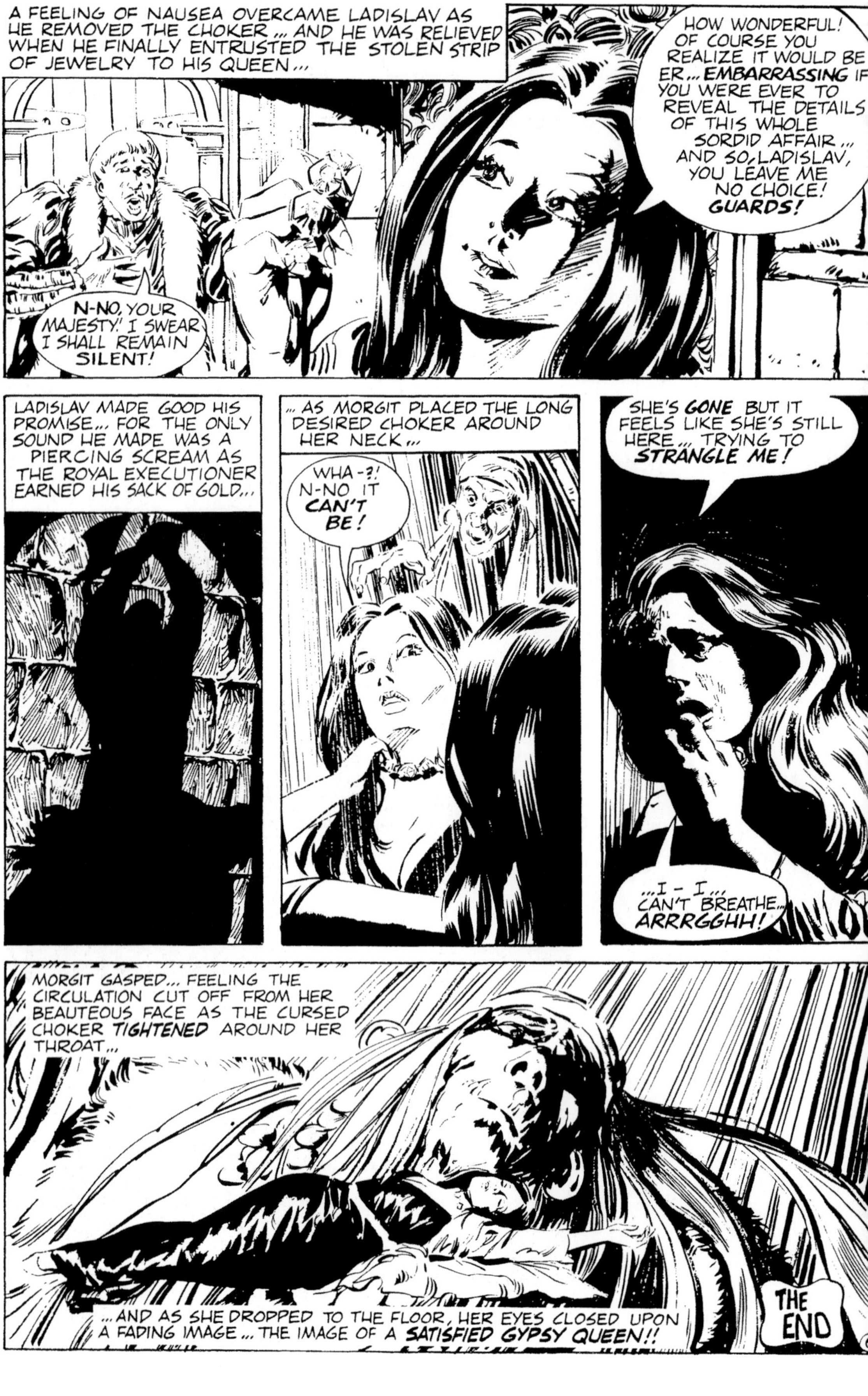

A FEELING OF NAUSEA OVERCAME LADISLAV AS HE REMOVED THE CHOKER ... AND HE WAS RELIEVED WHEN HE FINALLY ENTRUSTED THE STOLEN STRIP OF JEWELRY TO HIS QUEEN...
HOW WONDERFUL! OF COURSE YOU REALIZE IT WOULD BE ER... EMBARRASSING IF YOU WERE EVER TO REVEAL THE DETAILS OF THIS WHOLE SORDID AFFAIR... AND SO, LADISLAV, YOU LEAVE ME NO CHOICE! GUARDS!
N-NO, YOUR MAJESTY! I SWEAR I SHALL REMAIN SILENT!
LADISLAV MADE GOOD HIS PROMISE... FOR THE ONLY SOUND HE MADE WAS A PIERCING SCREAM AS THE ROYAL EXECUTIONER EARNED HIS SACK OF GOLD...
... AS MORGIT PLACED THE LONG DESIRED CHOKER AROUND HER NECK...
WHA-?! N-NO IT CAN'T BE!
SHE'S GONE BUT IT FEELS LIKE SHE'S STILL HERE... TRYING TO STRANGLE ME!
...I - I... CAN'T BREATHE... ARRRGGHH!
MORGIT GASPED... FEELING THE CIRCULATION CUT OFF FROM HER BEAUTEOUS FACE AS THE CURSED CHOKER TIGHTENED AROUND HER THROAT...
...AND AS SHE DROPPED TO THE FLOOR, HER EYES CLOSED UPON A FADING IMAGE... THE IMAGE OF A SATISFIED GYPSY QUEEN!!
THE END

# ESSAYS INTO THE SUPERNATURAL
# DRAGONS

IN PRIMITIVE TIMES THE HEROES OF VARIOUS TRIBES WOULD DRESS THEMSELVES IN THE FURS AND FEATHERS, TEETH AND CLAWS, SKINS AND HORNS OF THE ANIMAL MOST ADMIRED BY THE TRIBE. THIS TRIBAL REPRESENTATION WAS CALLED THE TOTEM.

THE TOTEM STOOD FOR IDEAL QUALITIES IN THE EYES OF THE TRIBE. A LION WOULD SYMBOLIZE COURAGE, AN EAGLE FREEDOM. A BULL STRENGTH. THE TRIBAL CHAMPION, DRESSED AS THE TOTEM ANIMAL, CARRIED THE FORTUNES OF HIS PEOPLE WITH HIM INTO BATTLE.

THE FEARSOME APPEARANCE OF THE ANIMAL-GARBED HERO WAS MEANT TO FRIGHTEN AND OVERWHELM ENEMIES. **ALL** TOTEMS HAD GREAT POWER, AND EVEN THE **LOSING** TOTEM WAS NOT ELIMINATED! IT WAS COMBINED WITH THE WINNING ONE, CREATING A SYMBOL THAT WAS **TWICE** AS POWERFUL!

THE NEW TOTEMS WERE MYTHIC ANIMALS WITH THE FEATURES OF **BOTH** TRIBAL BEASTS. THE **GRIFFIN** WAS EAGLE PLUS LION! THE **CHIMERA** WAS LION, GOAT, AND SNAKE - **THREE** TOTEMS COMBINED! AND PERHAPS THE MOST AWESOME TOTEM OF ALL WAS THE LION-HEADED, SNAKE-BODIED, EAGLE-WINGED **DRAGON!**

SEULING + GRAY MORROW

WHAT DID IT LOOK LIKE - THAT TERRIBLE APPARITION THAT MOVED OUT OF THE MORNING MISTS TO CHALLENGE **ST. GEORGE** ?

# ISSUE SIX

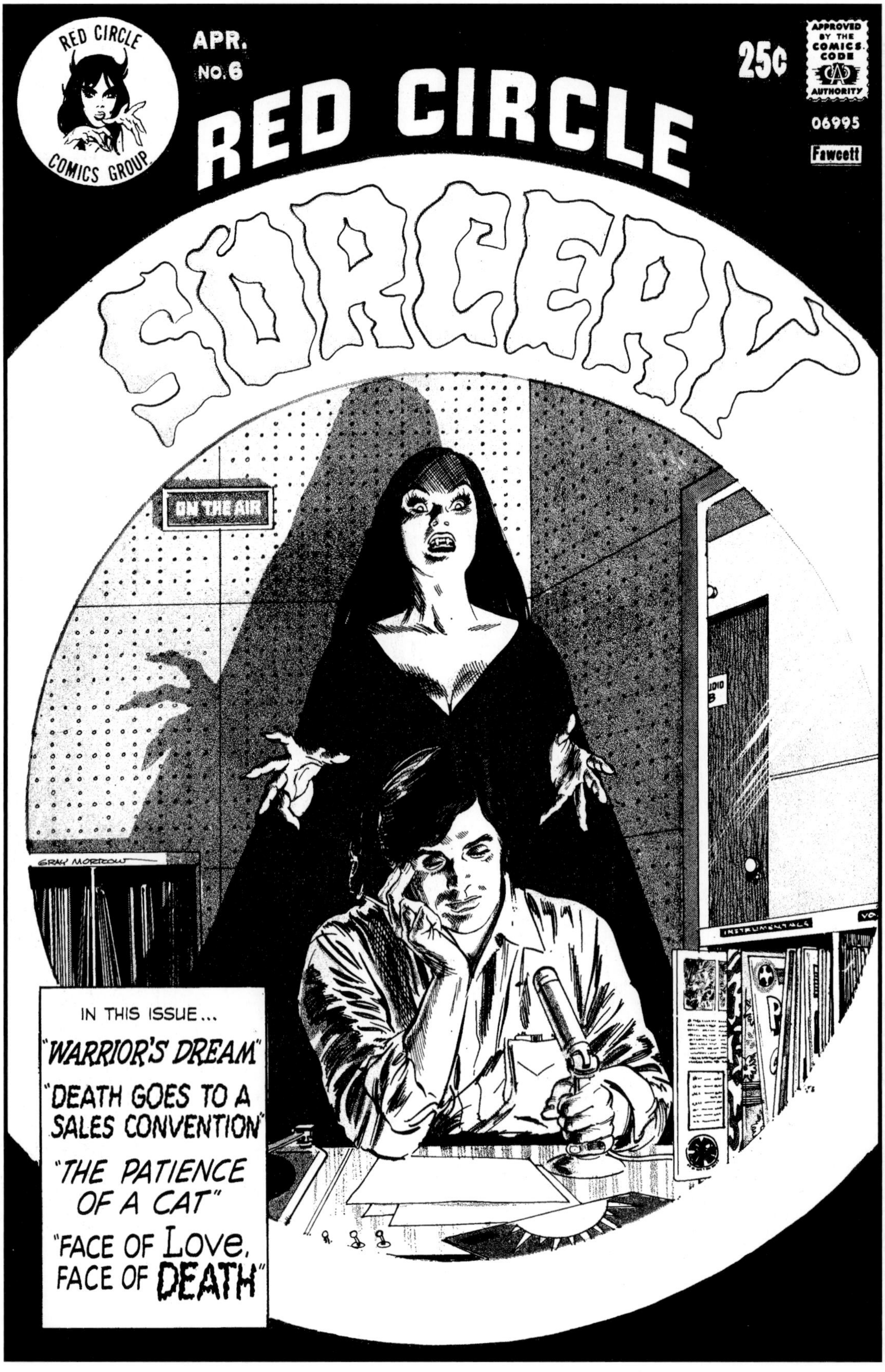
RED CIRCLE COMICS GROUP
APR.
NO. 6
25¢
APPROVED BY THE COMICS CODE AUTHORITY
06995
Fawcett
RED CIRCLE
SORCERY
ON THE AIR
GRAY MORROW
IN THIS ISSUE...
"WARRIOR'S DREAM"
"DEATH GOES TO A SALES CONVENTION"
"THE PATIENCE OF A CAT"
"FACE OF Love, FACE OF DEATH"

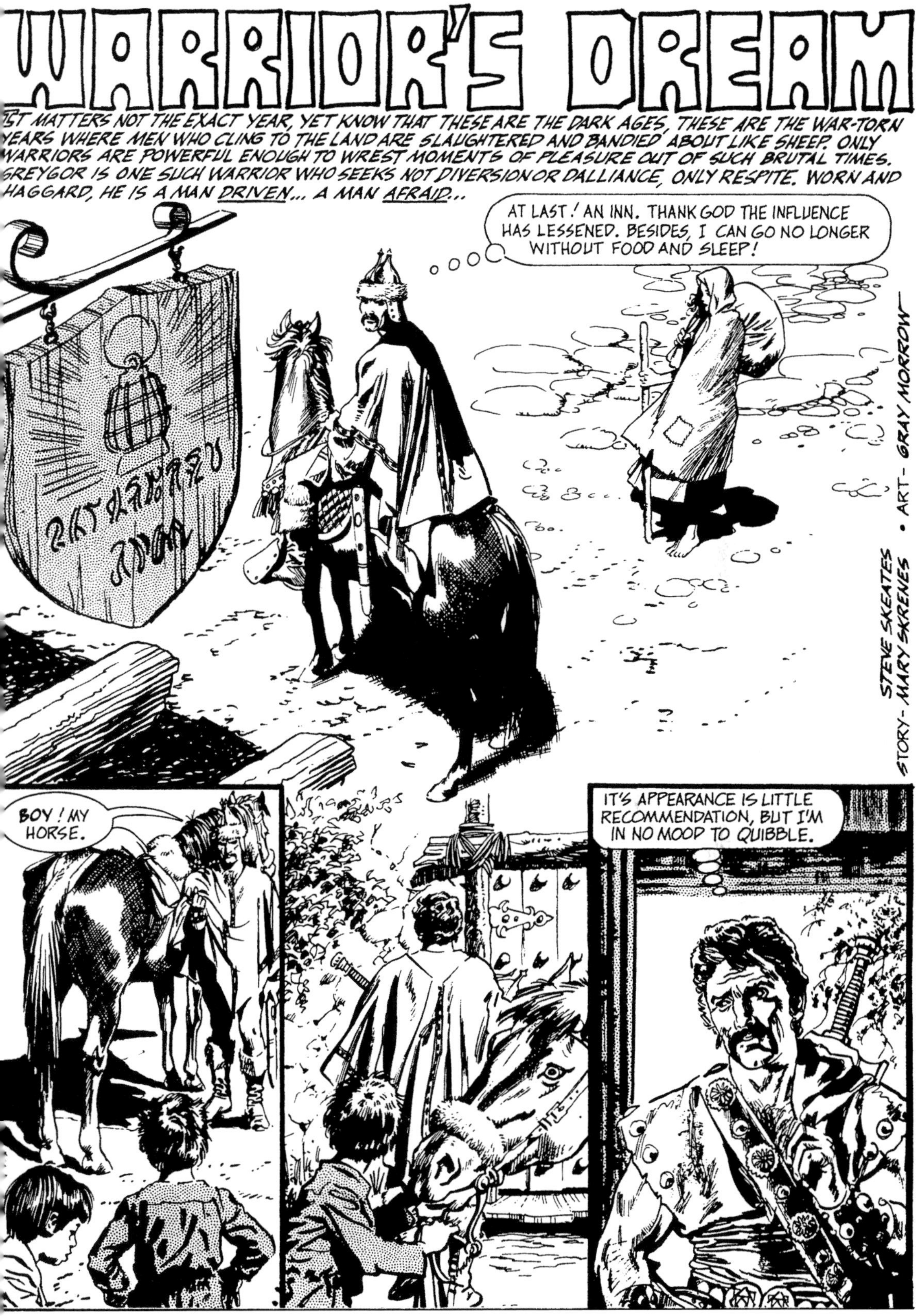
WARRIOR'S DREAM
IT MATTERS NOT THE EXACT YEAR, YET KNOW THAT THESE ARE THE DARK AGES, THESE ARE THE WAR-TORN YEARS WHERE MEN WHO CLING TO THE LAND ARE SLAUGHTERED AND BANDIED ABOUT LIKE SHEEP. ONLY WARRIORS ARE POWERFUL ENOUGH TO WREST MOMENTS OF PLEASURE OUT OF SUCH BRUTAL TIMES. GREYGOR IS ONE SUCH WARRIOR WHO SEEKS NOT DIVERSION OR DALLIANCE, ONLY RESPITE. WORN AND HAGGARD, HE IS A MAN DRIVEN... A MAN AFRAID...
AT LAST! AN INN. THANK GOD THE INFLUENCE HAS LESSENED. BESIDES, I CAN GO NO LONGER WITHOUT FOOD AND SLEEP!
STORY- STEVE SKEATES MARY SKRENES • ART- GRAY MORROW
BOY! MY HORSE.
IT'S APPEARANCE IS LITTLE RECOMMENDATION, BUT I'M IN NO MOOD TO QUIBBLE.

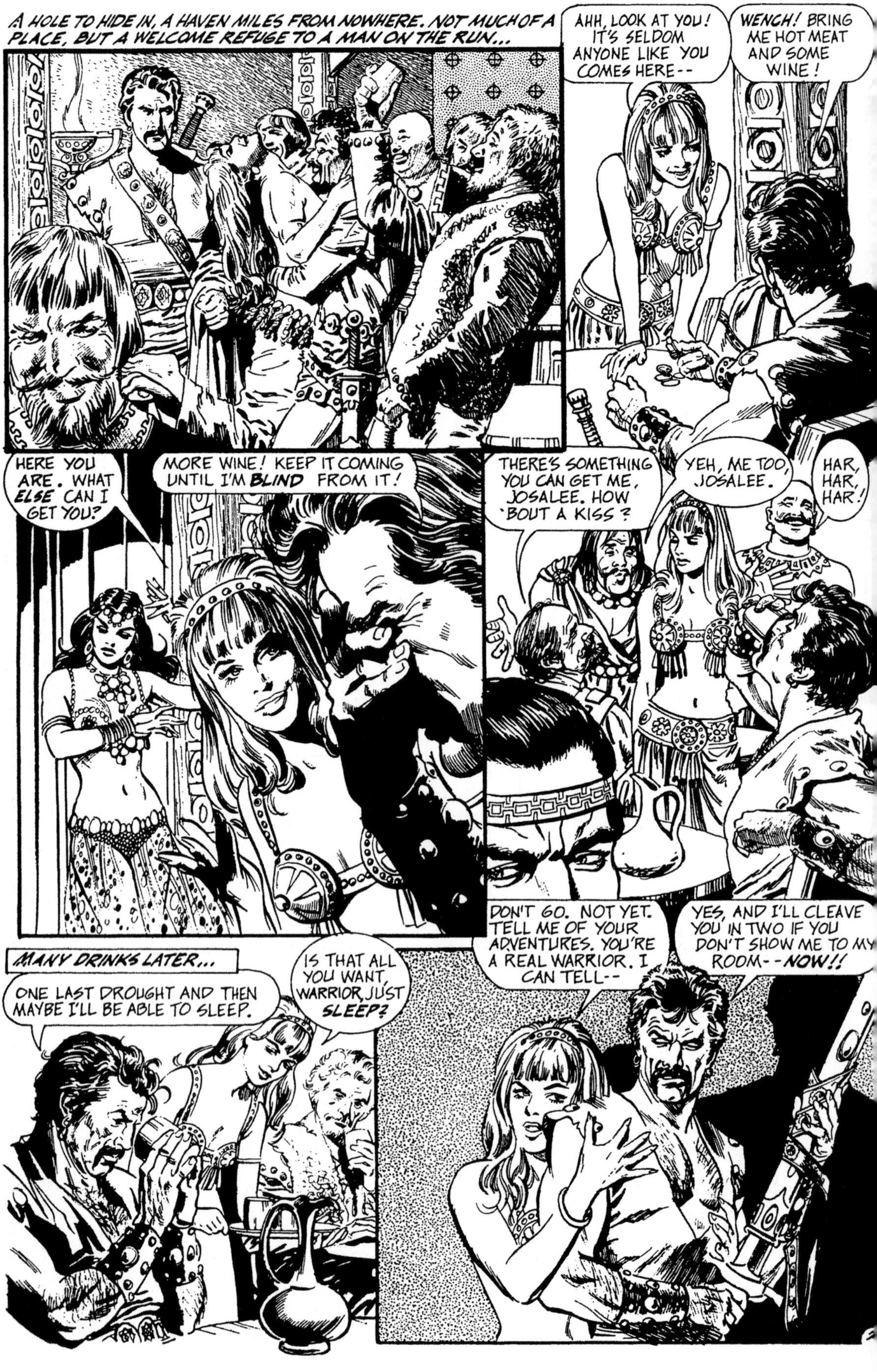

A HOLE TO HIDE IN, A HAVEN MILES FROM NOWHERE. NOT MUCH OF A PLACE, BUT A WELCOME REFUGE TO A MAN ON THE RUN...
AHH, LOOK AT YOU! IT'S SELDOM ANYONE LIKE YOU COMES HERE--
WENCH! BRING ME HOT MEAT AND SOME WINE!
HERE YOU ARE. WHAT ELSE CAN I GET YOU?
MORE WINE! KEEP IT COMING UNTIL I'M BLIND FROM IT!
THERE'S SOMETHING YOU CAN GET ME, JOSALEE. HOW 'BOUT A KISS?
YEH, ME TOO, JOSALEE.
HAR, HAR, HAR!
MANY DRINKS LATER...
ONE LAST DROUGHT AND THEN MAYBE I'LL BE ABLE TO SLEEP.
IS THAT ALL YOU WANT, WARRIOR, JUST SLEEP?
DON'T GO. NOT YET. TELL ME OF YOUR ADVENTURES. YOU'RE A REAL WARRIOR. I CAN TELL--
YES, AND I'LL CLEAVE YOU IN TWO IF YOU DON'T SHOW ME TO MY ROOM--NOW!!

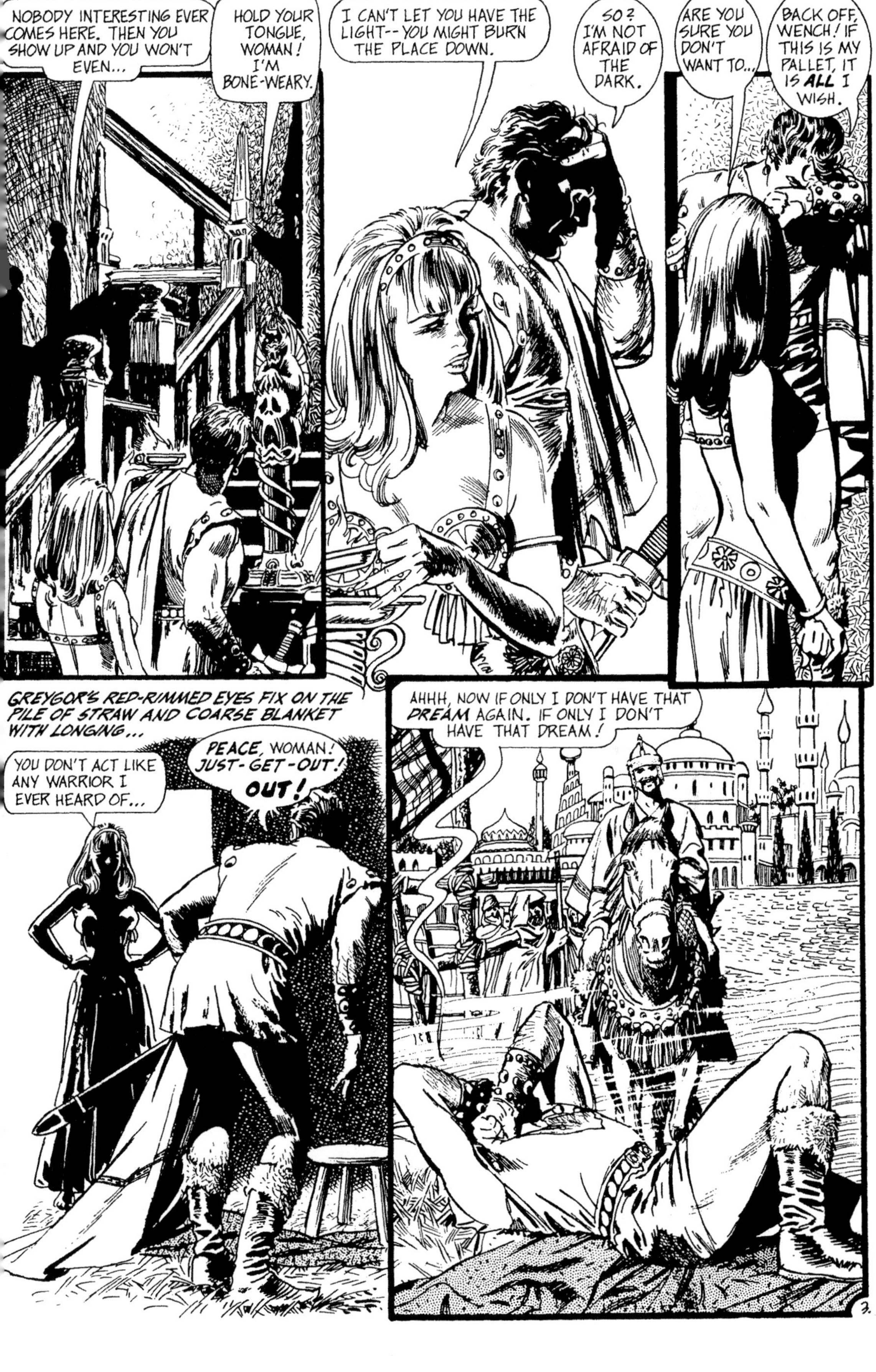
NOBODY INTERESTING EVER COMES HERE. THEN YOU SHOW UP AND YOU WON'T EVEN...
HOLD YOUR TONGUE, WOMAN! I'M BONE-WEARY.
I CAN'T LET YOU HAVE THE LIGHT--YOU MIGHT BURN THE PLACE DOWN.
SO? I'M NOT AFRAID OF THE DARK.
ARE YOU SURE YOU DON'T WANT TO...
BACK OFF, WENCH! IF THIS IS MY PALLET, IT IS ALL I WISH.
GREYGOR'S RED-RIMMED EYES FIX ON THE PILE OF STRAW AND COARSE BLANKET WITH LONGING...
YOU DON'T ACT LIKE ANY WARRIOR I EVER HEARD OF...
PEACE, WOMAN! JUST-GET-OUT! OUT!
AHHH, NOW IF ONLY I DON'T HAVE THAT DREAM AGAIN. IF ONLY I DON'T HAVE THAT DREAM!

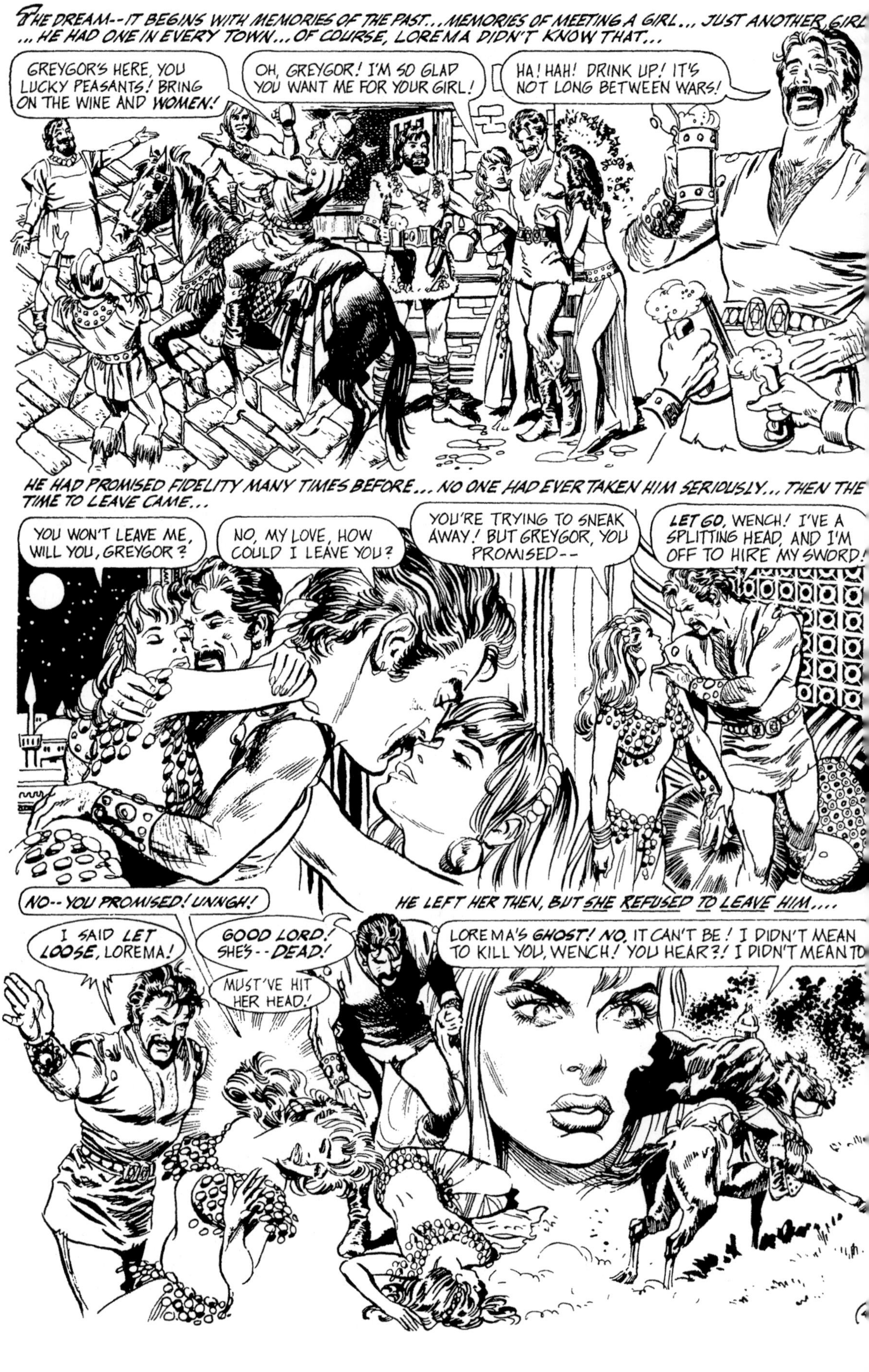
THE DREAM--IT BEGINS WITH MEMORIES OF THE PAST... MEMORIES OF MEETING A GIRL... JUST ANOTHER GIRL ... HE HAD ONE IN EVERY TOWN... OF COURSE, LOREMA DIDN'T KNOW THAT...
GREYGOR'S HERE, YOU LUCKY PEASANTS! BRING ON THE WINE AND WOMEN!
OH, GREYGOR! I'M SO GLAD YOU WANT ME FOR YOUR GIRL!
HA! HAH! DRINK UP! IT'S NOT LONG BETWEEN WARS!
HE HAD PROMISED FIDELITY MANY TIMES BEFORE... NO ONE HAD EVER TAKEN HIM SERIOUSLY... THEN THE TIME TO LEAVE CAME...
YOU WON'T LEAVE ME, WILL YOU, GREYGOR?
NO, MY LOVE, HOW COULD I LEAVE YOU?
YOU'RE TRYING TO SNEAK AWAY! BUT GREYGOR, YOU PROMISED--
LET GO, WENCH! I'VE A SPLITTING HEAD, AND I'M OFF TO HIRE MY SWORD!
NO--YOU PROMISED! UNNGH!
HE LEFT HER THEN, BUT SHE REFUSED TO LEAVE HIM....
I SAID LET LOOSE, LOREMA!
GOOD LORD! SHE'S--DEAD!
MUST'VE HIT HER HEAD!
LOREMA'S GHOST! NO, IT CAN'T BE! I DIDN'T MEAN TO KILL YOU, WENCH! YOU HEAR?! I DIDN'T MEAN TO

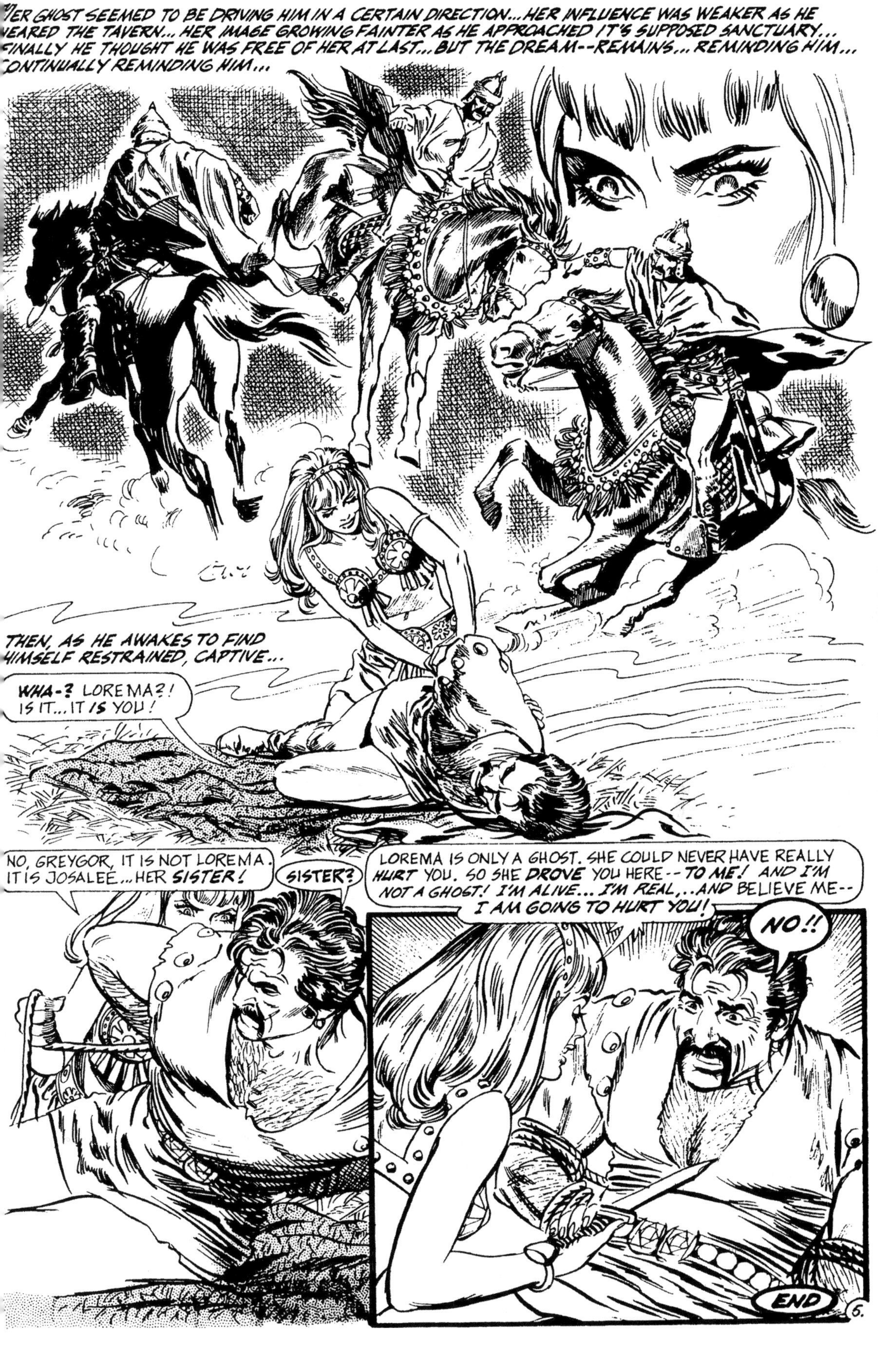
HER GHOST SEEMED TO BE DRIVING HIM IN A CERTAIN DIRECTION... HER INFLUENCE WAS WEAKER AS HE NEARED THE TAVERN... HER IMAGE GROWING FAINTER AS HE APPROACHED IT'S SUPPOSED SANCTUARY... FINALLY HE THOUGHT HE WAS FREE OF HER AT LAST... BUT THE DREAM--REMAINS... REMINDING HIM... CONTINUALLY REMINDING HIM...
THEN, AS HE AWAKES TO FIND HIMSELF RESTRAINED, CAPTIVE...
WHA-? LOREMA?! IS IT... IT IS YOU!
NO, GREYGOR, IT IS NOT LOREMA. IT IS JOSALEE... HER SISTER!
SISTER?
LOREMA IS ONLY A GHOST. SHE COULD NEVER HAVE REALLY HURT YOU. SO SHE DROVE YOU HERE--TO ME! AND I'M NOT A GHOST! I'M ALIVE... I'M REAL,... AND BELIEVE ME-- I AM GOING TO HURT YOU!
NO!!
END

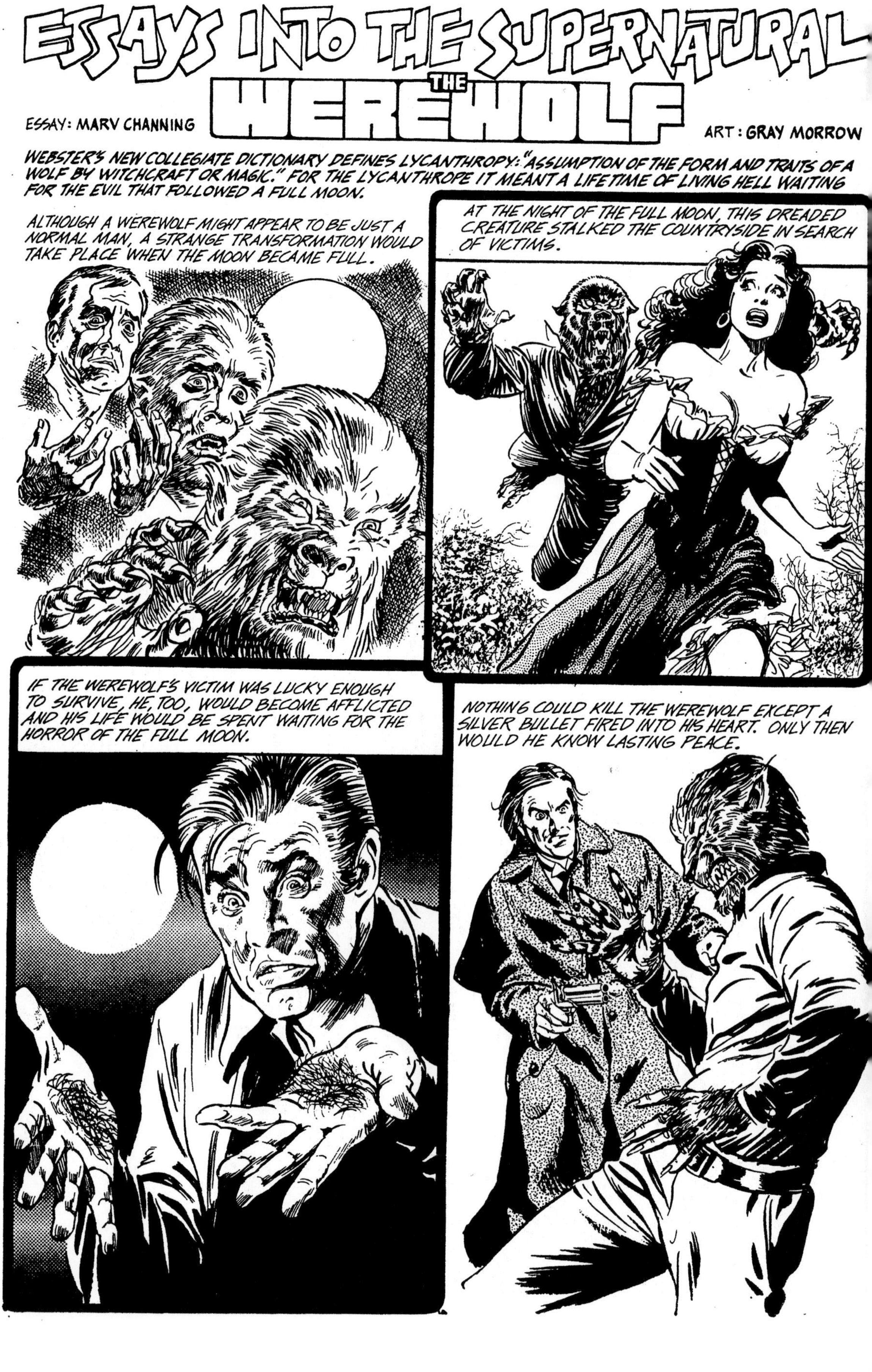
ESSAYS INTO THE SUPERNATURAL
THE WEREWOLF
ESSAY: MARV CHANNING
ART: GRAY MORROW
WEBSTER'S NEW COLLEGIATE DICTIONARY DEFINES LYCANTHROPY: "ASSUMPTION OF THE FORM AND TRAITS OF A WOLF BY WITCHCRAFT OR MAGIC." FOR THE LYCANTHROPE IT MEANT A LIFETIME OF LIVING HELL WAITING FOR THE EVIL THAT FOLLOWED A FULL MOON.
ALTHOUGH A WEREWOLF MIGHT APPEAR TO BE JUST A NORMAL MAN, A STRANGE TRANSFORMATION WOULD TAKE PLACE WHEN THE MOON BECAME FULL.
AT THE NIGHT OF THE FULL MOON, THIS DREADED CREATURE STALKED THE COUNTRYSIDE IN SEARCH OF VICTIMS.
IF THE WEREWOLF'S VICTIM WAS LUCKY ENOUGH TO SURVIVE, HE, TOO, WOULD BECOME AFFLICTED AND HIS LIFE WOULD BE SPENT WAITING FOR THE HORROR OF THE FULL MOON.
NOTHING COULD KILL THE WEREWOLF EXCEPT A SILVER BULLET FIRED INTO HIS HEART. ONLY THEN WOULD HE KNOW LASTING PEACE.

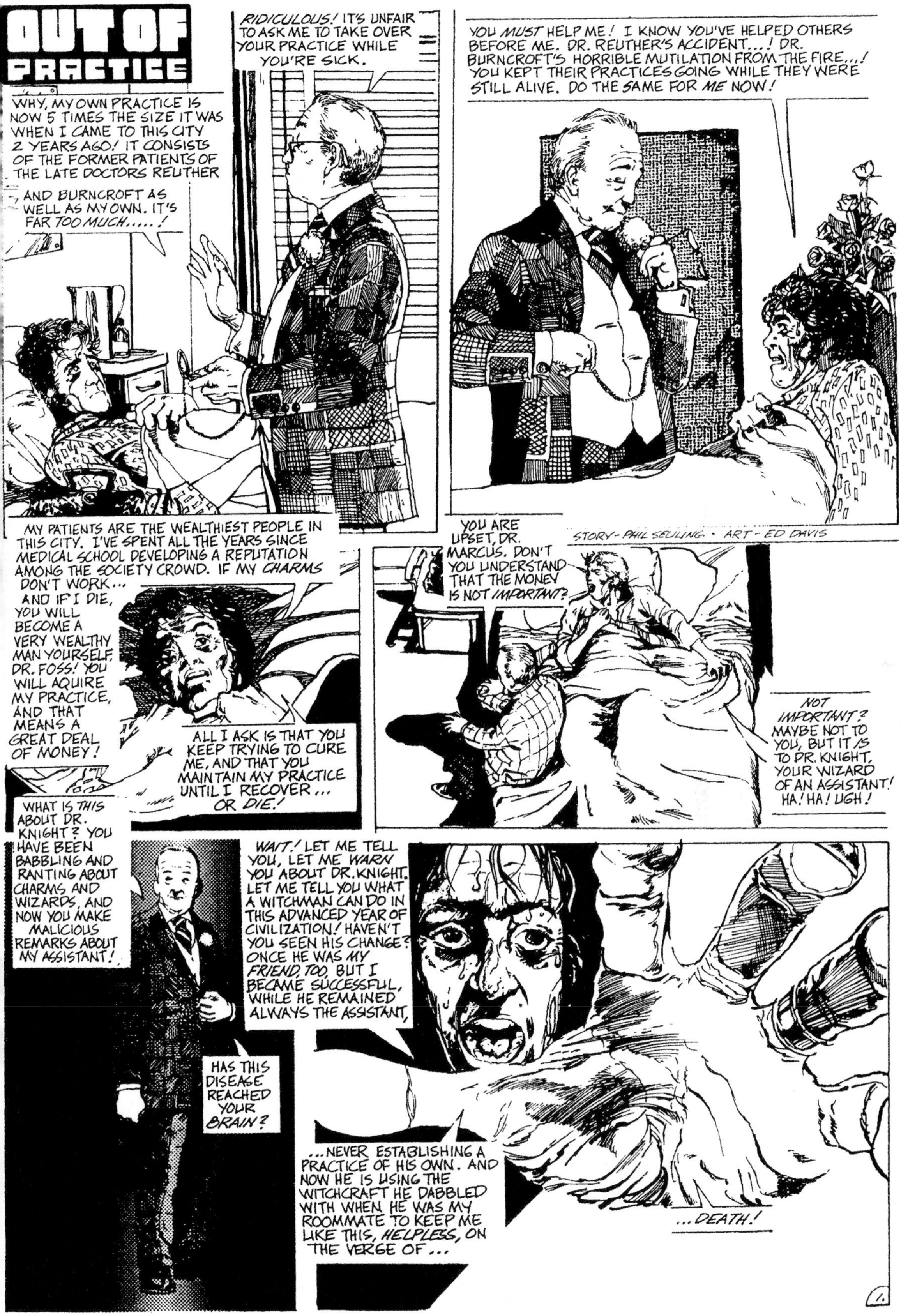
OUT OF PRACTICE
RIDICULOUS! IT'S UNFAIR TO ASK ME TO TAKE OVER YOUR PRACTICE WHILE YOU'RE SICK.
WHY, MY OWN PRACTICE IS NOW 5 TIMES THE SIZE IT WAS WHEN I CAME TO THIS CITY 2 YEARS AGO! IT CONSISTS OF THE FORMER PATIENTS OF THE LATE DOCTORS REUTHER
, AND BURNCROFT AS WELL AS MY OWN. IT'S FAR TOO MUCH.....!
YOU MUST HELP ME! I KNOW YOU'VE HELPED OTHERS BEFORE ME. DR. REUTHER'S ACCIDENT...! DR. BURNCROFT'S HORRIBLE MUTILATION FROM THE FIRE...! YOU KEPT THEIR PRACTICES GOING WHILE THEY WERE STILL ALIVE. DO THE SAME FOR ME NOW!
MY PATIENTS ARE THE WEALTHIEST PEOPLE IN THIS CITY. I'VE SPENT ALL THE YEARS SINCE MEDICAL SCHOOL DEVELOPING A REPUTATION AMONG THE SOCIETY CROWD. IF MY CHARMS DON'T WORK...
AND IF I DIE, YOU WILL BECOME A VERY WEALTHY MAN YOURSELF, DR. FOSS! YOU WILL AQUIRE MY PRACTICE, AND THAT MEANS A GREAT DEAL OF MONEY!
ALL I ASK IS THAT YOU KEEP TRYING TO CURE ME, AND THAT YOU MAINTAIN MY PRACTICE UNTIL I RECOVER... OR DIE!
YOU ARE UPSET, DR. MARCUS. DON'T YOU UNDERSTAND THAT THE MONEY IS NOT IMPORTANT?
STORY - PHIL SEULING • ART - ED DAVIS
NOT IMPORTANT? MAYBE NOT TO YOU, BUT IT IS TO DR. KNIGHT, YOUR WIZARD OF AN ASSISTANT! HA! HA! UGH!
WHAT IS THIS ABOUT DR. KNIGHT? YOU HAVE BEEN BABBLING AND RANTING ABOUT CHARMS AND WIZARDS, AND NOW YOU MAKE MALICIOUS REMARKS ABOUT MY ASSISTANT!
HAS THIS DISEASE REACHED YOUR BRAIN?
WAIT! LET ME TELL YOU, LET ME WARN YOU ABOUT DR. KNIGHT. LET ME TELL YOU WHAT A WITCHMAN CAN DO IN THIS ADVANCED YEAR OF CIVILIZATION! HAVEN'T YOU SEEN HIS CHANGE? ONCE HE WAS MY FRIEND, TOO, BUT I BECAME SUCCESSFUL, WHILE HE REMAINED ALWAYS THE ASSISTANT,
...NEVER ESTABLISHING A PRACTICE OF HIS OWN. AND NOW HE IS USING THE WITCHCRAFT HE DABBLED WITH WHEN HE WAS MY ROOMMATE TO KEEP ME LIKE THIS, HELPLESS, ON THE VERGE OF...
...DEATH!
1.

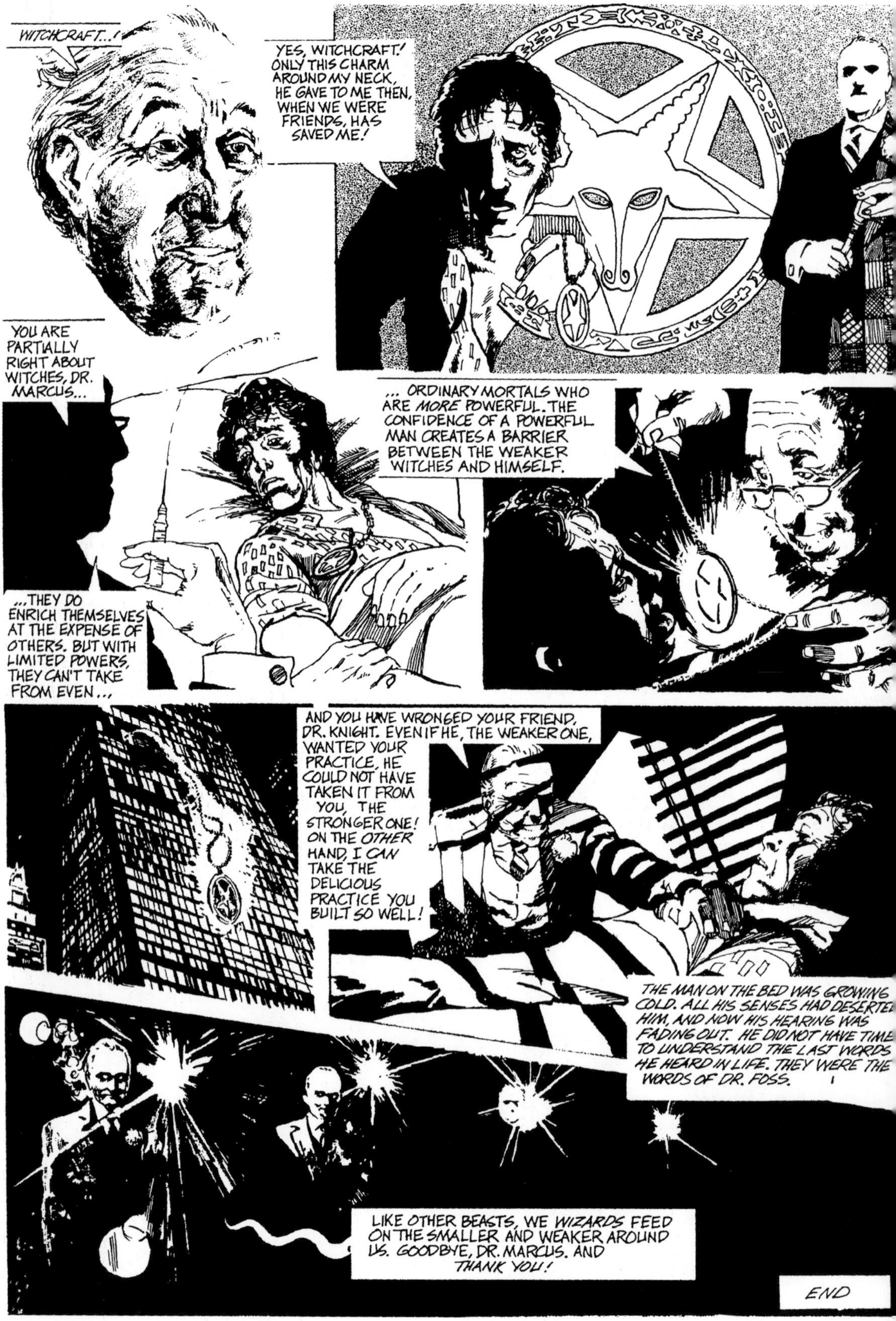

WITCHCRAFT...!
YES, WITCHCRAFT! ONLY THIS CHARM AROUND MY NECK, HE GAVE TO ME THEN, WHEN WE WERE FRIENDS, HAS SAVED ME!
YOU ARE PARTIALLY RIGHT ABOUT WITCHES, DR. MARCUS...
...THEY DO ENRICH THEMSELVES AT THE EXPENSE OF OTHERS. BUT WITH LIMITED POWERS, THEY CAN'T TAKE FROM EVEN...,
... ORDINARY MORTALS WHO ARE MORE POWERFUL. THE CONFIDENCE OF A POWERFUL MAN CREATES A BARRIER BETWEEN THE WEAKER WITCHES AND HIMSELF.
AND YOU HAVE WRONGED YOUR FRIEND, DR. KNIGHT. EVEN IF HE, THE WEAKER ONE, WANTED YOUR PRACTICE, HE COULD NOT HAVE TAKEN IT FROM YOU, THE STRONGER ONE! ON THE OTHER HAND, I CAN TAKE THE DELICIOUS PRACTICE YOU BUILT SO WELL!
THE MAN ON THE BED WAS GROWING COLD. ALL HIS SENSES HAD DESERTED HIM, AND NOW HIS HEARING WAS FADING OUT. HE DID NOT HAVE TIME TO UNDERSTAND THE LAST WORDS HE HEARD IN LIFE. THEY WERE THE WORDS OF DR. FOSS.
LIKE OTHER BEASTS, WE WIZARDS FEED ON THE SMALLER AND WEAKER AROUND US. GOODBYE, DR. MARCUS. AND THANK YOU!
END

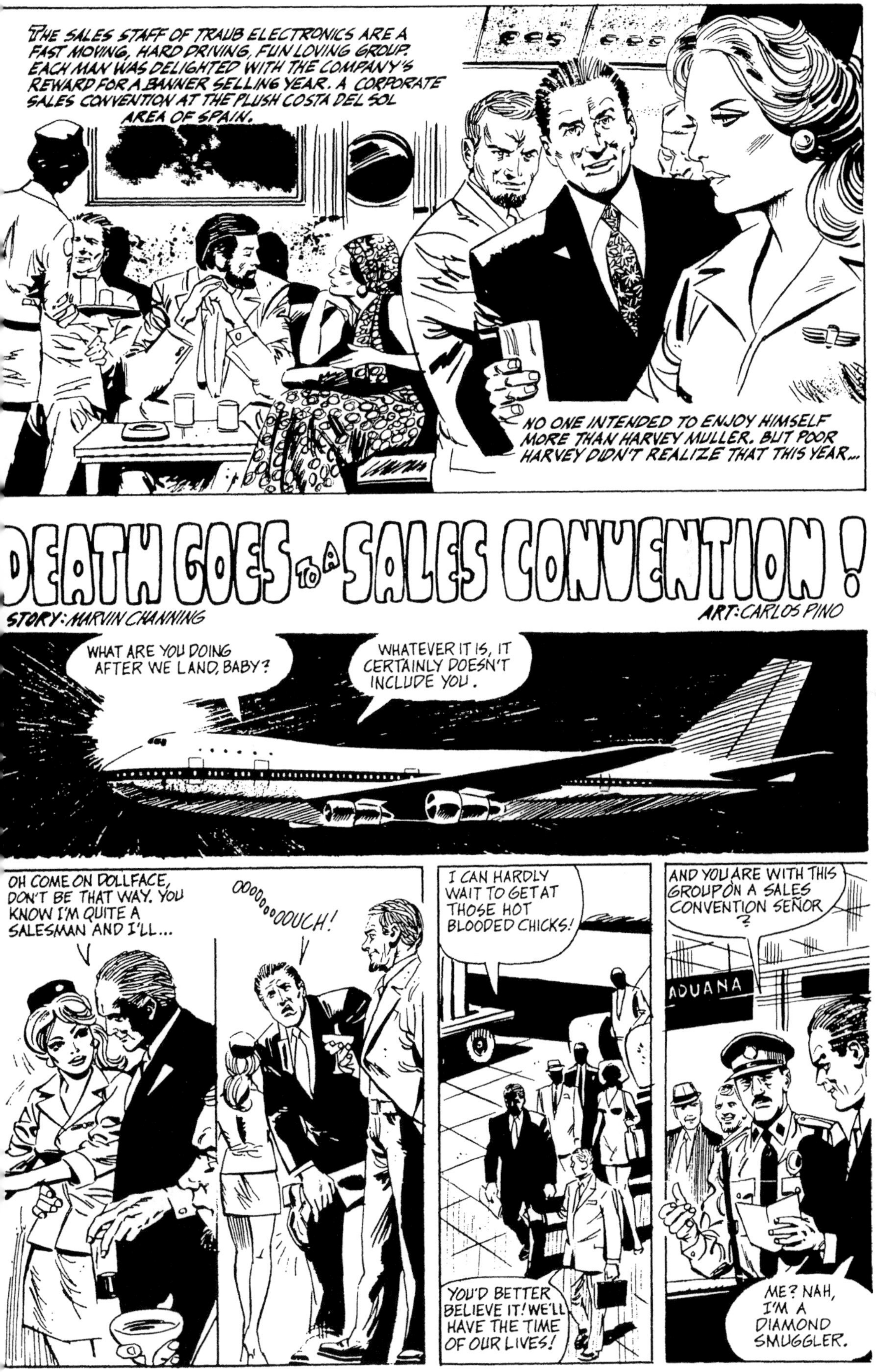
THE SALES STAFF OF TRAUB ELECTRONICS ARE A FAST MOVING, HARD DRIVING, FUN LOVING GROUP. EACH MAN WAS DELIGHTED WITH THE COMPANY'S REWARD FOR A BANNER SELLING YEAR. A CORPORATE SALES CONVENTION AT THE PLUSH COSTA DEL SOL AREA OF SPAIN.
NO ONE INTENDED TO ENJOY HIMSELF MORE THAN HARVEY MULLER. BUT POOR HARVEY DIDN'T REALIZE THAT THIS YEAR...
DEATH GOES TO A SALES CONVENTION!
STORY: MARVIN CHANNING
ART: CARLOS PINO
WHAT ARE YOU DOING AFTER WE LAND, BABY?
WHATEVER IT IS, IT CERTAINLY DOESN'T INCLUDE YOU.
OH COME ON DOLLFACE, DON'T BE THAT WAY. YOU KNOW I'M QUITE A SALESMAN AND I'LL...
OOOOOOOOOUCH!
I CAN HARDLY WAIT TO GET AT THOSE HOT BLOODED CHICKS!
YOU'D BETTER BELIEVE IT! WE'LL HAVE THE TIME OF OUR LIVES!
AND YOU ARE WITH THIS GROUP ON A SALES CONVENTION SEÑOR?
ADUANA
ME? NAH, I'M A DIAMOND SMUGGLER.

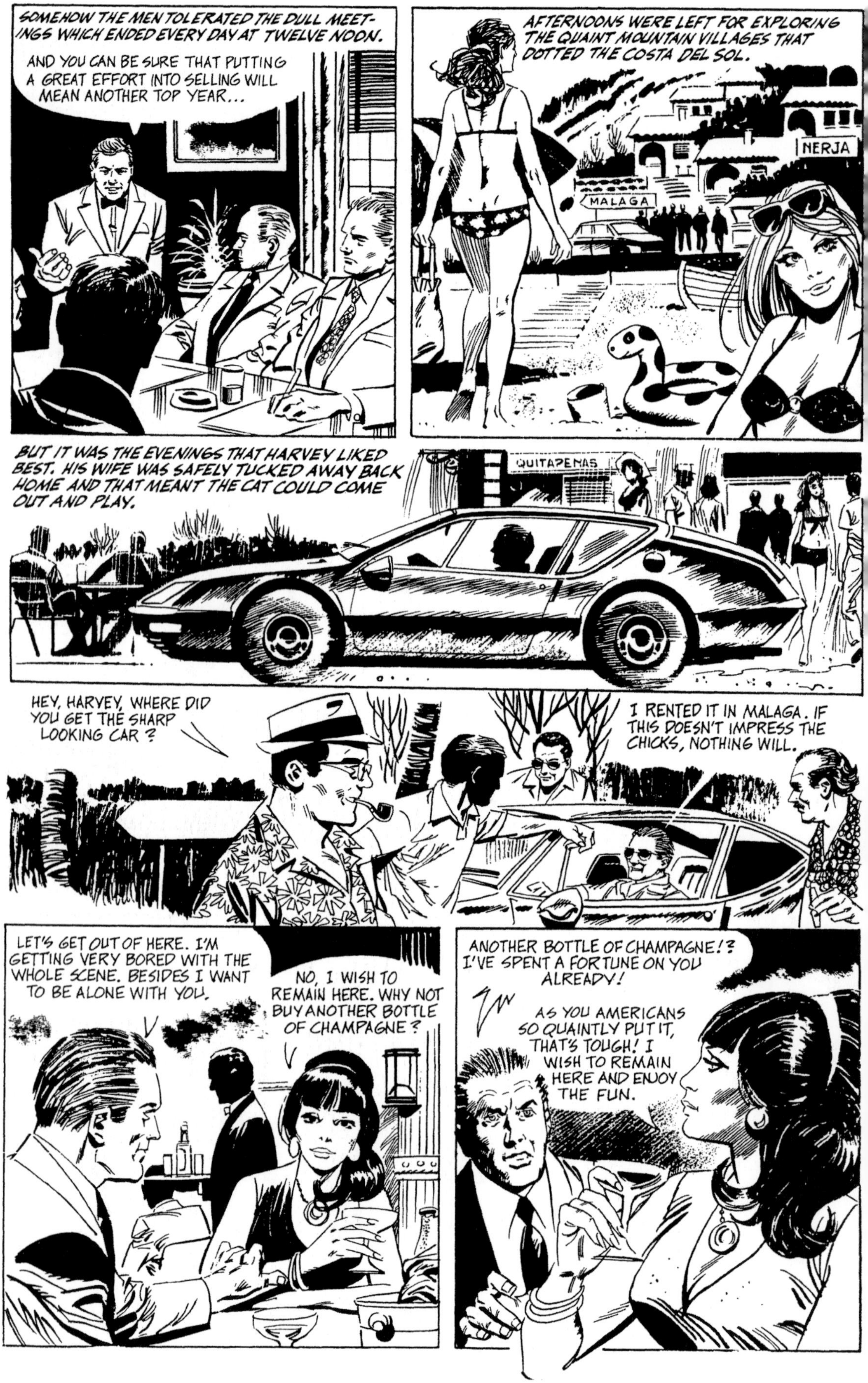
SOMEHOW THE MEN TOLERATED THE DULL MEETINGS WHICH ENDED EVERY DAY AT TWELVE NOON.
AND YOU CAN BE SURE THAT PUTTING A GREAT EFFORT INTO SELLING WILL MEAN ANOTHER TOP YEAR...
AFTERNOONS WERE LEFT FOR EXPLORING THE QUAINT MOUNTAIN VILLAGES THAT DOTTED THE COSTA DEL SOL.
NERJA
MALAGA
BUT IT WAS THE EVENINGS THAT HARVEY LIKED BEST. HIS WIFE WAS SAFELY TUCKED AWAY BACK HOME AND THAT MEANT THE CAT COULD COME OUT AND PLAY.
QUITAPENAS
HEY, HARVEY, WHERE DID YOU GET THE SHARP LOOKING CAR ?
I RENTED IT IN MALAGA. IF THIS DOESN'T IMPRESS THE CHICKS, NOTHING WILL.
LET'S GET OUT OF HERE. I'M GETTING VERY BORED WITH THE WHOLE SCENE. BESIDES I WANT TO BE ALONE WITH YOU.
NO, I WISH TO REMAIN HERE. WHY NOT BUY ANOTHER BOTTLE OF CHAMPAGNE ?
ANOTHER BOTTLE OF CHAMPAGNE!? I'VE SPENT A FORTUNE ON YOU ALREADY!
AS YOU AMERICANS SO QUAINTLY PUT IT, THAT'S TOUGH! I WISH TO REMAIN HERE AND ENJOY THE FUN.

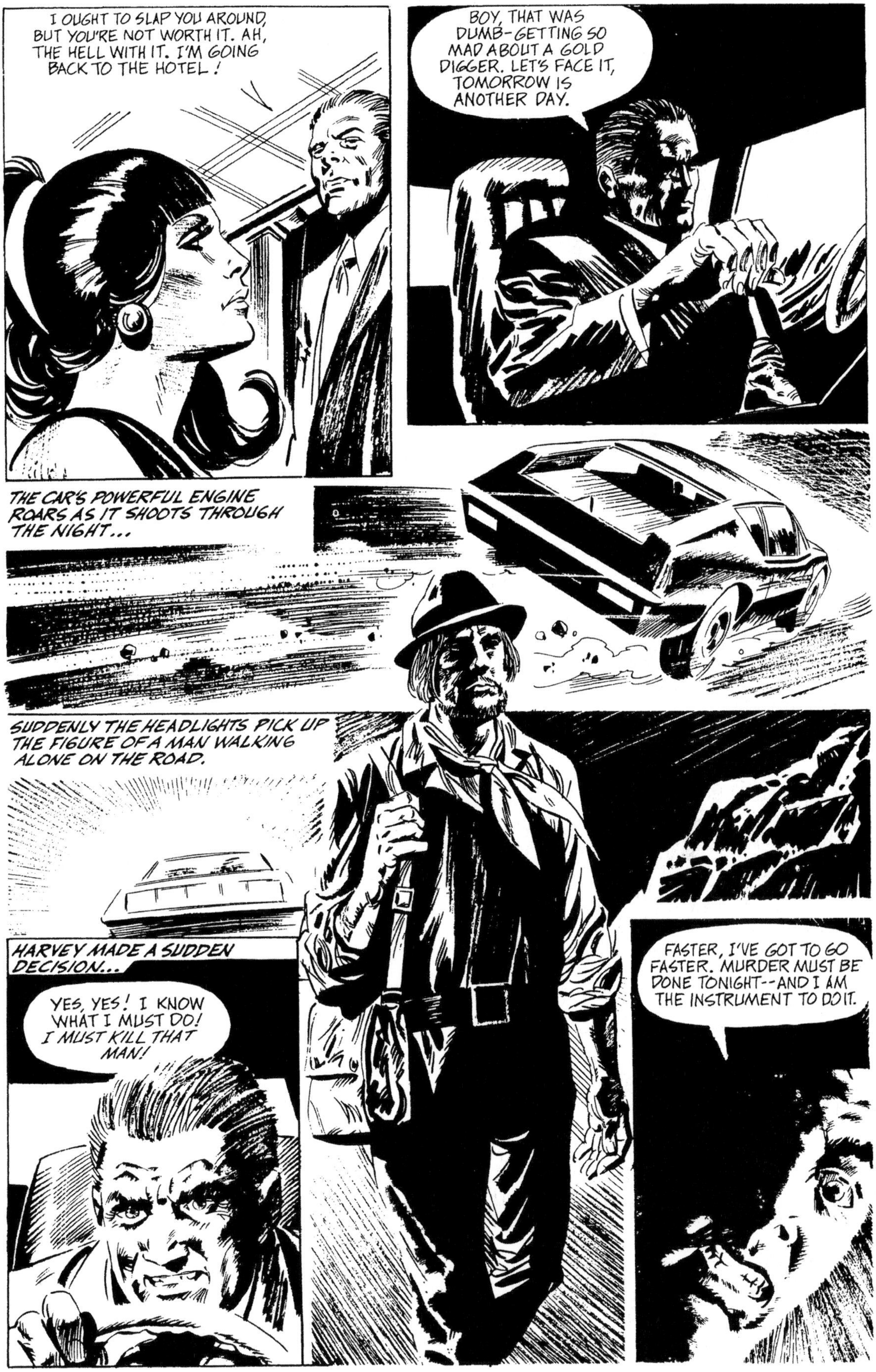

I OUGHT TO SLAP YOU AROUND, BUT YOU'RE NOT WORTH IT. AH, THE HELL WITH IT. I'M GOING BACK TO THE HOTEL!
BOY, THAT WAS DUMB-GETTING SO MAD ABOUT A GOLD DIGGER. LET'S FACE IT, TOMORROW IS ANOTHER DAY.
THE CAR'S POWERFUL ENGINE ROARS AS IT SHOOTS THROUGH THE NIGHT...
SUDDENLY THE HEADLIGHTS PICK UP THE FIGURE OF A MAN WALKING ALONE ON THE ROAD.
HARVEY MADE A SUDDEN DECISION...
YES, YES! I KNOW WHAT I MUST DO! I MUST KILL THAT MAN!
FASTER, I'VE GOT TO GO FASTER. MURDER MUST BE DONE TONIGHT--AND I AM THE INSTRUMENT TO DO IT.

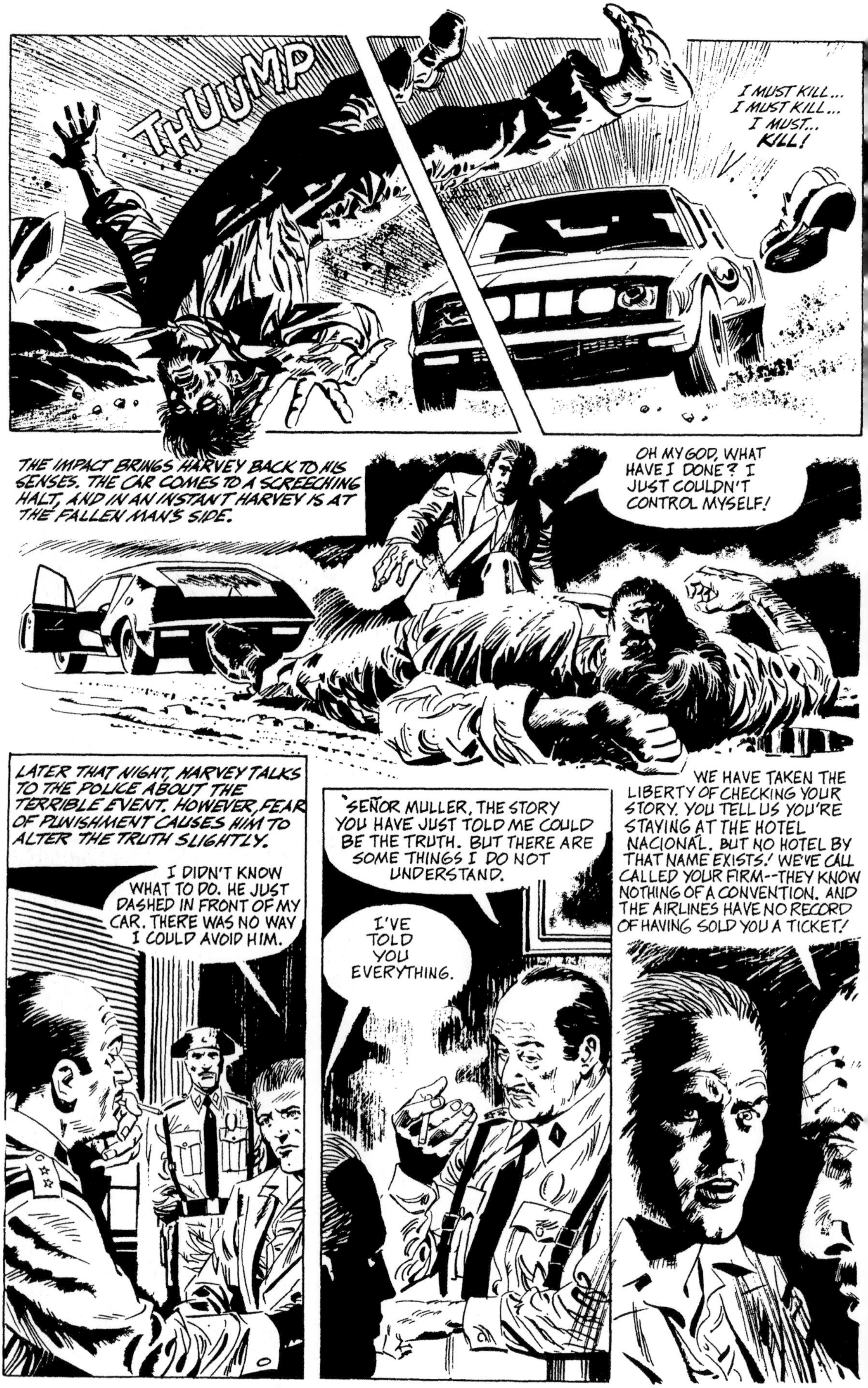
THUUMP
I MUST KILL...
I MUST KILL...
I MUST...
KILL!
THE IMPACT BRINGS HARVEY BACK TO HIS SENSES. THE CAR COMES TO A SCREECHING HALT, AND IN AN INSTANT HARVEY IS AT THE FALLEN MAN'S SIDE.
OH MY GOD, WHAT HAVE I DONE? I JUST COULDN'T CONTROL MYSELF!
LATER THAT NIGHT, HARVEY TALKS TO THE POLICE ABOUT THE TERRIBLE EVENT. HOWEVER, FEAR OF PUNISHMENT CAUSES HIM TO ALTER THE TRUTH SLIGHTLY.
I DIDN'T KNOW WHAT TO DO. HE JUST DASHED IN FRONT OF MY CAR. THERE WAS NO WAY I COULD AVOID HIM.
SEÑOR MULLER, THE STORY YOU HAVE JUST TOLD ME COULD BE THE TRUTH. BUT THERE ARE SOME THINGS I DO NOT UNDERSTAND.
I'VE TOLD YOU EVERYTHING.
WE HAVE TAKEN THE LIBERTY OF CHECKING YOUR STORY. YOU TELL US YOU'RE STAYING AT THE HOTEL NACIONAL. BUT NO HOTEL BY THAT NAME EXISTS! WE'VE CALL CALLED YOUR FIRM--THEY KNOW NOTHING OF A CONVENTION. AND THE AIRLINES HAVE NO RECORD OF HAVING SOLD YOU A TICKET!

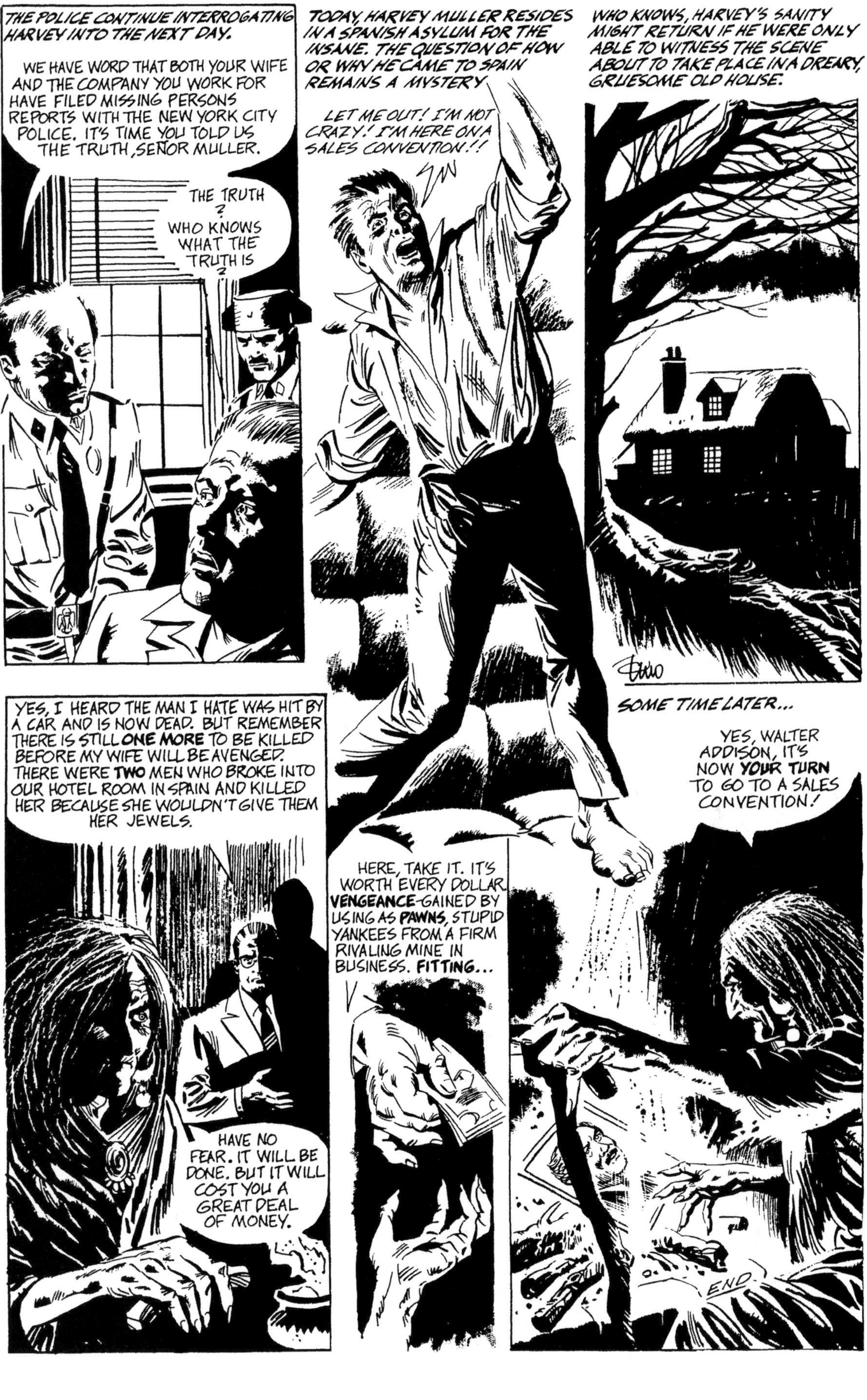

THE POLICE CONTINUE INTERROGATING HARVEY INTO THE NEXT DAY.
WE HAVE WORD THAT BOTH YOUR WIFE AND THE COMPANY YOU WORK FOR HAVE FILED MISSING PERSONS REPORTS WITH THE NEW YORK CITY POLICE. IT'S TIME YOU TOLD US THE TRUTH, SEÑOR MULLER.
THE TRUTH? WHO KNOWS WHAT THE TRUTH IS?
TODAY, HARVEY MULLER RESIDES IN A SPANISH ASYLUM FOR THE INSANE. THE QUESTION OF HOW OR WHY HE CAME TO SPAIN REMAINS A MYSTERY.
LET ME OUT! I'M NOT CRAZY! I'M HERE ON A SALES CONVENTION!!
WHO KNOWS, HARVEY'S SANITY MIGHT RETURN IF HE WERE ONLY ABLE TO WITNESS THE SCENE ABOUT TO TAKE PLACE IN A DREARY, GRUESOME OLD HOUSE.
YES, I HEARD THE MAN I HATE WAS HIT BY A CAR AND IS NOW DEAD. BUT REMEMBER THERE IS STILL ONE MORE TO BE KILLED BEFORE MY WIFE WILL BE AVENGED. THERE WERE TWO MEN WHO BROKE INTO OUR HOTEL ROOM IN SPAIN AND KILLED HER BECAUSE SHE WOULDN'T GIVE THEM HER JEWELS.
HAVE NO FEAR. IT WILL BE DONE. BUT IT WILL COST YOU A GREAT DEAL OF MONEY.
HERE, TAKE IT. IT'S WORTH EVERY DOLLAR. VENGEANCE-GAINED BY USING AS PAWNS, STUPID YANKEES FROM A FIRM RIVALING MINE IN BUSINESS. FITTING...
SOME TIME LATER...
YES, WALTER ADDISON, IT'S NOW YOUR TURN TO GO TO A SALES CONVENTION!
END

HAVE YOU EVER SEEN A CAT WAIT, STATUE-LIKE, OUTSIDE A MOUSEHOLE FOR HOURS? OR MOVE AN INCH A MINUTE, STALKING A MEAL ON THE WING? IN CONTRAST, LOVERS ARE NOTORIOUSLY IMPATIENT, ESPECIALLY WHEN THEIR LADIES ARE FICKLE. NO MAN LIKES BEING MADE A FOOL OF BY HIS LADY-LOVE, BUT... HE CAN EXACT HIS REVENGE, IF HE WILL EXERCISE...

STORY BY C. SEULING
ART BY HOWARD CHAYKIN

# The Patience of a Cat

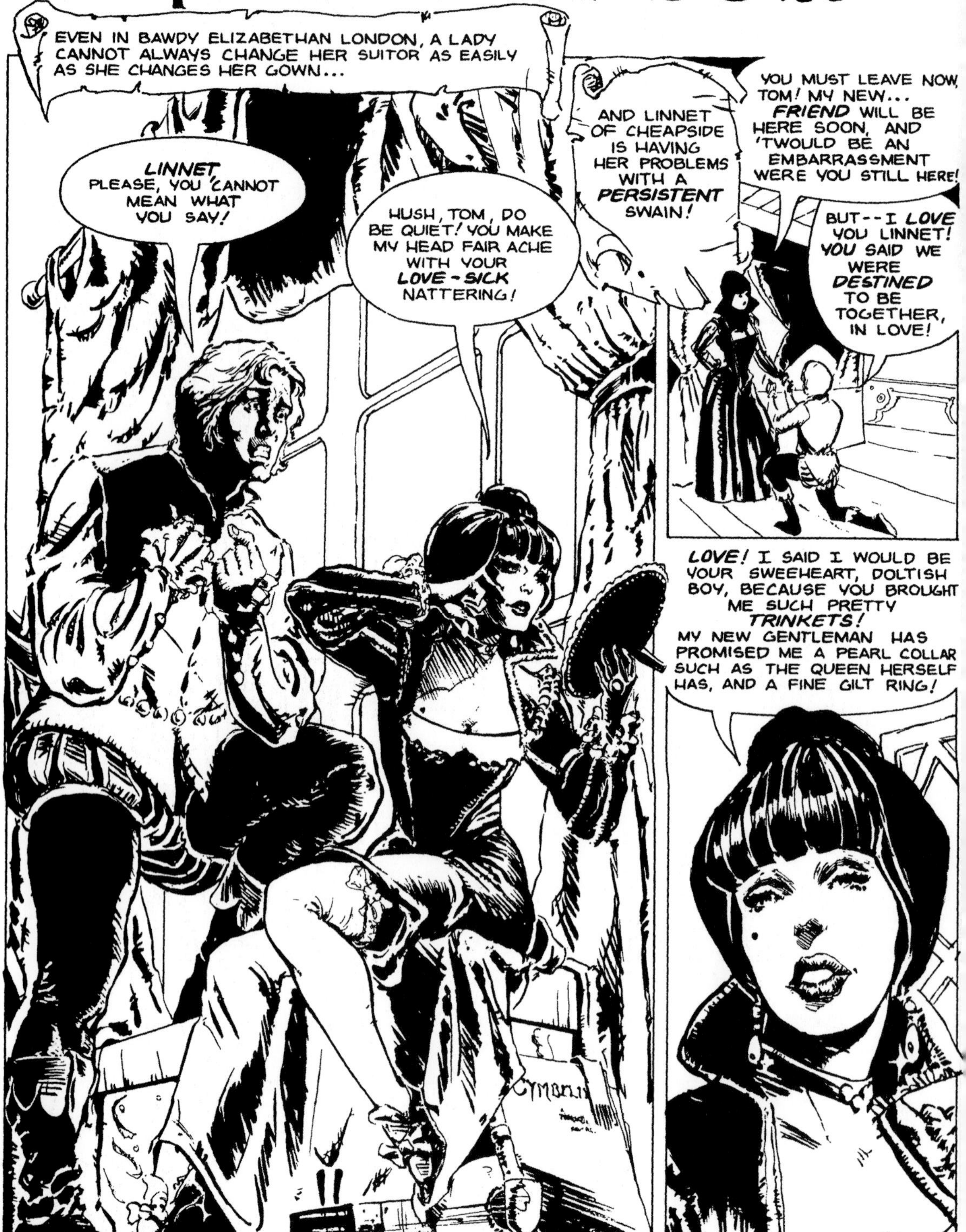
EVEN IN BAWDY ELIZABETHAN LONDON, A LADY CANNOT ALWAYS CHANGE HER SUITOR AS EASILY AS SHE CHANGES HER GOWN...
LINNET, PLEASE, YOU CANNOT MEAN WHAT YOU SAY!
HUSH, TOM, DO BE QUIET! YOU MAKE MY HEAD FAIR ACHE WITH YOUR LOVE-SICK NATTERING!
AND LINNET OF CHEAPSIDE IS HAVING HER PROBLEMS WITH A PERSISTENT SWAIN!
YOU MUST LEAVE NOW, TOM! MY NEW... FRIEND WILL BE HERE SOON, AND 'TWOULD BE AN EMBARRASSMENT WERE YOU STILL HERE!
BUT--I LOVE YOU LINNET! YOU SAID WE WERE DESTINED TO BE TOGETHER, IN LOVE!
LOVE! I SAID I WOULD BE YOUR SWEETHEART, DOLTISH BOY, BECAUSE YOU BROUGHT ME SUCH PRETTY TRINKETS! MY NEW GENTLEMAN HAS PROMISED ME A PEARL COLLAR SUCH AS THE QUEEN HERSELF HAS, AND A FINE GILT RING!

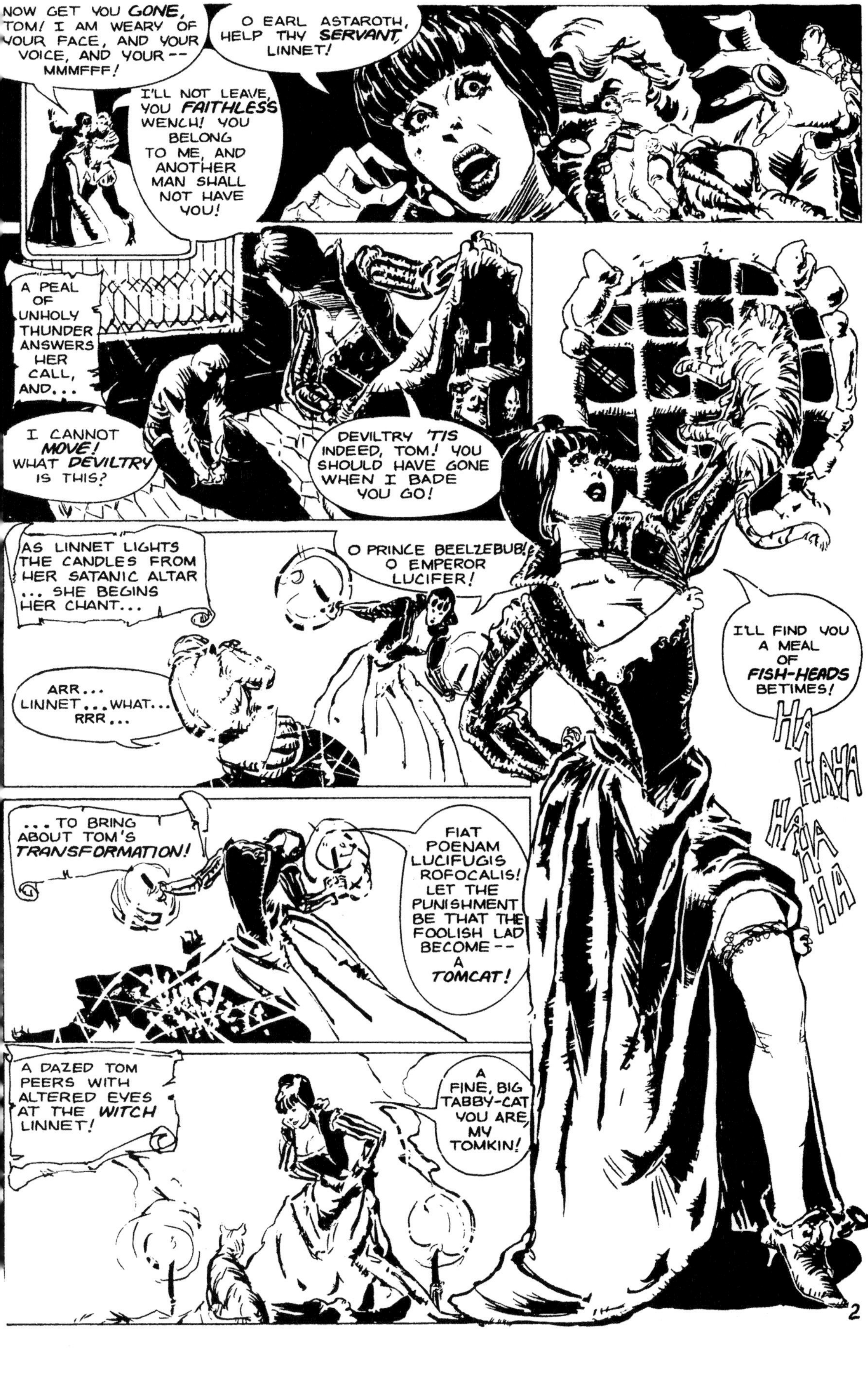

NOW GET YOU GONE, TOM! I AM WEARY OF YOUR FACE, AND YOUR VOICE, AND YOUR -- MMMFFF!
I'LL NOT LEAVE, YOU FAITHLESS WENCH! YOU BELONG TO ME, AND ANOTHER MAN SHALL NOT HAVE YOU!
O EARL ASTAROTH, HELP THY SERVANT, LINNET!
A PEAL OF UNHOLY THUNDER ANSWERS HER CALL, AND...
I CANNOT MOVE! WHAT DEVILTRY IS THIS?
DEVILTRY 'TIS INDEED, TOM! YOU SHOULD HAVE GONE WHEN I BADE YOU GO!
AS LINNET LIGHTS THE CANDLES FROM HER SATANIC ALTAR ... SHE BEGINS HER CHANT...
O PRINCE BEELZEBUB! O EMPEROR LUCIFER!
ARR... LINNET...WHAT... RRR...
...TO BRING ABOUT TOM'S TRANSFORMATION!
FIAT POENAM LUCIFUGIS ROFOCALIS! LET THE PUNISHMENT BE THAT THE FOOLISH LAD BECOME -- A TOMCAT!
A DAZED TOM PEERS WITH ALTERED EYES AT THE WITCH LINNET!
A FINE, BIG TABBY-CAT YOU ARE, MY TOMKIN!
I'LL FIND YOU A MEAL OF FISH-HEADS BETIMES!
HA HAHA HAHAHA HA

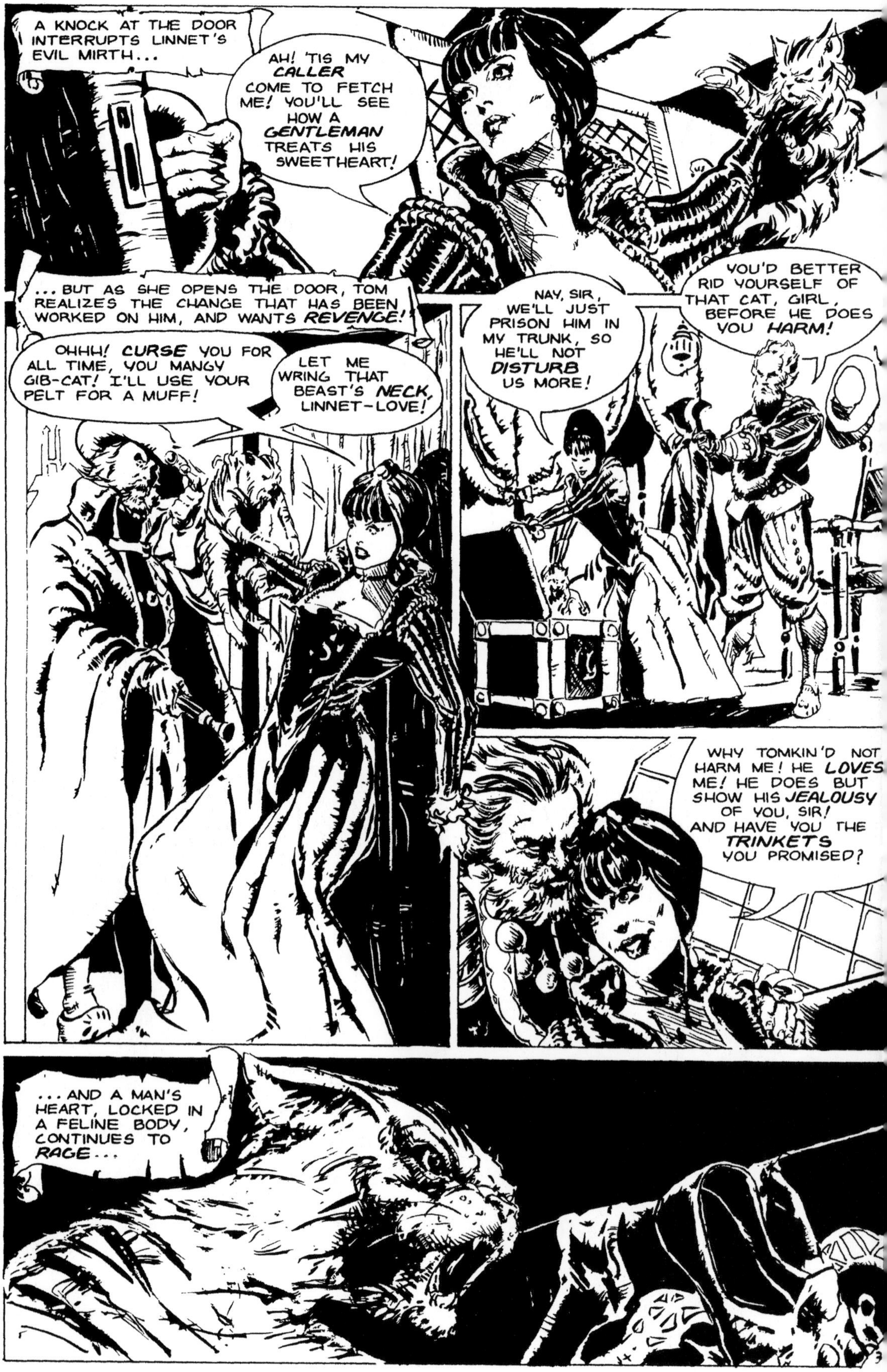

A KNOCK AT THE DOOR INTERRUPTS LINNET'S EVIL MIRTH...
AH! 'TIS MY CALLER COME TO FETCH ME! YOU'LL SEE HOW A GENTLEMAN TREATS HIS SWEETHEART!
...BUT AS SHE OPENS THE DOOR, TOM REALIZES THE CHANGE THAT HAS BEEN WORKED ON HIM, AND WANTS REVENGE!
OHHH! CURSE YOU FOR ALL TIME, YOU MANGY GIB-CAT! I'LL USE YOUR PELT FOR A MUFF!
LET ME WRING THAT BEAST'S NECK, LINNET-LOVE!
YOU'D BETTER RID YOURSELF OF THAT CAT, GIRL, BEFORE HE DOES YOU HARM!
NAY, SIR, WE'LL JUST PRISON HIM IN MY TRUNK, SO HE'LL NOT DISTURB US MORE!
WHY TOMKIN'D NOT HARM ME! HE LOVES ME! HE DOES BUT SHOW HIS JEALOUSY OF YOU, SIR! AND HAVE YOU THE TRINKETS YOU PROMISED?
...AND A MAN'S HEART, LOCKED IN A FELINE BODY, CONTINUES TO RAGE...

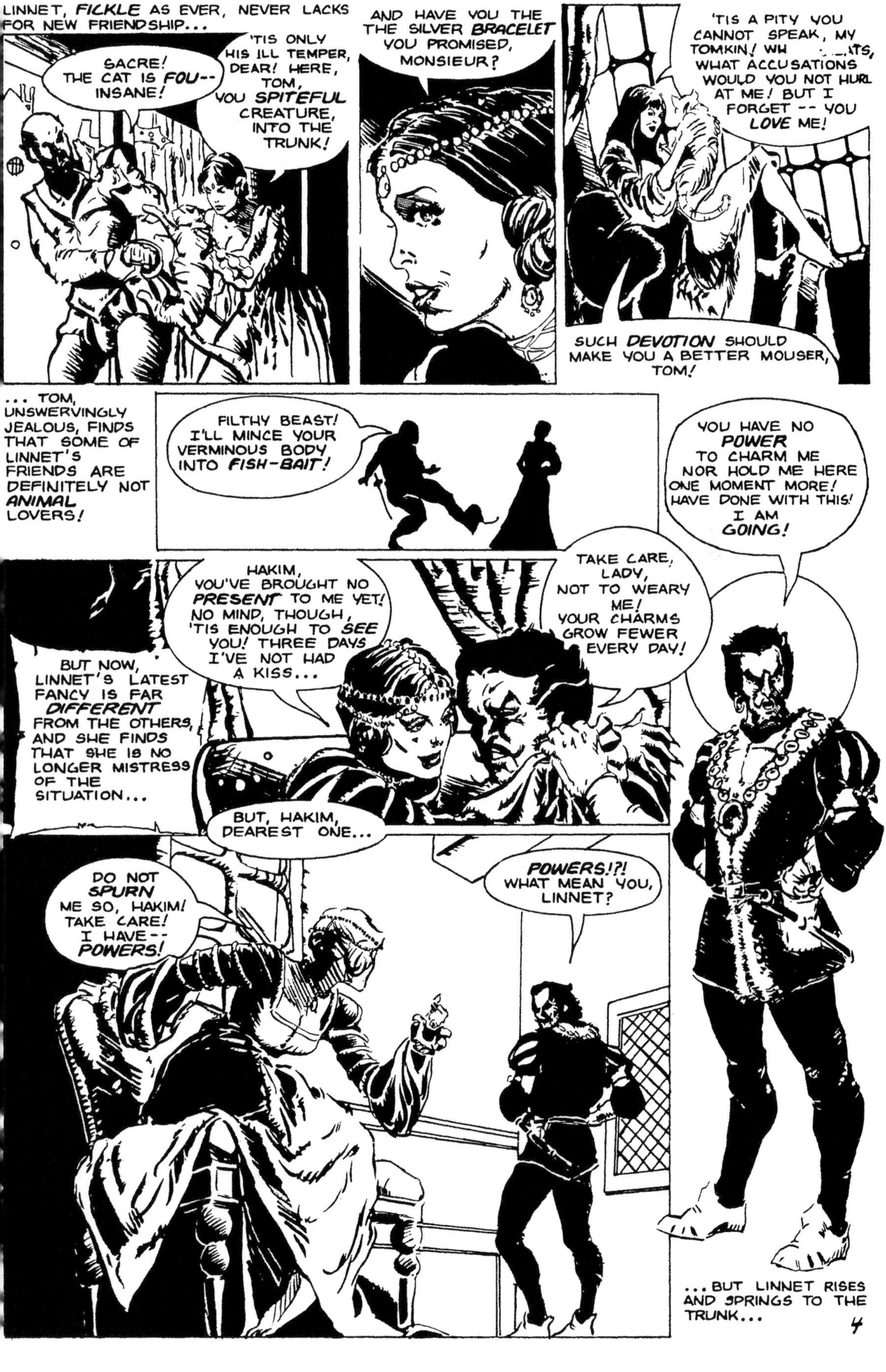
LINNET, FICKLE AS EVER, NEVER LACKS FOR NEW FRIENDSHIP...
SACRE! THE CAT IS FOU-- INSANE!
'TIS ONLY HIS ILL TEMPER, DEAR! HERE, TOM, YOU SPITEFUL CREATURE, INTO THE TRUNK!
AND HAVE YOU THE THE SILVER BRACELET YOU PROMISED, MONSIEUR?
'TIS A PITY YOU CANNOT SPEAK, MY TOMKIN! WH ATS, WHAT ACCUSATIONS WOULD YOU NOT HURL AT ME! BUT I FORGET -- YOU LOVE ME!
SUCH DEVOTION SHOULD MAKE YOU A BETTER MOUSER, TOM!
... TOM, UNSWERVINGLY JEALOUS, FINDS THAT SOME OF LINNET'S FRIENDS ARE DEFINITELY NOT ANIMAL LOVERS!
FILTHY BEAST! I'LL MINCE YOUR VERMINOUS BODY INTO FISH-BAIT!
BUT NOW, LINNET'S LATEST FANCY IS FAR DIFFERENT FROM THE OTHERS, AND SHE FINDS THAT SHE IS NO LONGER MISTRESS OF THE SITUATION...
HAKIM, YOU'VE BROUGHT NO PRESENT TO ME YET! NO MIND, THOUGH, 'TIS ENOUGH TO SEE YOU! THREE DAYS I'VE NOT HAD A KISS...
TAKE CARE, LADY, NOT TO WEARY ME! YOUR CHARMS GROW FEWER EVERY DAY!
YOU HAVE NO POWER TO CHARM ME NOR HOLD ME HERE ONE MOMENT MORE! HAVE DONE WITH THIS! I AM GOING!
BUT, HAKIM, DEAREST ONE...
DO NOT SPURN ME SO, HAKIM! TAKE CARE! I HAVE-- POWERS!
POWERS!?! WHAT MEAN YOU, LINNET?
...BUT LINNET RISES AND SPRINGS TO THE TRUNK...

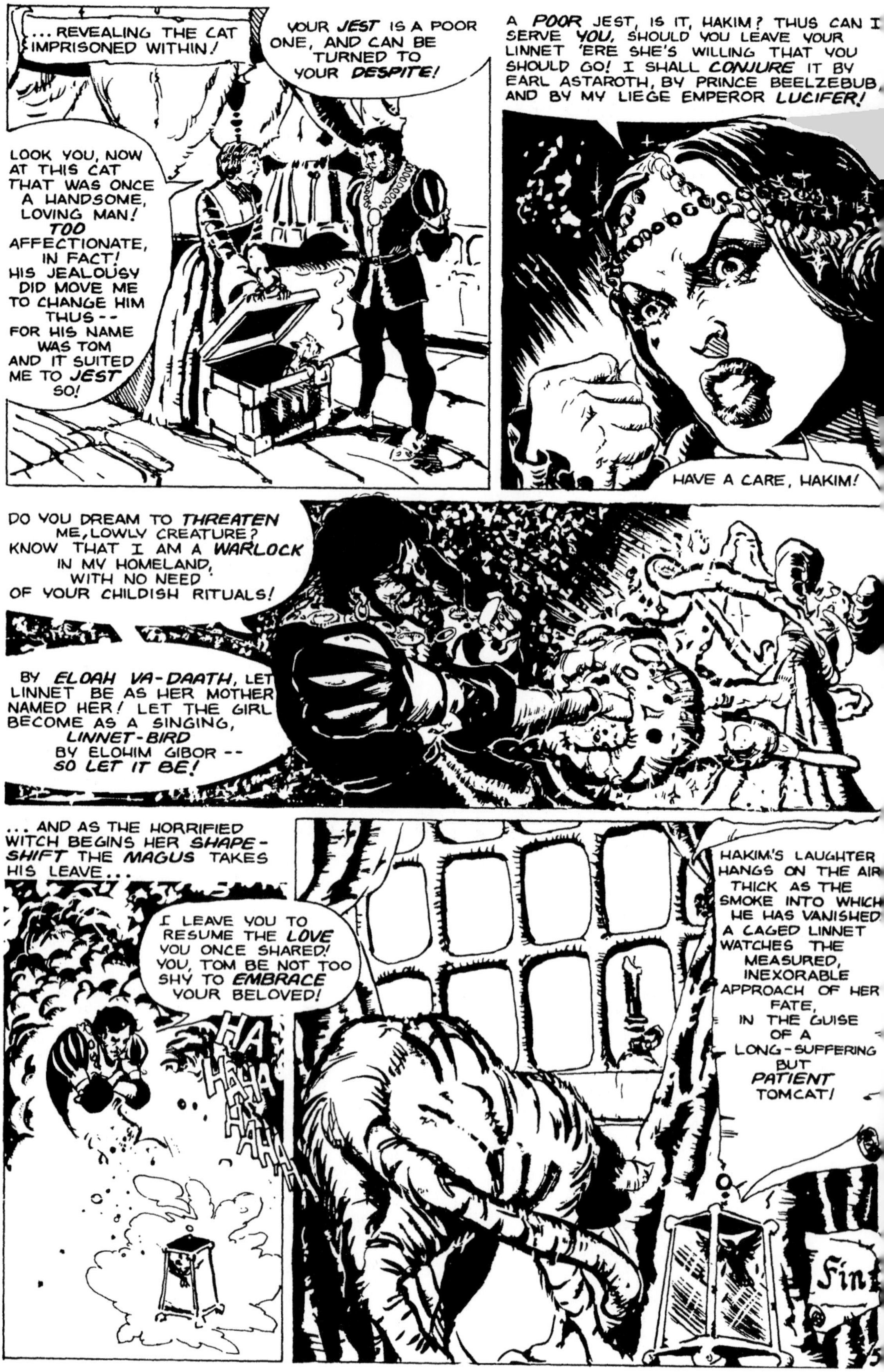

...REVEALING THE CAT IMPRISONED WITHIN!
YOUR JEST IS A POOR ONE, AND CAN BE TURNED TO YOUR DESPITE!
LOOK YOU, NOW AT THIS CAT THAT WAS ONCE A HANDSOME, LOVING MAN! TOO AFFECTIONATE, IN FACT! HIS JEALOUSY DID MOVE ME TO CHANGE HIM THUS-- FOR HIS NAME WAS TOM AND IT SUITED ME TO JEST SO!
A POOR JEST, IS IT, HAKIM? THUS CAN I SERVE YOU, SHOULD YOU LEAVE YOUR LINNET 'ERE SHE'S WILLING THAT YOU SHOULD GO! I SHALL CONJURE IT BY EARL ASTAROTH, BY PRINCE BEELZEBUB AND BY MY LIEGE EMPEROR LUCIFER!
HAVE A CARE, HAKIM!
DO YOU DREAM TO THREATEN ME, LOWLY CREATURE? KNOW THAT I AM A WARLOCK IN MY HOMELAND, WITH NO NEED OF YOUR CHILDISH RITUALS!
BY ELOAH VA-DAATH, LET LINNET BE AS HER MOTHER NAMED HER! LET THE GIRL BECOME AS A SINGING, LINNET-BIRD BY ELOHIM GIBOR -- SO LET IT BE!
...AND AS THE HORRIFIED WITCH BEGINS HER SHAPE-SHIFT THE MAGUS TAKES HIS LEAVE...
I LEAVE YOU TO RESUME THE LOVE YOU ONCE SHARED! YOU, TOM BE NOT TOO SHY TO EMBRACE YOUR BELOVED!
HA HAHA HAHAH
HAKIM'S LAUGHTER HANGS ON THE AIR THICK AS THE SMOKE INTO WHICH HE HAS VANISHED. A CAGED LINNET WATCHES THE MEASURED, INEXORABLE APPROACH OF HER FATE, IN THE GUISE OF A LONG-SUFFERING BUT PATIENT TOMCAT!
Fin

# Black Fog

*by* T. Casey Brennan

Slowly the black fog closed in, destroying his awareness, and then . . .

There was no doubt in Hal Thunder's mind that the scream had come from Linda's room. He quickened his pace, leaping up the stairs three and four steps at a time. His heart beat faster now, pumping adrenalin into his powerful body.

But he felt no fear.

With one violent motion, he kicked open the door to Linda's apartment. Linda was on the floor gasping, her clothes torn. But still alive, thank God, he thought.

"The window! Don't let him escape!" Her voice was hysterical.

Swiftly, but with great caution, Thunder stepped out the still-open window and onto the narrow ledge.

Then he saw the other man some three feet away. He realized that for the first time he was face to face with the masked arch-criminal whom he had sought so long—the Strangler.

In an instant, Thunder evaluated the situation. If they locked horns on this window ledge fifteen stories above the city, surely one of them would die, if not both. On the other hand, if he allowed the Strangler to escape, his next attempt on Linda's life might be successful. He could not take that chance. He moved toward the masked man.

The Strangler fought desperately, seeming to prefer death on the sidewalk below to capture by Hal Thunder. Summoning all his resources, Thunder fought to keep his balance under the force of his own blows, and the flailing fists of the masked man.

Like a madman, the Strangler moved in, grabbing Thunder by the throat. The movement threw them both off balance. Thunder's efforts to tear the powerful fingers loose were in vain, and they toppled together off the ledge.

In a split-second, the Strangler realized what he had done, and released his grip in mid-air. Free of the strangle-hold, Thunder's lightning reflexes took effect, and he grabbed the ledge with both hands as he fell. The shock might have broken the arms of a lesser man, but Thunder's body had long been conditioned for such things.

He dangled above the city fifteen stories, and then . . .

Then a strange thought hit him.

It hit him seemingly for the first time: Who am I, really? What am I doing here? What is happening?

It had suddenly become clear that the incident that had just taken place had a dream-like quality. And he had felt no fear.

There seemed to be a mist forming before him. Then the black fog closed in.

The black fog was lifting now. Just before it did, he realized painfully that he would have no recollection of it.

Linda was especially beautiful today. Thunder observed, eating his lunch. Perhaps it was because he was so grateful that she was still alive.

He felt her admiring eyes on him as he spoke.

"It looks as though this case hasn't been solved yet," he said.

Linda stared, wide-eyed.

"But the Strangler is dead now, isn't he?" she asked.

There was fear in her voice, Thunder noted. Understandably so, he thought, after her ordeal yesterday.

Thunder continued, "One Strangler is dead, yes! But these crimes now appear to be the work of an organized gang!"

He lit his pipe, arranged his thoughts carefully, then spoke again.

"You see, when this crime wave first hit the city, it appeared to be the work of a lone madman—a Jack-the-Ripper type. The victims were all women, and all brutally murdered.

"But there were too many flaws to the 'madman' angle. For one thing, all the victims were well-to-do. They were always stripped of their valuables. These crimes were very carefully planned out."

"You mean the killer tried to make the murders look like crimes of passion, when robbery was the real motive?!" Linda said.

"Exactly," Thunder replied, "that way, the police would be looking for a psychopath instead of a cunning band of ruthless killers!"

Linda's face grew sad.

"So now you won't get the reward money you were counting on," she said.

"Not yet!" Thunder corrected, "But I'm going to crack this case!"

He swore inwardly that he would get back at the Stranglers for their attack on Linda. He knew it had been meant as a warning to him.

And when he did catch them, it would mean a five thousand dollar reward. With that much money, he could make his private detective agency really amount to something, and more importantly, build a future for himself and Linda.

He watched Linda intently, then he noticed the mist forming all around. It became a deep black fog, and at first he didn't understand—then, he remembered.

The black fog cleared away rapidly, clearing with it all memory of what had happened.

He was in Linda's apartment now, holding her in his arms.

"Linda," he breathed, "I don't know what I would have done if something had happened to you!"

Her voice was a soft whisper. "How do you think I felt with you out on that ledge with that monster?! Oh, darling!"

Her voice continued, but he was no longer listening. He suddenly remembered that something else had happened on that ledge: What? Then he remembered—the questions. The feeling that something strange was happening.

He began to panic. Perhaps he could turn to Linda, he thought. He started to speak, but before he did, he had the strange feeling that he was doing something very, very wrong.

"Linda," he said, in an almost begging tone, "There's something strange happening here! I don't understand this! There's something wrong . . ."

He turned his face directly toward hers, expecting comfort. He was wrong. The warmth was gone from her face. The admiration in her eyes for Hal Thunder was gone. She wore a look of shocked anger.

"What's the matter with you?" she screamed, "Are you actually trying to ruin it for yourself?!"

The black fog closed in immediately.

Hal Thunder spoke with authority, as he smoothed the check between his palms. Close beside him, her hand on his arm, was Linda. And in front of him, seated at the desk, was his old friend, Commissioner Jensen.

". . . so you see," Thunder said, "It was a relatively simple job to outwit the killers!"

"You've done a fine job, Hal," said the Commissioner, smiling at them, "I'm glad to see you finally get that reward money!"

"We're so proud of you, Hal!" Linda purred, her eyes aglow, "And to think I almost lost you out on that ledge!"

*The ledge!* The words stuck in his mind. Then he remembered. The questions. The black fog. First he glanced around the room, wild-eyed. When he spoke, his voice was hysterical.

"What's going on here?' My name isn't Hal! What are we doing?!"

Commissioner Jensen was standing now, shouting. Linda was crying. The black fog closed in now, and as it did, he felt someone removing something from behind his right ear.

Someone said, "He's ruined another scene!"

When he woke again, it was with full realization of what had been happening. The director had his hand on his shoulder. Johnny Dorran, formerly Hal Thunder, hung his head.

The director spoke.

"I'm sorry, Johnny," he said, "We can't use you in the show! You just ruined two scenes. I don't think you can ever cope with twenty-first century acting methods!"

Johnny swallowed. He had expected this. Curse the psycho-acting devices, he thought. He had been a star when acting had been an art, not a superscientific trick.

But now, in modern Hollywood, nearly anyone could become an actor. That is, anyone without great sensitivity, those who might have genuine acting talent, in other words. It was merely a process of erasing all true memories, and replacing them with artificial memories, so that an actor could truly live his part. The mind usually recorded this erasing with a visual hallucination of black fog.

And Johnny Dorran's mind could not tolerate that black fog. He felt the director's eyes on him. So harshly, that he wanted to protest that these innovations had not advanced art—they had killed it. But he knew it would be no use.

He nodded, and turned to walk away. But before he reached the door, the girl who had played Linda, Janice, caught up with him and touched his arm. He turned around.

"Art is still alive somewhere, Johnny," she said, "Go find it! And when you do—"

She paused.

"When you do, come back for me! Because I want to find it too!"

Then she was gone, hurrying back to the set.

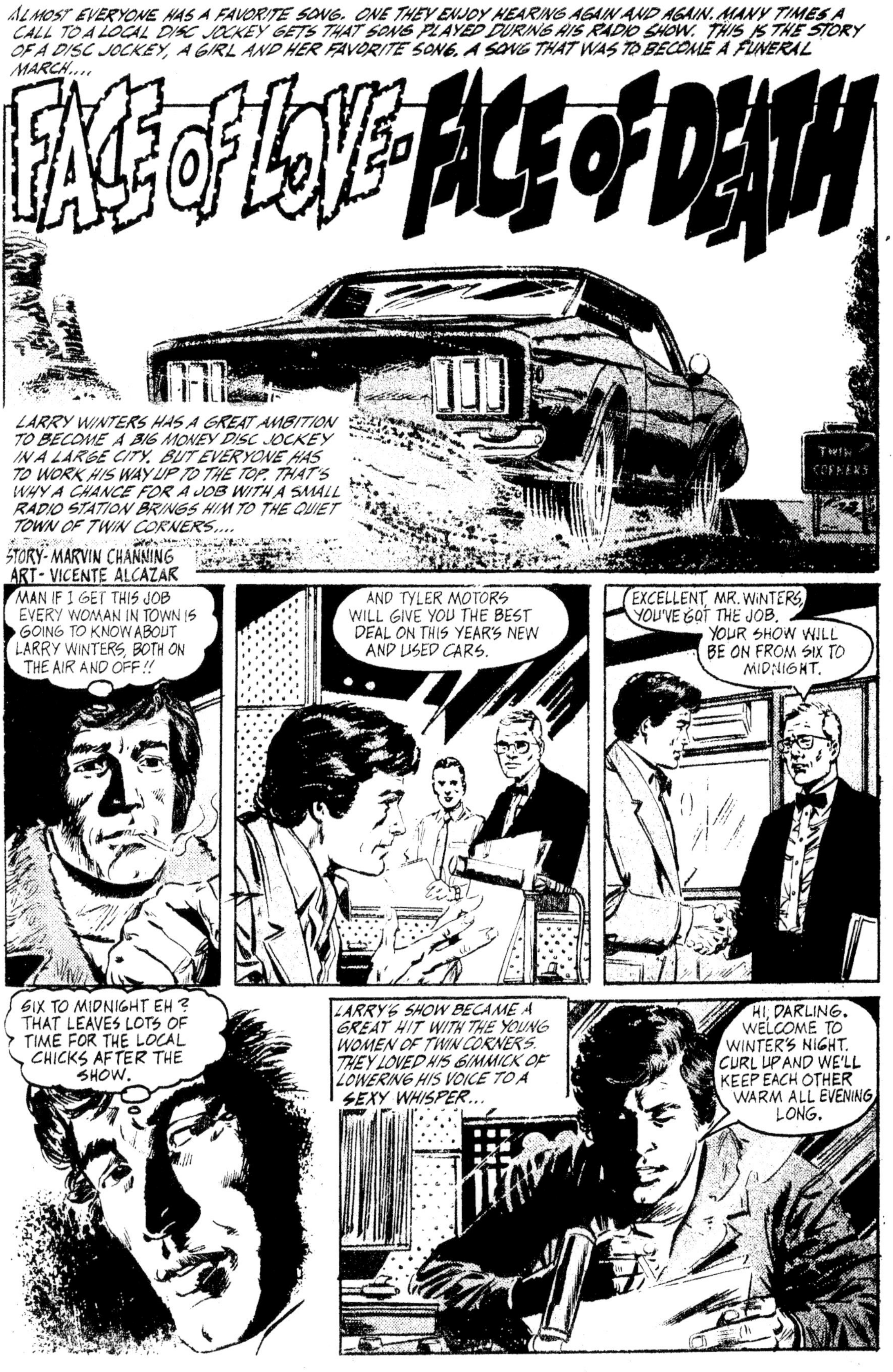
ALMOST EVERYONE HAS A FAVORITE SONG. ONE THEY ENJOY HEARING AGAIN AND AGAIN. MANY TIMES A CALL TO A LOCAL DISC JOCKEY GETS THAT SONG PLAYED DURING HIS RADIO SHOW. THIS IS THE STORY OF A DISC JOCKEY, A GIRL AND HER FAVORITE SONG. A SONG THAT WAS TO BECOME A FUNERAL MARCH....
FACE OF LOVE-FACE OF DEATH
LARRY WINTERS HAS A GREAT AMBITION TO BECOME A BIG MONEY DISC JOCKEY IN A LARGE CITY. BUT EVERYONE HAS TO WORK HIS WAY UP TO THE TOP. THAT'S WHY A CHANCE FOR A JOB WITH A SMALL RADIO STATION BRINGS HIM TO THE QUIET TOWN OF TWIN CORNERS....
TWIN CORNERS
STORY- MARVIN CHANNING
ART- VICENTE ALCAZAR
MAN IF I GET THIS JOB EVERY WOMAN IN TOWN IS GOING TO KNOW ABOUT LARRY WINTERS, BOTH ON THE AIR AND OFF!!
AND TYLER MOTORS WILL GIVE YOU THE BEST DEAL ON THIS YEAR'S NEW AND USED CARS.
EXCELLENT, MR. WINTERS, YOU'VE GOT THE JOB. YOUR SHOW WILL BE ON FROM SIX TO MIDNIGHT.
SIX TO MIDNIGHT EH? THAT LEAVES LOTS OF TIME FOR THE LOCAL CHICKS AFTER THE SHOW.
LARRY'S SHOW BECAME A GREAT HIT WITH THE YOUNG WOMEN OF TWIN CORNERS. THEY LOVED HIS GIMMICK OF LOWERING HIS VOICE TO A SEXY WHISPER...
HI, DARLING. WELCOME TO WINTER'S NIGHT. CURL UP AND WE'LL KEEP EACH OTHER WARM ALL EVENING LONG.

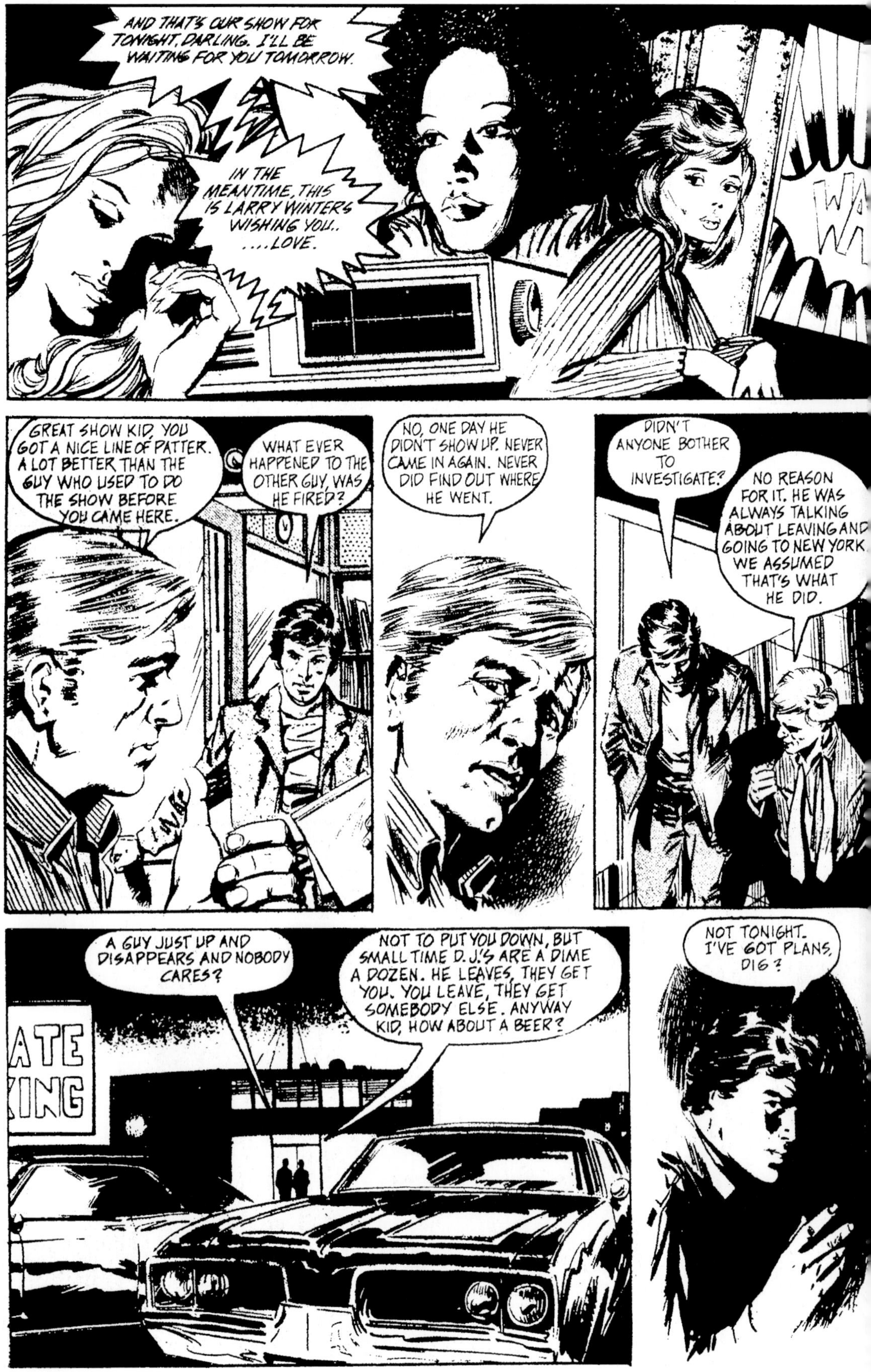
AND THAT'S OUR SHOW FOR TONIGHT, DARLING. I'LL BE WAITING FOR YOU TOMORROW.
IN THE MEANTIME, THIS IS LARRY WINTERS WISHING YOU.. ....LOVE.
GREAT SHOW KID, YOU GOT A NICE LINE OF PATTER. A LOT BETTER THAN THE GUY WHO USED TO DO THE SHOW BEFORE YOU CAME HERE.
WHAT EVER HAPPENED TO THE OTHER GUY, WAS HE FIRED?
NO, ONE DAY HE DIDN'T SHOW UP. NEVER CAME IN AGAIN. NEVER DID FIND OUT WHERE HE WENT.
DIDN'T ANYONE BOTHER TO INVESTIGATE?
NO REASON FOR IT. HE WAS ALWAYS TALKING ABOUT LEAVING AND GOING TO NEW YORK. WE ASSUMED THAT'S WHAT HE DID.
A GUY JUST UP AND DISAPPEARS AND NOBODY CARES?
NOT TO PUT YOU DOWN, BUT SMALL TIME D.J.'S ARE A DIME A DOZEN. HE LEAVES, THEY GET YOU. YOU LEAVE, THEY GET SOMEBODY ELSE. ANYWAY KID, HOW ABOUT A BEER?
NOT TONIGHT. I'VE GOT PLANS, DIG?

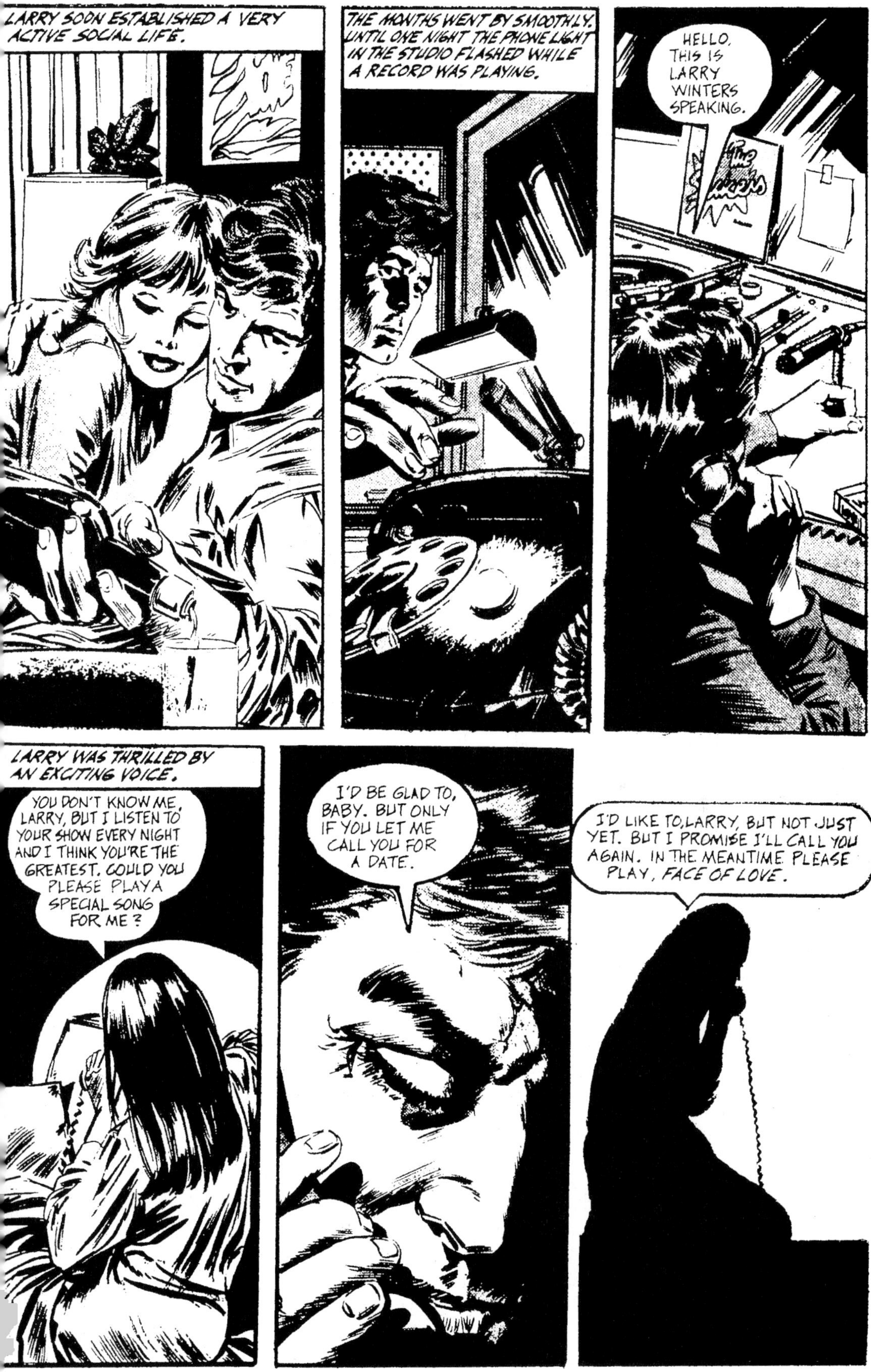
LARRY SOON ESTABLISHED A VERY ACTIVE SOCIAL LIFE.
THE MONTHS WENT BY SMOOTHLY. UNTIL ONE NIGHT THE PHONE LIGHT IN THE STUDIO FLASHED WHILE A RECORD WAS PLAYING.
HELLO, THIS IS LARRY WINTERS SPEAKING.
LARRY WAS THRILLED BY AN EXCITING VOICE.
YOU DON'T KNOW ME, LARRY, BUT I LISTEN TO YOUR SHOW EVERY NIGHT AND I THINK YOU'RE THE GREATEST. COULD YOU PLEASE PLAY A SPECIAL SONG FOR ME?
I'D BE GLAD TO, BABY. BUT ONLY IF YOU LET ME CALL YOU FOR A DATE.
I'D LIKE TO, LARRY, BUT NOT JUST YET. BUT I PROMISE I'LL CALL YOU AGAIN. IN THE MEANTIME PLEASE PLAY, FACE OF LOVE.

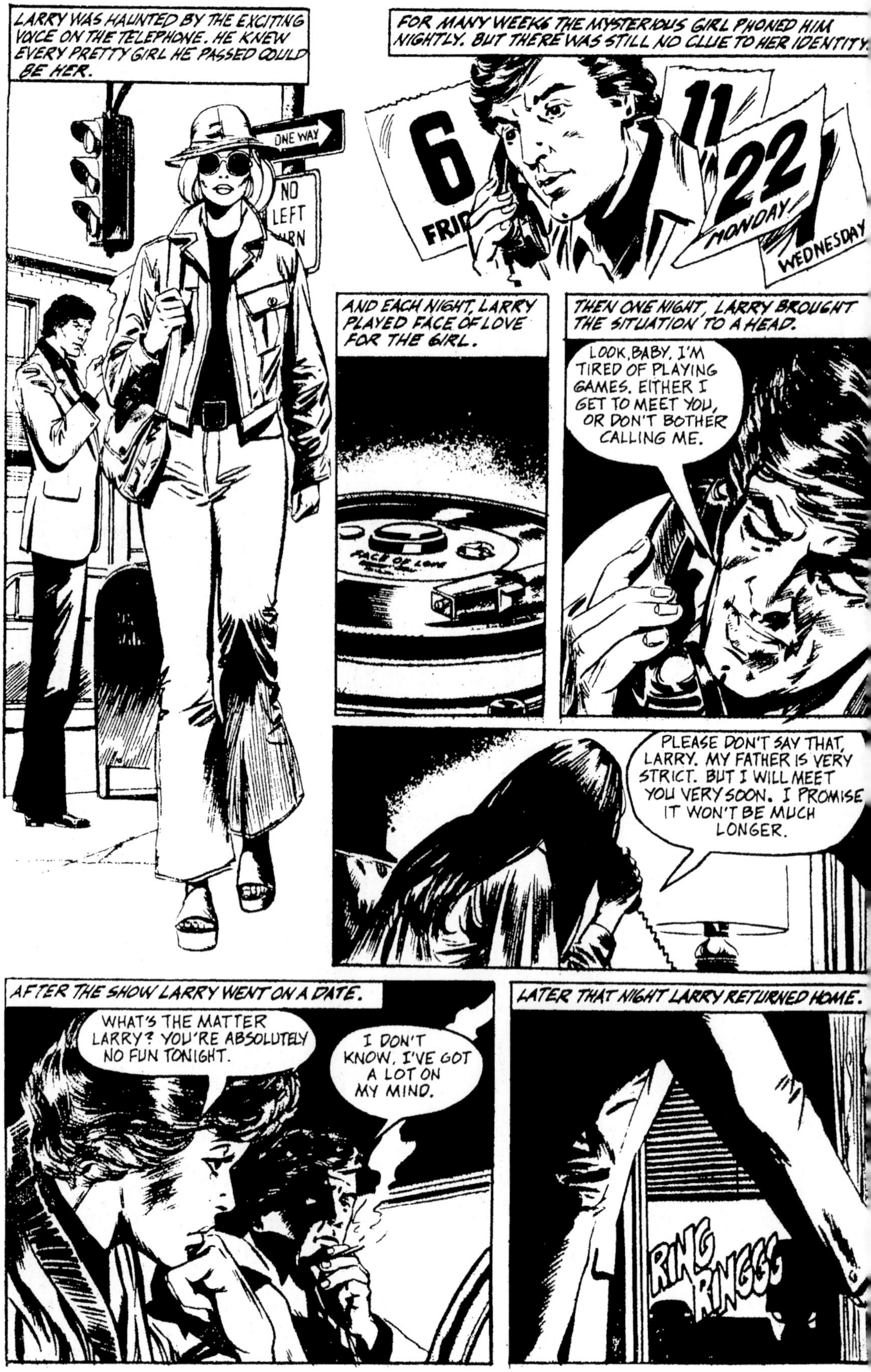

LARRY WAS HAUNTED BY THE EXCITING VOICE ON THE TELEPHONE. HE KNEW EVERY PRETTY GIRL HE PASSED COULD BE HER.
ONE WAY
NO LEFT TURN
FOR MANY WEEKS THE MYSTERIOUS GIRL PHONED HIM NIGHTLY. BUT THERE WAS STILL NO CLUE TO HER IDENTITY.
6
FRI
11
22
MONDAY
WEDNESDAY
AND EACH NIGHT, LARRY PLAYED FACE OF LOVE FOR THE GIRL.
FACE OF LOVE
THEN ONE NIGHT, LARRY BROUGHT THE SITUATION TO A HEAD.
LOOK, BABY, I'M TIRED OF PLAYING GAMES. EITHER I GET TO MEET YOU, OR DON'T BOTHER CALLING ME.
PLEASE DON'T SAY THAT, LARRY. MY FATHER IS VERY STRICT. BUT I WILL MEET YOU VERY SOON. I PROMISE IT WON'T BE MUCH LONGER.
AFTER THE SHOW LARRY WENT ON A DATE.
WHAT'S THE MATTER LARRY? YOU'RE ABSOLUTELY NO FUN TONIGHT.
I DON'T KNOW, I'VE GOT A LOT ON MY MIND.
LATER THAT NIGHT LARRY RETURNED HOME.
RING RINGGG

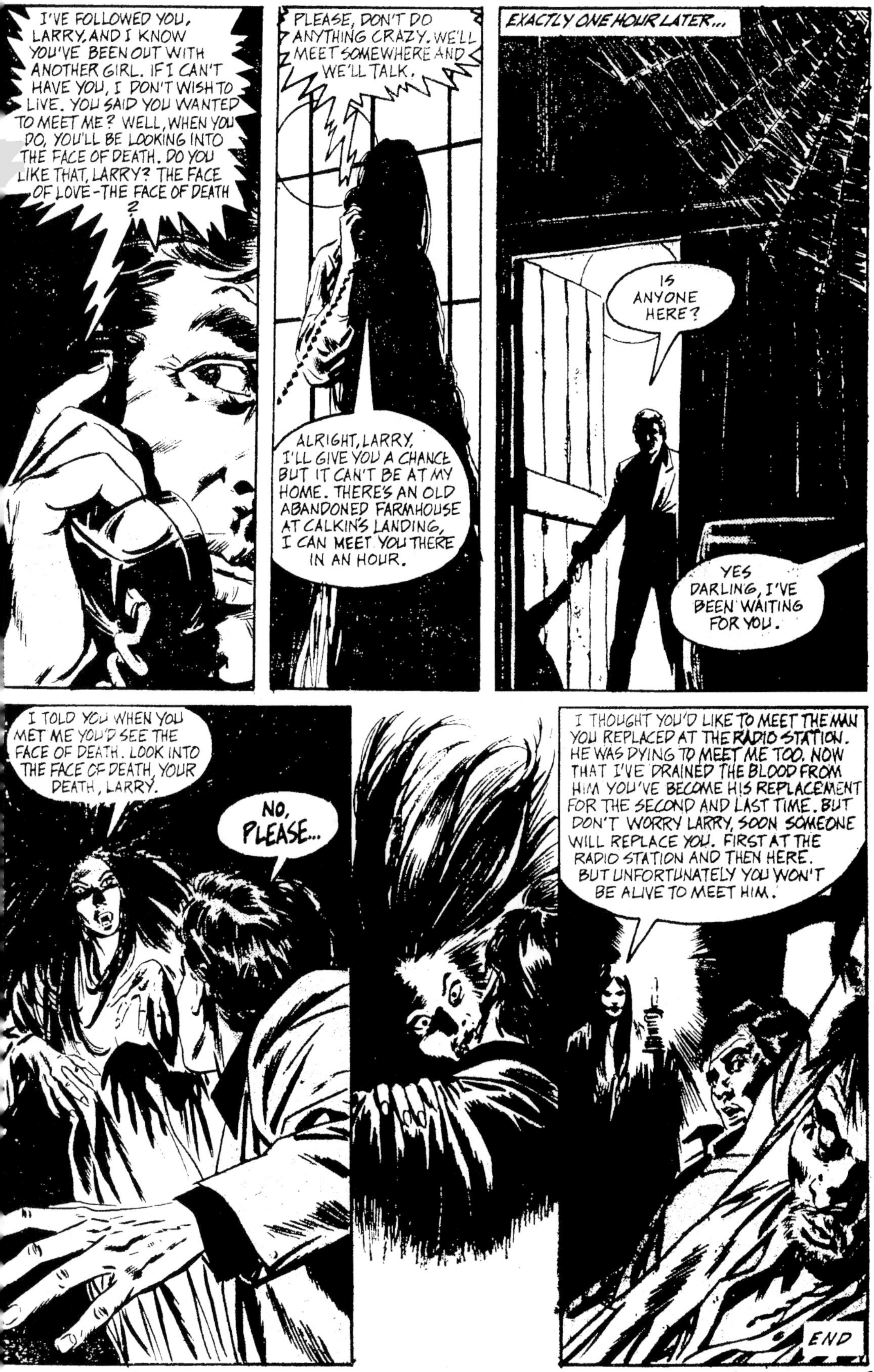
I'VE FOLLOWED YOU, LARRY, AND I KNOW YOU'VE BEEN OUT WITH ANOTHER GIRL. IF I CAN'T HAVE YOU, I DON'T WISH TO LIVE. YOU SAID YOU WANTED TO MEET ME? WELL, WHEN YOU DO, YOU'LL BE LOOKING INTO THE FACE OF DEATH. DO YOU LIKE THAT, LARRY? THE FACE OF LOVE - THE FACE OF DEATH
PLEASE, DON'T DO ANYTHING CRAZY. WE'LL MEET SOMEWHERE AND WE'LL TALK.
ALRIGHT, LARRY, I'LL GIVE YOU A CHANCE BUT IT CAN'T BE AT MY HOME. THERE'S AN OLD ABANDONED FARMHOUSE AT CALKIN'S LANDING, I CAN MEET YOU THERE IN AN HOUR.
EXACTLY ONE HOUR LATER...
IS ANYONE HERE?
YES DARLING, I'VE BEEN WAITING FOR YOU.
I TOLD YOU WHEN YOU MET ME YOU'D SEE THE FACE OF DEATH. LOOK INTO THE FACE OF DEATH, YOUR DEATH, LARRY.
NO, PLEASE...
I THOUGHT YOU'D LIKE TO MEET THE MAN YOU REPLACED AT THE RADIO STATION. HE WAS DYING TO MEET ME TOO. NOW THAT I'VE DRAINED THE BLOOD FROM HIM YOU'VE BECOME HIS REPLACEMENT FOR THE SECOND AND LAST TIME. BUT DON'T WORRY LARRY, SOON SOMEONE WILL REPLACE YOU. FIRST AT THE RADIO STATION AND THEN HERE. BUT UNFORTUNATELY YOU WON'T BE ALIVE TO MEET HIM.
END

# ISSUE SEVEN

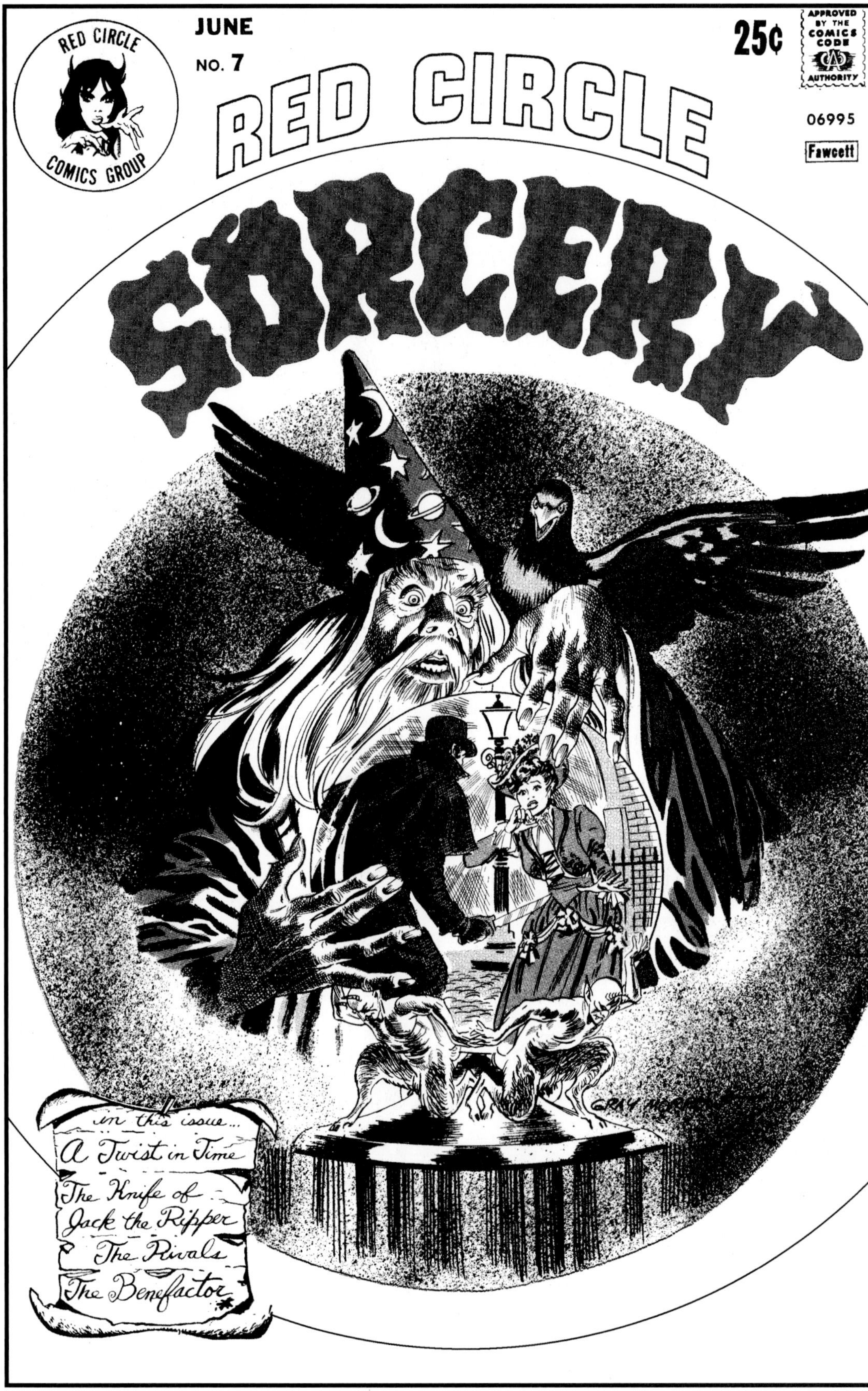
RED CIRCLE COMICS GROUP
JUNE
NO. 7
25¢
APPROVED BY THE COMICS CODE AUTHORITY
06995
Fawcett
RED CIRCLE
SORCERY
in this issue...
A Twist in Time
The Knife of Jack the Ripper
The Rivals
The Benefactor

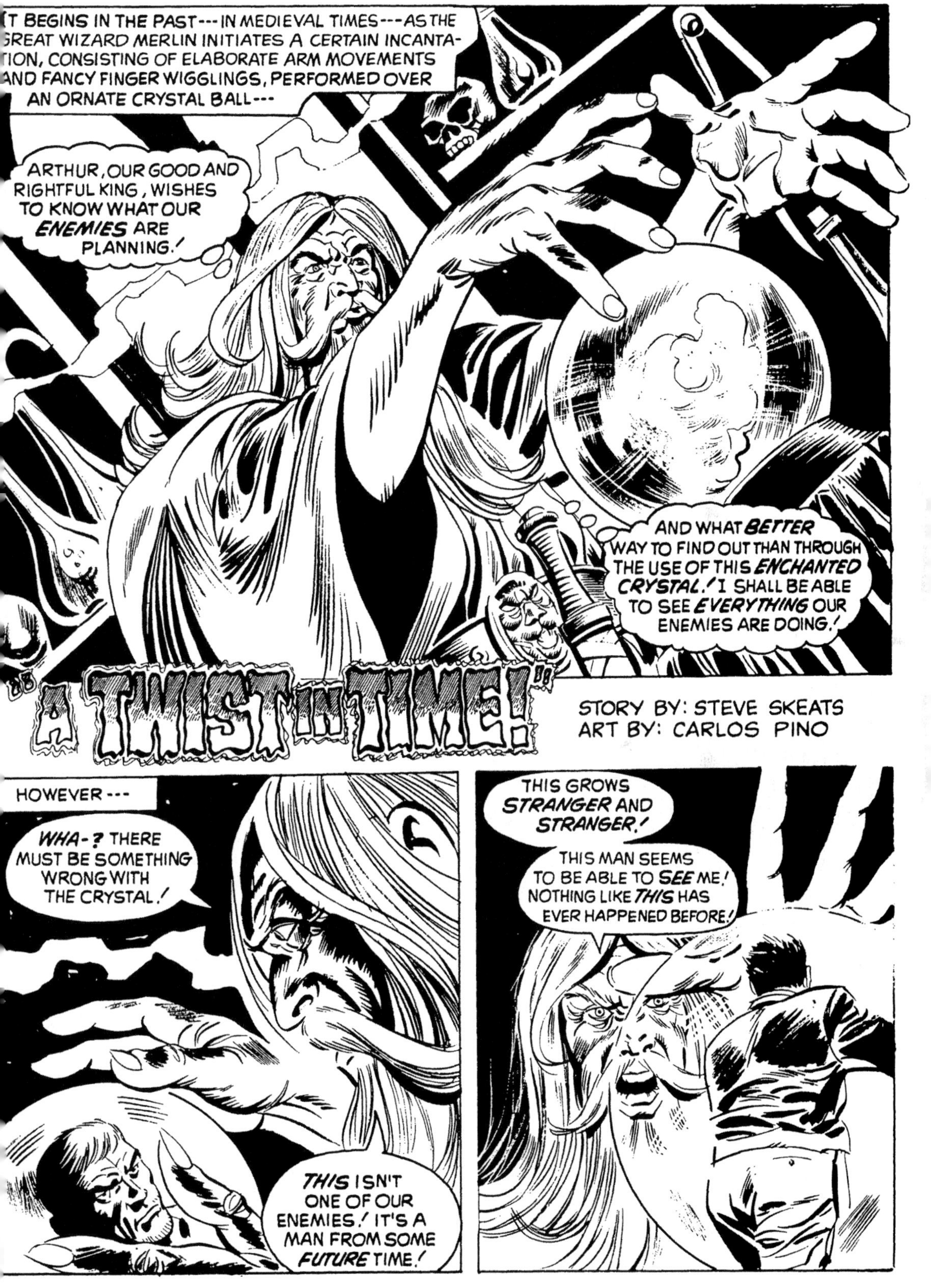

T BEGINS IN THE PAST---IN MEDIEVAL TIMES---AS THE REAT WIZARD MERLIN INITIATES A CERTAIN INCANTA- TION, CONSISTING OF ELABORATE ARM MOVEMENTS AND FANCY FINGER WIGGLINGS, PERFORMED OVER AN ORNATE CRYSTAL BALL---
ARTHUR, OUR GOOD AND RIGHTFUL KING, WISHES TO KNOW WHAT OUR ENEMIES ARE PLANNING.!
AND WHAT BETTER WAY TO FIND OUT THAN THROUGH THE USE OF THIS ENCHANTED CRYSTAL.! I SHALL BE ABLE TO SEE EVERYTHING OUR ENEMIES ARE DOING.!
A TWIST IN TIME!
STORY BY: STEVE SKEATS
ART BY: CARLOS PINO
HOWEVER---
WHA-? THERE MUST BE SOMETHING WRONG WITH THE CRYSTAL.!
THIS ISN'T ONE OF OUR ENEMIES.! IT'S A MAN FROM SOME FUTURE TIME.!
THIS GROWS STRANGER AND STRANGER.!
THIS MAN SEEMS TO BE ABLE TO SEE ME.! NOTHING LIKE THIS HAS EVER HAPPENED BEFORE.!

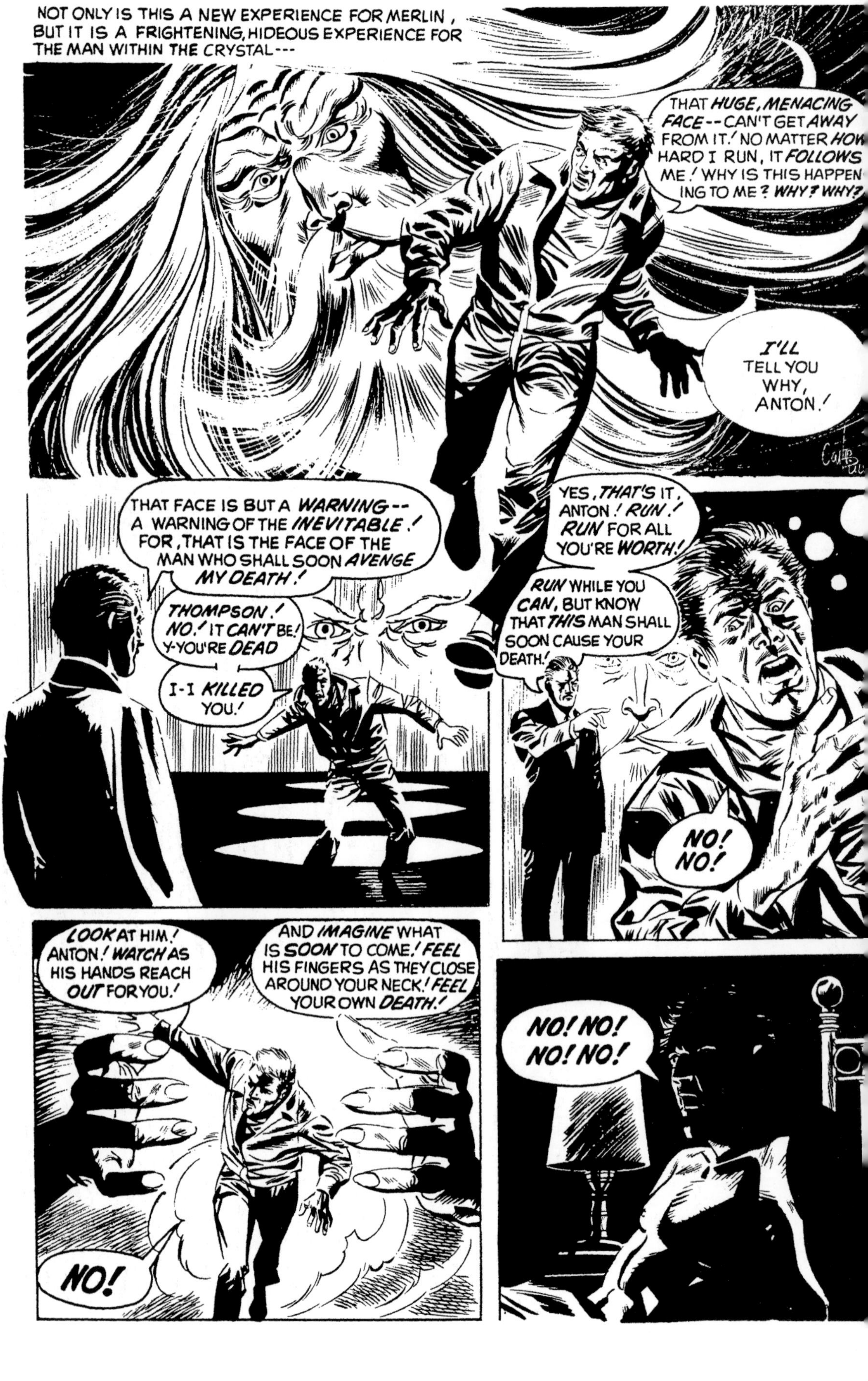
NOT ONLY IS THIS A NEW EXPERIENCE FOR MERLIN, BUT IT IS A FRIGHTENING, HIDEOUS EXPERIENCE FOR THE MAN WITHIN THE CRYSTAL---
THAT HUGE, MENACING FACE--CAN'T GET AWAY FROM IT! NO MATTER HOW HARD I RUN, IT FOLLOWS ME! WHY IS THIS HAPPENING TO ME? WHY? WHY?
I'LL TELL YOU WHY, ANTON!
THAT FACE IS BUT A WARNING-- A WARNING OF THE INEVITABLE! FOR, THAT IS THE FACE OF THE MAN WHO SHALL SOON AVENGE MY DEATH!
THOMPSON! NO! IT CAN'T BE! Y-YOU'RE DEAD
I-I KILLED YOU!
YES, THAT'S IT, ANTON! RUN! RUN FOR ALL YOU'RE WORTH!
RUN WHILE YOU CAN, BUT KNOW THAT THIS MAN SHALL SOON CAUSE YOUR DEATH!
NO! NO!
LOOK AT HIM! ANTON! WATCH AS HIS HANDS REACH OUT FOR YOU!
AND IMAGINE WHAT IS SOON TO COME! FEEL HIS FINGERS AS THEY CLOSE AROUND YOUR NECK! FEEL YOUR OWN DEATH!
NO!
NO! NO! NO! NO!

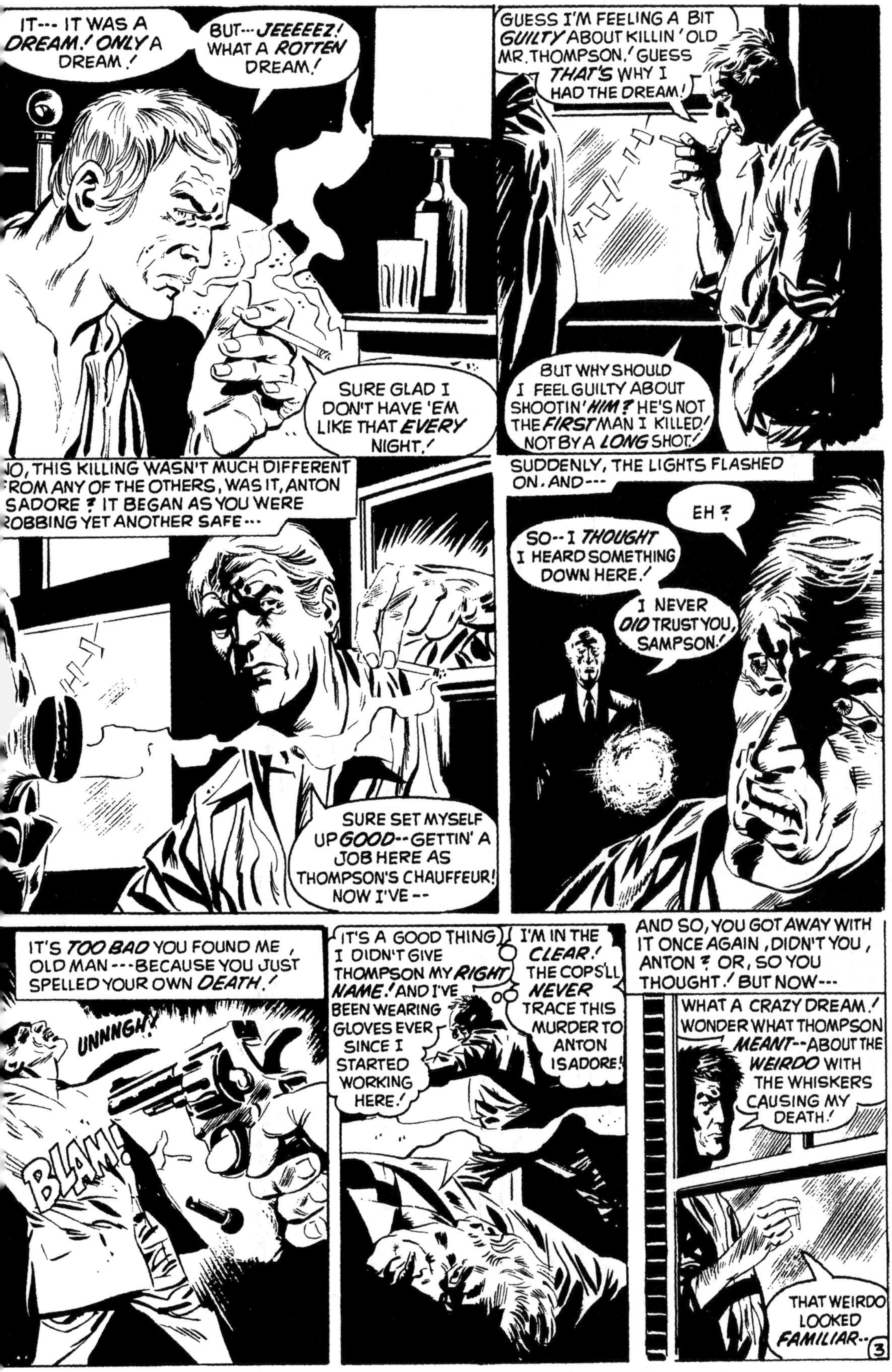
IT--- IT WAS A DREAM.! ONLY A DREAM.!
BUT--- JEEEEEZ! WHAT A ROTTEN DREAM!
SURE GLAD I DON'T HAVE 'EM LIKE THAT EVERY NIGHT.!
GUESS I'M FEELING A BIT GUILTY ABOUT KILLIN' OLD MR. THOMPSON.! GUESS THAT'S WHY I HAD THE DREAM!
BUT WHY SHOULD I FEEL GUILTY ABOUT SHOOTIN' HIM? HE'S NOT THE FIRST MAN I KILLED! NOT BY A LONG SHOT!
NO, THIS KILLING WASN'T MUCH DIFFERENT FROM ANY OF THE OTHERS, WAS IT, ANTON ISADORE? IT BEGAN AS YOU WERE ROBBING YET ANOTHER SAFE---
SURE SET MYSELF UP GOOD--GETTIN' A JOB HERE AS THOMPSON'S CHAUFFEUR! NOW I'VE --
SUDDENLY, THE LIGHTS FLASHED ON. AND---
EH?
SO--I THOUGHT I HEARD SOMETHING DOWN HERE.!
I NEVER DID TRUST YOU, SAMPSON.!
IT'S TOO BAD YOU FOUND ME, OLD MAN---BECAUSE YOU JUST SPELLED YOUR OWN DEATH.!
UNNNGH!
BLAM!
IT'S A GOOD THING I DIDN'T GIVE THOMPSON MY RIGHT NAME.! AND I'VE BEEN WEARING GLOVES EVER SINCE I STARTED WORKING HERE.!
I'M IN THE CLEAR.! THE COPS'LL NEVER TRACE THIS MURDER TO ANTON ISADORE!
AND SO, YOU GOT AWAY WITH IT ONCE AGAIN, DIDN'T YOU, ANTON? OR, SO YOU THOUGHT.! BUT NOW---
WHAT A CRAZY DREAM.! WONDER WHAT THOMPSON MEANT--ABOUT THE WEIRDO WITH THE WHISKERS CAUSING MY DEATH.!
THAT WEIRDO LOOKED FAMILIAR--
3

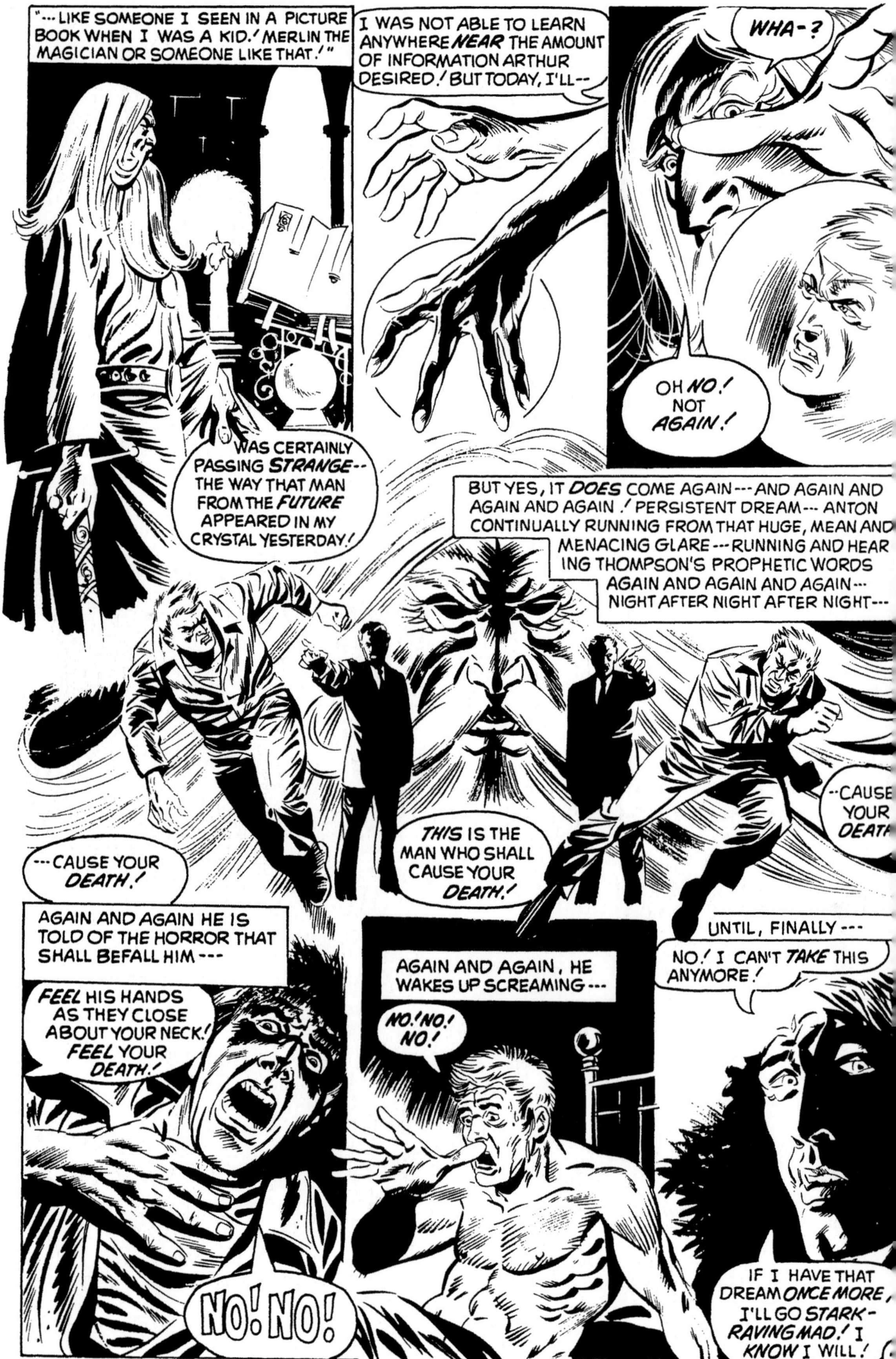
"--- LIKE SOMEONE I SEEN IN A PICTURE BOOK WHEN I WAS A KID.! MERLIN THE MAGICIAN OR SOMEONE LIKE THAT.!"
I WAS NOT ABLE TO LEARN ANYWHERE NEAR THE AMOUNT OF INFORMATION ARTHUR DESIRED.! BUT TODAY, I'LL--
WHA-?
OH NO.! NOT AGAIN.!
WAS CERTAINLY PASSING STRANGE-- THE WAY THAT MAN FROM THE FUTURE APPEARED IN MY CRYSTAL YESTERDAY.!
BUT YES, IT DOES COME AGAIN--- AND AGAIN AND AGAIN AND AGAIN.! PERSISTENT DREAM--- ANTON CONTINUALLY RUNNING FROM THAT HUGE, MEAN AND MENACING GLARE--- RUNNING AND HEARING THOMPSON'S PROPHETIC WORDS AGAIN AND AGAIN AND AGAIN--- NIGHT AFTER NIGHT AFTER NIGHT---
--CAUSE YOUR DEATH
--- CAUSE YOUR DEATH.!
THIS IS THE MAN WHO SHALL CAUSE YOUR DEATH.!
AGAIN AND AGAIN HE IS TOLD OF THE HORROR THAT SHALL BEFALL HIM ---
FEEL HIS HANDS AS THEY CLOSE ABOUT YOUR NECK.! FEEL YOUR DEATH.!
NO! NO!
AGAIN AND AGAIN, HE WAKES UP SCREAMING ---
NO.! NO.! NO.!
UNTIL, FINALLY ---
NO.! I CAN'T TAKE THIS ANYMORE.!
IF I HAVE THAT DREAM ONCE MORE, I'LL GO STARK-RAVING MAD.! I KNOW I WILL.!

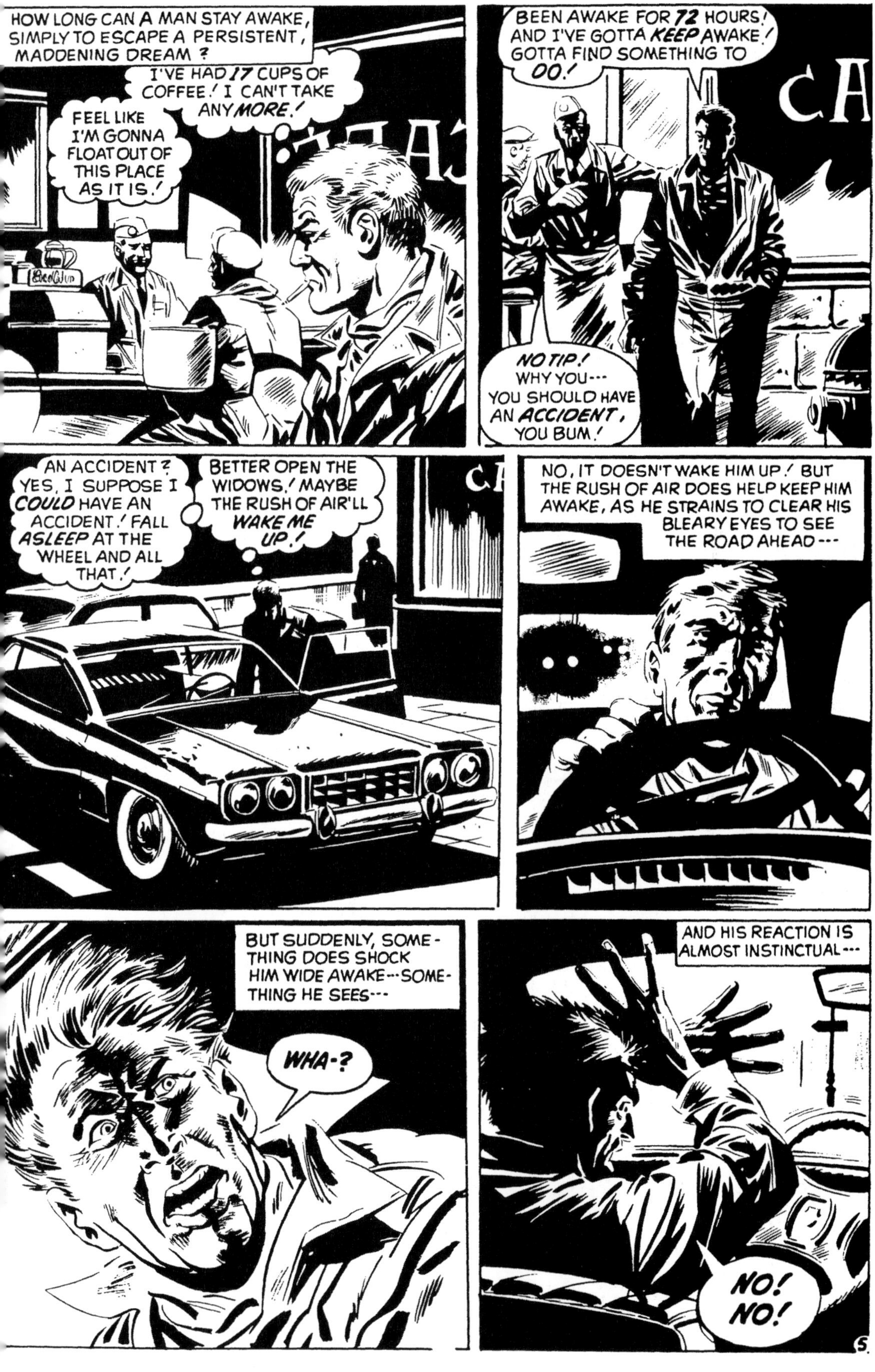
HOW LONG CAN A MAN STAY AWAKE, SIMPLY TO ESCAPE A PERSISTENT, MADDENING DREAM ?
I'VE HAD 17 CUPS OF COFFEE.! I CAN'T TAKE ANY MORE.!
FEEL LIKE I'M GONNA FLOAT OUT OF THIS PLACE AS IT IS.!
BEEN AWAKE FOR 72 HOURS! AND I'VE GOTTA KEEP AWAKE! GOTTA FIND SOMETHING TO DO!
CA
NO TIP! WHY YOU--- YOU SHOULD HAVE AN ACCIDENT, YOU BUM!
AN ACCIDENT? YES, I SUPPOSE I COULD HAVE AN ACCIDENT! FALL ASLEEP AT THE WHEEL AND ALL THAT!
BETTER OPEN THE WIDOWS! MAYBE THE RUSH OF AIR'LL WAKE ME UP!
NO, IT DOESN'T WAKE HIM UP! BUT THE RUSH OF AIR DOES HELP KEEP HIM AWAKE, AS HE STRAINS TO CLEAR HIS BLEARY EYES TO SEE THE ROAD AHEAD---
BUT SUDDENLY, SOMETHING DOES SHOCK HIM WIDE AWAKE---SOMETHING HE SEES---
WHA-?
AND HIS REACTION IS ALMOST INSTINCTUAL---
NO! NO!

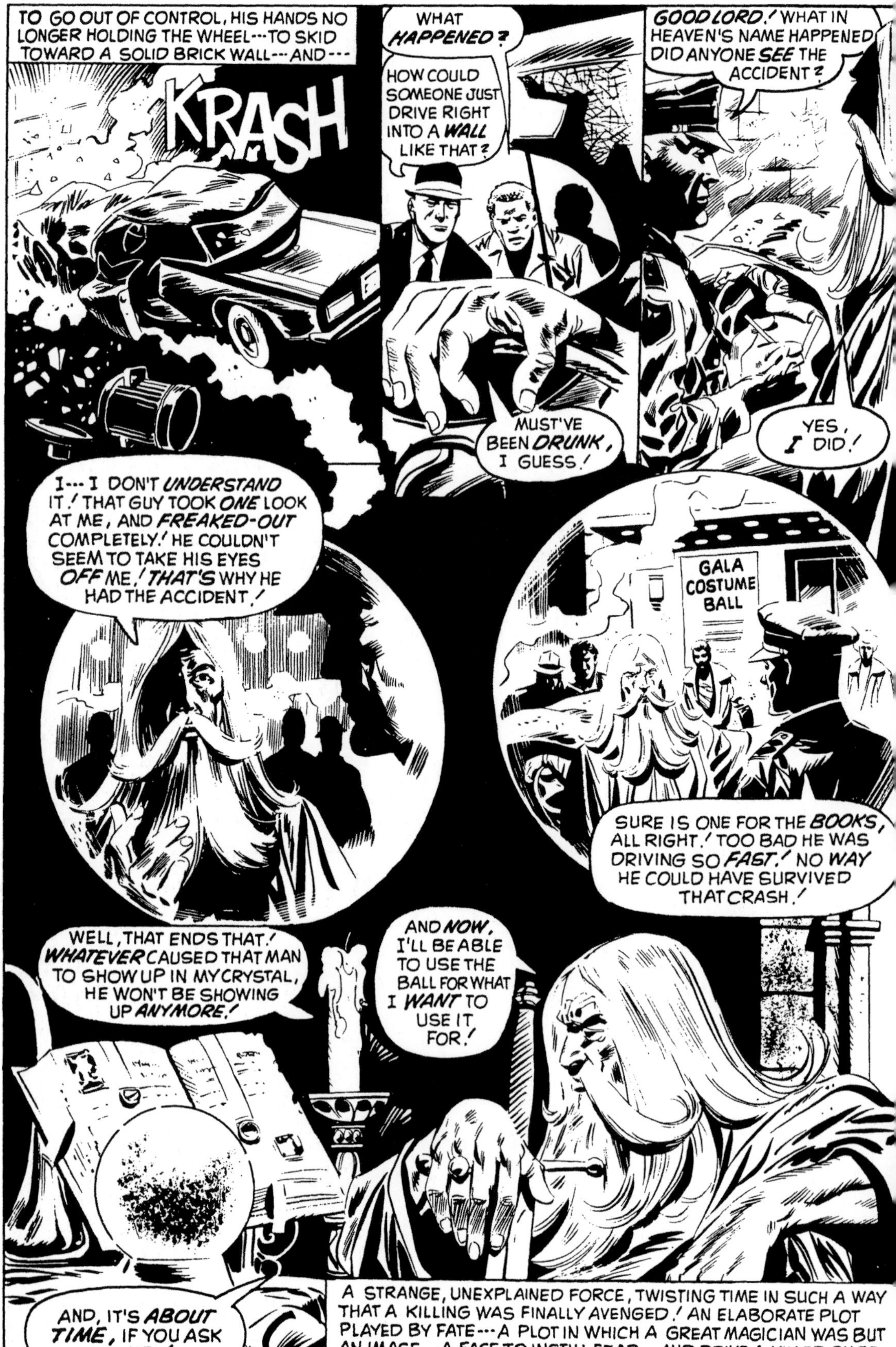

TO GO OUT OF CONTROL, HIS HANDS NO LONGER HOLDING THE WHEEL---TO SKID TOWARD A SOLID BRICK WALL---AND---
KRASH
WHAT HAPPENED?
HOW COULD SOMEONE JUST DRIVE RIGHT INTO A WALL LIKE THAT?
MUST'VE BEEN DRUNK, I GUESS!
GOOD LORD! WHAT IN HEAVEN'S NAME HAPPENED DID ANYONE SEE THE ACCIDENT?
YES, I DID!
I--- I DON'T UNDERSTAND IT! THAT GUY TOOK ONE LOOK AT ME, AND FREAKED-OUT COMPLETELY! HE COULDN'T SEEM TO TAKE HIS EYES OFF ME! THAT'S WHY HE HAD THE ACCIDENT!
GALA COSTUME BALL
SURE IS ONE FOR THE BOOKS, ALL RIGHT! TOO BAD HE WAS DRIVING SO FAST! NO WAY HE COULD HAVE SURVIVED THAT CRASH!
WELL, THAT ENDS THAT! WHATEVER CAUSED THAT MAN TO SHOW UP IN MY CRYSTAL, HE WON'T BE SHOWING UP ANYMORE!
AND NOW, I'LL BE ABLE TO USE THE BALL FOR WHAT I WANT TO USE IT FOR!
AND, IT'S ABOUT TIME, IF YOU ASK ME!
A STRANGE, UNEXPLAINED FORCE, TWISTING TIME IN SUCH A WAY THAT A KILLING WAS FINALLY AVENGED! AN ELABORATE PLOT PLAYED BY FATE---A PLOT IN WHICH A GREAT MAGICIAN WAS BUT AN IMAGE---A FACE TO INSTILL FEAR---AND DRIVE A KILLER ON TO DEATH!
THE END

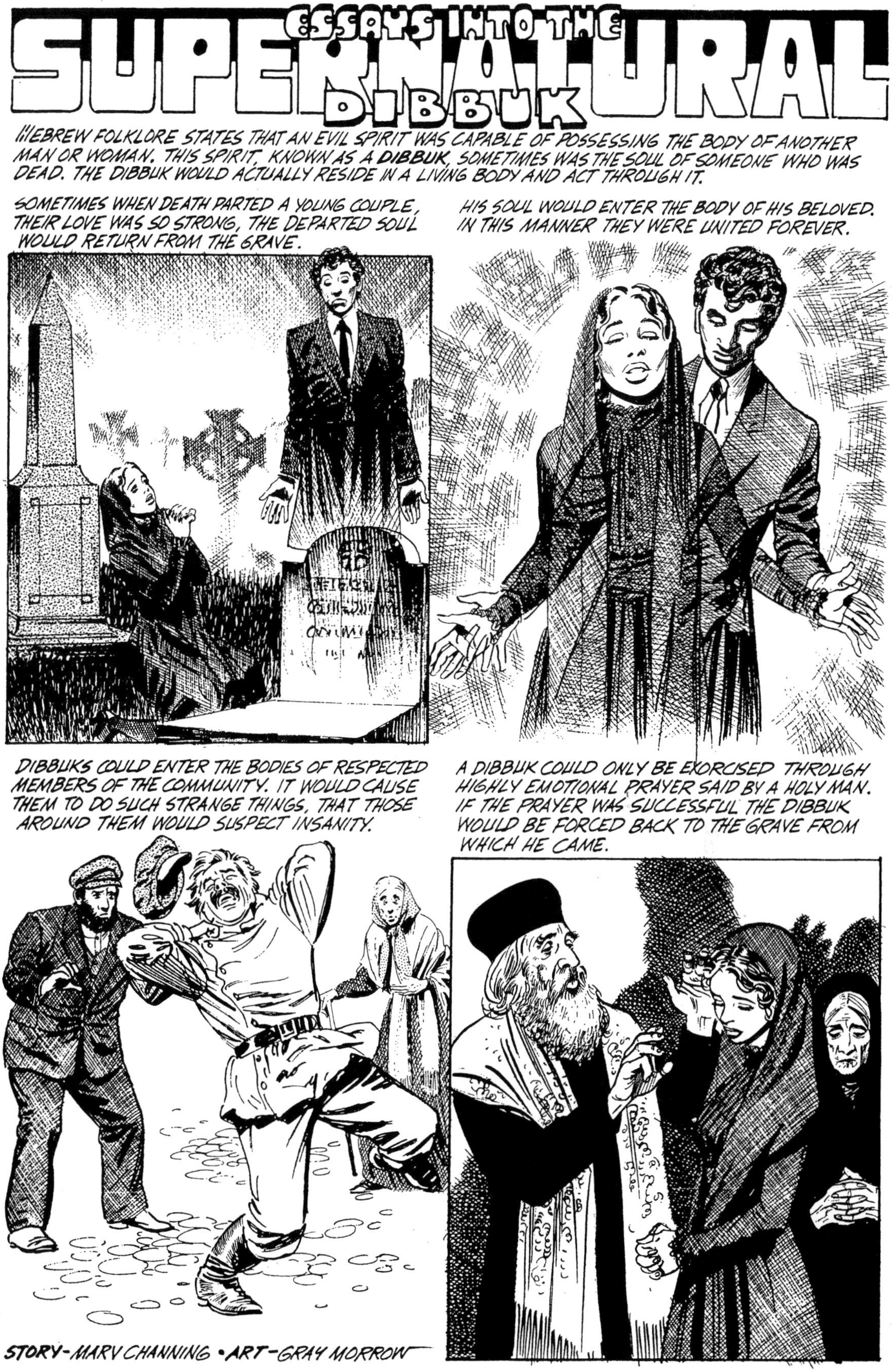
ESSAYS INTO THE SUPERNATURAL
DIBBUK
HEBREW FOLKLORE STATES THAT AN EVIL SPIRIT WAS CAPABLE OF POSSESSING THE BODY OF ANOTHER MAN OR WOMAN. THIS SPIRIT, KNOWN AS A DIBBUK, SOMETIMES WAS THE SOUL OF SOMEONE WHO WAS DEAD. THE DIBBUK WOULD ACTUALLY RESIDE IN A LIVING BODY AND ACT THROUGH IT.
SOMETIMES WHEN DEATH PARTED A YOUNG COUPLE, THEIR LOVE WAS SO STRONG, THE DEPARTED SOUL WOULD RETURN FROM THE GRAVE.
HIS SOUL WOULD ENTER THE BODY OF HIS BELOVED. IN THIS MANNER THEY WERE UNITED FOREVER.
DIBBUKS COULD ENTER THE BODIES OF RESPECTED MEMBERS OF THE COMMUNITY. IT WOULD CAUSE THEM TO DO SUCH STRANGE THINGS, THAT THOSE AROUND THEM WOULD SUSPECT INSANITY.
A DIBBUK COULD ONLY BE EXORCISED THROUGH HIGHLY EMOTIONAL PRAYER SAID BY A HOLY MAN. IF THE PRAYER WAS SUCCESSFUL THE DIBBUK WOULD BE FORCED BACK TO THE GRAVE FROM WHICH HE CAME.
STORY-MARV CHANNING • ART-GRAY MORROW

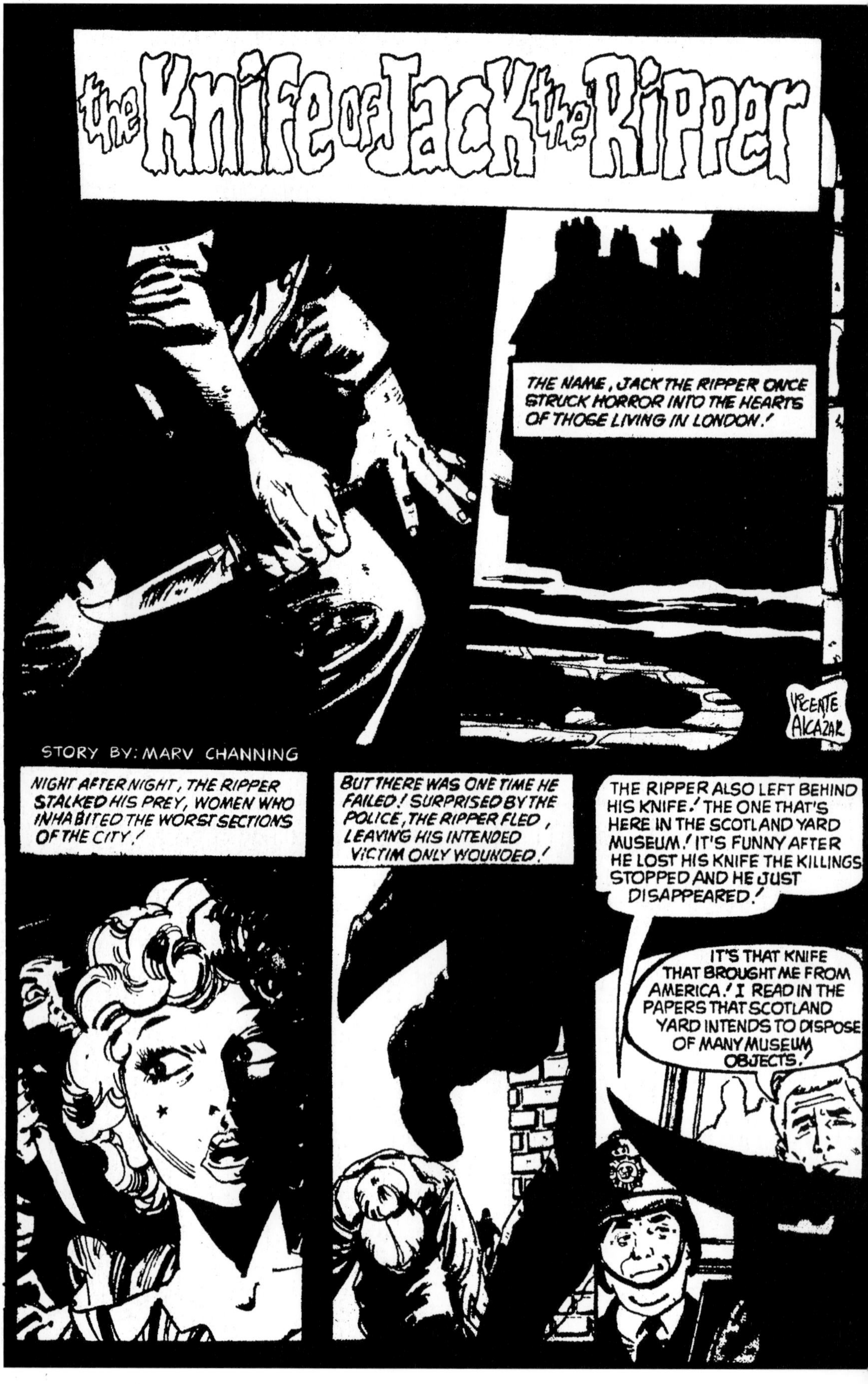
the Knife of Jack the Ripper
THE NAME, JACK THE RIPPER ONCE STRUCK HORROR INTO THE HEARTS OF THOSE LIVING IN LONDON!
VICENTE ALCAZAR
STORY BY: MARV CHANNING
NIGHT AFTER NIGHT, THE RIPPER STALKED HIS PREY, WOMEN WHO INHABITED THE WORST SECTIONS OF THE CITY!
BUT THERE WAS ONE TIME HE FAILED! SURPRISED BY THE POLICE, THE RIPPER FLED, LEAVING HIS INTENDED VICTIM ONLY WOUNDED!
THE RIPPER ALSO LEFT BEHIND HIS KNIFE! THE ONE THAT'S HERE IN THE SCOTLAND YARD MUSEUM! IT'S FUNNY AFTER HE LOST HIS KNIFE THE KILLINGS STOPPED AND HE JUST DISAPPEARED!
IT'S THAT KNIFE THAT BROUGHT ME FROM AMERICA! I READ IN THE PAPERS THAT SCOTLAND YARD INTENDS TO DISPOSE OF MANY MUSEUM OBJECTS!

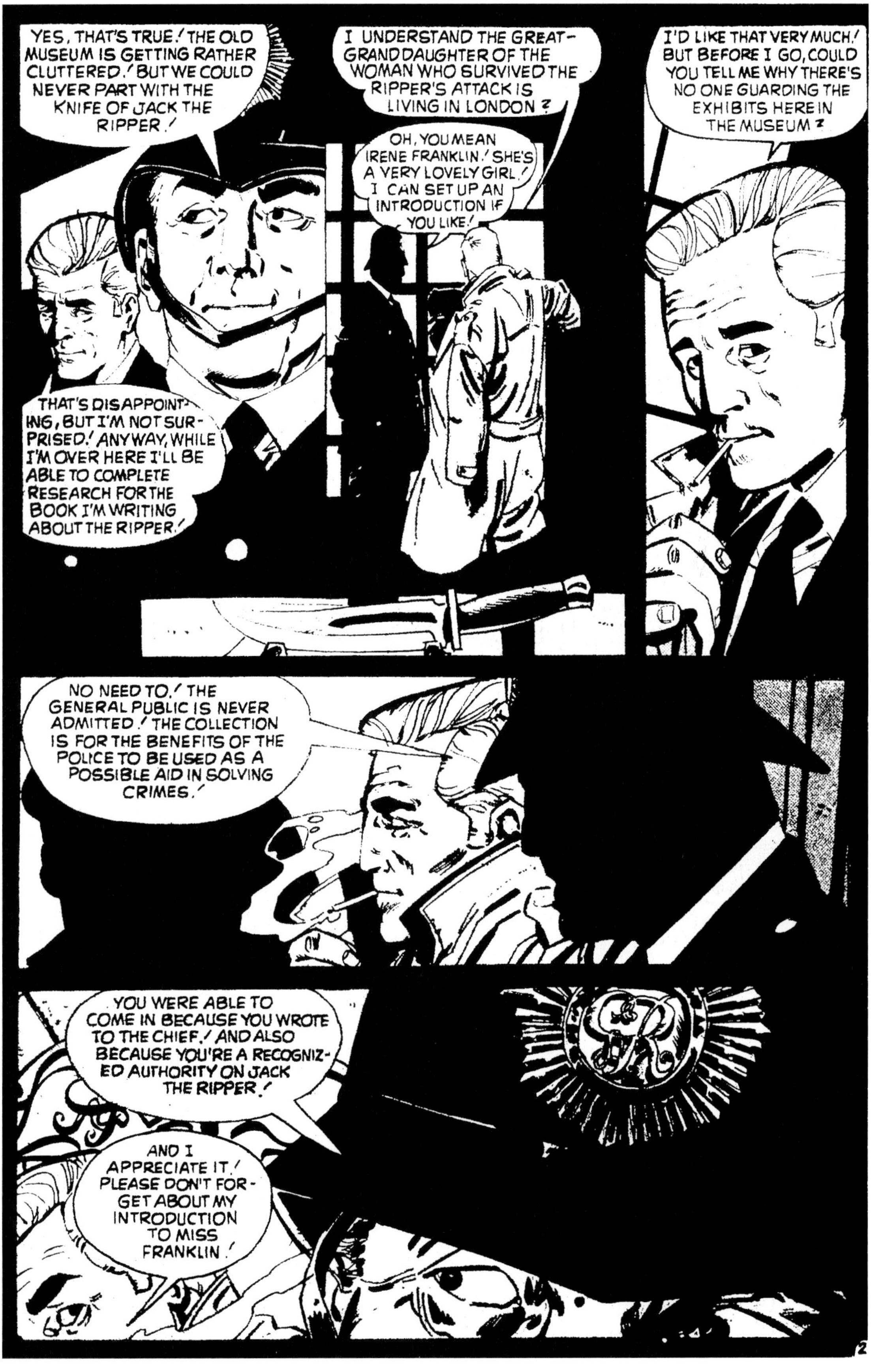
YES, THAT'S TRUE! THE OLD MUSEUM IS GETTING RATHER CLUTTERED! BUT WE COULD NEVER PART WITH THE KNIFE OF JACK THE RIPPER!
THAT'S DISAPPOINTING, BUT I'M NOT SURPRISED! ANYWAY, WHILE I'M OVER HERE I'LL BE ABLE TO COMPLETE RESEARCH FOR THE BOOK I'M WRITING ABOUT THE RIPPER!
I UNDERSTAND THE GREAT-GRANDDAUGHTER OF THE WOMAN WHO SURVIVED THE RIPPER'S ATTACK IS LIVING IN LONDON?
OH, YOU MEAN IRENE FRANKLIN! SHE'S A VERY LOVELY GIRL! I CAN SET UP AN INTRODUCTION IF YOU LIKE!
I'D LIKE THAT VERY MUCH! BUT BEFORE I GO, COULD YOU TELL ME WHY THERE'S NO ONE GUARDING THE EXHIBITS HERE IN THE MUSEUM?
NO NEED TO! THE GENERAL PUBLIC IS NEVER ADMITTED! THE COLLECTION IS FOR THE BENEFITS OF THE POLICE TO BE USED AS A POSSIBLE AID IN SOLVING CRIMES!
YOU WERE ABLE TO COME IN BECAUSE YOU WROTE TO THE CHIEF! AND ALSO BECAUSE YOU'RE A RECOGNIZED AUTHORITY ON JACK THE RIPPER!
AND I APPRECIATE IT! PLEASE DON'T FORGET ABOUT MY INTRODUCTION TO MISS FRANKLIN!
2

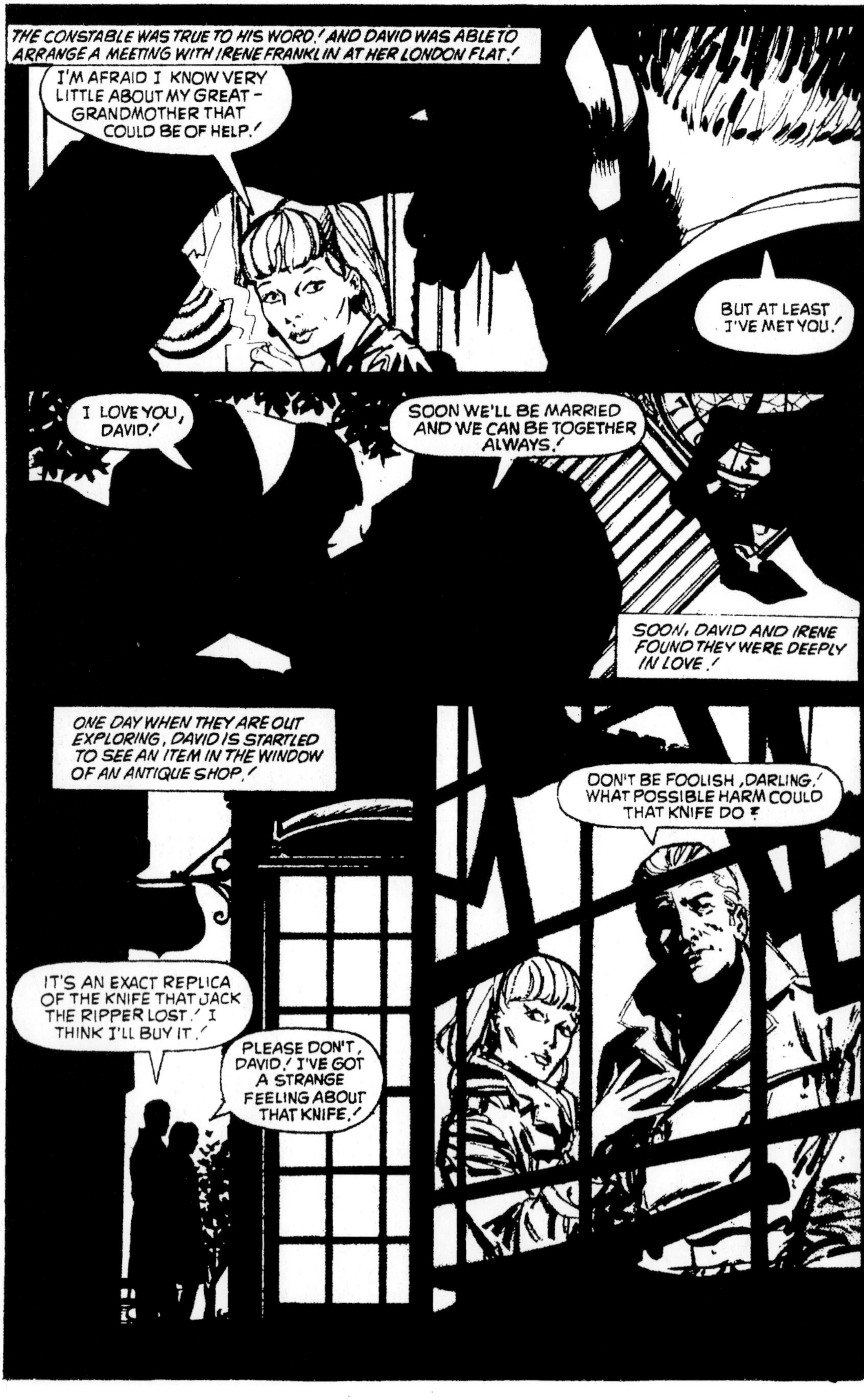
THE CONSTABLE WAS TRUE TO HIS WORD! AND DAVID WAS ABLE TO ARRANGE A MEETING WITH IRENE FRANKLIN AT HER LONDON FLAT!
I'M AFRAID I KNOW VERY LITTLE ABOUT MY GREAT-GRANDMOTHER THAT COULD BE OF HELP!
BUT AT LEAST I'VE MET YOU!
I LOVE YOU, DAVID!
SOON WE'LL BE MARRIED AND WE CAN BE TOGETHER ALWAYS!
SOON, DAVID AND IRENE FOUND THEY WERE DEEPLY IN LOVE!
ONE DAY WHEN THEY ARE OUT EXPLORING, DAVID IS STARTLED TO SEE AN ITEM IN THE WINDOW OF AN ANTIQUE SHOP!
IT'S AN EXACT REPLICA OF THE KNIFE THAT JACK THE RIPPER LOST! I THINK I'LL BUY IT!
PLEASE DON'T, DAVID! I'VE GOT A STRANGE FEELING ABOUT THAT KNIFE!
DON'T BE FOOLISH, DARLING! WHAT POSSIBLE HARM COULD THAT KNIFE DO?

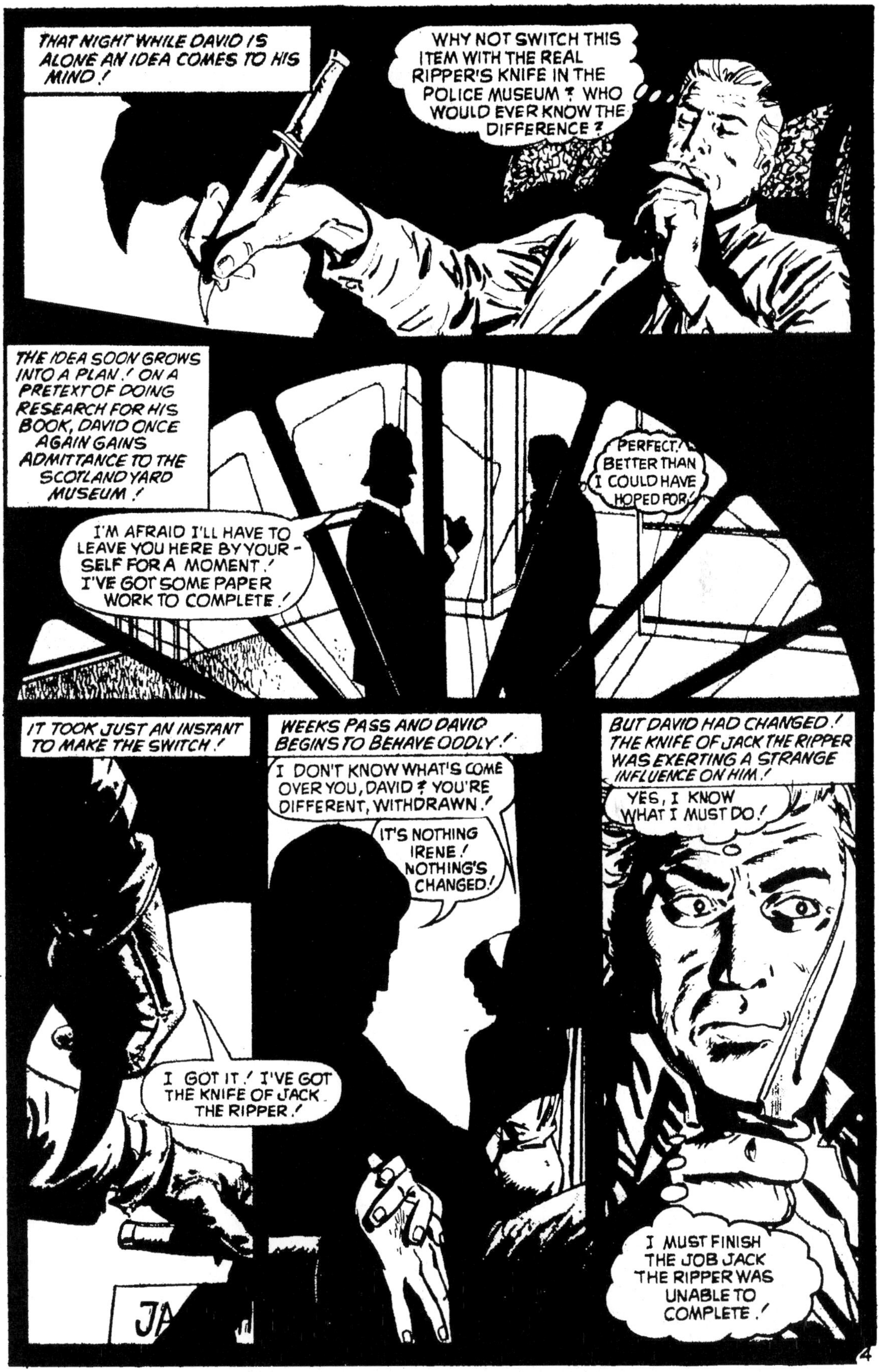
THAT NIGHT WHILE DAVID IS ALONE AN IDEA COMES TO HIS MIND!
WHY NOT SWITCH THIS ITEM WITH THE REAL RIPPER'S KNIFE IN THE POLICE MUSEUM? WHO WOULD EVER KNOW THE DIFFERENCE?
THE IDEA SOON GROWS INTO A PLAN! ON A PRETEXT OF DOING RESEARCH FOR HIS BOOK, DAVID ONCE AGAIN GAINS ADMITTANCE TO THE SCOTLAND YARD MUSEUM!
PERFECT! BETTER THAN I COULD HAVE HOPED FOR!
I'M AFRAID I'LL HAVE TO LEAVE YOU HERE BY YOUR-SELF FOR A MOMENT! I'VE GOT SOME PAPER WORK TO COMPLETE!
IT TOOK JUST AN INSTANT TO MAKE THE SWITCH!
I GOT IT! I'VE GOT THE KNIFE OF JACK THE RIPPER!
WEEKS PASS AND DAVID BEGINS TO BEHAVE ODDLY!
I DON'T KNOW WHAT'S COME OVER YOU, DAVID? YOU'RE DIFFERENT, WITHDRAWN!
IT'S NOTHING IRENE! NOTHING'S CHANGED!
BUT DAVID HAD CHANGED! THE KNIFE OF JACK THE RIPPER WAS EXERTING A STRANGE INFLUENCE ON HIM!
YES, I KNOW WHAT I MUST DO!
I MUST FINISH THE JOB JACK THE RIPPER WAS UNABLE TO COMPLETE!

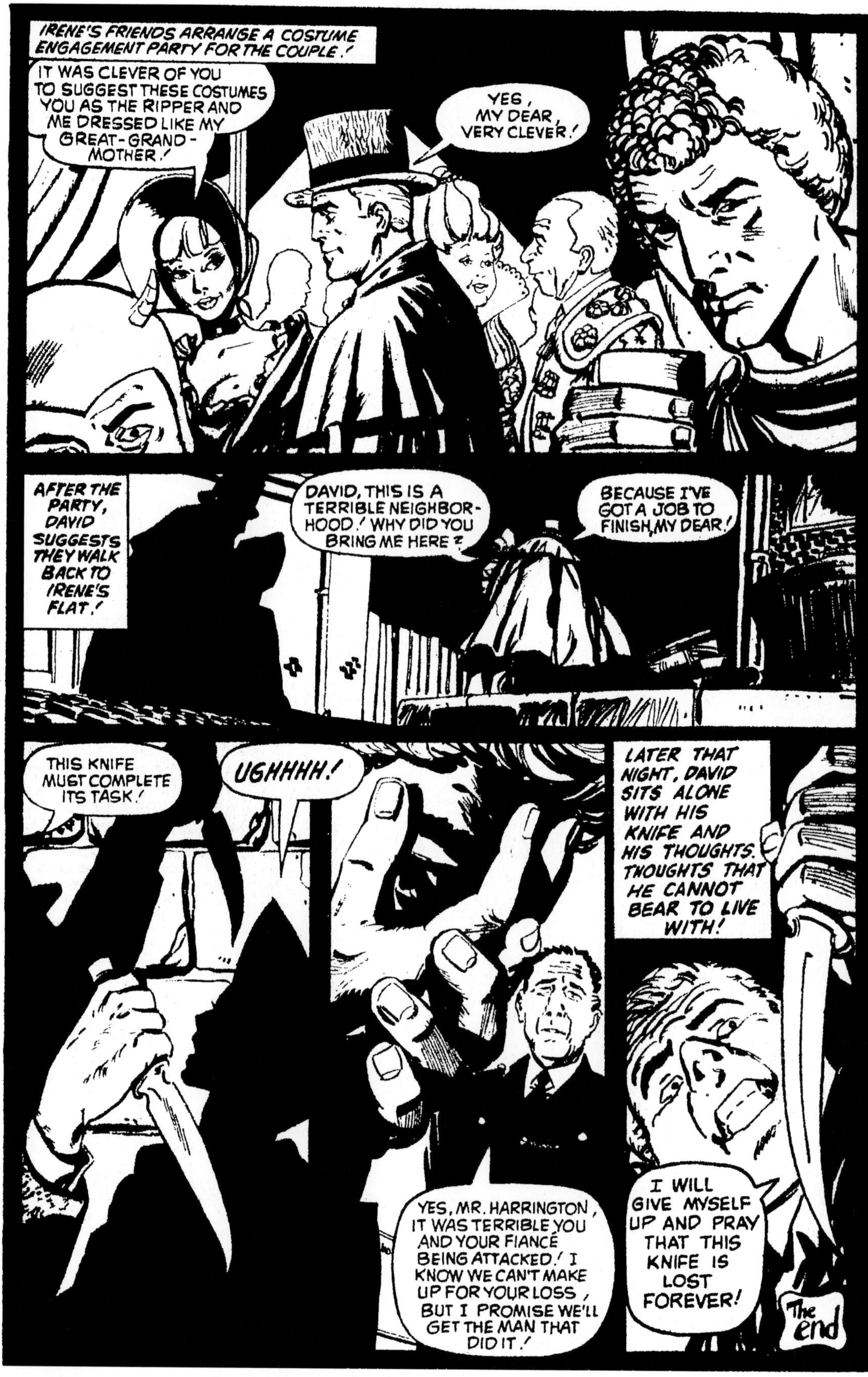
IRENE'S FRIENDS ARRANGE A COSTUME ENGAGEMENT PARTY FOR THE COUPLE.!
IT WAS CLEVER OF YOU TO SUGGEST THESE COSTUMES YOU AS THE RIPPER AND ME DRESSED LIKE MY GREAT-GRAND-MOTHER.!
YES, MY DEAR, VERY CLEVER!
AFTER THE PARTY, DAVID SUGGESTS THEY WALK BACK TO IRENE'S FLAT.!
DAVID, THIS IS A TERRIBLE NEIGHBOR-HOOD! WHY DID YOU BRING ME HERE?
BECAUSE I'VE GOT A JOB TO FINISH, MY DEAR!
THIS KNIFE MUST COMPLETE ITS TASK!
UGHHHH!
YES, MR. HARRINGTON, IT WAS TERRIBLE YOU AND YOUR FIANCÉ BEING ATTACKED! I KNOW WE CAN'T MAKE UP FOR YOUR LOSS, BUT I PROMISE WE'LL GET THE MAN THAT DID IT!
LATER THAT NIGHT, DAVID SITS ALONE WITH HIS KNIFE AND HIS THOUGHTS. THOUGHTS THAT HE CANNOT BEAR TO LIVE WITH!
I WILL GIVE MYSELF UP AND PRAY THAT THIS KNIFE IS LOST FOREVER!
The end

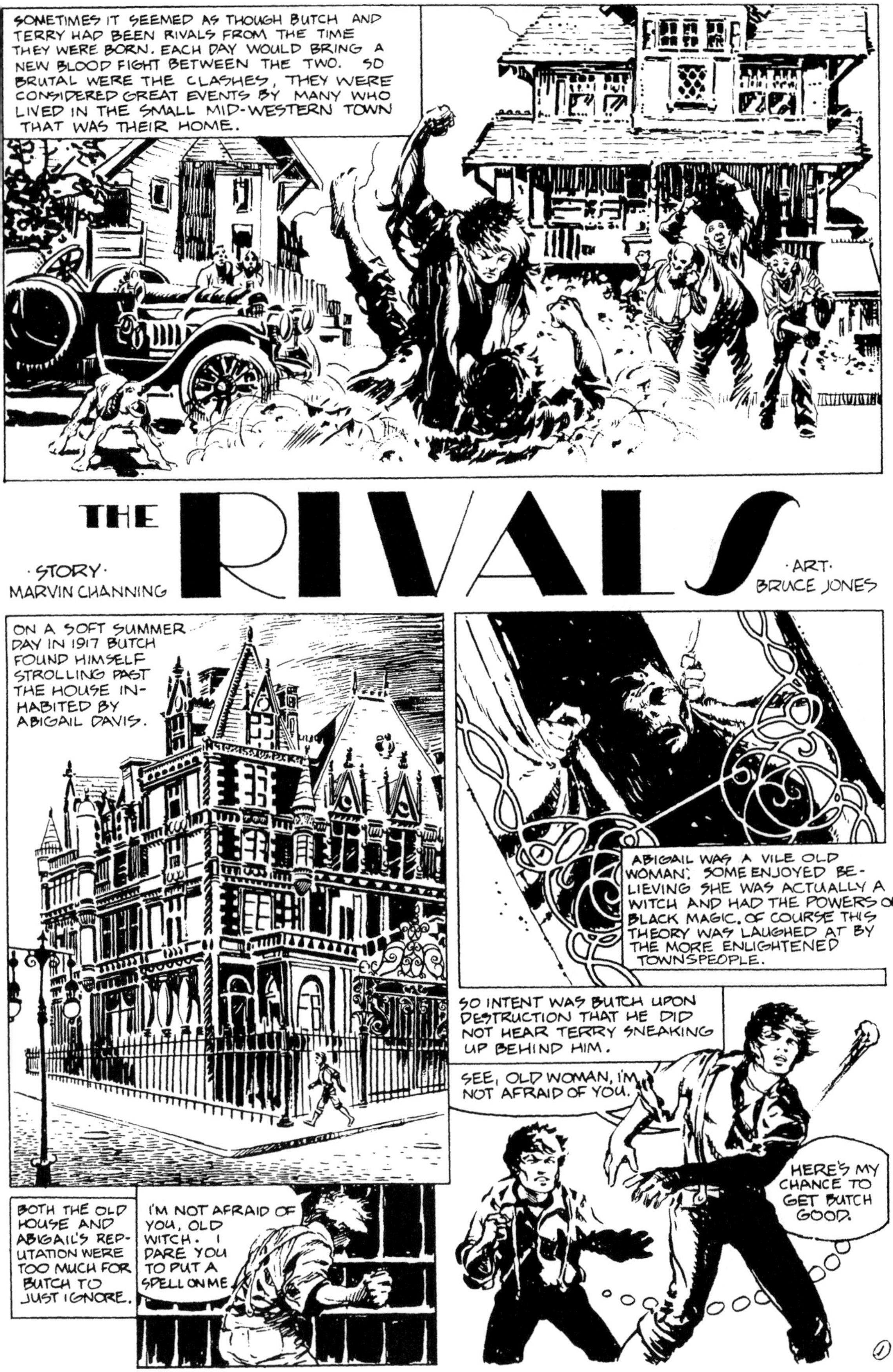
SOMETIMES IT SEEMED AS THOUGH BUTCH AND TERRY HAD BEEN RIVALS FROM THE TIME THEY WERE BORN. EACH DAY WOULD BRING A NEW BLOOD FIGHT BETWEEN THE TWO. SO BRUTAL WERE THE CLASHES, THEY WERE CONSIDERED GREAT EVENTS BY MANY WHO LIVED IN THE SMALL MID-WESTERN TOWN THAT WAS THEIR HOME.
THE RIVALS
·STORY· MARVIN CHANNING
·ART· BRUCE JONES
ON A SOFT SUMMER DAY IN 1917 BUTCH FOUND HIMSELF STROLLING PAST THE HOUSE INHABITED BY ABIGAIL DAVIS.
ABIGAIL WAS A VILE OLD WOMAN. SOME ENJOYED BELIEVING SHE WAS ACTUALLY A WITCH AND HAD THE POWERS OF BLACK MAGIC. OF COURSE THIS THEORY WAS LAUGHED AT BY THE MORE ENLIGHTENED TOWNSPEOPLE.
BOTH THE OLD HOUSE AND ABIGAIL'S REPUTATION WERE TOO MUCH FOR BUTCH TO JUST IGNORE.
I'M NOT AFRAID OF YOU, OLD WITCH. I DARE YOU TO PUT A SPELL ON ME.
SO INTENT WAS BUTCH UPON DESTRUCTION THAT HE DID NOT HEAR TERRY SNEAKING UP BEHIND HIM.
SEE, OLD WOMAN, I'M NOT AFRAID OF YOU.
HERE'S MY CHANCE TO GET BUTCH GOOD.

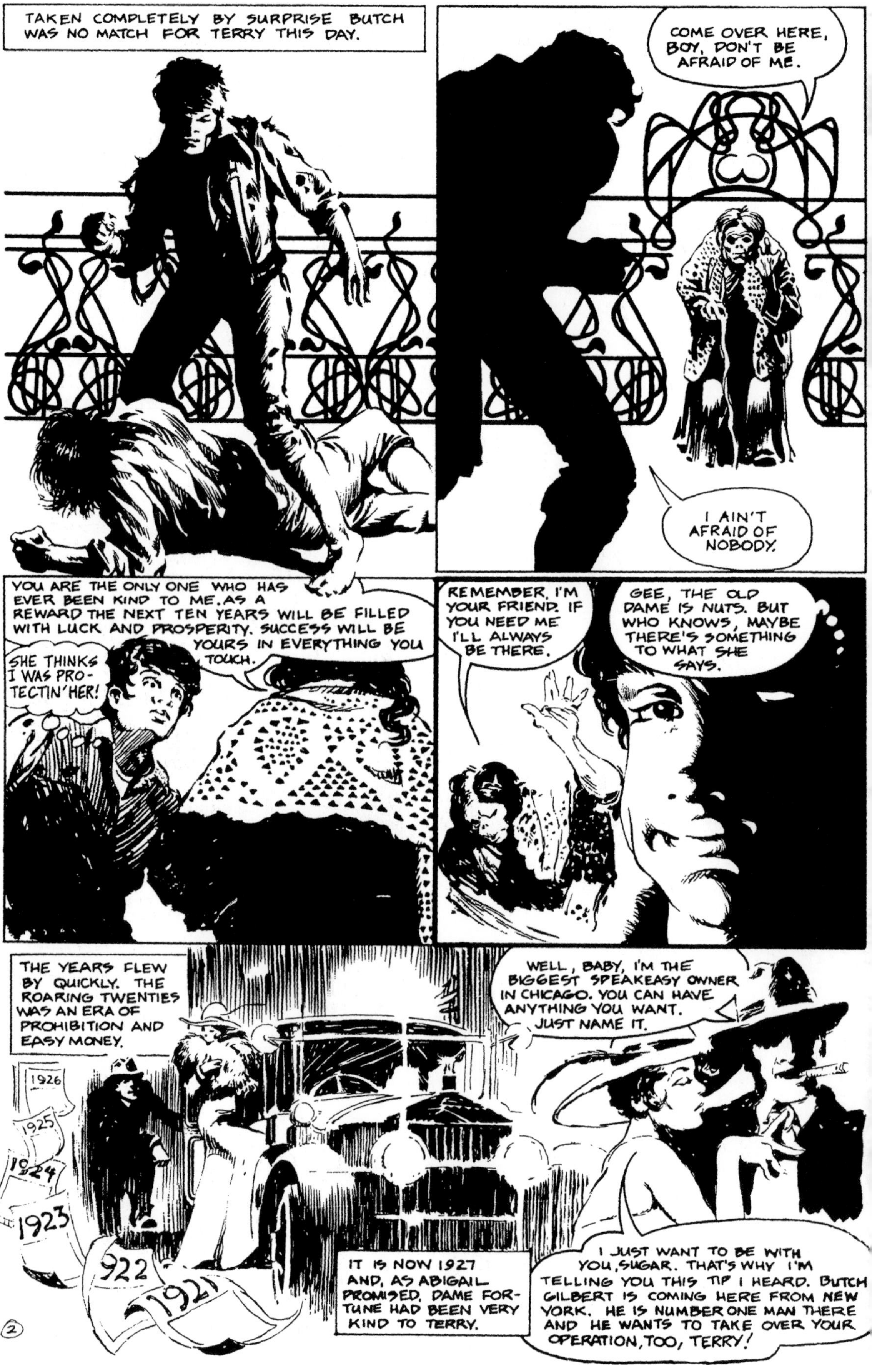

TAKEN COMPLETELY BY SURPRISE BUTCH WAS NO MATCH FOR TERRY THIS DAY.
COME OVER HERE, BOY, DON'T BE AFRAID OF ME.
I AIN'T AFRAID OF NOBODY.
YOU ARE THE ONLY ONE WHO HAS EVER BEEN KIND TO ME. AS A REWARD THE NEXT TEN YEARS WILL BE FILLED WITH LUCK AND PROSPERITY. SUCCESS WILL BE YOURS IN EVERYTHING YOU TOUCH.
SHE THINKS I WAS PROTECTIN' HER!
REMEMBER, I'M YOUR FRIEND. IF YOU NEED ME I'LL ALWAYS BE THERE.
GEE, THE OLD DAME IS NUTS. BUT WHO KNOWS, MAYBE THERE'S SOMETHING TO WHAT SHE SAYS.
THE YEARS FLEW BY QUICKLY. THE ROARING TWENTIES WAS AN ERA OF PROHIBITION AND EASY MONEY.
1926
1925
1924
1923
922
1921
WELL, BABY, I'M THE BIGGEST SPEAKEASY OWNER IN CHICAGO. YOU CAN HAVE ANYTHING YOU WANT. JUST NAME IT.
IT IS NOW 1927 AND, AS ABIGAIL PROMISED, DAME FORTUNE HAD BEEN VERY KIND TO TERRY.
I JUST WANT TO BE WITH YOU, SUGAR. THAT'S WHY I'M TELLING YOU THIS TIP I HEARD. BUTCH GILBERT IS COMING HERE FROM NEW YORK. HE IS NUMBER ONE MAN THERE AND HE WANTS TO TAKE OVER YOUR OPERATION, TOO, TERRY!

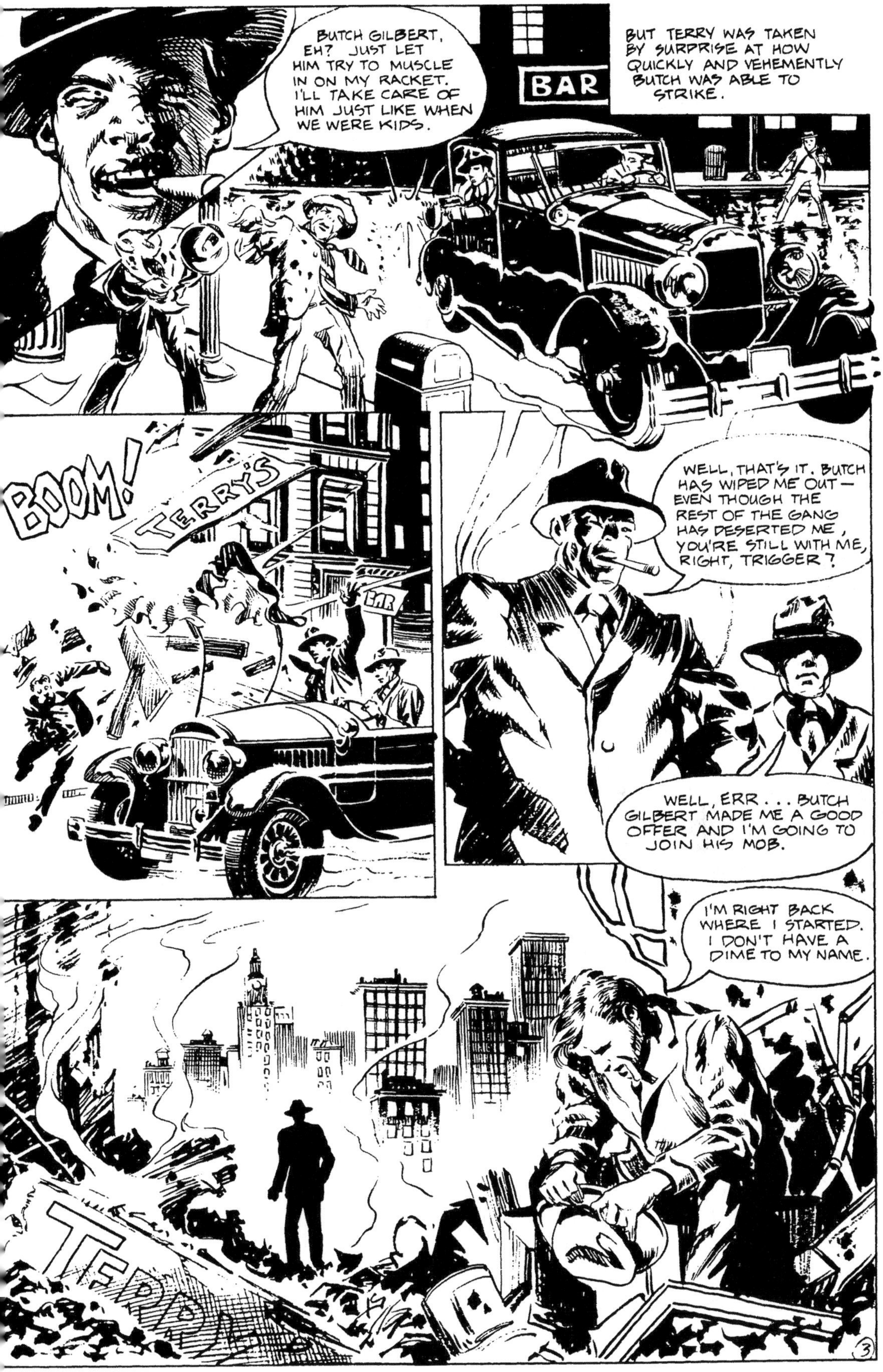

BUTCH GILBERT, EH? JUST LET HIM TRY TO MUSCLE IN ON MY RACKET. I'LL TAKE CARE OF HIM JUST LIKE WHEN WE WERE KIDS.
BAR
BUT TERRY WAS TAKEN BY SURPRISE AT HOW QUICKLY AND VEHEMENTLY BUTCH WAS ABLE TO STRIKE.
BOOM!
TERRY'S
BAR
WELL, THAT'S IT. BUTCH HAS WIPED ME OUT— EVEN THOUGH THE REST OF THE GANG HAS DESERTED ME, YOU'RE STILL WITH ME, RIGHT, TRIGGER?
WELL, ERR... BUTCH GILBERT MADE ME A GOOD OFFER AND I'M GOING TO JOIN HIS MOB.
I'M RIGHT BACK WHERE I STARTED. I DON'T HAVE A DIME TO MY NAME.
3

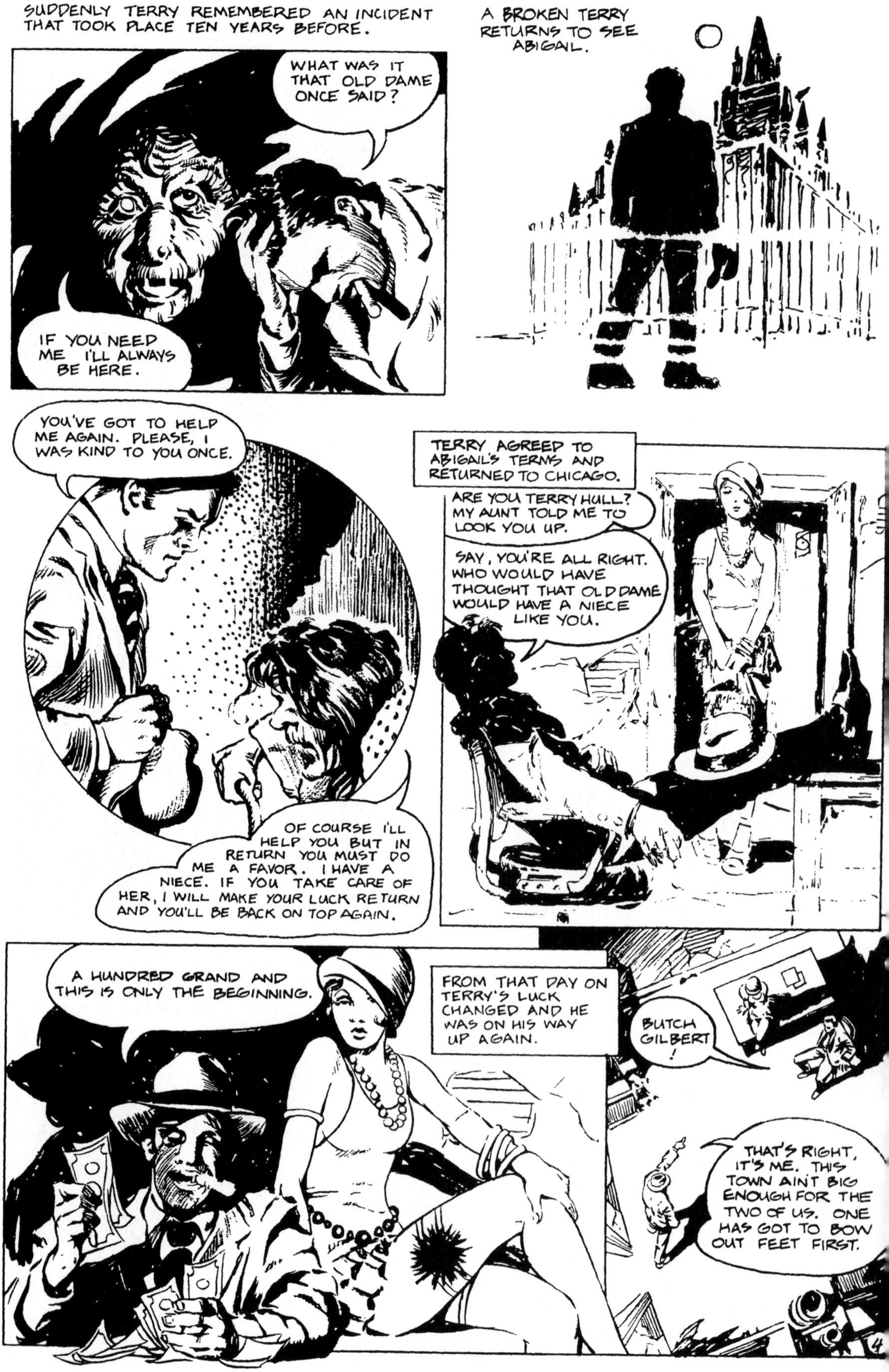

SUDDENLY TERRY REMEMBERED AN INCIDENT THAT TOOK PLACE TEN YEARS BEFORE.
WHAT WAS IT THAT OLD DAME ONCE SAID?
IF YOU NEED ME I'LL ALWAYS BE HERE.
A BROKEN TERRY RETURNS TO SEE ABIGAIL.
YOU'VE GOT TO HELP ME AGAIN. PLEASE, I WAS KIND TO YOU ONCE.
OF COURSE I'LL HELP YOU BUT IN RETURN YOU MUST DO ME A FAVOR. I HAVE A NIECE. IF YOU TAKE CARE OF HER, I WILL MAKE YOUR LUCK RETURN AND YOU'LL BE BACK ON TOP AGAIN.
TERRY AGREED TO ABIGAIL'S TERMS AND RETURNED TO CHICAGO.
ARE YOU TERRY HULL? MY AUNT TOLD ME TO LOOK YOU UP.
SAY, YOU'RE ALL RIGHT. WHO WOULD HAVE THOUGHT THAT OLD DAME WOULD HAVE A NIECE LIKE YOU.
A HUNDRED GRAND AND THIS IS ONLY THE BEGINNING.
FROM THAT DAY ON TERRY'S LUCK CHANGED AND HE WAS ON HIS WAY UP AGAIN.
BUTCH GILBERT!
THAT'S RIGHT, IT'S ME. THIS TOWN AIN'T BIG ENOUGH FOR THE TWO OF US. ONE HAS GOT TO BOW OUT FEET FIRST.
4

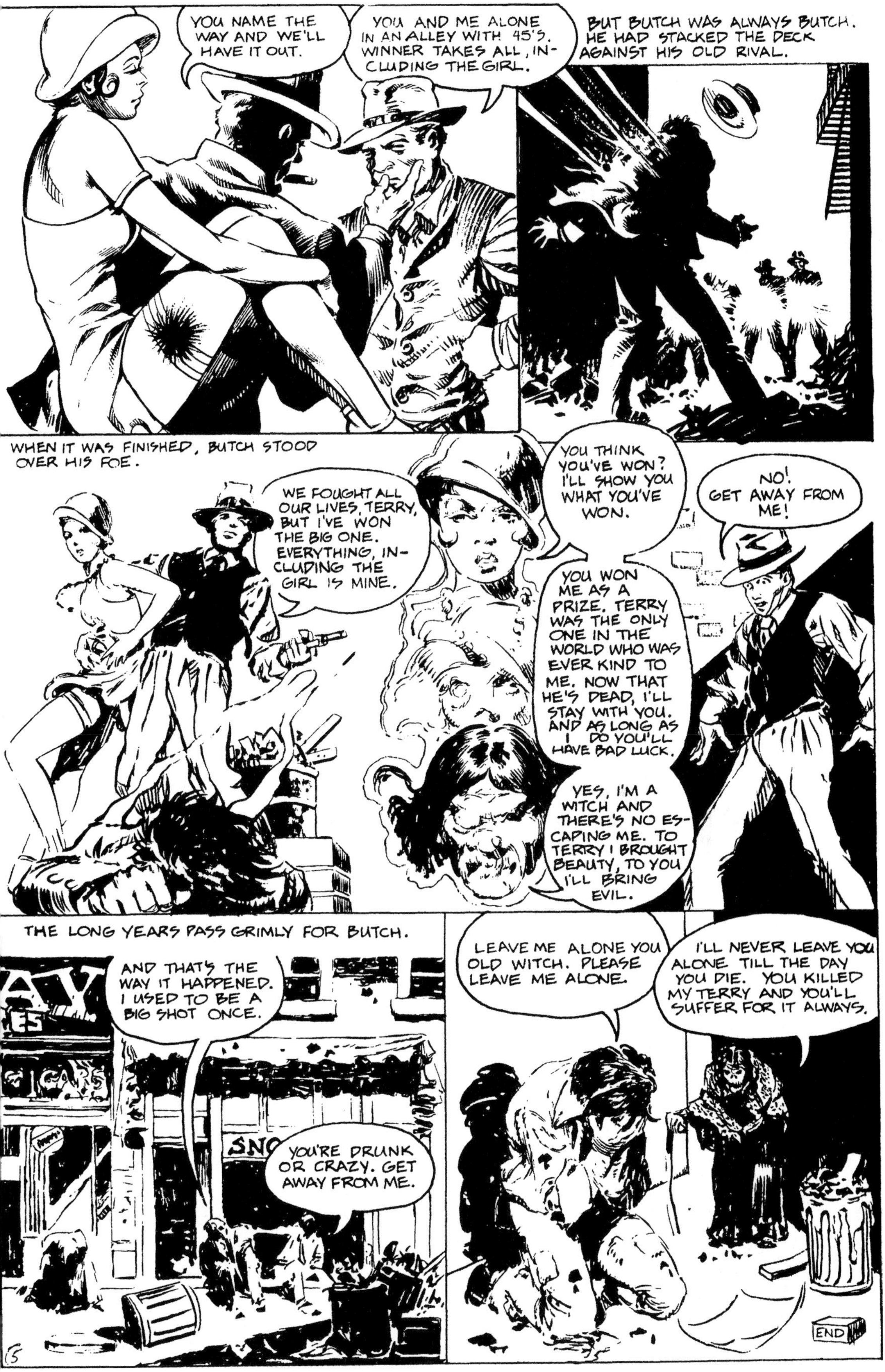
YOU NAME THE WAY AND WE'LL HAVE IT OUT.
YOU AND ME ALONE IN AN ALLEY WITH 45'S. WINNER TAKES ALL, INCLUDING THE GIRL.
BUT BUTCH WAS ALWAYS BUTCH. HE HAD STACKED THE DECK AGAINST HIS OLD RIVAL.
WHEN IT WAS FINISHED, BUTCH STOOD OVER HIS FOE.
WE FOUGHT ALL OUR LIVES, TERRY, BUT I'VE WON THE BIG ONE. EVERYTHING, INCLUDING THE GIRL IS MINE.
YOU THINK YOU'VE WON? I'LL SHOW YOU WHAT YOU'VE WON.
YOU WON ME AS A PRIZE. TERRY WAS THE ONLY ONE IN THE WORLD WHO WAS EVER KIND TO ME. NOW THAT HE'S DEAD, I'LL STAY WITH YOU. AND AS LONG AS I DO YOU'LL HAVE BAD LUCK.
YES, I'M A WITCH AND THERE'S NO ESCAPING ME. TO TERRY I BROUGHT BEAUTY, TO YOU I'LL BRING EVIL.
NO! GET AWAY FROM ME!
THE LONG YEARS PASS GRIMLY FOR BUTCH.
AND THAT'S THE WAY IT HAPPENED. I USED TO BE A BIG SHOT ONCE.
YOU'RE DRUNK OR CRAZY. GET AWAY FROM ME.
LEAVE ME ALONE YOU OLD WITCH. PLEASE LEAVE ME ALONE.
I'LL NEVER LEAVE YOU ALONE TILL THE DAY YOU DIE. YOU KILLED MY TERRY AND YOU'LL SUFFER FOR IT ALWAYS.
END

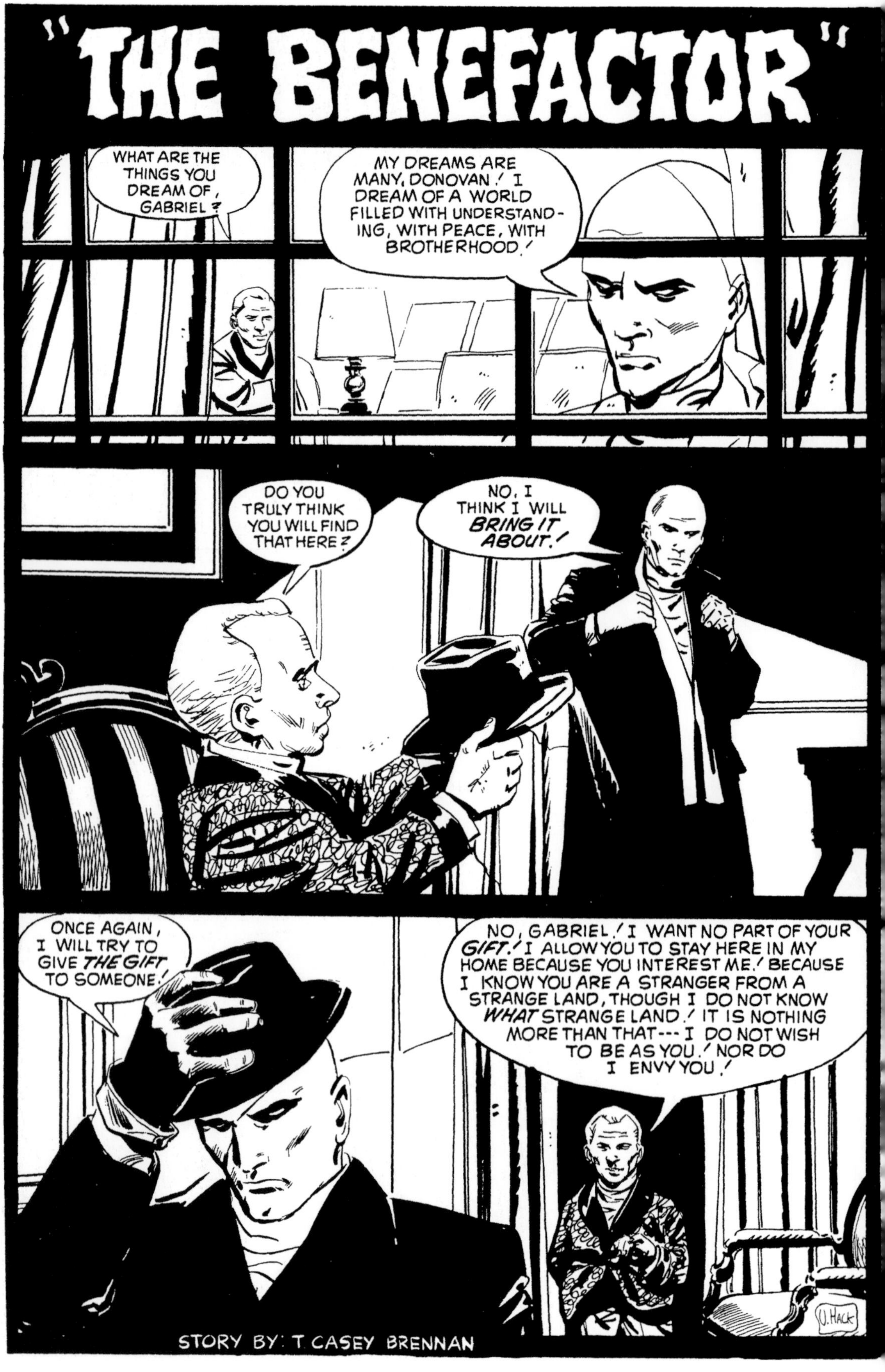
"THE BENEFACTOR"
WHAT ARE THE THINGS YOU DREAM OF, GABRIEL?
MY DREAMS ARE MANY, DONOVAN! I DREAM OF A WORLD FILLED WITH UNDERSTANDING, WITH PEACE, WITH BROTHERHOOD!
DO YOU TRULY THINK YOU WILL FIND THAT HERE?
NO, I THINK I WILL BRING IT ABOUT!
ONCE AGAIN, I WILL TRY TO GIVE THE GIFT TO SOMEONE!
NO, GABRIEL! I WANT NO PART OF YOUR GIFT! I ALLOW YOU TO STAY HERE IN MY HOME BECAUSE YOU INTEREST ME! BECAUSE I KNOW YOU ARE A STRANGER FROM A STRANGE LAND, THOUGH I DO NOT KNOW WHAT STRANGE LAND! IT IS NOTHING MORE THAN THAT--- I DO NOT WISH TO BE AS YOU! NOR DO I ENVY YOU!
U. HACK
STORY BY: T CASEY BRENNAN

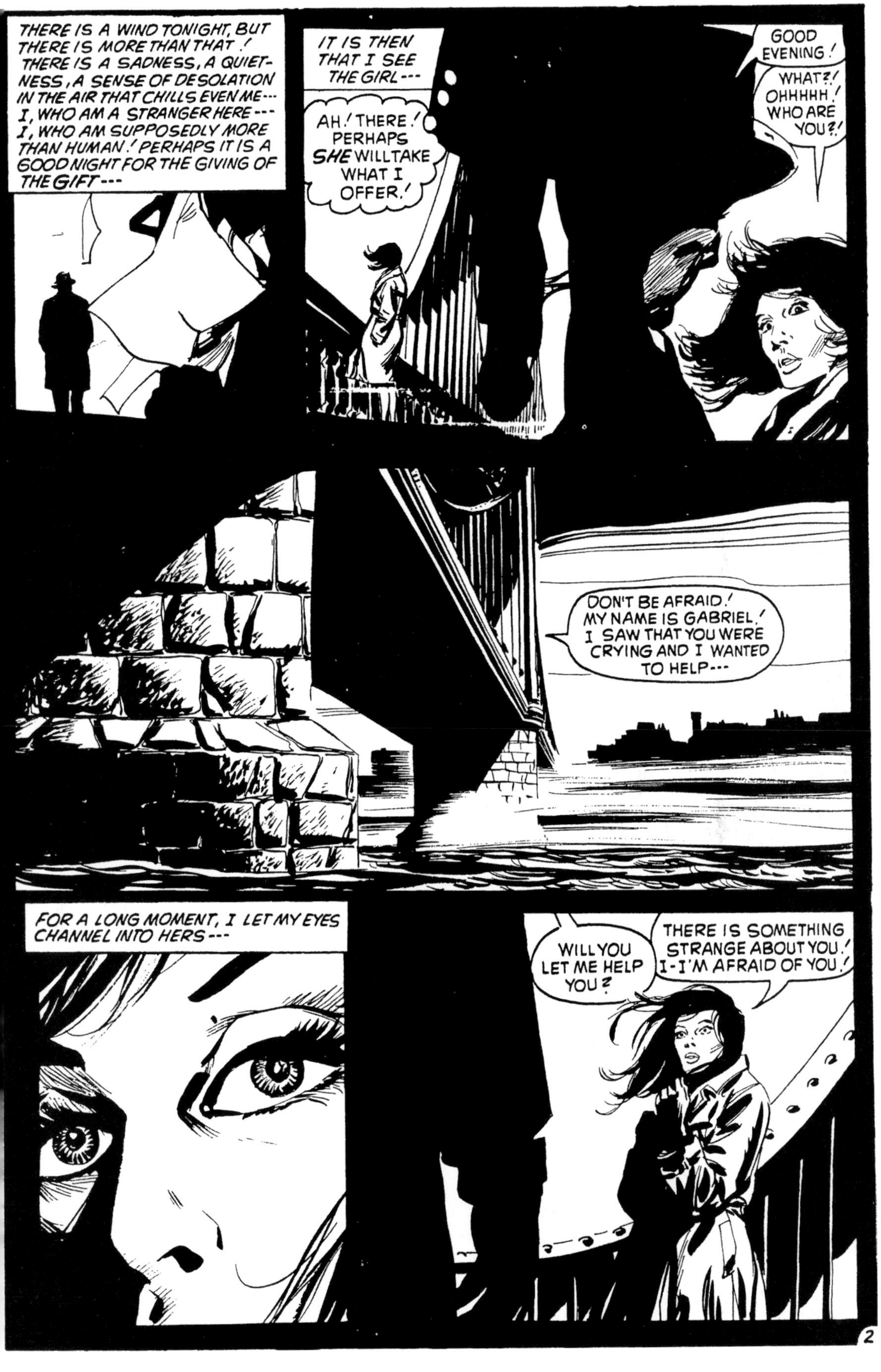
THERE IS A WIND TONIGHT, BUT THERE IS MORE THAN THAT! THERE IS A SADNESS, A QUIETNESS, A SENSE OF DESOLATION IN THE AIR THAT CHILLS EVEN ME--- I, WHO AM A STRANGER HERE--- I, WHO AM SUPPOSEDLY MORE THAN HUMAN! PERHAPS IT IS A GOOD NIGHT FOR THE GIVING OF THE GIFT---
IT IS THEN THAT I SEE THE GIRL---
AH! THERE! PERHAPS SHE WILL TAKE WHAT I OFFER!
GOOD EVENING!
WHAT?! OHHHHH! WHO ARE YOU?!
DON'T BE AFRAID! MY NAME IS GABRIEL! I SAW THAT YOU WERE CRYING AND I WANTED TO HELP---
FOR A LONG MOMENT, I LET MY EYES CHANNEL INTO HERS---
WILL YOU LET ME HELP YOU?
THERE IS SOMETHING STRANGE ABOUT YOU! I-I'M AFRAID OF YOU!

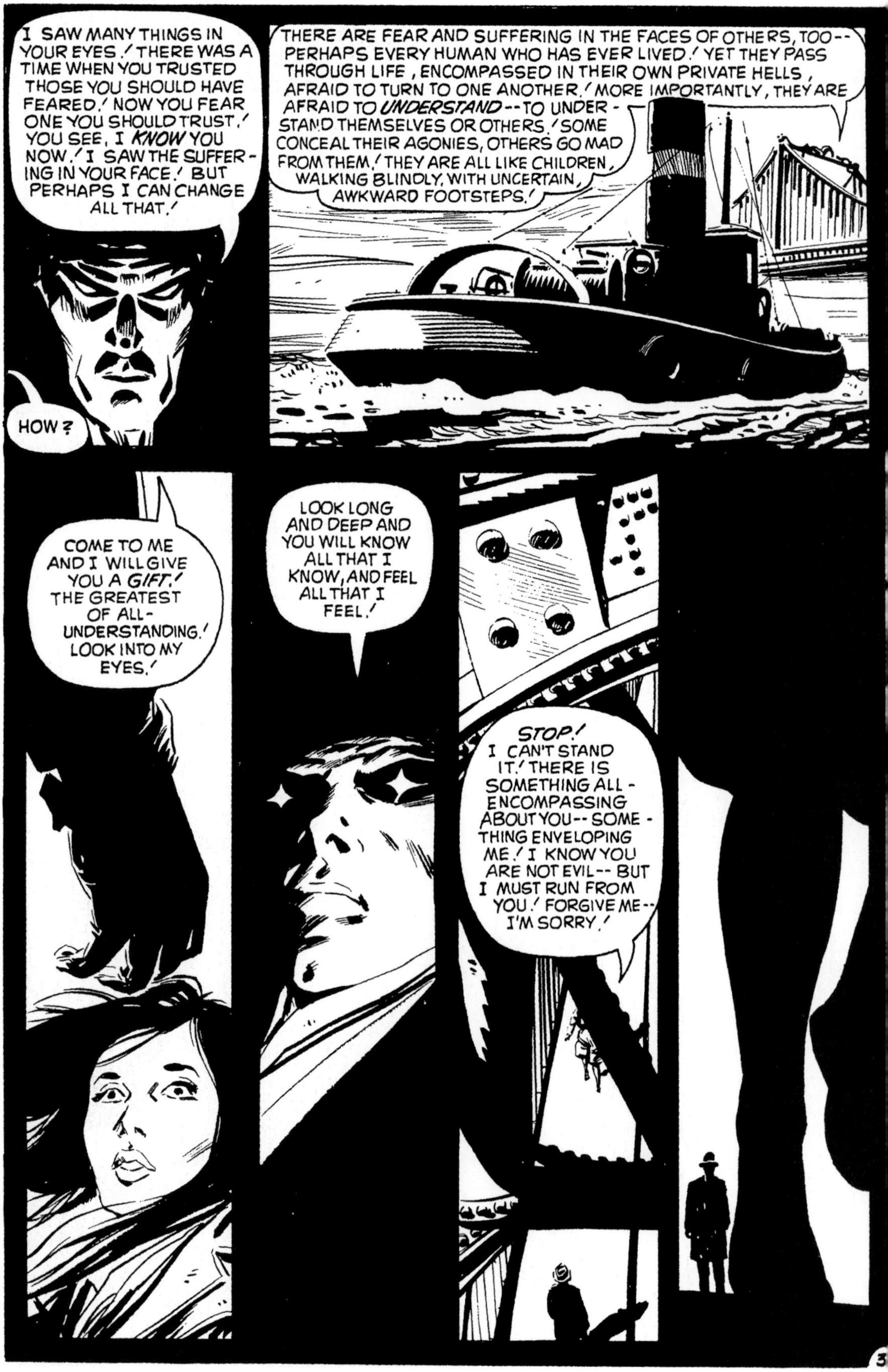

I SAW MANY THINGS IN YOUR EYES! THERE WAS A TIME WHEN YOU TRUSTED THOSE YOU SHOULD HAVE FEARED! NOW YOU FEAR ONE YOU SHOULD TRUST! YOU SEE, I KNOW YOU NOW! I SAW THE SUFFERING IN YOUR FACE! BUT PERHAPS I CAN CHANGE ALL THAT!
HOW?
THERE ARE FEAR AND SUFFERING IN THE FACES OF OTHERS, TOO-- PERHAPS EVERY HUMAN WHO HAS EVER LIVED! YET THEY PASS THROUGH LIFE, ENCOMPASSED IN THEIR OWN PRIVATE HELLS, AFRAID TO TURN TO ONE ANOTHER! MORE IMPORTANTLY, THEY ARE AFRAID TO UNDERSTAND--TO UNDERSTAND THEMSELVES OR OTHERS! SOME CONCEAL THEIR AGONIES, OTHERS GO MAD FROM THEM! THEY ARE ALL LIKE CHILDREN, WALKING BLINDLY, WITH UNCERTAIN, AWKWARD FOOTSTEPS!
COME TO ME AND I WILL GIVE YOU A GIFT! THE GREATEST OF ALL-- UNDERSTANDING! LOOK INTO MY EYES!
LOOK LONG AND DEEP AND YOU WILL KNOW ALL THAT I KNOW, AND FEEL ALL THAT I FEEL!
STOP! I CAN'T STAND IT! THERE IS SOMETHING ALL-ENCOMPASSING ABOUT YOU--SOMETHING ENVELOPING ME! I KNOW YOU ARE NOT EVIL-- BUT I MUST RUN FROM YOU! FORGIVE ME-- I'M SORRY!

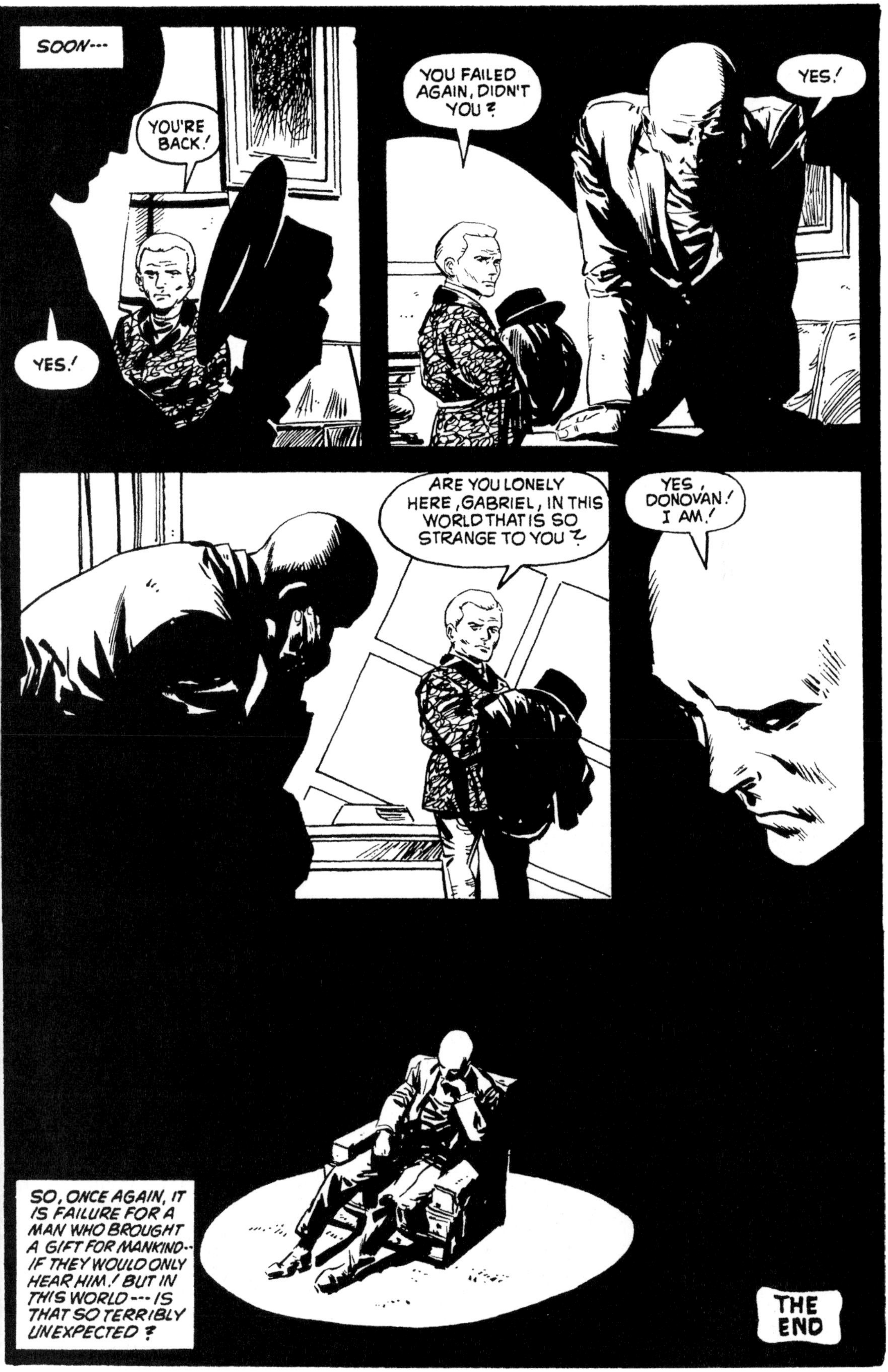
SOON---
YOU'RE BACK!
YES!
YOU FAILED AGAIN, DIDN'T YOU?
YES!
ARE YOU LONELY HERE, GABRIEL, IN THIS WORLD THAT IS SO STRANGE TO YOU?
YES, DONOVAN! I AM!
SO, ONCE AGAIN, IT IS FAILURE FOR A MAN WHO BROUGHT A GIFT FOR MANKIND-- IF THEY WOULD ONLY HEAR HIM! BUT IN THIS WORLD --- IS THAT SO TERRIBLY UNEXPECTED?
THE END

# ESSAYS INTO THE SUPERNATURAL
# POSSESSION AND EXORCISM

**TEXT AND ART** - GRAY MORROW

POSSESSION, WHEREBY A PERSON'S BODY IS "INVADED" AND "TAKEN OVER" BY EVIL SPIRITS WHO CAUSE THE SUFFERER TO BEHAVE IN STRANGE WAYS, IS A POWER ATTRIBUTED TO WITCHES. EXORCISTS IN THE MIDDLE AGES CLAIMED THAT WITCHES HAD MANY WAYS OF INFLICTING THIS CONDITION....

...BUT THE EASIEST WAY WAS TO CONCEAL A DEMON, SPECIALLY CONJURED FOR THE PURPOSE, IN AN APPLE AND THEN PERSUADE THE CHOSEN VICTIM TO EAT IT—SPIRIT AND ALL!

THE MOST EXTENSIVE RECORDS OF POSSESSION ARE FOUND TO BE IN EUROPE. NUNS AND SMALL CHILDREN BEING PARTICULARLY PRONE. FITS AND SEIZURES, SPEAKING IN UNFAMILIAR VOICES AND UNKNOWN TONGUES ARE EXAMPLES OF SOME TYPES OF POSSESSION.

CASES SHOW THAT THERE WERE SOME GRIM METHODS OF EXORCISM. WHIPPING THE VICTIM'S NAKED BODY TO DRIVE OUT THE DEMON AND THE EMPLOYMENT OF A WHEEL DEVICE, TO WHICH THE ONE POSSESSED WAS BOUND AND WHIRLED AROUND UNTIL THE DEVILS GREW DIZZY ENOUGH TO DEPART, ARE TWO MILDER ONES.

THESE DRASTIC MEASURES WERE SUPER-SEDED BY PRAYER AND THE LAYING ON OF THE HANDS, A TECHNIQUE WHICH IS STILL USED TODAY AMONG CERTAIN HOLY ORDERS.

# BONUS STORY

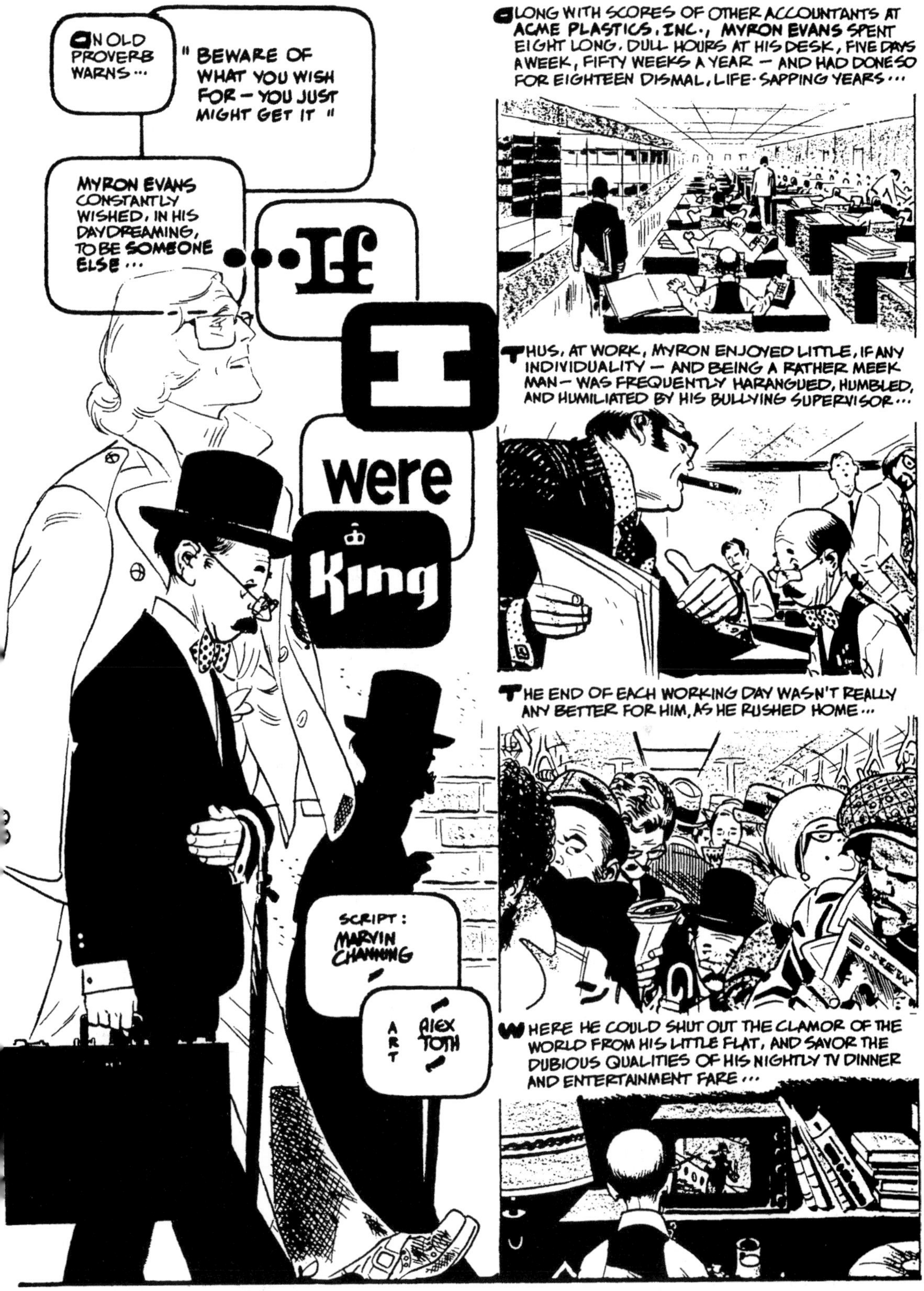

AN OLD PROVERB WARNS...
"BEWARE OF WHAT YOU WISH FOR – YOU JUST MIGHT GET IT"
MYRON EVANS CONSTANTLY WISHED, IN HIS DAYDREAMING, TO BE SOMEONE ELSE...
...If I were King
SCRIPT: MARVIN CHANNING
ART ALEX TOTH
ALONG WITH SCORES OF OTHER ACCOUNTANTS AT ACME PLASTICS, INC., MYRON EVANS SPENT EIGHT LONG, DULL HOURS AT HIS DESK, FIVE DAYS A WEEK, FIFTY WEEKS A YEAR – AND HAD DONE SO FOR EIGHTEEN DISMAL, LIFE-SAPPING YEARS...
THUS, AT WORK, MYRON ENJOYED LITTLE, IF ANY INDIVIDUALITY – AND BEING A RATHER MEEK MAN – WAS FREQUENTLY HARANGUED, HUMBLED, AND HUMILIATED BY HIS BULLYING SUPERVISOR...
THE END OF EACH WORKING DAY WASN'T REALLY ANY BETTER FOR HIM, AS HE RUSHED HOME...
WHERE HE COULD SHUT OUT THE CLAMOR OF THE WORLD FROM HIS LITTLE FLAT, AND SAVOR THE DUBIOUS QUALITIES OF HIS NIGHTLY TV DINNER AND ENTERTAINMENT FARE...

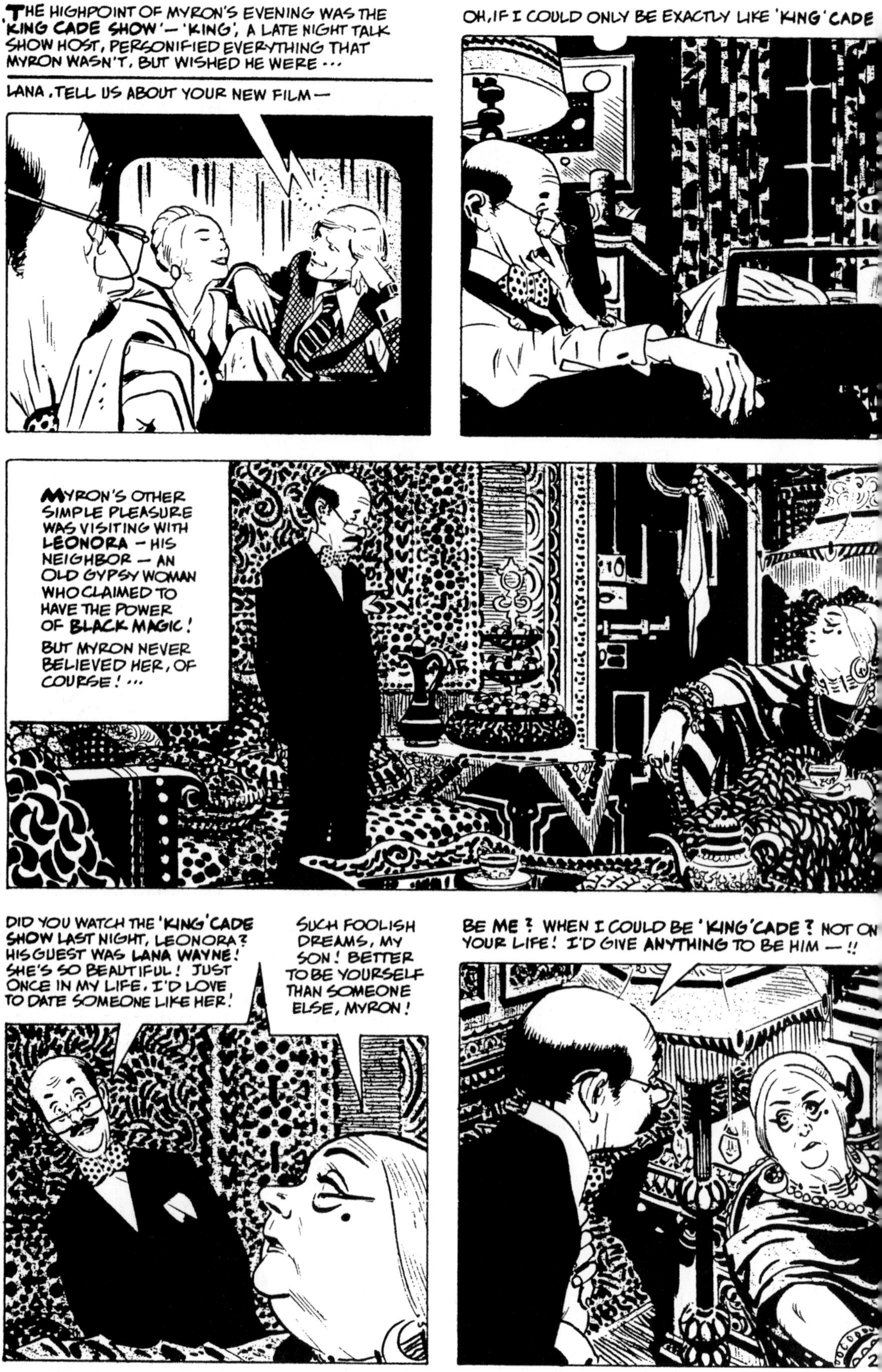
THE HIGHPOINT OF MYRON'S EVENING WAS THE 'KING CADE SHOW' — 'KING', A LATE NIGHT TALK SHOW HOST, PERSONIFIED EVERYTHING THAT MYRON WASN'T, BUT WISHED HE WERE ...
LANA, TELL US ABOUT YOUR NEW FILM —
OH, IF I COULD ONLY BE EXACTLY LIKE 'KING' CADE
MYRON'S OTHER SIMPLE PLEASURE WAS VISITING WITH LEONORA — HIS NEIGHBOR — AN OLD GYPSY WOMAN WHO CLAIMED TO HAVE THE POWER OF BLACK MAGIC!
BUT MYRON NEVER BELIEVED HER, OF COURSE! ...
DID YOU WATCH THE 'KING' CADE SHOW LAST NIGHT, LEONORA? HIS GUEST WAS LANA WAYNE! SHE'S SO BEAUTIFUL! JUST ONCE IN MY LIFE, I'D LOVE TO DATE SOMEONE LIKE HER!
SUCH FOOLISH DREAMS, MY SON! BETTER TO BE YOURSELF THAN SOMEONE ELSE, MYRON!
BE ME? WHEN I COULD BE 'KING' CADE? NOT ON YOUR LIFE! I'D GIVE ANYTHING TO BE HIM —!!

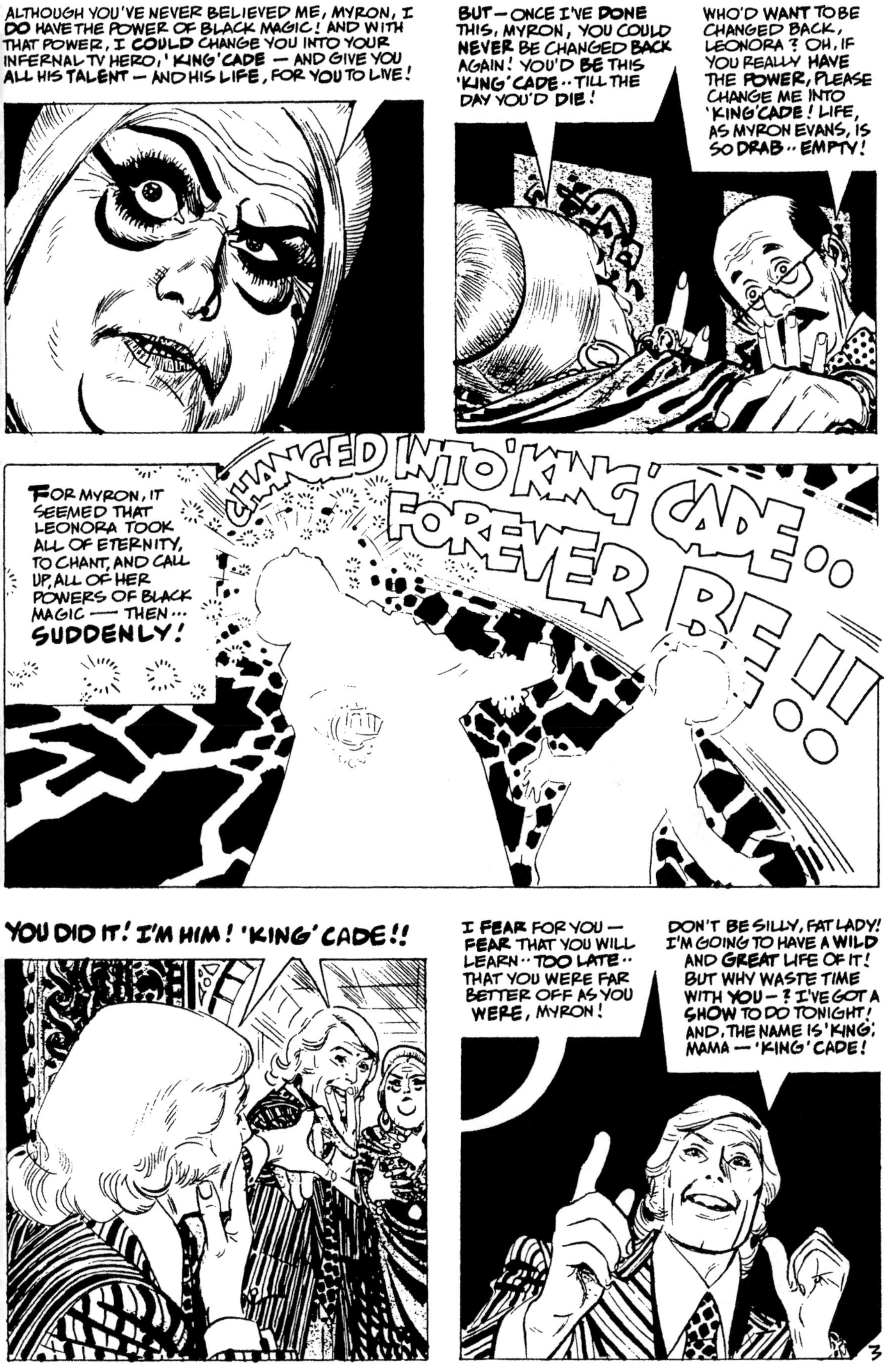

ALTHOUGH YOU'VE NEVER BELIEVED ME, MYRON, I DO HAVE THE POWER OF BLACK MAGIC! AND WITH THAT POWER, I COULD CHANGE YOU INTO YOUR INFERNAL TV HERO, 'KING' CADE — AND GIVE YOU ALL HIS TALENT — AND HIS LIFE, FOR YOU TO LIVE!
BUT — ONCE I'VE DONE THIS, MYRON, YOU COULD NEVER BE CHANGED BACK AGAIN! YOU'D BE THIS 'KING' CADE.. TILL THE DAY YOU'D DIE!
WHO'D WANT TO BE CHANGED BACK, LEONORA? OH, IF YOU REALLY HAVE THE POWER, PLEASE CHANGE ME INTO 'KING' CADE! LIFE, AS MYRON EVANS, IS SO DRAB.. EMPTY!
FOR MYRON, IT SEEMED THAT LEONORA TOOK ALL OF ETERNITY, TO CHANT, AND CALL UP, ALL OF HER POWERS OF BLACK MAGIC — THEN... SUDDENLY!
CHANGED INTO 'KING' CADE.. FOREVER BE!!
YOU DID IT! I'M HIM! 'KING' CADE!!
I FEAR FOR YOU — FEAR THAT YOU WILL LEARN.. TOO LATE.. THAT YOU WERE FAR BETTER OFF AS YOU WERE, MYRON!
DON'T BE SILLY, FAT LADY! I'M GOING TO HAVE A WILD AND GREAT LIFE OF IT! BUT WHY WASTE TIME WITH YOU—? I'VE GOT A SHOW TO DO TONIGHT! AND, THE NAME IS 'KING', MAMA — 'KING' CADE!
3

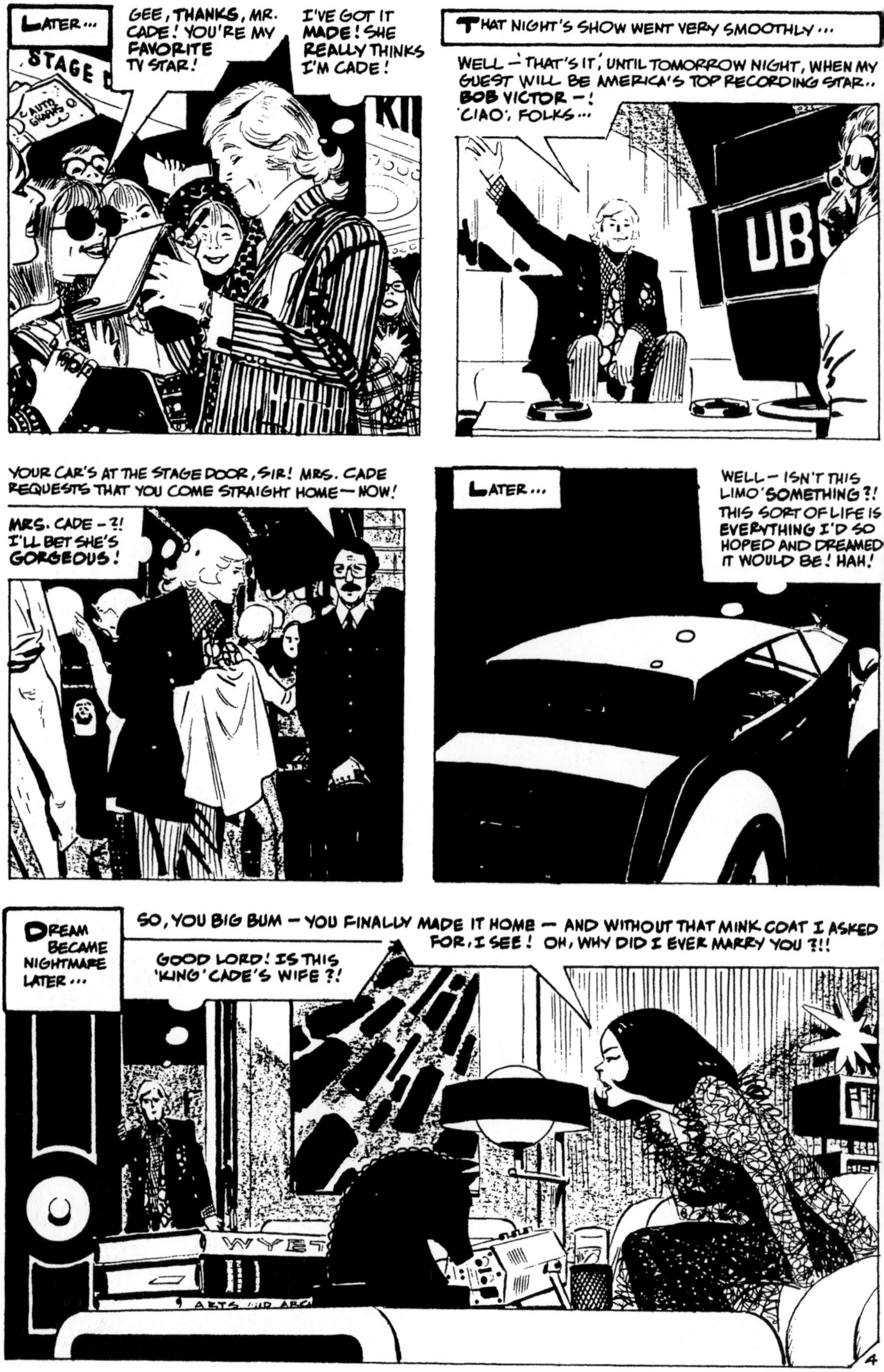
LATER...
GEE, THANKS, MR. CADE! YOU'RE MY FAVORITE TV STAR!
I'VE GOT IT MADE! SHE REALLY THINKS I'M CADE!
STAGE
THAT NIGHT'S SHOW WENT VERY SMOOTHLY...
WELL — 'THAT'S IT,' UNTIL TOMORROW NIGHT, WHEN MY GUEST WILL BE AMERICA'S TOP RECORDING STAR.. BOB VICTOR —! 'CIAO', FOLKS...
UBC
YOUR CAR'S AT THE STAGE DOOR, SIR! MRS. CADE REQUESTS THAT YOU COME STRAIGHT HOME — NOW!
MRS. CADE —?! I'LL BET SHE'S GORGEOUS!
LATER...
WELL — ISN'T THIS LIMO 'SOMETHING'?! THIS SORT OF LIFE IS EVERYTHING I'D SO HOPED AND DREAMED IT WOULD BE! HAH!
DREAM BECAME NIGHTMARE LATER...
SO, YOU BIG BUM — YOU FINALLY MADE IT HOME — AND WITHOUT THAT MINK COAT I ASKED FOR, I SEE! OH, WHY DID I EVER MARRY YOU ?!!
GOOD LORD! IS THIS 'KING' CADE'S WIFE ?!

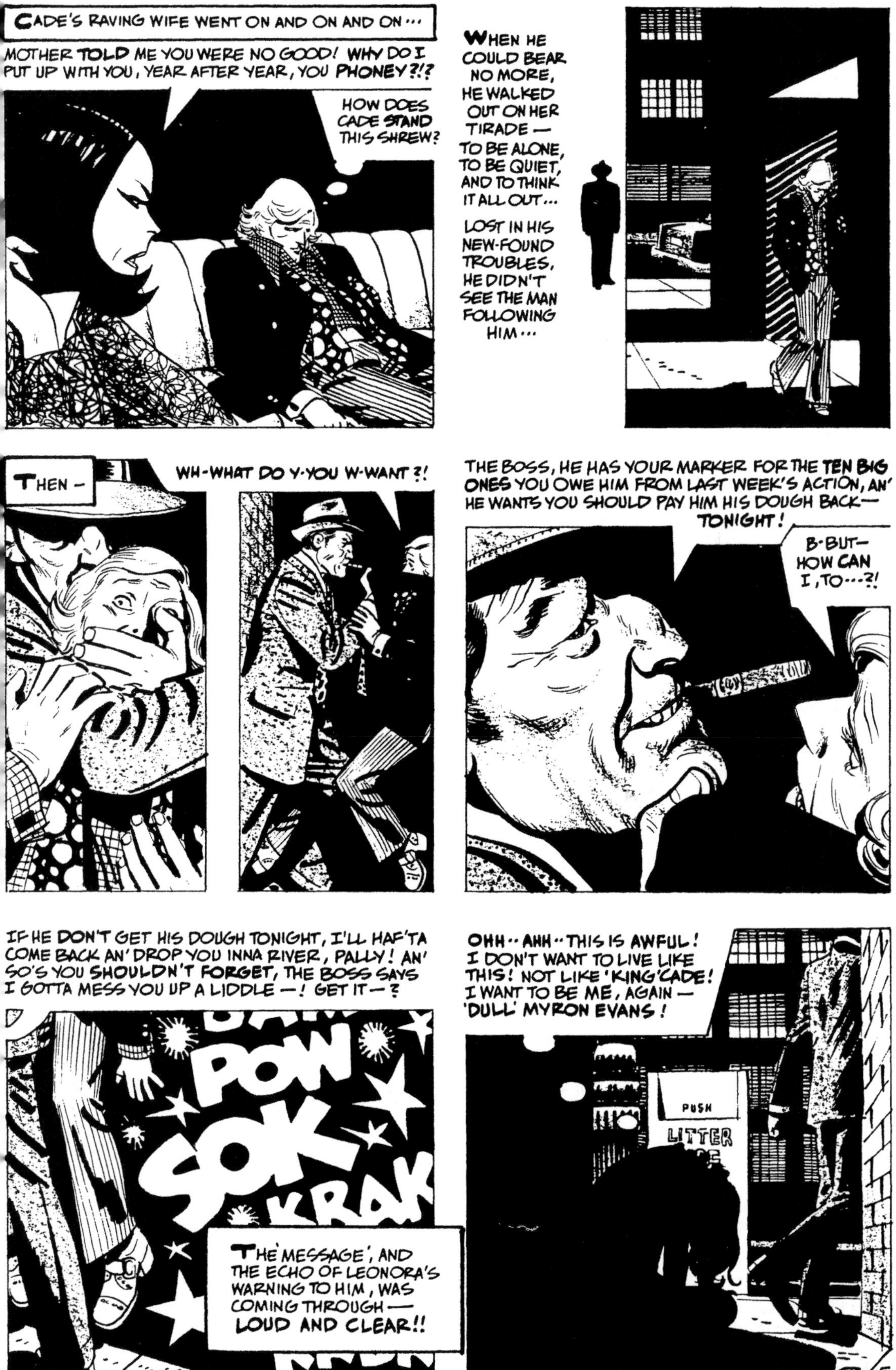

CADE'S RAVING WIFE WENT ON AND ON AND ON...
MOTHER TOLD ME YOU WERE NO GOOD! WHY DO I PUT UP WITH YOU, YEAR AFTER YEAR, YOU PHONEY?!?
HOW DOES CADE STAND THIS SHREW?
WHEN HE COULD BEAR NO MORE, HE WALKED OUT ON HER TIRADE — TO BE ALONE, TO BE QUIET, AND TO THINK IT ALL OUT...
LOST IN HIS NEW-FOUND TROUBLES, HE DIDN'T SEE THE MAN FOLLOWING HIM...
THEN –
WH-WHAT DO Y-YOU W-WANT ?!
THE BOSS, HE HAS YOUR MARKER FOR THE TEN BIG ONES YOU OWE HIM FROM LAST WEEK'S ACTION, AN' HE WANTS YOU SHOULD PAY HIM HIS DOUGH BACK— TONIGHT!
B-BUT— HOW CAN I, TO...?!
IF HE DON'T GET HIS DOUGH TONIGHT, I'LL HAF'TA COME BACK AN' DROP YOU INNA RIVER, PALLY! AN' SO'S YOU SHOULDN'T FORGET, THE BOSS SAYS I GOTTA MESS YOU UP A LIDDLE —! GET IT —?
POW
SOK
KRAK
THE 'MESSAGE', AND THE ECHO OF LEONORA'S WARNING TO HIM, WAS COMING THROUGH — LOUD AND CLEAR!!
OHH.. AHH.. THIS IS AWFUL! I DON'T WANT TO LIVE LIKE THIS! NOT LIKE 'KING' CADE! I WANT TO BE ME, AGAIN — 'DULL' MYRON EVANS!
PUSH
LITTER

RUSHING BACK TO LEONORA…

LEONORA – HELP ME!! IT'S TERRIBLE BEING 'KING' CADE! I WANT THINGS BACK THE WAY THEY WERE BEFORE! PLEASE?

I TOLD YOU THAT THIS MIGHT HAPPEN WHEN I CAST THE SPELL TO CHANGE YOU! REMEMBER, IT WAS TO BE… FOREVER!!

OH, NO! PLEASE! YOU MUST HELP ME! YOU'RE M–MY FRIEND!

I'LL TRY! —USING THE STRONGEST MAGIC I KNOW! BUT, IT'S UP TO THE SPIRITS TO DECIDE YOUR FATE…

LEONORA'S MAGIC WAS STRONG ENOUGH, AFTER ALL…

I'M BACK! I'M ME – MYRON EVANS!! OH, THANK YOU, LEONORA — THANK YOU, THANK YOU!! (SOB)

NEXT DAY: DURING MYRON'S ROUTINELY BORING SUBWAY RIDE TO HIS ROUTINELY DULL JOB, HIS NORMALLY CASUAL, UNOBSERVING EYES SHOT WIDE OPEN, IN SHOCK, AS THEY FOCUSSED ON THE JIGGLING HEADLINES OF THE MORNING NEWSPAPERS RINGING HIM…

New York Morning

'KING' CADE SLAIN!

TV STAR'S BODY FOUND IN RIVER

BEATEN, SHOT CORPSE A... GANGLAND-S... EXECUTION

SPECI...

the END

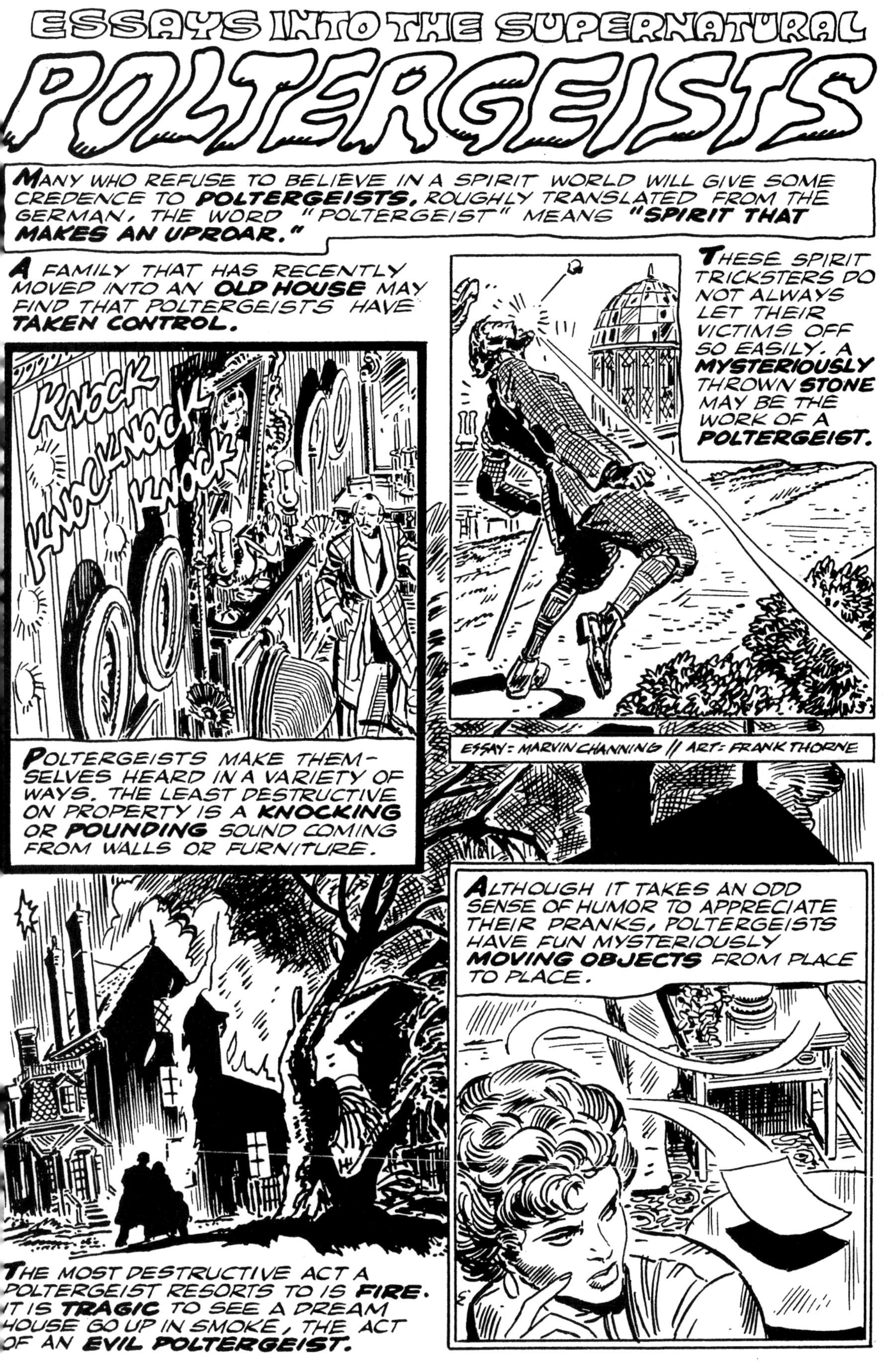

ESSAYS INTO THE SUPERNATURAL
POLTERGEISTS
MANY WHO REFUSE TO BELIEVE IN A SPIRIT WORLD WILL GIVE SOME CREDENCE TO POLTERGEISTS. ROUGHLY TRANSLATED FROM THE GERMAN, THE WORD "POLTERGEIST" MEANS "SPIRIT THAT MAKES AN UPROAR."
A FAMILY THAT HAS RECENTLY MOVED INTO AN OLD HOUSE MAY FIND THAT POLTERGEISTS HAVE TAKEN CONTROL.
KNOCK
KNOCKNOCK
KNOCK
POLTERGEISTS MAKE THEMSELVES HEARD IN A VARIETY OF WAYS. THE LEAST DESTRUCTIVE ON PROPERTY IS A KNOCKING OR POUNDING SOUND COMING FROM WALLS OR FURNITURE.
THESE SPIRIT TRICKSTERS DO NOT ALWAYS LET THEIR VICTIMS OFF SO EASILY. A MYSTERIOUSLY THROWN STONE MAY BE THE WORK OF A POLTERGEIST.
ESSAY: MARVIN CHANNING // ART: FRANK THORNE
THE MOST DESTRUCTIVE ACT A POLTERGEIST RESORTS TO IS FIRE. IT IS TRAGIC TO SEE A DREAM HOUSE GO UP IN SMOKE, THE ACT OF AN EVIL POLTERGEIST.
ALTHOUGH IT TAKES AN ODD SENSE OF HUMOR TO APPRECIATE THEIR PRANKS, POLTERGEISTS HAVE FUN MYSTERIOUSLY MOVING OBJECTS FROM PLACE TO PLACE.

# THE SPECTRE

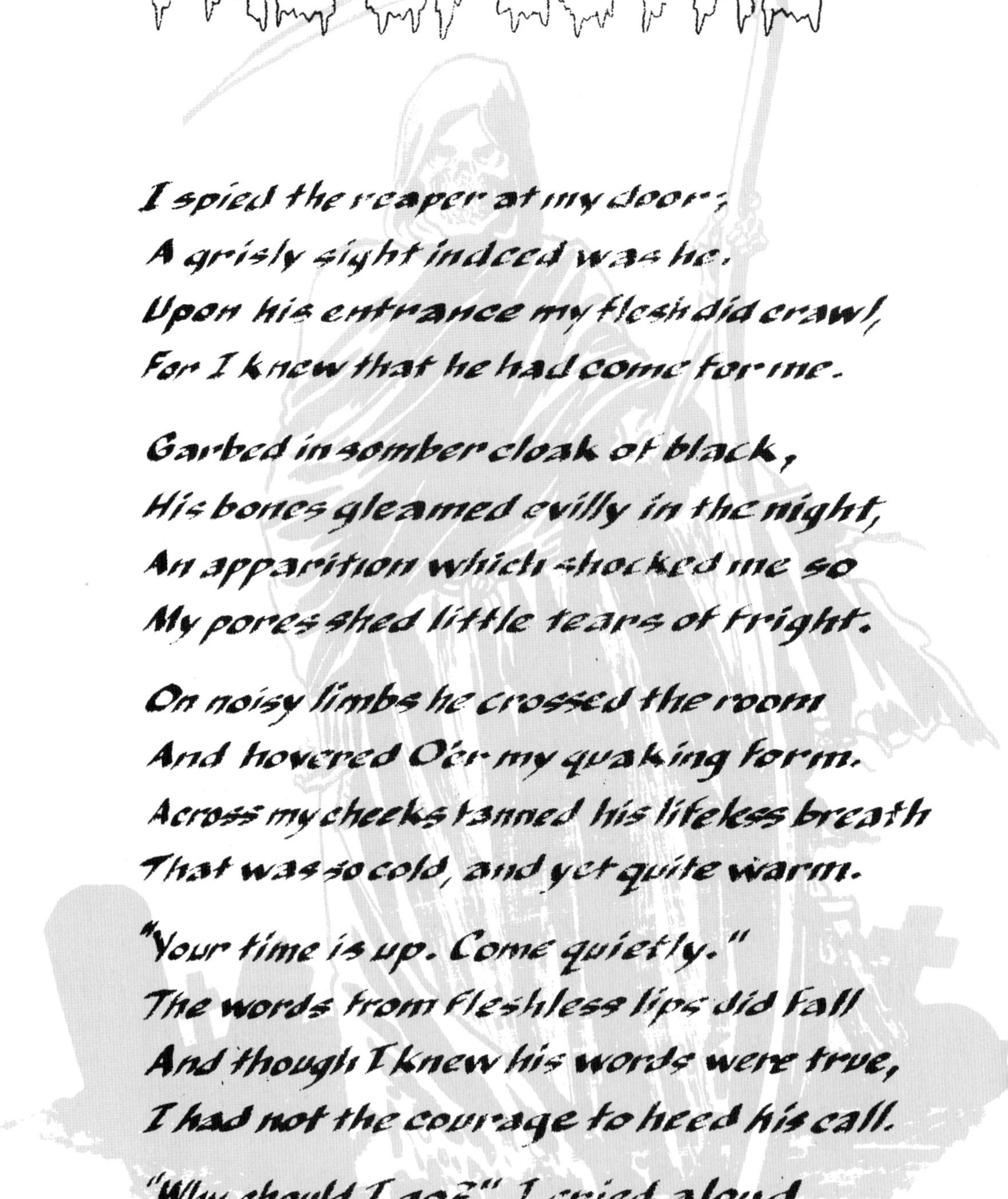

I spied the reaper at my door;
A grisly sight indeed was he.
Upon his entrance my flesh did crawl,
For I knew that he had come for me.

Garbed in somber cloak of black,
His bones gleamed evilly in the night,
An apparition which shocked me so
My pores shed little tears of fright.

On noisy limbs he crossed the room
And hovered O'er my quaking form.
Across my cheeks fanned his lifeless breath
That was so cold, and yet quite warm.

"Your time is up. Come quietly."
The words from fleshless lips did fall
And though I knew his words were true,
I had not the courage to heed his call.

"Why should I go?" I cried aloud
In anguish and despair.
"Have I done the world some awful wrong
That God should no longer care?"

The spectre laughed; a wicked laugh
That rattled raucously 'round my head.
A sound that echoed from the grave
and filled my heart with untold dread.

With bony digit he touched my breast,
A touch that chilled my soul with fear.
With gleaming sockets, hollow and deep
He looked at me, his meaning clear.

"Come, let us go," and with these words
His luminous rattling arms did reach,
And as he gathered me to his breast
My tears gave vent to a piercing screech.

I struggled wildly to free myself
From his cold and clammy grasp.
"You silly mortal, 'tis futile to fight,"
His coarse, unpleasant voice did rasp.

I fought him thus for quite awhile
But, alas, t'was as he said...
For as they look upon me now,
'Tis plain to see I'm quite, quite dead!

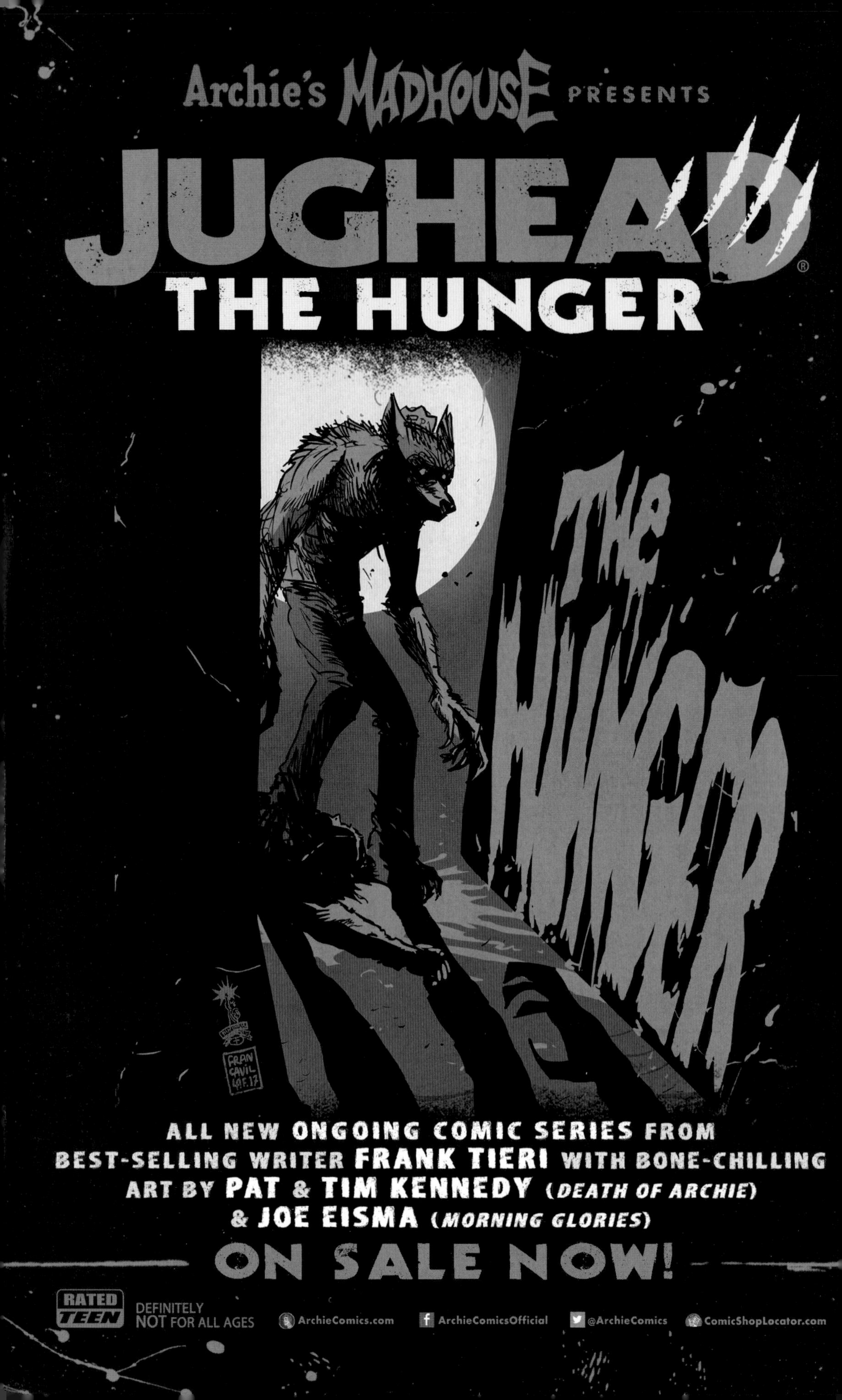
Archie's MADHOUSE PRESENTS
JUGHEAD®
THE HUNGER
THE HUNGER
ALL NEW ONGOING COMIC SERIES FROM
BEST-SELLING WRITER FRANK TIERI WITH BONE-CHILLING
ART BY PAT & TIM KENNEDY (DEATH OF ARCHIE)
& JOE EISMA (MORNING GLORIES)
ON SALE NOW!
RATED TEEN
DEFINITELY NOT FOR ALL AGES
ArchieComics.com
ArchieComicsOfficial
@ArchieComics
ComicShopLocator.com